Kim C Sturgess

another brother *Shakespeare*

Swimmer Publishing UK

Copyright

Another Brother Shakespeare

Paperback ISBN 978-1-0682687-0-0

For Catherine
tendre muse et encre de mes mots

another brother Shakespeare

0

During the year 2021 an old building in Carter Lane, Southwark, London was being demolished. In the rubble of the building a worker noticed a bundle of very old papers wrapped in goatskin. When inspected the writers name was still visible – Edmund Shakespeare

William Shakespeare was one of four brothers. In the year 1595 William was thirty-one and his youngest brother Edmund, just fifteen.

Part one

A brother

Chapter one

Edmund stood on the Southwark shore and looked back across the river to the city beyond. Bigger than the cities he had seen while on tour, but more chaotic and troubled. The religious wars in the Continental northern states were basically settled. One side had won. Here in London the struggles continued. The losers wouldn't accept defeat. As the winners still felt threatened they became more strident and unforgiving.

The city across the water appeared to be all warehouses full of merchandise imported to feed the tastes of new consumers who took more than they needed in a search for pleasure. Rising above the warehouses, Edmund could see the many Church steeples, all reaching up as if to connect to a divine energy that might save the faithful from their inevitable doom. From afar, the city in the year of our Lord 1599 looked to be a solid mass of man's triumph. From close up the reality was very different.

Edmund

Oh brother, it seems it has come to this. I'm doing the writing – words scribbled on scraps of paper. So many thoughts all tangled within places and times. Is it thoughts that stop me sleeping or this fear that, with each cough my life is being atomised into vapour. Droplets of soul that stain my shirt and the crusty sheets that hang about me. The nights are dark but not dark enough. Even when I close my eyes, the visitors come to torments me. They burst out of the gloom and demand I answer. 'Why' is the essence of their inquisition. Each time the me in my dream tries to speak I lose my place in the drama and instantly another face appears. I have known them all although now it is hard to put names to the lined faces streaked with stage paint and spittle.

That it should come to this. Me who had so many plans, me now desperate to be heard before the worms you love to invoke, burst pudding like from my guts. I needed a brother, perhaps a father but certainly a hero who would lead me to safety. You failed me just as you now believe, I betrayed you. I may be as you once said, 'an unperfect actor on the stage' but the role I have played was partly penned by you. I think this was when I was fifteen, but I had been practicing my scenes since I first reached for your hand. I expected much more, and my child hunger was fed with nothing but your neglect. Oh brother.

My lodging here in Carter's Yard, Southwark is for me a cell. I can smell the muddy river and the stink of the unlicenced slaughterhouse at the end of the yard. The cockroaches march out in lines from the wainscotting to then scatter in their hunt for some filthy meal. They feed on what drops from my plate and the skin dust from my unwashed body. Even alive I am food for unspeakable creatures. If I die here, you had better find me quickly or there will be nothing but my bones to bury. I am tormented by horror.

I escaped here from Shoreditch leaving my creditors to curse all men from Warwickshire. My poverty is the mark of Cain that all can see, and it will not stay hidden. I look poor – I smell poor. It is a curse that, like the plague, warns purse holders to stay away. Can you understand brother? You who have a fat purse full of coin and properties listed in the register. While I cheat to feed myself, you brother, are a money lender. Not for me a small share in this pecuniary safety. Each day I have to lie and cheat to achieve a little bread and pot of porter. We share a family name and all that our father chose to put on the table, but those times are long gone and there is now nothing for me in Stratford. I cannot go back and for me there is just London or rather these few narrow streets that drain away hope and bodily fluids. Beasts in a sty live better than I for they feast on a bucket of swill a day and have a fat sow to rut with when their strength allows. Here I lie alone and slowly rot while my mind traverses all the roads I have passed along.

What price a brother? Do you remember our life in Henley Street? You left when I was about eleven or twelve. You had been my big brother all through my brief childhood years. While I grew into my first pair of breeches, you thrust yourself into teenage manhood. As I struggled to climb trees and read my lessons from a horn ABC book, you climbed the thighs of the village beauties and wrote poetry. You strode the streets carrying messages of business from our father, I followed. I watched as you broke hymen and hearts. But you married someone an age away from where I played and the world I knew. Moonfaced giggling country girls still would raise their skirts as you passed by, but at home a stern and maternal woman dressed in black was your wife. This was the first time I lost you. I was alone and cast adrift in the infinite space of my mind, I felt a death so profound I wished my life would end. You were my hero and my first love. I saw you tall in my childhood small. I reached for you, but you had moved away. I couldn't understand and pain became my world where I acted out a boyhood with my now imaginary brother, always present like a Holyland faith that delivered me nothing but anguish.

The cracked mirror in my room presents a picture that is no longer mine. The one in my memory is fairer with a skin smooth and white. Eyes that sparkled, wide full of energy. Lips soft and ready to kiss or be kissed. A woman's face that captured many a woman's heart. Nature's own hand painted. This is the me of memory. But the yellowed square glass now reflects too much pain and bitterness – too much Rhenish wine and tobacco. I have become the living image of your Aragon as he opens the silver casket.

Last night I dreamt of our mother – can I call her mother? Not one dream of course, my night was a grotesque parade of apparitions, each more upsetting that the one before. But mother gave me moments of ease – how many moments I do not know. Dreams are not burdened by the turning of the glass. The scenes could last hours or perhaps just seconds, there is no way to tell. It is a febrile world of misrule with no limits or boundaries. In my dream Mother smiled at me and bowed down to kiss my forehead. How old I was I don't know but she walked tall beside me and the grasses parted tickling my cheeks as we walked toward the river. This was our river, the clean soft Avon not the turgid Thames, carrier of all things foul that city dwellers choose to excrete from the habitations.

Mother led me on to where the fat cows had lain while chewing their cud. The long grasses flattened into a bedlike bower and here we stopped, Mother settling down gently like a large goose on her clutch of eggs. I explored the matted grass with my fingers, pulling out thick stems, finding the cups of last year's acorns and the occasional smooth stone deposited by the winter floods. Mother was talking – I could see her mouth move but no sound could I hear. It was a peaceful, comforting dream. I felt safe there on the grass with mother.

You took this from me brother when you took her and when you poured your filth onto me. You soiled my past and my future.

Chapter two

Edmund

My first solid memories from my childhood probably date from when I was just five. I have vague impressions from before this I could speak of, but I fear perhaps these are just memories of stories I have been told by Mother. She told me colourful vignette sagas of what I did and, when listened to twice or three times, the stories become almost real. When spoken of twice more, they became part of my 'reality.' But true or not I remember the day Hamnet and Judith became more than a story. On that day the family was very agitated. People rushed in and out of rooms. Angry words were spoken and nothing to me made much sense. The house seemed full of women. Father had gone out early and you brother, where were you? I don't know and don't remember seeing you for days. I was being ignored and no one heard my pleas for food. Before noon I stole into the forbidden, wonderfully smelling pantry and found a chunk of hard cheese. This I stuffed into my smock, and I crept out of the house. No one seemed to notice and certainly no one cared for me that day. It was around the Holy-Day for the Purification of Virgin Mary and our Henley Street was all mud, straw and wheel ruts. Whatever the unannounced festival at home, I knew I wasn't invited so I ran down the street to the then bare orchard that lies above the Croft. What exactly I did for the rest of the day has disappeared into a mass of nothingness as is the fate for most of our past. But when I returned home, this is where clarity returns. The house was full of people chatting, smiling and looking pleased. Mother was firmly in control and people would disappear upstairs to return a few minutes later. After half a dozen or so such visits Nancy, the house maid, noticed me and grabbed me by the hand. I think I was forcibly washed, and my hair tied before it was my turn to climb the stairs. Although I had no idea of what awaited me. I was pushed forward through the throng into the doorway of the small back bedroom. Here I was confronted by two small bundles of cloth propped against a pillow made from washed rags. I was introduced to Judith and Hamnet, babies I was told, newly born, my niece and nephew, your two new children. William Shakespeare and father to twins. Aunt Anne (the title she preferred me to use) was in the adjacent room and I didn't see her for a week or more. I learnt later that giving birth to twins is a barbarous event and she had suffered terribly as if an occupant of room Little Ease in the Tower of London. You would only hear of all this several weeks later when, without warning, you returned home.

What I was soon to realise was that suddenly I was no longer the focus of the family. My position as the novelty had been usurped. People had less patience with me and certainly showed less interest in my exploits. I had become something somehow less, not that I ever remember being very important.

It was not that I was bad at my studies, I loved reading, and I could pen as well as the best in the school. But grammar school was not about discovering books and enjoying word play, it was more about learning by rote. Memorising pages and pages of text and declaiming this aloud for the master in front of the whole school.

Each and every mistake punished by the strap and then the process was repeated the next day. I was constantly forced to submit to the rule of the master without question or descent. I learned that I was not good at submission. I failed in this. So, father had decided that school should finish and my path ahead should follow the route he took. I was to become a glover. To him the future of seven years apprenticeship seemed the obvious choice. He needed help in the workshop and at the end of seven years I would be able to become a partner in his business. It would be Shakespeare and Son. I was faced with what seemed to me a bleak future. The glove making business held no interest for me. Just the endless process of manufacturing leather goods for the middle-class hands of Stratford, but also it meant all my future would be a repeat of my past – Stratford, Stratford and more Stratford. I felt as if I was going to trapped by my family and by the only town I'd ever known. I cried silently many a night as I struggled to understand what had happened and to devise how I might escape to a world of adulthood where I was no longer the 'boy', always being sent on errands and always being told to listen, not speak.

This was where you brother, led me astray. You who now were rarely at home. You who I wanted to share my exploits, my teenage games and my discoveries. Although you were not in Stratford, your name was frequently spoken. Mother of course and, occasionally father would talk about you and how you were now working with a company of stage players somewhere in London. You put on entertainments for rich people and even wrote some dramas that were performed for a paying audience. They are proud of their son who once a month sent them a purse of money. Lots of money, more than could ever be earned making gloves. People in Stratford knew that William Shakespeare was getting rich in London and had many rich friends. Envious gossips told silly tales of money and how the Shakespeare's were buying land and soon they would own the whole town. Giggling girls would call to me as I walked by. If my brother Will was famous, then I was famous for being his brother. Many a kiss I have been given and a sight of a plump budding breast, due to being William's little brother

Chapter three

The only person not impressed by William was William's wife Anne. From under her black bonnet, Aunt Anne would scowl and say the playhouse was the devil's work and nothing righteous could come from the wages of sin. Sinful it may have been, but Anne still took half share of the sinful money sent to the Shakespeare's home from London.

It was Aunt Anne's dislike of the money that led Edmund to stealing from the purse. Each week when William Greenaway's cart would arrive in Stratford from London, he would be sent to see if there was a package from son William. When there was something for the family, Edmund would take this to his father, and John would count the coins and write the amounts in a small dark covered reckoning book he kept in a large oak chest placed under the staircase.

But later, before returning home with the package from London, Edmund would carefully untie the string, unwrap the cloth and open the package. He would 'liberate' one of two coins and then rewrap the package and take it on to his father. 'My coins' as he called them, would be hidden under a loose floorboard in his bedroom. If Aunt Anne believed the money 'sinful', he reasoned he would save her from some of this sin. A game yes but he could use this argument to defend himself if he were ever caught. Edmund's share of the wages of sin gradually increased and a few coins this little pile bought him more than just the occasional kiss and feel of a breast. He was amazed at how much pleasure his share in William's wages of sin could buy.

So here lay the inspirational pathway out of an apprenticeship Edmund didn't want, and he knew he would abandon long before it was completed. If his beloved brother William was able to leave his family and escape to London, then perhaps Edmund could follow his example. If one brother was able to make what seemed to be a fortune to Stratford dwellers, then surely another could do the same?

At school the boys had been told of Sir Hugh Clopton and how, as a youth not much older than Edmund, he had travelled to London. He was portrayed as an admirable and worthy man, and Edmund decided to make Sir Hugh and his brother William his exemplars. Edmund had a scrap of paper with William's latest address in the hamlet of Shoreditch which lay close to Bishopsgate, and with this he was certain he would be able to find him. Before leaving Stratford, Edmund wrote a letter to his mother and father telling them he was going to stay with his brother, to see if he could learn a trade with him at the playhouse. Edmund told them he would send another letter when settled in London. This was not him running away. In Edmund's mind he was just changing one family residence for another; his wealthy brother was sure to have enough space for him at his London home.

At this stage Edmund had no idea where London was or how long it might take to travel there. As the journey he intended was a secret he chose not to ask others who might know. Edmund had watched the twice monthly wagon from Greenaway rattle across the

Clopton Bridge on route for London. It always seemed to return about ten days later so his assumption was that the journey took less than a week. The idea of walking all the way to London was not attractive. Edmund believed he could have done this but as he had a small purse fatted with my stolen share of the wages of sin, Edmund hoped he could buy a place on the wagon. Master Greenaway was a businessman and carriage was his trade. While a boy was not a box or bundle, he could travel in the same way. As Edmund had anticipated, Greenaway accepted the proposition, particularly as Edmund improved his story by telling him William had requested he join him in London and specifically recommended he should ride as his passenger. Edmund paid for his passage, and it was agreed they would depart the following morning.

Edmund had just turned fourteen years when he first saw London. 'Saw' isn't perhaps the right word. What he saw was London in the distance from the heath at Hampstead. Looking to the south-east, there was a wonderous vista of rooftops all wreathed in whispers of yellowy smoke leaking from the thousands of chimneys. Fires creating warmth and cooking meals for the invisible population. Chimneys in the tens of thousands all sprouting crookedly upwards towards the sky like so many blackened tree trunks after a late summer wildfire.

Edmund looked from the chimneys to church spires. Hundreds of tributes to the almighty reaching for the heavens to help the faithful dream of something better than a life in the here and now. All this his eyes took in as he gazed towards what for most country folk might seem to be a mirage. A sort of painting on the wall behind the church altar. A small, coloured promise of paradise above The Doom.

All this Edmund saw, but at the time, he didn't really get to see London, just Norton Folgate and Shoreditch. He had come to find his brother William and to escape the tedium of Stratford. His Father had pushed him to become his apprentice in the glove business. As by now it was already clear to all that Edmund was ill suited to school study and the master of the grammar school had made it clear that he was a bad influence on the other boys. Edmund would not be welcomed back for the Michaelmas term.

Chapter four

The journey from Stratford had taken four days to reach Hampstead, and a couple of hours after the brief breakfast stop, the wagon finally reached the road called Bishopsgate and this was where he was to leave the security of Greenaway's transport and start out on foot. The packages sent by William were always marked as being collected from the stairs behind the sign of the White Horse Inn. With this brief address Edmund hoped he would not have too much of a problem. After just two enquires from people he passed in the street, a man dressed in impressive mallard green coloured suit of doublet and breeches, directed Edmund to a narrow alley that ran from beside the White Horse.

A muddy alley led to a small yard with galleries on two sides. Edmund mounted the staircase that rose up to the first floor and there were three doors, once painted black although now much of this covering had long peeled away from the timber leaving the knotted deal bare. On the right-hand door, he saw a small piece of card with 'Shakespeare' written in an elaborate hand. This was it and Edmund put his soft bag down and knocked a fist on the door. From somewhere inside he heard a gruff, 'Hola.'

Edmund opened the door to the room and slowly entered. The room was large and lit by one window that appeared to face east, allowing the morning sun to silhouette the figure of a man seated at a table with his back towards the door.

'Who are you and what do you want?'

Said the voice using the Warwickshire accent that was a match to Edmund's own.

'Brother William?'

He asked, although he felt certain it was in the right room. The man's head raised and after a brief pause, he turned to face the visitor.

'Edmund? Edmund is that you. By all the saints, how is it you here in London? Is father with you?'

'No brother, it is just me, I came on my own to see you – to see the playhouse and all that is yours here in the city.'

William's face showed surprise and perhaps something else that was not exactly what Edmund expected. William didn't look pleased. Perhaps Edmund expected he would get up and embrace him and he would again feel the prickle of his beard on his cheeks, but no, William remained seated, and the embarrassing silence made Edmund pause close by the still open door.

At last, he spoke, and the sibling reunion commenced. Edmund told him about the journey from Stratford with Master Greenaway and about how his schooling had stopped. Edmund told him about how their father had expected him to become his apprentice in the glove making business. Edmund told William he preferred to come to London and join him and his company of players.

'How old are you, surely not yet fourteen years?'

'No not fourteen until next spring but I am old enough to work in the business of the playhouse and perhaps here I can make my fortune.' There was another pause and William put down the pen he still held, and he placed an ink spotted cloth over the scattered papers that covered the tabletop. William stared at Edmund and then, at last, he saw the familiar smile that for him had lit up his childhood and were part of his earliest memories. William, the man of business and a poet who then talked to the young visitor about the taverns of Stratford, was Edmund's brother and the person he most loved.

'Well Edmund, as you are here, put your bag in the hallway and I will get something to eat – it is nearly lunchtime, and I didn't have breakfast.'

William went out onto the gallery and yelled to a boy sitting unseen on a chair by the staircase. Food was ordered and, after a short delay, they both ate from a cold ham with hunks of warm bread. A jug of porter completed the fare and gradually Edmund felt reassured that all would be well. Following the meal, William showed Edmund the rooms that made up his apartments. There was the large sitting room with the table he had already seen, which appeared to double as William's writing room. Edmund had never before seen so much paper, some loose and some in rolls, some tied with blue ribbon, and some tied with string. From a narrow hallway there were two more rooms, the largest was a bedroom complete with a low slung double sized bed, curtained and covered by a dirty grey canopy. A large pottery basin and jug stood on the dark oak chest of drawers. Edmund also noticed a heavy round topped chest with brass bands and strong lock occupying the space at the foot of the bed. Although not mentioned by William, Edmund's thoughts immediately flew to possibility that here was the depository of the gold Sovereigns and Royals, William drew from before adding them to packages that made the journey to Stratford.

Edmund followed his brother, and he could not fail to notice that the playwright had become more rounded than when he last saw him. His belly pushed against his waist band and his hands seemed puffed and his rings dug tight into the soft flesh. William was not the country boy Edmund still saw so clearly in his nighttime dreams. William was now more something of this decedent city where men can become rich by sitting long hours before a desk. And the ink stains. Edmund had never noticed these before but now William's thumb, fore and index fingers of his right hand were stained black with pen ink. The sleeve of his linen shirt was spatted in the same colour, and Edmund realised this perhaps marked him out as one of the class of clerics who are paid to write out or copy words for others to read.

The siblings returned to the parlour room and William seated himself in the large captain's chair that seemed to be fixed on to a swivel base. A piece of heavy damask cloth loosely covered the seat. His throne where he commanded the room and anyone who was granted an audience.

'Well, Edmund, you have seen my residence and my place of work – they are one and the same. Not quite as spacious as our home in Henley Street.'

'No, brother but I like it and it seems you are comfortable here far away from tutting women and bawling brats.'

'Ha! you have it there, but there is a price to be paid when a reckoning is done. Here I have a certain liberty, but I continue to be bound by responsibilities to the family. But Edmund, why have you come? What do you expect to find here?.'

'Brother, I expected to find you – and I have. In Stratford I felt more and more lost. It was as if I was alone deep in the dark Warwickshire woods and although there were well trodden pathways leading from glade to glade, each one seemed the same as the last. None led me out. I didn't know which way to turn.'

'So, Edmund you have turned up here. But you must understand you cannot stay. You must return home to father in Stratford.'

This was not what Edmund wanted to hear and not the words of the brother he had loved from his first steps taken towards the world outside. The brother Edmund had mentally bonded with as he grew and for the days and nights of childhood. The William who took Edmund in a boat to punt on the river; the William who taught him to catch rabbits; the William who would let him drink from his tankard. His words were not what Edmund expected. Edmund started to feel an anger like a volcano churning hot inside a prison of granite rock. Edmund stared and thought of things he might say to change his mind. Clever things that might make a difference. Things that would hurt William and make him feel something of Edmund's pain.

Edmund didn't remember anything else from that day. The fatigue of the journey and the dark cloud that descended to choke his happiness combined and he slept on a cot bed that lay behind a curtain in the smallest room filled with boxes of musty smelling clothes that he took to be costumes from the playhouse.

In the morning when Edmund awoke, he found that he was alone. William had already left, and Edmund discovered a note propped on the mantle above the small hearth where there were the remains of a coal fire. William was perhaps at a rehearsal, and he left a silver shilling to pay for a breakfast from the Inn below.

Edmund had slept deeply and as he emerged from slumber; his dream had been of Stratford. The long days of jolting on Greenaway's wagon were lost somewhere in the future and the dreams were of soft grass and a slow-moving stream filled with hungry Tench. But the sounds coming from the courtyard and the smells – cleared his head of a rural home and the reality of Shoreditch made its presence felt. This was a brave new world and one still undiscovered although nearby. William's written note and his silver coin were tokens of the new order that awaited. While alone, Edmund was content to have the liberty to explore the rooms and poke into the cupboards and drawers. He opened stoneware jars and pine boxes absorbing all the little clues that might reveal part of the story of his playwright brother. This London brother was not quite the same as the one he had loved in Stratford. Here he seemed remote and old. The brother of Edmund's childhood was a teller of tales and a character of the forest full of light and sap.

After slowing sensing his way through the three rooms like a hound searching for a trail, Edmund decided it was time to see what a silver coin might produce in the way of breakfast. Edmund exited the apartment and walked down the stairs and through an open doorway that seemed to lead inside the Inn. The stone flags were well worn and scattered with dirty thresh that hadn't been swept from the night before. Edmund had to step over broken glass and the ugly contents of someone's stomach. The room was dark, and it smelt strongly of spilt ale, tobacco and stale sweat. On a large table of rough timber, he saw a collection of pewter tankards and a firkin cask, perhaps ready for the next herd of customers who would probably arrive in the afternoon. Edmund lifted a heavy tankard and looked at a name clumsily scratched into the soft metal. Kit? Perhaps but it wasn't clear.

'Hey boy, put that down. The man who drinks from it would sooner have it clean rather than befouled by your fingers'

The voice was sharp but tuneful – a woman's voice, strong and commanding. Edmund placed the tankard back into the ranks of grey soldiers and turned towards the unseen challenger. A woman with flashing wide eyes and a large mouth, like a golden carp in a pond, held a broom in her hand. Her strong arms were bare, and her hair was pinned up on the top of her head. This woman was not like the women of Stratford. She moved closer and Edmund wasn't sure what impressed him first; the smell of raw onions or the bounce of her barely covered breasts? She was both frightening and wonderous. Both a fantasy and a nightmare. This was no blushing maiden. This woman could devour Edmund whole.

He searched deep for courage and spoke with a voice of someone still uncertain of his status.

'I hoped I could have something to eat.'

'Breakfast, is it? We may have something left. Sit there and I will go find you something. Do you have money?

Edmund showed the shilling William had left, and he was promptly told this would buy both breakfast and a good dinner. Edmund realised that this London world was completely new to him and different from the life in Stratford. There he always had his meals at home. Edmund neither had money nor needed money. His Mother brought food from the market, and this was added to that the family grew in their gardens. Food appeared on the table, and Edmund ate his fill. His Mother, Aunt Anne or Joan prepared the meals. Susanna or Judith prepared the table. Sometimes they all sat together on the heavy settle with father at the head of the table. But mostly Edmund ate on his own as the school day measured the hours as much as the sun. And everyone used this excuse to bully him with sharp words and blunt thumps. Edmund was always being told he was late, or he needed to hurry. Edmund was told he was lazy. Edmund was told he wasn't as clever as brother William. The words and slaps were like horse flies in summer, ever present and annoying but not deadly. Edmund learnt to brush them off. But home was safe, it was always there, the thing he awoke to in the morning and the place he saw last as he blew out the bedside candle.

The madam of the tavern returned, and before Edmund, she placed on the table, a bowl of porridge, a chunk of coarse looking bread, a chunk of cheese and some butter. She told him to hurry as she had to go out before the lunchtime customers arrived. The words were just like home, but the food wasn't. There seemed to be grit both in the porridge and the bread and the butter appeared to be better suited to greasing cart axles. Despite this the woman took Edmund's shilling and dumped some dirty coins back as change. Edmund did as was instructed and ate quickly. There was nothing worth savouring in this place. London had to have more to offer me than this and London was out there somewhere.

Part 2

Players

Chapter five

Edmund lay back on the sagging cot, his head busy repeating the conversations of the past few hours. Things were not as he anticipated. He had expected his brother to have welcomed him and been pleased by his arrival. Edmund felt hurt and frightened. William of Shoreditch was not the same as William of Stratford. What had happened? What had he done to somehow lose his brothers love?

Stratford seemed far away, more than just by miles. Stratford was an old book, now closed, finished with and cast aside to lie on the dirty thresh, growing mildew and feeding small mice who live in the dark world behind the wainscotting. He couldn't go back: wouldn't go back despite the instructions of his brother. If London had provided opportunities for William, then surely the same London would hold similar prospects for him. They were both Shakespeares and had both learned their letters and grammars in the same school room, sitting at the same desks and they had both felt the same leather strap of encouragement. While William was undoubtedly the better pen man and poet, Edmund was the better orator. When Edmund stood before the class and was instructed to declaim memorised passages from Virgil or Ovid, he received praise and he believed, with this skill he could charm or corrupt a listener. If William now didn't see him as a beloved brother, Edmund believed he could still prove himself worthy of love. As he revolved all this over and over in his mind, the sound of the outside door opening forced the real world back into view.

'Who's there? Is it you William?'

There was no reply, but he could hear lightly trod footsteps approaching across the floorboards outside. The bedroom door slowly opened, and a figure stood silhouetted against the strong morning light.

'I beg your pardon sir; I didn't know Master Shakespeare had a guest. I merely came to return some pages to him and thought the apartments were unoccupied.'

The voice seemed young with a pleasant lilting tone that suggested the speaker was both well-schooled and friendly.

'Brother William has left for the day, and I don't know when he may return. But leave the pages and I will give them to him.'

The visitor seemed to pause before speaking, moving to lean casually against the open-door frame, neither leaving or entering the room.

'His brother! I know of no brother except Gilbert, and you are most certainly not he. You look too young to be a brother.'

'I am Edmund Shakespeare and William is my brother. My age is not fixed and will advance with his until one of us fall prey to disease or time. And who are you, page carrier?'

The visitor laughed and tapped his foot on the floor in a dancing beat.

'You have spirit sirrah Edmund and indeed you speak with the confidence of a Shakespeare. There is Warwickshire dirt on your tongue and fire in your chest. I am called Christopher Beeston, and I am a player on the stage.'

Edmund looked hard at this young man who now had brought something new into his life – a player on the stage. This was something from the world of William and it had arrived unexpected but just at the right time. This might be a gateway to a better friendship. Chris Beeson, at first sight appeared to be no older than Edmund. He was a slim youth with greasy lank hair, a small nose resting above a delicate wide mouth. He was dressed in clothes that appeared to belong to someone else being too long, too wide and too colourful.

'I am pleased to make your acquaintance Master Beeson. Meeting a friend of my brother is a happy occasion.'

'Friend! Ha, this is a bold suggestion to be sure indeed. Master Shakespeare is a playwright and soon to be a shareholder in the playhouse nearby. I am a mere boy actor who survives due to the roles written for those of us who can ape lady-parts. I serve his pen and occasionally do his bidding.'

Edmund saw his mistake and smiled as he digested the imagery created by the words he had just heard.

'Any friend or servant of brother William is welcome, and I hope you will tell me more about the stage and these 'lady parts.'

They both laughed and Beeson doffed his cap with a flourish. Edmund raised himself from the bed and, together they moved into the main room. Beeson quickly seated himself in the chair William had used the day before, there at the generous sized table, where layer upon layer of paper carpeted the surface. He had a broad smile on his face and Edmund could see he was relishing the chance to enthrone himself and assume the regal role of playwright. Edmund looked around the room and realising that this was the only chair, he drew the heavy, metal banded chest closer and perched himself like a frog on a Lilypad.

'Tell me about being a player on the stage as William has told me very little. I have only just arrived here in Shoreditch from Stratford, and William was seldom with us more than a couple of days at a time since he became successful. I am keen to learn about the playhouse and I hope perhaps there might be something there for me. I seek to escape a life of delivering silly gloves or trading greasy wool.'

Beeson studied this boy on the box. Like himself, slim with well-shaped legs and delicate facial features. Beeson was well skilled in assessing the qualities of a man, particularly one who matched his age and who had fair hair full of loose curls.

'As I told you, I am a jobbing player, sometime referred to as a boy actor. I live nearby in a house, close to Burbage's theatre. There are ten of us, all boys and ready to pull on a frock and wig to meet the needs of the afternoon audience. There is a good trade for us, as London now has many playhouses. The playwrights create the stories of power, blood and lust and we players are the flesh and breath used to fatten the thin black lines into visual drama. There are Kings and Queens, soldiers and lovers, women and girls. The latter are where we come in – we the boy actors provide the human shape that feeds the imagination – sometimes base but always tempting. Only last week I played the girl Lavinia in your brother's play Titus Andronicus. My performance made the audience gasp as I was ravished and my tongue was cut out. Some they cried for my pain – some just lusted enjoying the thrill of cruelty.'

This young man smiled at Edmund, and he felt his gaze peel away the layers of Stratford schooled naivety to find who knows what, beneath. Although of the same age, Edmund sensed Christoper had graduated from a type of college where books were only part of the lessons. Christopher was possessed of a knowledge which, like a tool in the hands of a craftsman, he shaped the external illusion others saw. He possessed a maturity that Edmund still the boy, longed to achieve.

'Are there many boy actors earning a living at the playhouse?'

'There are enough to play all the afternoon women twice over but the best of us are rarely without employment. We are valued both on and off the stage.'

'It seems strange to me that you and the other boys are happy to pull on a frilly frock and paint your faces, walking the walk like harlots on the stage in front a crowd of men.'

Christopher frowned and looked slightly annoyed by Edmund's comment.

'We are the living inheritors of the once enjoyed Coventry Mystery plays. We are skilled professionals who dress in coloured robes, wear powdered wigs, and perform with grace and poise for a paying audience. Other men dressed such as we, once did something similar, performing the Latin mass before the Anglican clergy outlawed such entertaining rituals. But we boy actors who take to the playhouse stage have nothing to seek forgiveness for, although when some of our number are defrocked, like with corrupted priests, temptation may sometimes triumph. A broad smile lifted Christoper's boy like face, and this broke the tension between them. Laughter releases so much healing.

'Edmund, you appear to need to learn more about what we boy actors do upon the public stage. Settle back and let me explain. Boys playing women is not some silly game performed for our personal amusement. We are as vital to the play as Burbage and Heminges, and although they appear as Kings and Lords, as in the real world, it is the Queens and Ladies who provide life's balance. The audience sees as well as hears and although most of the great speeches and soliloquies Shakespeare and the others pen are given to the male characters, it is often our presence that is remembered when the crowd leaves the playhouse. We boy actors playing Queen Margaret, girl Lavinia or Lady Anne are the pleasing spirit they see when they close their eyes. The powerful illusions we create are not reliant on the lines we mouth; it is the visual presence. The audience believe what they see, and our art is to paint a pleasing, moving image of girls and woman. We are living symbols of what men believe women to be. Not the real women they live with every day, but the imaginary women of men's make believe.'

'I think I understand Chris, although I find it hard to believe men are that foolish.'

'Oh, they are! Your brother knows this well. This is why whenever love between man and woman is the theme, the play is a comedy. Once man is in love with a woman, men are shown to be powerless fools who dance at the command of their desire and lusts. Man is easily seduced and seldom aware of what is happening. A real woman on the stage would be much too dangerous.'

Both boys laughed perhaps nervous that they were sharing secrets.

'Edmund, have you seen the Armada portrait of Queen Gloriana?'

'Yes, I have. One arrived at Stratford on tour, and we queued to see it at the Guildhall.'

'It is a fine brave painting of her Majesty, God bless her. But the painting is all symbols and dreams. The image is not of a natural woman or common place Lady, the type you might encounter at the market or praying devotions in a church. The Queen of the picture is an illusion, a performance that feeds our dreams and inspires love and sacrifice. Do you comprehend my lesson?'

'I think I am starting to, but now I fear I will be unable to play woman if my role is more than just a comedic diversion.'

'You will manage – you have all nature's gifts pleasing to the eye. What you now need to learn is how to move like woman. We will school you in all the hand movements, the head tilts, the expressions and smiles that represent a gentle woman. Remember this that although all the words we say on the stage belong to the playwrights, all the movements are our own. From today master Edmund, I want you to watch women, how they move: observe the arts of their gender.'

Chapter six

The following day Edmund accompanied Christopher for his first visit to the house of boys.

'Master Edmund, let me introduce you to my friends and fellow boy actors – know we here are all honest and true – with the exception of perhaps Charlie there.'

As Chris pointed out a small skinny boy, his smile broadened, and the group of boys laughed and playfully punched and pulled the Charlie targeted by the jest. Edmund blushed but did as he was expected, performing a deep bow with dramatic arm sweep worthy of the public stage. Chris continued as master of ceremonies.

'My fellow actors, I present to you a would-be apprentice ready for our schooling. Look to him and tell what you see – will a London audience accept him?'

There was a pause and the imaginary sound of many boys thinking. Edmund felt nervous and he avoided meeting the gaze of the group before him.

'My opinion sir is that Edmund has a 'woman's face with nature's own hand painted', a fair youth indeed, one worthy of Shakespeare.'

The boys hooted and laughed, and the speaker looked well pleased with himself. Edmund, relieved by the 'fair' comment, didn't understand the reason for the laughter and his frown signalled his puzzlement. Chris patted Edmund's shoulder giving him a necessary token of support.

'George there, was quoting a line from some private sonnets penned by your famous brother – we have had sight of them and the boys know several by heart. But the important judgement from this is we believe you my friend, if you study well, you will prosper. You have nature's gift of a pretty face and fair golden locks – We see a regular Adonis fit for the chase by any would-be lusty Venus or Apollo.'

The boys applauded and there were shouts of hurrah. They were a band of brothers and like all boys, they regarded life as a game and now there was a new player for the team. If life in London was dangerous, there was safety in being part of a gang and each one knew when a threat arrived, they would, together overcome.

After the introduction the boys settled back into the private chat that had been their activity prior to Edmund's arrival. Some boys grouped close to lit candles reading from rolls of paper that contained the written parts they needed to learn for tomorrow's rehearsals. A couple of boys moved off to a corner where they read aloud a dialogue between two characters. The room was now a workshop and salon where the boy actors lived and practiced their art. It was a community where the craft of acting was the constant and the energy of discovery united them in a fellowship stronger than any fierce schoolmaster or overlord could hope to produce.

'So, what do you think Edmund. Would you like to join us?'

Christoper appeared serious, perhaps knowing what might lay ahead for any new apprentice. But Edmund wasn't just any boy escaping a troubled home life. Edmund was Shakespeare's kid brother and William Shakespeare was the rising star playwright of the London stage. Shakespeare was friend to theatre owners and patrons of arts. He was known to socialise with Lords and Officers of the State. Shakespeare presented entertainments for the Queen. Edmund wasn't just anyone, he was someone with connections. Christopher assumed that Shakespeare would approve of Edmund joining the boy actors. An innocent mistake.

'Yes, is my answer. I wish to join you, and I pledge I will study hard to prance, lisp and sway – I will be woman, at least for all the afternoon hours at the playhouse.'

Christopher removed his glove and their handshake completed the deal. Two boys playing a man's game – tutor and student. Edmund felt a heady mixture of nervous excitement and purpose. He now knew what he wanted and how he was to achieve it. The doubt and chastisement of recent years would stop. No more grammar school. No more lectures from father about laziness or stupidity. No more gloves to deliver or bales of skins and wool to load on and off carts. If Stratford was childhood, Shoreditch was freedom.

Chapter seven

It was early evening when William returned to his lodgings in Shoreditch. Edmund was laying on the cot bed and trying to read by the light of a cheap candle that had neither the strength of wick nor quality of fat to burn brightly. He had found some pages of a play still in draft, something about Richard Duke of York. William banged the outer door closed and Edmund heard him feel his way to the table where he knew a lantern to have been left. Edmund could hear things fall as the hands, blind in the dark, struggled to light the wick. William was a little worse for having supped too long at the tavern. Either ale or wine now led him, and the alcohol proved to be a poor guide in a storm.

'William? Brother, how fair you?'

Shakespeare grunted as he recognised the young voice that pierced his privacy and reminded him, he had a guest – an unwelcome witness from his Stratford family home.

'You still here, are you? I thought by now you would either have returned to Stratford or be drowned in Shoreditch. What have you done with your day?'

'London is a brave new world for me. There are more people walking in the two streets below than I have ever seen in all of Stratford'

'Yes, people here are more numerous than ants on a Henley Street dung hill. The trick is to avoid all the ones that sting.'

'Christopher Beeson, I assume is safe?'

'Chris, safe! I wish you a better fellow for a playmate, but he is not a thief.'

'I will take that as a mark of approval from someone who makes his living by writing poetic judgement on his fellow creatures.'

Edmund then recounted the details of his day to his brother who appeared preoccupied and more than a little uncomfortable. Edmund told of his conversations and how Christopher had taken him to the boys' rooms at the tenement building alongside the ruins of the Holywell Priory. He had met with the old watchkeeper and been shown the outside of Burbage's playhouse. The boys had all been absent and Chris had told him rehearsals were held in the mornings and most of the boys had roles to learn and movements to practice. Edmund had been impressed at what he had heard, and he now understood that boys of his age here were free from parents and enriched by earnings as actors.

'Why, when you visited us in Stratford, did you not tell me of how I might here share in your good fortune? The playhouse seems an exciting life and if Christopher can play the woman and pay his way to fortune, I am sure I could do the same.'

'No Edmund, this is not for you. There are things you do not know and things best you avoid. I know all and you must leave these dreams and return to Stratford. This is not to be your life.'

Edmund responded to critical words of his brother in the way all younger siblings respond. Edmund fought and spoke with youthful passion only to find himself countered again and again by resolute blocking by a seemingly parental voice sixteen years his senior. Either the effect of the Ale or adult arrogance, moved William to ignore the pleas of the youth who had glimpsed what he believed to be paradise but was now told he could not enter. As Edmund's anger increased, William retreated behind a wall of disinterest. He picked up his pen and scratched word after word on a scrap of paper. After many crossings and ink blots, sixteen lines formed from the mind of Shakespeare. As Edmund sensed he had lost both the argument and his brother's attention, he noticed noises of a nasal snore had now replaced words of rebuke. William had fallen asleep at the table. Edmund lent over his older brother and removed the pen from his hand. He looked at the words and recognised them as a sonnet. Edmund took the sonnet, folded the sheet in half and placed it inside his doublet.

Another three days passed since Edmund arrived at his brother's lodging in Shoreditch. The daylight hours had been spent talking to Christopher and the other boy actors in the dilapidated tenement close by the playhouse. He had watched them learn their lines and their cues; rehearse their entrances and their exits. They had shared and laughed together. He now felt comfortable as one of their company. The comparison between their lives as a band of actors and his, a boy living as one of the Shakespeare family in Henley Street, was stark. The boy actors were free to choose how they spent their days. They had freedom and they expressed this by drinking ale, smoking tobacco and flirting with the pretty girls of the neighbourhood. In Stratford, Edmund was forced to attend school and when not learning lessons spoken by long dead voices from the Holyland, Greece or Rome, he was the servant to his father, commanded to unload, stack, deliver and fetch. One was a life for a gentleman of England the other that of a serf. Edmund knew the difference and now he had tasted the food of freedom there was no way he would accept the crumbs Henley Street provided. Edmund was now hungry for better, and he looked towards his new life.

He had not spent much time with his brother following their heated discussion about the boy actors. William left home mid-morning and didn't return until long after sunset. He appeared to have much business somewhere off in London as his shoes and stockings were always befouled with the animal waste of city streets when he returned. He ate his meals out and supped heartly before climbing the stairs to the apartment. As Edmund slept late each morning, he didn't observe how William spent each day. After waking, William would sit at the table and write line after line of dialogue between imaginary characters. The pens wore down quickly, such was the speed of the playwright. Words on paper scratched out by soft hands holding cheap goose quills. The floor beneath the table was littered with cuttings and scraps of crumpled paper. While Edmund slumbered, Kings struggled to save crowns of gold and brother betrayed brother for positions of power. Each morning's drama was quietly shaped in the ink lines until William felt himself drained and ready to put the pen back on the stained tabletop. He would then reach over for a square of muslin cloth and lay this over pages and table, signifying a pause in the process and allowing William to once more escape the world he alone had created. When Edmund shuffled into the room there was little evidence that his brother had been industrious. Edmund had little chance to understand the mind of a man haunted by his creative gift and tortured by the spirits of his own invention.

But this, the fourth morning since he arrived was to be different. Just before noon Edmund heard voices on the stairway, and he realised his brother was returning. The door opened and two familiar shaped men entered. The first, the stocky outline of William, the second a thin man smelling strongly of floral scent. Somewhere in Edmund's mind this smell triggered a memory. He had smelt this before.

'Infectum caput! Jump up lad and come embrace me.'

The man moved closer and now free from the silhouette; Edmund recognised the friendly face of Richard Field from Stratford.

'Wet-Head, it is good to see you here so far from the Avon and your home.'

Edmund gave the man a brief hug and he welcomed the familiar address of someone he had known since he was a small boy.

'What is this foolery, silly names that have no authority or logic.' William spoke across the two jolly friends, neither understanding nor sharing their joke.'

'Wet-Head is my nickname for Edmund. Many times, I have met Edmund heading home, all dripping with the water of our sweet Avon. During the long summer days, after school, Edmund would swim in the river just below the bridge. He would shake his wet hair as he passed me and hence the nickname. Many a day I would chase him off and cuff him with my glove.'

'Ah, I see now. I have spent so much time away from Stratford, the daily rituals and exchanges are a mystery to me. I didn't know you two shared secrets.'

Richard Field and Edmund laughed together and stood separate from the stern playwright as he settled himself in the chair and swivelled it to face them. After a few more exchanges, William coughed, and it became clear he wanted to talk of something heavier than summer swimming.

'I brought Master Field here as he has a task for you Edmund. Since his business as a printer keeps him in the city, I suggested you would carry an important letter for him back to Stratford. His uncle needs the document and it best be carried by someone we can trust.'

'Me return to Stratford? I hadn't intended to go back yet. I have only just arrived.'

'There is nothing here for you Edmund, I've already told you this. You will return to Stratford and complete your schooling. Mother and father will want you back and father needs your help with his business. It is all settled, and I have paid Greenaway for your place on his wagon. You leave tomorrow morning.'

Edmund listened to the pronouncement from his elder brother, and he clenched his fists as he struggled to contain his anger. His brother was dismissing him and shattering his hopes, throwing him back into the world he believed he had escaped. As William had recruited Richard Field as an ally, this had strengthened his position and made any rebellion by Edmund difficult. A public argument between brothers was not something Edmund expected or something he was prepared to cause. William had chosen the moment, and he was in a position of power. For Edmund to fight authority in front of a family friend from Stratford would be shameful and Edmund understood that for now he was beaten. This might be the close of Act One but there would be time for another two acts before the play would end.

Chapter Eight

Edmund

The road from London is almost reluctant to leave the city. The climb to Highgate and then Hampstead suggests terrors to come. Mud ruts and boulders combine to attack the wagon wheels. Casks and sacks roll together and then lean for security. What is proper for merchandise is an ordeal for me and the gentle citizens of the Commonwealth. A journey north creates an intimacy few would choose. We are jostled together, shoulder against shoulder - arms touching, hips touching hip momentarily until embarrassed, we struggle away. Breathing the expelled breath pungent from bad teeth and decaying pickled herring. Gaseous waste that insults the beautiful delusion that man is made in God's image.

Being back home in Stratford is a little like awaking after a wonderful dream. I look around and I recognise a familiar setting. It is all exactly as it was just before I shut out the light. I rub my eyes to clear the pillow dust of the night, and I try to focus on the nearest-most things, the remains of last night's candle, a half empty drinking cup of water. All this is mundane and a grey washed reality, instead of what still flashes colourful in my recent memory. Something else, not quite complete, but live enough for me to question if it was real. Another place, another time where I floated just moments before.

This is how it was after I arrived back in Henley Street. Shoreditch was still blazing like a fire inside my heart. I wanted to close my eyes and return to the dream.

I am still angry with brother William. What have I done to deserve his rejection? Last I saw him here we played together by the river. He sat on a tree stump and sang some song from a play he was writing. I hunted for frog's spawn amongst the reeds. He held my hand as we walked back along the winding path to Henley Street. I was happy. How long ago was this? It is difficult to know. I remember it so clearly but this, 'my' William, was slim and clean shaven. The William who sent me away was heavy waisted and had a lawyer's beard, sharp trimmed, marked with yellow stains of tobacco.

Why has my Stratford brother become the mean stranger of Shoreditch? What have I done to deserve being cast away like some mangy dog? I don't feel good, and I don't want to be the Edmund that mother and father demand. They seem to me ugly, unfeeling people. No, that's not correct. They do feel but that feeling is impatience and intolerance. They demand obedience and everything must be now. They don't want to hear me or share my wins or losses of the day. To them I am merely a servant who fails to do as they instruct. I am the bad boy who always gets it wrong. The twins Hamnet and Judith grin at me and get every kiss and warm cake while I get just the cold crust off yesterday's loaf. I won't stay here long. I deserve better and I refuse to be slave to a greasy wool dealer.

When I arrived back in Stratford, I delivered Richard's letter to his uncle in Tanners Street. He was happy to see me and grateful I had brought some deeds to a property that had been had purchased as a shared investment. He rewarded me with a golden sovereign and this I added to my secret purse. Brother William had also entrusted me with two of his leather bags. One was for father, and it contained money to purchase a couple of profitable tithes just outside of Shottery. The other bag was for Aunt Anne. This one contained money to fund household expenses. Before I handed it over, I removed two in every ten coins as my 'fee.' It was amusing to hear Aunt Anne curse her husband when she opened the purse and counted out the money she believed she had been given to fund the family over the next quarter. Anne accused William of wasting his earnings on high living and luxuries trying to appear a gentleman in front of his London friends. This while her costs for food in Stratford had all risen due to the continuing wars with Spain and poor harvests.

Chapter Nine

In the weeks that followed his return to Stratford, Edmund settled back into the routine of school, helping his father and performing errands for his mother. Had anyone of the family been observant, they may have noticed he seldom spoke and while obedient to the commands he had been given, he showed little enthusiasm or joy. Edmund, although just a boy of fifteen, seemed to have aged and he now appeared to carry a heavy emotional weight. The green shoots of knowledge that recently broke ground, could perhaps have inspired industry or a rush toward excellence. But in the soil of Henley Street, the sap was somehow blocked in his veins and any budding fruit dried up turning to dark canker. Boys at school chatted behind his back telling each other that Edmund was moody and no fun anymore. The fair youth who before had inspired sighs and giggles from the girls of Stratford, now acquired another male feature that made him even more desirable. The more melancholy he appeared to be, the more the girls chose to believe they alone could be the one who could make him smile. To the girls, Edmund was a deep vessel full of an exotic cargo of human emotion. The more he ignored their winks, their calls and teases, the greater their fantasy that Edmund was the boy of their dreams. A beautiful youth with a tortured, misunderstood soul.

At first Edmund was blind to how the girls watched him as he walked alone along the streets of Stratford. He sometimes saw them looking in his direction, but he failed to understand their animal responses to his dark mood.

It was about this time, fate intervened to light a pathway for him. One afternoon when the house was quiet and all the family occupied elsewhere, Edmund decided to explore some large wooden chests that were stacked, one on top of the other, behind a curtain in the bedroom used by Aunt Anne and his brother. He found the topmost chest was full of clothes, mostly items once worn by the twins but now all too small. Edmund had hoped to find money or something valuable, something saleable. Nothing there satisfied this desire. In the chest below he found papers, hundreds of papers, some loose and some held together by strips of leather – in the home of a glover there was always leather cuttings ready for unexpected usage. Edmund looked at some of the topmost papers and he recognised the penmanship of his brother. Here were the workings of another Shakespeare craftsman. Not gloves but verses and even some complete plays. One particular bundle of sheets looked interesting, and Edmund took them out and settled himself back on the floorboards to read. On the outer wrapper were the words, 'Henry the sixth' and this title kindled a remembrance of a sometime past winter evening when once, William read aloud to the family by the light of the fire. This was long before when William still shared his work and seemed to look for approval.

Edmund read a few lines on the first page and quickly turned the sheet over. Then the next and on and on, as he looked for anything he might remember. Kings, Dukes, battles; page after page. Then one name called his attention, Joan la Pucelle, a woman. As he read some of the dialogue between this daughter of a shepherd and the French Dauphin, in the gloom of the late afternoon, a bright idea formed in Edmund's mind. Here on this page was a role for a boy actor. Although in Stratford, Edmund was his father's drudge, perhaps he could use this near dead time to learn a female's part – something to help him towards a better life. He thought of Christopher and the house in Shoreditch.

Edmund, over the next few days, before sleeping, read the play pages he had found amongst his brother's papers. This handwritten play was a history, full of strutting nobles speaking words of anger before wildly swinging their stage swords. The part of Joan le Pucelle was an oddity in that, although she was introduced as a shepherd's daughter, she quickly pulled on a suit of armour and fought with the skill of a trained warrior. And despite the title of maid, in Edmund's opinion, Joan had been written more man than woman. Edmund regarded this as unrealistic but then the play script did suggest Joan was some sort of witch. This Joan was manly, and Edmund felt quite comfortable about this his first attempt at a woman's part. Both shepherds' daughter and witch were female and Edmund quietly mouthed her part as the candle flickered and the rest of the family slept. He easily imagined himself in armour heroically leading the French forces against the best England could muster.

His nightly study was just one element of his self-managed actor apprenticeship. If he was to present woman on stage, he would need to move like a woman and stand like a woman. Even as a fifteen-year-old boy, Edmund knew there was a difference between how he and the other boys appeared in front of others and how women and girls posed themselves like mobile statues. He knew there was a difference, but he couldn't explain it to himself. What to do? Edmund revolved the problem over in his mind. Perhaps this was where the ever giggling and love-struck girls of Stratford could be used as his study text?

The next day, following school and after he had delivered the gloves made by his father, Edmund went back to the High Street. There he seated himself on a broken, upturned barrel that had been discarded by the owner of the Angel Inn. From this position he held a commanding view of the main throughfare of the town. From here he could watch everyone and anyone as they passed by. The fat farmers and shuffling clerics were not of interest but just as he was becoming bored with the disappointing visual show, four teenage girls appeared, strolling arm in arm. They walked slowly by, chatting to each other and frequently glanced over in his direction. Edmund watched the girls, and the girls watched Edmund. To Edmund the girls had a movement like large cats on the prowl. They displayed the poetry of a fluid bodily sway, with heads held almost motionless. This was going to be difficult. For the girls, Edmund seemed a beauty too sad to move. He was a vision of Adonis just descended from Olympus. This was going to be difficult. Neither impression was very close to the truth. Both too much influenced by the colour of romance to render them clear or human. However, what was true, the girls were animals on the prowl though Edmund was the real predator.

Edmund returned to his seat the next evening and the next. Rather than just four girls promenading and returning his gaze, the passage of forty-eight hours had been enough for the number of girls to multiply. To the four girls of the first day were now added an additional two couples. Had the girls understood the real reason for the fair youth watching them so closely, perhaps they would have felt differently. But as animals on the prowl, to them the boy on the barrel was already in-love with each and every one of them. All they needed to do was to show themselves to be an irresistible, perfect beauty. Edmund studied the girls as they walked to the west, and then again somewhat later, the same girls returned heading to the east. At some point the group of four stopped and allowed one of the couples to catch up. The six then gathered in a circle, smiling to each other and appearing to socialise just as they might do after the Holy Trinity Church service on a Sunday.

The moment had at last come and Edmund stood up, and slowly walked towards the girls hoping that in some way he might find an excuse to start up a conversation. The 'cats' now recognised that the centre of power had changed position, from the barrel to the maids. As he approached, the girls drew closer together with their gaze fixed on one another. Edmund was not given the opportunity to catch anyone's eye. He stood motionless outside the circle not knowing what to do next. What do you say to break into a conversation when you haven't learnt the language? He felt awkward and he realised that he looked foolish. But just as he began to turn away to escape more embarrassment, one pretty girl wearing a white bonnet spoke his name.

'Edmund, do you remember me? I am sister to your friend George. You have many times picked apples from our trees. It is Lillian Combes.'

'Lillian? Yes, I remember you but the last time I collected apples you were, well, different.'

The girls giggled all as one and Edmund felt the blood rush to his cheeks. He was blushing and as his eyes welled with tears he looked down to the ground as he knew they were all watching him closely. Lillian was a pretty girl with curls of auburn hair peeking out from beneath her lace bonnet. She was nearly as tall as Edmund but with the swelling natural curves that proved she wasn't a boy actor. Her pinafore frock had no stiffening from whalebones or corset to restrict her girlish body from telling the innocent story of an Eve just after the apple.

'So, Edmund, how is it with you and your family? Are you still delivering gloves for your father?'

'My family are well, thank you and yes, I do sometimes help my father. But I have plans for better and I will soon start making my fortune.'

Once more the girls giggled and appeared to whisper to each other. Although not experienced in talking to girls, Edmund realised that trying to talk to a group of six was too much of a challenge and either he needed to retreat or try to get one to separate. If he could just get Lillian to join him to walk away, then his composure might be regained.

'Lillian, do you know if Mr Sadler the baker will still have some spiced buns. I thought I might buy some for my mother.'

This request was inspirational as it allowed Edmund to appear dutiful and happy to please a woman. It also showed the girls that he had money enough to buy little luxuries.

'A gentlemanly idea and something that might prove a boon to more persons than just you. Buns might still be had if the baker is true to his calling. Let us go and see. May I walk with you?'

'I hoped you might do just that as the baker has in the past abused my name and I have no desire to bear his insults. If I give you the money perhaps you can choose the buns for me.'

'My friend Beth here, will join us as it would not be seemly for me to be alone with a young man, particularly a Shakespeare.'

Edmund's face suggested surprise at this implied insult to his name. Perhaps Lillian had heard that his elder brother William, when just eighteen, had pursued an older woman and was now some kind of player on the public stage. But his annoyance passed in an instance as he sensed he had achieved a conquest, and he had separated two maids from the herd and he might now shepherd them to his will.

The two girls turned in the direction of the bakers and without a backwards glance at the unlucky four, they skipped confidently knowing they had won the attention of Stratford's melancholy youth. But it was really Lillian who now held the prize. It was she who had spoken first and she alone felt the heady thrill of having won

Edmund's attention. That the other girls would be jealous was the cream on the cake. As they walked off together, Lillian could sense Edmund was watching her closely and she took this as proof that the handsome youth found her attractive.

Nowhere was very far in Stratford and in five minutes they arrived outside the home of the Sadlers bakery. Even though it was early evening there was still a rich aroma of the morning bread. Although many families made their own bread, there was enough new prosperity in the town to provide a good business for a skilled baker who kept his ovens hot. Lillian stopped outside the open door and held out her palm towards Edmund. He looked at it seeing the delicate fingers and smooth pale skin. Instinctively he touched but the hand was hastily withdrawn.

'What's this? I wasn't asking to be stroked. Money, you said you had money for buns.'

Edmund apologised and opened his leather purse and removed a silver threepence. This he held out to Lillian.

'Will this be enough for four buns?'

'Perhaps, but if you have another threepence, it will save me from coming back for more.'

Edmund found another coin and with this Lillian and Beth entered the bakery leaving him alone. Edmund crossed the street, and he waited by a low hedge that marked the outer edge of a rough farm track. He still felt flushed with success although he wasn't sure of what he should do next. He had the company of two girls, but he would need to do something more if he was going to keep them. He watched the doorway and soon Lillian and

Beth reappeared. As they crossed the street, he noticed how both girls raised their skirts to avoid soiling them on the lumps of horse dung that created an unpleasant hazard. Men in thick leather shoes were usually oblivious to dirty streets but for girls in long skirts and thin slippers there seemed to be a technique Edmund would need to learn. Edmund looked at their ankles and calves then looked down at his own. Not so very different he thought and if his own coarse woollen hose was exchanged for the refined style worn by the girls, he was sure he could achieve the appearance of woman. Delicate steps, more toe than heel and the hem of the skirt held up in the left hand. He was learning.

Beth was shorter than Lillian, though very much more round. She had plump cheeks and what appeared to be a matching bosom barely concealed by a dress that seemed to be too small. The spiced buns, there were six, had been wrapped in loose paper and the smell of the bakery clung to the package making their walk to the riverside pleasantly fragrant. Once there they stopped, and Edmund offered each girl a bun. Lillian carefully chose one and delicately picked off small pieces and placed them one by one into her mouth. Beth chose the largest bun and bit into it, filling her mouth and chewing with unselfconscious enthusiasm. Lillian remarked that her bun tasted very nice. Beth didn't speak but it was quite apparent that she enjoyed her reward.

'I am pleased you are both here as I rarely have anyone to talk with. The boys from school prefer playing football to using spoken language and their minds.'

Lillian smiled at him and quietly finished eating her bun.

They then chatted about her family and various people in Stratford. Unlike Edmund, Lillian seemed to know everyone, and she was happy to retell their secrets or at least the things she believed to be their secrets. Edmund watched carefully, hardly contributing much to the conversation but accidently, his behaviour helped Lillian to believe he was really interested in her. Edmund had discovered the second-best way to a woman's heart was to make out you are listening. The first? To give her money to buy something.

Edmund saved a couple of buns for his mother as he remembered just in time that he had used this excuse to separate Lillian from the other girls. The evening had been a success and as they parted, he whispered into Lillian's ear that he would like to meet her again the next night. She said she would see if she was free. As the girls departed, walking back towards the town, past the Guild Pits, Lillian looked back towards Edmund and smiled. She would be back again tomorrow.

And so, it went on. After the school day where Edmund had borne the ordeal of learning to declaim passages from Ovid or Virgil, he attended a far better place of learning where he was both the master and the only pupil. Lillian willingly became his text and laboratory. He studied her as she arrived and as she left. During the period in between, he set her little tasks, such as picking up items dropped on the ground or feeding the swans with stale bread brought especially for the purpose. He encouraged her to explain to him about little details of her dress and how she prepared her hair. She loved all the attention from the still somewhat melancholy youth. She didn't sense the trap he had laid or recognise how she was in emotional jeopardy. To Lillian, Edmund was special, a sort of romantic lone prince walking straight off the page of an old fairy tale. Sadly, this fable was one written by a young man and the ending would not be 'happy every after.' Edmund was even saving himself the expense of buns or other little luxuries, as he soon learned that a kiss would 'buy' him all the indulgences he needed.

A new routine had somehow evolved, and Edmund settled back into the uneventful country life Stratford still offered the subjects of Queen Elizabeth. While elsewhere a struggle for spiritual clarity was being fought, religious faith for the town's folk of Stratford was still usually more personal than political. The state may now have become Protestant Anglican, but the old Catholic observances were still in the hearts of many people. In the Shakespeare family, William's father and mother had spent all their lives fed by rituals and pageants that told stories of saints and sinners and offered colourful images of heaven and hell. While they chose not to argue with the changes Elizabeth's ministers decreed, they quietly continued with their private beliefs. Daughter-in-law Anne wasn't of their generation and somehow a quest for purity seemed to her obvious and fresh, something that would improve life and satisfy the needs of her troubled conscience. So, Anne increasingly chose to wear black clothes and have her bodice buttoned tightly up to her chin. For the children granddad and granny were fun and easily persuaded to provide them with threats and tickles. Anne provided them with sharp words and warnings of damnation.

Susanna, Hamnet and Judith, like most children of their age, didn't take it too seriously.

For Edmund, the state sponsored struggle for the Christian soul was political. He could see that the new laws arriving from government ministers restricted freedoms and people occasionally died due to them breaking laws they neither knew of or really understood. Edmund heard told there were wars being fought on the continent and in Ireland. Boys of his age were seen occasionally practicing with long pikes and muskets before, one day they left, never to be seen again. Edmund decided this was not for him, fighting and dying for someone else or someone else's dream. The danger for him was, in Stratford, he was too visible. His name was on the town's list and at some point, someone would decide he was a number to be added to a bureaucratic reckoning. Edmund knew there were informers everywhere and they could earn a few shillings by simply whispering a name into the ear and pointing accusing fingers in his direction. Stratford, although ostensibly a quiet arcadian idyll, held threats to young men, in that its population was small and everyone knew everyone else. Edmund felt conspicuous. He reasoned that in London a young man could merge into the narrow streets and crowds. In London there was a kind of undergrowth of buildings. In London a young man could camouflage himself and there was a kind of freedom being one of the metropolitan herd.

In autumn of the year his brother's play Love's Labour's Lost was being performed on stage, Edmund decided it was time for him to leave Stratford. He would say farewell to family and the 'love' game with Lilian, would stop. After church one Sunday as the family ate their meal of mutton stew, Edmund announced that he would leave next morning. There was very little reaction from John and Mary. For them the boy leaving home was something natural and at this point three sons had already left to start their lives, and it was perhaps time. One less mouth to feed and more space in the crowded house. The loss of a delivery boy and labourer was just that, a loss, but Hamnet was growing bigger, and he could soon take over Edmund's duties. Mary said nothing and Edmund felt relieved he had escaped objections from his parents.

His Aunt Anne merely asked where exactly he was going and when he replied to her, she scoffed,

'To stay with brother William; With my husband? Then you will be joining an ungodly crowd. William enjoys the company of vagabonds and thieves and worse. It will be a descent into the bottomless mire that draws one down to damnation.'

Edmund laughed as he found this type of puritan outburst comic rather than threatening.

'Auntie, the players you slander are entertainers, and they perform before Dukes and Earls and even the Queen herself.'

'And that is no recommendation given the debauchery that is common amongst the aristocracy of England.'

'Be quiet Anne, not in front of the children. If Edmund can find lodging with his brother in London, then I for one wish him well.'

John gave his opinion. Hamnet broke the tension when he chose this moment to steal a piece of meat from his sister's platter. Judith slapped her brother with her spoon and, for a few moments there were shouts and tears, but all was quickly resolved. The meal was resumed without further discussion about Edmund's departure.

Chapter ten

Several days later Edmund walked along Shoreditch High Street, down past St Leonard's Church. The journey by wagon had been unpleasant as the roads had been deeply rutted and muddy due to much autumn rain. Master Greenway had been glad to have a paying passenger, particularly one who was young enough to often walk to lessen the load the horses had to pull. More than once, Edmund had been needed to help push the cart as the horses struggled and slid their way up the many hills that lay between Stratford and Hampstead. When he was not required to place his shoulder against the cart, Edmund had sheltered from the rain under some tar cloths, wedging himself between the various casks and baskets that made up the bulk of the load.

He was relieved that the journey was over, and he could nurse his bruised buttocks and stretch his legs. Shoreditch, although a small hamlet, just north of the far busier Bishopsgate, had more houses and Inns than the whole of Stratford. It also had more dirt; more smoke and more smells. If a person was looking to find a quiet refined place to live, Shoreditch wasn't it. But for Edmund, this place was exciting. The many inhabitants, though indifferently dressed, were more 'colourful' and alive than those seen in Stratford. It was easy to recognise the apprentices and tradesmen by their various liveries but there were also people more haphazardly attired. Some seemed to be wearing assorted ill-fitting clothes, perhaps acquired from street sellers, 'second hand.' There were also people who were perhaps entertainers of one type or another. Dirty ruffs, huge breeches complete with cod pieces and large brimmed hats with feathers, all suggested flamboyance. There were also women dressed in a style that Aunt Anne certainly would have strongly disapproved. They walked confidently and looked men straight in the eye, without a flicker of embarrassment or fear. Edmund avoided their piecing gaze, but he felt the thrill of knowing that these people were soon to be his neighbours, provided, of course, he could find the tenement house used by the boy actors.

It was after noon when he turned off into a side street hoping to find the theatre building, as he remembered the lodging house lay close by. He became aware that there seemed to be people, mostly men, walking in small groups towards the west. He rightly assumed that perhaps they might be heading in the direction of the playhouse, so he followed them along until the street opened out to a sort of yard area. This was the Burbage's theatre, and a crowd of people stood around perhaps waiting to enter. Play or no play, this was a place of entertainment as within the crowd there were jugglers and a man playing on a pipe accompanied by a boy beating on a tabor. There were the cries of pie sellers and a woman serving ale from a cask. Edmund paused to watch but as the bag he had been carrying all morning now seemed heavier, he decided it was time to find the house and take some rest.

As he left the yard, he could see a windmill and the mound by the remains of the Holywell Priory. He knew he had found the place and the tenement building leased by Burbage, stood close by. Edmund turned and approached the oaken door.

'Hola. You stop or you will feel the weight of my staff.'

The body of an old man rose up out of what appeared to be a large bundle of discarded rags piled by the doorway. The staff he gripped was taller than him and it wavered in his bony hands. Edmund stopped and measured the power of his adversary but quickly assessed he was perhaps just the watchman paid to guard the building. He was merely doing his job.

'I am here to meet with Master Beeson as I am to join the boys of the playhouse.'

The old man looked Edmund up and down then lowered his weapon.

'What is your name?'

'I am Shakespeare.'

'Shakespeare! I know a man of that name, but you are not he.'

'Perhaps you mean my brother, William Shakespeare?'

'He has a brother? You look too much of a country sprat to be brother to that fat cod but then as these are such strange times, it maybe so. You can go in but you will not find Master Beeson, he is out at the theatre.'

'Thank you kindly, I am in no hurry, and I will be glad to put down my bag as I have travelled far.'

The watchman moved aside, and Edmund entered into the narrow hallway and then climbed the worn staircase up to the first floor landing. He opened a door that had once been painted green, some of the colour still remained but the door was now scuffed and dirty by the passage of many bodies pushing through without much care for gentility.

The main room was large with an open fireplace at one end. There were a couple of small low beds which, through hard use, were shedding straw from their tired mattresses. The floor had several piles of cushions all bearing the imprint of their most recent occupant. The walls were covered irregularly by various hangings – some hand painted – probably scavenged from discarded scenery at one playhouse or another. It was all just as he remembered it from his previous visits, all those weeks ago. Edmund dumped his bag down, choosing one of the beds on which he settled himself back to rest and take in his new surroundings, so very different from those he had left four days before.

Edmund fell into a deep, dreamless sleep despite his nervous excitement produced by him arriving in Shoreditch. The journey by wagon from Stratford had been exhausting, even for a strong young man. It was late afternoon before loud noises emanating somewhere from the floor below, disturbed his slumber. He recognised bangs from boots as a number of feet stomped their way up the staircase. Then voices, full of youth and far louder than necessary, announced that the housemates had returned. Edmund just had time to raise his head before a heavy cushion was held down over his face. Something heavy and hard was on his chest and his wrists were being held tightly. Edmund struggled to free himself, but he had been successfully ambushed and he was outnumbered.

'Who are you and who said you could use my bed?'

A voice very close to his ear sounded none too welcoming or brotherly.

'Get off me! I can't breathe. I will explain but give me a chance.'

Reason prevailed and what turned out to be three boys released his arms and removed the cushion. As Edmund looked up, three faces looked down. Despite their shouts he noticed they were all smiling, and Edmund quickly sensed they were less of a mortal threat than he had feared. There was territory to be defended and the three had responded exactly as his school friends at Stratford would have done if faced with a new boy.

'I am Edmund and Christopher Beeson said I could stay here.'

'Edmund, Edmund? I remember Kit saying something about you. You're Master Shakespeare's brother, aren't you?'

'Yes, I am. And I want to become an actor at the playhouse. Kit, as you call him, offered to help me learn your trade.'

'But he didn't say you could use my bed.'

'I beg your forgiveness. I didn't know it was yours. No-one was here to ask, and I was very tired.'

'Humm, okay then. You are forgiven. But more so because you are Shakespeare's brother.'

All three boys laughed, and Edmund realised he had passed the first challenge. The three boys introduced themselves and the male ritual of handshakes was performed. Edmund was told to move his bag to a small room up on the floor above. This he quickly did, and he returned to find his new acquaintances drinking small ale from wooden cups. One of them had lit a fire in the grate and the flickering yellow light helped the place to become more welcoming. From within the shadows Edmund could see there had been more arrivals and warm voices murmured fragments of light conversation. John invited Edmund to sit by the fire and soon a toasting fork was found, and hot crumpets were piled on a trencher, one on top of another.

Sometime later, Edmund heard a voice he recognised. Christopher Beeson had arrived, and he quickly came over and welcomed Edmund. The group were now complete, and the eight boys shared the evening, shared some ale, shared crumpets and toasted cheese. Edmund's new life had begun well and if his life had ended then, he would have smiled contently as he passed through the gates of paradise. But this was not his time, and he wasn't called.

As boys fell silent laying on their chosen cushions or, they moved off into the shadows to find their bed for the night, Christopher drew Edmund apart to a small scullery area that led off from the back of the room.

'Does your brother know you have come back to London?'

'No, not yet, I haven't been able to tell him.'

'Will he be pleased or do you expect resistance.'

'When I was here before I did tell him I wanted to join you all as a boy actor and he forbade it. But I am old enough to make my own way and this is my decision. Mother and father were content that I should come, and I don't need my brother's permission.'

'Right you are, but his support would have been useful. He is your brother, and his plays are in much demand by playhouse owners. He can get a paying audience almost any day of the week. But so much for that. Your brother doesn't hire the players and the theatre managers, as with all businessmen, regard amassing silver shillings and golden coins, their ruling motivation.'

'Does my brother come to this house often?'

'Never. If a playwright wants to see a boy, we go to him either at his lodgings or at the playhouse. Your brother has now moved his lodgings closer to the city. He now resides in the Ward of St Helens Bishopsgate. You are unlikely to encounter him walking the streets of Shoreditch.'

This news seemed to please Edmund as he had no wish to open a battle with his brother so soon. He had a wish to settle and perhaps secure his place as an actor before facing any opposition from William. The playhouse was the business, and he felt sure that if he could prove himself of value to the theatre owners, then the Shakespeare brothers could unite and be friends again. He just needed to find this so-called woman's part.

Edmund slept well and it was mid-morning before he was awoken by the sound of laughter downstairs. He hurriedly pulled on a woollen shirt and went down to the large room; the boys jokingly called their court. It served as the boys' salon, dining and sleeping space. Edmund saw Christopher lounging back on some cushions, reading from a book, so he found a free stool and moved it closer so they could talk.

'It is time you heard a play and watched some of we boys practice our craft. There is a performance of Edward II at The Curtain playhouse this afternoon. The play was written by him that found a sharp quarrel in Deptford, the young Master Kit Marlowe. He is now dead, but the company of Pembroke's Men are still making money from his words. Robert Goffe here is to take the part of Isabella and Alexander Cooke will play the royal niece. The two nearest most boys nodded and smiled. There will be much plotting and some dirty deeds, but I am sure it will attract a full house.'

Later that day they walked together from the tenement house, down Holywell Lane. Edmund could see a tall timber framed building, that from its flag poles and the crowd of people, he took to be their destination. It was a building shaped like a pile of badly clipped gold coins. Not square nor circular but somehow in-between the two. It had three stories and a ragged fringe of straw from the steep roof. On one side Edmund could see a sort of turret structure and on this flew the several colourful flags. Christoper led Edmund to a small entrance at the bottom of the turret and, after a brief exchange with the watchman, they were permitted to enter.

'This is what we call the tiring house and in here the players gather their props and some change into their costumes. They also wait here and listen for their cues to go on the stage.'

Christopher made a theatrical sweep with his arm as if revealing a grandiose scene or biblical tableaux. Edmund's gaze followed where his eyes were directed, and he saw heads turn towards him as they started to thread their way between the half-dressed actors. Everyone was in a hurry to finish getting ready before the curtain was drawn open. A few men exchanged a brief; 'hola' with Christopher but no one was in the mood for pleasantries or chatter. Edmund saw a large hourglass placed on a table in the middle of the room. It was obvious that the sands were nearly run out and the actors needed to rush to complete their preparation. Christopher whispered to Edmund, and they squeezed themselves out of the tiring house and into the open yard. There Edmund was confronted by a mass of faces all magically turned towards the raised stage. No commandments were needed nor dark gowned clericals to shepherd the congregation to assigned pews. This audience all stood obediently, and they seemed to know the routine without needing to be told. Standing patiently like so many cows before a milking and, like cows, they were noisy with a bold hum of voices filling the yard. There was a small patch of blue sky above and several crows perched on the turret roof perhaps hoping for a meal of carrion. Occasionally voices called out, naming actors encouraging them to come out and get on with the play. It was all good humoured and Edmund sensed the crowd was ready to enjoy and together share an afternoon of entertainment. Suddenly there was the sound of a drum and a trumpet sounded. A player came out onto the stage and after a short announcement, the play of Edward II commenced. Edmund turned to watch the stage and, for the next two hours, all his senses became obedient subjects to the compelling drama.

'And so, Edmund, what did you think of your first London stage play? Did you take the side of Earl Mortimer or perhaps Gaveston?'

'I have been transported to a place where the well born act base and no-one deserves redemption.'

'Ha, be careful who hears you say so, some might judge words such as these, sedition. There were two Kings of England on that stage and although long dead, their descendants still live.'

'I will take your council and speak only of the art and not the morality. But if Edward as written has passed the test of the Master of Revels, it seems we have a lot of freedom in the playhouse, far more than my aunt Anne allowed us around the dinner table in Henley Street.'

'This may be truth, the best of playwrights have a way with words that create circles of reasoning that allow a myriad of mind images to form but without the sharp corners where a player might find himself with no escape, trapped by an inquisitor.'

'The love between the King and Piers Gaveston was not what I was expecting to be played out on the public stage.'

'Yes, but as Marlowe said in his play, The mightiest Kings have had their minions.'

'Some of the boys are prepared to play the 'minions' after the stage curtain has fallen. For those that choose this way, there can be a good reward. But that way is not for me and I doubt you will choose it either, although we may both smile enough to please those with rich purses and heads full of dreams of Hylas or Adonis.'

The next day had been assigned as the start of training for Edmund. He had a lot to learn if he was to become a player but living full-time in a house inhabited by boy actors meant he also had lots of opportunity. The house was a school that never closed, and the boys took great delight in showing off their skills and pushing Edmund to mimic their actions and gestures. He was coached by the best boy actors in London, each one ready to perform even if the audience counted no more than one.

Robert and Alexander, the boys who Edmund had seen perform in Marlowe's play, volunteered to teach Edmund how to dress as a woman courtier. They had both borrowed clothes from the Pembroke's Men, promising to return them before the next performance. Clothes worn by the wealthy and notable, were like their owners, 'richly left' and they represented the main physical asset of every company of players. The extravagant clothes were a key part of the visual spectacle and audiences took great pleasure at being free to stare at will, enjoying all the finery that the best dressmakers in London could produce. A well-dressed actor was theirs for the afternoon whereas, a real live Duke or Duchess would demand them bow their heads and lower their eyes in supplication. So, Edmund would be taught how to put the costume on and how to create the illusion that a real woman was up there on the stage.

After most of the boys had left 'the court' to attend the Bear Gardens in Southwark, Robert and Alexander called Edmund down from his room. He was a little nervous at the prospect of being dressed by the two boys. He couldn't really remember the time when his older sister Joan used to dress him and besides, he was still adjusting to the idea of a stage world where men helped each other become women, even if for a few short hours.

'Come Edmund, let us show you all the layers that just the other day helped Robert become Isabella. Just as The Pope dons robes of coded fabric to create and prove his authority, we players have to use fabric to become a painting that delights the eye.'

Alexander led Edmund to the centre of the room where there had been placed a large basket, full of clothes. He told Edmund to stand there and undress down to his slops. Edmund quickly complied and he then watched as his two teachers lifted out of the basket each piece of clothing, laying them, one by one on the bed. First came the Kirdle garment and he stepped into it before Robert showed how he should tighten the lacings on the front. Then came the padded roll, a strange circler device that was put around his waist. At first this didn't seem to make much sense but when Robert put the Farringdale over his head, he began to understand. The padded roll functioned like a wide curtain rail holding the underskirt away from his body. His lower half had been converted into some sort of tent structure with his feet disappearing underneath. The gown was then added, together with the triangular shaped stomacher. Richard and Alexander knew what they were doing and in minutes Edmund was quickly transformed from fair youth to beautiful young woman. The last touch was to add a dramatic standing collar and ruff. The alchemy was then complete.

'There Edmund, you are now Isabella or any other woman of breeding the playwright has written for us to perform.'

'Alexander, bring that looking glass over. Let Edmund view the result. From a born Adam he has become an Eve.'

Edmund looked at himself, not altogether believing the person he saw in the mirror. Edmund felt in himself the same male, but the layers of clothing had created the image of woman. He stared not quite accepting what he saw but then with his first movements, Lillian's movements now mimicked by him, he realised he had found the woman's part. Robert and Alexander smiled.

'Welcome Isabella. You are a fair maid, and London will fawn before your slippered feet.'

Edmund performed a slow curtsey before the two boy magicians.

'Do you really think I will do? Will the audience accept me as real? Will they love me?

'Oh yes Edmund, with a little face painting and with the right wig, you will be their Juliet, their Bianca or Lady Anne.'

Edmund looked at the image in the mirror. He realised he saw a woman. He smiled but the real smile was somewhere inside as he felt a new power. With this puissance what could he not achieve?

The remaining days of the week were filled with Edmund exploring the neighbourhood and chatting with the other boys after their early suppers. They introduced him to dominoes and the dice game Cent. Both involved wagers where the players all excitedly bet coins they had earned as jobbing actors. Edmund still had his hoard of coins pilfered from his brother's money bags so he was able to join the fun. He lost coin after coin, much to the delight of his new friends. But most of his time at the lodging was spent in 'the court', a student of acting and the social order of Elizabeth's England.

Just to west of the lodgings was an open area not yet settled by the growing population. Edmund had spent his childhood playing in the fields around Stratford and in some way this simple outdoor life still called him. Finsbury Fields, as the area was known became Edmund's morning walk and he would pass between the windmills and head south on a route to Moorfields. In the distance he could see parts of the old London Wall built by the Romans to keep the tribes of Britons from discovering their greatest secret. The Romans, underneath all their science and polished armour, were soft and vulnerable. Edmund was a descendent of the people who discovered this truth. Beyond the city wall was the high roof and tower of St Paul's cathedral.

Late one morning after he had returned from his morning walk, Christopher, Robert and Alexander beckoned him over and informed him that it was now time for him to choose a role and then fully learn the part. Edmund was ready for this task and he informed them that he had been learning the part of Joan from his brother's play Henry VI. Christopher laughed and pulled a face like he had just eaten a lemon.

'Joan le Pucelle! Merde, a monster of a woman, if dear William ever wrote such a thing. She is all iron and clanging rather than silk and sighs. Too many words and, to cap it all, she is a witch. This is not for you. Besides, with Joan you wouldn't win much attention from our patrons. Where would be the fun and money in that? With fair looks like yours you want to play roles that create desire in the galleries and yard. We want the audience to imagine warm thoughts and remember you when they leave the playhouse. Then they will watch for your name on play sheets and pay to see you in your next play. You, Edmund, have the gift of star quality and you can win over many followers, followers with fat purses. An Eleanor or Luciana or better still, Juliet. These are roles that will win the hearts of an audience.'

Edmund felt frustrated but this didn't stop him quickly grasping the logic of the lesson he was hearing. Christopher, although a craftsman, knew the stage and the playhouse were chiefly a business. If given a choice, an actor needed to select his roles with care. The best actors preferred parts that they knew would build their reputation and create a following. London had many stages and playgoers usually had a chose between new plays. They would follow their favourite actors, and Christopher was advising Edmund to be selective.

'Joan is also too big a part for your first appearance on the stage. I suggest perhaps as you have just seen Edward, a role from this play would be best. The King has a niece, Lady Margaret and her sweet part is far smaller'

The three boys laughed enjoying the lewd inuendo.

'I mean she speaks I guess, just twenty-seven lines. She would be good for you. She is young, attractive and doomed. Perfect!'

Robert agreed and then improved the proposition by him mentioning that he had heard there was to be a private performance of the play before the Lawyers of Middle Temple. The Lawyers always made a good audience and if they could once be won over; lawyers could afford to indulge in their play going habit. If the lawyers liked him, he would quickly become famous. With the plan agreed for Edmund's first public performance, there remained ten days for lines to be conned and hand gestures practiced.

Very soon Edmund felt himself thankful for the good advice of his mentors. Twenty-seven lines were quite enough for his debut. Robert and Alexander coached Edmund each morning and then again in the evening after supper. During the classes there were always other boys walking through 'the court', each in turn offering their personal style of encouragement or critique. Robert welcomed each intervention, explaining to Edmund this verbal banter was just like it will be when they perform. Members of the audience, and particularly an audience of lawyers, will always walk about and frequently voice comments while the actors perform on the stage. After all, they are learned men, and they have 'bought' the performance.

On the day of the play, Edmund took his morning walk as normal. He felt a little apprehensive about playing Lady Margaret, but he knew he was well prepared. He had watched Alexander wear the dress and play the lady. He had played the same, over and over again, mimicking each and every facial expression and hand gesture. He had been told repeatedly 'We give the audience, woman as a man imagines her to be, as man prefers her to be.

It is not realism, but our crafted illusion of the real.' He was sure this act was to be fun, and he felt the excitement that floods through a sixteen-year-old boy when he first believes he is an Apollo or Achilles.

The group of boy actors walked the road from Shoreditch to Bishopsgate and from there via the busy streets to St Pauls Yard. Then they left the city via Ludgate, walking down the hill and crossing Fleet River and up the other side, passing the Mitre and Old Cock Inns. The Middle Temple Inns of Court occupied the land once owned by the Knights Templar and the place was the home of ghosts and ancient ritual. The Hall where they had been booked to perform was an impressive Tudor building, built to last many centuries. The Hall's main function, other than for ceremonies, was as a dining room for Benchers and students. Three meals a day were served here but when the tables were cleared, the huge floor area was ideal for plays and the occasional Lute concert.

The boys had transported all the costumes they needed in a large basket carried on a hand cart. The hall staff led the players with their basket to an anti-room that lay alongside the kitchens. Robert pulled Edmund by the sleeve and beckoned him to follow.

'Come see the hall before the audience arrives. This place is special and so very different from the public playhouse.'

They entered the hall via one of the two carved oak archways. Edmund realised that Robert was right, this hall was more temple than playhouse. High up in the walls, two rows of huge windows spilled god's natural light down onto the heavy floorboards. On the west wall there was a stained-glass window and from here colours flew, mingling with the sunlight. As Edmund turned towards the way they had entered, he looked up at a huge carved screen that dominated the east wall. Climbing above this there ran a full width Minstrel gallery. As Edmund stood in awe, Robert pointed a finger up to the ceiling. Above the hall there was a crown of elaborate hammer beams supporting the roof. The Middle Temple Hall was perhaps rightly named as it was where of the men of Inns of Court assembled to worship all the finery their status and riches could afford.

Edmund suddenly felt very small in the face of all this man-made glory. But he knew words are also man-made and the right word spoken with art can be powerful and shake the strongest structures.

Soon after they returned to the dressing room and had settled themselves, the main company of adult actors arrived. If there had been order and friendship before, suddenly the mood changed. The professional players all regarded themselves as 'the stars' of London's theatre hierarchy. They took over all the best chairs and bullied the boys until they retreated to the kitchen. The atmosphere improved with the arrival of Edward Alleyn and he supervised the preparation of the play ensuring the boys were no-longer insulted or cuffed. As the sands in the hourglass ran out, the actors, one-by-one faced inspection and if approved, settled themselves to await the first scene. Edmund listened to the increasing noise emanating from the main hall. The student lawyers and Benchers were gathering, and each one seemed to have a voice fighting for attention. Then it was time and the play began.

For Edmund the next two hours were a bit of a mist in the otherwise clear afternoon light. But when the moving shapes of men reappeared, clapping was heard along with shouts and cheers. The performance had been a success. The lawyers approved.

As the players acknowledged the applause given freely by the audience, Edmund noticed a striking young man sitting passively, close by the actors. He looked to be about twenty years old, had long auburn hair and eyes of vivid blue. What seemed remarkable to Edmund was that, in a room of men dressed in dark woollen clothes, this young man was dressed in a tight doublet made of a cloth of silver adorned with, what at first sight appeared to be, many pearls. A fine dagger hung from his waist. The young man was not just well born, this fair youth was an English nobleman.

The players all exited the hall to congregate together outside under the trees where a table had been set, laden with various dishes, pies and a large cask of ale. The lawyers and actors all ate and chatted together easily irrespective of differences in formal status. It was obvious to Edmund that they had all done this many times before. The men spoke energetically of the play, of English history, of clothes and the market price of corn and butter. There was a kind of exchange where the freeborn spoke with ease, unconcerned about political diktats that the city fathers tried to enforce. Edmund listened more than contributed to the honest, and perhaps well-meant, radical discourse. Edmund was still wearing the clothing of young Lady Margaret, and any newly arrived witness would believe this was a social gathering of men and three women.

Edmund felt someone tap his arm and, on turning, he saw a liveried servant, cap in hand, asking for his attention.

'I beg your pardon sir, my master Earl Southampton requests you attend him in the hall. If you please, follow me.'

'An Earl wishes to speak to me? Are you sure there is no mistake?'

'If you are named Edmund Shakespeare, then there is no mistake.'

Edmund bowed accepting the summons but, before following, he leaned over to Alexander and whispered into his ear.

'Alex, I have been asked to meet with an Earl of Southampton. Do you know of this man?.'

'Ha, 'prince Hal', yes, we all know the young Earl, he is a patron of we players and your brother knows him well. Go boy, meet with him, there may be advantage in this.'

Edmund turned and quickly followed the servant back into the building, taking a staircase that led up to the Minstrel gallery. Once there he was escorted inside only to find the servant stop and nod in the direction of a man seated at the far end of the room. Edmund, still dressed as Lady Margaret, gracefully approached the young man in the silver doublet. The youth watched Edmund and Edmund felt the penetrating gaze of the blue eyes study his movements, his painted face and the very person that breathed beneath the layers of cloth.

'I have been told this was your first performance acting for a paying audience. You did well, but as a Shakespeare boy this is perhaps not surprising'

Edmund's face blushed and he did a small curtsey to help hide his nervousness. The Earl paused a moment and then began again.

'I know your brother, but in all our conversations he never mentioned you or gave a clue that he had such a fine-looking sibling.'

'My lord, I think my brother hoped I would make a life in Stratford and not appear here in the appearance of a lady. Perhaps it might be best if you will allow time to change out of these women's weeds.'

'No, stay as you are. I think I'd rather talk to Margaret than the younger brother of a poet.'

Earl Henry waved his hand in the direction of a brocade upholstered chair and Edmund, still moving in harmony with his stage clothing, carefully lowered himself on to the edge of the seat. Edmund looked at this nobleman, just a few years older than himself, and waited for the Earl to determine what should happen next. The young man appeared to be tall, slim and certainly handsome. His clothing all richly made and showing him to be a follower of fashion at the royal court.

'Your brother has recently done me great honour by dedicating two long poems to my name. Have you read them?'

'No, my Lord, I have not read them, but I will seek them out.'

'The two poems are the type of glorious art all great men would like to write. They represent 'the duty of poets' and I am content that in some small way I have inspired a poet such as your brother to create this beauty.'

The Earl paused and Edmund temporarily basked in the praise that had been offered to his brother.

'He has also written some poems of quite a different kind – sonnets – and, while still things of beauty, they are to me, not so welcome.'

Edmund sensed that the young Earl was embarrassed and was searching for the way to address the topic.

'I will tell you a story of a young man. This young man, of just seventeen years, was a ward of court, his significant title, a weight that would feel threatening until the day of his gaining majority. He enjoyed his studies at Cambridge and all the entertainment his wealth and status could provide. His guardian sought to persuade the young man to accept a marriage to his own granddaughter. The young man's mother welcomed the proposal and added her pleas for the union. But the young man was not ready to accept a marriage and besides, he intended to follow his own choice. Knowing her son was a lover of the arts, she requested a respected poet to assist her in winning over her son to accept the match. She argued passionately that her son's beauty should be passed on to children and an heir be provided for the family title. The poet as half lover and half apostle, wove these silken threads into a golden cloth tapestry of sixteen lines. Each sonnet carried the same heart felt plea of the mother. Many such sonnets were written, and each one was passed to the youth hoping his resolve would weaken. But this is now all in the past. Things have moved on; the twenty-first year has passed, and the youth is now free to decide his own future.'

Edmund listened patiently as the young Earl finished his story.

'The sonnets have all been kept, they were far too beautiful to be destroyed. However, it is best that they be returned to the sender – the poet your brother.'

'If I can be of any service to you my lord, please just request it.'

'If you can call at the rooms I keep in Blackfriars, my man there will give you the package. Here is my signate ring, my man will know you by this and exchange the ring for the sonnets.'

'I will do as you request my lord.'

'How is you brother? I haven't seen him for some time, although of course I have attended some of his new plays. I enjoyed them very much. There is more moist love in these than found in his earlier dry histories.'

'My brother is in good health although he is much consumed by his art and business affairs.'

'Affairs yes, I know something of these. Have you met Emilia? I believe she may be his most recent muse able to put fluid into his pen.'

Edmund

What a day! My world has suddenly been piled high with riches. Stratford is far in the past and it will never again be my burden. Here is the place. This city with its streets paved with dung but sprinkled with gold coins. I have knelt in the mire and plunged my fingers into the filth and plucked gold, clean and shining from amongst the thrown waste of the people. I am a player on the stage, and I can act a king, and I can act a queen. Even the anointed royalty cannot boast this. I Edmund, brother to a playwright, have felt the power of creation. I created Lady Margaret, and she lived by my art. I moved her and when I chose, she existed no more. There on those wooden boards, I felt the eyes of dozens of men hunger for the woman I had created. They lost their reason and became beasts ruled by their longings, their animal urges. They became fools who worship a craven image and hope they can please the heartless stiff idol. I had them and I can have them again. The applause was like gulps of the finest wine, it coursing through my veins filling my heart with fire. Sounds and a glorious fury of hands. Their eyes followed me, I could see into their souls, and I saw slaves.

But enough of this. There is more meat. This shining Earl, this man of royalty who is known even to Gloriana herself, he too gave a little of himself. He told me his story and it is now a shared secret. Its value is as yet unknown, but I will keep it and someday, in some way, it may prove more valuable than a few lines scratched on a piece of parchment. The revelation that my brother has been indiscreet, is caviar to my platter. He has to me acted so superior since I came to London. He has commanded me to go when he should have offered his hand to lift me up by his side. But now I know he has been close to a young man and in this he has risked all. And more, could there really be more? Yes, there is. My brother has a lover. He has strayed and perhaps not just the once. I will find this Emilia and if she has been free with my brother, perhaps she will be open to Edmund.

Chapter eleven

Edmund had a free day – no rehearsing – no performance, and by noon he decided to walk to the city and see what new pamphlets or books might be being sold. The summer sun had dried the usually muddy roads to uneven ruts, although puddles from the many morning piss-pots still needed to be avoided. The streets were full of people moving, baskets and carts of produce all heading to market at Cheapside. Along Bishopsgate, Edmund noticed women from the many brothels enjoying the sunshine, lounging on benches and chairs brought out from the now empty taverns. While the women enjoyed this short 'holiday', there were apprentices dressed by the various city guilds, seemingly hurrying towards the south. Edmund noticed their agitation but assumed it was perhaps something to do with trade or imposed military training.

Finally, he reached Cheapside with all its tables and stalls. Here Edmund slowed his pace and began to browse the items offered for sale. If he had been a cook, here were all the ingredients that would make many a meal. Eggs and heavy cheeses, huge dark hams and tarts, lots of tarts. He bought himself some apples to take back to the house. The boys ate their main meals at one of the many Shoreditch Inns, so food shopping was not something any of them bothered with. He did buy some tobacco, filthy stuff but it was part of the social life of the house, that and playing cards.

As he reached the top end of the street, he could hear voices raised in chants and the beating of drums.

Just before St Pauls Yard he could see in the distance a crowd of young men. This was where the apprentices had been hurrying themselves. There were placards and shouts. The rabble, as no doubt Mayor John Spencer would call them, were protesting something. It had been a summer of street protests. Edmund laughed at the crudely drawn images of City fathers being hung from gallows. A pamphlet was hurriedly pushed into his hand and from what he read, it seemed the boys were protesting about overcharging on the price of fish and butter. Edmund laughed again when he realised so many teenagers were about to riot because herrings had doubled in price. For a boy actor this seemed a poor use of energy but then his stage world was all castles and ancient cities. The daily struggles for citizens at this time of war, in this time and place, was somehow remote and unreal. Edmund absorbed the lively scene, and he became an audience to a drama being played out where the finale would be the painful death at Tower Hill for the ring leaders or those unlucky boys chosen from amongst the rioters as examples to the rest.

Edmund moved away from the crowd. There was anger here, misrule and a risk if the officers of the city arrived, tempers might flare, and blood could be spilt. And besides, there were informers everywhere remembering faces and collecting names. A filthy trade but a state fearful of its own people employed many rats. Edmund didn't want to find himself added to any such a list.

The bell of St Pauls tolled for what or for whom, Edmund didn't know but it's sound reminded him that he was now just a short walk from the Blackfriars Priory where he had reason to visit. Carter Street was pleasantly quiet after the crowds of St Pauls yard. He followed the blackened flint wall round until, from Water Lane, the old Porters Lodge gave entrance to the collection of apartments and houses that had now replaced the damp cells and chantries once used by the black robed friars. The porter directed him to some rooms used occasionally by the young Earl. Across the great cloister, turn right and the studded door at the end of the corridor. After a heavy knock on the door, it opened and the servant Edmund remembered from Middle Temple, asked him to state his business. Edmund showed him the Earl's signet ring and he was promptly ushered inside.

'Please be so good as to wait here. I will return with the package.'

The exchange was quickly completed, and Edmund placed the bundle of sonnets inside his bag, lacing its flap shut. This was not something he intended to lose to pickpockets.

Edmund retraced his steps but as he reached the junction of the cloister he recognised a familiar face walking quickly towards him. The thick set man stopped, blocking the way. It was James Burbage, far from his theatre in Shoreditch.

'Edmund, is that you? What are you doing here?'

'Yes, Master Burbage, its Shakespeare, here to collect something precious from the Earl Southampton.'

'Interesting. Two brothers but more alike in taste than I had expected. But begone with you. This is not a place for a boy, and I hope I don't see you here again.'

Edmund laughed and doffed his woollen cap to the man who had taken some of the main roles in his brother's plays. It was Burbage who provided the tenement house used by the boy actors, and he was the main shareholder and manager of The Theatre. If there was such a thing as playhouse royalty, then Burbage was it. Edmund walked on and with a broad grin on his face, he left the priory. Edmund knew this chance meeting had planted a seed of intrigue into the mind of Burbage, and this amused him. If they had just completed a scene in a stage play, the characters would now jump to conclusions that would serve to feed their suspicions. As Edmund then better understood, 'all the worlds a stage'.'

Chapter twelve

Something Southampton said was still unresolved. Who was this Emilia and what exactly was she to his brother? As Edmund took his morning walk, he revolved these things in his mind. He now had the package of sonnets hidden safely away ready for some future purpose, as yet uncertain. He had read them all and love for a fair youth was undeniable. The category of love was equivocal and might be argued, should any challenge be made. But what was certain, neither the Earl nor his brother would want these private poems published. So, Edmund had one valuable commodity in his keeping. If he could discover another, then he would not just satisfy his personal curiosity, he might possess enough capital to safeguard his material future. He needed to find out more about Emilia.

He had been told his brother had changed his lodgings and now lived closer to the city in the Ward of St Helens. This would be Edmund's task for the day, to find and observe his brother at his new address. Edmund returned to the tenement and while there, he borrowed an old, hooded cape from the basket of stage clothing. Once cloaked, Edmund walked the now familiar route down towards the Bishopsgate. Just south, there lay the church of St Helens. He walked to the churchyard and across to the alleys that led away into the thick woven mat of dwellings that had absorbed some of the new population who chose to flee to the safety of London. There were Huguenots and there were other spoken tongues unrecognised by Edmund. He felt these streets were foreign to a young man brought up in Warwickshire. Shoreditch was a gateway to the north of England. Houndsditch and the streets around St Helens appeared to be a gateway to the east.

Edmund decided his best option was to find a place to sit close to the front of the church and the main pathway to Bishopsgate. From here he could watch people come and go, and he reasoned at some point he was sure to see his brother. It was just a matter of time and of this he had plenty. People watching had become one of Edmund's amusements. Since arriving in Shoreditch, he had taken some pleasure in creating secret biographies for the many wildly dressed inhabitants of the quarter. When people chose to leave the town of their birth, they usually carried with them a story. Successful people who are content, stay where they are born. Those who leave the place of their family and chose to arrive somewhere like London, usually are escaping or searching. Edmund had learned to look at people like scholars do at books. There were plenty of people to practice upon.

After the sun had moved westwards to rest behind a large chestnut tree in front of St Helens, Edmund spotted the brother he had come to find. Dressed in what appeared to be a new black and white doublet and breeches, looking not unlike a large badger, William strode confidently out of a side alley and turned towards Bishopsgate. Edmund pulled the hood of his cloak forward and followed. William walked at a fast pace giving the impression he had business on his mind, not shopping. Edmund decided he would follow him on his trip and at some point, he reasoned, William would return to his lodgings and then Edmund would have the address he sought. Bishopsgate was busy as usual, and it became more difficult for Edmund to keep him in sight. At one point he seemed to disappear but as Edmund hurried to the corner of Folgate Street, he saw that his brother had turned off the main road. Edmund paused and watched his brother stationary about a one hundred yards further on, outside a tall house with dark brown window shutters. As he watched, the door opened, and William went inside. But before the door closed a glamourous woman leant out and glanced up and down the street. Edmund felt the excitement of success.

William was not at his home, and he wasn't going to a playhouse. Here he had arrived at a woman's house, and she appeared to be anxious about who might have been a witness to his arrival. Edmund considered what he had seen as 'interesting.' He lent back on the wall and took an apple out of his bag. This would have to serve as lunch today.

The sun continued on its track into the west, and he started to notice market traders slowly heading out of the city, their baskets and carts now empty, no doubt their thoughts on a hot dinner and hot bed. Such was the ebb and flow of the city. Then as he was about to give up his quest and follow the carts back up to Shoreditch, Edmund saw the house door open. William exited and bowed to the woman in the doorway. As Edmund watched, his brother began walking towards where he was standing. Edmund quickly turned away and joined the procession of traders. By the time he felt it safe to turn back, his brother had disappeared. Edmund retraced his steps to St Helens, but William was nowhere to be seen. This was a set-back but he felt sure he could find the lodging another day. Edmund strolled back to Folgate Street, and he easily found the house with brown shutters. This was the house, and he felt certain there was a secret worth knowing just behind the door.

Edmund took off the cape and brushed himself down. He believed he looked presentable and with his newly found stage confidence, he knocked hard on the door. After a few moments, the door opened and an old woman dressed in black, wearing a lace cap, stared back at him.

'I have a message for Master Shakespeare.'

The woman looked Edmund up and down and started to close the door.

'Madam, it is an urgent message for my master, and I must give it to him.'

She stopped and stared at the young caller.

'Wait there I will see if he is here.'

The door closed and Edmund's heart raced as he realised; he was no longer in control of the scene he had created. Then the door reopened, and the woman beckoned him inside. The hallway had polished red floor tiles and freshly painted wainscotting. A door to what might be a front parlour was open, and the servant signalled that he should enter. In the room, standing in front of the fireplace, was the glamourous woman. She wore a dark blue gown, white stomacher and a flamboyant neck ruff. Her dark curly hair was combed up into the fashionable heart shape chosen by lady couriers. Her eyes sparked.

'I am told you have a message for Master Shakespeare, but unfortunately for you, he is not here.'

'I beg your pardon my lady. I understood he had a meeting, and that I could find him here.'

'A meeting? Is that what he called it? No, not a meeting but he is an acquaintance, and he did call on me this afternoon. Perhaps you will find him at his lodgings, I believe it is close by.'

'I thank you; I will look for him there. Please may I ask, are you the Lady Emilia?'

'It is indeed one of my names although I am surprised Master Shakespeare has been so free with it.'

'My lady, I must make a small confession to you. My name is Edmund Shakespeare, and I am his brother.'

'That Shakespeare has a brother I knew. I believe he has a business, a haberdashery, somewhere in the city. But I don't know of an Edmund. You have the look of someone's son rather than Shakespeare's brother.'

'Well, I am sixteen years and now a player on the stage. William is my brother, and I hope perhaps I might be allowed to call you my friend.'

The woman smiled and what seemed to be a slight blush coloured her cheeks. Edmund smiled back and there was a very brief moment of shared intelligence, when two open spirits connect.

'I am sure friendship is possible and I would be amused to hear about Stratford and what you hope to achieve here in the city. Perhaps you would like to call on me, another day.'

'I would be honoured, my lady to visit again if you could tell me when it might be convenient to you.'

'Let us say tomorrow, late afternoon.'

'This would be perfect. I will sleep well tonight with thoughts of seeing you again.'

The lady blushed once more and then rang a small bell to summon the servant.

This was it, Edmund had found the woman mentioned by the Earl. Here was someone special and Edmund had reacted to her potent sensuality. She was beautiful, mysterious and seductive, he was already drawn towards her flame.

Chapter thirteen

The following day, Edmund spent the morning reading a new role he had been told he would take in the play Romeo and Juliet to be staged the following week. Robert had spoken on his behalf and secured Edmund the part of Lady Capulet. That he and Robert were of the same age and Robert was to play Juliet, suggested the audience might need to use their fertile imagination. But the boys were happy as they saw the possibilities for exploring sexual tensions – an attractive mother and her equally attractive teenage daughter both played by boy actors in dresses. It would be a lively performance and one likely to win them both greater exposure. Robert knew the part of Juliet well, having played her several times. Edmund believed that together they would be able to rehearse, and he looked forward to what promised to be a fun week.

The day sped on and by late afternoon Edmund found some clean hose and put on his best Jerkin and breeches. His preparation provoked some noisy ribaldry from his housemates. Several boys noticed his appearance and he was quizzed as to why he was preening himself.

'A girl! He's off to see a girl. Who is she? Do we know her?'

The questions, fired in from all directions, all missed their target as Edmund was not about to share this type of secret with his friends. He laughed as he fielded all their vulgar propositions leaving them in riotous excitement but no nearer the truth. Finally, he escaped and took his way along Holywell Lane past the Red Bull tavern, the closest refreshment house frequently used by the boys.

Half an hour later, Edmund stood outside the door in Folgate Street. Two hard knocks attracted the attention of the elderly servant, and she stepped back in to allow Edmund to enter. He was shown into the front parlour and then the servant left, closing the door behind her. Edmund was alone and for the first time this day he felt nervous. There was a lot of the unknown here and he realised he didn't have any lines memorised, or gestures practiced ready for this performance. He didn't have a costume or any counterfeited character to hide behind. For the first time since arriving in London, it was just himself. Would this be enough?

He heard light footsteps on the stairs and then the parlour door opened. There stood the Lady Emilia. This was her stage, and she made the most of her entrance. She paused to allow Edmund the time and distance to best appreciate the view. With her head slightly turned towards the light filtering in through the window, her womanly profile was at once a statement of femininity, with a power likely to enslave any red-blooded youth. It had worked before on William and the Earl. Now Edmund felt the power of the spell. She gave a slight curtsey and Edmund bowed in return and removed his cap.

'I am happy to see you again Edmond. I wondered if you might forget.'

'My lady, you have been in my mind constantly.'

'Let us break with one convention straight away. Please call me Emilia, after all, we are going to friends.'

'Yes Emilia, a beautiful name and so well matched to all I see.'

Emilia gave another pretty curtsey and then she closed the door and gracefully lowered herself on to a chair by the fireplace. Edmund noticed her perfect skin, not hidden by paints or coal. She wore a soft white gown and tight emerald- green stomacher. Her neck was bare, and Edmund tried not to allow his gaze to descend to seek where her breasts were squeezed by her kirdle. Edmund was lost.

'Well Edmund, tell me about yourself and why you are now come to London.'

'That I am a Shakespeare you know and with this name comes the family in Stratford-upon-Avon. My father is, no correction, was an alderman and he is in the glove and wool trade. My mother is from the Arden family although we have very little contact with her relations. I came to London several months ago to join the playhouse as an actor though I hope one day to be an owner.'

'You have ambition, this I believe is good, but I fear it may be a long time before you acquire enough property to invest in the playhouse business.'

'We will see, but I have hopes my brother will assist me with property and other funds to hasten my elevation.'

They chatted easily together, and her gentle demeanour encouraged openness from Edmund. She looked at him as he spoke, and she responded with smiles each time he exaggerated his position or his qualities.

'Tell me about your brother's wife. What is she like?'

'My Aunt Anne is a good woman, God fearing and strict. I believe she seeks salvation by choosing the puritan path.'

'That must prove very difficult for your brother given that he is busy making the family fortune by writing plays for the common stage. And now you Edmund are choosing the same playhouse, a place and occupation that any puritan must regard as an obscenity.'

Emilia laughed and looked quite pleased to have learned the tragic flaw in the Shakespeare crown.

'I have a light supper for us both although we will need to serve ourselves as my housekeeper has now left for the evening.'

'I do have an appetite so I will be happy to eat whatever you have.'

Emilia got up and walked over to open the room divider, revealing a table laden with an assortment of dishes. There were cold broiled fowls, beef tongues, potted meats, salads and a basket of figs. Edmund chose several items and carried his platter back to the parlour.

'I do have some wine, Malmsey I believe. I will just have a sip but please pour yourself a glass. Treat it carefully as it was my father's, very precious Venetian glass.'

Emilia ate her food delicately quite unlike the Shakespeare women back in Stratford. They ate heartily having prepared the meal and little caring if anyone judged them for their actions. Emilia seemed to savour each small morsel and Edmund was conscious that she expected him to notice her refinement.

'Tell me about your acting Edmund. You play women on the stage. Is this easy?'

'I do play women; I dress as woman; I move as woman. It is something I have learned to do by studying women. I think I do it quite well.'

'It sounds very, er, how do I say it, exciting?'

'Yes, our audience seems to be excited. I play woman but I think many in the audience want to play with the woman I play.'

Emilia laughed and reached to touch Edmund's hand. Her long fingers felt soft and although her touch was momentary, the effect was lasting.

'When will you play the woman again?'

'Quite soon, in fact late next week I will be on the stage as I have a role in a drama written by my brother. I will play a Lady Capulet. Perhaps you would like to come and see me?'

'Not in a public playhouse, no. But if you ever play before the court. I will certainly come.'

'Do you play women only or do they allow you sometimes to play the man?'

'On the stage I only play the lady parts.'

'And what do you know of lady parts?'

Emilia smiled and Edmund felt her eyes look through his eyes, into his soul.

'I know enough my lady, although I would welcome the chance to learn more.'

'And of kirdles and gowns? Are you skilled with these?'

'I believe I look well in both. Your gown is, I think, a lovely Flemish taffeta, yes?'

'And what about lady's under clothing. What do you know of this?'

'I confess, what lies beneath remains a mystery.'

There was a pause and Edmund believed Emilia could hear his heartbeat.

'I think I can help you with this. Stay here with me tonight and perhaps you can learn what is beneath the Flemish taffeta gown.'

Chapter fourteen

A routine had now evolved that, although not policed, seemed to be followed by all who lived in the tenement house. Edmund would return from his morning walk to find the other boys, one by one, joining the ad hoc breakfast of porridge and hot cakes. The porridge was supplied by an elderly widow who somehow survived by washing clothes and repairing damaged costumes. The hot cakes were delivered by a grubby, pock marked baker's boy, who stole if he was not watched carefully.

Following breakfast was the period when all the boys conned the lines written on the rolls of cheap paper. There always seemed to be a new play to be learnt and the boys understood their income depended on their industry. Smiles and coy giggles for the audience were not enough. If the adult players were to perform their parts, the boys needed to say the lines as written exactly when they were due. Each boy would study hard and then take turns to follow their cues in front of the others. The system worked well and baring a few slip-ups, when on stage they performed without suffering too many kicks or cuffs from the adult players.

When rehearsals were completed, the boys would go next door to the tavern and take a pie and a pot of ale for lunch before enjoying an early siesta. Plays usually commenced two hours after the noon bell and those who had a role, dressed themselves, performed and then joined 'patrons' to socialise on the cleared stage or occasionally, in a private lounging area beside the tiring house.

Those not involved in a performance, would usually be found in the court playing cards or dice. Gambling was one of the vices young men adopted as a safer alternative to risking the company of girls. It was difficult to judge which was the greater drain on their earnings. But with gambling, at least there was a chance of winning money on the roll of the dice or a turn of a card. With girls, winning meant a few moments of high pleasure but resulted in an empty purse and empty heart the next day. The boys generally alternated between these two vices not ever learning restraint and certainly not abstinence.

On the afternoon designated for the performance of Romeo and Juliet, Edmund dressed himself as usual, choosing the best gown and the many other garments that together were needed to create a woman for the stage. When he was ready, he joined Robert and Christopher in the tiring house. Here he was inspected as usual, but on this occasion, he received a sharp rebuke.

'Lady Capulet is a married woman and the mother to Juliet here. You look too much a young harlot for our scene to be believed. Christopher, go find a black shawl and cap for this strumpet.'

The players all laughed, mocking Edmund for their amusement. Christopher drew Edmund aside and they rummaged through several baskets of costumes until they found two items that served their purpose. A black mock lace shawl and black head cowl were added to Edmund's costume. To this new look, a heavy smear of Ceruse and Fucus was applied to his face hiding his boyish complexion, adding perhaps ten years to his age.

'Much better, you will do. Now listen closely for your first cue.'

The performance began and Edmund listened to all the Montagues and Capulets as they strutted the streets of fair Verona. He was surprised at all the shouting and clashes between the young characters. While supposedly they were fighting in some hot Italian city, the anger and passion seemed pure Shoreditch. This was the first time Edmund had heard the complete play as the boys had rehearsed all the woman roles without having a copy of the complete text. For Edmund, the clash between Tybalt and Mercutio was exciting and perhaps all too real. But Romeo was also an example of what he would try to avoid. Romeo was what happened when you lose at cards or dice and then risk girls. There were too many country Juliets ready to ensnare the boy actors and Edmund vowed under his breath, if given the choice, he would be Mercutio.

The audience were rowdy, but all were moved by the final scene. Many a man wept and stood motionless as the two young lovers lay together in the vault. Then a wild jig performed by the entire company, plus dog. It was pure London, and the crowd seemed well pleased with the entertainment. They would pay again, another day. The adult players left the stage and like true professionals, they quickly removed any clothing items not their own and returned all swords, daggers and whatnot to the props master. Within ten minutes the tiring house was clear, and the actors had departed, off to find a dinner, liquid refreshment or both.

The three boys, in their dresses, accepted what seemed to be the usual invitation to share some drinks with a few patrons of the arts. These gentlemen of substance, who while appreciating stage plays, also enjoyed the company of the women of the stage. The illusion the boys presented excited these gentlemen in such a way that they were often reluctant to say goodnight to their fantasies. Juliet may have died up there on the stage, but she still lived for the men who gathered to chat and drink after the epilogue. The boys now played on, not saying the lines written for them by the playwrights but saying all that they believed young women said when flirting with gentlemen of substance. It was a game and usually everyone accepted the conventions. Men were teased, kisses were blown, and bottoms were patted, small gifts were offered and quickly accepted. Usually but not always.

Edmund had played his part and chose his moment to curtsey and withdraw. Robert reached for Edmund's arm and spoke quietly into his ear.

'Stay Edmund, stay, there is money here and they like you.'

'Yes, perhaps, but I have better things to do than provide giggles and smiles on cue for these bored husbands, overdressed costermongers and merchants. But I wish you much profit and amusement. Until tomorrow my friend.'

With that Edmund left the playhouse. It was still early, and Edmund hoped he might have one more performance tonight. He remembered lady Emilia was to be home alone this evening. It was a pity he couldn't risk walking the streets of Shoreditch while still wearing the gown that had shaped lady Capulet, but amusingly, he had discovered he and Emilia shared the same taste and size in dresses.

Chapter fifteen

Shoreditch was a wild place. The City Fathers and even the Ministers of Queen Elizabeth, occasionally voiced concern about this suburb although neither authority chose to carry though any plans to tame the area. The suburb existed because land was cheap and far enough away from the city walls to be almost out of the sight of respectable citizens. As people arrived from the north, most escaping the reality of failed harvests and the hardships of farm work, more ramshackle buildings were hastily thrown together. There was opportunity here and in Shoreditch, it wasn't necessary to have a full purse or have completed indentures. If in England there ever was a frontier culture, Shoreditch was it.

When the working day was done or when work had finally been avoided, there was entertainment enough for everyone, although drinking was a feature of all of them except St Leonard's Church. The pinnacle of entertainment could be found in the two purpose-built playhouses. Neither the City Fathers or the Puritan activists would recognise this hierarchy but then neither group enjoyed or understood plays or the stage. What the City Fathers and Puritans did understand were the temptations of taverns and brothels. Shoreditch had many of both. On holy days the population of Shoreditch was boosted by visitors from the city. Apprentices walked up Bishopsgate Street hoping to avoid the risk of being observed by their city dwelling masters, or other members of their guilds or institutions who might report on their rowdy activities.

It was one such holy day evening that Edmund found himself briefly regretting leaving Stratford. There had not been a play that day, so the boys had relaxed and amused themselves with games of cards and dice. Generally, the bets were small and little damage was done to those unlucky at gaming. This was the normal, but on this day, there were in the house some outsiders. Adult players usually shunned boy actors but on this occasion several men joined the boys in the tenement house. Either because they wanted to show off or perhaps because their earnings were greater than the boys, the adults sought to increase the stakes. The large jug of ale they had brought with them didn't help the young minds to navigate the mire that gradually expanded from one game to the next. Edmund passed and declined to play the next hand, choosing to be just an observer as the visitors pocketed more and more of the boys hard earned coins. All but two of the adults then left. Gabriel Spencer remained. He was a onetime boy actor, not much older than Edmund, but as he had been a successful member of several actor troupes, Gabriel was now able to play adult roles. He boasted about his performances in Henry VI, Romeo and Juliet and other plays. Accompanying Gabriel was James Feake, the son of a Goldsmith and still apprenticed to his father. Happy with their winnings, Spencer and Feake proposed they should go out and visit a Shoreditch bawdy house run by Lucy Morgan. It was just a short walk away, opposite the church. The congregations of both houses probably pointed to the visitors to the rival building across the road, chanting their own sermons defending their preferred version of paradise.

Paying for sexual favours was not something the boys needed to do or could afford. The boy actors were in a special category of performer who, due to their age and handsome appearance, were seldom without admirers ready to share a bed or a brief liaison in an alley. But as the boys knew the girls who worked at Lucy Morgan's they felt sure they would be stood a tankard of ale without expense.

The boys were happy for any excuse to finish the game of Primero while they still had a few coins left so they followed Spencer and Feake out into Holywell Lane. A short walk later the men used some of their winnings to purchase ale and ten minutes upstairs with a girl of their choice. It was a riotous house and within the turning of an hour, they had witnessed two fist fights and various types of ugly bodily fluids being expelled. Spencer and Feake supped deeply and neither man won new friends with their boorish behaviour. Just as Edmund was about to slip away and escape, Feake suggested they should all leave and go back to his friend's house on Holywell Lane. He boasted he had more ale there and they could play cards again.

While this was perhaps not the most attractive invitation, at least it meant Edmund and the boys would be closer to home and any drinks would be free. Peer pressure won over the few dissenters, so they exited the stew and followed Feake to the house of a barber friend who was away for the night. More ale appeared along with a pack of dirty and well used cards. The boys' last few coins were staked but it quickly became clear they were not important. The two men were determined to beat each other.

After a couple of hands, the boys had all lost the last of their money. Spencer and Feake, both emboldened, raised the bids again and again, staring hard at each other trying to guess the cards and read the other man's mind. Tensions rose with both men becoming aggressive, grimacing like a pair of stone gargoyles. Spencer called the stake and triumphantly showed his four of a kind. Feake looked down at the cards on the table. All of a sudden Feake grabbed the candelabra and brought it down hard onto Spencer's head. Spencer with the blow, fell backwards and rolled towards his coat lying on the floor. Before Edmund and the other boys had time to move away, a large dagger flashed in Spencer's hand and Feake fell with blood spouting from his right eye. Both men were shouting, and Feake lurched to grab Spencer's throat. Together they rolled on the floor until Spencer broke free and scrambled away through the door and out into the lane. Feake quickly followed, calling for the watch. He managed a few steps and then he stumbled forward to lie in the animal dung on the road.

The boys looked at each other in horror but then it was all over so quickly. There was blood everywhere. Spencer had run off and Feake was lying in the dirt, cursing all the deities he still had the strength to remember. Edmund was the first to speak.

'We go, quick. This is not our fight. Out, run back home fast. Go!'

As if given a stage direction, all the boys stood up and rushed out of the door. Edmund paused and looked at the table. Using his hat for a bag, he scooped up all the money that had been the cause of the violence, then he quickly followed the boys out into the dark street. Within minutes they were all back safe in the tenement house.

The boys found their favourite seats and huddled together around one half of a used candle. There was the sound of heavy breathing and one boy began to weep. Christopher put his arm around the boy and ruffled his hair.

'It's over and none of us share any guilt. What had happened, happened and none of us can change the event. It was a bad performance but not ours.'

George sniffed and wiped his nose on his sleeve.

'Shouldn't we do something?'

'There is nothing we can do, and it is best we all forget we were ever there. That man Feake will be picked up by the watch, although I doubt, he will live many days. Spencer is the guilty one, but I will not be he who says his name again.'

'Agreed. It is best that none of us tell any story about tonight. This page is blotted and unreadable. Best we try to get some sleep and never mention this scene again.'

Christopher blew out the candle and each boy moved away to find his own dark space.

Chapter sixteen

It was now the month of August 1596, and the long days of sunshine had changed the landscape. Finsbury fields were less meadow and more like an arid savanna. Tall grasses waved in the breeze and bees hunted for any remaining flowers that had survived the daily broiling. In the evening, as the sun set into the west of Hounslow, makeshift canvas tents sprang up like morning mushrooms in autumn, as city dwellers tried to escape the hot narrow streets south of the old Roman Wall. Later, by the light of open fires, dark shapes could be seen silhouetted by the flames as people cooked themselves a snared rabbit or hare. The people of London were mostly country folk at heart and hot weather allowed them to return to their native roots, if only while the air was dry and there was small game to be found.

One morning before noon, as Edmund and the boys were at study, learning more lines for the latest indifferent play by Jonson or Dekker, a small, ragged boy arrived in the court. He announced to all he was carrying a message for Shakespeare. Edmund was not surprised as he quite regularly received brief notes from some admirer or other. And of course, he also sometimes received a one or two-line, unsigned note from Emilia. When she hungered for fun and the touch of an ardent youth, Emilia would send word of when her bower at Folgate Street was expected to be free of other callers. Edmund would then quietly fold the note and, without displaying any outward interest, set aside time for playing games of Ganymede to the goddess with pale slender fingers that so lightly played the Virginals while he chose a dress from her closet.

But on this occasion the message was signed and the senders name scratched large on the paper read, Shakespeare. Shakespeare to Shakespeare. Edmund had been summoned to the St Helens lodgings. This was the first time since he had come to London he had heard from his brother. The boy said he would wait until Edmund was ready, so it seemed William expected him to stop what he was doing and attend to his elder brother's command. Ten minutes later, after Edmund had put away the play role he had been memorising, he left the social security that the boys' home in Shoreditch now embodied. He followed the small messenger down to Bishopsgate and then through the alleys by St Helens. Here the boy led him to a terrace of houses built of flat London brick. The middle door of five with a worn step and brass knob polished smooth by all the many thousands of hands that had over the years, pushed their way inside.

There seemed to be four apartments, and the hallway had the lingering smell of fried breakfast herrings. The boy stopped outside a door on the first-floor landing. Here he knocked and a few moments later Edmund heard the single word, 'come.' The boy held out his palm and, without looking, Edmund gave him a coin and then he entered the room. The air was dull and stuffy but at least it was cooler than the street outside. The walls were lined in a heavy wood panelling, decorated only by one or two indifferent portraits with the type of eyes that appeared to follow you as you move by. In front of the window, in a large high-backed chair, sat the man who had commanded Edmund's attendance.

'Is that you Edmund?'

'Yes brother, it is me. I was happy to receive your message. Working I see. I hope you are well?'

The chair was pushed back, and William turned towards his visitor. Edmund didn't detect a smile or any gesture of welcome he had allowed himself to anticipate as he had walked from Shoreditch.

'You ignored my request and returned here to London. I thought I'd made myself very clear I wanted you to remain with the family in Stratford. You disobeyed me.'

'Brother don't say disobeyed. I merely made my own decision about my life. My decision, my choice. A life in Stratford is not what I wanted. You chose London and I have followed your lead. It is good here.'

'Yes, I have been told that you have found life here to your liking. You have used my name to gain entry to persons and places that a mere boy from Warwickshire should be barred.'

'But brother I am a Shakespeare too and nothing I have done or said used your name, but mine.'

'Stop this equivocation. Be quiet and listen, my patience has been long stretched. I know you have traded on my name to get acting work with Burbage, Henslowe and Alleyn, and there are others. I know you have spent time with Earl Southampton, probably telling secrets about me and mocking me with silly chatter – the man I still care for. I know you have wormed your way into the bed of my Emilia. You have soiled what I loved and thrust your dirty seed where I once worshipped. I can bear no more.'

'But brother.'

'Brother? Oh, how you trade on that borrowed title! But Edmund listen well, I am not your brother! You, Edmund, are a bastard. Mary is not your mother. At best you can claim me as half-brother in that my father is also your father. You are illegitimate. You are like the Bastard of Orleans that lived on my pages as an irritant to the English.'

'What are you saying brother? Why would you say such things?'

'Because boy, it is true. Back in the seventies father was often away from home buying and selling wool. He was a brogger trading illegally without a licence. He would be away from Stratford for many days staying overnight in Inn's and with relatives far from the prying eyes of my mother. Then one dark night, when I was 16, he returned, slightly drunk and carrying a basket. You Edmund were the babe in the basket. I later learned that he had been tupping some shepherd's daughter. She became with child and with your birth, she died. Father owed the shepherd money, so he was forced to bring you home to Stratford. You are a bastard. You are illegitimate and only half a Shakespeare. My mother was very hurt, but she had little option but to accept what father had done. Like a good woman she was kind to you, but she was never your mother, it was sister Joan who looked after you.

Edmund lurched over to his brother and grabbed the shoulders of his jerkin, shaking him hard and staring wildly into his eyes. William pushed him off and looked at him in disgust.

'I don't understand brother. I don't understand. Why do you say this? Illegitimate? That my real mother is dead and the mother I have known all my life has lied to me? You brother are the liar! You have betrayed me and I will not listen to anymore.'

With this angry outburst Edmund left the room of the St Helen's Bishopsgate apartment slamming the door as he left. William, now alone, slumped down into his chair. The tempest that had been building since Edmund first came to London had finally burst and the words spoken, like lightening striking a tree, could never be taken back. The damage was now done but the fires started might burn unseen for a long time to come. William felt both relieved but also guilty. He had lost his control over his temper. He had lowered himself to the level of a strutting character in one of his own plays. In his declaration of truth, he had vented his frustration but in the process, he had lost control of the narrative. The scene just played out between two brothers had changed the future and now the actions of the younger would determine the rest of the play. William, the skilled playwright, was no-longer the director of action. But he calmed himself and chose to dismiss the importance of the last scene. He told himself nothing had changed. Edmund was just a silly youth and after all he was William Shakespeare, a successful playwright and a poet, admired by lords and ladies. He had influential friends and his wealth was increasing. Edmund was just an irritating, minor side-show who could be forgotten.

Chapter seventeen

Edmund

What just happened? Can I believe these ears of mine? Did my brother just call me bastard? Did he tell me I am illegitimate? Somehow unlawful and less than him – less than Richard – less than Gilbert. He said these things – in anger – but William, this man of words, knew full well what he was saying. He hit where he hoped to hit, and my insides feel like they have been gripped by bloody hangman's hands and pulled out of my body. I am still breathing but all my substance has been hacked out, ready for the fire. Illegitimate. Bastard. Two words that lie heavy on a man's head. The word murder is lighter. With murder you can argue self-defence or that the slain deserved your knife. Soldiers murder every day in the name of the Queen. For this they are either rewarded or pardoned, never forced to walk the streets baring the brand of illegitimate.

A chasm has opened between my brothers and me. Without good natural reason they have an honour thrust onto their name. They are now legitimate and able to inherit all and anything John Shakespeare might own when he dies. Edmund, according to man-made law, is the opposite of legitimate. Edmund is outside of legitimate. But am I different? In what way? My father sired four sons. All four share his blood in our veins. All four carry his name and this name will be carved onto our tomb stones. Solid letters, Shakespeare. Why does the law judge me less, just because there is the lack of a marriage vow between my father and my mother? A silly ink line scratched into a church register is missing and because of this, the law claims I am base born. I feel full of rage.

And more, something more. Mother is now nothing. The mother who for sixteen years stood invisibly beside my days as a saint ready to salve my pain, has in an instant, been shattered like a holy statue at the hands of a puritan reformer. In my mind this mother watched over me in the darkness but now I learn that the darkness was my mother. Dead due to my birth. Never to be known and never to be named.

The lies I have been told. But wait, perhaps not. Was I ever told Mary was my mother? Perhaps I just presumed mother was mother. I adopted her, she never adopted me. The horror. I feel cheated, abused and degraded. But this cannot be left, this will not end well.

I am Edmund Shakespeare. I am loved by many. I will thrive. I will grow. I will prosper. I will have such revenges but as, yet I don't know what.

Chapter eighteen

Five days after the confrontation with his brother, Edmund crossed the Clopton Bridge, arriving back in Stratford. The town looked somehow smaller after his many months in London. The burnt-out buildings from the last town fire, still showed blackened timbers poking like ribs out of the chest of a rotting corpse.

The Shakespeare's Henley Street house was the same and at least this seemed welcoming. The house contained the memories of childhood, a fine time when Edmund knew nothing of secrets or deceits. The house was entirely innocent and for Edmund, it was still home. Too much of his childhood was played within the walls for it to be tainted by human duplicity.

The family was surprised to see him walk through the door, Anne immediately asking if William was with him. When he answered no, she vented her annoyance and then returned to the task of making pastry for a pie. At least the children seemed excited to see him, and they asked what London was like and if he was going stay in Stratford. He told them London was the size of a thousand Stratfords full of exotic people from all quadrants of the globe. This seemed to excite Judith, but Hamnet returned to playing with a wooden ball he had found in the Guild Pits. The rest of the day drained away and Edmund managed a few hours' sleep, woken occasionally by the shouts from the room below as the three women of the house prepared dinner.

At last, both the smells of cooking and the sound of John Shakespeare's arrival, heralded mealtime. The family found their usual places round the table and a Grace was said. Edmund looked at his father with less love and respect than he had before. Perhaps it was because of the knowledge he now had or just the passing of years, but John looked smaller and older. Edmund realised his father might not have many more years sitting at the head of the table. In between mouthfuls of good mutton stew, John asked about the business affairs of his two absent sons.

'Gilbert I never see. Perhaps he doesn't like the playhouse people or maybe he fears Shoreditch, I don't know. Trading in haberdashery keeps him busy in the city but I doubt if he finds the money comes easy.'

'And William, how is he?'

'My playwright brother seems able to keep the theatres full. But now there is a lot of competition for a paying audience. More playhouses are opening and there are many college men who provide scripts. I myself am a sort of actor apprentice for James Burbage and I hope one day to perform before the Royal Court.'

'It seems to me a dangerous business, speaking another man's thoughts out loud in front of an audience of thieves and informers. I'll tell you, no good will come of this.'

John Shakespeare had always opposed the idea of William being a playwright. For him either craftsman or merchant was the only respectable business for a gentleman. In this opinion, Anne concurred although for her there was the added issue of morality. She joined the debate.

'I wonder the city fathers allow these filthy degenerate places to continue to pollute the minds of the people. So many whores and catamites singing and dancing like demons in hell.'

'But quiet woman. Not in front of the children.'

John shut down the conversation and Edmund felt relieved he wasn't going to be chastised over his meagre involvement in the entertainment business.

The next morning the house was quiet. The children were at the school room and John was at his gloving. Mary and Joan were out gathering berries from the hedgerows. This left just Anne, and Edmund took the opportunity to stoke the fires of anger that simmered somewhere deep underneath the layers of black cloth. The combination of resentment towards her husband's absence and her religious fervour could easily be prodded and Edmund now possessed his own desire to punish certain wrong doers. The long uncomfortable hours spent on the road to Stratford had given plenty of time for fermenting malicious thoughts and now was the moment when he could put a match to the wreckage of his brother's marriage.

'Aunt Anne, I have long agonised over a secret that has weighed heavy upon my conscience. I do not wish to cause you pain, but I feel you have the right to know. I must share something with you. It is about my brother and the path he has chosen.'

Anne stopped sewing a torn shirt that Hamnet had discarded yesterday. She looked sternly at Edmund and asked him to 'go on'.'

'The playhouse you know of, and I believe I understand your objection to this place. But my brother's playwrighting for the public stage has led him into far worse vices. Aunt, it troubles me greatly to tell you, but my brother has strayed far from what any good Christian wife could accept. I cannot myself say the words, but I have here writings in his own hand that make it manifest how far he has dishonoured you.'

With that, Edmund passed to Anne several of the handwritten sonnets he had carefully selected and copied from all those intrusted to his seemingly safe hands by the young Earl and others he had stolen from a box in the bedroom of Emilia. Anne read the pages Edmund had given her. Slowly all the colour drained from her face.

'Can this be true? He wrote: 'A woman's face, with nature's own hand painted, hast thou the Master Mistress of my passion.' Then again here: 'and with his pleasure grace impiety, that sin by him advantage should achieve.' This, this is to a young man?'

'Yes.'

'And these lines to some woman? ' My mistress' brows are raven black.' And again here: 'Give then thy fingers, me thy lips to kiss.' Yet more: 'If snow be white why then her breasts be dun."

'Yes.'

There was quiet in the room, but Edmund could hear breathing. Then, as she struggled with her emotions, Anne looked up and spoke.

'Then William, my husband has betrayed his marriage vows, and he has betrayed me and our children.'

At this realisation, Anne put her hands over her face, and she began to weep. She sobbed deep emotional drops of loss. The long-held doubts that had troubled her during the years her husband had been an infrequent visitor to his home, now bubbled up to the surface.

Edmund quietly waited, seeing the effect of a few words, foolishly written and now maliciously given. But he didn't feel any guilt, as in his mind, William bore the full responsibility.

Anne gradually quietened herself and she dried her eyes. The strong woman, driven by religious piety, returned.

'Edmund, you can be of service to me. There is a large wooden chest of papers upstairs in the bedroom. Would you please help me to bring it down?'

Edmund said yes and together they went to find the storage box and bring it downstairs.

'No, not here. I would like to take it out into the garden.'

Edmund did as his aunt requested, and the chest was placed on a cleared patch of soil beyond the remains of this year's pea plants. Anne opened the lid and placed inside the sonnets Edmund had given her. She then walked back to the house and, a few minutes later, returned carrying a lighted piece of wood taken from the kitchen fire. This she placed inside the chest, setting fire to the piles of handwritten papers, all the poems and the plays of William. Anne watched the first pages curl, yellow and blacken as the flames spread within the chest.

'I must cleanse this house of these pages full of sin that stink all the way to the sulphury pit. Nothing must remain to pollute this family or blight our chance of salvation. Our very name must be purged.'

Edmund watched as his brother's writings burned to ashes. Anne had lit the flame, and it was she who was punishing William. He kept silent but if Anne had looked into his face she would have seen him grin. Anne used a rake to make sure the flames reached down to the bottom of the chest. Like someone at the inquisition, Anne stirred the fires until nothing remained but ash.

'As it is written in the book of Exodus, 'God will visit the sins of the fathers upon their children', and I fear the judgement that may still come. I vow to God, if he chooses that I outlive my husband, I will cleanse the world of anymore immoral writings he might leave behind. Nothing of his, will remain. I will cast them all into the flame.'

With this frightening ceremony complete, Anne turned away from the smouldering remains of the box and returned to the house.

Chapter nineteen

The next day Edmund rose early and walked along the riverbank, well before the town's folk awoke and commenced their daily commerce. The slow flowing Avon reflected the early morning light and Edmund stopped to watch the tiny but magical water-boatman, lighter than liquid, skate across the surface. The shiny river was pock-marked by rising Trout, feeding on unlucky insect lava. Waterfowl splashed and there was the sound of Sky Larks. All was calm and the world appeared to be in perfect balance.

Edmund continued on, walking back towards the town. When he passed the Guildhall Chapel, he pushed open the heavy studded door. The coloured glass in the windows blazed in the morning sunshine. On the walls it was still possible to see some of the paintings that, in the former Catholic times, told biblical tales of sin and redemption. By order of the State many had been covered with whitewash but some still remained untouched. Edmund stood for a while, and he read the poem on the wall that reminded the faithful that man comes from earth and to earth he will return. His head was full of words he had been taught but the voices were always his own.

Back in the house in Henley Street, eleven-year-old Hamnet had eaten his breakfast and was about to go to school. Edmund grabbed some left-over bread and accompanied the boy toward the schoolhouse. But as they walked together along High Street, Edmund suggested that as the weather was so warm, perhaps

Hamnet might miss the morning class. There was no objection from the boy. School was all tedious repetition and discipline and what boy would prefer that to a green meadow and the prospect of feeding ducks?

Edmund retraced his earlier route but when they came closer to the bridge across the Avon, he suggested they continue on and pass over to the other side where there were chestnut trees and willows.

'Do you play conkers at school Hamnet? Perhaps we can find some that will prove to be winners.'

Hamnet seemed happy at the suggestion and soon after they were both kicking through the fallen, spiked husks of horse chestnuts, selecting a few of the largest specimens from the hundreds of shiny brown conkers. Edmund gave to Hamnet the bread he had brought so he could feed the ducks, and they soon found themselves a space close to the water between the bull rushes.

As Hamnet concentrated on the energetic ducks, Edmund suddenly, playfully snatched away the woollen cap off Hamnet's head. For a few moments there was an excited tussle as the boy jumped and stretched trying to retrieve the cap from the much taller uncle. The game continued until Edmund tripped on an old log, this allowing the delighted Hamnet to strike back and grab his uncle's cap.

'Ha Ha, I've got yours, I've got yours.'

Edmund laughed realising that in this game he had been trumped. Hurriedly, a trade was agreed and Hamnet handed back the cap to his uncle. Edmund smiled and, then with a wide swing of his arm, threw Hamnet's cap up into a large weeping Willow tree that grew out over the river. The cap flew high and was caught by a branch.

'Oh uncle, my cap! I want it back. Mother will be angry if I lose it.'

'Then climb up and get it. That old Willow branch is slanted, and it should be easy for you to slide yourself along.'

Hamnet studied the tree branch and agreed that he would climb out over the water to retrieve his cap. Edmund sat himself down on the bank under the Willow and watched as Hamnet first climbed up and then pulled himself out along the branch. Further and further he went, the cap still just out of reach. One more effort and he had it. There was the sound of cracking wood and the far end of the branch broke off, falling into the water. Along with the branch, fell Hamnet. Deep below into the dark water, Hamnet plunged. The river bottom, muddy and thick with decaying leaves, quickly clouded as Hamnet's kicking legs stirred the sediment. His head popped up out of the river and he coughed out a throat full of water. He reached up both arms as if to grab something above him, but there was nothing. Down he plunged again, his woollen clothing soaking up the river, now all thick and heavy. There was one more burst to the surface, but it was weaker than the time before. Hamnet now gulped another lung full of river water and then he sank down below the surface. He didn't rise again.

Edmund remained passive, calm, watching from the riverbank. He never moved. The birds still sang, and the ducks returned, hoping for bread from the young boy who had disappeared. Edmund remained under the Willow tree for some time until he became aware that a cart was approaching on the nearby road. He looked up a saw a farm worker leading a horse as it pulled a heavy loaded cart of barley harvested from a field.

'Hola, Hola, I need your help! There is a boy fallen into the river. He can't swim!'

Edmund stood up and waved his arms to attract the attention of the farmer. He shouted again and the cart stopped. The man hurried towards him and Edmund pointed to the now still water that lay beneath the Willow tree.

'Run up to the cart and bring that rake here quick.'

With that instruction, the farmer waded into the water looking down for any sign of a boy beneath the surface. Edmund returned with the rake and joined the man in the water. The man raked around where Edmund told him Hamnet had fallen. After a few pulls, the rake caught hold of something and slowly Hamnet's now quiet body was drawn into the shallows. On the water, beneath the tree, floated the cap. It was all over.

Two days later the fine weather broke, and Warwickshire on that second Sunday in August 1596 felt the soft rain that brings life from the soil. But on this morning, while many of the town's folk were still breaking their night's fast, seven members of the Shakespeare family gathered around a small gap opened in the grass by Holy Trinity Church. The three main mourners stood solemn, their heads veiled in black cloth as their only son and brother was laid to rest. Behind them at the graveside, stood grandparents John and Mary together with their daughter Joan. A solitary youth stood at the foot of the grave. Edmund listened to words spoken calmly without emotion. The Reverend John Bramhall read from the approved book of Common Prayer.

'We therefore commit his body to the ground: earth to earth, ashes to ashes, dust to dust.'

A sexton stood quite apart from the mourners. His spade and barrow, the tools of his profession, ready for the final covering and completion of the rite. When all that could be done was done, the family, each in turn, made the sign of the cross and turned away to walk slowly back to the house in Henley Street. Edmund was the last to leave, As Anne passed him, he heard her whisper,

'The sins of the fathers upon their children.'

The next day Edmund joined the Greenaway wagon for his return to Shoreditch.

Chapter twenty

It was after dark before Edmund arrived back at the boys' house. There had been delays on the road from Stratford when a wheel on Greenaway's wagon cracked. They had to find a Smithy to do a repair, and this took many hours. But all was well in the end, and the wagon with its passenger arrived late but safe. Edmund found a candle in the stairwell and by this meagre light he negotiated his way through the sleeping bundles wrapped in blankets until he found his usual bed. Although old and inhabited by the normal colony of bugs, usual for a shared building in Shoreditch, the bed felt his and he quickly relaxed into a satisfying sleep.

It was mid-morning before he awoke to the sound of the boys already at their breakfast of porridge and hot cakes. Edmund lay for a time, warm under the blanket. He thought about the events of the last few days. Nothing could be undone, and fate had decreed the order of things. In his judgment he had been an agent of fate, releasing the landslide but he was not the cause. At least this was the result of that morning's deliberation. Yesterday his mind was different, full of revenge and justice. Tomorrow? How will the scales settle tomorrow?

He searched with his hand for something he knew should still be beneath the rag filled mattress. Yes, it was still there, and he felt re-assured that there was indeed honour amongst thieves or more correctly boy actors. The sock full of coins, he had savaged from the chaos of the evening at the barber's house, was still there. It was the gambling pot abandoned by Spencer and Feake as they fought, fell and fled. Edmund counted the money. Silver coins of many sizes and ages but, importantly, all accepted in exchange for goods sold by the purveyors in Shoreditch and Cheapside.

Edmund divided the 'spoils' into equal amounts. Equal except he did award himself a handsome 'finder's fee.' The boys were still eating as he joined them, sitting himself down on a cushion by the large pot that contained the remains of the porridge.

'It is best we not reopen the matter of the recent troubles in Holywell Lane. But I do have a small 'tribute' that was left by the combatants. It is the pot of coins that became the poison that inflamed their greed.'

'You have money?'

'Yes, it would have been foolish to leave it for the barber.'

The boys all laughed, and Edmund could see they were impressed he had been so quick witted at a time when most of them were bolting for the door and fleeing the scene. I have split the money between us, measure for measure. We can buy ourselves pie or tarts. The boys all patted Edmund on the back and joked between each other about how they might spend their share. Someone made the suggestion that perhaps they should all go to the Bear Gardens in Southwark. With whoops and shouts, it was quickly agreed for that very afternoon, the Burbage House boys would cross the river to the southern suburb. This would be the first time for Edmund to watch London bear baiting. As the boys prepared for their adventure, Christopher drew Edmund aside and quietly whispered in his ear.

'That James Feake died from his wound, but it seems Spencer has escaped any punishment. He is a lucky man.'

'Perhaps, but he is a man cursed and we best avoid him like the pox.'

The movement of six boys from Shoreditch to the riverside was all starts and stops as each boy in turn, took it upon himself to disrupt the progress of their march. First one then another but it was all good humoured and playful. Eventually they did arrive at the bottom of All Hallows Lane where many watermen with their wherries awaited their next fares. The tide was making and there was still a river beach showing, made up of shingle and broken pieces of Elizabethan manufacture discarded by a careless population. The boys couldn't resist their instincts and within seconds, stones were skimming across the watery surface. Those not skimming flat pebbles were hurling larger stones as far as they could. George was champion stone skimmer, and Christopher was declared a Hercules for distance throwing. These activities did not win approval from the watermen, and they made it very clear in crude Saxon language what they thought the boys next degrading activity might be. Things calmed down when money was shown, and a large wherry was soon pushed into the water. Six places and six boys plus one ruddy faced boatman. It was a heavy load, and the current was swift, but the waterman pulled hard and soon the boat crunched onto the sand on the Bankside shore, home to the Bear Gardens and The Rose playhouse.

The boys jumped off the wherry and bounded from the river to the narrow lanes that wove their way through the Southwark suburb. It was here that, outside the city and free from the controls of the mayor and his officers, were concentrated the various trades that fed the appetites of the citizens. Here on Bankside could be found brothels, bear pits and plays. Like Shoreditch, bankside was built on holy land owned by the church and therefore free from secular law. It was a Liberty and the Bishop of Winchester somehow managed to take a healthy percentage of the profits earned from catering to the pleasures of the flesh.

The largest bear baiting pit was on the ground known as Paris Gardens although the Manor house that gave it this name had long since been demolished. The boys pushed their way through the crowded alleyways and Edmund became aware of the noisy cheers of excited people. But the sound seemed somehow different from the applause at the playhouse. The noise from the bear garden had a wild almost angry tone. These shouts were the sound of a mob hungry for blood.

The building they came to visit was almost circular, three stories held up by heavy oak beams, supporting high galleries enabling the audience to look down into the arena. Once the entry price was paid the boys pushed their way to the front most row of seating. It seemed that a fight had finished, and many people had left their seats either to collect their winnings or to move on to another type of entertainment. Similar to the card games the boys played each evening, gambling was a key element and bear baiting was spectacle made more brutal by the wagers that were won or lost on the outcome. It was a sort of gladiatorial combat but where the winner or loser were animals instead of slaves.

The first thing Edmund noticed was the overpowering stench. It was a toxic combination of unwashed clothing, stale urine and animal excrement. Inside the bowl-like building, it was windless, and the air seldom moved. Edmund tried not to breathe deeply but it made little difference. Then a trumpet sounded and moments later a gate opened in the wooden wall of the arena. Two heavy set men entered, dressed in dirty leather robes, each holding an iron chain. They marched in unison dragging the chain towards the wooden stake sunk into the floor at the middle. The chains were then threaded through large iron rings at the base of the stake. Edmund watched as the men then hauled on the chains that first tightened, then jolted. Immediately there was heard the sound of fierce roaring coming from the open gate. The chains snatched tight and then all of a sudden, a huge bear rushed into the arena. The crowd all stood and shouted 'Sackerson! Sackerson! Sackerson!' The bear had both a name and a fan base of noisy supporters. He was huge with shaggy brown fur and a heavy brass studded collar into which the end of the chains were fastened. As the handlers tightened the chains, the bear was pulled closer to the stake. Each pull of the chain was matched by a roar from the bear.

The handlers then exited but returned moments later with two mastiff dogs on leads. At the sight of the bear the dogs snarled and barked, showing their vicious looking teeth. The noise grew louder. There were wild shouts from the crowd, roars from the bear and barking of dogs. The handlers walked the dogs around the perimeter of the arena keeping their leashes short so that neither dog nor bear was able to reach each other.

'This is when we place our bets, on which dog will last longest or the wildest bet, that Sackerson may lose. Make you choice.'

Alexander explained to Edmund the system and he said he would wager a shilling that Sackerson would kill the spotted dog first then the black one. Edmund looked first over at the bear and then at Alexander. He frowned and shook his head.

'No thanks, I'm not betting on this.'

Then the trumpet sounded again, and the handlers let slip the dogs and the fight commenced. Both dogs rushed at the bear. Sackerson roared and, with his huge, clawed paws, lashed at the air in front of the barking dogs. Being attacked from both sides at once inevitably led to one dog getting through the wildly swinging paws to fix its teeth into haunch flesh of the bear. Sackerson roared and pivoted trying to move away from the pain. The chains tight on his neck collar meant he could not escape. The mastiff hung on as the bear lurched towards the stake, in an instant, crushing the dog. The crowd roared, the bear roared and the dog with back now broken, crawled in the sand. With the next swipe of a fore paw, the cripped dog was flung across the pit to hit the wall. One loser down.

Sackerson now had the advantage of only one attacker. The black dog rushed the bear and leapt up towards his throat. But close above the throat were the powerful jaws and before the dog could sink his teeth into the flesh, its skull was crushed like a giant bloody hazelnut. The bear shook his powerful head, and the carcass of the dog hung down from his jaws. Twitching in the death throws. The second loser down. The crowd shouted their approval, Sackerson, Sackerson. The bout was over. If there were winners, coins changed hands and the gamblers felt the base glee that comes from petty triumph. The boys looked happy and those that bet on the loser cursed their luck and a now dead dog. The only thing that for the audience perhaps made this cruel spectacle pleasurable, was the gambling. Staking money on the strength of an animal tied to a stake or the baying mastiffs circling between a bear and the crowd, gave the cruel savagery some sort of meaning. Perhaps that, everyman's life and death is just chance.

Edmund shouted to Alexander, above the noise of the crowd.

'I'm leaving now. This is not for me. I will see you all later after I have been over to the playhouse.'

His friends all laughed and encouraged him to stay for the next fight, but he smiled and shook his head. Edmund took his leave from the bear garden and its spectacle of cruelty. In London, brutality was all too common. The frequent executions at Tower Hill and Tyburn drew crowds of watchers. Criminals being hung from the scaffold was somehow biblical in that it confirmed the verses that foretold that those guilty of sin would be punished and those not yet caught, were rewarded by being able to watch. Then there were the rarer but far grislier spectacle of beheadings, drawing and quartering. These punishments were reserved for those designated as traitors to the Queen and the State. These special events perhaps, less acts of punishment but more a very public warning to the onlookers as to what they would face if foolish enough to speak or conspire against the establishment.

But somehow for Edmund bear baiting was different. Here there were no scriptures or guilty parties or symbols of State. This was killing animals for no purpose but to satisfy a lust for blood and gambling. At heart, Edmund was still a country boy. For country folk animals represented a family's wealth. With good husbandry, a family used animals to produce food. Animals provided eggs, milk and cheese and regular wool for their clothing. Animal meat was considered special and eaten on feast days. No animal was wasted and certainly never tortured for amusement. The bear gardens were a product of hard people born in the city, between the bricks and grime, where the sunshine seldom reached. People who never knew the joy of seeing new lambs, calves, piglets or chicks. Edmund decided this would be his last visit.

Outside in the street there were still crowds, perhaps more now than earlier in the day. It became obvious that many were overcome by an excess of drink. The cobbles were wet from men voiding excess liquid that their bodies could neither process nor contain. Men sang. Women beckoned. Deals were done and commerce of the lowest kind was completed to no great level of satisfaction for any party. Edmund avoided the fallen and those that would have dragged him down to their level. He was looking for The Rose Playhouse. It was here somewhere and although he had visited it once before, Bankside was all alleys and buildings spawned from the same used bricks and timbers. But after a few wrong turns, here it was, taller than the other buildings and remarkable for Southwark, as it was neither a brothel nor church. As there was not a performance this afternoon, the doors were all barred. Edmund followed the wall looking for a way in. As he completed the perimeter, he noticed a tall man wearing a shoulder cloak, opening a small door and Edmund rushed towards him.

'Good sir, can you help me. I am looking for Master Henslowe. Is he here today?'

'I believe he may be somewhere close. Who's looking for him?'

'I am an actor, and I hoped Master Henslowe might be able to offer me some work.'

'An actor you say? Really, so many boy actors it seems the schoolrooms of London are all empty. Why would Henslowe want to talk to you when he has all the boys he needs?'

'I have played here once before in Romeo and Juliet and before that before a gaggle of lawyers at Middle Temple.'

'What is your name.'

'Shakespeare, Edmund Shakespeare.'

'Now that is a name for a playbill, but I fear it is not yours.'

'I am Shakespeare but perhaps you are thinking of my playwright brother. I am younger but we were sired in the same Warwickshire stable.'

'If you are a Shakespeare, you better come inside, and we can talk.'

The tall man led Edmund into the deserted playhouse. The yard smelt refreshing after the stench of the street and the bear garden. There was a smell of freshly cut wood chips and hazelnut shells. Gonfalons hung limp from the gallery and the empty stage lay like a huge box waiting for a pandora to open.

The man stepped confidently onto the boards and found himself a chair. He seated himself and looked out into the yard where, on play days, the groundlings pushed and jostled to find the best view. He removed his hat and smiled at Edmund.

'So, Shakespeare junior, what do you know of our craft?'

'I know the playhouse is where we hear the oracles of our time. In the church we hear only dogma and at the court, just law. These are two sides of the same blunt weapon used to frighten sheep. But here in the playhouse freemen talk the words of those who wish to be free.'

'Saints alive, you are a Shakespeare! But if you are to survive you need to learn your brother's skill at saying powerful things softly, so a listener is never quite sure exactly where you stand.'

The man laughed to himself and leaned back in the chair. He took a clay pipe from a pocket in his breeches. Edmund watched him and realised he still didn't know who he was talking to.

'Sir, will you please tell me your name?'

'I am Henslowe. This is my playhouse, and I know your brother although he has never mentioned to me your name.'

'My brother, for reasons I do not fully comprehend, has not welcomed my arrival in London. But I am here, and I wish to stay. I hope you will be able to employ me when you next have a play to cast. I have been learning to play the woman's part with Christopher Beeson and Robert Goffe as my generous tutors. We all live in Burbage's boys house in Shoreditch.'

'Kit and Bob are rising stars and if you make them your light you are sure to find your way. As to you performing here at The Rose, I can make no promises, but I am sure something may turn up. If so, I will send a message to the house'

'Thank you, sir. I will wait and I hope to hear from you.'

'I bid you good day Master Shakespeare.'

With that, the meeting was over, and Edmund found his way back to the door and he passed out into the busy street. Henslowe had a good reputation amongst the boys and although the few minutes of conversation was hardly an audition, Edmund felt sure something good would come from it.

Edmund now walked towards where he hoped he would find a route across the river and then on home. The sound of the evening Angelus bell rang out and he passed St Saviours Church that lay close to the southern end of London bridge. Edmund became just one small youth in the stream that moved slowly towards the only road that led across the river, back to the city. The bridge and its towering houses funnelled the human traffic like a drain. There was movement and the bodies seemed to be carried forward, passive and inevitable. But as Edmund was drawn along, he looked up, straight into the blackened faces that once had eyes that cried. There were heads on spikes on the first pillars of the bridge. Unhappy heads, condemned traitors, who had once laughed and kissed, as all do when they think they will live forever.

Edmund saw this sorry sight and he stopped. Those behind pushed but he moved out of their way. He suddenly felt ill, and this was not the road he wished to tread. He looked back towards the church, and he pushed his way to a side alley and a narrow path that led along the shore to St Saviours Stairs.

Here the wherries rode the ebb tide, awaiting passengers wanting to return to the city. Edmund stepped aboard the upstream boat and took the stern seat. The waterman followed and held out his hand for the fare. Like Charon on duty at the river Styx, the man used a single oar of pine to first push his boat out into the wide river. He had been doing this all the years of his life and he did not look at his passenger or towards the far shore. He just lent to his oars and pulled with a steady rhythm. The lantern lights on the bridge reflected in the water. What had looked merely unpleasant when the boys crossed several hours earlier, now as the daylight fled with the hour, the water looked dark and threatening.

Edmund looked at the ferryman and then far across towards the north bank, wishing for the safety of the shore. As he stared into the distance, suddenly, he thought he saw something. Something up ahead in the water. Was there somebody there? In the water, a head and two arms reaching up.

'Boatman, I think I saw someone struggling in the river up ahead.'

The man turned his face towards where Edmund had pointed. His eyes were well used to the dark and the river held no mysteries.

'Nothing there, just water.'

The boatman continued his steady rhythm, stroking neither faster nor slower. The boat continued on its course. Edmund once more stared out into the dark. Nothing. Then again, he saw someone in the river. A head disappearing and two hands reaching out of the water.

'There boatman, there, I can see it again.'

'Settle yourself, or it might be you in the river. There is no one there. I can see nothing.'

Edmund closed his eyes, but he still saw. A boy drowning.

A few minutes later and the wherry made the landing and Edmund quickly stepped out on to solid timbers, relieved the crossing was complete. Had he left Hades, or had he arrived? Edmund strode rapidly up the street, eyes forward, not looking back. In less than an hour he was home, and the friendly faces cheered his arrival. There were hot pies to eat and a game of Nine Men's Morris.

Chapter twenty-one

Edmund resumed his Shoreditch rhythm. A morning walk across Finsbury Fields and then time spent memorising parts. There was a new play to be learnt, and Edmund had been told he could have the role of Helena. Another boy had been given the same part and it had been made very clear to both that they were in competition. The best performer would have the role on stage, the other boy would be the understudy. As usual Edmund had not seen the whole play script, but it seemed to be set in Athens, Greece. The boys all enjoyed themselves pulling from their memories, stories from Homer, learnt during long school day lessons. A strange fusion of imaginary characters and centuries, created in the minds of young boys who had never left English shores. All inspired by an ancient Greece that still dominated school rooms of England and the writings of romantic poets.

Helena loved Demetrius but he loved Hermia. Just an everyday teenage drama and one that well suited Edmund with his good looks and growing stage confidence. He felt happy that this time he would be centre stage and play a girl of his own age.

After several hours study Edmund decided he needed to perform an errand and make one social visit, both in the city close to Bishopsgate. It had been a week since Edmund returned from Stratford and as, yet he hadn't seen his brother to give him the news. Burbage had mentioned he believed William might be in Kent with some players touring the larger towns. Edmund assumed he would by then have returned to his St Helen's lodging. It would be the first time the brothers met since William declared Edmund to be a bastard and merely his half-brother. A chasm had opened between them and resentment ran hot under the skin. William had harboured this for sixteen years and now the sharp crack in the Shakespeare family vessel had been revealed. For Edmund, his brother's ambush had been sudden and traitorous. He felt betrayed and his anger at his brother bubbled like volcanic larva barely concealed under the crust of a smile. But Edmund now directed events and the scenes at Stratford had been penned by the young actor and not the playwright.

Edmund chose the scenic route to the city walking down Curtain Road and then across Moorfields until he met the old London Wall. Here, he passed by St Botolph's Church and the Dolphin Inn, before entering the gateway to the city. From there it was just a short walk to St Helen's where he slowed his pace. He looked at some of the gravestones that, though veiled by lichens, marked the passing of residents with enough riches to buy a piece of stone. This in the hope that their bones might be spared the sexton's spade and the fires used to clear ground for the reselling of church yard plots. As Edmund passed the corner of Winding Lane, he noticed a thin man, wearing a large, brimmed hat, leaning against the wall. From where the man stood, he could see the entrance to his brother's lodgings. Was the man watching the building? Edmund wasn't sure but he felt there was something sinister about him. Edmund walked on and he pushed at the door to the house. Up the stairs to the landing and then he paused, before knocking hard on the door.

'Come if you must.'

Edmund entered the room and found his brother as usual, seated at a table, spread over with pages, discarded quills and several open books. This was the workplace of a playwright, and this playwright was much in demand.

'Who is it? Can't you see I am working.'

'The globe turns many times while you have your back to the multitude of stars. Your eyes are fixed low searching for words that are read by the few.'

'So, Edmund, you came back again.'

'Yes, I did. Brother do you owe anyone money?'

'Only the City Fathers, no one else. Why?'

'I think there may be a man watching this house. A thin man with a swarthy complexion and ugly black gloves.'

'I don't recall seeing such a man, but it is possible. There are spies and plotters everywhere.'

Edmund slowly walked around the room choosing the best moment to deliver his Stratford message.

'When did you last see your son Hamnet?'

'When I was in Stratford, perhaps four months past, but why do you ask?'

'I saw him last just seven days ago. He was in the river Avon, sinking. I watched as he struggled, reaching out, trying to grab a Willow branch or a hand. I watched as he drowned. The day after, I was there as prayers were said by that Puritan John Bramhall, and your son was buried in the cold earth of the churchyard.'

William stopped writing. He turned to face this bringer of dark news. Edmund watched as his brother suffered. The man so full of words for his characters, seemed to find it impossible to find something for himself to say. Strangely, there was no doubting or questioning of the news, how it had happened, who did what. Although an enormous shock, in a second, deep inside William felt he knew the truth. William's head slumped forward, and he shielded his eyes with ink-stained hands. William wept.

Edmund seated himself and picked up a book that was lying discarded on the floor. It was the play, The Jew of Malta by Marlowe. A tragedy and as Edmund turned the pages, he felt the room darken with unhappiness. Edmund looked from the open book to his brother, a man closed and deep in thought. After many minutes, William lifted his head and turned around, back to face the table. He picked up his pen and found the unfinished line he had been working on before Edmund spoke, and once again, he began writing.

'I will be travelling up to Stratford soon and I may stay there several days. When I return here, I will send you a message. Go now.'

Edmund stood up and waited a moment but as his brother did not turn around or cease writing, he walked to the door and left. The street was empty, but the thin man was still there standing on the corner. Edmund left the scene with its solitary mourner up there in his room, dealing with loss in his own way. What he felt, he never said out aloud but, his pain found its way into voices as yet unheard and faces unseen.

Edmund walked on; this dark theatre closed but a better one was waiting close by. Emilia was the social visit Edmund intended when he left the boys house, and he now walked swiftly to the street where she lived. He hadn't seen her for quite some time, and he wasn't sure if today he would be welcome. He stood outside the door for a moment, listening for any voices from within but hearing nothing, he knocked. A few moments later there was the sound of the bolt being drawn and the old servant woman peered around the door.

'Ah, it is you. My lady has a visitor at the moment. She is not available.'

Edmund heard Emilia's voice from the parlour asking the servant who had come calling. The servant glanced at Edmund and told him to wait. She turned around and went to the parlour door. Something was said and briefly he saw the face of Emilia. There was a quick smile and then she disappeared. The servant returned and informed Edmund that the mistress would send a messenger tomorrow. Edmund bowed and turned away. For now, he was disappointed but there was a promise of another day and for this, he felt a flush of male excitement, imagining the pretty woman and the touch of her lips. As his body anticipated pleasures to come, Edmund noticed a well-dressed man walking towards him. Fine silken hose and bejewelled doublet, the handsome young man held his head high as was fitting for his rank. It was the Earl Southampton. As he drew closer, the young man recognised Edmund although the last time they had met Edmund had been dressed as a pretty woman. Both men smiled at each other and Edmund doffed his cap in greeting. Nothing was spoken between them, but each man knew they shared a friend in the Lady Emilia.

Chapter twenty-two

William Shakespeare appeared, as usual, confident and an immovable authority in his own world of drama. After all, he wrote peoples' lives, determining their entrances and their exits. He decided their level of joy or their pain. And on this occasion, he had decided it was time for Edmund to leave. William had written what he intended would be Edmund's final scene in London. The recent tragedy up in Stratford had taken place while William was away in Kent with the players on a tour of the larger towns. He had watched as the players took their bows and collected fees from smiling crowds of people not used to the theatre. He returned to London to face the news that brought personal grief as any father would feel it, but for him death was all part of the plot. In his time, he had experienced so many deaths. Ink lines scratched out on paper, quickly closing a life and opening a new scene for those that were left in the narrative. Stratford was all familiar but somehow still distant. For William, life went on. New pages, new stories and new lives. There undoubtedly would be more tragedies and his pen would provide sentence to characters cursed with flaws so contagious that whole families would bleed and weep. But at this moment, as he looked at this brother Edmund, William held on to the hope that for the Shakespeares, more tragedy might be avoided.

'Edmund, I want you to leave England.'

'What? Leave? To where and why?'

'Listen and try not to react until I have said my piece. What has happened cannot be undone but it can be forgotten. Well, not forgotten but certainly it must be left behind us. You and I must move on, and as I have estate and family in London and Stratford, it must be you Edmund who moves furthest.'

William paused and looked hard and tried to read any response in the eyes of Edmund. Nothing could be detected so he continued,

'I know a man, Robert Browne, a good theatre man who was born here in Shoreditch. He has for many years moved between London and the protestant city of Cassel on the near continent. He is in the service of a wise Hessian Prince of that city, and he has a company of actors who tour from there to many rich courts and states. The actors all live in a fine castle and are paid handsomely by the Prince for their craft. The man I know is now here in London recruiting and I can secure you a place in the company.'

'And if I won't go?'

'You are a cunning boy and ambitious. The offer I am making you is a good one. I will pay your passage and let us call it an apprenticeship fee. I will also give you a purse of 400 Crowns meaning you will be able to live in Hesse as a gentleman. This is a wonderous boon, and I know you will think well on it and choose wisely.'

'And if I won't go?'

'If you were to refuse my good offer and stay on here in London, I will use my influence and power to have you shunned from all employment in every playhouse.'

Edmund felt a flush of anger course through his veins, but he was now learning a little more self-control. He took a deep breath and moved over to the table where

William had been working when he arrived. Pages, pages, so many pages. He picked up one sheet and started to read.

'Iago. Now that is not a name from Warwickshire!'

'Put that down please. That is something in progress that still needs more work.'

'Another foreign play? Why do you set so many plays in places and times that are not ours? Jonson, Dekker, Massinger all write plays of today.'

'And their plays are weaker because of this. They attempt plays of 'now' but in doing so they can never reach the timeless essence that lives deep within man. We playwrights are all struggle and search and for written words to raise questions that force the listener to better understand themselves. I believe it is best not to be distracted by the superficial that is 'today.' My plays offer a portal into everyman and for this I must unlock the imagination.'

'It seems I am back to the school room, but I will think more on it. Both your philosophy of playwriting, and your Cassel proposal.'

Edmund realised there was more to his brother than he had thought. It didn't change how he regarded him, but it warranted more reflection. He made his excuses and left his brother to continue his work, telling him he would return with his answer in seven days.

Edmund

What is this new plan of his? He is still giving me orders and treating me as a child. When I first came to Shoreditch to spend time with him and see the London world where he spent so much of his life, he rejected me. He refused to be my brother and share with me what he himself had found. It was as if he had secrets, and he would not allow me to see them. I was told to go. He told me I had to return to Stratford and the life he had already rejected. Being a glover or wool trader had been too mundane an existence for my brother, but he was sending me back to do exactly what he shunned.

But I am no fool and I didn't obey commands that he himself would never have accepted. So, I came back without his help. I found a home here with the boy actors and I have learned their mysteries. I have found the woman's part and can now play woman for men on the stage. And much more, I can play woman for woman. This is a precious craft and something that unlocks hearts and thighs. So, I now too have secrets and in these my star is ascending.

But my brother's new plan for me is of interest. To travel and see the world – well perhaps not the world but more than just England. This Robert Browne I must meet to learn something about his players. Is there money in this? My brother says yes and of course there is his purse of 400 Crowns. What could this amount buy me? I don't know but perhaps it could buy me a share in a London playhouse. Perhaps.

What is it like on the continent? These foreign shores where men speak in tongues not ours? Brother said they are protestants so perhaps we share something already. So many questions for me and I must seek and find answers before I meet with brother again.

Chapter twenty-three

The day agreed for the meeting between Edmund and Robert Browne arrived. William had organised this and it was to be held at his lodgings in St Helen's. The playwright intended to write the next scene, the one in which his brother Edmund goes into exile, never to return.

Edmund arrived and walked up the stairs and he found the door to the apartment open. There was his brother and the man he had come to meet. Robert Browne was dressed all in black, but the cloth had a silk like sheen. This was a suit of clothes not made in England. His beard was sharp trimmed and had the gloss of henna. Robert had all the appearance of a man who collected his look from tailors in Antwerp, Amsterdam or other continental cities. He had dark brown eyes and auburn hair, cropped short.

William performed the introduction with a cool efficiency but quickly Robert took control of the meeting.

'I am happy to make your acquaintance Edmund. One Shakespeare is a boon and, to the playhouse, he has brought great riches. I now I discover there is another, a brother. I watched you perform on stage the other afternoon as Helena, in that play, what was it called William, 'Summer dreams?'

'That is close enough for now. A first version that I will improve before it plays before the Court.'

'I enjoyed the play, but it is quite ambitious and difficult to stage well, although I would like a copy to try it with my company before the Prince in the great hall at Cassel.'

Robert asked Edmund to seat himself and he then spoke at length of his past, his present and the future. Robert told the two Shakespeares that he had been born in Shoreditch to a family involved with the early days of Inn yard performance. He was an actor, but his skills went beyond treading the boards. He had a flair for production and management. He toured with the Earl of Leicester's Men and quickly gained a lot of experience. Shoreditch at that time received many visitors from the Court of the Queen. Foreign emissaries and ambassadors, all reporting back to their Princes and Kings about the virgin monarch and England. The new English style of theatre attracted their attention, and Robert met a young prince from Hesse. The Prince decided his father's court might be improved by stage entertainment and he asked Robert to form a company of players and bring them to his father's palace in the city of Cassel. The money offered was good and he also offered a legal contract. Since that time Robert had been based in Cassel although the company of players toured many cities from Zeeland to Prague. Life was good working for Prince Maurice, Landgrave of Hesse who now had inherited his father's title and riches.

Robert was in England to recruit more actors and to buy certain items for the Prince. He would be returning to Cassel by the end of the year.

'I would be very happy to have a Shakespeare in my company and the Prince can offer you a twelve month renewable contract. You will receive a handsome wage, two sets of livery, your accommodation and food. This is a good opportunity for a young actor.'

Edmund smiled and his head span with all the things he had heard. There was a lot to take in, not least that he would have to leave England, the land of his birth, and live in a country he had never heard of.

'What you have told me suggests a bold new life. Although one where I will perform on stage as I do now. I still need a little time to consider it all and think over your gracious offer.'

'A wise boy who chooses to tread carefully when offered a golden calf and a pathway leading off into the dark. I would do exactly as you intend if I were to be offered a map to Solomon's mines. Shall we say seven days?'

'Yes sir, seven days will be long enough. Where can I find you to give answer?'

'I am staying with a merchant friend of the Prince. You can find me or leave a message at Goldsmith's Hall, Foster Lane.'

Edmund got up to go but Robert waved his hand to signal he should remain.

'It is I who must take my leave as I have business in the city. Thank you, William, it has been good to see you once again and to meet your brother Edmund, who I hope I will hear from soon.'

Robert departed, leaving the brothers alone. Neither one welcomed more conversation but there were still matters of the deal to be clarified.

'Brother, you mentioned a purse of money you would give if I was to leave England. I think you said 400 Crowns?'

'Yes, that is my offer. Provided you leave England and do not return, I will give you 200 when you depart and there will be 200 waiting for you to collect at the port of Flushing.'

'And if I don't choose to accept the exile you propose, what then?'

'As I told you before, if you refuse my offer and that of the employment given by my friend Robert, I will use all my influence here in London to ensure you never work in any playhouse, ever again.'

Edmund stared at his brother, this playwright, this poet. The richness of his soul that allowed him to put fine words into the mouths of Kings and Queens, somehow didn't surface as love for his family. Edmund sensed that he alone saw the hard man before him, everyone else saw the gentleman from Stratford. Edmund picked up his cap and nodded farewell to his brother as he left the room.

Chapter twenty-four

Edmund packed his bags, ready to leave the boys' house. When he had arrived there, he had one small shoulder bag and just the clothes he was wearing, nothing else. That arrival seemed a long time ago. Since then, he had learned many things, and it now seemed that along with knowledge came physical baggage. He had learned about women, how to play women on stage and how women off stage, like to be played. He had learned friendship, and he now felt a slight sadness to be leaving the other boys with whom he had shared so much. But then there was also that monstrous thing he wished had never been told. His one-time loving brother had forced him to learn something of his birth. It was knowledge, but of a kind that stole from him his family and birthright. His head was now cluttered with thoughts, all jumbled together. During his moments alone, Edmund had to 'shuffle the pack', find his Aces and bring them to the front.

So today it wasn't just a small shoulder pouch, but two large leather bags. He was moving and all he possessed, he would carry. Along with a few choice pieces of personal clothing he had acquired by trading with other boys, there were two gowns that Emilia had given to him. They still bore her scent, and she had judged he looked better in them than she did.

But not everything he owned was in the two bags. He had a bundle of incriminating sonnets, written by his brother, but 'salvaged' by Edmund. This bundle he had wrapped tightly in cloth and carefully sewed the seams together to make a secure package. With a makeshift wax seal on the join, this precious parcel had been entrusted to Christopher Beeson. Although leaving England, Edmund was already planning for his return. Christopher promised to keep the package secret and safe, only to be given up to Edmund in person.

Edmund's departure had all been arranged and he had already said his farewells. The other boys were jealous of his good luck. A monthly salary and the chance for travel to royal palaces and rich cities where who knows what he might achieve. In the world the boys created between themselves, Edmund was off to make his fortune. He promised them, if fortune came, he would send word, and they could all join him somewhere in the Germanys over the Rhine. It was all boys talk, of course. The future for men would always be different.

It had been agreed with his brother that he would send a man to accompany Edmund to Flushing. The other boys saw this as a gesture of a loving brother. Edmund thought differently. The man was his jailer, paid by his brother to guarantee Edmund went into exile as he had instructed.

So it was, that just before noon, Edmund and his brother's man, were walking down Bishopsgate heading for the Tower. They carried one bag each and little was said as Edmund was deep in thought. He was not happy at the deal he had been forced to make by his brother. To Edmund it felt like a new betrayal, and another hurt to be borne like a new scar on his back, unseen by everyone else, but still felt deeply.

The man walking beside him, was named George Bull, a man of his brother's age. Bull was William's factotum, and someone entrusted to fetch and carry business matters, matters outside anything remotely romantic or creative. His brother had business affairs where the profits from the playhouse were 'worked' to provide more profit. Properties and Leases were bought and sold, loans were made, and debts collected. Bull was the man who dealt with matters the playwright sometimes wrote about but seldom touched with his own ink-stained hands.

'Never fear boy, with me you are safe. I have made this trip many times. Flushing is, how do you say it, my second home? I was with the Earl Dudley when we fought the Papists and their Spanish slaves.'

'I am surprised you want to return if you have memories of battles and death.'

'Both are part of being a man. The playhouse is for fops and boys.'

'Well, I am one of those boys and you, soldier, are carrying my bag.'

'Ha, you speak the truth. You have metal in your tongue.'

'As much as my brother though perhaps not so silvery. How long will it take to reach Flushing?'

'Maybe two days. First, we have to find a ship at Deptford and then voyage down the Thames with an ebb tide. Once at sea, with God's provenance, it will be just another day.'

The prospect of two days in the company of George Bull, didn't please Edmund but he needed his skills, even if he stank like a boar and had the same conversation. The two mismatched travellers passed by Leadenhall where they stopped to eat pies and toasted cheese before continuing on towards the Tower of the

Conqueror. A castle built on the east wall of the city. Built to defend the new lands the Normans claimed. Defend from their Scandinavian cousins, who with their long ships, threatened to sail up the Thames and settle family arguments. The walls were high, but their main use had been to keep rebels inside rather than keep invaders out. Englishmen have always hated the building and feared an invitation to visit. Some who lodged there lost their heads behind its stone walls or, like the apprentices taken at the recent 'price of food' riot, hung by the neck on gallows outside on Tower Hill.

The two travellers walked, and George Bull navigated the streets until they arrived at St Katherine's Stairs. Here he negotiated passage with a waterman, to have them rowed down river to Deptford. The bags were put aboard the wherry and in a few minutes the boat was out in the stream and slowing moving eastward past low suburbs bearing names Edmund had heard spoken of but had never visited. These were home to communities of seafaring people where ships and cargo were the meaning of life. Here the sole institutions of the Elizabethan state were a few excise officers and armed watchmen, there to guard against invasion or foreign threat. England's enemies came out of the continent, exactly the place where Edmund was about to start his exile. Rotherhithe, Wapping, Redcliff, all slipped by as the waterman rowed his boat using the outgoing current to assist their progress. All along the shore there were ramshackle wharves and low timber buildings, full of casks, canvas and ropes. There were ships of all kinds. Some at anchor and others clearly resting in the mud as the tide dropped down. This was the real gateway to London. Not facing the green counties of England but leading out into the world. Across the seas lay empires, all rivals to England, although most accepted trade ships and these floating arks built of oak, carried riches, some bought, some stolen, back to the motherland, England.

It was mid-afternoon before the boat approached the shoreside at Deptford. The waterman steered his craft into a water gate set into the river wall. Here the boat would wait while George Bull went ashore to find a ship and agree onward passage to Flushing. Edmund waited aboard the boat, pulled his cap down over his eyes and tried to sleep. How long passed, he didn't know but he was awoken by a heavy jolt of the boat as Bull stepped back aboard.

'All done. We have passage to Flushing. The ship is anchored close by and may leave with the tide sometime during the night. It is good for you I have a sister here who knows the captains and was able to give me a name.'

'That is good. Is it a big ship?'

'No, just a Hoy but she is large enough to get us across the estuary and out to the east.'

Instructions were given and the waterman pushed the boat out from the stairs, and they began the search for the ship.

'You see that house Edmund, close by the stairs? That is the house my sister keeps. Same house where, about four years past, Marlowe was stabbed to death.'

'Marlowe. Do you mean Christopher Marlowe the playwright?'

'Right enough. But it wasn't playwriting that got him killed. He had been playing a dangerous game for that man Walsingham. There were papists everywhere and Marlowe got himself caught between the hunters and the hunted. Sister said it took her hours to clean up all the blood.'

Edmund was not comforted by the story although he didn't know how much of it was true. Either way, the man who had negotiated his passage to Flushing and with whom he might be forced to share a cabin, had a past that suggested violence and thuggery.

The waterman rowed downstream, and they hailed five ships at anchor before they found the Hopewell bound for Zeeland. She was moored within sight of Greenwich Royal Palace and the hunting grounds behind. A young seaman dressed in a heavy wool jacket and cap, helped Edmund to climb the ladder and then Bull handed up the two bags. This ship, one of the many, that regularly made the passage between London and Zeeland. There was trade enough for all of them to have full holds of cargo, both ways with the occasional passenger serving as a bonus source of income. They were hard working ships with few concessions to comfort. Edmund could smell tar, sisal ropes, wood and bilge water. Despite the river air, to Edmund the ship conveyed a foul humour. The seaman threw Edmund's bags down the companionway, to land on the floor of the saloon below. Edmund followed quickly to check for breakages and find somewhere safe, and hopefully dry. The dark cabin smelt worse than it had on deck. As he stepped forward, within three paces, he twice cracked his head against the cross beams supporting the deck above. To Edmund, the ship appeared to have been built for a crew of dwarfish, ricket suffers. Edmund began to realise there was something mysterious about the men who chose the sea as a way of life. Living on a farm in the county was simpler and a man could stand up straight on solid ground that didn't constantly shift underneath him. It was going to be an uncomfortable night, and he wished it was over. Another sailor appeared from out of the dark holding a dim lantern.

'You be a passenger for Flushing? If so, get aft to that starboard cabin.'

'What? Where?'

'Starboard side, aft.'

The sailor pointed in the direction he had instructed. Edmund looked around for any clue as to what the man had meant. His puzzled look was noted, and the sailor grabbed the two bags and slouched his way towards the back of the saloon, stopping beside a door with a brass handle. This door was slid open to reveal what seemed to be a small cupboard with a mattress lying on a shelf. The sailor threw the bags onto the mattress and left. This cupboard was to be Edmund's cabin for the passage. Edmund heard a laugh, and he recognised the heavy shape of George Bull who had joined him below.

'Nice and snug ah. Just like a coffin. You will fit like a fat worm in a hole. Best it be like this, so you won't roll too much as the ship rocks her way over the waves.'

'This might be a good time to ask for the first payment. That money my brother gave you for me. Just in case I don't survive the crossing.'

'Ha, you'll do. Here, take the purse.'

With that George moved away into the dark and disappeared. Edmund went back up on deck and looked around the ship. It was bigger than it had first appeared, and this helped relieve some of his nervousness. This would be his first time at sea, and he had heard enough stories of shipwrecks and Moorish pirates to make a boy from land locked Warwickshire, very anxious. Being born on an Island with a wide watery moat between it and the continent, made ships an inevitable necessity for anyone forced into exile. Edmund looked up at the huge black mast with its impossible tangle of ropes that held it upright and pulled out the sails. This ship was far more complicated than any horse drawn wagon or piece of farm machinery.

There were just six crew, all solid men with faces as weathered as a blacksmith's was burnt. They were all Cornishmen and seemed to speak a private language between each other that neither Edmund nor George could understand. But they all had smiles and seemed to know their trade. The sun set in the west and a large cauldron of rabbit stew was taken off a fire burning inside a box lined with bricks. Crew and the two passengers sat on the deck and ate from wooden bowls. Bread and cheese completed the meal and then everyone, smoked their clay pipes. Not Edmund, as this was one London habit he had still not adopted. The captain told them that as soon as the tide turned, the ship would up anchor and set sail.

As it grew dark over the river and the birds noisily discussed their day, there were little spots of light marking where before, Edmund had noticed houses. Over to the distant northeast, there was a very faint glow in the sky and this he was told was London, rebelling against nature and marking itself a place where God's laws didn't apply.

Part Three

Travels

Chapter twenty-five

Edmund

'Our father which art in heaven', thrice I have said the Pater Noster. May God help me!

This ship will throw me into the cold waters, and I will be food for fish. It rolls and pitches, like a demon trying to throw me off its back. Here below inside its belly, I fall and bash from timber to timber, all unseen in the dark. The floor is slippery with the filth that slops up out of the bilges. There must be a monster down there regurgitating all the liquid blackness that unfortunate passengers of the past have vomited out.

Oh, there it goes again. Worse this time. The ship must break up. I can hear the timbers growling and fighting with each other. I can hear bangs and crashes as casks and crates move about down in the hold. And water, water everywhere. Pouring through the hatchway and leaking through the deck. The noise I hear is of banshees and mad demons all loose inside this timber drum. And my stomach! Nothing like this before. Not after rotten food or even poison could make me feel this bad. Ugh, it comes again. I will go back on deck although that evil mouthed captain doesn't want me there.

Is there no place on this ship of torture I can find relief? Here on deck the rain beats down, if it is rain and there is still a sky above. The sea comes straight from the wind and water batters me from all sides. I crouch down here behind an overturned punt to try and shelter from the wind, so heavy that it could lift me if I did not grasp hard on the rope lashings. Oh, and here it comes again.

My stomach should be empty. I have long since purged anything left inside but still something ugly heaves its way up into my mouth. And I am so cold. So cold. My muscles won't move, my blood seems to have set hard within me and although I still breathe, nothing wholesome moves through my heart.

This is hell. I think I will die but I no longer fear it. Surely death would stop it all. Bring on death.

The morning approached and a small red sun appeared, rising above the horizon. The vast grey waters stretched to the edge of the world, with the ship Hopewell somewhere in the middle of the void between England and Flushing. The captain smiled and lifted Edmund's head that had sunk low down onto his chest.

'The wind has backed, and the sea is down. We are running before, and we are making good speed. From now it will be better.'

Edmund looked up but he said nothing. He heard the words, but they were something external. For Edmund everything that mattered was what he felt. The cold, the wet, the sickness, none of this felt 'better.' But he was still alive. The new day had arrived, and it was getting lighter. Perhaps he had been saved. Edmund dozed between the state of exhaustion and hypothermia. But each time he awoke, the ship seemed to move less violently, and the sun had risen higher in the sky. He was not as cold as he had been before. Another hour, and another. With each hour, marked by the sound of a bell, Edmund regained something of himself.

By early evening a grey streak of land could be seen on the horizon. The ship Hopewell had come unflustered and safely across the Southern Bight of the North Sea. The crew had done their job, and all was well. Only the passengers had suffered, one more than the other. As the sea flattened, the motion of the ship eased into a slow sway and the crisis of the night, while not forgotten, was a memory that would gradually fade like ink on a page. Edmund slowly found himself feeling better and he even managed a turn or two around the deck, before fatigue led him back to his chosen, miserable private sanctuary.

At last, the ship approached the outer harbour wall and the captain gave orders for the sails to be lowered and furled. The anchor was let go and the crew made everything once again, ship shape. The captain informed the passengers that they would have to stay aboard until the next morning. The ship was safe, lying still and ready for another day. Edmund looked at the companionway and considered his options. Down below there was a small and perhaps warm cabin. On deck there was the chill of the evening and cold wet boards. He would go below to the cabin. In just ten minutes Edmund was asleep and the voyage, forgotten.

Dreams cannot be chosen as they are unruly spirits born from our past and our fears, timeless and careless. Edmund dreamed and there were people everywhere and water, lots of water. As he awoke, he could almost feel the dream, but it slipped out of his grasp, and in an instant, it was gone. He puzzled for a few moments trying to get back there, wherever 'there' was, but without success. He felt uncomfortable, slightly unnerved that there was a place inside his mind he could not control.

He could hear banging above, somewhere very close to his head. He remembered he was onboard a ship and the crew were up on deck, doing whatever sailors do. His clothes were still damp from the tempest of the day before and what was dry, was stiff and stained by salt. He slid the cabin door open and dismounted the narrow bunk. The saloon was orderly, and the hatchway was open allowing the soft morning light to enter. Everything was wood. It was like a huge box and Edmund imagined toy soldiers lying waiting for their owner to raise the lid. The voyage and the sea had freshened the air, and the ship no-longer smelt like a dung heap. He climbed the companionway steps and put his head up out into the day.

'Hola, someone has slept long. If you are now hungry, there is porridge and biscuit.'

The captain pointed amidships, on the tar sheet covering the hold, where the pewter cauldron had been left. Edmund took a bowl and helped himself to the lumpy, grey substance. He added salt and a large knob of butter and then seated himself on the hull of the upturned punt; the same boat he had crouched behind for much of previous day. Off to the east he could see the town of Flushing with its fortified walls looking angry with a row of back cannons pointing out to sea. Behind the walls there was a forest of masts with their coloured pennants flapping in the breeze. The ship Hopewell was anchored perhaps three cables offshore. Just far enough so that it had sea room if a storm suddenly arrived, but perhaps still within range of the cannon. As Edmund started his second bowl of porridge, George Bull arrived, coughing muck out of his lungs. He walked to the side of the ship and, after a rough fumble, urinated a bladder full of spent ale consumed during last night's meal.

'That's better. It has been pressing on me since I awoke but I couldn't find a piss pot down below. Ah, porridge, I'll have some of that.'

George filled himself a bowl and noisily shovelled the contents into his mouth. In the five minutes since he came on deck, he had completed three activities vital for his start of any day. He looked out over towards the town and pointed to the harbour wall.

'The captain will hoist a signal flag when he is ready and the harbour master will send out a boat to collect those who are going ashore. I'll not be going unless the ship is staying a few days. I have things waiting for me back in London. But you will be okay on your own. Master Shakespeare has written a message for his merchant friend here and if you show this to the harbour master, he will direct you to the house.'

'Is it far, this merchant's house?'

'No, in a street just behind the harbour. An easy distance.'

Edmund understood the arrangements that had been agreed. He would stay with this merchant, a Franz Kugelmann, and await the arrival in Flushing of Robert Browne. Browne would bring Edmund the rest of the money his brother promised him. Then he will arrange the transport for him and any other actors hired. They would all travel together to the Schloss Wilhelmshöhe, Cassel. How long he would stay here in Flushing, he didn't know, but he had Crowns in his purse, the promise of adventure and the ship had stopped rolling. It was a good day.

About mid-morning Edmund watched as a sailor hoisted the signal flag and he went below to collect his bags. Not long after a low sided boat with two oarsmen could be seen exiting the harbour walls, making towards Hopewell. Soon they tied up alongside and one of them spoke at length with the captain. Papers were passed over and then the call came for Edmund to go ashore. George helped with the bags and passed to Edmund the sealed message for Master Kugelmann.

'I wish you good luck, Edmund. These Hollanders are friendly people, and you will be fine here. When you arrive on the harbourside, just show that message I gave you to someone and they will direct you to the house.'

'Thank you, George. I am not sorry to leave this ship. A sailor's life is not for me and whatever the land holds for me, here my stomach will stay put.'

With these farewells, Edmund jumped ship and seated himself on the harbour boat.

Chapter twenty-six

Letter, October 1596, Stratford upon Avon

Dear brother Gilbert

I hope my letter finds you well and that your business is proving successful. These are troubling times with the bad harvests and rising food prices, so I fear people may have less money to spend on fine buttons, lace and fabrics. But perhaps things in the city are different from those here in Stratford? I don't know if perhaps sister Joan writes to you, but I thought I would share with you some news of the family.

The family are all well, though of course, we all still miss Hamnet. Anne has been very strong, but she now rarely smiles. She says she feels betrayed although what exactly she means, I don't know. She spends long hours reading her bible and her closest confident seems to be the Puritan John Bramhall, the preacher at Holy Trinity Church.

Father's health has suffered, and he seems to cough much more than before. He walks badly and his hands are becoming painful.

I have concerns about William and Edmund. It was several weeks after the funeral of Hamnet that William arrived home. He had heard about the accident from Edmund. What concerned me about William was that, in addition to sadness over Hamnet, he seemed angry at Edmund. Several times I heard him blame Edmund for Hamnet's death. I haven't seen Edmund since the funeral. I wondered if you see him in London?

I wonder what he is doing there. I do fear his relationship with William has become full of rancour.

Other news from here. William has bought a run-down pair of barns on Chapel Street, opposite the Guildhall. The buildings are in a bad state, and they seem to need renovation before anyone might live there. A strange purchase, I think. William is almost never in Stratford and Anne and Judith don't need a big house and garden.

The other news, I am sure you know this, Father has now the title and Arms of a gentleman. William arranged this for him at the College of Heralds in the City. There is a family Crest and a Motto. I doubt if he will have long to use either. William's business in the London playhouse, seems to be very profitable if he can lavish such expenditure on luxuries. Who could have thought it, our brother making money from silly poems and plays.

I hope to see you back here in Stratford soon.

Your brother,
Richard

Chapter twenty-seven

When seated in a rowing boat, looking from the sea, the town of Flushing appeared like a floating fortress. The walls were high, and the town seemed to be almost circular, surrounded by water. The small entrance was hidden behind two low moles that jutted out into the water like strong builder's arms. It was only as the boat turned between these rubble breakwaters, could Edmund see the narrow entrance to the harbour. This was a place born of wars and it guarded the entrance of the wide Scheldt River that led inland to the important city of Antwerp. The riches of many a Prince had been lavished on its defensive ramparts. The strange politics and treaties of rival empires had resulted in an English garrison being stationed here to keep the Spanish out, so Edmund was arriving in a foreign country but where his nationality was accepted if not quite loved.

The small boat passed into the harbour and Edmund was amazed to see there were canals and docks leading far into the town. There were ships, not anchored as with the Thames, but alongside solid stone wharves with paved unloading areas. Cobbled streets ran along the dockside. It was a marvellous sight, suggesting industry, wealth, and above all this, civilisation. The oarsmen brought the boat alongside some stone steps and Edmund felt the solid land again after three days on the moving water. His first steps were unsteady, the motion of the ship was still with him and he felt as if drunk on ale. The oarsmen laughed as he staggered, well knowing the signs of men returning to land after a sea voyage. His bags were unloaded, and he was directed across the dockside to a desk where, an official in a broad brimmed felt hat, was seated.

'Goedenday.'

Just one word and the reality of his arrival in Flushing rose up, like the fortress wall, before Edmund. Here they spoke a language of sounds that bounced in his ears like rolling thunder. The civilisation he had just marvelled at, was the achievement of people who did not speak the good Queen's English.

'Do you speak English sir?'

'An Englander! Yes, I speak. You are welcome here. What purpose you come?'

'I am here to visit Master Franz Kugelman and then after, travel on to Cassel.'

'Ja, good. Do you have money?'

'Yes sir, I have money.'

With that, Edmund shook his purse, this being the universal signal that he was not a beggar, and he could pay for lodgings and food. The harbour official smiled and signalled to a group of boys who were playing a game of skittles on the quayside. The smallest of which came over and awaited instructions. Words were spoken, none of which Edmund understood and the boy quickly shouldered the two bags and staggered off under their weight. Edmund bowed to the official and then hastened to follow the boy who was rapidly disappearing behind some wagons that stood in a line on the quay.

The streets were all clean and the cobble stones, shiny. The sound of wooden sabots clattered as the townsfolk went about their business, unaware that for one man at least, they appeared as exotic and amusing.

The house address he had been given by his brother was Hellebardierstraat and the boy, now carrying, half dragging the bags, skipped along Smallekade lined with sleeping ships awaiting their next cargo. The boy turned left into a street of tall, well-built brick houses, all very different from those Edmund knew back in London. Although a terrace, each separate house had a gable roof facing the street. The edges of each gable were stepped, climbing one after the other to the topmost flat stone. There was a Dutch architectural style here and Edmund felt there was also something fable-like in these buildings.

The boy shouted something to Edmund and then stopped outside a green painted door. The boy indicated that Edmund should knock here. There was a heavy brass knocker shaped like a jumping fish and Edmund nervously banged it three times. The sound echoed along the street and the few people, all turned as one to see the stranger. The door opened quickly, and a young serving woman dressed in black, wearing a strange stiff white cotton cap on her head, stood looking out.

'Ja, kan il je helpen.'

Sounds spoken by an intelligent native but sadly all lost on an alien from Warwickshire.

'Master Franz Kugelman please.'

'Meneer Kugelman, Ja.'

The woman looked expectant, perhaps assuming Edmund would then explain the purpose of his visit. Edmund thought quickly but the only idea that sprang to the front of his mind was to thrust his brother's letter towards the woman, as though it was a magic key or a weapon. The woman took the folded paper from him and read the name there written.

'Wacht alstubleft.'

This was becoming more and more like a scene from his brother's play Comedy of Errors. A young woman, a boy and a confused youth, all good Christians but now stage comedians, miming on the streets of Ephesus. The woman smiled and closed the door slightly then disappeared back inside the house. A few minutes passed then the door reopened, and Edmund was waved inside. The boy placed the bags on the floor in the hall, and two silver sixpences, bearing the head of Queen Elizabeth were forced into his hand. He didn't recognise the coinage, but his doubts were ameliorated by the fact that there were two not just the one he was expecting. The door closed behind Edmund, and he realised the trials of the day were far from over. The hallway had a floor of red tiles, and the furniture was heavy and carved with animals and birds suggesting some Eden or other wonderous hunting grounds. There was a strong smell of smoked herrings, and this served to remind Edmund that his stomach had recovered, and it was long since his last decent meal. As this basic need filled his mind a large, clean shaven pink faced man appeared from a doorway.

'Welcome, welcome, you are welcome, Master Shakespeare. I have met your brother many times when in London. We have had business together and I have been able to put into his hands several stories and papers I believe he may have used for his playwriting.'

'Sir, I am happy to meet with you and I hope my arrival will not put you to any trouble.'

'It will be no trouble at all. I am happy to have a guest from England in my home. You will be able to tell me the news and what is happening in the city and of how the markets stand. A merchant must read the Runes if he is to stay ahead and profit from events, both good and the not so good. But I forget myself. You must be hungry after your sea voyage from England. Come, let us sit in the kitchen and I will get Jolanda to find you something good to eat.'

'Thank you, sir. I will be happy to eat. The Cornish ship served only porridge and sea water.'

Jolanda seemed happy to prepare food for the young, handsome Englander. Perhaps having a fresh new person about the house was a form of entertainment. She cooked a special type of pancake. This was one word of Dutch that Edmund managed to learn, Pannekoeken. This word would prove to be very useful in the coming days. It was quickly agreed that they should all use first names and Franz then proposed a small toast to be drunk to summon good luck for his new life as a touring player. Unfortunately for Edmund, Franz chose a traditional drink made there in the Hollands. From a brown stoneware bottle came Jenever. This was taken out of the large kitchen dresser and a generous measure was poured into three pewter cups. Jolanda joined in the salute to fate and Edmund quickly discovered Jenever was a foreign spirit with fire. The host and Jolanda both laughed as Edmund spluttered on his enthusiastic first gulp of the clear liquid. Had he stopped at just one cup full he probably would have had a more productive evening. But hospitality was offered, and Edmund willingly accepted. Edmund's first day in Flushing ended in a bit of a blur and quite how he came to be undressed and between clean cotton sheets, he didn't remember.

When the morning light filtered into the room through the window shutters, Edmund had a headache and no recollection of the latter half of yesterday. But in his defence, he could have claimed the three days at sea had been very draining. He was also dehydrated and lacking food. The combination of all this plus the relief at his arrival on land, the good food and the brown stoneware bottle, all worked their magic upon him and sleep came very easily.

When Edmund did raise himself from his pillow and swung open the window shutters, he saw a new city. Rooftops with red clay tiles, their gables marching skyward in all directions. Flushing was a pleasing view, and Edmund studied the scene from his top floor bedroom. When he had explored with his eyes this impressive little town, he was surprised to discover that the clothes he had worn when he arrived had disappeared. Luckly, he had a change of clothes in his bag, and he put on a clean shirt, slops and breeches. The second bag contained the two gowns Emilia had given him, but this was not the time for a theatrical entrance for breakfast. When properly dressed, Edmund descended the four floors to the kitchen. Jolanda was nowhere to be seen. He explored the room and the well-stocked pantry. Behind the house was a small, enclosed yard and here the mystery of his missing clothes was solved. The clothes were all hanging on a line stretched between two apple trees. Someone had kindly washed the salt out of them, and they were now drying in the breeze. As Edmund realised his good fortune to have been welcomed into such a friendly household, he heard someone behind him. He turned to see Franz coming out of the kitchen.

'Good day Edmund. How do you feel?'

'Good morning, sir. Much better thank you. But I think from now, I will be more careful with that bewitching drink. I fear I may need to seek your forgiveness for my behaviour last night.'

'Ha, no need for that my friend. And remember we agreed, you call me Franz. Here in Flushing, we are very used to Jenever but perhaps for Englanders, our spirits are too strong and more like the Gaelic whisky than your watery ale.'

'A weapon against our weak heads but I will learn from my mistake. I see I have someone to thank for washing my clothes. I was surprised to find them all gone when I awoke.'

'That was Jolanda. She is a good woman. She is my cousin's daughter, so family and since my wife departed this world, Jolanda has kept house for me. She is out at the market at the moment.'

'I will thank her when she returns. But tell me Franz, how was it I was put to bed in a clean night shirt.'

'That was also Jolanda. She has many brothers, so she is well used to see boys in their Adam state. She noticed your clothes were still wet, so she decided to get them off and wash them. We are both lucky men.'

'Most certainly.'

Edmund smiled broadly. Perhaps he was going to enjoy the customs of the continent. Franz and Edmund chatted together for a few minutes before Franz took his leave. Business required his attention.

'Ah Edmund, before I forget, your brother requested I advance you some monies, he will repay me when I next visit London. It is best I give you this in Guilders as these will be accepted both here in Zeeland and in the Hessen States.'

On the kitchen table Edmund found some fresh bread, a type of local jam and an unusual orange rinded cheese full of holes. He ate breakfast quietly while he planned his day. It was time to explore the town. He put on his shoes and was about to leave when Jolanda returned carrying a wicker basket covered by cloth full of food.

'Goedenday Edmund. Ik hoop dat je goed geslapen hebt.'

The problem of yesterday suddenly returned. A smiling, friendly person in front of him but this Englander couldn't understand a word she said. Perhaps one word was recognisable, and Edmund smiled and tried his best to say it.

'Hod-er-dack.'

That was it. Panic set in, he smiled and started to mime, trying to communicate that he was going out for a walk. Jolanda quickly understood but just as rapidly she noticed Edmund didn't have a jacket as his was still drying outside on the washing line. She signed to him to wait, and she went into the kitchen and opened a large cupboard. Here she selected a spare coat of blue wool and offered it to Edmund. Though too large in size, he took it. It would do for the time being and he didn't want to seem ungrateful. Once out into the street, Edmund decided he would start by retracing his route from yesterday. He wanted to see if the Hopewell was still at anchor or if she had left to return to England. The streets were busy with people, and he noticed the clopping sound of many sabots on the cobbles. He noticed many women and they mostly wore heavy skirts, white aprons, and a type of white cap with wings or at least this was what Edmund thought they looked like. They looked healthy and happy perhaps both more so than the working women of London.

Edmund looked at all the ships, some being unloaded by workmen, some being repaired by sailors. This was a town for merchants and their trading provided the wealth that seemed to be fairly distributed amongst the townsfolk. It was a short walk to the main harbour and there he found steps up to the ramparts of the sea wall. He looked out to sea and watched the many ships sailing along the coast. He looked hard, searching for the Hopewell but without success. She had left. Although he felt quite content in Flushing, knowing that there would now be no easy return to England, caused him a moment of doubt. From his position up on the wall, he could see what appeared to be soldiers gathered in small groups. Their swords, belts and large boots made them conspicuous. As he returned to the dockside, he could hear them speaking English. This was reassuring. He wasn't the only English man in Flushing.

Then as he studied the faces and people around the harbour official, still there at his desk, he noticed someone who looked familiar. There, leaning on a wall, was the thin man with a swarthy complexion and ugly black gloves. The same man who he believed had been watching the lodgings of his brother in St Helen's Bishopsgate, was here in Flushing. How could this be?

Perhaps he was mistaken. There must be many men with similar looks although he did look very familiar. Edmund watched the thin man who seemed to be watching some men disembarking from the harbour boat. They appeared to have just arrived, as he himself had done yesterday and were about to show papers to the harbour official. Edmund left the wall and slowly walked around the harbour, occasionally glancing back towards the thin man. He was still there.

To allow the large ships to enter the inner dock areas, there were several wooden bridges with lifting mechanisms to allow the central spans to raise up when required. Edmund crossed over two of these on his way to the far side of the harbour where there appeared to be a large Guildhall. Outside there were tables and benches and several stalls selling food and drink. As it was now nearly lunchtime, Edmund decided he would try to spend one of his new Guilders. After looking closely at all that was on offer, he selected a soup with the attractive cypher of Erwtensoep chalked on a board. Edmund took his bowl of soup together with a chunk of rye bread, to a table to eat his lunch. The soup turned out to be made of peas with bits of sausage. It was good and he felt satisfied that he had managed to buy food without speaking a word of this puzzling language. As he basked in the glow of self-satisfaction, a man joined him at the table. The thin man.

'Good day sir, Are you from England?'

Without any polite gestures of introduction, the man asked his question.

'Yes, I am from England. Do I know you?'

'I doubt it. I would have remembered. Have you been long in Flushing?'

Edmund looked hard at this man. It was definitely the man he had seen in London. He suddenly felt the chill of anxiety as he thought, perhaps he had been followed to Flushing.

'I arrived here yesterday. Do you too have business here in Zeeland?'

'Of a sort, yes. There is someone in Flushing you should meet. It will profit you. Can you meet him here after the evening bell? He is an Englishman and in the service of the Queen.'

'Perhaps. An Englishman you say. Yes, I could meet with him this evening. What is his name?'

'Poley. His name is Robert Poley.'

With that, the thin man stood up and left. Edmund watched as he walked back across the two bridges to return to the harbourside where he took up his previous position leaning against the wall. Watching.

Edmund finished his lunch and then spent the rest of the afternoon exploring the town. He walked the city walls and viewed the fortifications and windmills.

In the late afternoon, Edmund visited St James the Great Church. As in England, the church was originally Catholic but became Protestant at the time of the Reformation. This religious conversion had caused much pain for the people of both nations and was the catalyst for wars. The English garrison in Zeeland was the latest manifestation of this conflict. For Edmund, the possibility he might be forced into an army, any army, was horrible. He didn't want to kill, or risk being killed in someone else's war. He had hopes of a better life and having escaped Stratford, he would do everything possible to avoid fighting a holy war.

The church bell sounded, and Edmund went towards the place of his meeting. The tables were still there as were a number of men in small groups, drinking out of large tankards made of pottery, just chatting. There was one man on his own. He wore a large, brimmed hat, from underneath spilled long greasy hair that fell onto his collar. He wore a short dagger in his belt and a black jerkin. Edmund looked about and then approached.

'Is your name Poley?'

'Yes, I am he. Sit down. You look like the youth my colleague mentioned. Are you English?'

'Yes, I am English, but I don't know why you asked for me to meet you here.'

'Patience, I will explain. But first I will get us both beer. It is good here. Very different from English ale.'

The man named Poley got up and walked over to a stall and bought two tankards of beer. He came back and seated himself down.

'I like Flushing. It is very compact and civilised. Too small for an ambitious young man such as yourself but it is a gateway to the continent. Many Englishmen pass this way and then there are men going in the other direction.'

Edmund listened but he had no interest in friendly conversation. He didn't know this Poley but he knew he was connected to the thin man. And this was not a good recommendation.

'What is your name?'

'Shakespeare, Edmund Shakespeare.'

'We know of a Shakespeare. A playwright in London. Are you related to him?'

'He is my brother. But you say 'we.' Who are the 'we'?'

'The government of the Queen. I work for Lord Cecil, and he works for the Queen.'

'The other man, the thin man, he was watching my brother wasn't he. Why was he watching him?'

'We were watching your brother because your brother knows people we are watching.'

'I still don't understand. Who are you?'

The man then told Edmund a sort of story. He made it sound reasonable and patriotic. In reality, it was neither. His name was Robert Poley and he was an agent of the Crown. The Crown was under attack by people who claimed to be followers of the Catholic religion, and they took their orders from the Pope. These orders included murdering the Queen and putting a Catholic onto the English throne. There were many conspirators and a few assassins all plotting to change the regime in England and Poley was employed to find the plotters and stop them. In London there were high ranking people who were under suspicion, some of whom knew Edmund's brother William, so he was being watched. Here in Flushing, agents of the Crown watched the port, noting who arrived and who left. Everyone who travelled through Flushing was watched. Edmund now understood although this story wasn't a good story.

Poley then explained he wanted Edmund to be an informer. To report to him if certain people spoke against the Queen and her government. He would pay for any information received.

'Who do you expect me to report on?'

'There are many people. I can give you a list of names later. But for now, remember the name Percy. Anyone of the Northumberland Percy family are of interest to me. If you meet any, talk to them. Let them talk. They will condemn themselves by their words.'

Edmund didn't like this man Poley but it seemed more dangerous to reject his proposition than to accept. He didn't believe he would meet any enemies of the Crown, but he would accept money, if money was offered just to listen to tavern chatter. Edmund realised to refuse would make himself a target. The only option he now had was to appear to have agreed but then do nothing. So that was it. Edmund became an agent of the Crown, albeit a sleeping agent. Edmund was happy to leave grubby Poley and walk the clean, civilised streets of Flushing. Back in the house in Hellebardierstraat, Edmund found his clothes were in his bedroom. All dry and neatly folded.

Chapter twenty-eight

Breakfast was always a fun time. There was the magical smell of freshly baked bread that Jolanda brought back from the bakehouse before Edmund awoke. On the kitchen table there was always a collection of cheeses and hams. The difference between England and the Hollands was subtle but breakfast was a portrait of what the two nations had in common, with the little distinguishing marks on full show. In the Hollands, breads had exciting seeds, cheese had holes and hams were dried or smoked. Edmund enjoyed breakfast.

Franz and Jolanda would talk as only members of families can do. Edmund would watch their facial expressions, trying to divine any clues as to the subjects of their discussions. Sounds rather than words, it was a language that mystified Edmund and kept him somehow always a voyeur. But without the means to join in the daily conversation, Edmund was forced to analyse and thoroughly digest everything his eyes consumed. The solitude forced upon him by the absence of external language, enriched his comprehension of every small thing around him. At these moments it was as if he transcended the normal to touch a monk like contemplation.

'Jolanda and I have just been speaking about your clothes. You only have one jacket and perhaps it would be better for you to have a spare one before winter arrives.'

'That is an idea Franz. I have heard told winter in the east maybe colder than in England, so perhaps a thicker jacket would be useful. But I fear I will have difficulty with a tailor as I cannot speak your language.'

'We have thought of this, but Jolanda can go with you to a local tailor I use for my clothes. You have your Guilders, so you can buy yourself a good Hollander's coat.'

They both smiled broadly, and it was all agreed. Later that morning, Jolanda made herself ready for the town, and after a few phrases and mimes, Edmund joined her to go visit the tailor. They walked out together and immediately Edmund politely offered to carry Jolanda's large basket. With nods, smiles and blushes, Jolanda accepted the offer, and the odd couple walked the route, via the bridges, to the far side of Flushing. It was soon apparent to Edmund, that Jolanda was a well-known and liked member of the community. Nearly every second person offered her greetings in some form, either by nodding or speaking as they passed. On two occasions, women of her age, stopped and longer conversations took place. Edmund realised that he was the topic. It seemed the females of Flushing wanted to know more about this young foreigner carrying Jolanda's basket. The short journey to the tailor took longer than could have been anticipated. But they did arrive and once inside the tailors, Jolanda took charge. Edmund stood in his shirt sleeves and was prodded and turned. The tailor measured him for the new jacket. Several fabrics were shown and rejected by Jolanda. Finally, one passed her test. Buttons and linings were chosen as were the number of pockets and belt. Edmund listened, watched but understood very little. At last, after what for Edmund felt like an age, it was complete. The tailor had his instructions, and they left.

On the way back to the house, they passed by several small fishing boats tied up alongside the quay. The boatmen had returned from a night at sea with their catch and now they were enthusiastically hawking the fish to the townsfolk. There were fish of all types and sizes. There were baskets of black shelled mussels and huge frightening crabs. For Edmund who lived most of his life as far from the sea, as in England it was possible to get, the huge selection of silvery fish was wonderful. Unlike the sad, dull eyed smelly causalities of the sea that were transported up the Thames to Billingsgate Market, in Flushing the bounty offered by the harbour boats was like treasure. Jolanda bargained and finally selected two fat Halibut fish and a heavy quantity of shiny mussels. Edmund now had something significant to carry.

Later that day, the front door boomed as the brass knocker announced a visitor. Edmund was in his top floor room, but the noise still reached him. A few moments later, he heard the sound of Jolanda calling his name. Three flights of stairs later, Edmund saw the shape of a large man standing by the closed door. For a moment Edmund slowed his descent as he suddenly thought perhaps it was Poley or one of his minions, arrived to demand some sort of service. But as the visitor turned his head, Edmund recognised Robert Browne. They greeted each other in the style of Englishmen everywhere. A brief handshake and question, where the answer was always the same, 'very well thank you', then the weather, and it was all over. Jolanda showed Robert and Edmund into the front parlour and then she left the men to discuss their business.

'How have you been getting on Edmund. Do you like Flushing?'

'I have been very well looked after here. Spoilt in fact and I will be sad to leave. Flushing has been a pleasant surprise. If the cities of the continent are all like this, I wonder why so many people leave and journey to London.'

'Flushing is special but by no means not equalled by some other cities. Flushing is by the sea, and this gives it an advantage. But remember, many of the people who struggle their way up the Thames to London are fleeing religious zealots or from vengeful Princes.'

'The politics that control the lives of we believers are a mystery to me. Perhaps one day I will make a study of the subject but for now I am a student of people.'

'A goodly statement Edmund and I wish you well in your studies. But are you ready to head east to a new classroom?'

'Certainly. I can be ready to go whenever you decide.'

Robert then explained it would be several days before he would have made all the arrangement for their travel to Cassel. Hesse was a distance of ninety-eight leagues, and this would require several river crossings and long stages on wagons. In addition to the six players he had recruited, Robert had brought a quantity of goods Prince Maurice had ordered to be brought from London. The journey would be slow, but it needed to be completed before the first snows of the winter. Robert described how they were unable to take the shortest route due to the city of Antwerp being under the occupation of the Spanish. Because of this war they would need to travel north before turning to the east and then on to the Germanys.

Chapter twenty-nine

The day arrived when the Robert Browne Company of players were to leave Flushing. Together with Robert, they were eight in number. All were experienced stage performers, but this didn't stop them feeling slightly nervous about the challenge they faced. Firstly, there was the journey of ninety-eight leagues. Only Robert knew the way, though he had completed the journey many times and everyone put their trust in him. Robert told his players, when on the road to Cassel he would try to get a few paid performances. Not of full plays but some well-chosen scenes and comic entertainments. They would perform in English, and this would mean probably only the elite classes and aristocrats would be able to appreciate the spoken dialogue. But then performance of music, dance and mime were all key components of English theatre. Edmund was the only boy actor, but Robert told him of an Anthony Jeffes who was waiting in Cassel for them to arrive. He had been part of the former Browne Company but had chosen to remain in Hesse when Robert had returned to England to recruit new performers.

Robert hired two waggoners to carry the eight persons plus the six large crates of items for the Landgrave. The first stage of the journey was to travel the length of Zeeland and then board river boats to cross the Oosterschelde to Holland. The boats were Scules, a type of flat-bottomed river boat. Edmund was relieved to see, although passage by river was required several times, the waters were flat, friendly and his stomach could hopefully remain quiet. The land they passed over was as flat as the rivers. This was a country without hills, few trees but lots of windmills. Edmund noticed there were many dykes, and the Hollanders were busy engineering their landscape, stealing acre after acre from the jealous Neptune. They were creating a solid country from a water world where, before man, there was just mudflats and sand banks. The wagon route was along the tops of the dykes and every few miles there would be a small village or town. They would stop and buy bread and sausage to eat on the next leg. Most evenings, they would sleep inside one of the many red painted barns that farmers had built to house their cattle during the winter months. The actors would sing and tell stories and one or two would always perform speeches from their favourite stage characters. Edmund recognised several passages performed in the barns were from his brother's plays. He thought it best if he didn't make it known he was the playwright's brother. There would be time for this when the company started to rehearse for the first full length play. He wanted to avoid rivalry during this period when everyone was forced to deal with the stress and the difficulties of travel.

From Holland they passed into Utrecht. Robert told Edmund; these countries were all part of the new Dutch Republic. There was much change here as the war with Spain dragged on. But somehow the conflict on the southern border had brought commercial benefits to the people. Merchants and their money that used to work in Antwerp, Brugge and Ghent, chose to escape Spanish rule and moved along with their skills to the Republic. The coastal ports were all booming due to Dutch flagged ships that, with each rising tide, arrived in harbour with their holds full of exotic goods from the East Indies or the Americas. Other cargoes were stolen nearer to home from fat Spanish ships. The economy was good and artists of all types in the cities benefited from the surplus wealth.

Next on the player's route was the mighty river Rhine and this needed to be crossed before the wagons could turn eastwards. For Edmund, one river looked much like the next and there were a lot of rivers. But there did seem to be a city in the centre of the area where crossing the Rhine was possible. On arrival, Arnhem was visually striking with its high fortified walls. In England, city walls were common, but many dated back to the Roman occupation or the thirteen-century periods of chivalric combat. The walls of the Dutch Republic were modern structures speaking loudly of recent war and cannons. For Edmund, it looked similar to Flushing but without the softening effect of the sea. More rows of tall, terraced houses, all topped by the distinctive gable ends and red tiled roofs. The two wagons entered the city via the Sabelspoort gate and then rolled their way over the cobbles to the grand Stadhuis. Robert had performed here before, and he knew the Burgermeester and several of the city officials.

Robert was soon successful, and the Browne Company were offered rooms and food in a guesthouse just behind the hall. The city administrators quickly produced play bills and the players from England were announced in a style that suggested they were a famous institution, and Arnhem was honoured to have them visit. All morning on the day of the performance, the small troupe chose and rehearsed excerpts from plays they all knew. Robert asked Edmund to play Juliet and the Verona window scene. Philip Kinsman, one of the other adult actors had played the part of Romeo before and the audience were sure to enjoy watching young aristocrats discovering the comedy we call love. Edmund had seen the play when he played Lady Capulet at Middle Temple before the lawyers, but he hadn't played Juliet. It was to be a challenge to learn the scene in just a few hours, but Edmund was prepared to try. Edmund worked hard and Philip helped by writing out some lines from the longer passages, so Edmund could have these prompt sheets placed around the window and on the inside of a large fan. If he became stuck, he could hold the fan up and read. For the performance, Edmund chose one of Emilia's gowns. The effect was breathtaking, so much so, two of the new players proposed marriage.

The public meeting chamber in the Guildhall was the venue for the entertainment and the townsfolk of Arnhem all seemed to turn out to watch the players from England. Perhaps some of them remembered attending plays during the previous visits by the Browne Company, but either way the chamber was full, with some people standing at the back. The Burgermeester delivered a short speech, although what he said was a mystery to Edmund and the other players. The fun then began, and the seven performers worked hard to entertain. Edmund was pleased to witness his new colleagues tumbling, juggling and playing music on recorders and tabor. There was a comedy routine which involved a Queen like character being surprised by huge mice as she prayed to a picture of what appeared to be the Pope complete with devil's tail. And then it was time for Romeo and Juliet.

'But, soft! What light through yonder window breaks?'

Philip made his entrance from the back of the hall and delivered Romeo's lines as he arrived in the middle of the audience. Fair Juliet stood behind a large frame, denoting the open window. She was a picture and there were sighs from some in the audience.

'O Romeo, Romeo! Wherefore art thou Romeo? Deny thy father and refuse thy name.'

Juliet spoke the lines together with maidenly facial expressions and hand gestures. She was a sweet girl and believable. Few in the audience, were probably able to understand the words spoken but the dramatic effect was powerful and transcended the language barrier. If few understood every word, it is certain, even less noticed that during the longer passages Juliet was ad-libbing. The fan device had worked initially as a prompter but, William's poetry was too elaborate for Edmund's memory. As a true profession, Philip played along without a pause and the star-crossed couple fell in love as they were destined to do.

The audience clapped and stamped their wooden shoes when the scene was over. Then, as a finale, Romeo and Juliet danced a volta accompanied by Recorders, Voils and Robert playing a Hurdy Gurdy. The show had been a success and Robert came back onto the stage and thanked the mayor, officials and the audience. As the players cleaned off the face paint, and Juliet metamorphosised back into Edmund, he thought, well if this is touring, I can do this.

The following day was a day of rest and Edmund played tourist. He visited the churches and walked the city walls. In the evening, the players visited a town Inn, and they all ate and drank well, although this time Edmund avoided Jenever. Soon after dawn the next day, the players climbed back aboard the wagons, and the tour rolled on east into the Deutsch speaking countries.

After the success at Arnhem, all the players found their energy levels were boosted and the trials of the road journey became less important. They were performers and they fed off their craft. An audience was everything and the applause they received was food and drink for their body and souls. Their confidence gave them strength and each league covered drew them closer to the palace of Cassel where they all believed their destinies lay. The road ahead went via Brunswick, then on to Breme. From Heldesham to Hamel and then to Zappenburch Castle, built on a hill just three leagues from Cassel. From the tower flew the Red and White colours of the Landgrave Maurice and Robert informed the players they would rest here before travelling the final journey leg to Cassel. Robert was known by the castle staff and its steward, and he felt sure they would be well looked after. Master Mazenburgh greeted the company warmly as they entered the courtyard. He had a brief discussion with Robert then he addressed the Company. He told them that he had spent some time in England, and he was happy to have the players under his care at Zappenburch. He would instruct the castle servants to treat them well.

Edmund learned the castle was now used as a hunting lodge and as a place to entertain official guests of the Landgrave of Hesse. For a young man from Stratford upon Avon, all this spoke of Royalty and fortune. Edmund was dazzled by the glamourous world he had entered. That he was just a hired servant or at best, a temporary guest, didn't lessen the glister of his position. The phrase penned by his playwright brother, 'All that glisters is not gold', was forgotten or disregarded.

The next morning, as Edmund walked the castle grounds beyond the walls, he looked to the south and saw what he believed was a horseman in the distance. The mist was still veiling the ground and far off between a break between the trees, someone was coming. Edmund watched and gradually realised there was something different about this rider. The shape and the movement was not normal. The rider was seated very high, and the animal walked as if lame in two of its four legs. But still, the rider came closer. Edmund was hypnotised by this vision, the dramatic theatre of the lone rider approaching a castle through the morning mist. The rider drew still closer but at last Edmund questioned his own eyes. The rider had a black face, and the animal was not a horse. Although not a Catholic, Edmund made the sign of the cross several times.

The rider was now parallel with Edmund. He was swathed in heavy robes and wore cloth wrapped around his head. The animal was huge and had a large hump in its back, a long neck and fur the colour of tanned glove leather. As he passed Edmund, the rider looked down and with a small turn of his hand, signalled a greeting.

Edmund touched his own cap and the two travellers, passed in the quiet of the morning.

Edmund sat down on the turf and watched the rider, and his animal enter the castle gate and then disappear towards the stables. Edmund considered what he had just seen. Was this real or some phantom from the forest. He rushed back to the servant quarters, flustered and unsettled. He strode into the small dining room where the other players were eating their breakfast. Robert was there and he quickly noticed Edmund seemed perturbed.

'What ho Edmund. How is it with you? You look like you have just seen the ghost of Clarence.'

'Ghost, maybe but certainly a rider straight from Hades. A black faced man on a giant yellow beast.'

Robert roared with laughter, spitting out bits of bread and toasted cheese in his joyful response to Edmund's revelation.

'You, Edmund, must be speaking of Emmanuel and his camel Fadila!'

'The spectre has a name! This vision from the underworld?'

'Yes, the man has a name, and he serves Prince Maurice.'

After Robert had settled himself down and took another portion of toasted cheese, he explained to the still wide-eyed youth, that Emmanuel was an African sailor, now in the employment of the Landgrave. He had arrived in Amsterdam on a Portuguese trading ship. There were many Africans working for wealthy Merchants. The Prince heard of him and then bought his contract and since then, the man and his camel lived at the palace. At special events, Emmanuel would lead the processions and sometimes escort high ranking guests from Rappenburch to Cassel. Robert believed this perhaps was just such an occasion. The Browne Company was to arrive in procession at the palace with Emmanuel as herald.

Chapter thirty

Edmund was with Robert and Emanuel, and they were sitting together in the servants hall. Robert and Emanuel were smoking their pipes, and the rest of the actors were at another table playing dice. Edmund was thoughtful as there were several questions he wanted to ask their black skinned companion.

'Emanuel. Please tell me how you came here and where you are from?'

Robert paused his puffing and smiled.

'Edmund, if you want to talk with Emanuel you will need to speak Dutch. He doesn't understand English. But if you will permit me, I could try to interpret for you.'

'Thank you, it would be very helpful. Please ask him where he is from.'

Robert appeared to think hard and then he spoke the question Edmund had asked, using the best Dutch he could manage. Emanuel gave a broad smile and looked at Edmund.

'Ik ben Berber uit Salé.'

Edmund recognised two words from this answer. Emanuel was a Berber from the west African port city of Salé. In England there were many stories told of ships from Salé. They were feared as they attacked merchant ships and captured many crews.

'How did you get from Africa to Amsterdam?'

Once again Robert paused while he translated this into Dutch. The reply was much quicker in coming.

'Portugees schip. Vele jaren van huis.'

The story Robert had originally told Edmund was confirmed. Emanuel had been taken by a Portuguese ship off the coast of Salé and he sailed with them as one of the crew until it docked at Amsterdam. There he left the ship and spent time with some other Africans who lived there and in the nearby town of Haarlem. Later he was hired by a merchant to serve in his Amsterdam house. Some years later, when the steward of Prince Maurice was dining with the merchant, a deal was done between them and Emanuel was transferred to the Prince's staff at Cassel.

'So, Robert, is Emanuel a slave?'

At the word slave, Edmund saw Emanuel stiffen and his eyes flashed with anger.

'Not slaaf!'

Robert reached out and put his hand on Emanuel's arm.

'No, he is not a slave. Emanuel is a freeman, like you. He works for the Prince. The Prince is a wise and wealthy man and he collects many precious things. Paintings, sculptures and arts of all kinds.'

'Are you saying, the Prince added Emanuel to his collection of rare, precious things?'

'Yes, perhaps I think you could say as much. Emanuel has a small wage, and he eats and lives here as a servant to the Prince.'

Edmund thought about what he had just learned.

'Have we players been collected? Are we Englishmen part of the Prince's collection of beautiful things?'

Robert laughed heartly and then rose from the table and left the room. Edmund looked at Emanuel. The two proud examples of God's creatures, deep in their own private thoughts but both men felt a new fellowship.

It was another seven days before the steward informed the Browne Company that they should start their move to Cassel. The accommodation had been prepared and the Landgrave Hesse-Cassel would now have leisure time to receive them.

The wagons were reloaded, and the players climbed aboard for the last stage of the journey. Emanuel would ride ahead to lead the way. The proud camel was persuaded to leave the stable, and she would walk with a stately but relentless pace, the wagon horses following a safe distance behind. The distance of three leagues would take most of the day to cover. The route was along a well-trodden pathway through a large forest. The path led along a ridge and, about at the halfway point and the small town of Holzhausen, it was possible to see the city Cassel in the distance. The route then dropped down from the heights to the valley below. Here was the river Fulda and they followed its course until they could make out the city walls and the castle tower, this being the highest point of the town.

Cassel proved to be another city shaped by wars. The fortified walls were built with all the additional defensive ingenuity the engineers could devise. But the town had one more formidable barrier for any would-be attacking army. Before they reached the walls they would need to cross a liquid obstacle, as water from the river had been diverted to completely encircle the city. The only entrance to the town was by crossing over the stone bridge with its four arches. Edmund looked in awe at this picture-perfect Hessian city. The houses were tall, sometimes of five stories and all timber framed. Many were decorated with painted panels and carved figures. There was wealth here. Not just the Landgrave but the merchants and townsfolk benefited from the palace and its status as the home of one of the four sons who inherited the lands and riches of the Duchy of Hesse.

The townsfolk going about their business, stepped out of the road and watched as Emanuel and the camel Fadila made their stately progress across the bridge. There was no surprise shown. Clearly, they had seen all this before. The two wagons, complete with their eight passengers, were considered just traffic and probably no one imagined the travellers had come all the way from England. A couple of street corners and then, in front of them was a gatehouse for the castle, complete with narrow drawbridge crossing a deep moat. The castle guards stood to attention and somewhere a trumpet sounded. The Browne Company had arrived at their new residence and touring base. Edmund was excited. This was something new. The Stadtschloss Cassel was grand, more like a Parisian palace than any weapon of war. The wagons turned into the large quadrangle with the wings of the palace on all four sides, climbing a full four stories above ground, but above this was a steep roof, housing more floors with dormer windows. Emanuel stopped by one of the four spiral staircases, this one winding in curves up to the first-floor gallery. The camel gracefully knelt, first the two front legs and then the hind ones. Emanuel dismounted and stood by the camel's head.

Two finely dressed men arrived on the gallery and looked down from there at the new arrivals. Robert climbed off the wagon and then mounted the staircase to meet with the two gentlemen. There were handshakes and bows, and Robert showed his respect to them, confirming for Edmund his supplicant position within the hierarchy of service. One of the gentlemen accompanied Robert down the stairway, and walked towards the waiting players. In broken English, he introduced himself as Master Brackenburie. The players were welcomed and told their accommodation was ready and an early dinner would be served.

His highness the Landgrave of Hesse-Cassel was otherwise engaged with visiting ambassadors, but he had been informed of their arrival. Edmund was much amazed at the splendour of the palace. White stone and tall windows. Exotic trees, shrubs and baskets of flowers. This was not just home to a Royal Court; it was a celebration of renaissance refinement. Edmund felt the grandeur, created by generations of princes, each one adding to this picture of artistic achievement.

Master Brackenburie returned to the stairway and left an under-steward to escort the players across the quadrangle and through a small archway that led to the servant's lodgings.

Chapter thirty-one

The next morning, everyone slept late, except Edmund. As soon as light filtered through the small dirty window in his bedroom, he awoke. Everything was silent except Edmund's mind. Somewhere within the many levels of subconscious, the arrival in the palace had been registered but the images not dimmed. His mind was excited like a shaken bottle of cyder, and the cork was ready to pop. He quickly dressed and found his way along the corridor to the servants dining room. In a palace like Stadtschloss Cassel, servants didn't seem to sleep. Though early in the morning, the palace below stairs was busy with livered men and women arriving and leaving, all delivering or collecting. There were commands and complaints all shouted in the language of the Hessians. There was a highly developed system here, but Edmund was an outsider from both worlds. To the household staff he was neither master nor servant. The performers of the Browne Company didn't fit into either category. They were aliens in the true sense of the word.

Edmund stood awkwardly trying to comprehend how best to find some breakfast in a room where all the staff were ignoring his presence, and he couldn't speak Deutsche. Correctly he realised that to enter the kitchens would not be a wise idea. As he was about to give up and go outside for a walk, he heard what he thought was his name being called.

'Edmund. Are you Edmund?'

He turned in the direction of the sound and saw in the corner of the room a young man sitting at the end of a long table.

'Yes, I am Edmund.'

'I thought as much. I can see you are lost and that by the style of your clothes, you are English. This means you must have arrived here yesterday with Robert Browne. He told me there was a seventeen-year-old boy actor named Edmund. So, by a process of deduction, you must be he. My name is Anthony Jeffes.'

'I am pleased to make your acquaintance Anthony.'

This was the other boy actor in the Browne Company. He had chosen to stay on in Cassel when Robert returned to England on his mission to recruit more players. Edmund smiled due to the relief he felt at finding another English-speaking person in the Palace. But also, because as the only two boy actors in the company, Edmund and Anthony would be taking all the stage roles of girls and young women. Friends or rivals, they would be working together. Edmund quickly assessed his competition. Anthony was a little older than Edmund, perhaps eighteen. He was shorter than Edmund and had straight fair hair. Clean shaven, of course, and with big eyes, narrow lips and clear skin. To Edmund, he was no beauty, but he could see how, with dressing, Anthony would pass any stage test for becoming a woman. The audience would believe what they saw.

'How long have you been with Robert as a touring player?'

'It has been three years. He knew my father in Southwark and as I had already been on the stage there, he convinced father that it would be good for me to come out here. Since then, we have toured from country to country, all under the patronage of the Landgrave. Have you toured in England?'

'No, this is all new for me. I have been a player on the stage in London, at The Rose in Southwark, The Theatre and Curtain in Shoreditch and at Middle Temple in front of lawyers. I have had good teachers, and I have studied hard. But the life on the road touring will be very different. I do have a brother who is a playwright.'

'What is his name? Perhaps I may know one of his plays.'

'William Shakespeare.'

At this name, Anthony's wide eyes grew a little wider. He paused as if he was trying to remember something.

'I think I may have heard of him.'

Edmund began mentioning titles of some of his brother's plays. Anthony had a broad grin on his face.

'Stop. I was joking. Of course I have heard of the playwright Shakespeare. His Henry plays and his Titus were filling the playhouses when I was just starting on the stage. Robert has several playscripts of your brother's work although, on the road, we usually just perform single scenes.

'Yes, I understand. While we were traveling here to Cassel we stopped in Arnhem. I played a scene as Juliet beloved by Romeo.'

The two youths chatted as if they were old friends. They were both happy to be with someone who shared their experience of being a boy playing a woman in front of an audience. Most of the other actors had not started on the stage as boys so they didn't appreciate the mind games a boy must master to live on the inside with at least two external persona.

Anthony, as a long-time resident of the palace, knew the system operating within the downstairs world. He understood the hierarchy adopted by the servants and how they lived by rules they themselves developed. Each person had their place in the household and identifiable responsibilities. No-one should dare to overstep their role or intrude upon their territory. If Anthony wanted something to eat, he must ask the right level person and, of course, not attempt to get it himself. Anthony realised that Edmund would probably like to eat some breakfast. He began to watch the door leading from the kitchens and, at last he saw the person he was looking for, the scullery maid.

'Helga, Bitte sei so nett. Meine freundin und ich möchten gerne jrühstücken.'

A pretty young girl, dressed in a pinafore and apron, smiled in his direction and nodded. Breakfast would be brought when she had a free moment in her duties. Edmund was impressed that his new friend had learned enough German to be able to organise food. Having Anthony as a friend would mean one of the main problems for Edmund might be lessened.

A few minutes later, Helga returned to the room and placed on the table a jug of milk, some breads and a fat smoked sausage. Anthony collected knives and pewter plates from a cupboard and now they were both set. Brothers at breakfast, their relationship had started very well. Sharing a meal and friendly talk are part of rituals of family life and the two boys, far from home, needed family. Together they could become a team and although never spoken of, they would feel benefit by being together.

After breakfast, Anthony offered to show Edmund around the palace. After three years, he knew where the private family rooms lay within building, and he could open doors to the public halls and galleries with confidence. Edmund was happy at the suggestion, and he followed closely his guide who enjoyed displaying his knowledge to this new boy from England.

The tour began in the courtyard. The four wings of the main palace building stood on each side, and, in the corners, there were four spiral staircases rising to the floors above. On the wing that lay opposite the narrow entrance, there were three galleries, rising like tiers on a wedding cake, running the full width of the building. Edmund felt that in all his life he had never been inside so beautiful a building. Anthony led Edmund up a staircase to enter what he described as the guest dining hall. The walls were all covered in grey marble. Antony counted off twenty-seven carved panels, the important ones depicting events from the Christian Bible. Edmund recognised The Passion, Resurrection and Judgement. Anthony pointed out the carved escutcheons of the various Electors of Palatine and local notables.

Together they walked through room after room, all hung with tapestries and some with beds covered in rich damasks and crimson taffeta. One bed chamber had been decorated with a huge painted fruit tree, its branches spreading down each of the four walls. Edmund marvelled at the beauty. This was clearly the palace of a wise Prince and at this moment, Edmund felt very privileged to be in his service. After viewing the highlights of the interior, Anthony led Edmund out into the enormous gardens. Here there were fountains and ponds full of fish. There were lemon trees, pomegranates and ornamental trees of all kinds. If Anthony intended to impress Edmund, he had succeeded. Could it have been any better? Perhaps not.

Chapter thirty-two

Robert Browne informed his players that it was time to start rehearsing. Since hiring the men in London, he had only seen them perform once on a public stage. He had brought with him a small number of playscripts, and Robert needed to match his actors to the parts. Master Brackenburie agreed the company could use the main hall in the palace for the day. The six actors and two boys trouped out of the servant quarters and climbed the spiral staircase to the first floor. Robert, as stage director, lined up his players and stood back to consider his options. Many of the plays he had bought included fifteen or more characters so some actors would be required to play two or three parts. This practice of doubling was a normal aspect of English staging although more necessary with a small touring troupe. Anthony and Edmund would find their special skills vital to the success of any performance. The actors were all in good spirits and each person used the time to test themselves against their colleagues. It was a noisy morning.

Several times a grim faced and gloved servant appeared at the doorway and gave instructions for less noise. It was as if the actors had all returned to the days of the schoolroom, with Robert playing the role of the pedant.

When the door opened on the fourth occasion, the man who appeared looked very different from the uniformed servants. The man was tall and heavy set, with a high forehead and fine facial features. He wore a short, sharp trimmed beard and moustache. His clothes were large and lavish. The shoes had heels and were of cream colour leather decorated with leaves of green. Robert immediately raised his hand and signalled to the players to halt everything they were doing. He then gave a deep bow, slowly and with reverence. The man in the doorway was Prince Maurice, The Landgrave Hesse-Cassel, their patron and employer. Robert rose from his bow and walked quickly towards the Prince, addressing him in the formal manner normal for the Hessian court.

'Eure Durchlaucht.'

'I heard from my steward the players from England had arrived and it appears from all the noise, you have now settled in.'

The Prince spoke in English with the natural confidence that came from his position of authority and years of experience of intellectual pursuits.

'We are pleased to see you here Master Browne and look forward to watching your first play. Since you left on your travels, it has been too quiet here. I have had few people to argue with as my courtiers are all dutiful and too full of respect. It takes the presence of the unruly English to disturb our still waters and force we Hessians to question life.'

'I thank you for your compliment, sir. I hope we can prove worthy of your expectations. We are but humble players for the day.'

'I am sure Master Browne you will, as always, amuse the court and greatly annoy the palace servants.'

'I will do my best sir.'

'And what play shall we have from you, perhaps for the new year eve?'

'Sir, we have recently played scenes from a new play straight from the Court and playhouses in London. A Midsummer Night's Dream, and although not of the correct season, I am sure this comedy will prove amusing.'

'Let it be so. Now I will leave you to your exercises.'

Robert bowed low and the seven players followed this cue. The Prince, with a small nod, turned and left the room.

Rehearsals for the New Year's Eve entertainment commenced the following day. In addition to the play, there would be some songs, a comedy routine and music. The eight players would be stretched and more than earn their wage. Edmund would play Helena with Anthony as Hermia. Philip Kinsman, the Romeo in Arnhem, would take both Hippolyta and Titania. Robert's skills were fully utilised as not only did he have to devise the best system of doubling for the play's seventeen characters, but he would also take the part of the Duke. If the play was sold by the playwright as a comedy due to the humour and three weddings, the rehearsals were certainly comic. Eight Englishmen transported all way to ancient Greece to perform as seventeen characters. At times it was chaotic, there were some tears and tantrums but mainly smiles and laughter. Edmund pouted and played the spurned lover with an uncanny perceptive quality, worthy of any spirited teenager.

Robert had planned out the days in detail to ensure everyone was ready precisely in time for the New Year's Eve revels. They had a full-dress rehearsal, and the women were subject to a close inspection by Robert and the senior members of the troupe. They all understood that for the audience to embrace suspension of disbelief, the women must be convincing. The illusion must be complete if the audience were to be seduced and won over. Edmund dressed carefully and he and Anthony did each other's hair. Two sisters making ready for the Palace ball where they would try to catch the hearts of many a would-be prince charming.

On the day of the performance, Robert commanded the entire company to be dressed and fully ready a full two hours before the entertainments were due to start. As the hourglass was turned, and turned again, Robert anxiously looked at all the empty seats in the great hall. The Palace seemed very quiet for the eve of the new year. The only people who walked through the hall, didn't sit and they all looked puzzled. The actors gathered behind the thick blue arras. The tension increased as the minutes drained away and still the audience hadn't arrived. Suddenly the Palace Steward entered the hall and approached Robert.

'Master Browne, we are surprised to see you all, dressed and ready to perform.'

'Sir, we need only his highness and an audience and we can begin.'

'I fear you will have a long wait, eleven days to be precise. It is not yet new year.'

Robert looked shocked and very confused. Today was, by his calculation New Year's Eve. It was New Year's Eve in London. In London! Suddenly, he had an epiphany. The calendar in London was not the same calendar they used here in Hesse. Protestant following princes such as Queen Elizabeth, chose to follow the old Julian calendar not the new more scientifically correct Gregorian version. New year in London was eleven days ahead of Cassel. The Steward followed Robert's mental deliberations and quickly reached the same epiphany. The two men burst into laughter although only one of them felt himself a prize fool. When Robert confessed his error to his players, there was first disbelief then wild hilarity. Robert funded several jugs of beer that night at dinner.

Chapter thirty-three

The audience in the Palace great hall, clapped their hands enthusiastically. There were cheers and salutes spoken in polished Deutsch. Robert had been correct. The Midsummer Night's Dream play had been a success. Edmond dressed as Helena, curtseyed gracefully and he continued to play the woman's part despite the play being over. He looked at all the excited faces, so many girls and ladies all chatting and sharing the joy that comes from beautiful words performed beautifully. The boy actors held hands and took one final bow and then a curtain was drawn. Edmund walked out into the main section of the hall and immediately found himself surrounded by young girls. He curtseyed again and blew kisses all around. One very pretty girl in a white silk gown and embroidered stomacher took his hand and led him over to the side of the hall.

'What is your name miss.'

'My name? I am Shakes: err, I am Helena'

The girl giggled together with her four friends who had formed a circle around him. Delicate hands stroked his gown, and they inspected his white ruff and silver trimmed sleaves. This was a fashion show but one where the model was possessed with a little more than just feminine beauty. As Helena, Edmund was a girl, as Edmund, he was a handsome youth in a beautiful dress. For the five girls, it was like a Christmas dream.

'My name is Anna. I am happy to meet you, Helena. You played your part very well. Do you enjoy having the attention of the audience?'

'Yes, my lady, I do. To give pleasure to so many is exciting. But Anna, if I may call you thus, you speak English very well.'

'I thank you. I have a very good tutor. In fact, I have many tutors here in the palace. My uncle is very wise, and he is also generous.'

Edmund looked at this girl. She had perfect skin like alabaster and wide eyes of China blue. Beneath her bejewelled cap, her blond hair was plated into a bun. She was perhaps sixteen and overflowing with Naiad like energy. As he waited, the girls all bent their heads together and whispered to each other. Then with feminine sounds of delight, he discovered his hands seized and they led him out of the hall and to a broad stone staircase that rose to join a corridor, running the length of the building, entering the east wing of the palace. The now six girls, swept their way along, their gowns all rustling and the excited chatter echoing off the stone walls. Edmund played along. His audience expected more than just the memorised words written by his brother. He had created Helena and Helena had been invited to the apartments of the Prince's niece.

In a few short minutes, a door closed behind them and Edmund was the centre of attention in the large salon where the girls enjoyed all the pleasure only riches and maidenhood could offer. There were richly coloured tapestries, thick silken rugs and piles of soft cushions. There were assorted musical instruments and an ivory decorated Virginal standing in one corner. The scene was completed by a large blue and yellow Macaw bird standing on guard on his silver perch. This was not the 'flowery bower' of Titania but something more material.

The girls led Edmund over to a long velvet covered couch where Anna seated herself and then invited Edmund to sit beside her. They then talked, with many questions asked about England, its Queen and the fashions of the English court. Edmund did his best to answer all, although more than once he found the need to invent, trying to satisfy his delightful but insatiable interrogators.

Suddenly the door opened and a mature woman wearing a dark gown, entered the room. She looked quite stern and moved with authority.

'My girls, it is time you had your rest. I have told you before, in mid-afternoon, ladies sleep a little so they can look pretty and fresh for the evening.'

Edmund started to move but Anna squeezed his hand tightly and winked at him.

'Shssh. Don't worry she sees only girls.'

The woman in the dark gown glanced at the six girls and then continued to draw back the curtains on a huge bed that lay against the far wall. She turned down the coverlet and quickly turned to go.

'Thank you, Hilda, we will follow your instructions. You may leave us now.'

Anna once more squeezed Edmund's hand and they both watched as the woman swept quickly out of the room, closing the door behind her.

Edmund's eyes widened as he watched the four girls help each other to step out of their gowns and stomachers. The cloth of their delicate kirtles were just as effective as the gowns for covering their thin slips but Edmund felt the excitement of a boy who was in a wonderland. Anna took his hand and told him she would help him off with his gown. Hands unseen unlaced it for him and like the girls, he now stood gracefully in just a kirtle and hose although, it was becoming more and more noticeable that he was a boy. The girls blushed and feigned embarrassment but then he was led by the hand over to the large bed. Anna closed the curtains and joined her now five friends for their afternoon rest.

It was in the new year of the year 1598 there came an eclipse of the sun. The tour went on and on.

Chapter thirty-four

In summer of the year 1599, Flushing was much as it had been before. Tall red roofed houses with gable ends, standing like dragon's teeth in rows high above the cobble stone streets. The town's defensive wall still standing proud ready to repel even the most persistent attacker. The docksides still teemed with valiant little ships that went and returned as directed by their owners or the demand of markets for exotic foods and materials.

Edmund noticed little change. If anything had changed it was Edmund. He was now nineteen and he had been living away from any real home for four years. These were the important years, if perhaps there is a hierarchy in the ages of man. But for Edmund, these four years, when he became a man, were spent far from any guidance that might have been expected. He was neither subject to rules imposed by parents or benefiting from sibling advice. He was not subject to military regulations or apprenticeship indentures. He had lived his life as a free boy and now a free man. His role models, if they existed at all, were stage performers and musicians. His meals were most usually eaten in Taverns and Inns. He was used to spending time amongst harlots and punks and others who were part of the entertainment business. He had become used to drinking strong liquor and playing games of chance where young men bet their wages on the turn of a printed card. He had travelled on tour as a performer, night after night, dressing as a girl and speaking lines written by poets and seducers. As a glamourous girl up on the boards, many girls and a few men, pledged their bodies to him and, as a teenager, he accepted their offers, well at least the ones from girls and women.

Edmund had seen countries on the continent and lived the life of a stage idol. He had survived but he was not unscathed. Edmund didn't know who he really was. He could now be anyone. He spoke memorised lines. Sometimes a few were his own but he no-longer really knew if there was any such thing as Edmund or truth. If truth did exist how did this differ from performance? Edmund was a performer. He drank too much. He consumed too many women, and his purse was empty having squandered his money on cards and dice.

Edmund

My journey back to Flushing has taken the last few coins that remained of the money brother paid me to leave England. It has all gone, all four hundred crowns. I don't have money to pay for a room and certainly nothing to pay for my passage back to London. But this is my plan – to return. Perhaps I can get some money from Franz Kugelman and if this doesn't work, there is always Robert Poley. I have done with travelling and being a servant of the Landgrave of Hesse-Cassel. It was great time for me, but the wheel has now turned, and I want to walk the streets of home. Home? Well, a place big enough for me to get lost in but still feel comfortable. That I gave my word to my brother I would not return, well enough of that. It was a cruel thing for him to demand. Exile! He gave me four hundred crowns to disappear. And I did, for two years but I feel I don't need to accept his terms anymore. If my brother felt it was worth four hundred crowns to get me to leave, how much will he pay to have me stay 'disappeared' in London? I am now deemed to be a good actor, and I can tread the boards of the London stage for an honest wage.

I have had enough of wagons, touring and foreign towns. And I fear I now have a sickness, Lord let me not be poxed. Let it not be that.

Chapter thirty-five

The streets of Flushing felt very familiar despite Edmund not being in town for over two years. Edmund soon found Hellebardierstraat and the green door belonging to the house he was looking for. Three knocks and then the sound of wooden sabots approaching along the hallway. And then a face he remembered. Jolanda looked surprised but the broad smile revealed what her verbal greeting could not. Jolanda was pleased to see him. This hadn't changed and neither had the fact that Edmund was still unable to understand her Dutch language, so communication was all facial and mime. But this was enough to allow Edmund's entry to the house and then into the kitchen. He left his one bag in the hall, the second one that had contained the two gowns given to him by Emilia, had been sold to pay off some of his gambling debts.

In the small yard behind the house, Franz Kugelman was tending his fruit trees. He heard the voice of Jolanda calling his name, so he put down his pruning knife and came back to the kitchen.

'Edmund! It is very good to see you again. I think it has been perhaps, two years, yes?'

'Two years, yes, but it feels like more.'

'How do you enjoy being a touring player? What was it like to live at the grand Palace of Cassel?'

'The Palace was, is, a wonderful place. Sheer beauty set withing amazing ornamental gardens. There were some drawbacks, but I can tell you my stories a little later perhaps. I do need to speak on another matter. I hoped that perhaps I could stay with you here for a couple of days while I try to find passage on a ship?'

'Most certainly you can stay. The guest room is free, and I am sure Jolanda will not take many moments to air the room for you.'

Franz and Jolanda then spoke together, and it seemed to be all agreed. Edmund felt relief. He could now stop travelling for a few days and he knew with Jolanda, he would eat well. Once settled comfortably at the large kitchen table, Edmund told some of the story of the last two years. He explained how life as a player with the Browne Company had many benefits but, as it is said in England, there was a fly in the ointment. Edmund told them about the flies. Living in the servant quarters meant he had a small bedroom that was shared with another player, and this meant he had no private space. Between play performances, there were long periods of inactivity, when the players had no duties or any need to do anything. The palace staff had a routine which they followed with impressive efficiency. But the players merely watched them while they lounged about smoking and gambling, until the Prince called for another evening of revels.

When the Prince was absent from the Palace for any extended period, Robert would arrange for the company to go on the road. He would plan out a route and the wagons would be loaded and then head off to find a new audience. The road journeys were uncomfortable to say the least. Long hours being jolted and bruised when the roads were dry. When it was wet, the players were wet and frequently they would be needed to put their shoulders to the wheels. Mud and hills are the enemy of waggoners and if you chose to live on a wagon, you learned to hate both.

When finally, the tour arrived at a town or palace, Robert would negotiate with the town's officials or the local Lord. Sometimes, they were well received and well housed. They would perform at Fairs outdoors and in town squares. When at Manors or Palaces, they would be allowed the use of great halls. But sometimes they were ejected and then treated like vagabonds. And there was always another town, then another. Life on the road was all comings and goings with too short a time in between. Edmund lost his enthusiasm for the road.

It has been two years, and he now felt he couldn't face another tour. He wanted to regain the freedom to sleep in the same bed every night. To gather his precious things around him. To make some sort of home. His home. He had decided he needed to return to London and see what life he could make for himself.

He didn't of course mention to Franz and Jolanda, he owed money to some of the other players. He had gambling debts he now hoped he could escape. He didn't mention his drinking problem, so bad, even he recognised he had one. He didn't mention the illness he feared he had contracted. Franz and Jolanda listened to his stories, and they enjoyed hearing all about a life they themselves would never experience. It sounded glamourous but somehow at the same time, empty. Both of them knew that contentment can only come to a person who has a safe home. They had one, Edmund did not.

Edmund confessed to them he was now without money and could not pay for his return passage to

England. Franz immediately offered to loan Edmund enough to buy a ticket and for food. As a friend of William Shakespeare, Franz believed the brother would pay any debt and consider him loaning money as an act of friendship.

Edmund felt more relaxed now he was back in the upper bedroom. He slept late each day and the mental maze he had been battling during the last few weeks, was gone. Having made the decision and now started action on his plan, he found a kind of peace. Perhaps not the everlasting kind but then any ceasefire is better than endless war inside his head. He had been debating with himself the problems for a long time. Touring was draining his resolve but there was a wage to be had. Leaving Robert Browne would mean he would need to find money from another source. Leaving the tour and returning to London would also inevitably lead him into conflict with his brother. He didn't fear this, but his brother had age and reputation to his advantage. That Edmund knew things about his brother that his brother wanted kept secret, perhaps gave Edmund the upper hand.

Edmund had the name Shakespeare, and this might unlock doors and some purses. There was money to be made in London. His brother was vulnerable, and Edmund felt a flush of pleasure as he turned over in his mind the hand he had been dealt. He had all the picture cards and if he played them well, he would win the game. But the game was in London. Now he had visited several continental cities, London no longer looked such a Grand Lady. The reality he now recognised, she was dirty, fly blown, and pock marked. But what London offered Edmund was access to rich people who had appetites and spoke to him in the Queen's English. Edmund ticked off his strengths. He was young, handsome, talented, and he was Shakespeare's brother. That brother was a married man and had a reputation he wished to protect. His brother had wealth. His brother was legitimate. Edmund had nothing to lose. The decision was taken, and he was pleased it was done.

Franz asked his business associates on the Mart about ships. As a merchant he frequently learned the ship names and the cargoes expected in Flushing and those about to leave. He quickly found that The Christofer, a Dutch ship was loading and would be leaving for London soon. The captain, Joos de Moor, was agreeable to taking another passenger as he already had one Englishman who had paid for the use of his cabin. The deal was done, and Franz was happy in his belief he had been able to assist the much young brother of his friend.

Two days later, when the tide was right, the little ship was towed out of Flushing harbour. Once at sea, the sails were set and a westerly course towards the Thames, was given to the helmsman. There was one other passenger onboard, and he gave his name as Thomas Lodge. He was a tall man, although Edmund could see little else as he was wrapped in a large, heavy cape and wore a Hollander's style woollen cap. Edmund nodded a brief reserved greeting and told him his own name of Shakespeare. Edmund was in no mood to make polite conversation as he felt a rising anxiety due to the prospect of the coming sea voyage. When Lodge understood that Edmund was not a good sailor, he turned and spoke a few words in Dutch to Captain Joos, who then smiled and quickly disappeared down to his cabin. When he returned, in his hand he carried a black leather bottle. Lodge pointed to the flask.

'This is what you need. Drink. With this you could sail around Cape Horn.'

The captain than handed the bottle to Edmund, who took a large swig. The heavy liquor rushed down his throat, forcing a path of spreading fire through the pipe, boiling the blood in his chest. Edmund coughed and his eyes filled with tears.

'What was that?'

The passenger Thomas Lodge and Captain Joos laughed at the question.

'Goede Caribische rum. Mother's milk, if your mother was a zwarte witch! Drink more of this and the sea will be smooth and the wind, have the touch of a fairy.'

Edmund shared the captain's joke and took the flask of rum down below to find a warm bunk. The captain's remedy for sea sickness was true and Edmund was to know little of the voyage from Zeeland. He missed the sight of Foreland Head that marked the entrance to the Thames estuary. He missed the seaman using a lead line to sound the depths as the ship passed over the many shoals that hazard the channels leading towards London. He missed Tilbury Ness where Robert Dudley, Earl of Leicester massed English troops when the Queen feared a Spanish invasion back in the year 1588.

The 125 sea miles from Zeeland were for Edmund, just a dream. It was only when, sometime the next day, the ship's anchor was being raised did Edmund return back on deck. The captain had anchored off Gravesend to await a flooding tide and the song of seamen and clanking capstan awoke him.

The decks were wet from condensation but there was some weak sunshine burning through the early morning mist. Edmund stretched himself and looked at the water, shiny and creeping slowly inland. Small tuffs of seaweed and driftwood rode the current to later be abandoned, high and dry on some isolated shore. There were gulls and terns searching for an easy meal. All was peaceful but the tide wouldn't wait, and Captain Joos wanted his ship up river before the next ebb began.

Edmund's head hurt as he looked for a water barrel so he could slate his thirst.

'Goedemorgen, Englishman. There is biscuit and cheese, if your stomach can take it. Our other passenger has already left the ship.'

The captain smiled and pointed towards a basket placed on the afterdeck. Edmund sat himself down and watched as the crew hoisted sails, and the ship begin to glide gently with the current. The river Thames winds its way through many miles of marshy land. There was very little farming being done close to the river. Too much water and too much salt in the soil. The Dutch engineers would have made something of this soil but perhaps the English had easy land elsewhere. There were signs of a few fish traps and sour basins where live oysters were stored, awaiting boats to take them up to Billingsgate market. Edmund knew this was England but there was very little to be seen that suggested he was home.

The journey upriver took up most of the day and it was mid-afternoon before the ship rounded the last bend in the river just before London, opposite Ratcliff and the Hamlet of Wapping. The ship was brought inshore, closer to the north bank and then the anchor was dropped. London lay just a couple of miles to the west and Edmund could see the White Tower of the castle and in the far distance, St Paul's cathedral. The crew knew their job and it wasn't long before the sails were stowed, the deck cleared and The Christofer swung to her anchor. Edmund collected his bag from below deck and went to say his farewells to the captain.

'Captain Joos. Thank you for getting me here so smoothly and without my stomach turning inside out. I wish you well for your next voyage.'

'One of the deck boys will take you to the shore. I hope you fare well in this country of mad people.'

'There is much truth in that, but at least here, my madness will not be seen.'

They laughed together and shook hands. The ship's punt was lowered into the water and the skinny deck boy rowed Edmund ashore. The gravel and broken shells groaned under his boots as he walked the few paces to the Wapping bankside. Somewhere far off in the city, church bells tolled. It was too late in the day for a funeral, but tomorrow maybe. As Edmund walked along the rough road that followed the river to St Katherine's hermitage, he was sure he could smell something in the air. It wasn't the wholesome odour of freshly baked bread. It wasn't the scent of wildflowers or the reek of fishing nets. It was something that came from having too many base people living unnaturally too close together. He could smell the city before he even arrived. If this was really England, he had forgotten the unpleasant details. He remembered the good bits but the everyday detail was lost beneath a heavy layer of nostalgia. By the time he reached Tower Hill, the rainbow blanket of hope had dissolved. From a wooden scaffold, hung two bodies, The Tower ravens took it in turns to peck out the soft bits that once saw and spoke. If this place was ever truly home, he had arrived and he remembered.

Edmund turned to the north and headed towards Bishopsgate. Nothing had changed about the buildings or about the people who walked on the streets. To a city where people first chose to settle more than 1600 years ago, the two years Edmund had been absent were like rain drops in a pond. For a city, two years are imperceptible.

The taverns were all busy and men who had no work, stood idle with half-filled mugs of ale. Edmund would have liked to stop but he had spent the last few coins of the money Franz had lent him or rather, had lent his brother. He walked further, knowing that the only place he might be sure of a welcome, was the boys' house in Shoreditch.

Part Four

Reckoning

Chapter thirty-six

It was dark when he arrived in Holywell Lane but there was a full moon and this was enough to guide him to the scuffed door. He stepped lightly on the stairs and went up to the first-floor room the boys jokingly referred to as The Court. Just one candle was burning next to a mattress in the corner. Someone was awake, reading, perhaps learning lines for a play to be on stage tomorrow. The face turned towards the noise of the opening door, trying to recognise the person who had just entered. Edmund tiptoed across the room and as he walked, studied the young boy who showed no fear. It was Alexander, two years older than when Edmund last saw him, but still fresh faced and very much a small boy.

'Hola Alexander. It is me, Edmund, I'm back. We can talk in the morning but for now, is there a spare bed I can use?'

'Edmund! A ghost from Stratford. Are you here to join us again?'

'Tomorrow we will talk. Is there a bed?'

'Yes, back where you came in, near the door. Kevin went away last week.'

'Thanks, now sleep.'

With that, Edmund moved away from the light and lay down on the spare bed. As he settled himself, he could hear the sound of the sleeping boys' rhythmic breathing. A soothing sound for a boy looking for a home.

The night was short and a restless owl hunting somewhere out on Finsbury Fields, interrupted Edmund's slumber. When he awoke he was conscious he was somewhere he had been before. He recognised the odour of dirty socks and unwashed boys. The smell was different from that of fat, sweaty unwashed men. Hormones of youth make a difference. He lay for a while listening to the subdued chatter and the sounds of the scraping of spoons in the wooden bowls they used for porridge. He faintly heard the sound of his name. Alexander must have been sharing the news that an adventurer had returned.

The smell of bread and porridge awakened Edmund's appetite and he forced himself to leave the warmth of the bed to join the others at breakfast. There were four boys sitting on the floor by the unlit fire grate. Christopher, Robert, Alexander and someone Edmund didn't recognise.

'Hola Edmund! Good to see you still alive and now back in Shoreditch. It has been a long time.'

Christopher sounded friendly and he led the welcome in the understated way teenagers speak when they don't want to show their enthusiasm or betray an interest. But of course, they were interested. Not so much in wanting to hear of Edmund's success but rather to delight in his mistakes. Edmund tried in a few words, to boast of how well he had done on the continental tour. He painted a colourful canvass, full of triumph and wonders. Within five minutes, one by one the boys switched off and changed the theme to matters of

Shoreditch and the London stage. Edmund's moment of stardom was short, and he accepted he had been drawn back into a more mundane and routine existence.

Edmund learned from the boys that the playhouses were all open and the audiences still ready to pay their pennies to stand in the yard to hear a play. Some actors had died either due to fights, sickness or the effects of excess drinking. But there was always someone new to take their place. The road down from the northern shires was busy with men arriving, seeking a better life than the one they knew at home. Few ever returned to tell the truth about what they found in the ever-spreading suburbs that hung to the sides of the bloated City.

When breakfast was over, Edmund drew Christopher aside so they could talk privately.

'Are there any plays due to be staged soon? I need a wage, and I am ready to take any part offered.'

'All the plays I know of are already cast but I will spread the word you are available to work. Perhaps you should go speak to Henslowe, he may have something.'

'Good. I'll do that. I have no money at all. Could you lend me something, anything?'

Edmund noticed his friend seemed to shrink a little when he heard the words 'lend money.' The boys might share their food and their beds, but coins were cold and not part of friendship. Christopher remained silent.

'I understand, don't worry. I know someone who might still have a heavy purse and may spare me a few crowns. That package I asked you to keep for me. Could I have it please?'

Christopher got up and went into the rear room. A few minutes later he returned with the package, still ribboned and with its seal intact.

'This package may one day prove precious. If it does, I will repay your past kindness. Do you know of any lodgings available nearby?'

'Perhaps you could try Parsonage Yard, just behind St. Leonard's Church. There is a widow who sometimes has a spare room.'

The two friends parted, with Christopher moving off to help the other boys learn lines for the next play at The Curtain. Edmund put the package of sonnets into his bag and then left the house to try to find the widow of Parsonage Yard.

Later that day Edmund lay himself down upon an old truckle bed inside his first solo lodgings. The room was large with a single window opening onto the yard below. There were just three pieces of furniture, the bed, a chair and table, but there was space enough for more if he chose to buy some. The widow had been easy to find. She lived in the house and passed her time seated in a turned chair placed by the front door. From there she could watch her three tenants come and go, while, importantly, deter them from stealing her furniture. A deal was done for the room without any money being paid. Edmund had given his brother's name as surety against the unpaid rent, and as the widow was a playgoer, she knew the name Shakespeare and that he was a wealthy playwright. During the negotiation for the room, the widow told Edmund something interesting. His brother was now a shareholder in a new playhouse soon to open in Southwark. The Theatre in Shoreditch that two years ago was a thriving business for the Burbages, had been dismantled timber by timber and rebuilt on a site close to The Rose in Southwark. His brother was now a man of property, and the name of Shakespeare had risen in value. Edmund dozed in his new lodgings, filled with feelings of self-satisfaction and hope.

While he had managed to secure lodgings without money just by using the name Shakespeare to gain credit, for buying a meal, cash was an imperative. Late in the afternoon, Edmund readied himself for a social call. He brushed off the travel dust from his most presentable jerkin and breeches. He found a pair of hose that didn't disgrace his calves. His clothes were well tailored and the best he could buy when he still had money left from the 400 crowns paid him by his brother. As a stage actor he well knew that good presentation could win over an audience. He put on his hat and adjusted the angle to create the image he hoped would catch a lady's eye. The lady he had in mind was Emilia.

It was a short walk from his lodgings to Folgate Street and his pace quickened as he drew closer. It had been two years since he told her he was going away. Two years during which time he had travelled many roads and found pleasure in the kiss of many pretty women. It had been a period when he became accustomed to women looking for him rather than the other way round.

He knocked on the door and waited for the sound of a bolt being drawn. Slowly the door opened and the elderly servant whom he recognised from his previous visits, looked out at him with an expressionless face.

'I wish to see Madam Emilia.'

'Who should I say is calling?'

'Shakespeare, Edmund Shakespeare.'

The woman retreated back into the dark hallway. Minutes went by and Edmund began to feel anxious. Could it be that Emilia was not alone or she didn't want to see him again? Could it be her husband had returned?

At last, the servant reappeared and with a small move of her hand, beckoned him inside. The front parlour was just as he remembered it. There was one new addition, a portrait in a gilt frame. Emilia looked down on him from the wall. The look was haughty and seemed to question his intent. What was his intent? Was he merely there to borrow money or did he want to renew the relationship they had before. Three years ago, he had been a naïve sixteen-year-old, unaccustomed to the ways of married women. His time on the continent touring with the players had destroyed any illusions about purity or chastity. He was no longer a boy in awe of an angel. The act of love was neither paradise nor a step on the path to comedy, so often portrayed in the plays of his brother. To Edmund, women were a fine food. He chose where and when he ate and then moved on to another dish.

Emilia kept him waiting. She knew this would signal her position of dominance and, if Edmund waited, it signalled his acceptance. When she arrived at the doorway, it was an entrance worthy of Cleopatra. Edmund saw what he had forgotten. Emilia was a sensual feline who looked on men as wanton fools. She would allow a chosen few to stroke her or, she could toy and claw them until they scurried away bloodied. Edmund removed his hat and bowed low, as he would have done if in the presence of any Queen.

'Edmund, how good it is for you to come to see me. You have been away, yes?'

'You know I have. I took my leave of you in this very room just a little over two years past.'

'Has it really been that long? I am surprised. Please, sit and tell me what you have been doing.'

Edmund played her game and told stories from his days as a touring player. He created a tale that began and ended in the Royal Palace of Cassel. The glory of Cassel lived again, and he spared no detail that might help boost the impression that he Edmund, was a star and a favoured courtier to the Royal family of Hesse. In exchange for Edmund's colourful entertainment, Emilia mentioned her husband and confirmed that he was away from London again. She implied, or though did not directly state, she no longer saw his brother. She also told him she believed William had moved lodgings and was now resident in Southwark. The topic of his brother was timely as it allowed Edmund to mention that William owed him money, which he would receive sometime soon. This was of course a lie, but it was believable. Emilia smiled when he asked if she could perhaps lend him, say twenty crowns to cover his expenses until he was able to cross the river and meet with his brother. He was now in her debt and this, plus her seductive charm, gave their new liaison added frisson.

The evening was then brought to a close. Emilia gently dismissed him but as he came close to kiss her cheek, she whispered in his ear that if he came again the day after tomorrow, perhaps he could put on a private performance.

Chapter thirty-seven

William Shakespeare lent forward; his elbows heavy on the rough table that bore the marks of many years use. The tavern was dimly lit by a number of fat tallow candles – their yellow light flickered as each new customer entered or left via the door to the alley. A soft murmur of voices, men of all sorts, talking between puffs on their short clay pipes. The air was thick, full of smells and gritty with soot. This was not a place for persons of refined taste or pretention. This was the city and trade between men hungry for business seemed better conducted without bright light. William moved the joint stool to try to find a level flagstone. He had already spilt some of soup that today would have to be his lunch. Money was short this week as the playhouse was closed and he had not seen Burbage for several days.

Across the room through the gloom, William became aware of someone watching him. Dressed as a gentleman, his hat, sword and gloves suggested wealth and status. His well-trimmed beard concealed much of his face and mouth. William liked his look and briefly imagined that he should ask his tailor to find him a similar hat. William was still searching for a style that would create the right impression. William hoped women would notice him and men would show him respect.

The stranger moved closer, the man realising William was noting his presence.

'Good day sir, I perceive we are like fellows in that we are not regulars to this place. My name is Thomas Lodge.'

With this introduction he gently nodded his head and touched the brim of his beaver hat.

'My name is Shakespeare, William Shakespeare.'

'The playwright? Ah, a man I have heard of and someone who has filled my afternoon with poetic words both potent and dangerous.'

Shakespeare smiled.

'I am happy to know, you at least understand my lines as I fear many remember little, but a stage littered with bodies and my Titus bellowing his rage.'

Both men grinned and let out a brief laugh suggesting a shared moment of levity.

'But let me say, I think I have just met your brother, Edmund. He was on a ship travelling back to London from Flushing.'

William frowned and looked up to the ceiling as if seeking strength from some spirit above.

'So, he has returned to London, has he? Are you sure the man said his name was Edmund?'

'Yes, I am sure. Perhaps he hasn't found time to visit you yet.'

William took another full spoon of the soup.

'But William, I know a little of what it is to pen the spoken thoughts of newly imagined people and so I feel kindred with you. The writer gives birth to misshapen claylike fools who never refine themselves enough to deserve the name human. But I should beg your forgiveness – your Henrys come so close to royalty.'

William studied this man from the shadows. Who was he? Writer or spy? These were dangerous times to reveal too much to strangers in a tavern. In fact to reveal anything might lead one to the steps of the scaffold. The written word possessed the potential to transport a friendly soul to high thoughts nearing paradise but for the plotters or the constables of the State, the lines on a page could condemn even the pure of heart to hours on the rack.

'We try sir, to direct our children of clay to speak true and present a mirror to what it is to live without falsehood.' The stranger nodded his agreement.

'Do you live here in the city sir?'

William asked.

'Not now but I was born just to the east and I spent my youth hereabouts. Recently I have found myself somewhat an adventurer having chosen the sea life for many a year. I have spent time in the Brazils and got as far south as Patagonia, and you Master Shakespeare, have you seen foreign shores?'

'Ships I do fear, so being born on an island surrounded by a sea cursed by tempests and pirates, I travel only from page to page. I read and salvage stories wherever I can discover them. It is enough.'

William felt relieved as there was little to suggest this gentleman was concerned with the stewpot of London life. Sailors and adventurers blew with the wind, rarely settling long enough to commit themselves to civic causes.

Thomas Lodge saw he was being studied and he sensed this man Shakespeare was reluctant to say more of his craft or business. Lodge looked to the tavern door as, yet another ill-dressed carter pushed his way into the smoke filled room.

'I have to take my leave sir, business awaits, and I have much to do before I leave these shores again. But before I go, I do have something for you that might serve as a story for a play. It is something I wrote for my friends and to occupy the long tedious days at sea. As a love story, it will soon be forgotten by them but perhaps you might 'salvage' something from it. It is a retelling of the old tale of Gerismond, lawful King of France who has been exiled by his brother into the French forest of Ardenne. His fiesty daughter Rosalynde is much plagued by love for a Prince. I have an idea that if it could be fattened with poetry it might played upon the stage, but I fear I will never have the time to move it forward. If you are interested, I could have my man deliver you a fair copy. Accept it as my gift. I hope perhaps one day I might hear it much improved by your own greater skill.'

William looked up from watching a fly float to the surface of his half-eaten soup. He noted the bright eyes of the stranger, and he saw what he recognised as sincerity.

'I will gladly accept your gift and if your tale be pregnant with possibilities, I will consider how it might be given a birthing. I thank you and wish you good health.'

Chapter thirty-eight

Edmund stood on the Southwark shore and looked back across the river to the city beyond. Bigger than the cities he had seen while on tour, but more chaotic and troubled. The religious wars in the Continental northern states were basically settled. One side had won. Here in London the struggles continued. The losers wouldn't accept defeat. The winners still felt threatened and they became more strident and unforgiving.

The city across the water appeared to be all warehouses full of merchandise imported to feed the tastes of new consumers who took more than they needed in a search for pleasure. Rising above the warehouses, Edmund could see the many Church steeples, all reaching up as if to connect to a divine energy that might save the faithful from their inevitable doom. From afar, the city in the year of our Lord 1599 looked to be a solid mass of man's triumph. From close up the reality was very different.

London was an unnatural place where waste accumulated as if it had a life of its own. It was so different in Stratford, there everything manufactured had a practical use or could be reworked into something else. Redundant vegetable waste or flesh was fed to chickens, pigs or dogs. Nothing was thrown into the river. The river Avon was revered by the town's folk and its water was a home of swans and fish, both understood for their beauty and for their welcome place on their celebration tables. Food for spirit and for bodies

Edmund watched as dozens of wherries moved to and fro, carrying city dwellers from the place of a thousand laws, to Southwark, where seemingly there were none. Edmund laughed to himself at the folly of it all. He had come south on a mission. He hoped to find Henslowe at The Rose playhouse and also learn the whereabouts of his brother's lodgings. Before Edmund had left London, Philip Henslowe was considered to be the most prominent of theatre owners. He had business interests in nearly every street in Southwark. There was his Rose playhouse and the Bear Garden. He also had interests in several Stews and Taverns. He had, as they say, 'a finger in every pie.'

Edmund walked quickly through the alleyways towards The Rose. He remembered the route but before he had gotten very far from the shore, a huge new building blocked his way. A playhouse had been built, larger than any he had seen before. It was tall, with a roof of new yellowed thatch and between the supporting timbers, walls still soft, their plaster yet to fully dry. So, this was the new playhouse his brother had helped to finance. It wasn't as big as St Saviours Church, but it would entertain more people in one performance than the church might see over seven Sundays. The old order was being challenged and money was being earned. His brother was part of this secular transference. Edmund was pleased. As his Shakespeare name rose in value, his own opportunity to prosper increased.

He found Henslowe at his business in a room behind the stage at The Rose.

'Good morrow Master Henslowe. Do you remember me, Shakespeare?'

'Now there's a name to force a canker on any tree bud. But though you bear an ill name, I can see you are but the pup.'

'A pup perhaps but certainly a player who is freshly arrived from the stages on the Continent and the Royal Palace of Cassel.'

'Ah, now I remember you. Young Edmund who joined Browne and his Company to pay service to a foreign Prince.'

'Yes, and I am returned in good spirit, and I am ready to play the woman for you here at The Rose.'

'A rose by any other name, but there are parasite flies blighting her blooms. Have you seen that great monstrosity your brother and the Burbage brothers have built across the way? They are stealing my audience.'

Edmund wasn't expecting this. Henslowe was angry at the new competition built just yards from his place of business. Edmund quickly realised his brother's activities might create obstacles for him to vault. He now learnt what his brother already knew, that having a brother carried some risk along with opportunity.

'But Master Henslowe, you have the Admiral's Men, and everyone knows of The Rose. You will prosper as you have always prospered.'

'Perhaps boy, perhaps. We are not beaten just a little chaffed. You say you are ready to act?'

'Most certainly. I can be ready with a day's notice.'

'Humm. I will think on it. Where can I find you?'

'Close by St Leonard's Church, Parsonage Yard.'

'Begone with you. I have things that require my attention. And mind, say nothing to your brother about what I have spoke on.'

Edmund left the room somewhat piqued that his hope for a wage had not been satisfied. He wandered back to the new playhouse that so irritated Henslowe. Workmen were still finishing the building. As he watched, a long wooden pole arrived, carried by two men. A door opened and the men with their pole, disappeared inside. Moments later, the same door reopened, and a portly middle-aged man with receding hair, exited. Edmund knew this man to be his brother. William walked quickly away turning into an alley that led to Clink Street. Edmund followed keeping a safe distance behind so he wouldn't be seen. His brother wasn't looking around as he walked. He appeared to be in haste and have his mind preoccupied elsewhere. Another turn and his brother stopped outside a heavy door above which was the Crest of the Bishop of Winchester. William went inside and closed the door behind him. So, this was his new lodgings, here in the heart of the Liberty of the Clink and close to the new playhouse. His brother was living on the job. This discovery brightened Edmund's mood. He knew where to find his brother and in knowledge, there is said to be power.

Edmund was about to leave when he noticed someone not unfamiliar. There was a thin man, wearing a large, brimmed hat, leaning against the wall. This was Robert Poley's watchdog, stationed there at the end of the street. In his mind he replayed the conversation with Poley when they met in Flushing. 'We watch Shakespeare because he knows people we watch.' The dirty game continued, played by people who all claimed to be patriots. Edmund thought for a moment, and he quickly decided there was advantage for him to know the players of this game, particularly those who had Crowns to spend. Edmund walked slowly over to the man and then gave a little cough to attract his attention. The man's dark sunken eyes studied Edmund's face. He turned back and continued his quiet task of watching people in the street.

'I want to meet with Poley.'

'That maybe possible. Tomorrow evening, at Ludgate. There is a tavern named The Bell Savage. He will be there.'

Edmund turned away without speaking anymore. He didn't want to be seen in conversation with this man. As Edmund retraced his route, back to the new playhouse, he noticed a boy carrying a heavy bag on his shoulder. He was handing out what appeared to be a leaflet of some kind. Edmund held out his hand and a small, yellowed piece of paper was thrust towards him. It was a playbill for a performance on the coming Thursday. The Globe Playhouse presents the Tragedy of Julius Caesar. It seemed, from this announcement, Henslowe was right to mark the arrival on bankside of a new theatre. This new play about a Roman ruler would be sure to attract a paying audience. Edmund smiled and pushed the paper into his jerkin and continued his way towards the river shore to find a wherry back across to the city.

Chapter thirty-nine

The Bell Savage Inn lay close to one of the ancient gateways to the city. The building was large with two courtyards where guests could be safe from any disorder that plagued the common streets. The innermost court had from time to time been used to stage plays. Edmund entered via the archway leading off Fleet Street and he then explored the public rooms. There was no sign of the man he searched for. The inner court had two stories, fronted by balconies, allowing any guests to look down on performers in the yard. Edmund again searched but without success. He was about to leave when a Tapster approached him.

'How can I help master? What would you like, Ale or Wine?'

'I am looking for a man who said I might meet him here. His name is Robert Poley.'

'The man you seek is in room seven on the first floor.'

The Tapster quickly turned away. It seemed the name Poley, while known, was not a name the man wished to speak, and he had no desire to dally with anyone seeking his company. Edmund found the staircase and then down a dark corridor, he stopped outside the door. He knocked.

'Who is there?'

'Shakespeare.'

'Come Shakespeare.'

The room was small, but it contained a narrow bed, a washstand and a table. In a large chair facing the door, Edmund recognised Robert Poley.

'Ah, Shakespeare the younger. I wasn't certain your brother hadn't found a reason to pay me a visit. But I am pleased to see you again. Flushing, wasn't it?'

'Yes, in Flushing but two years have passed since then.'

'The year counter may have moved but times have not. The enemies of our Queen still huddle in their dark holes and plan how they might reclaim England. Did you hear any such talk when you were travelling on the continent?'

'Nothing that concerned the matters you speak of. But I am now here in London, and I wished to know if you will still pay for information.'

'Do you have something?'

'Nothing at present, but I have ears and eyes, and I could use both in the service of the Queen. If I can secure enough currency to pay for my food and lodging in the city.'

'A payment on account I will make to save you from the pederasts or debtor's prison. For this I expect you to visit me here once a week, on Monday evenings.'

Poley opened a large purse that lay on the table and counted out five shillings. He slid the coins across the table towards Edmund who reached down and scooped them up into his palm. Nothing more was said, and Edmund concluded the meeting was over.

Edmund

I prosper! I have made progress. Before I left Flushing, I thought hard about what I should do. Touring with Robert Browne fed me and provided a bed to sleep in. There was safety in this but everyday a different bed, but the same people and the same performance. The trumpet sounded and I was Helena, Juliet or Lavinia. I didn't know who I was and I'm not sure anyone really cared. I pulled on a gown and a wig, and the slobbering audience put me into their private fantasy. I said the lines and the plays rolled on around me. It never stopped. When I closed my eyes, the plays continued. All eyes in the dark. It was only with Gin or Sack, could I get the stage to stop turning. And then in the morning, I would awake to the realisation the play was about to start again.

To escape became my only wish. Even if it meant returning to England and uncertainty. But here I am. It has been a good two days. I have lodgings. A space where, for the first time, no-one is looking at me, where I can be myself, if such a person still exists. I have some money in my purse, enough to last me this week if I don't play Dice or Primero. Emilia welcomed me and perhaps she will still share her body. It is a warm and moist place. She is more to me than all the silly girls who waited for the plays hoping to climb the thighs of Helena, Juliet or Livinia.

London has stages enough. Here I am free to choose. I have found two men here who are hungry for the downfall of my brother. Henslowe has reason and perhaps the means to put poison in the big apple that is The Globe. Poley is the dark spider in the web, and he waits in the corner for my brother to stumble within reach of his fangs. The enemy of my enemy is my friend. I will prosper.

Chapter forty

Augustine Philips welcomed another card player to the Chamberlain's Men.

'Ah, the pretty boy is back, I'm not sure your birth stars are your friend Edmund, given your lack of luck at cards. But perhaps tonight the heavens will smile for you.'

While Edmund, the boy actor, had been blackballed by his brother, stopping Richard Burbage from casting him in any play at The Globe, as a player of cards, he managed to avoid any prohibition. On many an evening, after the audience had departed, the players bought themselves a flagon of ale and the playing cards would come out. The men relaxed, enjoying challenging the fates, puffing their pipes and betting on each hand of Primero. Edmund became a regular attendee joining the party whenever he felt the irresistible pull of lady luck. But this flirty lady seemed to be jealous of the handsome youth who won so many hearts while dressed as a woman.

Edmund was popular with the actors. He was a lively character, and they took a certain delight in leading astray the brother of their principle playwright. He also gambled heavily, and his losses enriched his new friends. Each time he arrived he had more coins to cast into the pot and the players were happy to take his silver coins or his markers. The promissory notes were written by a Shakespeare and the actors felt confident that if the need arose, William would settle his brother's debts.

The Globe playhouse was proving a good investment for its shareholders. It seemed the playgoing habit was addictive. London had an ever-increasing population of males who enjoyed the verbal wordplay offered by the playwrights of the day. There was shared pleasure in joining several thousand like-minded free men. The crowds on Bankside gathered to enjoy a play, a joke, a few drinks and, if they felt they could risk it, a few moments of delicious lust with one of the enticing Winchester geese. Bankside fully deserved the criticism hurled its way by Puritan Preachers and City Fathers. Business was good.

Henslowe fumed as his audience decreased. His takings were down, and he could see and hear the cause. The noise from The Globe groundlings could be heard in The Rose. As the Admiral's Men performed plays that were full of tragedy and pathos, the shouts from the audience at The Globe would intrude and signal to one and all, there was other entertainment next door.

The success of The Globe ensured the card group regulars had plenty of share cash to feed their gambling habit. On this particular evening, As Phillips, Pope, Cooke and the others enjoyed their card game, men with graver matters on their minds, entered the backstage room. Edmund saw them first as he was seated facing the door. Six gentlemen, all expensively suited and, as a mark of their rank, carrying swords and poniards in their belts, strode confidently into the middle of the room. The card players continued their game. Although anxious looks were exchanged as each in turn privately considered the possibility that someone, or maybe even all of them, were about to be arrested. Augustine studied his cards and took his pipe from his mouth.

'Gentlemen, I regret to tell you, this is a private game, although if you have a mind to gamble, perhaps we could invite you to join us on another day.'

'It is not cards we are here for. If you be the players of The Globe, we would have words with you.'

'This is indeed The Globe, and we are some of its players. We will listen.'

'I am Sir Charles Percy, and this gentleman is Sir Jocelyn Percy. We are minded to hear a play this coming Saturday.'

At the name Percy, Edmund's interest in these six men was heightened. He remembered the town of Flushing and a conversation with Robert Poley. He had then suggested anyone bearing the name Percy was of interest to him and there was money to be earnt for reporting their words. And here tonight, two years later, two Percys marched into the playhouse demanding a play. There was perhaps more to this than just an interest in stage drama. Augustine signalled to the card players that the game should be paused while these armed intruders were dealt with.

'And is there a particular play you are hoping to hear?'

'Yes, we would like the play, Richard II. The whole play, nothing left out.'

'Richard II? An old play. Good, yes, but now unlikely to attract an audience. We have better, newer plays we could perform.'

'We want to hear Richard II this coming Saturday.'

Edmund listened as Sir Charles Percy gave what appeared to be instructions rather than a request. The Globe players should stage Richard II on the coming Saturday, and he was prepared to pay forty shillings above the money collected on the door for this performance. The six gentlemen, with their swords and poignards, made it very clear they would not accept any refusal. Augustine Phillips negotiated and agreed the deal. A purse was handed over and the six men, turned and left the playhouse. Edmund picked up his cards and the game recommenced.

There were three more hands of cards and then Edmund retreated, having lost the last shilling he possessed. His lack of money was the primary reason for leaving the game, but there was something else on his mind. There was something unusual about the visit by the six gentlemen. It was mysterious this request made by Sir Percy. A new play was being written but Edmund didn't know if this was to be a history, a comedy or tragedy. It was certain this play had a setting in the future, the coming Saturday. Edmund left The Globe and walked to the Southwark shore to find a boat to take him back to the city. He revolved in his mind all the clues that he gleamed from the muddy lines that had been spoken. The wherry slid across the dark waters of the river and Edmund stared into the blackness. Small balls of light reflected on the surface but there was too little for him to make out anything solid. Halfway across the river, Edmund told the wherry man to steer the boat west, towards Blackfriars Stairs.

Edmund had decided that he might profit by a visit to Ludgate. There, waiting in the corner of his sticky web, was Poley, the spider. There was also a fat purse. Although this was not the designated day, he thought it might be worthwhile seeking out Poley. One half hour later, Edmund knocked on the door at The Bell Savage.

'Who is there?'

'Shakespeare, Edmund Shakespeare.'

'Come in Shakespeare.'

Robert Poley was sitting in the chair at a table. There was one other person present, the thin man, who, without speaking, turned and exited to the adjoining room.

'You were not expected. This is not your day.'

'No, but I have heard something I believe it might be worth you hearing. Something important. What would you pay for information about Sir Charles Percy?'

'Without knowing what it is I don't know what it is worth. Tell me what you have heard, and I will figure you a reckoning.'

Edmund then recounted what he remembered about the visit by the six gentlemen. Poley appeared deep in thought without showing any outward response. He silently picked up a knife and peeled an apple.

'Richard II, you say. Tell me Edmund, do you know what this play concerns?'

'It is a history play written by my brother, like the Henry cycle or Richard III. Not much fun really.'

'England has had so many Kings. Tell me, what in the play happens to this one?'

'Richard is murdered after he has yielded his crown to Bolingbroke.'

Poley looked up at his young visitor, and aggressively cut the apple in half.

'Murdered and yielded. Play to be performed this coming Saturday. On the instruction of two Percys.'

Edmund said nothing. Poley had distilled a concoction down to a drop of thick poison worthy of a skilled apothecary. It appeared it might be deadly for someone. Edmund felt a cold chill run down his spine. He now realised what might be at stake.

'Master Poley. You understand, my brother wasn't at the meeting, neither does he know anything about the visit by the Percys.'

'Humm. Yes, I see. You want me to protect your meal ticket. It is not in your interest to have your brother arrested.'

'No. It would not be good for me.'

'So, my report will not name the playwright.'

With that, the leather purse was opened, and Poley's dirty fingers flicked their way through the contents. He slid eight crowns across the table towards Edmund.

'You have done well. You know where to find me if you hear more.'

Edmund left the room and quickly walked back to his Shoreditch lodgings.

On the Saturday, The Globe Playhouse managed to find an audience for Richard II but the crowd were not the usual, light hearted and rowdy playgoers. There were some serious faced men who arrived together and spent as much time watching the other playgoers as they did the performance up on the stage. When the play was over, the stern looking men trouped out together as if just dismissed from a military parade. Edmund wasn't on Bankside to see the play. At his meeting with Poley, Edmund realised that the staging of Richard II was being used as a sort of public signal, prior to some form of insurrection. He wanted no part in whatever might follow. On the following Sunday, Edmund awoke in a clean, soft bed, curtained with lace. It wasn't his bed. Emilia had permitted him to stay the night after he performed for her and showed what he had learned during his two years touring with the Browne Company. Had he chosen to get up and attend the morning service at St Paul's Cathedral, he might have witnessed the arrival of the Earl of Essex together with the Earl of Southampton at the head of a nervous troupe of heavily armed men. They came to St Paul's Cross after the sermon. Not finding the masses of would-be rebels they expected, within minutes they departed, back towards Essex House. Seventeen days later the Earl of Essex was beheaded at the Tower of London. The Earl of Southampton's death sentence was commuted to Life Imprisonment. Edmund learned of these events and well understood the danger of getting too close to political struggles.

Chapter forty-one

The summer of the year 1601 was hot. The narrow streets of the city felt as if airless, and the animal dung baked hard, long before the street rakers were able to clear it. There were flies and biting insects that bred happily in the river mud. For Edmund in Shoreditch, it brought to mind the time of his first summer in London, living at the boys' house. Finsbury Fields was once again dotted with makeshift canvas tents set up by city dwellers seeking relief from the heat and flying bugs. Edmund was now twenty-one and his days as a working boy actor had become more difficult. For many theatre owners, he was considered too old. There were younger, more fresh faced boys queuing to audition for every female part.

Although he regularly visited the boys' home near the Curtain Playhouse, he increasingly found their games and conversation, trivial. He was now perhaps too much a man to share the boys' joy at discovering themselves free of parental diktats. He no-longer was amused by their delight at being the centre of attention for all the middle-aged patrons of the arts who took sly pleasure from the company of pretty boys. He found it annoying that the boys easily found paid work when he found it difficult.

And there was another form of competition that created problems for jobbing actor Edmund. In a hall at the old Blackfriars Priory, a company of young boys, all choristers with sweet voices and angelic bodies, now performed plays for wealthy Londoners. They were just a fashion, but all the adult companies found themselves forced to compete. Edmund was neither young enough for the best girl roles nor humble enough to accept the parts written for older women. He felt bitter that the London stage had moved on, and his special attributes were no longer so marketable. In the evenings he drank more and with a muzzy head, gambled away his meagre earnings.

On the days when he felt strong enough to stand, plead for work and then face the humiliation of rejection, Edmund would visit each playhouse during their period of the morning rehearsals. There were many playhouses, but the managers seemed to have their favourite actors, and Edmund was no longer someone they valued. He would do the rounds, north of the river and then take a wherry across the river to Southwark. On this day he found Philip Henslowe in his usual place of work and in his usual bad humour.

'What again? Another player begging for work when I have had ten here already this day.'

'You mistake me for someone else, Henslowe. I am Shakespeare, Edmund Shakespeare and no beggar.'

'Your brother will make us all beggars if that dammed Globe is not set a fire. My Rose is half empty while the Burbages pile up profits from the pen of your sibling. He has managed to put some fool life into that dreary old Hamlet piece from Kyd. The Globe has been full, and I hear the streets all a chatter about ghosts and grave diggers.'

Edmund listened to Henslowe moaning and cursing his luck. Two of his bears had just died and he feared that there might soon be an outbreak of the plague. It appeared the life of a successful playhouse owner was not to be envied. Edmund quietly laughed to himself at the pain of the self-obsessed wealthy. While many men and women in England were struggling to feed themselves and their families, here was a man who owned pavilions, theatres and stews, whining about his falling ticket sales.

He left Henslowe and walked next door to the Globe, where he could hear the sound of rehearsals underway for what he assumed would be the afternoon performance. The gateman recognised Edmund and allowed him to enter. On the stage he saw a number of men waiting their turn to audition. Richard Burbage was seated at the side of the stage, and on his lap were the pages of the next play. Edmund doffed his cap when he saw Burbage notice his arrival.

'Players auditioning for the role of Malvolio, a mean faced puritan, who lusts after his mistress. Step forward, one by one, and say the lines as written on the paper. Remember, it is a comedy.'

Edmund watched as the first man spoke a dozen or so lines. Burbage shouted 'Next.' Six more hopefuls followed, until Burbage, raised his hand and pointed to the side of the stage. The player nodded and stepped over to an underling who was taking names. One lucky man and his family might eat tonight.

Edmund moved across to the tiring House and found some of the regular acting company. Alexander Cooke was there watching the auditions, and he smiled when he saw his friend.

'Hola Edmund. You are too early for the game or perhaps you were hoping for a part in the play?'

'I would, if my mean-hearted brother would but allow it. You know he has barred me from acting at The Globe. But what is this new play?'

'A comedy still in need of a title. Set in some place called Illyria. But it is not for performing yet. We still have an audience for Hamlet and also that French Forest comedy.'

'I have heard tell that the Hamlet play is popular. Do you have a role in it?'

'Yes, a good part but short. I play Ophelia who is jilted by the Danish Prince when he becomes mad and haunted by his dead father. She dies in the river.'

Edmund listened to Alexander as he explained more about his part in the play, but his mind was off somewhere else. He was sitting by a clean river full of fish. There are ducks and he can hear someone calling his name.

'Edmund! Are you listening to me? You look as if you have seen a ghost.'

'No, it was nothing. Your performance put me to sleep.'

Edmund's face broke into a broad grin, and he playfully punched Alexander's shoulder.

'Do you have the whole play written out, perhaps something I could read?'

'Not the whole play we are performing, no. But I think there is an earlier version somewhere. I guess you could read that. Shall I see if I can find it?'

'Yes, why not. If I cannot have a role in my brother's play, I might still read it.'

Alexander got up from his stool and went to the back wall where there was a row of pegs hammered into an oak beam. On each peg hung a bundle of well-thumbed pages tied together with string. He looked at several before he found the one, he was seeking.

'Here it is. As I told you, it is an early version. Shorter than the one we now perform. Probably best, if you put it inside your jerkin as I don't want to be accused of helping a Shakespeare to a Shakespeare script.'

Edmund did as Alexander suggested. The heavy bundle of pages, discarded by the Chamberlain's Men, now pressed close to his heart. Edmund said his farewell and he left by the small back door. He stood outside the playhouse for some moments, deep in thought. He still didn't have a part in a play but he did have a play. Edmund walked towards the river shore. He stood and watched as the little craft crossed the outgoing stream. Some laboured hard to make progress, while some turned with the flow of the current, the boatmen accepting the slight change of direction. Edmund turned around and walked back up the alley in the direction of The Rose. He found Henslowe still at his table, noting down in book, all the receipts for that week's performances.

'I see I cannot get rid of Shakespeare no matter how hard I try.'

'What if this Shakespeare can fill The Rose with a paying audience?'

'Jove might succeed in this but you, my boy, are not he.'

'I have a business proposition for you. I want a part in your next production. You want an audience to fill your playhouse.'

Edmund then explained to Henslowe about the play script he had inside his jerkin. He had a fair copy of the play Hamlet, that had been filling the Globe next door. A play by William Shakespeare. In the play there was a character named Ophelia. On the condition that Henslowe cast Edmund in this role, and for the price of just forty crowns, this same Edmund would sell the play to The Rose. Henslowe's eyes widened and he had the look of a fox when he finds an open hen coop. He quickly turned over the pages Edmund had offered him. He hadn't seen the play at the Globe, so he wasn't able to recognise the copy he had in his hands was a shorter, early version. But what of this. In the entertainment business, there were usually several versions of each play, and a skilful manager would select the one that best suited the audience and the venue. The opportunity for profit was clear to Henslowe. The Rose could stage Hamlet when the Globe was playing something else. This was too good to miss and although he attempted to horse-trade down the asking price, he knew he would accept Edmund's proposition. The deal was done and both men drank a mug of sack wine to seal their bargain. Edmund departed The Rose chuckling to himself. He had money in his purse, a part in a play and he had again punished his brother. A good day for a bastard.

Chapter forty-two

Philip Henslowe collected together a company of actors to perform the play, Hamlet. Not all the usual Admiral's Men were willing to work with this play as they knew it had been pilfered and was part of their competitor's repertoire at The Globe. London actors were all friends, to some degree or another. They met in the same taverns; the same Stews and they shared in the fellowship of playhouse life. Excuses were made. Certain persons had to visit family out in the shires. Some others had business commitments meaning they had to be away from London on the dates Henslowe had decreed The Rose would offer Hamlet to the public. Henslowe took it all in his stride. Players were plentiful, as were playhouses. Different stages, like costumes, were part of the life. Performers came and went and few in an audience marked named individuals as vital to a fun afternoon.

The available players were assigned their parts and, with the usual meagre few hours of rehearsals, they assembled at The Rose on the day of the first performance. The key role of the young Danish Prince was given to Anthony Jeffes, Edmund's former colleague in The Browne Company. He had returned to London from touring, having felt the need to settle and cease the nomadic life that drained the human from a man, leaving just a painted mechanical, dressed in someone else's clothes. After the stage performance and the audience departed, a pale cadaver was all that remained. Anthony knew some of Edmund's off-stage secrets. He had been there with him on the road, he had seen Edmund do things that no man would want revealed to his family at home. Edmund looked into the eyes of his former friend, searching for any sign that somewhere inside, Anthony remembered indiscretions or might be judging him. But there was no need to fear. Not everyone in London was like Edmund. Plotting and backstabbing might be his special skills, but Anthony was a good-natured man who chose to ignore the dirt under another man's fingernails or a brand on someone's thumb, if they offered a hand in greeting.

The Rose attracted a full audience of young men who, on that afternoon, either had no work or chose an excuse to avoid it. Many playgoers knew the entertainment advertised offered them a foreign castle, brother murdering brother, deaths galore, and the ghost of a dead King. This was a play that promised much amusement for an audience that longed for diversion that allowed their escape from the reality of life in England; well at least for a couple of hours.

The opening scene was well received and, as usual, the players found themselves competing with many witty comments offered up by the groundlings. There wasn't just one ghost below the stage talking to the young Prince but a few dozen gallants who had already drunk deeply from their flagons. It was a fun afternoon, and Henslowe counted his receipts with pleasure. Edmund had the appearance of his old self, dressed there in the pretty gown of Ophelia, the Lord Chamberlain's young daughter. The lewd wordplay between Anthony and Edmund provoked much ribaldry and laughter. A beautiful young woman spurned by her former lover was a story for the males and the males responded in the way males always did. Edmund enjoyed the effect and the lecherous gaze of those who hungered to deflower a pretty young maid.

All went well and the first of the bodies fell. The murder of Ophelia's father, on the sword of Hamlet, caused her rapid descent into the type of extreme grieving, more stage dramatic than any mirror to life. Edmund took his part well and towards the end of Act Four, as Ophelia, he spoke the lines of grief written by his brother.

> 'And will he not come again?
> No, no, he is dead,
> He never will come again.'

The emotion was well played. The words choked the player and tears streamed down his face. He spluttered and sank down to his knees as if struck by some hand of judgement. The audience stared in amazement, at last silent and absorbed by the emotion of the scene. The other actors looked shocked and glanced nervously from one to another. Here was something raw, a performance of wonder. As Edmund sobbed uncontrollably up there on the stage, somewhere in a graveyard in Stratford-upon-Avon, the cold earth trembled.

The audience shouted and clapped their appreciation, none of them knowing that Ophelia's distress was, this time not an act.

It was several months after Edmund's performance at The Rose, and he was at this time resting between roles. This was the euphemism used by players to explain their current status. While the term resting, might usefully disguise the reality of being out of work, the lack of money meant rent couldn't be paid and meals were obtained on credit or by abusing the hospitality of acquaintances. Edmund allowed himself just one meal a day, although quantities of cheap Ale helped blunt his hunger pangs.

One morning in early September there was a knock on his door at the St. Leonard's lodging. A boy stood at the threshold, saying he had a message from Master Richard Field for W.H. Edmund took the note from the boy, who then held out his hand for the expected coin. Edmund slammed the door shut and went back to lie on this bed. He turned the note over and examined the red wax seal that secured the message. Richard Field was a printer and as such, even trifling notes were given a professional touch. Edmund broke the seal to open the neatly folded paper. The penmanship was perfect. The content was less so. John Shakespeare, Gent., of Henley Street, Stratford upon Avon, was dead. He was already buried. Richard had been staying in Stratford at his family home at the time and he had attended the brief service at Trinity Church.

Edmund, stared out of the window watching the clouds moving slowly across the sky. The world still turned; day still followed night. Edmund was still without money or property. He was the youngest of John's four sons and, as he had recently learned from his brother, for them he bore the additional title of bastard. The passing of his father would bring him nothing, but perhaps his last weak connection to Stratford had just withered away. Edmund found his last silver coin and went out to buy some ale.

Edmund

I am not sure what I expected. Perhaps more than this. Father is dead and slowing rotting, being consumed by the worms that await us all. I am alive. I expected to feel something huge but there is barely a tremor. He was, I think, three score years and ten, so his death is not really any surprise. He was always there at the head of the table but now he is gone. His secrets have gone with him. That secret he never shared with me, that of my mother. She died twenty-one years ago bearing his child. Me, Edmund, mother killer. Both people responsible for my birth and blood are now gone. Of her, I know nothing except the slight shadows I sometimes see in the mirror. Something in my face that is not all Shakespeare. This must be mother. Was she an only child? Or did she have sisters and brothers? Are there others somewhere out there that share a little of my blood? The secret my father kept from me, stole any chance of my knowing my mother's family. Do I really care? Perhaps. The Shakespeare clan gave me very little. Certainly, no love and no property. Joan tried. No, that is unfair. It was only Joan who showed me love and human kindness. The others were cold and distant. I was always the last, the black sheep at the back, following the sullen flock of Saxons. Now I know why but for years I just felt their cold glances. The Shakespeare's were like mangy sheep.

They followed each other to the feeding table without expression. We ate together in silence and slept alone. I saw them, and did as they did, but I never truly felt one of them. Perhaps they all had secrets? But now father has taken his with him to the grave and I am the last. The sins of the father as Aunt Anne said.

Chapter forty-three

The morning after Edmund received the news about his father, he rose early, just as he did in the days when he first arrived in Shoreditch. He lifted a floorboard in this room and removed the package of papers he had hidden when he first arrived. He dressed himself in the best of his clothes and set out to walk to the city via Finsbury Fields. The grasses were dry and spent, the summer heat now over and the autumn rains yet to arrive. He walked steadily and with purpose. The fields reminded him of his childhood but his focus was on the present.

He entered the city via Cripplegate and walked on past the church of St Giles. His destination was Blackfriars, the place now fashionable and known to all who relied upon any playhouse for their income. The Children of the Chapel were still performing stage plays and although only frequented by a small audience of wealthy playgoers, their existence was nevertheless an irritant to other owners and players alike. But it wasn't the old Hall at Blackfriars that drew Edmund down from Shoreditch. Blackfriars was the location of the London home and office of Richard Field.

Edmund found the street he was looking for and stood before the handsome door bearing the name Field. A servant opened the door and asked for his name and the nature of his business. He was ushered into a small waiting room. Edmund seated himself down on a polished bench and listened to sounds of a press being worked in a printing room at the rear of the house. A short while later, a deep floral scent heralded the arrival of Richard Field who appeared at the doorway and beckoned Edmund to follow him down the hallway. He turned into a large parlour, comfortably furnished with a number of leather covered chairs. Richard stepped to the side allowing Edmund to enter and, as he did so, he immediately saw the room was already occupied.

Two elegantly dressed women stood together by the stone fireplace. They were wearing finely styled hats and gloves, suggesting they had either just arrived or were about to leave.

'Edmund, let me introduce you to my wife Jacqueline and her good friend and country woman, Marie Montjoie.'

Edmund removed his cap and performed his best stage bow to the ladies.

'This young man is an old friend of mine from Stratford. He has been a boy actor, but I believe he has now graduated to be a player. I understand he has recently performed at The Rose on Bankside.'

Edmund smiled at the introduction and made eye contact with both women. Madam Field seemed to note him, perhaps herself being an occasional playgoer.

'The Rose owned by Master Henslowe. And what part did you play?'

'A small role but one of great importance to Hamlet. I played Ophelia, the young daughter of the murdered Lord Chamberlain.'

Both women smiled and a blush came to their cheeks. Madam Field whispered something to her friend. Edmund recognised the language although he wasn't able to understand exactly what was said. It was French.

'I have always been fascinated by men who are able to become women, on a stage before a large audience. Perhaps one day Marie and I will be able to watch you perform. But for now, we must take our leave as I am sure you both have business to discuss. We were just going out when you arrived.'

Richard and Edmund both bowed and the two women went out into the hallway, Jacquline closing the door behind her.

'You are very welcome here Edmund. Quite a young man about town and very different from the small boy in Stratford I used to tease with the name Wet Head.'

'That seems a long time ago. I know my hair misses the clean waters of the Avon.'

'But forgive me, I forget myself. I should first say how sad I am at the death of your father. I am sorry it was I who had to write you such news. By chance I was in Stratford that week when he died. I knew both you and William were in London and probably unaware of the news. So, when I returned here yesterday, I sent a note to you both.'

'I am grateful to you for this act of kindness. Without you it might have been several weeks before I could have heard.'

'Do you not visit Henley Street to see the family?

'I haven't been for a long time, and now father has gone, I will have even less reason to make the long journey. But may I ask, were you at the funeral and was there a Will read?'

'Yes, to your first question, but no to the latter. To my knowledge your father didn't leave a Will. Your

Mother Mary, as surviving spouse, will inherit any property he owned.'

'I understand. It is as I expected.'

There was a long silence, broken only when Richard asked Edmund about his life in Shoreditch and the work at the playhouse. Edmund explained his status, being that of a jobbing actor but with few jobs. Richard was perhaps closest person to a friend, and Edmund didn't feel the need to try to put a mask over his current difficulties. Edmund was out of money; his father had just died and acting work on the stage was increasingly difficult to find. But there was method in all this. Edmund wasn't just being truthful; he came expecting to ask for a loan and this he then did. Richard had known him since he was a small boy. He knew his family and of course, he had published his brother's two most successful poems, Venus and the later Lucrece. As Edmund had anticipated, Richard, although a little embarrassed, went to a locked cabinet and took out a soft leather bag. He counted out twenty crowns and asked Edmund to write a brief note of receipt.

'Thank you, Richard. I appreciate the money, and I will of course, repay you when I next have regular work. But in the meantime, I do have a business proposition for you.'

'This, I am pleased to hear. Have you been playwriting?'

'Me? No, but my brother has, err, entrusted me with something from his pen. I have some, perhaps more than one hundred, very interesting Sonnets that I am sure, if published, would sell well.'

Richard's eyes widened and his face showed surprise. He confessed he had heard chat about some private Sonnets. He himself had not read any of them but, if offered, he would be very happy to consider publishing. Edmund opened the bundle of papers he had brought with him from Shoreditch. From the bundle, he took out several sheets and, one by one, passed them to the printer to read. As Richard finished each one. He returned them to Edmund.

'I am certain they would sell very well although I doubt your brother would be content to have them made public. He must realise that the Sonnets contain the form of words that, any literate person possessing half a wit might use to jump to the conclusion that the poet was unfaithful to his wife. Not just with another woman but also, perhaps a fair youth.'

'But good poetry, yes?'

'Certainly, but dangerous to the poet. If I were to publish them, I would first need your brother to give me his authority.'

'That he will not do. He has entrusted me with this matter, and I believe he now wishes to forget about their existence. He cannot bear the thought of destroying poetry, nor does he wish to personally profit from their publication. But I can.'

'I might have a solution for you. Myself, I am too closely associated with your brother's work to link my name to publishing these Sonnets. But I know of someone else who might. His name is Thomas Thorpe.'

'Is he trustworthy and you know him to be able to produce good work?'

'Yes, Thorpe has published several such works, and I can certainly vouch for his skills. Would you like me to speak to him on your behalf?'

'Yes, please speak to him. Sound him out and ask how much he might be willing to pay. I will await to hear from you.'

The mood had now changed, and the two businessmen shook hands, with Edmund carefully re-wrapping the bundle of Sonnets. With his purse now full of Crowns, and with the Sonnets, Edmund left Blackfriars.

On Thursday 24, December there was a portentous, full eclipse of the sun, visible to all the citizens of London.

Chapter forty-three

In the summer of the following year, Edmund decided he would attend morning rehearsals at The Curtain playhouse in Shoreditch. He had heard Tavern chatter, suggesting Christopher Beeson had recently left the Chamberlain's Men company of actors following pressure from some of the senior players and he was now again working at the Curtain. The story Edmund was told, was that a young woman had accused Christopher of rape and of him leaving her pregnant. He had been arraigned before a magistrate, but no criminal charges were agreed upon or filed.

Christopher had been Edmund's first friend when he arrived in Shoreditch, and from him, he had learned many of the skills required to become a boy actor. The arrival of Christopher at The Curtain served to buoy up Edmund's sinking humour. It had been many months since he last was offered a part in a play. Though the same age as Edmund, Christopher had been one of the playhouse community since his early teens. He had a good reputation with playhouse owners, and he knew many of the actors who trod the boards throughout London.

Edmund entered the playhouse yard and stood unobserved for several minutes. The scene in the playhouse was characteristically Shoreditch. Actors, bare headed and in just their shirtsleeves, stood in small groups, chatting. There was ale and a pie seller. Up upon the stage, two actors were rehearsing a sword fight. The wooden blades clattered, as thrust after thrust was parried, all under the watchful eyes of Christopher. To stage right, a boy actor was having a gown fitted by a seamstress. Perhaps too many pies had been eaten, as the woman scolded the boy about his fat tummy and complained she was going to have to let out the Kirdle. Here was a healthy, creative chaos and Edmund immediately felt quite at home. It was sometime before Christopher noticed his presence.

'Hola, Edmund! You are a welcome sight. At last, a player who knows how to get down on his knees to please an audience.'

'Better that than to have to play a soldier. But fighting with swords is a trifle old fashioned. Pistols are the future.'

'Come up here, take a seat while I finish schooling these two ruffians.'

Edmund climbed the steps and briefly embraced his old friend, who smiled and joked just as he had once done when they shared the boys' house in Holywell Lane. Edmund found himself a stool and settled down to watch as the rehearsals resumed. His gaze moved quickly from the legs of the fighters to the breast of the seamstress. The woman was pretty and had loose, fair hair. She was elegantly dressed and, as she fussed over the gown of the boy, Edmund enjoyed the brief sight of her legs and a bosom that seemed to be struggling for freedom from the tight stomacher she wore. An attractive woman and he soon realised he had seen her before. When the boy stepped out of the tight gown, Edmund walked over to pick up the collar that had been dropped on the floor.

'Let me help you mistress. I can see you have your hands full.'

'Boys are careless with what is to a woman, precious.'

'But some of us have learnt, a woman's precious parts need to be held.'

Their eyes flashed with the energy of seduction, and she shook her head in mock protest.

'I knew you Master Edmund when you first tried on a lady's bodice. Do you not remember me?'

'At the time I was still very new to dressing in front of a woman. I was nervous so hopefully you will forgive me for not marking your name. But I do remember your smile.'

'Your eyes tell me it is not just my smile you admired. Look up here please. I'm Alice, Alice Sly.'

'Ah, yes. Now I remember, Alice. You dressed me many times.'

The playful flirtation continued, and Alice enjoyed the attention of the handsome young man, still a glamourous, desirable male despite him being absent from the paid cast of most new plays. Alice was three years older than Edmund and she was married to the player William Sly, a boorish man who, unlike Edmund, seemed to be constantly working at one playhouse or another.

As seamstress, she had her own business, and she knew the dimensions of all the men and boys who entertained on the public stage. Edmund told Alice, he hoped to be offered a role in the next play at The Curtain.

'Then I wish you luck Master Edmund. Perhaps, I will have my tape measure around your middle in the future.'

With this and a cheeky wink, she bundled the discarded gown in her arms and carried it to a worktable in the tiring house. Edmund felt his old confidence return. Acting was his chosen profession. He was a performer and although he had perhaps, a habit of choosing the wrong parts for himself in the offstage world, at twenty-two, he could still charm a public audience and win hearts.

When Christopher finished supervising the sword play, he walked across the stage to speak to Edmund.

'Are you working at present? I have not heard your name mentioned for some time.'

'No, I am between roles. I hoped perhaps you might have something for me.'

'That, I might. I have a play or two from Thomas Dekker we might be performing. There may be a part for you in these. But I also intend staging the Night's Dream. It is the right season after all. Would you like to reprise your Helena? I realise you are now a little old for the part but perhaps with a little painting you can still play a girl.'

Both men laughed. They were easy together, unburdened by the rivalry or malice that had infected so many of Edmund's relationships. Terms were agreed and Edmund was told to come back the following week when the playhouse calendar had been prepared.

The prospect of work, while perhaps torture for many listless apprentices in the city, for a jobbing player it brought sunshine after rain. Crafting a performance wasn't arduous as it combined intellectual activity with social bonding. An actor needed to get to know the character he was to play. To play a role, first the actor needed to discover the human lying beneath the black ink scratched upon the paper. Edmund embraced the task, and the task gave in return, good humour and a sense of worth.

Early each morning, as Edmund scraped away any signs of a beard from his face, he looked into the mirror and saw Helena looking back. He spoke her words to her image, pouted her lips and smiled her smile. When at the tavern, he watched the serving girls and the whores, learning again how a woman moves and responds to men around her.

Each morning, he walked to the playhouse to meet with the other actors and share a laugh with the workers who, behind the stage, provide the props, and stage effects expected by the London audience. Christopher was happy at the visits made by his old friend. The success of a playhouse depends upon a team effort and Edmund had now joined the team.

The up-and-coming performances of Midsummer Night's Dream were discussed, and a play bill approved. A dress for Helena was chosen by Christopher then rejected by Edmund, who preferred another. Alice the seamstress, offered yet another option. Each person, in-turn, argued for their preference, and if Helena had been present, she would perhaps have feared she would be asked to run naked through the forests outside Athens. In the end, Alice prevailed. Edmund was encouraged to parade across the stage holding each dress against his body as the other actors amused themselves by shouting and awarding points for each. Perhaps because the actors understood that to oppose the seamstress, was not a wise move and might have consequences, her choice of dress achieved most votes. Following the comedy of the dress selection, Edmund was led into the tiring house by Alice.

'Now Edmund, we have chosen the dress, our question is can you wear it without splitting the seams.'

'I have grown a little since I last played this part.'

'Grown? Perhaps the Ale and pies have thickened what was once thin. Take off your breeches and we will see if the dress will hang prettily.'

Edmund did as he was asked. He took off the quilted, loose breeches and his tight jerkin. He stood there in just his slops and stockings. Alice looked at the man in front of her and smiled. She took her measuring tape and wrapped it around his waist. She noted the number. Then she let the tape slip down lower to encircle his hips. She then knelt on the floor behind him and slid the tape lower until it caught on the protuberance of his penis.

'This has grown. Helena cannot have this lump swinging to and fro beneath her dress.'

'Mistress Sly, please control your speech. I may be now more man than boy but your teasing me won't help.'

'No, perhaps not, but we will have to do something, or the dress will not hang correctly. Perhaps some strapping. Yes, we, or rather you, can try this.'

Alice got up and walked over to her work basket. She found a long length of muslin cloth and handed this to Edmund, together with two pins.

'Before you arrive her tomorrow, wind this cloth over your err, your, well you know what I mean. Use the strapping. Do you understand?'

'Yes, I do. I will do as you suggest.'

'I will let out the seams of the dress and we can then see how it fits.'

Alice stood smiling as she watched Edmund put on his breeches and jerkin. Once presentable he bowed to Alice, took his strappings and left.

Chapter forty-four

The dark omen portended by the eclipses finally came to pass. On the fourth Monday of March, in the year 1603, the main woman of the age, Queen Gloriana died in her Richmond palace. Soon after, many more people started to die as a pestilence moved across the city from the east.

It was a sombre gathering of the hitherto carefree players. Over the second half of the year 1602, things had been good. Plays had been well received with full audiences at the playhouses. Receipts were healthy and all the players and workers had money to spend on luxuries. They were anticipating a profitable summer season. But all this optimism dimmed behind a thick cloud as external events exploded like a cask of powder. The death of the only Monarch most of the players ever knew, was a severe emotional blow. Elizabeth was a mother figure for the nation, and no one feels good when their mother dies. Yes, there was mourning and for many, an outpouring of grief. There was a palpable sadness in the people, but all businessmen knew, this would end and the pent-up emotions would bust out in an attempt to buy some joy. People would drink, eat and visit the playhouse to cheer themselves, once the natural period of grief passed.

Beyond the death of their mother figure, there was the spectre of uncertainty. What would the new Scottish King be like? Who would come with him to govern the English and would Taxes and laws change?

No soothsayer could accurately predict the whims of those in the ruling elite. The players had been told the Scottish court were all Presbyterians. This suggested they were another type of Puritan, and this was not good news for the entertainment business. But the players and team had prospered under Elizabeth, even with her stern-faced ministers, and there was reason to suppose the playhouses could prosper under James.

But a graver external event arrived, that of the plague. The Bills of Mortality issued by the City authorities started to show deaths from the plague to be rising. Week on week, the numbers rose higher. First in the Hamlets and Suburbs out in the East, but everyday there was a westerly movement, as death crept nearer. The plague was seeping across the City Walls and bloodied bodies were thrown onto the city streets. Orders for the closure of the playhouses had just been issued. For the players, it seemed that if they escaped the black death, then starvation would be their reward. Everyone was fearful. The stories were a nightmare and the threat of a horrid painful death, real. Every man and woman said their prayers and counted the coins in their purse. Would money last until the playhouses reopened?

Edmund couldn't believe his bad luck. He had just re-established himself as a performer able to achieve a regular wage, and then, suddenly the doors of the playhouse were nailed shut. He was back where he had been when he first returned from the Continent. Long days of unemployment and evenings of dizzy Ale and costly futile card games. Debts upon debts. He felt himself betrayed by the wheel of fortune. He had allowed himself to believe he was a winner but now all this had been snatched away.

'Gentlemen and lady. This is bad but we have survived the like before, and, as with a football, we will bounce up out of the dark slough.'

Christopher tried to encourage his team, using fine words, the currency of their business. They might not be able to stop the plague, but they needed to deny the possibility of defeat. Provided they were alive, the plague was an unpleasant setback, not the final Armageddon. They needed to talk themselves out of despair and try to rationalise to find a solution.

'I propose a tour. It is time the provincial masses had the opportunity to see us perform. While they may not have the disposable income to feed a regular playgoing habit, they can afford to buy tickets to see a visiting spectacle. Civic Authorities in the past were happy to prove their towns equal to that of London. Public funds exist to entertain their townsfolk, and we are ready to take their purse. On the road we will go.'

Edmund groaned and put his head between his hands.

Edmund

I am not sure what is worse, dying of the sickness or being dragged like a beast on tour around the dung pits of England. At least with the sickness, I would suffer for just a few days but on the tour my torture may stretch for many months. Foolish to think this way. In truth, the plague is my greater terror. I hear told it turns your skin black and your organs to liquid. You writhe in agony but, for the sick, there is no cure. When the bilboes first swell, you know you are one of the soon to be dead. Images from the Doom, painted in colour on the wall of Guildhall Chapel in Stratford, fill my mind. Demons await me. The plague hunts the streets for victims and no matter what I do, it will be the fates that mark me out to die or to live on in fear. I have heard told, some so stricken, although abandoned by friends and family, do survive. But what of this, I do not trust to bet my life on chance. Each person I meet may be my assassin; the sickness hidden within their flesh waiting for the moment to strike me down. Their breath, their touch may pass me their contagion, Our Father, please save me from this.

Chapter forty-five

Christopher and his team organised things for the departure. Wagons had to be bought, and horses hired. Costumes and props were assessed for their worth and then, the chosen items packed up into boxes. Space on the wagons was limited, so the players could only take on the road the bare minimum from the playhouse. The rest of their precious stage possessions would have to be locked in a room to await their return.

Christopher briefed the chosen players as to his intentions. They would first head west to Oxford where he had distant family members. They were tenant farmers and perhaps the troupe could use one of their barns. They might help with the animals or in the fields when needed. He could then visit Richard Browne, the City Mayor at the Oxford Guildhall. Hopefully they would be allowed to perform in the city square.

From Oxford they might travel north to Leicester and Coventry. Other actors of experience spoke of York and Norwich. Even Stratford upon Avon was mentioned as a possibility. Optimism grew like a weed in damp earth. Soon the team were smiling and joking about what fun they would have on the road. Memory is a funny thing. Those players, who like Edmund had toured before, somehow forgot the hours of misery, trudging through deep mud while being soaked by the cold rain. They forgot the biting wind, scouring skin and turning eyes bloodshot. They somehow misplaced memories of sleeping on straw in drafty barns or drinking rank Ale that had been discarded as undrinkable by farmers or owners of roadside Inns. They forgot the endless, sameness. One day's travel, a scrappy performance and then another day's travel, over and over again. Everyone they will meet will be a stranger and all the strangers will want something from them. The visits to the Cities excepted, for many provisional townsfolk, the players were nothing more than vagabonds. Edmund didn't forget. He remembered.

It turned out to be a thirteen-month sentence served, despite Edmund not being convicted by any legal court. The tour did at last come to an end when reports from London reached the players, that deaths from plague had fallen sufficiently for there to be talk about reopening the playhouses. Out of the ten actors who set out on the tour, all had survived although two had dropped out and it was presumed, they were now husbands of some, soon to grow fat, country girls. Edmund owed money to seven of the eight. Christopher always declined to lend so his friendship has survived Edmund's foolishness. Sadly, the others had been unwise and, in consequence, they no longer spoke or broke bread with Edmund. But while there was much enmity, the thirteen months away from London achieved its primary purpose. None of them had been stricken down by the plague and none of them had starved.

The prospect of returning to the individual emotional thing we all call home, blunted any anger and helped sooth feeling of resentment. The return to

London had arrived just in time to suppress a rebellion or worse. Edmund thought fondly of his lodgings in Shoreditch. Before leaving he had agreed with the widow that, for five crowns, she would hold his room until the plague passed. No specific period was mentioned as neither of them had any advance notice of how long the pestilence would persist with its attack on the population. In the end, the bravery of city dwellers, together with perhaps an inherited resistance to plague, a gift from their ancestors who might have encountered a similar disease in centuries long passed, combined to beat the pathogen. Those who were marked to die, had died. Those who fate decreed would win the genetic lottery, survived. The city looked the same although there were far less people. There were vacancies and soon country folk from the shires made their way south and east to take the places of the fallen. Memories are short. The wheel of life turned again, and few considered the possibility that the good times were temporary and that the jagged fracture in the wheel rim would at some point, arrive to leave its mark again.

Being on the road had left its mark on Edmund. He was thinner although not slim. He had lost his youthful shine, and his face showed the hollows of a young man who had struggled to outrun his own personal demons. He was still considered handsome although those who judged him so were getting older.

There was another eclipse of the sun on 12 October 1605. Some people talked of the times being cursed.

Chapter forty-six

When Edmund returned to Parsonage Yard, close by St Leonard's Church, he found the widow outside in her chair, guarding her property. He wondered if she had been there every day since he left. For her, each day was an exact repeat of the last and this was good. She didn't want any changes because, at her time of life, any changes inevitably would be bad. When one reaches three score and ten, change usually equates to loss, illness or worse. Same equals good and when Edmund arrived, the widow saw continuity. She smiled with her dry shrunken lips and watery eyes.

'Good morning, Madam. I am pleased to see you looking well.'

'Better than some, yes. But I don't complain. My knees do ache something terrible and at night I feel my heart pounding like a May Day dance.'

'But there is no sickness here in the Yard?'

'Plague? No, not here. Out there maybe, but I don't go there much. It was all over when last I heard but doubtless, it will visit us sinners again.'

'Let us not provoke the fates with talk of that. My room is ready for me?'

'You have money?'

'Some, yes. But my brother has a purse for me that he has kept safe while I was away.'

'Does he by Jupiter. Well, see you get it soon and pay me my rent by this Sabbath.'

'That you can be sure of. I bid you a good day.'

Edmund hastened away in fear she might change her mind and demand money now. There was no purse, and his brother wouldn't be lending. Edmund climbed the staircase to the room he had last seen thirteen months before. The door creaked and the sound of fleeing mice, told the story of how no one had been there since he left. He opened the casement to allow the air to change, and then slumped himself down onto the bed. The dust didn't bother him, as didn't the cobwebs and dead flies. He had a home again and, tomorrow and tomorrow, God willing, he would awaken in the same bed.

The following day, Edmund visited several nearby taverns, not so much for the food and drink, but more for the news. He needed to learn the current state of the city and who might have returned and who never left but survived. With his enquiries he discovered that the playhouses were awakening after the many months of slumber. He was told the playwright Shakespeare had moved lodgings and now lived in Silver Street, just south of the Wall and St Giles. Oh, and a new King had paraded himself through the city, bathed in pomp and vainglory.

Several days later, Edmund found the Junction of Silver Street and Monkwell. In the churchyard of St Olave's were signs that there had been some type of earth works. In the space between the flagstone path and the low wall, the soil was banked high and Edmund realised this was perhaps the result of burials. He shuddered to think of the layers of rotting corpses, submitting to the inevitable corruption and worms. He found a dry piece of stone wall and made himself comfortable. What was happening underground behind him was not his current concern. In front of him was the street and he had a good view of the Montjoie residence.

Christopher Montjoie and his wife Marie were French protestants who had chosen London over a life trying to avoid Catholic mobs and rabble-rousing Priests. They had transportable skills in that they were both makers of silver and jewelled tiaras, much in demand by the wives and daughters of the wealthy. But this was not the primary reason why Edmund watched the house. Along with several servants and apprentices, the house contained a lodger, one William Shakespeare.

It was not long after Edmund took up his position perched on the wall, the door of the Montjoie house opened and the familiar figure of his brother appeared. He was getting fatter, and his cheeks puffed out as he hurried himself along the street, heading towards Cheapside. Edmund watched him go. The man he saw no longer inspired feelings of admiration or sibling love. The term brother was now just a painful title, not any statement of healthy relationship. Once upon a time, it had all seemed simple. He held his brother's hand, and he gazed up at his smiling face. Now his brother was false. When William chose to use his claim of legitimacy as a weapon against Edmund, any relationship they once had become poisoned. They were now rivals to a name and Edmund watched his brother as a tiger does when he comes upon a tethered goat. His calculation was his brother could be expected to move regularly between here and The Globe playhouse. All was well and his brother's business success meant more opportunity for Edmund to purloin money and raise loans against William's estate. While his main interest was financial there was also the chance of pleasure. Marie Montjoie was a fine-looking woman and Edmund had already learned, his brother seemed to always seek out a closeness to beautiful people.

The next day, Edmund returned to St Olave's Churchyard, and at about the same time as in the morning before, his brother left the house and marched off in the direction of the river and towards his business in Southwark. Soon after his departure, the door opened again, and he saw Marie Montjoie leave the house, carrying a small wicker basket. She was elegantly dressed with a small cape draped over one shoulder and wearing a delicately coloured Catholic style veil over her hair. She walked gracefully, like a dancer with a rhythmic sway that appeared natural rather than an affectation. Edmund who was still a student of all things feminine, could recognise the allure of this woman. He left his perch and followed at a discrete distance behind.

Marie walked on, along Noble Street, until she arrived at Cheapside. Here, as usual, there were tables and awnings, where farmer's wives and costermonger arranged their produce for sale. Marie was shopping. Edmund watched as she moved from table to table, inspecting the items on display. It was obvious to Edmund that many of these traders remembered this French woman, and she appeared to have brief conversations with several of them before she reached a table laden with strawberries. Here she stopped. Edmund seized the moment and approached the table as Marie tasted the fruit to make sure they were ripe. As Marie's hand reached across to pick another strawberry, Edmund lent forward and matched her action.

'Please forgive me Madam. I didn't mean to fight you for the best fruit. They look very good but tell me, are they sweet?'

'They promise to be, but the only sure test, is with the tongue. You should try one.'

'I have known promises made with the tongue to be false, perhaps I could ask you to choose some for me?'

'If it really be strawberries you seek, I will try to please.'

Marie let her hand wander across the fruit, selecting the most promising and rejecting those that had already been tasted by the worms in the field. Her eyes sparkled and the rouge on her cheeks decorated what was already most appealing. And her voice gave to English words the taste of France, playful and seductive.

'I am in your debt madam. But you have perhaps forgotten me. We have met once before.'

'Is that so? The city has so many new people, I struggle to remember everyone.'

'I know you as a friend of Madam Jacqueline Field, and we met briefly at her home at Blackfriars.'

'Ah yes, perhaps we did. What is your name?'

'Shakespeare, Edmund Shakespeare.'

Marie turned around to face Edmund and she studied this handsome young man who was paying her attention.

'Let me pay for my strawberries and perhaps we could move over to that tree to find some shade.'

He smiled again and looked deep into her large brown eyes. He was close enough to see his reflection, like a small round ball but sharp enough to pierce like a bullet of lead. Marie spoke with confidence and a voice that sounded like the colour of fine Burgundy wine. He decided to sip her if he could. He took off his cap, bowed slightly and stepped back to let her pass. Marie gathered her purchases and placed them into her basket. She found a coin and the seller wished her a good day. He heard her laugh and after two or more steps she turned her head slightly as she walked, nodding a coded feminine approval. Edmund walked behind her as she stepped the few paces before stopping under a large Lime tree that shaded the south side of the street.

'If your name is truly Shakespeare, I doubt you were really shopping for ripe strawberries. Now, tell me the truth.'

'I confess, you have caught me out. But we did meet some time ago at the Field's house and I have looked for you ever since. By chance, I came to where I heard my brother has lodgings, and, to my great pleasure I saw you. My heart raced.'

'So, the playwright is your brother?'

'A very much older brother, yes. I too am involved in the playhouse, but I am an actor on the stage.'

Marie smiled as she inspected this handsome man, more than ten years her junior. She enjoyed the attention he was giving, and she felt the slight excitement of an animal sensing his display of courtship. He danced the dance of a potent male, when in presence of an available female. And although married, Marie was available.

'You must tell me some secrets about my lodger. He seems to write a lot but he says very little. It might be to my advantage to know more of him.'

Edmund bowed and then laughed. In his head he knew the game was going well and he realised that Marie, like himself, enjoyed using her beauty to charm those who might prove useful.

Chapter forty-seven

As the widow landlady had foretold, the plague returned to ravish the people of the city. Deaths continued to mount although the authorities judged the numbers acceptable; those who suffered the disease or loss of family members probably didn't share their opinion. Business was business and The City, to make wealth, consumed people as and when it served the needs of the markets. There were always more people ready to come and fill the places of those who had ceased to exist. The impersonal names written on a list, were just statistics. The dead could be replaced. The preachers exploited the continued presence of the pestis, to argue that sin was the problem and the curse of the poor and, plague was their punishment. Most accepted the risk and for them, life went on. The summer of 1606 brought the city hot weather and, the rats prospered. As the rodents multiplied, not coincidentally, the numbers of plague deaths increased. At last, the City Authorities began to worry, and their first response was to close the public playhouses again. The actors packed their costumes and locked the playhouse doors. The lucky ones accepted the call of managers to go on Tour and they soon followed the wagons as they left the city, bound for the distant Shires. London's loss was to the benefit of country towns of England. The hard sun-baked roads were to be criss-crossed by touring companies and players performed in town squares and Guildhalls.

Edmund didn't go. He didn't get an invitation for any tour. He was now twenty-six and no longer in demand to play pretty women on stage. Physically, he was ready for roles where sharp-tongued mothers and wives commanded boys and men, but his pride and ambition railed against reality. He was also considered by some other players as difficult to work with. The best players, with their resident playwrights, left the city. Edmund remained, accepting unemployment with resignation and bad humour. Money was hard to come by and his luck at cards was as poor as ever. He borrowed from everyone who still believed the name of Shakespeare to be a mark of security.

There were many theatre people still resident in the city. Touring was just for the few. The backstage workers, such as seamstresses, carpenters and stagehands, had been abandoned with a few token gestures and promises. Alice Sly remained in the city while her boorish husband William, left with The King's Men to perform for the rural folk.

Alice possessed skills always in demand. The wealthy citizens, while choosing fashionable tailors to make their clothes, needed seamstresses to repair and mend items already part of their wardrobe. Men grew fat and their clothes needed to be let out. Women grew pregnant and this too provided paid work for Alice. The service she offered wasn't well paid but it at least it was paid, which was just as well as her husband didn't send her any money. The rooms she rented, just off Hog Lane, were both home and workshop. Edmund was an occasional visitor. Alice sometimes shared her dinners with him, as he was again penniless.

'You look like you haven't eaten a decent meal for days. Ale is not enough to keep that young body of yours strong.'

Alice as usual, spoke the truth, though she received little gratitude for either the food or advice.

'Ale is plentiful and if I am to win at cards, I need to help my friends feel content to lose.'

'Win! Is that what you do? Whenever I see you playing, it is the others who are winning.'

'Enough of this. You are not my mother. I don't need to be told what to do.'

'Perhaps this is just what you need. Your mother or perhaps a wife.'

Alice smiled ruffled Edmund's hair. She was always good humoured, and Edmund felt comfortable being with her.

'A mother I would like but none was left for me. A wife is something I might play upon the stage but if in real life they match what is written for them, it is best I stay as I am.'

'There is some truth in what you say. Playwrights like your brother, create many bad wives. There are few up there on the stage who deserve the love of a kind man.'

'Happily, Alice, my brother didn't write you. If you weren't already married, I might plight you, my troth.'

Edmund playfully pattered her behind and laughed as she smacked away his hand.

'Me married? Only just and to a man who is seldom here and then rarely solid enough to do me much good.'

Alice winked at Edmund and served him another bowl of the thick soup she had been heating in a pan on the fire. As she leant forward to give the bowl to Edmund and watched as his eyes caught hers and then lowered his gaze, to her breasts. Alice was a hungry woman, and Edmund always rose to signals of appetite.

Over the following days, Edmund became a regular visitor to Alice Sly. She worked during the daylight hours when small stitches could be seen, and the servants of her clients made their visits. During the evenings her visitor would amuse her with his stories of childhood in Stratford and his time on the Continental Tour. He would share her bed, and this made her remember what it was to be a woman. They both took what they needed from the visits. In this game, they both won, although their contributions were not equal.

Alice had a sister named Beth, and Beth regarded Edmund as baseborn. Not that she knew the story of his parentage, but that she saw past the performance and into the man beneath. For Beth, Edmund was a cheat who fed himself by exploiting the vulnerabilities of gentle people. Beth was married to a Shoreditch shoemaker and although they had low income, she felt respectably content. She hoped the same for her sister. This resulted in her frequently judging those who Alice chose to love. Beth disliked William Sly and Edmund. No man was good enough for her sister. While possibly correct in her opinion, this did nothing to help Alice live in harmony with her men.

On most evenings, when Edmund settled himself down on the one large chair scavenged from the old priory, Beth would find a reason to visit the lodgings.

'The wandering Shakespeare, here again I see.'

'Mistress Beth; yes here again, as are you. We have much in common.'

'I doubt that. I am here to protect my sister.'

'Exactly my intent, it is just I do not share your method.'

'Method! What method do I have.'

'You Beth plan for my downfall and with your constant visits you seek to hasten my end.'

'Balderdash. Your head is full of lines from the playhouse. Silly words that weave confused patterns over the dark void that is your life.'

Exchanges like this were normal. Once done, Beth would turn her back and chat with Alice. She would ignore Edmund's presence although her heart was always full of malice for him. The dialogue between the sisters told each of their day and each woman, in her own way, took pleasure in the sharing. Edmund was an observer, never a participant. When Beth finally took her leave, Edmund would feel a flush of satisfaction. Not only had the irritant left, but he had again triumphed. Alice was his once more, a least for a few more hours when the cycle would be repeated.

During his afternoons, before Edmund wandered towards Hog Lane, he would search out old acquaintances in the taverns and Inns of Shoreditch. He kept a mental record of all those who carried his marker and needed to be avoided, plus those who were, as yet unburdened. The former list grew longer, the latter, shrank. Edmund felt pursued although this was due to his own actions. On more than one occasion, a creditor caught him unaware, and he received a thick lip or black eye to help him remember the debts he owed. The occasional battering he received bought him much soothing and gentle attention from Alice. She would bathe his face and kiss his bruises. Of more value to Edmund were the coins she found in her purse, given to him to help pay off the attacker and save him from further concussion. Sadly, for Edmund, her purse wasn't nearly big enough to hold the amount of coins needed to pay off the debts he owed.

As the city dwellers lived with their dark fears over the continuing plague outbreak, for some the fear was well justified. As October closed, a small group of family friends at St Olave's Churchyard, watched as the body of Marie Montjoie was laid to rest.

Then, it was a little more than a month after the first Fifth of November Thanksgiving celebration, a day when Edmund found himself in a pew St Leonards Church, listening with the others to a sermon about conspirators, foreign plots and threats to English way of life, that Edmund started to realise he was losing control of his narrative. The days were short and the nights long and, as if to make matters worse, one evening when Edmund arrived at the lodging of Alice, his routine suffered an unwelcome change. When Edmund opened the door he found Beth already in the room, enthroned upon the only chair. Alice was working by candlelight on a large white linen garment. She raised her head and smiled at Edmund as he entered the room.

It was obvious to him that the sisters had been together for some time and that his usual evening of relaxation was already lost.

'Better a Tapster than a Player, I've always told Alice, but now she has two of them attached like ugly cankers on a vigorous limb.'

'We are fated to have the benefit of your twisted wisdom Beth, although I doubt a dose of the plague could bring me anything less welcome.'

'More blotted lines from a Warwickshire bumkin who has nothing but foul seed to spread.'

'Don't you have a husband you can tend to rather than sit here pecking at me like an old harpy?'

'Do not talk of my husband, it is Alice's husband you must mark. What will he say?'

'What will he say about what?'

'Tell him Alice. Tell this motley fool how his scabby pizzle has stained us all.'

Edmund looked from the gurning face of one sister to the loving smile of the other. He waited for Alice to speak.

'Edmund, I am with child. I didn't think it could happen. My husband and I have been married for so long, I thought I couldn't conceive. But now, because of you, I am going to have a baby.'

The news, although seemingly joyous, was totally unexpected. This was part of woman he had not rehearsed for. He could dress like a woman, move like a woman and talk like a woman, but the biology that, since Eve had given life, was a mystery to him. He had lived as if both he and Alice were merely characters and as such, when the curtains closed, they could take off their costumes and the leave the stage. Sans everything. Nowhere in his brother's Seven Ages of Man speech, did it mention fatherhood. Edmund found a stool and sat down heavily.

Chapter forty-eight

When Alice grew round bellied, Edmund left. Shoreditch had become somehow less than it was before. He had already stopped his nightly visits to Hog Lane. The sights and sounds of the sisters were for him, too much to endure. What was once a comfort, became a test he failed to pass. Alice was happy to be with child and bravely ignored the possibility that her husband might soon return and not share her joy. Beth took control of the lodgings and with vigour, she voiced her predictions of more travails. She cared for her sister but seldom missed any opportunity to repeat the tedious mantra of 'I told you so.' Had Edmund even chosen to share Alice's trials, Beth would have prevented him. Edmund was exiled for the second time in his life although he regarded this as a release rather than a punishment. He had lost his evenings of comfort and any future access to Alice's purse. The playhouses were still closed, and the widow became more insistent that he should pay the rents owed. His creditors, the inhabitants of taverns and Inns of Shoreditch, were now so numerous he couldn't risk visiting any of the local places of food and drink. His solution to the pyramid of problems he himself had built, was to flee Shoreditch during the hours of darkness when one more cloaked stranger threading their way through the alleyways, would not be noted or remembered.

Edmund moved his lodgings from Shoreditch to St Giles, Cripplegate, just outside the old Roman wall to The City. He found two small rooms off Redcrosse Street, at the rear of a storehouse building that was used by Christopher Montjoie living in nearby Silver Street. Here he thought, he might be invisible. Here he could escape his creditors and any consequence of Alice's condition. He travelled light but one small precious bundle of sonnets went with him. He determined that it was now perhaps the right time to transform these thin lines of poetry, written on mere paper, into potent golden Nobles coins.

It was another hard winter and what with the plague and rising food prices, life in the city was grim. The once happy times were memory and each citizen lived from day to day, trusting in God that things would improve. Even Edmund found himself on his knees, mumbling a few prayers as the preacher in St Giles Church led the Sunday service. But the days were getting longer and the recent cold weather, combined with the decreasing host population, served to disperse the colonies of rats. Spring was in the air and fresh green buds brought colour to shrubs and trees. Little messages of renewal to cheer those who allowed themselves the freedom to raise their eyes from the ground.

Edmund took his bundle of papers to Blackfriars, home and printing office to his Stratford friend, Richard Field. Edmund was admitted and asked to wait in the front room while Richard supervised his workers operating the press. It seemed apparent, that despite the plague, the market for the written word was healthy. The citizens of London sought answers to their questions and the church preachers had nothing new to say. But there were poets, philosophers, alchemists and astrologists, who offered solutions for a few pence a time. Richard printed pamphlets that sold well at the many stalls in St Paul's Yard.

The waiting brewed anxiety within Edmund. Like a sealed flask of tainted wine, he felt the pressure building. He needed money and the Sonnets must provide. The room felt smaller than it had when he last visited the house. Suddenly he noticed a strong perfume of a flora scent.

'Edmund, you are welcome. It has been a long time since I saw you. How are you?'

'Better than many, but not as good as some.'

'Equivocal, but I think in these times, few people might answer more truthfully. I understand from my wife Jacqueline, you became acquainted with her friend Marie, now sadly passed on.'

'Yes, Marie helped me with some err French, although I doubt now I will have much chance to use what she taught me. But Richard, I am here for more weighty matters. You remember I showed you some special Sonnets?'

'Yes, I remember them. I also remember saying that printing them would be a problem for me.'

'But not perhaps for your friend Master Thorpe?'

'Like your brother, Edmund you have a good memory. Yes, Thomas Thorpe might be prepared to publish poetry of that kind. I did mention the Sonnets to him, and he showed an interest. Do you have them with you now?'

'Yes, they are here, ready if Master Thorpe has gold enough to purchase them.'

Richard Field looked sternly at the shabbily dressed, young man who had once seemed full of promise and vigour. He seemed changed and in these few short years, the look of youth had gone, and a cynical veneer now hid what might still be left of the boy he knew in Stratford. Richard could see this, would-be, vendor was desperate to find a buyer. Edmund was not in a strong position but, as they used to say in Warwickshire, 'for old times' sake', Richard felt he might help. Besides, Edmund still owed him money and if the Sonnets could be sold, Richard might recover some of the debt.

'If you will trust the affair to me, and leave your bundle here, I will meet with Thomas and get the best deal possible.'

Edmund looked at his friend, a friend from Stratford but also a friend of his brother. Could he trust him? Did Edmund now trust anyone? He felt uncomfortable but he also understood he didn't have much choice. To refuse to trust Richard might mean Richard would decide not to help Edmund sell the Sonnets. Edmund didn't know this Thorpe person and he feared more hunger, his creditors and what he saw in his sleep when closed his eyes at night. Money could make all this go away. He had to trust Richard.

'I will do as you suggest. The Sonnets here must be worth at least twenty pounds as I am sure a good printer could make more than thrice this sum when the book is sold with my brother's name on the cover.'

'I will do my best for you Edmund. Where can I send my man to let you know when the deal has been done?'

'No need to send for me. I will come back here to see you, say in seven days?'

'It will be as you choose Edmund. Seven days.'

The farewells were conducted with polite process but little of the warmth that had once typified their previous meetings. Edmund retraced his route, back to St Giles, along the streets that were the homes and thoroughfares to the many threatening faces that Edmund now hoped to avoid.

Edmund

I think I can hear blood pulsing in my ears. My head aches and my throat! Tight, and sore with each breath. I am afeared that each night might be my last. And if I don't wake tomorrow? What of it? Would anyone notice or remember that I once lived? I have seen nameless bodies collected from the street each day. They are tossed onto carts and wheeled away. Somewhere there are shallow pits in the earth where the once living, are thrown huggermugger. Piled. Mixed. To rot. To become foul vapours and yet more food for rats. This will be my end. The horror, the horror. But will this be the complete end? As my body rots will my soul fight on in some accursed level of hell? What will come next? I fear the dreams, but I fear not to have them. Only ale and sack sooth the tempest of my hours.

My brother's sonnets have been bought but the money paid me was a paltry sum. Thorpe and Field cheated me. I know it but they both abused my poverty. Now they will profit as I count my few gold coins. But there is enough here to keep me in food and drink, for now. How long I will need it I can't tell.

Chapter fifty

It was a summer's day in July and to Edmund, the lodgings off Redcrosse Street, felt stifling as the morning sun cooked the walls like a pie in an oven. The bugs left their deep cracks in the plaster, perhaps hoping to find somewhere damp and dark under the floorboards. Edmund watched them go but he knew they shared his hovel and would not go far. He was their host and provider, and they fed themselves on his continued decline. This annoyed him. Why should they profit and thrive merely because he lay all day in his own dirt.

Today would be different. Edmund chose sunshine over gloom. Sunshine, he reasoned, cost nothing and perhaps the fire in the heavens would prove to be physic for whatever illness had taken up residency in his bones. Edmund raised himself and pulled on a jerkin and his cap. For the first time in several days, he left his lodgings. The workers in the yard nodded as he passed by, out into the street. The city was more alive again and the dark plague times almost forgotten. The citizens hustled and traded, earning themselves enough to buy their food and pay their rent. The city economy, like the bugs in the wall in Edmund's room, prospered on the sweat and industry of the people. And there were people.

Edmund bought himself a cake from a stall on Cheapside and wandered on towards the river. Down All Hallows Lane, until he saw the water and the wherries lined up against the shore, awaiting passengers. He remembered another day, a long time past, when he and friends, the boy actors, skimmed stones across the surface of the water. It was the time of his first visit to the Bear gardens and a time when he truly enjoyed life. So much had changed.

The tide was falling and the wet sand below the strand line, sparkled with tiny pieces of quartz and broken glass. Edmund sat himself down on a length of driftwood. He put his head back and felt the hot sun on his face. Behind his closed small eyelids, the red glow spread deep into his senses, the small space became a vast hall of colour. He removed his cap, and for a few moments, everything felt new. His skin tingled and the noise of the gulls flew him to a far-off foreign shore. An island where he alone was king, exiled once more from the common rabble. In the distance a castle stood proud upon a hill and there was sweet music carried on the flower-scented wind.

Somewhere, someone was shouting. From the rabble, a voice.

'Hola, you there! Get up you fool before you be drowned.'

Edmund opened his eyes, but the glare hid the skyline and the far bank where church spires and playhouses poked up above the line of low buildings. The voice was still there, now laughing. And there was something else. Wetness. He was sitting in water. The tide had returned while he slept. Edmund got himself up and he stood ankle deep in the river as he embraced the real and regained his balance. Two wherry men were still chuckling at his folly but nothing else noted his existence. He took a few steps and retrieved his cap that had been washed away and was lying a few yards further along the shore. The comedy of the scene suddenly became clear, and Edmund smiled, not to anyone but just in response to his own internal dialogue, now bursting through the wall of reserve that is built by man as he leaves boyhood behind.

Edmund walked up the beach and tried to squeeze out some of the water from his breeches. His hose and shoes were sodden and as he trod the cobbles stones he left behind a wet trail of foot prints. It was an uncomfortable journey but he still chuckled to himself as people stared at the bedraggled man padding his way up from the river like a Sebastian escaping the shipwreck on Illyria. When, sometime later, Edmund opened the door of his rooms, there was someone there. Sitting on a box by the window, was Beth. On her lap was a small bundle of cloth. Edmund spoke.

'I won't say it is good to see you, but I am surprised you found where I live.'

'Even in a big city, a cockroach will leave a trail. Shoes wear out and a cobbler's wife will deliver even to the houses of Redcrosse Street. You were spotted.'

'What news do you bring from Shoreditch, for I guess you haven't come to pass the time of day with me.'

'Alice has died. The fates never wanted her to bear a child or permit her the joy of motherhood.'

Edmund was silent. The story was an old one and nothing could be said by him that could improve its ending. He looked at Beth and he felt the anger she bore him. Medusa like, her stare paralysed him. Beth's hand moved and she pulled open the cloth bundle that lay in her lap.

'This is what you left inside my sister. This is what killed her. Part of you grew to kill her. I had him baptised in St Leonards Church. His name is Edward Shakespeare. Take it. It is yours. May God have pity on him, I have none left to give.'

With that, Beth stood up and placed the now moving bundle on the box. Edmund stepped aside, and she left the room.

Chapter fifty-one

Edmund looked down at the child wrapped in cloth. Edmund didn't move, his mind churning in a dizzy spin, as he tried to focus on the bottomless void. Things were unsteady and he had lost his hold on any solid ground. Somewhere, swirling there in the fog, he saw himself in a basket. A motherless child, cast down on the floor in Henley Street. Edmund's eyes grew blurry, and he wept.

Sometime later, when the tears ceased having drained all his self-pity from its source, Edmund began to manoeuvre his thoughts. The child was something he hadn't planned for and was a creature that needed things he felt unable to provide or even understand. Edmund was twenty-seven years old, and a former boy actor and the player trade was all he knew. The child in the bundle needed someone in the mother trade.

Edmund, looked again at the bundle of cloth, then he went outside into the yard. From there it was a short walk to The Sun tavern, a place where since he received the proceeds from the sale of his brother's Sonnets, he had been taking his meals. The bar room was already busy with customers refreshing themselves with drink and boisterously occupying the period between work and sleep. The serving girls herded the men like cattle and brought them their feed. They ate and drank standing, as cattle always do. Edmund searched the faces looking for one certain woman he believed might have the skills he needed to hire.

'Rosy, Rosy! Over here, come.'

Edmund called over a young woman, older than himself, but not yet matronly and safe to be with. Rosy was a spirited woman born in the city and well used to the habits of men and of making her own way, free from their entanglements.

'Edmund, a strange sight indeed. You look like you have just kissed the devil. Your face is all aflame.'

'My face? Yes, perhaps a Lucifer has been at work. I fell asleep in the sun, and I maybe have been given the colour of a ripe apple.'

'Frightful, I'd say. I'll bring you a tankard of cyder to quench the fire in your cheeks.'

'Stay, Rosy, I need to have words with you on a matter of some import.'

Edmund pressed a shilling into her hand and pointed to the doorway leading out into the street. Rosy looked at the silver coin and then at the customers in the bar. She looked at Edmund. She then nodded her head and followed him outside. Edmund explained the barebones of his new situation. There was no flesh, no fat or any attempt at justification. A newborn baby needed to be cared for. It needed mother's milk. He had money enough and he would pay the cost. Simple. Rosy didn't need to hear all the past and future. The present events were common enough and a wetnurse could easily be found from within the neighbourhood of St Giles. Two shillings a week should be enough, and Rosy stated this money must be paid in advance. The coins were handed over, plus a further shilling for Rosy. She told Edmund she would bring someone to his rooms by nightfall to collect the baby. Edmund returned to the tavern and supped several tankards of cyder, calm and detached from the tragedy he had just escaped.

Less than four weeks later, three days before the Ides of August 1607, tragedy returned. Edward Shakespeare, baseborn, was buried in the churchyard of St Giles. His life hadn't really started. He wasn't noticed when he lived, and his death brought just a few words written on paper in a mildewed register.

Soon after, Edmund packed his one bag and left the sad lodgings in the yard off Redcrosse Street. He put the river Thames between him and his recent past and found a rundown lodging in Carter's Lane, Southwark, not far from the playhouses he once believed would be his pathway to fortune. His money now nearly exhausted, he sank lower into the pit of poverty that suffocates all unfortunates along with the guilty.

Edmund

Today I awoke with something heavy upon my chest. Today again I am Edmund. Why can I not be Gilbert, Richard or better still William? Sheets of dun colour paper rustle as I turnover in this bed trying to avoid the noon sunlight piecing the rags of cloth draped over the window frame. Papers covered with words written in a strange shaky hand, my hand. Words I have found in my conscious; words perhaps I can sell. Words from me now shunned by those who own the suburban theatres. Being me hurts.

I looked for Alice but, like always, with the morning light, she is gone. She was here in my mind last night as I blew out the candle but she faded away as I fought over words and imagined foggy bogs and the dialogue of old kings. Although alone, I only feel really lonely when I allow myself to be angry with her.

This writing is because of him; that brother and all the other brothers I will never know. I am now writing, because no one will listen to me and there is still something that must be drained out of this vessel before it sinks completely. But yes, I Edmund was once loved. I lacked money enough to buy a suit fine of clothes, but I shone through my eyes, a light bright enough to touch a woman's heart. Truth be told there were more than one but less than enough. Touching them more than they touched me. There was Emelia of course. And then Marie, soft and with a body that talked silently of French blood and mystery. Marie loved me for a while. And then Alice.

It has been a bleak year, and my strength is now at a low ebb like a tide that keeps falling, sucking at the grey shingle on the riverbank, perhaps never to return. I am tired of watching things drain-away. I am tired of the pestis that haunts the city alleyways and suburbs like the foul witch's fog swirling on Forres heath. I am tired of the pox that infects my veins and makes me feel unclean no matter how many times I wash. Things of this room that should create light feel leaden and I'm haunted by the dread that I may be a contagion, cursing anyone I touch.

I have dreams of little Edward wrapped in his cloth as his body was placed into the cold earth just four short weeks from his birth. A small space between the decaying corpses of St. Giles Churchyard. Something tiny that will never grow and will never understand. I remember the words Aunt Anne once said to me, 'The sins of the fathers upon their children.' Words seem not enough but then words are all we have. I write these, my lines and shuffle the scenes. Try as I might only the bones are taken, broken up, scavenged and inserted into dramatized bodies that might be spoken on a stage but without acknowledging me as author. Collaboration is just another word for spinning my lines woven into a tapestry, flapping a mere hour in the afternoon sunlight, sometimes heard but never remembered.

It feels like the stars have always been wrong for me. Someone wrote of recent eclipses, how things would end unhappily. Unnaturalness between the child and the parent: death, death, dissolution of ancient amities and I know not what. Someone wrote these lines.

I don't remember having a birthday. Sister Joan had celebrations. Richard received honey cakes. For reasons, I now understand thanks to brother William, mother didn't mention a day for me. The Saints had their days, but not me.

My fear is, that to love a mortal person, or a moment in time or a beautiful place, can only lead to an emotional collapse. An attack that could prove to be incurable. Perhaps this is where the human desire to love God comes from. God is without end, God cannot die. God cannot leave. To love God and allow emotions to run unchecked is safe. Where's the risk? When finally, the body decays and one dies, a God lover can feel content for he or she is at last going to become closer-to their real love, that is God. A nonbeliever who is subject to strong unchecked emotional forces can only lurch through pleasure and pain. As the new loves in life become less frequent and the number of lost loves increase, the balance between pleasure and pain shifts. The growing confusion, fear and mourning for lost love is intolerable. Perhaps God is love without risk, love without end. It now sounds attractive. But there must be a drawback, a catch? While the chance of love without risk is a great boon, could I possibly block out all the years of belief in material pleasure and ignore the huge number of unanswered questions that litter the fields of our religion? Words that a player might speak upon the stage. Words of character.

As with a plug of soft wax, I bear your imprint my brother. A Shakespeare's mark is on my soul. I am a moving shadow of what you hide from your wife. Your lines, so well composed, lead to where I hide. I am little Edmund, but I bubble and churn within you as you sleep. Your nightmare is, one day I will be known as your brother.

Chapter fifty-two

The winter of year 1607 in London had been bitterly cold. By December, beggars froze in the streets where they lay, the short day pleading for Alms, not enough to achieve coins for food let alone a place to sleep away from the cold. Fires were lit on the streets, but the Officers of the City quickly extinguished them, in the fear wooden buildings would catch aflame. Priorities required the city be protected above the needs of the people. As many beggars lost the battle for life, the cold was an opportunity for the strong. As the Thames River froze solid and the wherries lay immoveable, seized by the ice, man's spirit of enterprise triumphed. The city founded by the Romans and bound by law, gave birth to a free city built by the people. Traders built temporary stalls and booths out on the ice. There were tents and braziers, tables and benches. Traders sold hot food and drinks to the crowds delighting in the new sensation of walking on frozen water. Children played games and, for the adults, there was music and dancing. The Puritan fathers of the city were horrified. Preachers warned their congregations that the ice and the recent eclipses of the sun, were signs sent from God. Sinners should repent and prepare for the end of days. While many people privately voiced their fears, few sinners chose to reform their ways. London was London and the populace were neither meek nor mild. If the air temperature was all haw frost and snow, the blood in the veins of Londoners was still hot with a passion for any stolen life of pleasure. Those with the financial means to purchase a place to lodge themselves and sea coal for the fire grate, enjoyed the time of the Thames frost fair and life went on.

Edmund was in his lodgings in Carter Lane. The fat bugs still thrived while his body shrank from the poor diet he consumed, and the silent disease that ate away his energy. His small room in the attic was his whole world and his bed, a rack. The day and the night were as one. The room stank of unwashed clothes and an unemptied chamber pot. He lay in his own filth, unattended and abandoned, just as he had discarded all those who had shown him any love during the better times when he still walked the streets and strutted upon the playhouse stage. His dreams were full of a strong Edmund, feeding off the weakness of others. He had once triumphed in the world he chose for himself and now his dreams mixed times and places into a collage of moving frames. He was looking at pictures formed from his past although no calendar ruled. In sleep, man's life is just chaos before the final curtain and any tolling of a bell.

Once a day Edmund received a small visitor. Not a friend, there were none of these, but a boy who, for a few coins, would bring bread, ale and piece of coal for the fire. The boy was named Tom, and he was a boy of the street. He had bright eyes and a quick mind. London was all he knew and the Playhouses and the Stews, for him offered the promise of food and better clothes. Edmund before his sickness, was a man of all the things Tom aspired to achieve for himself. Edmund had told him of the good times when he played the woman's part upon the stage. Tom hoped to do the same. The daily visits to the top room of the tenement building, were merely steps towards his dream of a life of smiles and applause. There were no childish dreams of actual financial success because Tom didn't know he was poor. His world was to him, infinite, measured only by the feeling of a full belly and warmth of one suit of woollen clothes. The sick man up in the room, was a step towards all he knew of and all he wanted.

On this Wednesday morning, Edmund was asleep when Tom entered the room. The remains of yesterday's bread lay on the floor and the flagon of ale, untouched. At first Tom thought his employer was no more. His face was a grey colour and the pustules, all crusty and brown, his thin lips streaked with spittle. This was not an image of life. Tom stood beside the bed fearing to touch what he believed to be cold flesh. But as he studied what was once the picture of man, the impression of a corpse coughed.

'Edmund! It is Tom. It is another Wednesday.'

'Another day? What's that to me?'

Tom didn't attempt to answer the question. He quickly reached across and picked up the mug of stale ale.

'Here, Edmund. Take a drink. There is still some left from that I brought yesterday. You must drink. Do you have more money so I can go find you some food?'

'Go find my brother. The man William Shakespeare, he of The Globe Playhouse. Tell him to come. He has money. He can help.'

'I will do as you ask. The Playhouse is closed today but he may be there.'

Tom felt relieved to escape the dark room full of stale air. The streets outside were very cold and empty of people, the frost fair still in full swing providing all the entertainment and commerce necessary to satisfy the commonwealth body. It was a sunny day outside in Southwark.

It wasn't until the evening that the sound of footfalls of a heavy-set man, broke the silence of the house in Carter's Lane. The worn stairs creaked a protest as each foot shuffled forward, blindly searching by touch, for the next step. The cold air from the street followed the man as he rose floor by floor. The casements on each landing were open and a silvery light from the moon revealed un-swept floorboards and a solitary mouse out hunting for food. Tom had told of the room being on the top floor and William Shakespeare cursed his luck to have been bidden to visit this squalid tenement. Why did he feel the need to answer this call? He had ignored many before. In fact, he avoided any contact with this Edmund, baseborn son of his own now dead father. What was he to William, this bastard who used the name Shakespeare to gain favours from any and all who knew of the playwright.

The stairs stopped abruptly on a small landing, leading to one single door. William didn't knock but opened it and went inside. The smell of decay and degradation assaulted his nose, and he instinctively retched before he quickly pulled a handkerchief out from his sleeve to cover his mouth. There was something living here in the dark. Something breathing, unseemly and unpleasant.

'Edmund? Are you here?'

'A piece of him, yes. Edmund Shakespeare, son of John. Your brother.'

'A claimed title hitched by a thread to a strong family name.'

There was no candle, but the glow of a small fire there in the grate, revealed enough of the room to present it as a place of doom. William saw more in the dark, than most people would have seen in the glare of noontide sun. The room held what was left of twenty-seven years of living. A man, nothing more. Nothing remained of the Stratford boyhood, the Continental touring or the recent years of London scavenging. Edmund was here, now a broken vessel stranded on a muddy shore.

'So, I came. What do you want from me?'

'Just your love, brother. All that is my due.'

'Your due? You jest! You have had all that could be pilfered from the half claim you were given by my father's foolish thrusting into a milkmaid. You are due nothing from me, although charity might push me to leave you a groats worth of bread.'

'A playwright with no heart although words a plenty.'

'Yes, words I have. And here are some you might own. You Edmund came to Shoreditch when I had forbade it. You stole money from my purse that I had earned to be sent back to my wife and family. You traded on my name to gain favours from those who knew me. I gave you money, lots of money, for you to leave England and start a new life on the Continent, a player on stages I would never tread. You spent or gambled it all and then came back here to plague me again. You bedded my Emelia, and your filthy seed gifted her the pox you had earned in Utrecht or some Hessian pit of foreign temptation. You did the same to Marie Montjoie. Any muse I once embraced, felt your lascivious tongue and the push of your dirty fingers. You borrowed money using my name and your debts pursued me as I moved from one lodging to another. Wherever I went, your markers followed. And there was Hamnet. You let him drown!'

William stopped talking. The arraignment had been made. There was silence. Both men breathing. One in anger, the other in amusement.

'Brother, what you have charged me with, that I have done and more, much more. I have your sonnets. Well, had your sonnets as they are now sold and will soon be published. Your wife Anne knows all as I have told her. But she will soon feel the disgrace as the public reads of your betrayals.'

In the dark room, William clenched his fists. This brother, though diseased and of weak flesh, had once again written a new scene and hit him when he least expected another blow.

'But brother, I need your help. Just a few crowns. Or maybe some food and coals for the fire. Not much to ask for from my wealthy brother. Do this for me. I feel very, very tired.'

With that, Edmund drifted back into his dreams. What he saw there and what players performed, as usual, he would not remember. William Shakespeare walked across to the casement. He opened the window wide to the freezing night air. As he moved back by the grate, his foot knocked over the flagon of undrunk ale, spilling the contents and extinguishing the last weak flames of the meagre fire. He exited the room and closed the door behind him. William slowly descended the staircase that led to the empty dark street and the night beyond.

Afterword

The funeral of Edmund Shakespeare took place at St Savior's Church, Southwark on 31 December 1607.

Early in 1608 Shakespeare's version of the play known as King Lear was published in Quarto. Here, for the first time, there is a character named Edmund – he is a villain and described as a bastard.

When William Shakespeare died in 1616 at home in Stratford, Anne was true to her vow. Nothing handwritten by her husband, no papers or poems, plays, letters or diaries have ever been found.

Acknowledgements

Thank you to Terry Insull and John Insull for their help in close reading my manuscript.

Printed in Dunstable, United Kingdom

75918784R00190

Printed in Dunstable, United Kingdom

79977922R00211

Acknowledgments

Thank you to my dear family for your encouragement and constructive ideas, and for being my number one supporter since day one.

Message To Reader

Thank you for reading my story until the end.

You may have enjoyed it and may be keen to find out what happens next. Or you may not!

As an author, I love to tell stories. But there will be no point in my stories if there is no one around to listen. That is why, you, as the reader, matter a lot to me.

I humbly ask for a few minutes of your spare time, to write a review on your thoughts. Not only will it mean a lot when I see in which hands my book may have landed into, it will mean even more to hear what you thought about it. Please, be honest!
I promise I will not be offended.
cries in a corner

Once again, thank you, from the bottom of my heart.

CHAPTER ONE

The Kingdom of Shinrin

INSIDE THE TRANQUIL PALACE OF Shinrin, Prince Satoru Takashi sits in his study as he works on a new piece of artwork.

He watches the ink from his calligraphy brushstrokes absorb onto the parchment, expanding the branches of a cherry blossom tree, and waits to see if the stress weighing him down decreases any less.

With a sigh, he puts down his brush.

Satoru leans back in his chair and closes his eyes. An irritating tug pulls at the back of his mind, constantly

reminding him of the Mutoren.

For the past three years, he has been trying to capture the infamous masked thief who has been stealing the most powerful treasures in his kingdom.

Satoru has a feeling his necklace will be the Mutoren's next target. There is a loud knock at the door. "Prince Takashi!"

Satoru jolts in his chair, causing it to swing onto its back legs briefly. He briskly grasps his desk, pulling himself forwards as he just about recovers from the less-than-graceful moment. A sound of surprise and embarrassment escapes his lips before he hastily adjusts his position, and his facial expression returns to one of seriousness.

With a firm tone, he says, "Yes, come in."

The door flies open as his first-hand guard, Albert, half stumbles inside. "Prince Takashi, I have serious news."

Satoru looks at Albert, whose sapphire eyes are wide with worry. His pale forehead glistens with beads of perspiration.

"What brings you such concern?" Satoru asks. "Is it the Mutoren?"

"No, no, it is not, Your Highness. This is much more serious." Albert's blonde hair falls in front of his eyes.

He appears out of breath. He wipes away the perspiration from his forehead.

How fast had he run to deliver this news?

"Your Highness, seven more villagers have been found dead in the North. Again, their eyes were gouged out and their internal organs are missing."

Something inside Satoru's heart sinks. Last week, three villagers were found dead in the same condition by a river down South. The week prior to that, there had been two reported, identical cases.

Something is not right.

"This is alarming," Satoru answers, his emerald eyes reflecting Albert's concern.

"Very much so, Your Highness. I worry for the safety of our people. This is unlike anything we have heard of, and I fear it is unlike anything we have ever encountered," Albert says between breaths.

Satoru's eyebrows turn downwards. Since the increase in the number of cases last week, he has begun looking into the possible methods of protecting his kingdom to possibly reduce the number of casualties until the perpetrators are caught. Perhaps this is the call to begin strengthening the kingdom's walls right now.

"Albert," Satoru says, "we need to strengthen the defensive walls of our land. Please begin to look for the

greatest artisans you can find. Seek out the strongest, finest materials, and command our constructors to get to work."

Albert raises his eyebrows in surprise and points at himself. "You want *me* to go?" he exclaims.

"Yes."

"As in, leave the palace?"

"Yes, Albert," Satoru repeats. "If we are doing something as important as changing the infrastructures of Shinrin's walls, I will need you as my first-hand guard to go and ensure this is being done correctly. You know I trust no man more than I do you."

"But who will be here to defend you?" Albert asks, looking uneasy. "As your first-hand guard, Prince Takashi, I must always stand close to you. You are like a brother to me—"

"I understand your concerns," Satoru says, "But we have many guards in our palace. I know you worry for my safety, but remember, I am a skilled fighter myself." Satoru smiles as he tries to reassure him.

". . . Very well, then," Albert answers reluctantly, his voice gradually diminishing. First, there'd been the Mutoren, and now this. It really does not feel like a good time to leave the prince's side. "I shall do as you say and begin locating artisans on this land. I will plan my

departure and embark on this journey soon."

Satoru nods, although he can see Albert's reluctance. "Thank you, Albert," Satoru says as he watches his first-hand guard bow and exit his study.

Satoru turns to face the window. A small gust of wind blows against his face and he catches a glimpse of a shadow just as it disappears out of his sight. He blinks and rubs his eyes. Perhaps he is tired.

✾

That night, Satoru sits in front of his dressing table as he prepares for slumber. He opens the drawer, takes out a wooden comb, and peers into his grand mirror.

He sees himself looking back: eyes as deep green as the leaves of the magical forests of their land. Hair as charcoal as the feathers of a raven.

He pulls his comb through the silky strands that reach his lower back. His soft facial structure and high cheekbones give an outward expression of poise and confidence, but it is something which he does not feel about himself.

His mind wanders. Is this the face of a king? As a young man of six-and-twenty, becoming the sole and lone ruler of a land as large as Shinrin was something he never thought would fall upon him. Not this soon, at

least. The weight of having yet to formally take on this title sinks a little in his chest.

He hastily shakes away this thought.

Satoru's mind drifts towards his family as his hands entwine into the long strands of his hair, gracefully twisting them into a long braid. He thinks about his mother, father, and dear older brother. Where are they now? He is grateful he has Albert. He is the only person left by his side who he can call his family.

The familiar weight of heavy responsibilities he carries on his shoulders expands. He knows what he must do. He opens the right-hand drawer of his dressing table and reaches for the wooden box encasing his flute but stops abruptly.

Sitting next to this wooden box is a pile of parchment, bound together with a rope: his collection of materials on this ongoing case of the infamous thief. Satoru's eyes linger on the pile of parchment for a second longer before he picks it up.

Mutoren. The 'wooden man.' The stealer of treasures. The spider creature, whose face has never been revealed.

Satoru traces his thumb over the sketch of the notorious figure. A rectangular wooden mask with two spirals carved in dark green ink for the eyes and a

straight line for the mouth. A very odd expression, to say the least.

Mutoren, what are your motives? Satoru ponders, thinking about the most guarded treasures which have been stolen by this creature. *How are you able to get past the traps every single time?*

The two green spiral eyes stare back at him, like two spinning voids. These voids remind Satoru of the gouged-out eyes of the dead bodies who have begun appearing all over Shinrin.

He frowns and stands up briskly before lighting his lantern, grabbing it by the handle, and striding towards his bedroom door. As he pulls it open, it creaks slightly.

"Master Takashi!" his main doorman guard, Ryota, exclaims before bending forwards into a deep bow. "What may keep Your Majesty awake at this late hour of the night?"

"I must go to the library," Satoru answers.

Ryota nods and bows again. "Yes, Your Majesty!"

Satoru takes long strides down the corridor. Various other guards bow to him as he walks past. He turns a few corners until he reaches the library. With a firm pull on one of the metal rings on the door, the library door slowly opens.

"Would you like me to awaken Sir Koberic, Your

Majesty?" the guard standing by the library door asks. "He is asleep at this hour."

Satoru thinks of the well-respected man of nine-and-eighty who acts as the palace librarian and guardian of the wisdoms. "There is no need," he says.

He pulls open the door wider and steps one foot inside. He holds up his lantern amidst the darkness of the library. The scent of old scriptures fills the air.

He can barely see anything. "On second thought," Satoru says, looking back at the guard, "yes, please do wake him."

The guard nods. "Yes, Your Majesty." He rushes off to a small side room adjacent to the library and knocks on the door.

A few moments later, a small, old man dressed in a brown robe, hobbles out of the room, holding onto a small lantern. The light from the lantern flame reflects off the wrinkles on his aged countenance as well as his old, wizened pale blue eyes—eyes which are struggling to stay open. "Young Master!" Koberic says as he rubs his eyes. "What keeps you awake at this late hour, my child?"

Satoru has always liked and respected Sir Koberic, for he taught knowledge and much of his wisdoms to him since he was a child, making him into the well-

educated young man that he is today.

“Sir Koberic,” Satoru says. “I apologise for waking you at this hour, but I require your help to navigate this library.”

Sir Koberic hobbles behind Satoru as they both enter the vast library, which houses thousands of ancient books and centuries-old scriptures. It smells dusty and nostalgic.

Sir Koberic removes the candle from his lantern and starts lighting up a few candles along the library wall.

“The killings,” Satoru begins. “You must have heard about them.”

“Oh, yes.” Sir Koberic nods as he puts his candle back inside his lantern. “Gouged eyes and missing organs . . . frightening, isn’t it?”

“Very much so.”

“I take it you want to know if we house any more information on these unfortunate events, my child?”

“Am I that predictable?” Satoru asks.

“Well, I was thinking about it actually,” Sir Koberic continues. “Looking back, many years ago, something similar happened in the land of Qieta.”

“Qieta?” Satoru asks, the name of the unfamiliar and distant island taking him by surprise.

"Yes, Qieta," Sir Koberic repeats, as they walk between shelves and shelves of books. "A tragic tale it was. The disaster wiped out most of their people."

"How come I have not heard of this?"

"You were young, my child. You were, if anything, but a boy of five or six years old. And Qieta is very far. We do not have much information about that place." He stops walking and looks up. "Ah, there are the volumes on Qieta. We have five."

Sir Koberic begins pulling on a rope attached to a small wooden lift, a simple invention he had built himself. A rectangular box slowly descends towards the ground. Sir Koberic waddles inside and starts to wind a metal handle in a clockwise motion. Slowly but surely, the wooden box with the old man now inside rises next to the towering bookshelves.

Satoru ponders at how an old man of nine-and-eighty could see five books in near complete darkness that are on a shelf twenty feet high up. Before he can reach a conclusion, however, the old man has returned to the ground with five heavy volumes next to him.

Sir Koberic pulls them out onto the floor and picks up the first volume. With a *thump*, he drops it onto the wooden surface in front of them. Specks of dust bounce off the aging cover.

"Although we do not know much about the island of Qieta," Sir Koberic begins, "in my mind, it was one of the greatest disasters in living memory." He flicks open the book, examines the script, and then flicks over a few more pages. "Ah."

Satoru looks at the page. His eyes widen and he jumps. A sketch of the attacks is depicted in detail, very much as Albert described: two hollow and bloody voids where the eyes should be and internal organs missing from the bodies.

Satoru looks away, then reaches towards the book and closes the cover.

"Their land suffered greatly. It took them a long time to rebuild what they have lost. I am unsure if they ever found out what was behind these killings. We probably have to speak to the people of Qieta themselves," Sir Koberic comments.

"Is that so?"

"I believe so," Sir Koberic answers. "The island has dealt with the disaster once. They should hold valuable information on how best to deal with this before Shinrin experiences as great of a tragedy as they did."

Satoru ponders this thought. *I will have to find out more information on this disaster first,* he thinks. "I will take these back to my chamber," he says. He puts the book

back onto the pile and picks up the stack of volumes.

Sir Koberic picks up both lanterns and waddles in front of Satoru—who is struggling to balance himself with the heavy books in his arms. They exit the library and Sir Koberic closes the door behind them.

"Prince Takashi!" the guard at the library entrance exclaims as he notices the prince wobbling with the books in his arms. "Please allow me to carry these for you. You must not injure yourself!"

"No, no," Satoru replies, "it is quite all right. I apologise for bothering you all at this late hour. Thank you, Sir Koberic. I bid you goodnight." The prince smiles.

"Goodnight, my child. Do not stay up reading too late." The old man chuckles, yawns, and disappears back into his little room.

Satoru carries on walking unsteadily towards his chamber, trying to balance his lantern on top of the books. The guards watch in slight amusement as the prince struggles and wobbles back towards his chamber.

Upon reaching his room, Satoru drops the pile of books with a loud *thud* next to his bed, before making his way to the bathroom and washing the dust off his hands. He climbs into his bed and blows out the candle before pulling the covers onto him.

Upon closing his eyes, he finds the green spirals of the Mutoren mask staring back at him. His eyes snap open and a sudden burst of adrenaline releases inside him.

He examines the room, gaze darting around, but there is nothing there. Perhaps he is feeling tired? If Albert is going to leave his side, he really must prepare himself, for he is sure the Mutoren will be appearing again soon.

Satoru ponders about why he has been feeling a bit strange lately. There have been multiple moments where he felt as though there was someone there, yet each time, there had been nothing. He then wonders about why the mask of the Mutoren has such a weird looking expression before drifting off to a deep sleep.

CHAPTER TWO

Albert's Duty

FOR THE PAST FEW DAYS, Albert has been working hard on locating the various artisans of Shinrin. Prince Takashi asked him to find the strongest and finest materials and to command the constructors to strengthen their defensive wall.

Albert sits at his desk, finalising the map of his journey, even though he disagrees with Prince Takashi. Will the wall, even after being strengthened with the finest materials, really be able to defend Shinrin against these attacks? Whoever—or whatever—is behind these

killings may be living amongst them already, so why did Prince Takashi decide to send away his first-hand guard at a time like this?

He sighs. As clever and smart as the prince is, sometimes, Albert really struggles to understand the reasoning behind his plans. He decides he will have to speak with him again. He will try to convince him to let him stay. He looks at his map, rolls it up, and sets it aside.

Albert gets up from his chair and walks out into the courtyard. It is another bright day. Despite it being still very early in the morning, the blazing heat is already rising off the gravel underneath his shoes. The sunlight reflects off his short, sandy hair. He squints against the sun, raising a hand over his eyes to orientate himself in the right direction. He then makes his way towards the other end of the palace.

As he approaches one of the rooms in the opposite courtyard, he looks about, trying to make out if anyone is inside. "Akalin!" Albert shouts. "Are you there?"

"Behind you," responds a light and playful voice.

Albert turns around to face the forest on the side of the palace. He looks up.

Sitting on one of the branches, with one leg bent and the other dangling, is a young athletic man in a purple robe. Hair long, silver, and held in a high

ponytail, and with eyes the colour of amethyst that starkly contrast against his bronze skin. He stands up on the tree branch, leaps into a forward somersault, and lands effortlessly on a lower branch. It barely sways underneath his weight.

"What brings you here today, my friend?" Akalin asks.

Akalin Kinali is only a few years older than Prince Takashi and Albert himself. The Kinali family were well known for their exquisite skills in the arts of defence, and Akalin's father had been their trainer when the prince and Albert were younger.

"Prince Takashi wants to send me away to find a suitable material to strengthen the defensive walls for the land," Albert says. "This means I will be away from the palace. You will need to step up as his second-hand guard."

Akalin laughs. "What is this outrageous plan? What is Satoru thinking?"

"Please, do not address our Highness so informally," Albert says.

"Royal Highness or not, he is still our naive little Satoru," Akalin replies. He pauses. "So, you are telling me that the time has come for me to step inside *Prince Takashi's* royal grounds, I gather?"

Albert looks disapprovingly at him again.

"Why is he asking you to do something so ridiculous?"

"I am sure our Royal Highness has his reasons," Albert replies. "You must have heard about the killings which began a few weeks ago."

"Ah. Yes. I better watch my eyes and my intestines, for it appears someone is out here to steal them."

"Akalin, please. Will you be serious for once?"

Akalin shrugs. He then appears deep in thought. Albert cannot tell whether or not he is being sincere.

"A wall to keep these perpetrators out will need to be made of some very extraordinary material indeed," Akalin comments as he strokes his non-existent beard.

"You should practice a few duels with the prince to start with," Albert suggests. "He needs to refresh his skills. I worry about him if I am not here to defend him."

"Satoru is not a bad fighter, you know," Akalin says.

"I didn't say that he was, what I meant was—"

"I'm *joking*." Akalin laughs. He flicks Albert on the forehead, taking him by surprise. "Are you always so serious? You are such a worrier. All right. Message received. I will go and see Satoru today."

"Thank you." Albert nods. "Please do your best to defend our prince in my absence."

Akalin winks and salutes, and with that, he somersaults backwards, disappearing into the trees. The branches sway in the light wind and Albert struggles to contain his laughter.

Akalin is such a bizarre man.

Albert begins to make his way to the main palace. He tries to think through what he will say to Prince Takashi. As he approaches the main entrance of the ornate ivory and charcoal building, the two guards standing on each side of the door simultaneously bow.

"Sir Leon," they say.

"Good day, my gentleman." Albert nods in return. "May either of you know the whereabouts of the prince on this fine morning?"

"Our Majesty is training in the Central Training Ground," the guard on the left replies.

"I thank you," Albert says. "Make sure you keep yourselves well hydrated, for what a scorching day it is!"

The guards bow again, and Albert continues on his way.

He spots Prince Takashi from afar. The prince's movements are often described as dance-like. He is light on his feet and moves gracefully as if he is being carried by the wind. He leaps from a branch, and as he somersaults forwards, his left hand lets go of something.

He delicately lands on the ground, and a split second later, three small swords hit the bullseyes of three of the standing targets. One misses and falls to the ground.

"Prince Takashi!" Albert exclaims. His heart begins to thud slightly inside his chest. Will he be able to convince Prince Takashi to let him stay in the palace?

The prince looks up. "Good day, Albert!"

"I see your skills are still exceptional."

"Not at all," the prince replies. "I feel I am very rusty."

"I am certain it will come back in no time," Albert says encouragingly. "Prince Takashi—may I have a word?"

The prince walks towards the targets, picks up the small swords, and walks towards Albert. "Yes, certainly. How is the search for the artisans coming along?"

"Prince Takashi, I have sought out the main artisans of the land and finalised my map. However, I must ask . . . do you really think strengthening the wall will protect us from these events?" Albert pauses and debates how to discuss what he is feeling. "And must *I* go? I feel now is a time of grave danger. I believe it is not a wise time for me to leave the palace."

"I met with Sir Koberic a few days ago," Prince Takashi replies. "He let me borrow a few books. It

appears these killings occurred many years ago, in Qieta."

This does not answer Albert's question. "Qieta?" he asks, wondering where this is going.

"Yes. It was one of the greatest disasters in living memory, according to Sir Koberic."

"I believe a material called malachite would be suitable for strengthening the walls," Albert replies as he attempts to shift the topic away from the island.

"I agree," Satoru answers. "I remember reading about it. When enough of them are placed adjacently, it is said to have the ability to form a defensive barrier. If we make these an addition to our wall, then we will be making a good start."

"But what if the perpetrators are already on our land?" Albert asks. He wonders if strengthening the walls would be enough to protect the kingdom.

"I doubt it. In those books about Qieta, they described that the sky would turn crimson before the attacks occurred. No one on our land has reported this sighting. If this case is anything like what happened on the island, it leads me to believe that attackers must have done this elsewhere."

"But what makes you so sure that this is like what happened over there?" Albert asks.

"The description of the victims' bodies was identical, Albert," Satoru replies.

There is a pause.

"So far, these new victims have remained unidentified," Satoru continues. "As such, my theory is that these were not citizens of Shinrin. They must have arrived here from somewhere else."

"But how can this be?" Albert asks. The topic is drifting further and further away from where he wants, and he is uncertain how to redirect it.

"Unfortunately, the books did not say much else in regard to the killings. For now, we need to begin strengthening Shinrin's walls whilst I investigate how this could have happened."

"Perhaps this is not a good time for me to leave the palace, Prince Takashi," Albert tries again. "And won't it take too long to strengthen these walls?"

"Not if we awaken the Hakkan."

Albert gulps. The Hakkan—colloquiality known as the forest giants—have not been woken in over a century. Things are really beginning to escalate.

"I believe that the next step will be for you to journey to Qieta to find out more information after you meet the artisans. I will ask for the victims' bodies to be examined further," the prince continues.

Albert blinks in alarm. “Prince Takashi—Qieta is rather far.” The prince wants to send him even *further* away? “I still believe it is unwise for me to be so far from the palace at a time like this.” Albert’s eyebrows furrow with concern.

“We really are in unprecedented times,” Satoru says wistfully. “We will need to find out as much information as we can in order to protect our kingdom before it is too late.”

Albert sighs a little as he realises that his plan of convincing the prince to let him stay is going in the complete wrong direction.

“And—if I was to say—reach the land of Qieta, how will I keep in touch with you?” Albert asks.

“Send a bird from their land, the Kaidara,” Satoru replies. “Their feather is the symbol of their land.”

Albert’s eyes drift towards the ground as he takes in this information.

“You are a good man, Albert. I will always be grateful for you,” Satoru says.

Albert’s eyes drift back up towards the prince at the sudden compliment. “It is my honour,” he answers quietly. However, his mind continues to run in different directions.

“Please come and see me again before you depart,”

Prince Takashi says.

Albert nods. It appears that the likelihood of him being able to stay in the palace is now even less than before. He sighs silently, bows, and heads back towards the palace.

CHAPTER THREE

A Brother's Promise

AKALIN SITS ON THE FLOOR inside his chamber. His fingers work intricately with a needle and yarn as he finishes crocheting a little leg of his little creature.

He looks at his creation. Brown with green patches and black beady eyes that reflect Akalin's concentrated face. It is a Vedeir—magical deer-like creatures that live in the forests of Shinrin.

It now has three legs. One more to go.

He thinks of Aiyla. His little sister is turning ten years old soon. He had promised her that one day, he will show her a real vedeir in the forests. She has always wanted to see one. Akalin planned to turn up at home on her special day as a surprise with his handmade gift.

He has always been very fond of his little sister, but since accepting the role as the second-hand guard, he has not been able to return home to visit very often at all due to the distance.

Akalin imagines the surprise on Aiyla's face and her beautiful smile when she sees him. Like Akalin, her eyes are of deep violet, but her hair is a lighter silver.

He wonders how she is doing.

Before he left home, Akalin often took care of Aiyla while their father trained other students in the arts of defence and their mother worked hard in making the most exquisite textiles and attires. He often braided her hair, helped to sew her clothes, and cooked dinner for the family.

People usually do not suspect this side of Akalin due to his slightly quirky personality and active lifestyle, but he enjoys a peaceful family-oriented life. Whenever he thinks of Aiyla, his heart bursts with love and pride. He would do anything for her.

Akalin puts his three-legged creature down. He will

need to go and see Satoru soon. It has been a long while since he has been inside the heart of the palace. He decides he should make his way.

He exits his chamber, and strides towards the palace.

The sun is beginning to set. It appears large and orange in the sky, like the yolk of an egg. He reaches the main entrance and as the two guards bow simultaneously, Akalin's eyes catch onto the intricate carvings on the door frame; the fine wooden scales of a dragon gleam back at him.

"Sir Kinali!" the guards say.

"Good day, good day. Or shall I say good evening?" He points at the carving. "I wonder how long it took to carve this?"

The guards look at each other and blink. One shakes his head slightly and the other semi-shrugs.

"We are not sure, sir!" one of the guards says. He bows again.

"Never mind. My guess is that it took a very long time." Akalin chuckles. "So, where is our lovely leader of the land?" he asks, half humorously.

"Our Majesty is in his study," the guard on the right replies.

Akalin pauses for a moment as he tries to remember

where the study is. He taps his finger on his chin as he thinks. "Ah," he says, "up here, isn't it?" He points to a few stories above where he is standing.

"Yes, sir," the guards say in unison.

"Thank you, my lovely people." Akalin salutes.

He strides towards the palace wall, leaps onto a branch of a neighbouring tree, and somersaults up each level of the building until he reaches the top. He jumps down and lands on the balcony outside the prince's study, giving the two guards who are standing there a fright.

"Sir Kinali!" they exclaim. "Our Majesty would prefer if you entered from inside the building!"

Akalin laughs. "Ah, no such thing!" He walks towards the window and taps on the glass. "Yoo-hoo!" he says as he forms binoculars with his hands against the window and tries to peer inside the room. He notices the prince staring intensely at a book by the light of a candle.

The prince jumps in his chair as he turns around. His eyebrows raise into a look of surprise. "Akalin!" the prince shouts. He opens the window.

Akalin balances himself on the windowsill. "*Prince Takashi*," he says in an overly formal manner as he does an over-exaggerated, elaborative bow.

"What brings you here, my friend?" the prince asks.

"Our friend, Albert, has summoned me to you—" He crosses an arm in front of his chest and begins to speak dramatically. "—for I *must protect you in his absence!*"

"Ah, Albert."

"How do you do, Satoru? Are you king yet? Saving our land as usual?"

"I am grateful you have come, Akalin. Our land is in danger."

"Or so I've heard. I hear you need a refresher for your combat skills. Why don't we start with a duel in the Showman Training Ground tomorrow?"

Satoru is surprised at the sudden invitation. He narrows his eyes. "Was Albert behind this?" he asks suspiciously.

"Who knows?" Akalin replies mischievously. "Anyhow, I'm always up for a duel."

"Well, a duel it will have to be, then."

"At sunrise. Showman Training Ground." Akalin extends a fist towards Satoru, expecting a bump in return.

Instead, Satoru nods, and Akalin retracts his hand with disappointment.

"A duel it is," Satoru repeats.

Akalin salutes, turns towards the edge of the balcony, and backflips back down the building before disappearing into the night.

CHAPTER FOUR

The Showman Training Ground

EIRLYS LOOKS OUT OF THE window of the cart as she journeys with her father towards the village of Ajisai. The sun is rising and the sky is a beautiful mixture of cerulean with streaks of orange like the flames of a fire.

She listens to the horses' hooves as they trot along the gravelly tracks in front of their wagon. Her butterscotch-coloured hair is tied neatly into two braids and secured with a white ribbon. The rising sun reflects off her honey-coloured eyes.

She notices her father, sitting opposite her, dozing off. They had to depart very early this morning, as the central village of Ajisai is quite some distance from their home of Akamatsu.

Eirlys is a young lady of four-and-twenty, and her intelligence earned her place at Furukawa Academy—one of the most prestigious institutions of Shinrin—to learn Healing. Since completing her studies, she had often been busy travelling to various villages to help treat the sick and the wounded.

Today, however, she was not called for that matter. She and her father have come to Ajisai in search of the flowers this village was named after.

These beautiful flowers are well known for their colour-changing ability that ranges from white to pastel blue to pink, depending on the status of the soil. Not only are they beautiful, but they are also one of the most important remedies in healing, as they have strong purifying properties, important in the cleansing of any contaminated wound.

The supply of the Ajisai petal elixirs has been running low at home, and as such, Eirlys and her father, Delwyn, have come to look for more. The village of Ajisai has their beautiful flowers blooming in its rich grassy fields. Situated in central Shinrin, this village sits

very close to the palace.

Having set off so early in the morning, her eyelids fall heavy as the wave of sleep drifts over her, too. Soon, Eirlys falls asleep like her father.

As the cart approaches Ajisai, the sound of a bustling crowd cheering and celebrating can be heard. Eirlys and her father open their eyes and both peer outside. Villagers are running towards a large open ground situated in front of a splendid ivory building with layers of slanting charcoal roofs. The building exudes a presence of power and nobility. The crowd is cheering and jumping.

"My goodness, father. That must be the palace," Eirlys says.

"The palace it is indeed," he agrees.

"What are they cheering about?" she asks, cocking her head to one side. Perhaps there is some sort of celebration?

"It appears there is an event today," he replies. "It is not often that you see live action in the Showman Training Ground."

Eirlys continues to watch the crowd, curious as to what is happening.

The trotting of the horses stops, and the cart comes to a halt. They have arrived in Ajisai. Delwyn opens the

door and they both step down. Eirlys shields her eyes from the sun, which is now bright in the sky. Her attention is still focused on the crowd.

“Go and join them, my child,” Delwyn says as he notices her daughter’s fixation. “It is not often one gets to witness this. Go and have a look. I will start preparing the tools back here.”

Eirlys’s mouth breaks into a wide smile. “Yes, Father!” she says as she starts running excitedly towards the crowd. As she nears the congregation, she starts to overhear some conversation.

“My goodness, aren’t they handsome?”

“The prince is as beautiful as I heard.”

“Is that Sir Kinali? How exquisitely he moves!”

Eirlys reaches the fence surrounding the showground. She notices a group of village girls who are particularly loud, screaming and cheering at the top of their lungs. She shields her ears with her hands and turns towards the two figures who are at the centre of everyone’s attention.

Both have long, spear-like instruments in their hands. They are in some sort of duel, which looks more like a dance. They both move the spears swiftly and effortlessly. She notices one of them has long, shiny black hair held high in a ponytail. His movements are

graceful. He uses the length of his spear to balance himself as he swings his legs around to kick his opponent.

That must be Prince Takashi, Eirlys thinks. *His face really is of true beauty.*

His strong facial structure and deep emerald eyes give a compelling look to him, but his facial expressions have a certain softness to them, which surely makes him very attractive.

If only Sana was here too, Eirlys thinks. Her younger sister would have loved to see this.

Eirlys's attention drifts towards the prince's opponent. His long, moondust hair is tied up high and his bronze skin glistens under the sunlight. His movements are soft but more agile than the prince's, often incorporating acrobatic flips and somersaults as he advances.

"Who is the one with the silver hair?" she asks.

The girl on her right looks at Eirlys briefly before her attention snaps back towards the duo. She holds her face in her hands and smiles dreamily. "Sir Akalin Kinali," she replies. "My, isn't he beautiful?"

Eirlys blinks at the girl and looks back towards the showground. It appears these two men have the whole village's girls completely spellbound.

Suddenly, Sir Kinali manages to kick the spear out of the prince's hands, and, with one swift movement, he strikes it aside with his own. The prince falls backwards onto the sand and Sir Kinali points his spear towards the prince's face.

The crowd bursts into a huge round of applause.

The prince smiles. "Good match," he says.

Sir Kinali extends a hand towards him and helps the prince to get up. He turns towards the crowd. Eirlys is struck by his eyes. They look lavender underneath the sun.

"Thank you for joining us, my lovely people," he announces. His voice is silky with a mischievous edge.

"Thank you, my dear citizens of Shinrin. It was a pleasure to have you all with us this morning," Prince Takashi follows. He is soft-spoken.

"We love you, Prince Takashi!" the crowd cheers.

"Shinrin is lucky to have you as their leader!"

"Sir Kinali, you are amazing!"

The prince holds a hand to his chest and bows. Sir Kinali sees this and does the same, however he twirls his arm forwards three times elaboratively before bowing.

Eirlys laughs.

The crowd starts to disperse, and the two figures turn their backs as they start heading back towards the

palace, their long silky ponytails swinging from side to side. Eirlys remains standing, her hands holding onto the fence. It was such a shame that Sana wasn't here to see this spectacular show. She is sure her sister will be very jealous when she hears about this next time they meet.

As Eirlys starts to make her way back towards the cart, she sees that her father has already plucked a basket full of Ajisai flowers and is busy grinding some petals with a pestle and mortar. He looks up and waves with both his hands.

Eirlys waves back before she goes to join him.

✾

Later that day, Satoru sits at his study, once again studying the books of Qieta Sir Koberic had lent him. He looks at one of the pages depicturing the symbol of their land: a circle with a feather of a Kaidara inside.

He reads again about this messenger bird of Qieta—it is a small, azure creature that can fly for thousands of miles, that has the ability to retain information without fault, and that can re-transcribe the sender's message to the receiver by stamping out a few characters with their feet.

For the past few days, Satoru has learnt more about

the land of Qieta. However, he still does not have much information about what is causing the killings.

There is a light knock at the door.

"Come in," Satoru says.

The door opens slowly, and Albert appears. "Prince Takashi," he says as he bows.

"Albert."

"Prince Takashi, I have finished preparing for my journey. I will depart tomorrow at noon and begin looking for the artisans who have a good supply of malachite."

"Very well, Albert."

"A-And with regards to Qieta, do you still believe that I should journey to the island?" Albert asks, wondering if the prince may have changed his mind. "Could we not obtain the information from their people through the messenger birds of their land?"

Satoru shakes his head, much to Albert's disappointment.

"The messages sent by their Kaidara are limited to only a few characters. They do not carry scrolls like our Ketu, but rather, they read and transcribe. It would take much too long. I believe it would be best for you to journey there and back with the information whilst I work on sorting things out from this end."

Albert sighs internally once again. He pauses for a moment. "Before I depart, Your Highness, there is something I must draw to your attention," he begins.

"And what may that be?" the prince asks.

"I know this may not be on your mind right now, but the Mutoren may be making an appearance soon."

Satoru is surprised by this sudden mention, for he had been thinking about this the past few days as well, despite everything else going on. A rather unsettled feeling begins to creep inside him as he pictures the green spirals on the wooden mask of the spider-like creature.

"In a few days, we will be reaching a full moon," Albert continues. "If our calculations are correct, he will appear, for he relies on the moonlight to perform his doings."

"I agree," Satoru replies, deep in thought. "It is highly likely."

"I know you have insisted on keeping the Emerald Necklace of Takashi on you as your personal possession, but I urge you to reconsider placing it into the palace safekeeping chambers," Albert says.

"I thank you for your concerns, Albert," Satoru replies, rather flatly.

"Prince Takashi, the Mutoren has already stolen

four of the greatest treasures in our Kingdom. He has been able to take down every single guard and get past every single trap we have designed. He is a dangerous and unpredictable creature—"

"I am certain that if I am to come into contact with true danger, the necklace will protect me," Satoru states. He is aware that he must be coming across as stubborn, but the necklace is too important to leave his side.

"Your Highness—" Albert continues, the concern in his voice increasing even more. He places both his palms onto the prince's desk and leans in towards him. "—we have never yet seen it glow. How can you be certain it will protect you?"

"Albert, this necklace has belonged to my family for generations. I shall not let it leave my side. If that means that I shall come face to face with the Mutoren, then so it shall be," Satoru states firmly, hoping that Albert cannot tell he is in fact, feeling rather unsettled about the idea.

"Your Highness—" Albert tries once more as he leans in even closer. "—please, I urge you. We do not know the reasons behind the Mutoren's motives. I fear you are putting yourself into great danger unnecessarily."

"I have been analysing this case for the past three

years, Albert," Satoru says. "I am grateful for your concerns, however I have said my piece."

There is a small silence.

"Ve–very well, Your Highness," Albert says, sighing. "I will inform Akalin before I depart, for we must ensure he is close at hand to help defend against the Mutoren when the time comes."

The prince nods in acknowledgement. "Please, send me updates via the Ketu during your journey," he says, sincerity returning in his voice.

"Of course," Albert agrees.

"I wish you a safe journey and hope to see you again soon, my friend," Satoru says. He smiles and embraces Albert, and with that, Albert turns and exits the prince's study.

That night, Satoru climbs onto the roof of his chamber, his special place of tranquillity. The haunting images of the killings and the possibility of the Mutoren making another appearance linger at the back of his mind. He closes his eyes and begins to play his bamboo flute, trying to clear away these thoughts.

Satoru's jet-black hair glistens underneath the moonlight as the soulful tune is carried into the night. In the distance, someone amongst the trees watches as the wind sways the branches from side to side.

CHAPTER FIVE

Hinoki Village

AKALIN PLUCKS THE SMALL SCROLL from the burrows of the Ketu's wings and scans the message quickly.

Dearest Son Akalin,

Aiyla has fallen quite ill the past few days with a fever and cough. As you know, it is difficult to get hold of a healer in good time these days. We wonder if you may be able to ask the palace

healer to pay her a visit for us? In the meantime, we are doing everything we can to heal this ailment.

Regards,
Mother & Father

Akalin's eyes widen. He immediately begins to pack his belongings into a cloth bag under the light of the moon. As he does so, his mind races.

Only a few days ago, Albert had told him that he is to be by Satoru's side on the night of the next full moon, for they believe that is when the Mutoren will strike again. Albert urged him to be extra vigilant and to protect Satoru at all costs.

But this unexpected news about his sister means that he will need to make the long journey back to Hinoki—his home village—with the palace healer . . . and tomorrow will be the night of the next full moon.

As a second-hand guard, he shouldn't be leaving the palace at a time as important as this. He sighs and shakes his head.

I will have to inform Satoru, he thinks. *I will explain what has happened and aim to be back before nightfall tomorrow.* This way, he will ensure to be back before the Mutoren potentially strikes again.

Akalin gathers his things and ties a knot onto his cloth bag. He sighs as worry seeps inside him. He wonders what has happened to his dear sister.

Hang in there, Aiyla, he thinks. He throws the cloth bag over his shoulder and makes his way towards the main palace to find the prince.

✾

The moon, a little more than a waxing gibbous, is shining brightly in the night sky. Akalin is back in his chamber as he readies himself for the journey ahead. He informed the prince of what happened and will journey straight to Hinoki. The palace healer will follow as soon as he finishes dealing with an emergency case for one of the palace guards. He should be able to reach Hinoki around two hours after Akalin.

Akalin pulls on a cobalt-coloured robe and a thick outer layer, for the air is cold during the night. He makes his way outside.

"Hello, Leia," Akalin says to his horse, a beautiful steel-coloured creature with a black, velvety mane. He takes a wooden bucket and fills it with water from a neighbouring well, then holds it in front of his horse as he watches her drink. He pats her head.

"Good girl, Leia," he says. "We have a long journey

ahead. Aiyla will be happy to see you."

Akalin readies his saddle and fixes it onto his horse. With that, he leaps onto her back and rides off into the night.

The journey is smooth, and the cold wind breezes against Akalin's face as Leia gallops away into the forests. The sun starts to rise, and slowly, the air starts to warm up.

As the day progresses, the sun rises higher into the sky, and the temperature rises even more. As Akalin starts to spot cypress trees, he knows that his home of Hinoki is nearby. The pace of his heart quickens as he thinks about his sister. Is she getting better?

Leia slows to a trot as they approach a clearing and Akalin sees his village from a distance. His eyes narrow. Something does not seem right.

His village is usually orderly and neat, but even from afar, he notices that there appears to have been some sort of destruction. When they get even closer, his eyes widen into a look of horror. There are doors hanging off their hinges and shattered glass from broken windows. Pieces of fresh fruit and vegetables scatter in a mess on the ground and some have been trampled on. The houses have been completely ravaged and the shops and stalls have been looted.

Villagers lay scattered on the ground, lifeless. A wave of sickness rises from inside Akalin's stomach. His heart and mind begin to race. He looks around his hometown whilst Leia walks carefully amongst the bodies.

Akalin notices a man lying on the ground, severely wounded. The man reaches his arm outwards as he tries to drag himself along the ground using his elbow.

"Help . . ." He can hardly manage a whisper.

Akalin leaps down from Leia and runs towards him. "Sir, what happened?" Akalin asks, his heart beating so hard it is as though it is about to burst out of his chest. He looks at the man, whose eyes are in absolute terror as they meet his.

"Please . . . save us, young man," he says. "They . . . they took our . . . children . . ." He coughs and splutters, vomiting up a large amount of blood onto the gravel, before his head falls lifeless towards the ground. He lies motionless.

Akalin's eyes remain wide. What in the world is going on? The nausea in his stomach triples as he thinks of his family. He leaps back onto his horse and gallops towards his home. His heart is ripping apart.

Akalin catches sight of the front of their house and it, too, looks like it has been ransacked. His lungs are

bursting. He runs inside in such a panic he nearly trips over.

The main room is empty. His eyes dart left and right, up and down, but he cannot see anyone. Their beautiful home has been turned upside down. The tables and chairs have been smashed and broken; the curtains are torn. Is this some sort of nightmare?

Akalin squats, squeezing his eyes shut. His hands press on the sides of his head as he tries to understand what is happening.

He stands briskly and runs through his home, opening every door. The destruction is the same—he notices the broken splinters of his favourite wooden chair which his mother had built for him as a child. The luxurious robes she had made for him to wear on special occasions are ripped and torn unforgivingly, thrown across the floor. Aiyla's dear stuffed white bunny lays limply next to them, cotton protruding from the side of her head. Akalin cannot find his father, mother, or sister anywhere.

He runs out to the back of the house.

No one is there.

There is something on the ground: a little brown shoe. Aiyla's shoe. He picks it up and his hand trembles. He falls to the ground and screams. He arches forwards

as he howls in anguish. Sharp daggers stab at his chest and his throat closes up so sharply, he is at the point of suffocation. He has never felt such torment and heartache in his life.

Akalin grasps onto the little shoe as he cries painfully, his insides ripped into a million pieces. He kneels on the ground, lost in complete sorrow, anger, and grief. Leia approaches him slowly from behind and lays her head on his shoulder in an attempt to comfort her owner.

✻

Akalin sits emotionlessly on the ground behind his home. He is unsure how long he has spent looking all around the whole village of Hinoki. He has found nothing but lifeless bodies of villagers and destruction of homes. Not only could he not find his parents or his sister, but he also noticed that all of the children have disappeared; their bodies are not amongst the dead.

He sent a Ketu back to Satoru to inform him of what happened, but the bird will take quite some time to get to the palace. The healer had already arrived and had to return to the palace grounds. Perhaps he will bring this tragic news to Satoru faster.

Akalin shakes his head. Leia is sat curled around

him, trying to keep her owner warm. The night had already fallen and the full, round moon shines brightly in the sky.

Akalin looks down at his hands. He is still holding onto Aiyla's shoe. The sole is worn and there are wrinkles along the surface, lines created from where she had run along fields joyfully and gone on her own little adventures. He takes the small shoelace and traces it gently with his fingers as he remembers teaching her how to tie them for the first time.

Suddenly, Akalin's blood begins to boil. How could someone do something as unforgivable as this? He looks up from the ground, and something in his eyes changes. He feels a rush of determination to find out who did this and to take revenge. He reassures himself that, as he did not find the bodies of his parents nor his sister, they must be still alive.

This fills him with a newfound strength. He stands up suddenly, giving Leia a fright. She looks up at him and cocks her head to one side before standing up beside him.

Akalin suddenly notices how cold it is. The wind is harsh and bites at his skin. His stomach growls with hunger. He had not eaten all day. Nor had Leia. He puts Aiyla's shoe into his robe as he reaches into his cloth bag,

taking out a carrot.

Leia's head plunges forwards as she sniffs the carrot on his palm. Her big nostrils create mist amongst the cold, night air. Akalin feeds it to her, watching her gobble it up.

He strokes her forehead. "Let's go, Leia," he says, before climbing onto her back. She slowly walks through the village of Hinoki, now barren and isolated.

Akalin's heart is heavy. He turns to look at his village one last time as they slowly make their way out.

CHAPTER SIX

The Night of the Full Moon

BACK IN THE HEART OF Shinrin, Satoru sits on the bed in his chamber, peering out at the full, round moon that is starting to rise in the night sky. The flame of the candle by his bedside table flickers.

Will the Mutoren turn up tonight?

He clutches onto the small, emerald leaf of his necklace, which dangles from a thin, golden chain on his neck. Every time he hears even the slightest of sounds, his eyes dart towards that direction. Each time, there is nothing there.

Satoru had thought long and hard about where he would locate himself on this very night. Previously, the elaborate traps he had spent so long meticulously designing had always failed. No matter how much he trained his guards, the Mutoren still got past them.

Will tonight be the night we finally come face to face?

This time, Satoru decided he will not set up any elaborate traps. Since the Mutoren's first sighting three years ago, Satoru has been studying and analysing his behaviour on each reported case. If his predictions are correct, the Mutoren will appear tonight in an attempt to obtain the Emerald Necklace of Takashi.

Rather than hiding this piece of treasure in a guarded vault, Satoru had decided that, by keeping the necklace on himself, the Mutoren will have to face him. According to his calculations, the Mutoren—although frightening and unpredictable—will not attack unless it is inevitable. As such, Satoru will utilise this to his advantage, and, with the help of his guards and Akalin, they will trap the Mutoren in his chamber.

Satoru will unmask him at last. They will place him into palace confinement until he confesses his plans and returns Shinrin's treasures.

There is a light tap on the window. Satoru's eyes dart towards the glass.

One of the guards on his balcony quietly slides the window open. "Your Majesty," he says anxiously. "It is long past night fall. Sir Kinali still doesn't seem to be here."

Satoru nods. Akalin had informed him of the need to journey back to Hinoki, but he was due to return before nightfall.

He is not a man to not stay true to his words. Did something happen? This is odd.

"Send another Ketu to find his whereabouts and obtain another message from him," Satoru replies.

"Yes, Your Majesty." The guard bows and slides the window shut.

✾

As the night goes on, the moon starts to rise higher in the sky. Silver, round, and magnificent, it shines over the palace of Shinrin. It must be well past midnight.

Satoru remains fully alert. He holds onto his necklace and carries on listening for the slightest sound. He glances away from the window briefly. His eyes move around his chamber. His desk, bookshelf, closet, door—

Satoru's chamber goes completely dark.

A burst of adrenaline surges through him. He jolts

and stands up briskly. His candle flame has gone out. For a moment, his eyes are unable make out a single thing. His head snaps back towards the direction of the window as he hears it slide shut. His eyes are darting around and he feels each heavy thud of his heart inside his chest.

Satoru waits for his eyes to adjust to the darkness. It is still difficult to see his surroundings. He raises his head slowly—

"Agh!" A small sound of shock escapes him.

A creature hangs upside down from his chamber ceiling. It begins to crawl slowly towards him, movements spider-like. The two green spirals for the eyes almost glow. It has a straight line for a mouth, just like the reports have described. The wooden face looks at Satoru and he tilts his head slightly to one side, as if trying to understand what he is seeing.

Satoru stares wide-eyed back at the Mutoren. *He is really here.*

A chill runs through his spine as he takes a step backwards. The Mutoren continues to crawl towards him, his limbs poking out at odd angles, covered in black from head to toe. Satoru looks at the upside-down wooden face, in disbelief that this is really happening. The Mutoren is in his chamber.

Satoru holds onto his necklace tightly. The room remains dark. It does not glow.

Suddenly, the Mutoren scurries like an insect at the speed of lightning along his ceiling, taking Satoru by surprise. His movements are inhuman and unlike anything he has seen before. He disappears over Satoru's head and by the time he turns around to look behind him, the creature has disappeared into the darkness.

Satoru gulps. His heart is now beating so hard against his chest it almost hurts. He looks around, but he cannot see anything. His breathing is heavy. He tries to suppress the feeling of fear that is rising in his stomach. Should he alert his guards? Are they still outside? Did the Mutoren get past them once again?

Another rush of adrenaline flows through Satoru, along with a slight tinge of fear. However, there is also an odd feeling of excitement that, at long last, he has finally come face to face with the infamous Mutoren.

He turns around once more and finds the wooden mask staring up at him from the ground, making him jump again. The Mutoren, now on the floor, is starting to crawl towards him on the ground. Satoru cannot tell what his next move will be. He blinks hard and tries to remain calm.

The creature, now only inches from him, stands. Satoru readies himself for defence. The Mutoren's silhouette is more evident as he stands in front of the moonlight entering the window. Satoru can see now, that the Mutoren, most definitely, is a human. One with a small form, in fact.

But nonetheless, he is very terrifying.

The masked man lifts an arm, which Satoru instinctively attempts to grasp to throw him over his shoulder. However, Satoru's arms only briefly brush past the Mutoren's before the creature leaps into the air and, with one swift swing of his leg, kicks Satoru on his right shoulder with such force it causes him to fall and tumble across the floor. The Mutoren lands back onto the ground without causing a sound.

He is fast, Satoru thinks, as his mind races, and he jumps back up from his fall, balancing himself. His adrenaline rush intensifies. The lack of light is making it extremely difficult for him to anticipate the Mutoren's moves. It is extremely unhelpful at a time like this.

The Mutoren stands again. This time, he maintains his distance. Once again, he raises his arm. Satoru looks at him. Covered in black fabric from head to toe, the odd mask stares back. The Mutoren stays still. His right

arm is raised, palm facing upwards.

Satoru looks at the Mutoren's hand, and then down at his necklace. It still does not glow.

He looks back up at the wooden mask. "No," Satoru says. "You will not obtain my necklace. You shall return all the treasures you have stolen." He maintains a firm tone, despite the fear that is pulsating through him.

The Mutoren barely moves. Instead, he edges his right arm further forwards, fingers spreading wider in persistence.

Satoru attempts to lunge towards the Mutoren, closing the gap between them. He lifts his right leg into a roundhouse kick, which easily reaches the height of the Mutoren's head. However, it is difficult to make out the Mutoren's exact location in the dark, and before his foot makes any contact, the Mutoren ducks out of the way, leaps up into the air, and extends his left leg out into a side kick towards Satoru's chest. His movements are sharp and precise, like a snap.

Satoru tumbles once again and somersaults backwards to balance himself back onto his feet. The Mutoren disappears. Satoru looks up. He can just about see that the masked man is now back on the ceiling.

Will he now attack? Satoru thinks, his breathing heavy.

The Mutoren lunges from the ceiling towards him. Satoru jumps out of his way towards the side and attempts to strike the Mutoren with his hand. The Mutoren swiftly blocks the strike with his forearm and flips backwards.

I may not be able to see as well as you in the darkness, Satoru thinks, *but I should think that I know the layout of my own chamber better than you.*

Satoru sees his chance. As the Mutoren falls towards his landing on the ground, Satoru swings a kick at the vase on his table. It tumbles to the ground and surprisingly, does not break. The akaibara flower which stood inside falls onto the floor as water spills out, right by where the Mutoren's foot is about to land. The clear liquid glistens as it spreads onto the floor.

It is too late for the Mutoren to dodge. His foot makes contact, and he slips and falls sideways as Satoru launches himself towards him. The Mutoren crosses his arms in front of his mask. The two of them roll across the floor and, using all his strength, Satoru pins the Mutoren to the ground.

To Satoru's surprise, the Mutoren is unable to overpower his force. The creature may be fast, nimble, and agile, but he appears surprisingly slight underneath him. Satoru can feel the Mutoren struggling to get up

off the ground.

"Tell me," Satoru urges. "What do you plan to do with the stolen treasures?" His heart is racing.

The Mutoren remains silent.

"You lay before the Prince of Shinrin," Satoru demands. "I order you to speak!"

The Mutoren does not respond.

"What you have done is unlawful! I shall reveal your face at once!"

Satoru removes one hand from the Mutoren's shoulder and reaches towards his infamous wooden mask. He grabs it briskly and throws it to one side. Instinctively the Mutoren moves his forearm up to cover his face.

Satoru reacts immediately and seizes his arm. His eyes widen in shock. He finds himself looking at a pair of innocent eyes, dark round and beautiful like a vedeir. Pale skin reflects off the moonlight and rosy lips complete an expression of shock, one that mirrors his own. He stares at her delicate face, struck by her look of innocence.

"You're a . . . *girl*?!" Satoru exclaims in disbelief.

A sudden pressure thuds behind his eyes and a shadow flashes through his mind. His grip loosens as he moves his hand towards his forehead.

"A *lady*," she replies. Her voice has a melodic ring to it. Her look of shock vanishes instantly, and swiftly, she reaches out towards Satoru's necklace, grabs it, and sends a powerful kick towards his stomach.

The golden chain snaps from Satoru's neck. The Mutoren picks up her mask.

Satoru is still in a state of shock as he tumbles over and over towards his bookshelf before hitting it. A pile of books fall onto him. He braces an arm above his head to protect himself. By the time he looks up, he sees the silhouette of the young girl just as she disappears out of his window.

Satoru stays laying on the floor, under his books, panting. He is in complete disbelief. His brain is sloshing around inside his skull. He blinks and blinks. He then manages to sit up and crawls like a child towards his window, feeling the ache in his stomach. He looks outside to see his guards lying on the balcony. They look like they are asleep.

The sun is beginning to rise and his guards start to stir. They appear confused. Satoru turns around to look at his chamber. His necklace is gone.

Something on the floor catches the light from the rising sun. Satoru gets up slowly and walks towards it before picking it up. The item is a copper emblem of a

circle with a feather inside.

Satoru's eyes widen. *Qieta?* he thinks.

He looks up from his palm. The akaibara flower is still on the floor. His mind snaps back towards her look of innocence and shock just as he removed her mask.

His heart skips a beat.

CHAPTER SEVEN

Tanaka Inn

ALBERT SQUINTS AS HE STRUGGLES to see the path in front of him. He is in the midst of a storm and the rain is splattering against his face. Night has fallen. His outer cloak is drenched and the cold from the rain seeps into his skin as he and his horse brace themselves against the howling wind.

For the past week, Albert had managed to visit the artisans as he had planned, and—of those who had stores of malachite—all were keen to help protect Shinrin by supplying as much as they could.

Journeying to the very outskirts of Shinrin over the last few days has been tiring to say the least, and he is looking for a place to reside until the weather improves. He thinks of Prince Takashi and whether the Mutoren had turned up on the night of the full moon as they predicted.

Ahead of him, Albert spots an orange glow. “Slow down, Erwin,” Albert says as he tugs gently on the reins. “Good boy.”

Erwin, the magnificent ivory creature that he is, slows down to a walk obediently. As they approach the glow, Albert sees that it is a light coming from inside an inn. Erwin stops, and Albert looks at the engraved writing on the wooden sign flapping in the wind above the building’s door.

Tanaka Inn.

He peers through the window and faintly makes out a very cosy-looking interior through the rain-splashed glass. He hops down from Erwin and lightly taps the knocker against the door.

A few minutes later, the door creaks open. A burst of warm air blows against Albert’s cheeks. A friendly, jolly looking old man appears. He is a round little man, whose height reaches about the level of Albert’s elbow. His thick, grey eyebrows are so broad that Albert cannot

make out where his eyes are. His mouth is surrounded by a matching thick, grey beard. Something about his manner makes him very endearing.

A friendly and welcoming voice comes from him. "Hello, young man. Are you looking for a place to stay?"

"Please." Albert nods.

The old man notices Erwin behind him, soaked in the rain. The horse blinks back at him with his round, beady eyes and shakes his head, trying to get rid of some water.

The old man's thick, bushy eyebrows raise in surprise. "My, my! What a divine creature you have!" he says. "Emiko will take care of him. She adores horses very much. Come! Come on in." He turns and shouts, "Emiko! We have a guest! He has a horse!"

Albert bends to remove his shoes and tries to squeeze out some water from his cloak before stepping inside. He places his shoes on a wooden stand by the entrance and removes the hood of his cloak.

Erwin cocks his head to one side as he is left out in the rain.

The old man's bushy eyebrows raise in surprise once again. "My, my, for is it Sir Leon who stands before me?"

Albert's eyebrows raise up, mirroring the facial

expression of the old man standing before him—he still has not become used to the fact that, outside the palace, he is a recognisable figure. He is a little flustered.

"Please. Albert is all right," he replies.

"What an honour it is to welcome you to our inn." The old man bows.

A young girl appears. She walks quickly towards the old man, throwing on a cloak. Her long, apricot-coloured hair flows behind her as she moves.

"Good eve—" Her amber-coloured eyes meet Albert's. "—ning," she finishes, seeing how his heavy cloak drapes over his broad shoulders and a few drops of rain run off his golden hair onto his handsome face.

Her face stiffens, she blushes, and her eyes snap to the floor as she marches awkwardly outside into the storm. She takes hold of Erwin's reins and guides him towards the back of the building.

"We have a farm behind the house," the old man reassures. "Emiko is taking him to our stables."

Soon after, the young girl returns, her cloak soaking from the rain.

"My name is Kenta," the old man introduces himself. "This is Emiko, my granddaughter. My wife, Shizuko, is around the back. It is our honour to have you." He turns to his granddaughter. "It's Sir Leon!"

"I know," she barely manages a squeak. "Welcome, Sir Le–on," she whispers.

Albert wonders if he has frightened the poor girl without realising. He looks at her curiously, but her eyes stay fixed on the floor.

Kenta leans towards her and covers his mouth. "Tell Grandma to come here. Tell her Sir Leon is in the house!" he whispers too loudly.

The young girl disappears in a flash.

"Please, let me help you with your things," Kenta says to Albert kindly. He reaches to help him take off his cloak. It drips with water as he places it on a stand by the fire.

Soon, an elderly lady appears. "Sir Leon!" she exclaims. Her grey hair is tied into a bun and the aging lines around her brown eyes deepen as she gives a warm, friendly smile. "Please, make yourself at home. I will tell Emiko to run a hot bath for you while I prepare you something to eat. You must be hungry, young man. Hurry and make yourself warm. You must not catch a cold!"

"It is quite alright," Albert replies. He is feeling overwhelmed by the kindness from this humble family. After all, he was only looking to have a roof over his head tonight.

Kenta opens the drawer at the front desk and hands him a large, metal ring with a key dangling from it. "We have quite a few guests tonight, and you make a wonderful addition. Make yourself at home, Sir Leon," says Kenta.

"Thank you so much," Albert replies.

Shizuko leads him upstairs and shows him his room. As they reach the landing, she points down the hallway in the opposite direction. "The baths are that way," she whispers. "Emiko is getting one ready for you. Please make yourself comfortable while we prepare your meal." She winks and waddles back down the stairs.

Albert looks at his key. It has a wooden tag engraved with the number II. He finds his room, inserts the key, and the door slides open as he unlocks it.

He finds himself looking at a humble room lined with olive-coloured tatami flooring. The refreshing scent of cherry blossoms fills the air. He lowers his cloth-tied bag onto the woven rush and hemp floor and heads towards the baths. As he approaches, he notices the sound of running water.

Emiko dips her hand into a large bamboo tub, checking the temperature. Her eyebrows frown with concentration as her eyes settle into the middle distance.

Albert decides to say something to make her aware of his presence. He doesn't wish to scare her again. "Excuse me—"

The young girl jumps and squeaks.

His idea failed.

"Sir Le–on," she manages to say. "Your bath is nearly ready." She pauses to breathe. "Please let us know if you ne–ed anything else."

She turns off the bamboo lever and briskly runs away before Albert can thank her. She returns a few seconds later, plops a towel and a robe on a large stone by the side of the tub, nods at Albert, and disappears again.

Albert watches curiously as the girl runs away and wonders how he keeps scaring her somehow.

He gets ready and lowers himself into the bamboo tub. The warmth of the water seeps around his body and a feeling of relaxation sweeps over him. He slides lower until the water is at the level of his ears and closes his eyes.

I will need to send a Ketu to Prince Takashi tomorrow, he thinks to himself.

He needs to start planning the supply of malachite. Will he need to depart to Qieta straight from here? Has Prince Takashi started investigating those victims he

mentioned? He wonders if the Mutoren had made an appearance at all. Is Prince Takashi alright? Is he hurt?

He leans back with these thoughts on his mind. Soon, the tapping of rain against the windows reaches his ears. It brings him a sense of calmness and, slowly, his mind begins to empty as he enjoys the tranquillity of soaking in the warm water.

✾

Emiko flops onto the bed in her chamber above the guest rooms with a pillow over her head. Her heart is thumping inside her chest. Who knew one day *Sir Leon* would be residing *here?* She punches her bed a few times to calm herself down.

She flips over, holds onto her pillow tightly, and stares at the ceiling, thinking back to four years ago.

When Emiko was fourteen years old, she went on a trip whilst studying botany at school. They were learning about all the different plants and flowers in Shinrin. That day, the school had taken their class to the village of Ajisai, which was situated near the Palace. They were told to pick the various plants and flowers in the village to learn about them in their natural habitat. Then, once picked, they would contribute said plants to the various elixirs made in the School of Healing, at

Furukawa Academy, the most pristine institution in Shinrin. Her teachers had mentioned that if they were lucky, they might spot the royal residences of the palace, or even Prince Takashi himself!

Emiko remembers taking her task very seriously. She studied her piece of parchment with the various plants very carefully and put the flowers into her basket as she wandered across the fields. Before she knew it, she found herself separated from her class, lost amongst the greenery and the forests. She panicked.

Soon, out of nowhere, there came the sound of a horse's hooves. A pure white stallion appeared through the forests, and on his back, sat a tall, striking young man in a navy-coloured robe. He spotted her and stopped his horse as they approached.

She remembers that moment very clearly.

Emiko dropped her basket of flowers. The young man hopped off his horse and landed lightly on his feet. He towered above her, so bent forwards into a bow.

"Are you lost, my child?" she remembers him asking.

He looked like an elf prince from the fantasy books she loved to read. His short, golden hair shone so beautifully and radiantly that he almost blinded her, and she found herself completely lost in his deep,

sapphire eyes.

Emiko remembers being very flustered, for she had never seen anyone so dream-like. She hurriedly scrambled on the ground, trying to pick up all the flowers she dropped. The beautiful man helped her gracefully, and with one swift movement, he easily picked her up onto the back of his horse.

"You are from the visiting class today, are you not?" he asked gently.

Emiko was unable to say anything, so she nodded. The young man climbed back onto the horse behind her, and she felt like she was flying as the horse cantered through the forest. She felt safe between his strong arms and clutched onto her basket as she wondered if what was happening was real.

Soon enough, she found herself back on the main field where her classmates were scattered around, searching for plants. Her knight in shining armour hopped back down and carried her down from his horse.

"Stay safe, my child," he said to her as he patted her on her head. "Stay close to your friends. Enjoy your trip." His smile dazzled her before he climbed back onto his horse and disappeared into the palace grounds.

Emiko later came to know that her saviour was Sir

Albert Leon, the first-hand guard of the Palace of Shinrin. She felt like she had fallen in love with him that very day.

Since then, she made a promise to herself that she would study very hard. She wishes to be accepted into Furukawa Academy, which is situated close to the palace, for she hopes to see Sir Leon once again to express her gratitude.

She cannot believe that right at this moment, her saviour is under the same roof as her. Her heart is going to burst. She suddenly thinks of him in the bathtub downstairs and nearly faints.

✾

Albert makes his way back down the stairs, following the delightful and enticing scent of food. His stomach grumbles.

Shizuko appears. “Come here, my child,” she says, beckoning him to follow her.

Albert enters a common room where many wooden tables and chairs are laid out. Further ahead, there is a warm fireplace with a few surrounding maroon couches. Kenta sits snugly on one of them, reading a book. A furry, golden dog is curled up next to him. A bowl of fluffy rice is placed on one of the tables, next to

a plate of the most scrumptious looking curry.

"Please help yourself." Shizuko smiles.

"Thank you so much," Albert says, his mouth watering as he sits down and prepares to tuck into this delightful meal.

Kenta notices him and waddles over. The golden dog follows. The old man sits down. "So, what brings a royal Sir such as yourself to the outskirts of Shinrin?" he asks curiously.

The golden dog sniffs around Albert excitedly, his tail wagging. He pokes Albert's leg with his slimy nose and rests his head on his lap.

"Excuse Kiiro," Kenta says. "He always gets excited when guests are around."

Albert strokes the dog's fluffy head and beams. He is fond of dogs.

"Hello, little Kiiro," Albert says. He then takes a spoonful of the delightful food, and his eyes widen and sparkle. "My goodness," he says. "This is divine!"

Kenta laughs. "My wife is quite a cook," he says.

Albert takes a further three spoonfuls before answering. "I was sent by Prince Takashi to look for materials to help strengthen our defence walls," he says. "You may have heard that our land is in danger."

"Ah, yes," Kenta replies. "Those killings. It appears

the disaster of Qieta has come to Shinrin."

Shizuko walks into the common room, wiping her wet hands on a towel. "How is the food?"

"Oh, it is wonderful," Albert replies. "I am speechless."

Shizuko laughs. "Eat up, Sir Leon. A young man like you will need to maintain his strength." She sits down beside her husband.

"You know about Qieta?" Albert asks, returning to the previous conversation.

Kenta continues, stroking his beard. "Ah, Qieta. The island which lives in the night. I sure do know a thing or two about that enchanting land. I may not be a Qietian myself, but I have spent many years there."

Shizuko nods in agreement.

Albert leans in, intrigued. He wonders if they know the details about the disaster. "Please, tell me more," Albert says between mouthfuls.

"I was an explorer, back in the day," Kenta explains. "In my younger years, I was one of the few who got sent to the lands outside of Shinrin, to learn, discover, and bring knowledge back home. I was sent to the furthest land—to Qieta. The island where sunlight does not exist."

Albert listens intently.

"So was my wife," he continues. "That is how we met," he chuckles.

Shizuko nods again and smiles.

"Anyway, we spent a good many years there. Qieta was an undiscovered treasure. For such a small population, it turned out to be one of the most established lands. Fascinating place. We discovered new materials and new ways of living and sent a Kaidara to Shinrin with some news from time to time. Over the years, we settled there and had a son." Kenta's bushy eyebrows rise up.

Albert sees his warm, brown eyes glisten with emotion, and he slows his eating in sudden dread.

"We named him Arwel. What a lovely boy he was. Grew into such a charming young man. He married a beautiful lady. Ceri, her name was. Then they had baby Emiko. That was when the disasters struck. The skies were turning crimson red and the harmonious population of Qieta were under attack. No one knew or understood how or why it happened, but numerous dead bodies kept appearing along the shores. It was horrific."

Albert takes a sip of water, engrossed in the story.

"The King and Queen of Qieta started sending boats out in distress, telling the citizens to escape. The older

and the vulnerable had priority. There came a never-ending storm, and it was a battle between the sea and the land. I remember that day very clearly." Kenta pauses and wipes his eyes.

"It was the very last boat, and Shizuko and I were some of the last people to board. We had baby Emiko. Arwel forced us to get on. He and Ceri promised to go back to take the small boat my wife and I originally journeyed to Qieta in, but I told him that boat was too old and unsafe. We departed from the land amongst the storm, and as our boat set sail, the biggest and most unforgiving wave I have ever seen crashed over the land. I never saw my son or my daughter-in-law again."

Kenta is quiet. Shizuko holds his hand tightly.

Albert sits still, gripping onto his wooden spoon. "I am so sorry," he says quietly.

"That is quite alright," Shizuko continues for her husband. "The journey was quite unrelenting. Many of the boats were lost or wrecked on the way. I am unsure if anyone else apart from the three of us managed to reach Shinrin." Shizuko exhales. Painful memories reflect in her eyes.

"Did they ever find out who or what may have been behind this disaster?" Albert asks.

"It is a shame—I do not know what happened after

we left. My guess is that half of their land is now under water. We do not know what could have been behind this." Shizuko falls quiet.

"Anyhow, Emiko is very fond of you, Sir Leon," Kenta says, breaking the silence after a while.

Albert raises his eyebrows. "She is?" he asks. He thought he had been somehow frightening the poor girl up until now.

"Most certainly," he replies. "You helped her when she was a little girl. She was lost in the forest."

Albert cocks his head to one side as he tries to remember this. He suddenly recollects a memory of a little girl with a basket. He remembers taking her on Erwin back to a class who came to visit the fields.

"Oh! So, I did!" he exclaims.

"A sweet girl she is," Shizuko says. "A hardworking one. Very good with animals, too. She adores them."

"She is trying her best to get into Furukawa Academy this year," Kenta says proudly. "Animal studies."

Albert nods in acknowledgement. "I see." He beams as he looks down towards his plate. "Thank you both. You have been ever so kind. Thank you, Shizuko, for the lovely meal, and thank you both again, for sharing your experiences with me. You have been through a lot."

"It is our pleasure," Kenta replies. "Please, Sir Leon, get ready for bed now. It is late."

Albert helps to take the dishes to the kitchen and cleans them despite Shizuko trying to bat him away. He makes his way back upstairs into his room and gets himself ready for bed before taking out the mattress from the cupboard and rolling it flat onto the tatami. He takes out a small piece of parchment, a brush, and ink from his cloth bag, scribbles a message to Prince Takashi, and leaves it by his side for tomorrow.

He lies down and listens to the rain tapping on the window, thinking about the things he will need to do tomorrow. He will need to send his message via a Ketu to Prince Takashi.

He ponders about the mysterious killings and then feels grateful that he had stumbled across such a lovely, gracious inn. Soon enough, he drifts off into his dreams.

✾

The sunlight pours through the window and onto Albert's closed eyes. He stirs. There are birds chirping outside. He has not had such a comfortable night's sleep in quite a while. Being so far out in the countryside and being surrounded by the sounds of nature reminds him of his home when he was still a child.

He gets up, rolls up his mattress, puts it away, and gets himself ready. Albert picks up the small piece of parchment he left yesterday and walks towards the window. As he pushes it open slightly, the fresh morning breeze generates a light sound from the wind chimes hanging from the top. He peers out to see a beautiful warm day and grassy fields.

He checks his message again.

Prince Takashi,

I have sought out the artisans who source malachite. All of them will supply as much as they can. I have met a humble family who lived in Qieta for many years. They may have helpful information for you. Would you like me to journey straight to Qieta or return to the palace?

Regards,
Albert

Albert whistles a short, simple tune. Soon enough, the flap of wings can be heard. A scarlet bird with an orange underside lands on the windowsill. Her shiny black eyes look at Albert and she chirps.

A Ketu.

Albert rolls up the small piece of parchment and tucks it into the burrow of feathers between her wings. "Please send this message to Prince Takashi," he says to the bird.

She hops once, twice, and then off the windowsill, expanding her wings and revealing the characteristic white tips of her feathers.

Albert watches as she swoops in the breeze and flies off into the distance. He then pulls on a fern-coloured robe and makes his way downstairs to check on Erwin.

✾

Emiko pours grains into the metal feeder for the chickens on their farm—they hurry over and begin pecking at the seeds.

Today, her hair is tied into a single, thick braid. She had trouble sleeping last night. She could not stop thinking about what to say to Sir Leon if she sees him. What if he leaves today? What should she say? She wants to express her gratitude.

She usually isn't a flustered kind of person, but for some reason, in the presence of Sir Leon, she has turned into someone else. She tries to divert her attention as she approaches the pigs and sees them rolling in the mud, damp from yesterday's rain.

She collects a bucket of fresh water from the well and heads towards the stables. Their horse, Lucille, appears to still be sleeping when she peers into her stable compartment. She is curled up on the straw in a wheat-coloured ball.

Emiko walks further down and sees Sir Leon's brilliant white stallion poking his head out into the sunshine. His tail swishes from side to side and he turns to munch on some hay which hangs in a basket beside him.

Emiko pours fresh water into a large metal container in his compartment. She opens his door, takes a brush which hangs on the wall, and enters. "Hello, royal horsey," Emiko says. "Do you remember me?" She starts to brush his hair.

The white stallion blinks at her while he munches. Some hay falls to the floor. Emiko strokes his forehead. Erwin continues chewing.

"You and Sir Leon saved me when I was little," Emiko continues as she pulls the brush through his ivory mane. "You are a beautiful horsey. I wonder what your name is."

"Erwin," comes a courteous, warm voice from behind.

Emiko jumps and squeaks. She turns to see Sir Leon

standing outside the stables. His tall frame is dressed in a fern-coloured robe, which compliments his blue eyes. Emiko looks at his handsome face and remembers seeing him for the first time in the forests.

Her heart flutters. “Good morning, Sir Leon,” Emiko says. She didn’t expect to see him. Her heart beats wildly inside her chest.

“Please, Albert is all right.” He smiles as he looks at his horse. “You are spoiling him! I will have to bring him back to you to be groomed in the future. I see you are quite the specialist with animals.”

Emiko laughs and then is horrified at how manic she sounds. She isn’t sure where to look. “Sir Leon, I—”

He looks at her curiously with his mesmerizing eyes.

“I–I wanted to say–I mean–I’m not sure you remember me, but. Thank you–for coming to save me when I was younger,” she manages to finish.

“That is quite all right. I didn’t do much,” he replies modestly. “For a small child, you really wandered quite far into the forests.”

The warmth inside Emiko’s heart increases. He remembers!

“I–I am grateful for what you did,” she replies.

“I hear you want to enrol into Animal Studies at

Furukawa Academy?" Sir Leon mentions.

Emiko's eyes widen. *Did grandpa tell him that yesterday?* "Oh! I–yes, I mean! I will try my best," she answers.

"We need people like you," Sir Leon says kindly. "Our creatures of Shinrin are of great importance. And people who can interact and understand them are exceptional." He smiles at her. "For all you know, you could be the next Queen Saeya."

Emiko's eyes widen again at his comment. She is honoured. Queen Saeya is one of her biggest inspirations. "That is–very kind of you," she whispers.

"I am sure you will do very well, Emiko," Sir Leon replies.

A burst of happiness releases inside her when she hears him say her name. "Sir Leon—" Emiko begins.

"Albert," he corrects.

"A–Are you departing—today?"

"Perhaps tomorrow," he replies. "I am waiting on a Ketu."

A wave of relief sweeps over Emiko when she hears this. She will need to cherish the time she has left with her saviour. A feeling of warmth spreads through her heart and she bursts into a huge smile.

Albert cocks his head to one side as a sparkle lights

up Emiko's eyes. He turns back to Erwin to see him staring at them both; he is greeted with a puff of warm air from his nostrils.

CHAPTER EIGHT

The Medical Examiner

IT HAS BEEN A FEW days since the night Satoru encountered the Mutoren.

He sits at his desk in his study with the first volume of Qieta from Sir Koberic's collection laid open in front of him, depicting the symbol of their land: a circle with a Kaidara feather inside. He flips the small copper emblem round and round between his fingers.

She most certainly has an association with this land, he thinks to himself. *Perhaps she is Qietian.*

On the morning after the incident, Satoru found all

his surrounding guards in a sleep-like state. He still has no idea how the Mutoren managed to do what she did, but it appears that none of his guards had any recollection of what happened. Nor were they hurt. When they woke, there was a frenzy of panic when they found out that the Mutoren had encountered the prince in his chamber and that the necklace had been stolen. Satoru can tell by her fighting that she must not be as youthful as she appears. It must take quite some years to reach such a substantial level of expertise. A very odd style, not to say the least.

He had also found out that there had been a massacre in the village of Hinoki—Akalin's hometown—around the time of the Mutoren's appearance. Most of the villagers had lost their lives, and the Hinoki children were stolen. The victims' deaths were of a different description to the killings by the rivers, and he had launched an investigation into this new tragic case. He prays that Akalin is doing alright.

Satoru has decided that he will keep the details of his encounter with the Mutoren sealed. Since the unmasking, he has been feeling a little strange. He has also decided that, if the Mutoren is Qietian, she must hold some essential information about the killings by the rivers. He wishes to meet her again to find out more

but has no idea how.

There is a knock at the door. "Prince Takashi!"

"Come in," he answers as he tucks the copper emblem into his robe.

Ryota appears by the door. "Professor Asante has some news for you in the examining chamber. He asks if you may join him." He bows.

"Very well," Satoru replies. He gets up from his chair and makes his way towards the examining chamber in the palace. He wonders what news Professor Asante will bring him.

Each day, the weight of these killings weighs him down more and more. This case is proving itself to be difficult, and the discovery of each new piece of information is taking a lot longer than he expected. If the number of killings continues to rise at this rate before he can offer decent protection for his kingdom, the citizens are going to start to lose faith in him as a leader.

Since receiving the news of these killings, Satoru sent a message out for the victims' bodies to be retrieved. He also sent a message via a Ketu to Professor Dimak Asante, a medical examiner, to ask for his expert opinion—he would be the specialist for gleaning more information from the bodies.

Satoru reaches the far end of the palace and pushes open a heavy stone door. A few stone tables lay in front of him, each with a large white sheet covering what is underneath. A man in his forties, who is dressed in a grey robe, puts one of the white sheets back into place and looks up at Satoru. His umber skin glistens with perspiration as he wipes his forehead. He adjusts his round spectacles and places a wooden box of lenses down by his side.

"Prince Takashi," he says as he bows.

"Professor Asante," Satoru replies. "I thank you for your dedication and your time. I have come to see what news you have for me."

"Yes, Your Majesty," the Professor answers.

Professor Dimak Asante is a renowned figure in Shinrin. He was one of the most outstanding scholars of his age whilst enrolling in the Studies of Healing when he was a young man. After travelling across the various lands of Neputa and contributing to saving the lives of many, he went on to specialise in Medical Examination. He has now reached a level of expertise regarding the causes of death higher than anyone else.

"My prince, I believe you are right," Professor Asante begins. "I do not think these are victims of Shinrin. These are not recent killings. I believe the

bodies are at least fifteen to twenty years old." He pauses to adjust his spectacles. "I do not understand how it is possible, as the bodies should, most definitely, have decomposed by now, at least to a certain extent. I cannot fully work out the ethnic background of these victims, but some of them appear somewhat Qietian. This is bizarre."

"This island is becoming the centre of this mystery," the prince answers, deep in thought. Could it be possible that history is repeating itself?

"As for the cause of death, I believe the victims were likely drowned," Dimak continues. "The pattern on their skin and hair is most consistent with drowning. However, the missing eyes and organs are odd. The way they have been removed appears deliberate, as if a creature has devoured them in a very particular way."

"Could humans be behind this?" Satoru asks inquisitively.

"The wound edges have remnants of saliva, Your Majesty," the professor replies. "Although I cannot be sure yet, I am more inclined to say that the victims' bodies were ripped open by the jaws of a creature. I have never seen a case like this, Your Majesty," Dimak answers. "Keep in mind that all of these are my best guesses, and even then, many things are not quite

adding up."

Dimak lifts one of the white sheets slightly, and a pale, mottled arm falls limply to the side, giving Satoru a fright.

"My goodness!" Satoru exclaims.

"Please excuse me, Your Majesty," Dimak warns the prince. "I understand this sight must be unsettling, but there is something I must show you." The Professor takes one of the round lenses from his wooden box and hovers it over his own arm. "Look here," he explains. "This is what a healthy piece of human skin should look like."

Satoru peers through the lens and sees a geometric pattern of the Professor's umber skin. The Professor then hovers the lens over the lifeless arm. Satoru notices a disruption of the pattern, along with a strange, blue-mottled colour. He is unsure at what he is looking at.

"You see," Dimak continues, "although I said these patterns are most consistent with drowning, it does not quite match the typical picture. I have never seen these mottled patterns before. But they appear on all of these victims."

"Does it resemble any of the diseases you have come across during your various travels?" Satoru asks.

The Professor shakes his head. "This is a new

mystery to me, Your Majesty. There are many other findings which baffle me, but I will not show you further. I understand this is distressing."

"Your level of expertise never ceases to impress me, Professor Asante," Satoru says.

Dimak bows in honour. "I will continue to investigate, Your Majesty."

"I am very grateful for your contributions, Professor. Please keep me updated on any new findings."

"Of course." The Professor bows again.

Satoru thanks him and exits the examination room.

✾

Satoru peers out of the window of his chamber as the large, orange sun sets in the sky. His mind flashes back to when he saw the Mutoren's silhouette just as she escaped from his room. He exhales and closes his eyes.

I must take back my necklace, he thinks. This treasure, which had been handed down for many generations, must remain with a member of the Takashi family. He looks at the trees in the distance, the branches swaying in the breeze. *I also need to find a way to see her again. She must hold more information about the disaster of Qieta and what may be behind these killings.*

Satoru feels for the copper emblem in his robe. He holds it between his thumb and index finger and examines it again.

Just then, there is the sudden sound of wings flapping in the wind. A scarlet bird lands on his windowsill. Her pointy beak taps on his window; it is a Ketu. He opens his window and she hops inside, bending her head and parting her wings slightly to reveal a tiny scroll of parchment.

The prince takes the scroll, and the Ketu immediately takes off into the sky. It is a message from Albert. His eyes glance quickly at Albert's script, and he nods as he thinks.

Satoru decides that he shall ask Albert to journey straight to Qieta. He will need Albert to find out exactly what happened in the disaster, how the people dealt with it, and whether they ever found the perpetrator.

Once Albert returns, they will use this information to protect the kingdom of Shinrin and track down the perpetrator as fast as possible.

Satoru takes out a brush and some parchment from his drawer before scribbling a response.

CHAPTER NINE

Behind the Wooden Mask

ON A ROOFTOP AMIDST A building in the forests, a girl sits and watches the sun rising. She glances at the small, emerald leaf on her palm, one that is attached to a thin, golden chain. She throws it up in the air, watches the small jewel as it glimmers, and catches it again. Each time she does so, the same thoughts run through her head.

The prince will reveal my identity to the whole of Shinrin.

She flings the small jewel into the air once more before it lands back into her palm.

The prince will keep my identity a secret.

The girl sighs. What *will* the prince do?

She places the jewel in her pocket, crosses her arms behind her head, and lies down on the roof as the clouds drift by. She cannot get rid of her unsettled feelings.

Her medium-length black hair, as dark as midnight, is tied into a thick braid. The rising sun reflects off her round, obsidian-coloured eyes. Her soft facial features give her a youthful look of innocence.

It has been a few days since she met Prince Takashi in person. She enjoyed coming face to face with him at last, after having observed him from afar for so many months whilst she planned her next heist.

The thrill of their one-on-one duel—not to mention that it was with the great leader of Shinrin—gave her a surge of adrenaline, the type she enjoys the most. But the fact that he managed to reveal her face was the last thing she would have expected.

She shakes her head.

His face is sure as charming as the scriptures have described. High cheekbones and deep, forest green eyes. A face so perfectly proportioned that it is as if he was hand sculpted to be particularly pleasing to look at.

The girl sits up and scoffs. She grabs a pebble lying by her side and throws it off the roof.

I can't believe I lost my emblem, she thinks as she reaches for the copper chain around her neck. The part where the emblem would normally hang is now empty. It must have somehow come off during her duel with the prince. Perhaps it came loose.

At least I got the necklace, she thinks to herself, before taking said item back out of her pocket, throwing it in the air once more, and catching it again. She tries to reassure herself that the loss of her emblem is outweighed by the necklace. Its magical power of protection against evil is probably the most important ability any of her stolen treasures have.

Today is the beginning of the academy break, a time when the various academies of Shinrin focus on entrance exams and the enrolling of the next generation of students. This means that she has a few days to go home and visit her family.

Swiftly, she makes her way off the roof, jumps onto a branch on the tree standing opposite, and lands onto the ground. Her movements barely make a sound. She makes her way back into the academy dormitory and packs up her belongings.

✾

The young girl makes her way to the bustling central of

Shirakaba village. *Do people recognise me as the Mutoren?* She avoids looking anyone in the eye, standing as far away from people as possible.

As she stands by the carriages and awaits the next one available, she overhears some conversation from the two ladies standing in front of her.

"Haven't you heard? The Mutoren apparently turned up at the palace a few nights ago!" the middle-aged woman gossips to her friend.

The young girl blinks as something in her heart sinks. News sure travels fast.

"Heavens!" the friend replies.

"He is pretty frightening, is he not?"

"Did anyone get hurt? How does he manage to get past the guards every time?"

"He is not human. I am certain. There has been a lot of writing about it. I am sure he is half spider. He must possess dark magic."

"Terrifying! Did they manage to find out anything else?"

"The palace hasn't yet issued any announcements. At least, none that I know of yet—"

One of the women notices the young girl standing behind them and looks at her curiously.

She stiffens up immediately.

"My, what a young girl you are!" the woman exclaims.

Wait, do they recognise me as the Mutoren? She manages an awkward smile.

"Are you travelling by yourself?" the woman continues.

"Yes, ma'am," the girl answers, avoiding her eyes.

"My child, you are too young to be out here alone. Is your mother not close by?"

The girl shakes her head. "I am twenty, ma'am," she replies.

"Oh!" The woman's eyebrows raise in surprise. "My! You certainly have a youthful face."

Why are they talking to her? She edges away from them as far as she can manage. Just as she tries to think of how to shake them off, a carriage arrives, and the two women get ready to board.

"Travel safely, young girl!" The woman waves through the carriage window.

Not long afterward, another carriage pulls up. An elderly man gets down from his horse and opens the carriage door.

"Hello, my child. Where are you travelling to, today?"

"To Akamatsu village, please," the girl replies.

"Very well. That will be fifteen kudon, please."

The young girl hands over a few silver coins and boards the carriage. The door closes behind her.

As the horses begin to trot, the carriage moves. She lets out a sigh and closes her eyes. The noise of the town centre is giving her a slight headache.

✽

The large, wooden house of Harlande is situated in the village of Akamatsu, known for its lustrous forests of red pine trees. Eirlys wipes her forehead with the back of her forearm as she takes a small break from kneading the dough in front of her. She has not been called recently to tend any ill or wounded patients. As such, she has been at home the past few days, making the most of her free time and creating delicious meals for her parents to enjoy.

Today, she is making steamed buns, one of her mother's favourites.

Eirlys looks up from the countertop and spots a small figure through the window. As the figure approaches, her eyes widen into a look of surprise excitement. She hastily pats her hands on her apron, runs out into the courtyard, and around to the front gate.

"Sana!" Eirlys shouts.

The mouth of the young, approaching girl turns upwards into a small smile. "Sister," she says as she walks towards Eirlys. Her cloth bag falls from her shoulders onto the ground as Eirlys pulls her into an embrace.

"I did not expect to see you!" Eirlys exclaims.

"Yes, it is the academy break. Good to see you, Sister," Sana replies.

"Hurry, Mother and Father will be so pleased you are here," Eirlys says as she heads back towards their home. "Mother! Father!" she exclaims.

Soon enough, Delwyn and his wife, Elian, rush to the front door. Their arms widen welcomingly.

"Welcome home," Delwyn says.

Sana blinks as a warmth flows through her heart during their embrace.

Eirlys gets back to work as Sana follows her into the cookery and fetches a cup of water.

The soft, white dough sits on the countertop next to various bowls of delicious fillings. Sana hovers her head above the bowls and eyes each one. "Wow, what are you making?"

"Red bean, taro, custard." Sana nods as she counts each one.

Sana's mouth waters at the sight.

"And I will keep some plain dough to make some mantou," Eirlys says to her sister.

"Would you like some help?" Sana asks, knowing that she will be told to sit down.

Eirlys laughs. She does not trust her sister around her when she is cooking. "Go sit down, little sister," she says.

Sana holds her cup of water and sits down on one of the cushions by the dinner table. She drinks in large gulps.

"Oh—Sana! I saw Prince Takashi a while back!"

Sana chokes. She splutters and coughs, hardly able to breathe.

Eirlys's mouth falls open in horror. "Are you alright?"

Sana gestures to her sister that she needs a moment. "Sorry—went down the—wrong way—" Sana coughs. Why, out of all times, is the prince being mentioned *now*?

Eirlys laughs. "Anyway, as I was saying, I saw Prince Takashi a while back. I saw him in a duel against a man with silver hair at the Showman Training Ground. I think his name was Sir Akalin Kinali, and it was so exciting! It was such a shame you weren't there." She finishes rolling out a piece of dough into a long rod

before chopping it into small, equal pieces.

"Very—nice," Sana manages.

"You wouldn't believe the sight! The girls were so loud, but I guess both men are very handsome. Especially Prince Takashi."

Sana's eyes water between the coughs. She wipes them with the back of her sleeve. "You must have—had a great—time," she says.

"It is a shame you were not there," Eirlys replies.

"Not at—all."

✤

That night, Sana sits on the tatami floor of her room, staring at the fan on the ceiling going round and round. She suddenly decides to get up. She crawls on the floor to the corner of her room and picks at the tatami mat. Sure enough, it comes away easily, revealing some space underneath the flooring. She reaches her hand inside and picks up a small, wooden chest before placing it on her lap as she crosses her legs and opens it.

She admires the items inside, a gleam reflecting off her round, dark eyes.

The Ruby Eye of the Dragon, Century's Amulet, Queen Saeya's Phoenix Feather, and Atlanta's Ribbon. She reaches into her pocket.

And now, the Emerald Necklace of Takashi, she thinks, as she plops it inside the box. She looks at the treasures, deep in thought. After eyeing the treasures some more, she leans back against the wall and her gaze softens.

She closes her eyes. *I wonder how much time I have left.*

Sana puts the box away and climbs onto her mattress before pulling the covers over her head. She closes her eyes and her mind drifts towards Prince Takashi. Part of her wants to stay as far away from the prince as possible, but if she does that, how will she reclaim her emblem? Or perhaps she could find a way to make the prince forget what he saw? She ponders on this thought.

Slowly, the feeling of slumber drifts over her and the image of Prince Takashi's surprised facial expression lingers on her mind as she falls asleep.

CHAPTER TEN

The Cellar Maker's Son

HOURS BEFORE THE HINOKI VILLAGE massacre, Aiyla lies in her chamber, propped up in her bed.

"Drink, my dear," Aiyla's mother, Yasmina, says. She sits by her bedside and feeds her some soup with a spoon.

"I wonder where brother Akalin is," Aiyla says quietly. She takes a mouthful and swallows.

It has been five days since her mother sent the Ketu, but they have not yet heard back from her brother. She still feels rather weak, but her cough has since

improved, and her fever has subsided.

"Perhaps something happened with the Ketu," her mother replies. "It is rare for there to be issues. I have never heard of Ketu getting lost before."

Aiyla leans back and closes her eyes. She misses her brother. She wonders if he's received the message yet.

"Mother, where did Father go?" Aiyla asks as she opens her eyes. She heard him exit the front door a little earlier.

"He went out to look for some more Sadore, my dear," Yasmina replies. "In case your fever spikes again."

Aiyla nods. Her parents have been brewing her some tea made from this flower for the past few days. It seems to have helped quite a lot.

Suddenly, there is the sound of screaming and shouting. Yasmina gets up from Aiyla's bedside and walks towards the window.

Aiyla's eyes widen and her heart begins to beat slightly inside her chest. "What is happening, Mother?"

Yasmina is alarmed. Some masked men arrive at the village on horses, carrying large lances. A villager is slashed right across his chest and falls lifeless to the floor as blood splatters onto the ground.

Immediately, Yasmina turns around and lifts Aiyla up from her bed. She runs into their back garden,

carrying Aiyla in her arms.

"Mother—" Aiyla gasps. She begins to tremble and her heart rate accelerates rapidly.

Yasmina puts her daughter down on the grass and hurriedly pushes a large, mossy rock to the side, revealing a wooden door. Her husband had asked someone to help build an underground cellar for more storage space to store their homemade pickles, and it had only recently been completed.

She puts her hands on her daughter's shoulders and looks her straight in the eyes. "Aiyla, I do not know what is happening, but you need to hide."

Aiyla cannot speak. She looks at her mother with wide, frightened eyes.

"Hide in this cellar. Do not come out. I will move the rock back over the door. If you need to get back out later, open the small flap, and push the rock aside. But for now, stay quiet and hide." Yasmina opens the larger wooden flap and hastily picks her daughter back up before lowering her onto the wooden step ladder.

Aiyla climbs two steps down into the darkness, feeling the cold. "But Mother—where is Father?" she asks, her voice faltering as she shakes.

"I will go and find him," she answers. "Hurry now, Aiyla. Promise me you will stay safe."

Tears well up in Aiyla's eyes. She is frightened and she does not want her mother to leave her side. However, she does as she is told and makes her way down into the cellar using all her strength. She looks up and sees her mother's face one last time before the hatch closes over and she hears the rock sliding back over the top.

Aiyla sits on the dusty floor in complete darkness. Her heart is bursting through her chest. She starts to hear screams, shouting, and people running. The sounds become louder and louder. She shuts her eyes tightly and trembles as she places her hands over her ears. She prays that whatever is happening outside will end soon and that everyone will be safe and stay in one piece.

Aiyla thinks about her brother, Akalin, and how fearless he is. Whenever she finds something difficult or challenging, the thought of her brother always brings her comfort and gives her strength. At a moment like this, Aiyla wishes nothing more than for her strong brother to be here and for his arms to be around her.

Brother Akalin wouldn't panic. Brother Akalin would always find a way out and he would ensure that everyone remains safe.

✽

Aiyla is unsure how long she has been in the cellar. Her head rests on her arms over her knees as she keeps her eyes firmly closed, not making a sound.

Suddenly, she hears the rock sliding on the hatch. A spark of fear bursts inside her. She jumps up and her heart races. Her eyes dart upwards towards the cellar entrance, but she cannot make out anything.

Are bad people going to come into the cellar?

Suddenly, a slit of bright light appears. She can hear her own heavy breathing. Someone is coming down. She backs towards the end of the cellar and does not dare make a sound as she watches a figure slide the rock back over the closing hatch. She is back in complete darkness.

Aiyla hears the striking of a matchstick. Suddenly, a bright flame appears as the figure lights a candle. A gasp escapes Aiyla and she covers her mouth with her hand. The young boy sees her and jumps, clearly not expecting there to be anyone inside.

Aiyla bursts into tears.

A small sound of shock and surprise escapes the young boy's lips. He looks around frantically, not knowing what to do.

He raises his hands like she is a startled animal. "I'm sorry—I'm sorry, don't cry," he says. His kind facial features tell Aiyla that he is not someone who will hurt her.

"I'm scared," Aiyla manages to say. She then realises she has met this boy before. He and his father were the ones who came to design and build the initial part of this cellar.

"Do you know what is happening outside?" Aiyla whispers between tears.

The boy shakes his head. "I do not. I was rowing on the river behind the houses. I heard screams and saw a few men rampaging through the village. I recognised your back garden because I have been here before, and I couldn't think of anything apart from trying to hide. I am scared as well," he whispers back.

The flame wobbles as his hand trembles.

He sends her a shaky smile. "Thank goodness I have these matchsticks and candles. As cellar makers, we always carry them," he continues.

"I'm worried about my parents," Aiyla says, her eyebrows furrowed with fear. She takes a breath. Her chest still hurts when she does so.

"I am, too," the boy replies. He slowly sits down next to Aiyla. He notices that she is trembling as well. He

reaches out and holds her hand tightly. “What is your name?” he asks her kindly.

“Aiyla,” she replies.

“Oh, moonlight,” he answers. He is quiet for a moment.

“Our parents named me that because of our silver hair,” she answers. “My brother is Akalin.”

“I know. He’s Sir Kinali of Shinrin,” he says, his eyes gleaming in awe as he forgets what is happening outside for a brief moment, “and your father is Master Erol Kinali. Your family is quite famous, Aiyla,” he says.

The atmosphere lightens ever so slightly.

Aiyla looks at him, unsure what to say. She rubs her nose and wiggles her toes in the dirt.

The young boy nods. “My name is Sako,” he says. “It means gentle.” He manages a laugh. “I am the opposite, though. I tend to accidentally break things, actually.” He looks at Aiyla. “How old are you?” he asks.

“Nine,” Aiyla says. “I am turning ten soon.”

“I am thirteen,” Sako replies, nodding.

The two children continue to sit in silence, tightly holding hands. They barely know each other but feel a strong sense of connection. Somehow, this sudden, startling tragedy has brought them together, so they will need to stick together.

They both watch the flame of the candle and, after what seems like forever, the flame suddenly reaches the end, and diminishes. The cellar is pitch black.

Sako fumbles in his pocket for another candle. “Oh, no. That was my last one,” he says. He cocks his head to one side as he tries to listen for any sounds coming from outside. “It sounds quiet,” he whispers.

Aiyla does not say anything. She squeezes Sako’s hand tightly.

“I am not sure how long we have been in here,” Sako continues, “but perhaps we should have a look outside. It sounds like whatever has happened has come to an end. Perhaps we can go and look for our parents.” He stands up briskly, pulling Aiyla to her feet.

She struggles to stand up. “I can’t see—anything–” Aiyla whispers between shaking breaths.

“It is alright,” Sako answers. “Hold my hand tight. I will guide you. I am used to working in the dark.”

Sako takes a few slow steps forwards as Aiyla stumbles behind him. He moves her hand towards the wooden steps.

“Hold onto this tightly and be careful as you get up,” he says. “Stay behind me.”

The two of them ascend slowly, and Sako reaches to open the small wooden flap before pushing the rock out

of the way. He pokes out his head slowly, squinting his eyes against the sunlight. He looks in all directions, making sure the coast is clear. He then steps out onto the grass, and offers a hand to Aiyla, helping her to get out.

Aiyla is still trembling and stays behind Sako as the two of them slowly make their way around to the front of the house.

The horrific sight of lifeless bodies and blood scattered across the paths suddenly crosses Sako's eyes. He immediately turns to Aiyla, wraps his arms around her eyes and shields her from the devastating scene.

"Don't look," he says. He carries on walking slowly, keeping his arms around Aiyla.

"There's more!" a loud shout comes from nowhere. There is the sudden sound of trotting hooves. Soon, a few masked men on horses appear and charge towards them.

"*Run*!" Sako shouts, turning Aiyla back around as they both scramble back towards the cellar in the back garden.

The horses are incredibly fast and, before they know it, the two children are picked up easily by two of the masked men. Sako kicks his feet as he is lifted off the ground. He panics, and soon, Aiyla is being lifted, too.

"Aiyla! Bite him!" Sako shouts, before attempting to bite the big, bulky arm in front of his neck. He barely manages to sink his teeth into the flesh before a hard blow strikes him across his face. The pain of the man's punch is excruciating. Sako flinches before the man shoves a cloth over his nose and mouth. Seconds later, he falls unconscious.

Aiyla is squirming in the arms of the second perpetrator, kicking her legs with all her might despite not yet being fully recovered. It is taking a lot out of her.

"This small one's a tough one," the man laughs. He catches her foot on her next attempted kick and as Aiyla continues tussling, one of her shoes falls to the ground.

Suddenly, the man slaps a cloth over Aiyla's nose and mouth. She feels suffocated. Seconds later, she too, falls unconscious and her head falls limply to the side.

The men carry the two children and laugh wickedly before leaving the devastated village of Hinoki behind.

CHAPTER ELEVEN

The Children on the Boat

A HAND FALLS ON AIYLA'S shoulder.

"Aiyla!" Sako says. "Aiyla! Wake up!"

Aiyla stirs slightly and opens her eyes slowly. The sound of children crying rings in her ears and the stench of uncleanliness and seawater infiltrates her senses.

She tries to sit up, but a deep pain aches through her stomach and into her back as she looks around.

It is dark, but gradually, she manages to see that there are many children surrounding them.

Aiyla attempts to get closer to Sako but is

immediately met with a large, heavy resistance that tugs on her wrists. She realises in horror that her hands and feet are attached to metal cuffs which, in turn, are attached to heavy, metal chains.

“Sako!” she exclaims. “Where are we?”

“I think we are on a boat,” he replies. “It smells like the sea.” He looks around and realises they are locked up in a metal cage.

“I feel sick,” Aiyla replies as the thick, heavy stench of seawater mixed with what Aiyla believes is the stinky smell of farm fertilisers hits her. She lifts her arm to cover her nose, causing the chains to clink and clank. “It stinks,” she whispers.

Sako shuffles next to Aiyla and holds her hand tightly. “We will stick together, no matter what happens,” he says to her reassuringly.

Suddenly, the boat hits something and the children jerk forwards. The screams and cries become even louder. A bright light blazes through as the large, heavy cloth covering their cage is lifted. The sound of chains clank as the children scramble to shield their eyes.

A frightening-looking man appears outside the cage. He is wearing a red cloth that covers his nose and mouth. Sako and Aiyla recognise his uniform—it is the same as the men who attacked their village of Hinoki.

The man unlocks the cage.

Sako and Aiyla happen to be the closest to him. They breathe heavily, their eyes wide with fear.

"Get out," the man commands.

Aiyla's legs tremble. She stands but falls back down.

"Hurry up," the man says harshly. He grabs onto Aiyla's small wrist and yanks her arm, forcing her out of the cage.

Sako winces at the unkind gesture he just witnessed. He quickly follows and stands after Aiyla, obeying the man's commands. His legs are also trembling.

One by one, the children get up and step out of the cage, their chains clinking as they struggle to walk. Aiyla recognises some of them as other children from her village. Some are from her school, although she does not know them very well.

The children look around, their eyes wide with fear as they are dragged off the boat. They see that they are on the shore of a very rocky-looking place. Above them towers the tallest cliffs they have ever seen. The cliffs are as black as midnight and, as the sunlight falls upon them, it reflects specks of glitter like diamonds and stardust. The wind is harsh and bites at their skin.

Something prods Aiyla in her back. She turns to see the man pushing her with the back of his lance.

He gestures with his weapon to the path in front of her. “Move,” he commands.

Aiyla stumbles forwards. There is a large cart housing another cage waiting in front of them. There are more men with red facial coverings standing around.

A chill runs down her spine.

Obediently, Aiyla follows their gestures and realises they are being forced into the second cage. She sits and Sako sits next to her. She is grateful he is here with her.

Once all the children are loaded into the cart, there is a loud, commanding shout and soon, they jolt sideways as horses begin trotting and carry them across the land.

Aiyla peers out of the cage and notices that they are being carried up the cliffs they saw when they arrived. The waves crash against the shore unforgivingly and she shivers in the cold temperature. She holds onto Sako’s arm tightly and their worried facial expressions reflect each other’s.

Aiyla wonders what is going to happen.

Where are they being taken to? Are they going to die?

✾

After a long time, the cart comes to a halt. The children are offloaded, and Aiyla and Sako are the last ones to get down. They are frighteningly high up and see a long, wooden bridge without any barriers, one that stretches out in front of them to connect one side of the rocky cliff to another.

Being now last in line, Sako and Aiyla realise that they will have to cross that bridge. The children in front are crying again.

"Get moving," one of the men commands. "Walk. If one of you falls, all of you will fall," he says, pointing to the metal chains connecting the children. "Now, you don't want that to happen, do you?" He smirks.

The children shake and tremble. The first child in line glances down at the crashing waves onto the rocks below and gulps. She bravely looks forwards and carries on walking. The children next in line follow, each of them swallowing their fear.

Sako steps onto the planks. It does not seem safe on these beams. Will it be able to take the weight of what is being loaded onto it? He has no choice and carries on forwards. Aiyla follows and glances down at the waves. Her legs wobble, but she takes a deep breath, and walks ahead.

Soon, Aiyla notices that they are being led to a large,

central ground. There are many children already there. They look unkempt and dirty. Somehow, the line has switched backwards again, putting Aiyla first and Sako second.

Aiyla and Sako both look around and notice there are children dotted around the entrance to some caverns in the distance. On the other side of the space, there is a gigantic, wooden, turning wheel. Each wooden beam has one child pushing it, forcing it to go around in a circle.

One of the men unlocks the cuffs around her wrists and ankles and pushes her harshly towards the central ground towards another man. This one is frowning.

There are red marks embedded in her skin from the rough, heavy metal cuffs.

The frowning man looks at Aiyla and inspects her. It doesn't take a second for him to harshly push her towards the left with the back of his lance. Aiyla stumbles towards the group of children who are already standing on the left.

She turns back around to see Sako looking between the two groups of children—one on the left and one on the right. He fixes his eyes on her.

Sako's cuffs are next to be unlocked. He is pushed towards the frowning man. The man takes one look at

him, and moves to push Sako towards the right.

Sako bravely speaks. “Wait,” he says.

The frowning man’s eyes turns into a look of surprise. He then smirks under his mask. “How amusing. A child speaks,” the man says, looking Sako up and down. His eyebrows then turn back into a frown.

“I know what you want,” Sako says. He is trembling. He looks the man straight in his eyes. “If you want workers in the caves, put me there,” Sako continues. “I am a cellar maker. I work well in the dark.”

Aiyla looks at Sako from afar.

“Is that so?” The frowning man sneers at Sako. He laughs. “We have a volunteer!” he announces. “Well, that’s a first, isn’t it?” He puts his face frighteningly close to Sako’s and glares. “Well, kid, you better bring back double,” he snarls, before shoving him hard towards the left.

Sako stumbles slightly but quickly regains his balance as he rushes towards Aiyla.

“Are we going to die?” Aiyla whispers. The intensifying fear inside her decreases ever so slightly as Sako returns to her side.

“No matter what,” Sako whispers back with determination. “We will try our best to get out of here.”

CHAPTER TWELVE

A Young Girl's Love

EMIKO SITS AT THE DESK in her chamber, glancing through the notes she has made. For the past few months, she has been studying very hard. Her entrance exam into Furukawa Academy to learn Animal Studies is soon. She tries to look at the words on the parchment in front of her, but the lines blur and squiggle.

She is struggling to concentrate because Sir Leon is on her mind.

She was so pleased to hear that he will stay another night. She wants to make the most of the time she has

left with him, but at the same time, just the thought of him makes her panic. She gazes at the sky through her window into the distance. It is so blue, just like Sir Leon's beautiful eyes.

She smiles and daydreams about her saviour. Suddenly, there is a knock at the door. Emiko jolts in her chair. Her chamber door creaks open.

Her grandma pokes her head through the door. "Emiko, my child," she says.

"Grandma!" Emiko exclaims.

"I know you must be very stressed," Shizuko says, "but I think you should take a break. Grandpa and I want to make mushroom stew tonight for the guests at the inn, but we have run out of mushrooms. Sir Leon insisted on helping to pick them, but he doesn't know where to go."

Just the sound of her saviour's name sets off a flutter inside Emiko's chest.

"Why don't you go with him, my child? It will be good to get some fresh air as well," Grandma Shizuko says. She then winks.

"Grandma!" Emiko shouts, taken aback.

"Come on," Shizuko answers and turns her back as she starts to make her way down the stairs.

Emiko hurriedly jumps off her chair and stumbles

behind her grandma. The wooden floorboards creak under her feet. They make their way down to the ground level. Emiko spots Sir Leon straight away. He is standing outside the front door next to his horse Erwin, holding onto his reins.

"Emiko will show you the way." Shizuko smiles, a bit too broadly, as she hands over a large basket to Sir Leon. "She knows the forests here very well."

"I didn't mean to trouble you—I just thought to help out whilst I'm here—" Sir Leon begins.

"It's not a worry at all!" Emiko replies. Her voice sounds a bit too loud and firm.

Grandma hands a basket to her as well, and Emiko hurriedly runs towards the stables to fetch her horse, Lucille.

Soon enough, Emiko returns on her horse, ready to go. She cannot quite look Sir Leon in the eyes. She notices him swing his legs over his white stallion and cannot help but be reminded once again of the elf princes in the fairy tales she read when she was younger.

"Stay safe and come back soon!" Grandma Shizuko waves happily at the pair.

Emiko's heart will not stop fluttering. She accidentally sends Lucille off briskly in a gallop. Erwin follows but stays a few paces behind.

✾

Emiko and Albert arrive at a lustrous green forest. Lucille slows down to a trot and Erwin does the same.

"We're here," Emiko says, hopping from her horse.

Albert hops down next to her. He looks around and notices some semi-destroyed stone buildings and structures surrounding them, many with moss climbing on their walls. It looks like a ruin. A very beautiful one.

"So," Emiko begins, "you have to pick the round white or brown ones." She bends down and picks up a plump, white mushroom to show to Sir Leon. "Like this one," she continues. "But be careful. Some of them look very similar, but they are poisonous." She feels like she is rambling. She takes a few steps forwards and looks around, spotting another. "Ah—this one!" She points to it as she tries to calm her nerves.

Albert sees a round, white mushroom. To him, it looks identical to the one Emiko just picked up.

"You see, with this one, the stem has grey creases in it. These are poisonous. Same goes for the brown ones."

Albert nods, but the truth is, he cannot tell the difference. He spots another round, white mushroom, and crouches down to examine it. The stem looks plain and white.

"Emiko, is this one alright?" he asks.

The young girl jumps at the question and draws near to Albert. "Certainly," she replies.

The pair pick mushrooms in silence. Albert is concentrating extremely hard, whereas Emiko is too nervous to say anything else.

Suddenly, a drop of rain lands on Emiko's cheek. She looks up at the sky. Thick, dark grey clouds loom over them, and soon enough, heavy rain crashes down onto the ground. Albert looks up in surprise and stands briskly. He immediately runs towards Emiko, takes off his cloak and holds it above both of their heads.

Emiko's cheeks start to burn. "Let's go there!" she shouts over the rain, pointing towards one of the stone ruins.

She holds onto both baskets and the two of them slosh across the muddy ground towards the shelter. The two horses trot behind them.

Albert sits on the stone step underneath the shelter as Emiko plops down beside him. There is a strong hand on her shoulder as Albert pulls her closer towards him. It makes her jump.

"Come closer," Albert says. "Keep yourself out of the rain."

Emiko isn't sure where to look. She is sitting so close

to him that their thighs are touching. His warmth is radiating through to her. This causes her to blush, and she looks away.

Albert looks at the sky with a confused facial expression. “It is certainly storm season here, is it not?” he asks.

Emiko doesn’t answer. She thinks about how she was in such a hurry earlier that she completely forgot to put on her cloak.

“It rained so heavily on the night I arrived, just like this,” Albert continues.

The two of them sit huddled under Albert’s cloak, staring at the rain. Emiko notices the two baskets of mushrooms in front of them. Hers is a mixture of brown and white, whereas Albert’s are white only.

She suddenly struggles to contain her laughter. “Why don’t you have any brown mushrooms?” Emiko laughs. Her laughter releases some of her nerves. It is contagious.

Albert finds himself laughing along with her. “I am no mushroom expert,” he admits.

Emiko catches her breath. “They look so sad!” She struggles to contain herself. The round fungi sit lifeless in the baskets under the rain.

“Yes,” Albert agrees. “They’re drowning.”

His short statement causes Emiko to burst into more laughter, and Albert starts to find it amusing at how the young girl can find something so simple so funny.

As she calms down, Emiko turns to face Albert. His face is so close to hers. She looks at the rain running down his golden hair, just like it did on the night when he first arrived. Her eyes meet his, and she looks at how they glisten like deep sapphires. There are butterflies fluttering inside her stomach. She wishes that this moment will last forever.

Just as she is lost in his eyes, Albert gives her a soft smile, and she is dazzled.

She snaps her eyes away and inhales. "So—so—how did you come to be in the palace?" Emiko says out of nowhere, breaking the silence. She then worries that this question is too personal.

"I grew up with Prince Takashi," Albert replies simply.

Emiko nods. "Your parents and the King and Queen are good friends?" she asks.

"Sadly, I do not have parents," Albert replies.

Emiko is taken aback. "I'm sorry," Emiko says.

"That is quite alright," Albert answers.

There is a small pause. She thinks about her own

parents.

"Actually—me too," Emiko says. "I don't have parents either. I know how it feels."

Albert remembers the stories that Kenta and Shizuko told him last night. He looks at the young girl and a slight pain aches in his heart.

"You have wonderful grandparents," Albert says. "You are very lucky to have them."

"I know," Emiko agrees. She pauses. "And you are a wonderful person," she finds herself saying. Her eyes then widen with shock at what she had just said. She glances over nervously at Albert.

He laughs radiantly. "That is very kind of you."

The rain starts to lessen slowly and soon the clouds disperse, revealing a brilliantly blue sky.

Albert uncovers the cloak. "Thank goodness it stopped," he says. He then notices his basket of mushrooms. "You might want to check mine," he admits to Emiko.

Emiko smiles and takes out each mushroom—one by one—checking them over. She then turns around to Albert and smiles at him playfully. Her braided, long, fiery hair flows around her. "Well done. You have passed the mushroom exam," she says to him.

"I have?" he asks with genuine surprise.

"Indeed!" Emiko replies cheerfully as joyfulness radiates out from her.

The two of them then hop onto their horses and head back towards Tanaka Inn.

✾

Upon arriving back at the inn, Albert helps Emiko put the horses back into the stables, carries the baskets into the kitchen, and enters his room to dry off.

Not long after he steps inside, there is a *tap tap* on the window. He walks towards it and slides it open. Two Ketu sit there; one on the windowsill while the other swoops down towards the ground floor.

Albert unfolds the scroll quickly and his eyes skim over Prince Takashi's elegant script.

Albert,

Thank you for your hard work. I will command the artisans to begin their supply immediately and awaken the Hakkan. Meanwhile, please journey straight to Qieta. Send a Kaidara when you arrive. Please gather as much information as you can on the exact details and timeline of the disaster, how the Qietian people dealt with it, and whether they ever found the perpetrator. Journey straight back to Shinrin after this.

I will invite the Tanaka family to come to the palace soon. I also believe the Mutoren is linked to Qieta. Please keep me updated and stay safe.

Best wishes,
Satoru

CHAPTER THIRTEEN

Purple Eyes

AKALIN SPOTS ONE OF THE boats from a distance. It wobbles in the water. He watches it rock from side to side even more as it takes the weight of the frightened young children as they are loaded aboard.

The silver moon shines as a glowing crescent above the water. Two men wearing red cloths around their faces cover the large cage with a cloth, dampening the children's cries. As they start to unravel the rope connecting the boat to the dock, Akalin makes a move

and silently darts through the darkness towards them.

For the past few days, Akalin has been travelling across Shinrin in search of anyone who knew about the kidnapping and massacre of his village. After staying in various inns and gathering as much information as he could, he gained enough bits and pieces of information to find the location of these boats a few nights ago.

Frightened villagers had noticed men wearing black armour and red masks and riding horses with large carriages while travelling towards Neril, a tiny land just North-West of Shinrin. Neril is well known for its fishing villages and is a major site of trade and transportation due to its location and proximity to the sea.

Akalin had been staying in Hafier for the past few days—a tiny, secluded dock right on the edge of Neril. Local fishermen spotted the masked men offloading carts containing children onto boats every few nights. However, on the one occasion when a brave fisherman approached them to challenge their actions, he was killed on the spot. Since then, villagers have been too frightened to do or say anything about what is happening in front of them.

Akalin had sent his horse, Leia, back to the palace and sent a Ketu to Satoru to explain what he had found

out and what he is planning to do.

He lands on the boat. It barely moves as it takes his weight. He notices a few crates and drops down in the gap between them. He watches as the docks drift further away. The boat has set sail.

He hears the two men talking.

“Honestly, I could do with being in bed right now. I am exhausted,” one of them says.

“Samuel, you are useless,” the other replies unkindly.

“Are you always this mean, Lucas?”

“Samuel, if you don’t shut your mouth, I will actually kill you.”

Akalin hears Lucas swinging his lance towards Samuel. There is a pause.

“Sorry,” Samuel replies.

Akalin remains hidden in between the crates. He looks up at the night sky. The constellations glimmer, and a faint, starry band stretches across the sky. His breath creates some mist in the night air. It is cold. The muffled sound of children crying comes through the large cloth draped over them.

“These stupid kids are doing my head in,” Lucas comments.

“I feel bad for them,” Samuel replies. “I mean, it is

pretty traumatising—" Samuel cuts off abruptly and groans.

It appears Lucas has struck him across his face. Akalin peeks between the crates and sees Lucas lean close towards Samuel, pulling on his collar threateningly.

"Speak again and I'll kill you." Lucas's stone-cold voice drifts through the air. He lets go of Samuel's collar and watches him slump to the floor of the boat. Akalin frowns as he eyes what is unfolding in front of him. Who are those soldiers and who are they working for? Why are they abducting all these children?

Hours pass by. Akalin is still sitting between the crates. The cold night air bites at his skin. His nose is running but he is afraid to sniff lest he make a sound. He debates wiping it on his sleeve and then feels glad no one is here to witness it as he does so.

Akalin pokes his head out between the crates and looks around. He cannot see either of the two men. He emerges slowly between the gaps and takes a few light, soundless steps.

He turns a corner and suddenly notices one of the men curled up on the floor. The man's chest rises and falls; he is fast asleep. Akalin looks around in all directions to make sure the coast is clear. He takes

another few small steps forwards then turns back around to check behind him.

Suddenly, the pointed edge of a lance swings towards Akalin's face. He instantly moves his head back and dodges it just by a few millimetres.

Lucas swings the lance around again to trip Akalin, but Akalin jumps up just in time and aims a kick towards Lucas's stomach. It connects, causing him to stumble backwards a little.

Akalin notices the man turn his head towards Samuel. Although Lucas has half of his face hidden behind a red mask, it appears he is about to shout for his comrade. Akalin leaps behind Lucas in a flash and—with his left hand—smothers the man's red mask over his mouth.

Lucas attempts to strike Akalin with his elbows and the two of them fall onto the deck, rolling towards the crates as they struggle against each other.

Lucas reaches for his lance and manages to detach the blade from the end of the stick. He strikes towards Akalin's face just as he briskly turns his head to his right. The blade misses his face by an inch and embeds into the wooden floorboards of the deck. Lucas pulls the blade out of the floorboards with anger, but before he can do much else, Akalin strikes him on his chin, causing

him to lose his balance and fall.

Lucas stretches out his left leg towards Akalin's ankle and trips him. He clambers onto his hands and knees like a wild animal and throws his weight towards Akalin. He kneels on top of him and, using all his might, strikes the pointed blade towards Akalin's chest.

Akalin just about manages to grasp onto Lucas's wrists before using his strength to resist the force that is being pushed towards him. The silver, pointed edge reflects the moonlight as their hands tremble against each other's and Akalin's eyes move towards the frightening man who is sitting on top of him.

The man's eyes are piercing and full of rage. They look empty. There is no remorse—only pure hatred and fervour.

Akalin frowns in concentration as, for a fleeting moment, Aiyla's face flashes before his eyes. His grasp on Lucas's wrists tightens and suddenly he overpowers him, knocking him to the side.

Lucas drops the blade.

In a flash, Akalin grabs the blade before clambering on top of Lucas, holding him in place with his weight. He looks at the man beneath him. He does not want to kill him, but he nearly lost his life to him only a split second earlier.

There is no other way.

He holds the blade forcefully against the man's neck before ripping the red mask off his face. A trickle of blood oozes as the blade cuts into the man's skin ever so slightly.

"Tell me why you are taking these children," Akalin states with a harsh whisper, not wanting to wake the children inside the cage.

"They will work until they die," Lucas replies slowly. He looks almost manic. He then smirks. "Go on. Kill me, purple eyes," he says.

Akalin takes a breath. He does not want to do it, but he has no choice. Either himself or this man will have to die tonight. He winces and then slowly sinks the blade into Lucas's neck. A sickness pulsates in his stomach. Lucas's emotionless eyes suddenly widen in shock before he splutters and coughs up some blood. His head falls back limply.

Akalin's breaths are hard and heavy as he takes in what has just happened. He looks up and notices the other man still sleeping. He wonders if he should throw them both overboard. However, someone will have to navigate the boat.

He thinks for a moment, then gets up quickly before dragging the dead body to the side of the boat.

He takes off the black armour Lucas is wearing as he keeps his eyes fixed on Samuel's prone form. Samuel turns briskly, then snores.

Akalin hastily puts on the armour. It is still warm inside. He then puts the red mask on his face; his stomach turns vigorously as the stench of the man's breath hits him. He retches.

He grasps onto the body in front of him, wipes the blood from the blade onto Lucas's clothing, and throws him overboard. The splash makes him wince. The body drifts out into the cold dark waters of the ocean.

Akalin walks slowly towards the stick of the lance that lays on the deck. Just as he reaches for it, Samuel sits up from the far side of the boat slowly and rubs his eyes.

"Lucas? Is it my turn to navigate?"

Akalin freezes. His mind races as he decides what he should do next. He makes a quick calculation. From his observations, Samuel should be a lot less threatening than the man he just threw overboard.

"Yes," Akalin says simply.

Samuel yawns through his mask. "Alright, boss." He gets up and plods towards the front of the boat before peering at the stars in the sky. He appears to be calculating the whereabouts of their location. "Righty-

ho," he says as he starts to pull on the ropes of the sail. He then looks towards Akalin and cocks his head to one side. "You alright, boss?" he asks. He looks at the blade in Akalin's hand.

"Yes. Just sharpening this," Akalin replies as his heart hammers inside his chest, and he tries to mimic Lucas's harsh tone voice. He reattaches the blade onto the stick of the lance.

"You can sleep. It's my turn to navigate the rest of the journey anyway," Samuel says.

Akalin pauses. "It's all right. Better for both men to be awake."

Samuel blinks. It is as if he cannot quite believe what he just heard. "Boss, are you sure you're feeling alright?"

Akalin is unsure if this man really cannot tell it is not his comrade standing in front of him, if he really is that clueless, or if he is just not fully awake yet. He nods and sits down slowly, resting his back against the side of the boat. He stares into the distance and suddenly senses there are eyes on him. His eyes snap towards Samuel.

Samuel has his hands on the ropes of the sails but is looking at Akalin very curiously. Akalin gulps behind his mask.

"Boss, don't hit me, but honestly, I never noticed

how pretty your eyes are," Samuel says innocently. He smiles underneath his mask.

Akalin looks at him and does not respond.

"They are so purple. Wow." He blinks a few times. "Wow," he says again. Samuel turns his head back towards the direction the boat is sailing. He starts singing. "Keska! Keska, here we come!"

Keska? Akalin thinks to himself. *Where is that?* He ponders in silence. Has he heard of this place before? He tries to picture the map of Neputa in his mind but cannot pinpoint its location. *Who are these soldiers and why are they stealing children?*

"God forgive me," Samuel says quietly.

Akalin looks in his direction. The man appears to be saying a prayer. His eyes are closed tightly.

"One day I will save these poor children," he says. "It is not I who wanted this. I pray for the day we can get out of this."

Akalin watches him curiously. "Samuel." Akalin tries out a firm tone. "What are you doing?"

Samuel's eyes snap open abruptly. "Nothing, boss!" he says. He then continues to sing. "Keska—the wonderful land of Keska . . ."

Akalin turns to face the sea. The sun is beginning to rise and creates a shimmer on the surface of the gentle

waves. He then looks towards the strange man as he continues to sing.

Something tells Akalin that the man singing in front of him has a good heart.

CHAPTER FOURTEEN

Sir Leon's Departure

THE SUN IS ROUND AND orange as it sets in the sky. It casts a shadow on Albert and his horse, Erwin, as he stands outside Tanaka Inn and gets ready to depart.

Kenta and his wife, Shizuko, have received a Ketu from His Royal Majesty, Prince Takashi, inviting them to stay on the palace grounds for a few days. While there, they should try to offer more information that may help with solving the case of the killings. Emiko will travel with them and undertake her entrance exam at Furukawa Academy.

"It has been a pleasure to have you," Kenta says kindly as he and his wife bow towards Sir Leon.

"You have been the kindest towards me," Albert says and bows in return. "I will be forever grateful."

The old couple had refused to take any payment from Albert for his stay, but little did they know that he had left three times the amount of kudon behind their front counter as a gesture of thanks. He had snuck it there whilst they were busy making the mushroom stew.

Kiiro suddenly appears and runs towards Albert, jumping up towards him, his tail wagging. Albert reaches down and pats his head.

"Ah!" Kenta says. "Kiiro has come to say goodbye!"

"Goodbye, little Kiiro," Albert says, beaming towards the dog.

Emiko stands behind the door of the inn. Her heart is aching. She never thought that she would see Sir Leon again, at least not in her own home. The feelings she has had for Sir Leon over the past four years have catapulted through the roof in the few moments they have spent together in the last two days. She does not want him to leave and seeing him about to depart is breaking her heart.

She looks up at her saviour. His tall silhouette stands

out against the sunset and his brilliant, white horse. She feels a sudden rush of adrenaline—if she wants to say something to Sir Leon, she will have to do it now, for she may never get the chance to see him again.

Albert notices Emiko standing behind the front door. He looks in her direction, smiles and nods a little. "Emiko, thank you for the past two days as well. Best of luck in your exams, I am sure you will do very—"

Before he can finish, Emiko takes a leap of faith and runs towards him, throwing her arms around him. Her grandparents' heads move in unison as they watch their granddaughter fly towards the young man. Kenta's thick, bushy eyebrows raise in alarm and Shizuko's mouth widens into a gasp before she covers her mouth with her hand.

Albert stumbles backwards from the unexpected force, his eyes widening in surprise as he lets go of Erwin's reins to catch Emiko.

Emiko trembles as an overwhelming number of emotions sweep over her—anxiety, sadness, and heartbreak. She is worried that what she is doing may be crazy, but it is now or never. She looks up at Sir Leon, straight into his eyes.

Albert is taken aback at the intensity of her emotions. Her amber eyes are burning straight into his

own—burning with a determination he has never seen before.

“Sir Leon,” Emiko says firmly.

Albert blinks.

“Sir Leon, I am sorry if this comes across as too forwards, but I have to say this now that I may never see you again. I do not want to regret anything.” Emiko’s heart beats wildly inside her chest. At this moment, standing under the sunset, she feels as though they are the only two people left in the world. “I do not know if you have anyone in your life already, but I have been in love with you since the day in the forest four years ago.”

Albert’s sapphire eyes widen even more.

“My heart aches with so much love for you, and now that you are departing, I feel so much pain. I do not expect anything back, but I just want you to know this is how I feel.” Tears begin to form in Emiko’s eyes. She loosens her grip as she takes a breath and steps back.

Kenta and Shizuko are frozen behind her. Kiiro sits still and sniffs the air. Erwin’s nostrils widen behind Albert. Albert looks at the young girl in front of him and blinks a few times.

“Please. Don’t forget me,” Emiko whispers. More tears well up.

Albert takes a step forward and pulls Emiko into a

gentle embrace. He pats her on her head before putting his hands on her shoulders and bending down so that their eyes are level.

Emiko looks up at him with overwhelming emotion, unsure at what he is about to say.

“I won’t forget you,” Albert replies softly. He looks at her with a gentle expression. “Emiko, you are very kind and gifted. You are still very young, and you have a very bright future ahead of you. I will never forget the kindness you have shown me, and I am grateful we have crossed paths. For now, concentrate on achieving your dreams. I am sure we will cross paths again.”

Emiko’s eyes are locked on Albert’s as she takes in every word. She cherishes the warmth of his embrace and wishes again that this moment will last forever.

“Please have a safe journey, Sir Leon,” Emiko whispers.

Albert nods and smiles. “Albert,” he says.

“Stay safe, Albert,” Emiko replies. His name rolls off her tongue smoothly. She blushes at how it sounds to say his first name out loud for the first time.

Albert takes hold of Erwin’s reins as he turns him a little before hopping onto his back. Emiko wipes away a few tears, before walking to stand back next to her grandparents. They wave towards Sir Leon. Erwin

begins a slow trot and Emiko watches as her saviour slowly begins to depart.

"Goodbye, Albert!" Emiko shouts.

She watches as Albert turns back around one last time. He nods at her before giving her a soft smile which makes her heart flutter. He lifts a hand and gives a small wave before he turns back around.

Emiko watches as the golden-haired man on his stallion disappears into the distance.

CHAPTER FIFTEEN

The Palace Announcement

FOR THE PAST FEW DAYS, Satoru has been thinking constantly about how to meet the Mutoren again. He is sure that she has connections to Qieta and that she holds important information about these killings.

But why is she stealing Shinrin's most powerful treasures?

Albert had brought him news that an elderly couple he had met may be able to help him with the case. Akalin had also brought news that the lost children of

Hinoki were likely being stolen and traded off the shores of Neril.

His mind is filled with too many things. He closes his eyes and lets out a sigh. Both his first and second-hand guards are away from his side.

His mind shifts back to the Mutoren. Now that he has unmasked her, he can focus more of his attention on the killings, but he will need a way to find her again.

Suddenly, an idea pops up in his mind. His eyes light up, but then he laughs slightly at his own idea.

What if he makes an announcement that all young women with dark hair and eyes are to be brought to the palace? Heavens, the land will think that he is looking for a wife, which is the last thing on his mind!

Who has time for a wife when there is a whole kingdom under your rule?

Not to mention—it will take him a century to filter through all these women to find the Mutoren. And, knowing how the Mutoren is, she likely will not even turn up. This plan is outrageous.

But . . . surely the Mutoren will have to be a citizen living amongst the rest of the population in Shinrin. No one can ignore commands or requests which come from the palace. At a time like this, one may be charged with withholding information to the palace and

hindering the kingdom's safety.

Satoru lets out another sigh and turns to face the window. Whilst looking at the mountains in the distance, he ponders about how to see her again. He must meet her.

Satoru turns back to face his desk. He cannot think of another way. He gets up and strides towards the door.

"Master Takashi." Ryota bows deeply as the door opens.

Satoru turns towards him. "Ryota, please gather all the palace scribes. Command them to send a Ketu to every household of Shinrin stating that every young, petite woman between the ages of sixteen and six-and-twenty who are highly skilled in combat and have dark hair and dark eyes are to come to the palace to meet me," Satoru says without any changes to his tone of voice.

Ryota is alarmed. His eyebrows raise in response to what he just heard, for this is something he would never have expected to come out of the prince's mouth.

"Master Takashi," Ryota says in surprise. "Are you . . . looking for a Queen?" he asks slowly and carefully, then blinks a few times.

Satoru tries to keep his face straight. "Ryota, my first- and second-hand guards are thousands of miles

away. We are in unprecedented times, and I do not know how long this will last. I need to appoint a new first-hand guard in their absence."

Ryota cocks his head to one side.

"I need someone with a similar build to the Mutoren. A highly skilled fighter and a potential opponent for the creature to help defend the kingdom against him while I concentrate on the case of the killings."

"And they must have dark hair and dark eyes?" Ryota asks, raising an eyebrow. The corner of his left lip turns up into a mischievous smile.

"Correct. These people are more likely to have a trait which allows them to see well in the dark." Satoru makes it up as he goes along. "This is very important as the Mutoren does his deeds in darkness." He is beginning to struggle to keep a straight face.

"Is that so?" Ryota asks, the corner of his lip turning up even further. "And it must be a lady?"

"Indeed."

Ryota isn't buying it. "Master Takashi, there is no precent for a lady taking on the role of a guard. If you are looking for an Empress, there is no need to hide it. The land will be joyous to know."

"Ryota—" Satoru begins, "ladies can be just as good

at fighting as men. If anything, they are lighter. More agile." His mind works quickly. "It is time to change these old, concrete rules. There is no such thing as whether someone can or cannot. We look at the skill, not the person. My kingdom shall not have such ridiculous rules."

Satoru is aware he is really pushing it. His nose twitches as he struggles to hold himself together.

Ryota nods slowly, deep in thought. "Master Takashi, your way of thinking never ceases to impress me. You are very ahead of your time."

Satoru gives a nod. "I know." His insides are roaring with laughter. "Please pass my message along to the scribes."

"Yes, Your Majesty." Ryota bows and takes a few steps forwards. He then stops and turns back around. "Dark hair and dark eyes, was it?" he asks. He struggles to hide his mischievous smile.

"Correct," Satoru replies, holding onto his straight face which is about to break any minute now. He watches as Ryota makes his way and he closes the door.

Satoru returns to his desk and holds his hands out onto the surface to steady himself as his laughter explodes loudly. He is sure the whole kingdom is going to think that he is looking for a wife. He tries to shake

the thought out of his mind. His outrageous idea is worth a try, for it will give him the smallest chance of meeting the Mutoren again.

He reaches into his drawer and takes out the small, copper emblem to trace the Kaidara feather with his thumb, before flicking it into the air and catching it again in his palm.

"Mutoren," Satoru says to himself, smiling. He pauses. He thinks of her weird mask, and laughs. "You are really bad at art."

✽

Over the next few days, the households of Shinrin receive big news from the palace—Prince Takashi is looking for a young lady! A young lady to act as the first-hand guard in the absence of Sir Leon and Sir Kinali. Something no one has ever heard of before.

The citizens are gossiping that, in fact, Prince Takashi is actually looking for an Empress. He must finally be looking to take on the title of an Emperor! It appears that the prince has an eye for ladies with dark hair and dark eyes!

✽

Back in the House of Harlande, the family are sitting

around the dinner table, when there is a *tap tap* on the kitchen window. A red bird with beady eyes peers into the warm light coming from the dining room.

"A Ketu!"

Eirlys puts down her chopsticks and gets up from the table. She opens the window and takes out the small scroll from between the bird's wings. It is lined with a crisp, golden border, tied together with a golden string.

"A message from the palace," Eirlys says.

Sana stops mid-chew and her nostrils widen. *What now?* She looks at her sister and swallows. That mouthful was particularly dry.

Delwyn reaches for some steamed vegetables and plops some onto his bowl of rice. "Read it for us."

"Dearest citizens of Shinrin," Eirlys reads. "Prince Takashi is looking for a young lady to act as his first-hand guard in the absence of Sir Leon. The young lady should be between the ages of sixteen and six-and-twenty. She must have a strong background of combative skills and have dark hair and dark eyes—" Eirlys stops mid-sentence and looks at Sana.

Oh, Sana thinks. She relaxes a little. Perhaps this means he is not planning on revealing her identity after all.

"Is it just me, or is he practically describing you,

Sister?" Eirlys laughs. "More like the prince is looking for a *wife*," she continues.

"Heavens," Elian chimes in. "Is our prince finally looking for a lady? About time."

"Why would a guard need to be a particular age and have a particular hair and eye colour?" Delwyn asks innocently. "Surely it can be anyone as long as they can fight."

Eirlys scoffs. "Like I said, it's more like he is looking for a *wife*."

"What—what else does it say?" Sana asks. Perhaps she can use this chance to meet the prince, actually. Then, she shall use her Mutoren ways to make him forget their whole encounter after she reclaims her emblem.

"If a young lady meets these criteria, she must sign her details on this script and return it via the Ketu which delivered this missive. A carriage will be sent to these households in two weeks' time and each young lady will meet with Prince Takashi to undergo a series of interviews and combative demonstrations. This is a gentle reminder that every household must remain truthful and requests from the palace must not be ignored. Warmest regards, the Palace of Shinrin." Eirlys finishes and looks at Sana again. "Who knew my sister is

the prince's ideal type?" Eirlys comments quietly.

Sana pretends to look offended for she is not someone who would jump at this sort of opportunity. She does not want her family to get suspicious.

"I'm not going," she states firmly.

"Sana, it is not every day you get an invitation from the prince," her mother says gently. "It is a rare opportunity to secure a place on the palace grounds."

"What about my studies?" Sana replies.

"There will be a way around it," her mother reassures. "Anyone who has a place amongst the palace will have all their needs catered for. You know how it is."

"I—I can't," Sana replies.

Although . . . *should* she be flattered that the prince is still looking for her, despite her having attacked and injured him? Anyway, she will make him forget all of this.

"You are a gifted girl. What is worrying you so much so, my child?" her mother asks.

"This is also a gentle reminder that requests from the palace must not be ignored," Eirlys whispers. She blinks and looks from her mother to her sister.

"Elian, give the poor girl a chance to digest. Come here." Delwyn beckons to his daughter.

Sana gets up slowly and shuffles towards her father

before plopping down next to him.

Delwyn puts a comforting arm around her. “Sana, I know how you are, but you know we cannot ignore the palace requests. Go and see how it is. If you do not like it, I am sure you can leave. Shinrin is a fair kingdom and Prince Takashi is one of the greatest rulers we have ever had. If you don’t try it out, you will never know how it will be, right?” He smiles reassuringly.

“Give me some time to think about it tonight,” Sana whispers. Her facial expression is blank. She gets up slowly and leaves the dinner table.

Her family watch her in silence.

Eirlys blinks. “Will she be alright?”

“Of course, she will be. The palace is the safest place in the kingdom,” Delwyn replies. “Knowing her, she will excel in whatever she is asked of when she gets there.” He looks towards the red bird who is trying to peck at some rice grains which have fallen onto the dinner table. “Looks like you’ll be staying with us tonight,” Delwyn says.

✾

Sana lies on her bed and stares at the ceiling in the dark. The fan goes round and round. She tucks her hair behind her ears and sighs.

Prince Takashi. The righteous ruler of the land with a handsome face. What does he want from her? Is he going to naively ask her to return his necklace? Is he going to capture her and throw her into palace confinement?

Sana flips over and buries her face in her arms. She had become the Mutoren and set herself on a mission. Her unmasking has really made things turn. Now, the prince is becoming a rather large hindrance, and things may be becoming more serious.

Sana reassures herself that, after she manages to make the prince forget all of this, she shall continue with her mission as if this encounter never happened.

Sana sighs and flips back around as she stares at the ceiling once again. She thinks about how, over the years, she has made a name for herself and has become one of the most wanted beings in Shinrin.

The *Mutoren*. The half-spider creature, feared by all.

The *man* who has stolen five of the most powerful treasures in the Kingdom. The *creature* who can get past any guard. The one who always outwits the prince and the case which the population of Shinrin are always hungry to hear more about.

Little did her family know, that the very Mutoren of Shinrin is sitting right underneath their roof.

CHAPTER SIXTEEN

Remembrance

SINCE THE TRAGEDY OF THE Hinoki Village Massacre, Satoru commanded for the body of every victim to be carefully retrieved, cleansed, and laid to rest. He also started village restoration.

His royal cart comes to a halt. Tonight, two months on from the tragedy, he has come to the village himself to give a formal send off to the victims.

Satoru can see many civilians from various other villages of Shinrin have already gathered here in Hinoki

at the site of the newly laid cemetery.

As he steps off the cart, the villagers who have gathered immediately bow towards him. He can see that candles have been lit at the front of the cemetery. Many of the villagers also hold candles in their hands. They look solemn, and some have tears falling from their eyes. It is a heart-breaking sight.

"Good evening, my dear citizens of Shinrin," Satoru begins. The heaviness pulls at his heart. How can such an awful tragedy like this happen in his very own land? The kingdom of Shinrin had always been peaceful, safe, and harmonious.

He thinks of his dear friend, Akalin, and his family—of Master Erol Kinali, who was his main trainer, the one who helped hone his combat skills. Satoru's heart sinks further and his throat dries up.

What has happened is so unexpected; it has shocked the whole kingdom.

He takes a moment before beginning to speak again. "I thank all who have come to join us in person tonight." He pauses to light himself a candle. "What has happened here in Hinoki Village is an awful tragedy. I am sure many of you are frightened, confused, and angry."

He notices the look of despair and sadness in the

villagers' eyes.

"Shinrin is a land of peace and harmony, and what has happened is extremely unjust. Since the unfolding of this tragedy, I have sent soldiers from the royal grounds to patrol, protect, and bolster the security of each village. I have launched further investigations to find and locate the perpetrators and I will ensure they are rightfully punished for their crimes."

"Prince Takashi," a middle-aged woman speaks up, tears in her eyes. "Do we know who did this yet, and where the children have been taken to?"

She begins sobbing. Her husband pats her on the back.

"As of the moment, milady, we have found some evidence. However, there is much left unknown. We will disclose the news to our citizens once we have more confirmation."

The woman sobs harder.

A little boy standing next to her speaks up. "Prince Takashi," he says, wiping some tears from his eyes. "My friend was from Hinoki. Will I ever see her again?"

"I have sent many of my soldiers to the places that may have additional information to investigate this further," Prince Takashi answers. "We aim to find the children and to rescue them. I understand this is

distressing."

"Oh, Prince Takashi." An elderly man's voice wavers and cracks as his grief overspills. "My heart is broken. Please, we need you, as our leader, to solve this catastrophe."

"We will do our very best," Prince Takashi answers. "I hope that, for now, my dear citizens can feel reassured that Shinrin will continue to be a safe land and that we will bring justice."

"Prince Takashi—" a middle-aged man starts. "I fear Shinrin is becoming unsafe." He trembles slightly. "Aside from the Hinoki village massacre, there are dead bodies appearing along our riverbanks. Have we found a cause for this? I've heard there is an evil spirit amongst us. We dare not let our children play near the riverbanks anymore."

This mention of the killings and its exacerbating threats causes Satoru's heart to sink. His fear of his citizens losing faith in him as a leader is beginning to play out.

"As the leader of Shinrin, I am responsible for maintaining the safety of our land," Satoru says as he acknowledges the man's worries. "We are working our hardest to protect our kingdom. I understand our investigations are taking longer than expected, but I've

already implemented some additional safety measures."

Satoru sighs internally, disappointed in himself at how he handled this response. His mind is not working as well as it usually does tonight.

"Oh, Prince Takashi," the man replies. "You are our great leader and we have utmost faith in you. We are just so frightened with everything that is happening. Please, do your best, Your Majesty!"

Hearing the encouragement from this citizen eases the anxiety inside Satoru just a little. He takes a moment before placing his candle onto the altar at the front.

"Our hearts are with the victims and their families. Let us take a moment of silence to remember our dear citizens of Hinoki village. May they all rest in peace," Satoru speaks.

He crosses his right arm over the front of his chest, and immediately, the villagers surrounding him do the same. Satoru closes his eyes and leans forwards slightly. There is pain clutching at his heart. He thinks of the Kinali family, as well as the many innocent civilians who had their lives so unjustly taken from them.

This gesture, the *Saludel,* is an expression of mourning, loss, and grievance. He performs it again, and the villagers mimic it a second time.

The flames of the candles flicker in the evening

wind as a sorrowful atmosphere drapes over the desolate village of Hinoki.

CHAPTER SEVENTEEN

The Knight

SATORU WAKES UP. HE OPENS his eyes and looks up at his ceiling. It has been fourteen days since he sent out his major announcement in search of the Mutoren.

The whole population of Shinrin are bustling about how the prince is looking for a wife. He tries to swallow the feeling of discomfort and reminds himself of why he is doing this. It is for the greater good. Yes. The greater good.

There is a knock at the door.

"Come in," Satoru answers, without moving an

inch.

The wooden door creaks open slowly. The top of Ryota's head pokes through. "Prince Takashi—" He then notices the prince laying in his bed clothes and his eyes widen with shock. "My apologies!" His head disappears as he tries to shut the door.

"Ryota, tell me," Satoru says. He sits bolt upright and, as Ryota's head pokes back around, the prince looks him straight in the eye.

"Master Takashi—please excuse me. There is already a trail of carriages outside the palace. I know you said the day will begin at noon but . . . there appears to be quite a lot to get through—"

Satoru turns to look out the window. The sun is just rising. He closes his eyes for a moment as a feeling of dread flows through him. There is so much happening recently that he is starting to get a pounding headache. He has an urge to let off some steam, but somehow manages to suppress this feeling.

He then turns to face Ryota. "That is fine. Is all the combat skill equipment in the forests prepared?"

"Yes, Your Majesty. Exactly as you have planned."

"And the guest rooms are all set for every lady that will turn up?"

"Yes, Your Majesty."

"Please, do not forget the Odeen."

"The Odeen are very much prepared and ready, Your Majesty."

"Very well, Ryota. I will be up and ready soon. In the meantime, please command the palace servants to serve all those who have arrived in carriages some light refreshments. Thank you."

"Of course, Your Majesty," Ryota replies and bows as he closes the door.

Satoru gets up and strides towards his dressing table before sitting down and peering at himself in the mirror. He looks tired. His emerald eyes look dull and his hair appears to have lost its shine. Why does he look so miserable? Perhaps it is because he is indeed miserable.

He pulls open the drawer and as he reaches for his comb, he notices the stack of parchment on the Mutoren. He blinks.

Will she be here today? He takes his comb and starts to pull it through his raven-coloured hair. His hand motions become more and more ferocious until he suddenly frowns and looks back at himself in the mirror.

Of course, she will. One cannot ignore requests from the palace. He nods to himself.

He has a sudden impulse to make himself ultra-presentable today, although he is unsure why.

He pulls his long hair into a high ponytail before locking it in place with a gold and azure ring. He picks out one of his most lavish robes, those made with the finest arctic blue silk, trimmed with golden seams, and embroidered with hand sewn sapphires. The colours bring out the green in his eyes and almost make them look turquoise. To finish, he pumps a few sprays from a small glass bottle onto his neck. He now smells like the birth of Shinrin's finest forests.

He looks at himself again in the mirror. The frustration he felt a moment earlier has disappeared and he now feels like he can take on the world.

✾

Satoru strides out towards the main entrance of the palace. From afar, he can see a long queue of carriages and some guards are helping the ladies step out of them. There is already a line of young ladies standing outside. There are servants serving them light refreshments, just like he has requested.

Satoru shields his eyes from the sun with his hand as he walks closer.

One of the ladies notices him and gasps. "Oh, it's

Prince Takashi!" she exclaims, before putting her hand over her mouth.

In unison, all the ladies turn to face him. The extra effort he put into his appearance today appears to have dazzled them completely, so much so that they appear to be struggling to keep eye contact with him. He notices one of them wobble on her feet before her eyes close. She collapses backwards.

He quickens his pace and just in time, catches her as she falls into his arms.

"Are you alright, milady?" Satoru asks her. His gentle voice flows out of his slightly parted lips as his face graces with genuine concern.

The young lady opens her eyes and tries to fan herself with her hand. She suddenly gasps and a small, strange noise escapes her mouth as she looks at the most perfectly sculpted face she has ever seen.

"My dear lord, an angel has fallen from the heavens," she whispers before the prince's scent hits her, making her swoon. Within the next second, she falls completely limp in his arms.

Satoru blinks at the lady. He looks up, his eyes wide. "Please, may we have some help—"

The other ladies look at him in awe and, soon enough, two others become weak at the knees and

slowly drop towards the ground.

Satoru looks around and turns his head briskly from left to right. "What is happening?"

"Please, Your Majesty," one of the guards says hurriedly as he bows to the prince. "Please wait inside. It appears your presence is too much for the ladies to handle. Leave this to us."

Satoru's eyebrows raise in confusion as the guard gently carries the lady from his arms to the side.

This is going to be a long day.

✾

Due to the overwhelming number of ladies that have turned up, Satoru has had to start the day a lot earlier than he expected. He sits on his grand throne at the top of the royal crimson carpeted stairs in the main hall. Ryota stands close next to him.

There are guards lined around the perimeter of the room. The palace artist stands in a corner and begins to paint the scene, for the prince looks even more strikingly handsome than usual—he has already caused three ladies to faint before the day has even begun.

This is the news that the whole of Shinrin will be dying to know about over the next few days.

✽

The line of young ladies begins near the entrance to the grand hall. Rows and rows of lavish, red chairs are set out for each lady to take a seat.

A guard starts the announcement. "Good morning, ladies," he begins. "It is an honour to welcome you all to the great palace of Shinrin today. As we all know, our Majesty, Prince Takashi, is looking for a new lady to stand as the first-hand guard in Sir Leon's absence."

He takes a breath before continuing.

"You are to bow as you enter, stand on the golden cross marked in the centre of the room, and say your name. Do this in the following order—your surname, followed by your first name, and then surname again. After this, please bow and wait, and then answer any questions that Prince Takashi may have. You will be asked to drink a small amount of Odeen, which will reveal one's original eye and hair colour."

The guard pauses and extends his arms in front of him, checking how much of the announcement is left on the scroll.

"When the prince nods, please make your way towards the exit. A guard will then escort you to the ballroom, where you may wait and have any

refreshments you may like. Stay there until you get called for the interview or combative skills demonstration. This may or may not happen today."

The guard pauses and takes another huge breath.

"Please bear in mind there are many candidates. As such, the prince has many ladies to assess. This process may last several days, during which we thank you for your patience. Each candidate has a guest room to stay in inside the palace. If you require any amenities, please do not hesitate to ask. We hope you enjoy your stay, and we wish you the best of luck for the selection process. Any questions?"

The guard wipes his brow after finishing his extraordinarily long announcement. He looks at the scroll of parchment and amusingly turns it upside down, checking if he had missed anything.

"Oh, Prince Takashi is so kind to us," one of the ladies comments.

"Isn't he just wonderful? We are so lucky to have this opportunity," another agrees.

"I've been practicing my archery skills. I cannot wait to show him," a third chimes in.

The guard looks around the room at all the ladies, overwhelmed by how many there are; the queue goes all the way outside the palace and servants still have not

finished laying out all the chairs.

"Please take a seat, ladies," the guard says, before gesturing to another guard standing by the entrance to the great hall.

This guard bows and offers a hand to the first lady by the entrance. "Milady," he says.

The first young lady takes his hand as he leads her out into the great hall. She nervously enters and is immediately overwhelmed by the number of people inside. Sure enough, she sees the golden cross in the centre, steps onto it, and looks up towards Prince Takashi before falling into a deep bow.

✾

Ryota stands next to Prince Takashi, fiddling with the tassels on his uniform.

He sniffs. "Your Majesty, you smell nice today."

Satoru looks at him. Ryota cannot tell if his look is threatening or bewildered.

"Thank you," Satoru replies. He looks down at the golden cross in the middle of the room and wonders how long it will take him to get through this crowd of people. Just thinking about it makes his core sink.

He notices the palace artist in the corner frantically flipping his brush away at the canvas. The scribe in the

other corner is scribbling away on a piece of parchment. Satoru adjusts his headpiece and takes a breath as he readies himself for what is to come.

A guard steps out into the room, bowing as he gestures a young lady towards the cross.

"Oh, here we go," Ryota says.

Satoru blinks.

The first young lady wobbles a little as she walks. She is dressed in a beautiful, rose-coloured robe and adorned with glistening jewels around her head and neck. Her dark hair is braided and twisted gracefully around her head. She looks up nervously at Satoru and quickly bows.

"My, isn't she beautiful!" Ryota comments.

Satoru turns to glare at him.

Ryota gathers that this look is more threatening than the last. He closes his mouth tightly.

Satoru thinks to himself. *Why is she dressed like that? I thought I said I am looking for a guard, not a ballroom dancer.*

"Fay. Adrienne Fay," the lady says quietly.

"Your age, milady," Satoru replies.

The young lady looks up nervously. "Eighteen, Your Majesty."

Satoru leans back in his throne and waits. Soon

enough, one of his guards appears with a small drinking glass in his hand. He walks towards the young lady and hands it to her as he bows.

"Miss Adrienne Fay," the guard says to her, "please take a sip of this Odeen. It is a palace requirement to ensure that all participants have been truthful about their appearance."

The lady nods a few too many times as she stretches out her hands and receives the glass. It nearly slips out of her palms, which are sweating. She looks at the liquid inside. It is of the darkest blue, with specks of glitter like midnight.

Miss Fay takes a small sip and hands the glass back to the guard. The crowd is silent. Satoru peers at her and waits for a few seconds. Suddenly, her braided hair transforms into the lightest of blonde. Satoru cannot see her eye colour as she is standing too far, but it most definitely appears lighter.

"Hm." Satoru grumbles through his fingers as he rests his chin on his hand.

He had a feeling some ladies would try to alter their appearance. Perhaps he should have asked his guards to give them the Odeen before they appeared in front of him. He sighs, thinking about how he had put together this plan too hastily.

This is going to be a very long day.

As soon as Miss Fay is escorted out of the room, the second lady comes through. She, too, is dressed very exuberantly.

"Masaki. Yamane Masaki," she says.

Satoru leans back in his throne once again and sighs.

This really *is* going to be a very long day.

❦

As the day rolls on, Satoru forgets how many ladies walk through the door. Most of them are dressed like they are attending some sort of ball or wedding, and Satoru is unsure if half of them can even lift a feather.

Do these ladies truly believe he is looking for a bride, despite that he made it clear he was looking for a guard?

Satoru shakes his head. He asked for their ages here and there, just to appear engaged, but deep down he cannot help but wonder: where is the Mutoren?

The scribe has written a pile of drafts to publish the next day and the artist is now working on his fifth portrait. They have had to stop the day twice for lunch and dinner already, and the palace kitchens are exhausted from a full day's work of providing constant meals and refreshments. Satoru is starting to feel like he is losing the will to live.

✽

Sana sits on one of the many puffy red chairs, swinging her legs as she tucks her hands under her thighs. She thinks about the elaborate scheme the prince has had to create just so he can find her again.

How many kudon must it be costing him to host this entire thing?

Although, it shouldn't be a problem for him. After all, he is the royal leader, and the richest man in the land.

However, is Prince Takashi just using this elaborate plan to hide his true intentions? Is he using this to put up a kind and righteous façade, when, in reality, he might lock her up and punish her for stealing the kingdom's most guarded treasures?

"Milady," a guard's voice interrupts her trail of thought.

Sana looks up and suddenly realises she is the only one left in the room. The chandelier above her head glistens brightly and it appears to be dark already outside. She looks at the guard, who bows towards her.

"Please." He holds out a hand.

I am the Mutoren, Sana thinks. Will they attack as soon as she steps out into the room? Will the prince

order all his guards to come at her all at once?

Sana takes a breath. She is prepared for anything. She strides towards the guard and is led into the great hall.

✾

Satoru rests his chin on his hand. Why does his head feel so heavy? Maybe his hair is too long. Or perhaps it is the headpiece he is wearing. It feels like his head is about to fall off his neck.

"Last but not least," the guard at the entrance says.

Satoru looks up. He does a double take. His eyes widen and, suddenly, his neck is strong enough to hold up his head once again.

Mutoren. You're here.

A surge of adrenaline rushes through Satoru and his heart begins to beat hard against his chest. A feeling of pressure suddenly overwhelms him, and he closes his eyes as he waits for it to pass. He then opens his eyes.

Her face is shining. It is a different feeling seeing her in the light. She stands right before him.

He has found her again at last.

Her slight frame looks like a breeze as she swiftly advances towards the golden cross. She is dressed in deep, teal fabric from head to toe. Her dark, shiny hair

is braided neatly, tied with a red ribbon, and falls in front of her left shoulder. This is what a real fighter looks like.

“Your name, miss,” the guard at the entrance whispers, trying to catch her attention. “Please tell the prince your name!” he whispers, slightly louder.

Sana doesn’t hear him. She kneels onto the golden cross on one knee, like a knight. Her eyes are fixated onto the ground. She looks so confident; the room falls silent. The palace artist pauses and pokes his head from around the canvas to catch a second glimpse at her.

“Wow. That is cool,” Ryota comments next to Satoru.

Satoru is still struck and speechless. “Show me your face, milady,” he manages to say, after a while.

Sana looks up and looks him straight on, dead in the eye.

Satoru is taken aback by the intensity in her eyes. She has round, innocent, dark eyes, like a vedeir.

“Your name, please?” Satoru asks. His ears perk up as he prepares to hear her name.

“Lishuah. Gudeya Lishuah,” the Mutoren replies confidently.

Ryota raises his eyebrows. “Interesting,” he comments, cocking his head to one side. “Never heard a

name like that before."

Satoru, too, is surprised. It sounds somewhat familiar.

"Your age, Lishuah," Satoru asks.

The Mutoren smirks a little—it is the mischievous smirk Satoru remembers, the one she sent him just before she struck him in his stomach.

"Twenty, Your Majesty."

"And where are you from?" Satoru queries.

Ryota raises his eyebrows. Up until this point, the prince had only asked, at most, one question to each lady throughout the day, if not, none at all.

"Shinrin," she answers simply.

Satoru narrows his eyes. He decides to stop here before he appears suspiciously interested. Soon, a guard steps out and Satoru watches as the Mutoren takes a sip of the Odeen. Nothing happens.

He nods, as the Mutoren breezes past him.

Gudeya Lishuah, Satoru says again inside his head. Interesting.

✾

Satoru is exhausted after a long day of looking at a crowd of people he cannot remember. The process took a lot longer than he expected. However, a part of him is

chuckling victoriously at the fact that the Mutoren really turned up.

He lies in his royal bathtub, enjoying the warm water against his skin. Cherry blossom petals float along the surface. He closes his eyes and leans back, allowing himself to relax for a moment.

His long, silky hair flows around him. His mind is stuck on one thing and one thing only. The Mutoren. At last, he has found her. He is sure she holds the answers to many of his questions. She shall help him with this case of the killings.

But he is going to have to calculate things very quickly; from his limited interactions with her, he can tell she is very quick witted.

Gudeya Lishuah . . . her name drifts into his mind. Why does it sound so oddly . . . familiar?

He says it a few times in his head, enjoying his newfound knowledge. He suddenly cocks his head to one side and says it out loud so that his own ears can hear.

"Gudeya. Lishuah," Satoru says aloud.

Li . . . shuah. His eyes widen as he realises. He stands up from the water, so abruptly that a wave gushes over the sides of the bathtub and petals scatter onto the bathroom floor. He realises why it sounds familiar.

It is the ancient tongue of Shinrin.

Li. Shuah. You lost.

"Oh, you little—"

Satoru catches his bare reflection in the grand mirrors in front of him. His face is twisted into a look of shock and his mouth hangs from his jaw. There are petals stuck to his skin like the crumbs on the cheeks of a child who just ate a messy meal, and his wet hair is splattered across him like a drowned rat. It is an absolutely ridiculous sight. He plops back down into the bathtub, sending another gush of water over the rim. He hits his forehead with his palm.

He cannot decide whether to be offended or impressed. Not many people in today's age know the ancient tongue of Shinrin. It is largely historical, and barely used. Yet this girl has simply made a fool of him right in front of the palace. This Mutoren is something else.

"Twenty, is it?" he asks himself, wondering if there was any truth in what she said.

He hastily dries himself off and pulls on a robe before stepping into his chamber. He strides towards his bookshelf and pulls out a dictionary on the ancient tongue.

Gudeya . . . Gudeya . . . Satoru thinks as he flicks

through the pages, searching for its meaning. His eyes dart left and right. The ancient tongue is so rarely used that he is struggling to remember what this word means.

His eyes catch onto it. *Stomach ache.*

Satoru shakes his head in disbelief. "You—"

Stomach ache. You lost.

Satoru repeats this again in his mind as he remembers the small smirk on the girl's face. *Mutoren, you are something.*

CHAPTER EIGHTEEN

Gullna

"MOTHER, WHERE ARE WE GOING?" an eight-year-old Satoru asks. He wobbles from side to side as the wheels of the carriage they are sitting in turn over the gravelly road they are travelling on.

Satoru looks at his mother and father—the Empress and Emperor of Shinrin—who are sitting opposite him. His mother, Empress Ruolan Takashi, is a beautiful and powerful woman. Although she has an outward demeanour of utmost poise and elegance, her heart is of the purest kindness and she is nothing short of demure.

Her long, raven locks are tied up delicately underneath her royal headpiece. Her eyes are of the deepest crimson, and they look like rubies against her pale skin. Despite her beautiful countenance, it was her humble heart that the emperor fell for.

Her husband, Emperor Miyahira Takashi, is sitting next to her. He is the great ruler of Shinrin and a proud man, standing at six feet and three inches tall. He boasts a muscular build and a face with a handsome, sharp jawline, dark spiky hair, and a trimmed beard. A scar crosses over his left eye, a remnant from the many battles he fought through and survived. His eyes glisten the colour of emeralds, just like his son's.

"We are going to meet a special friend today, my child," Satoru's mother responds.

A friend? Satoru thinks. He isn't interested in making any friends. He has his brother Satoshi, and that is all he needs.

Satoru leans out of the window of the carriage and watches as the trees go by. He hears the *trot trot* of the horse's hooves and thinks about how brother Satoshi would let him sit in front when he rode his stallion, and Satoru would feel like he was flying. He is too small to ride big horses like his brother and has only just started to practice riding ponies.

The carriage comes to a halt. The door opens and the old man who steered the carriage pops down before bowing to them deeply. Satoru's mother and father step off in front of him. Satoru follows.

"Your Majesty. Young prince," he says.

Satoru finds himself standing in front of a large, cobbled cottage in the middle of the countryside. The entrance looks warm and welcoming, and a friendly looking, middle-aged lady hurries down the stone steps towards the King and Queen. Satoru stands close behind his mother.

"Your Majesty!" The woman bows deeply. "I thank you sincerely for visiting us today."

She looks at Satoru. He is dressed in an amethyst-and-golden-coloured robe with his black hair tied up high in a ponytail.

"Oh, and don't you look charming today, young prince!" the lady comments. She hurries back up the stairs and opens the old, wooden door of the cottage.

Satoru follows his parents up the stone steps as they head inside. There is a friendly, cosy atmosphere. A few soft couches surround a warm fireplace. Satoru notices a wooden sign hung on the wall with a flower and some writing etched onto it: *Daisy Farm*. A small, brown dog with a long torso and short legs runs towards Satoru, his

tail wagging.

Satoru notices and points at the creature. “Sausage dog!” He then crouches down and pats the dog on his head. “Hello, Sausage.”

“Please, take a seat, Your Majesties,” the lady says.

Satoru’s mother and father sit down by the fireplace.

“Thank you, Lady Jane,” his mother replies.

Lady Jane comes back with a large book and starts flicking through the pages. “Ah—”

Satoru’s mother politely interrupts. “Please. Satoru, my child, why don’t you go and have a look around the place with that lovely young lady over there whilst we have a chat?” She gestures to a friendly looking young lady standing by the counter.

Satoru does as he is told and plods towards the lady who politely bows towards him and leads him away from his parents.

“Is this a farm?” Satoru asks the lady.

“Yes, my prince, but it is also an orphanage. We care for children who do not have parents until they find a new home.”

Satoru nods. He has no idea why he is here. He peers out the large windows and notices a large, green field. Children are running around happily, playing.

"It is their playtime," the lady adds. She smiles at Satoru. "Can I get you anything to drink, my prince?"

Satoru shakes his head. "I am fine. Thank you, miss," he replies.

The lady gushes over at how adorable he is before going off to get him something to drink anyway.

Satoru looks at the children running around. It reminds him of when brother Satoshi was practicing his combat skills in the forests and Satoru would run around pretending to be his brother's target.

Satoru then notices a young boy sitting on a stone ledge next to the slides. His back is turned. Satoru wonders what he is looking at. He seems to be very far away from the rest of the children. His short, golden hair shines brightly even though he is sitting some distance away.

Satoru hears Lady Jane talking in the background.

"Your Majesty, I thank you for travelling all this way, but are you both sure you would like to meet the boy imminently? The poor boy doesn't speak. Perhaps we can try something more gradual once he has had more time to work with our psychiatrist? It has been three months but the poor boy has yet to mutter a word."

"Remind me of how this boy got here, please?"

Satoru hears his father reply.

"He was rescued from Cerne, My Lord. His family home was destroyed by a bear. He was discovered a week later, malnourished and in critical condition. His mother, father, and what appears to be an older sister were found dead at the scene, My Lord. For the past six months, he was in the care of an orphanage in Cerne, but due to their shortages of food and supplies, they contacted the services in Shinrin for help. They were running low on fuel and there weren't enough supplies to keep the homes heated," Lady Jane continues.

"Poor boy," Satoru's father replies. "And, my dear, how did you come to know about this child?" he asks his wife.

"I have been looking into finding Satoru a new friend for a while now, my dear," Satoru's mother answers. "You know how he is—such a well behaved and studious boy. But without interacting with the world outside the palace, he is not getting the opportunity to make many friends. And since we broke the news to him that Satoshi will be leaving soon, he has become a lot more closed in on himself. This boy is around the same age as our Satoru."

I don't need a friend, Satoru thinks to himself.

"Is the boy mute?" his father asks. "Or does he just

not speak the common language?"

"We do not know, my lord," Lady Jane replies. "But according to the staff at the Cerne orphanage, the boy has never spoken. The child psychiatrist believes the boy is suffering from post-traumatic stress disorder and that his loss of speech is a severe reaction to the event."

"And how is his health physically?" Satoru's mother asks.

"Physically, he is in a much better condition now," Lady Jane reassures.

"Do we have any more information? What is his name?" Satoru's father asks, peering over at the large book in Lady Jane's arms.

"I'm afraid not," she replies. "We do not know his name. But here, we call him Gullna. At Cerne, they called him that—it means 'golden' in their language. He appears to respond to it."

The young lady who showed Satoru around earlier suddenly reappears with a glass of orange juice and a plate of doughy mochi. "My prince, I'll leave these here on the table for you!" She smiles at Satoru.

Although Satoru declined earlier, he peers at the plate; the round, beige-coloured mochi look quite appetising. He picks one up and plops it into his mouth. It is peanut flavour. He then takes the glass and sips on

the orange juice, still looking at the golden-haired boy in the distance.

They must be talking about him, he thinks, linking the word "Gullna" with the boy's hair.

"Let's introduce Satoru to the boy today then," he hears his mother say. "We can see how they get on."

Satoru pops another mochi in his mouth. He thinks. *Cerne is quite far away, is it not?*

From his geographical knowledge, Cerne is some distance up in the north, with a sea separating it from Shinrin. It has a sparse population and is a land of snowy mountains and glaciers. He has studied this country quite a bit—amongst others—and is familiar with the country's basic culture and etiquette. However, although, he already speaks five languages fluently at his age of eight, he has only started learning Cernese not too long ago and feels only intermediate at his current level.

His parents suddenly appear next to him and Satoru sees Lady Jane step out onto the fields and walk towards the golden-haired boy. Once she reaches him, she takes him gently by the hand and leads the boy back inside.

"Satoru, be ready to meet your new friend," his mother says to him gently.

"I know," Satoru replies quietly. "I heard." *But I don't*

want a new friend, Satoru thinks.

His father nods and gestures to him to introduce himself to the boy.

Satoru looks at the boy standing in front of him. They are the same height and appear to be around the same age. He has short, golden hair and solemn, sad, sapphire eyes. His skin is pale and his sombre expression makes him look tired. He is wearing a simple, white cloth shirt and brown trousers.

"Hello. I am Satoru," Satoru says, and holds out a hand, expecting a handshake.

The golden-haired boy looks slowly from Satoru's hand to his eyes. He remains silent.

Satoru looks back towards his mother, who is smiling and nodding at him encouragingly. Satoru takes back his hand and decides to try a different approach.

"*Ciena, Gullna,*" Satoru says. *Hello, Golden.* Satoru holds the back of his right hand flat against his own forehead, showing the boy his palm and bows slightly. He speaks in Cernese and gestures their way of greeting, hoping he is doing it right.

Gullna lifts his eyebrows slightly and his blue eyes glisten with slight surprise. He looks at Satoru.

"*Mei ileumya Satoru,*" Satoru continues. *My name is Satoru.*

Gullna blinks.

"*Jinaye sota Shinrin. Mei mag tono gullna tomen,*" *Welcome to Shinrin. I like your golden hair.*

Satoru's mother and father are smiling and nodding. Lady Jane has a pleading look in her eyes, as if hoping everything will be all right.

Gullna blinks a few times, looks at the floor, then looks at Satoru. He rubs his nose a few times with his sleeve, to which Satoru is unsure what to make of it.

"Perhaps we should step aside?" Lady Jane whispers. "To give them some space."

Satoru's parents and Lady Jane go back around the corner and Satoru finds himself alone with the boy. His father peeps at Satoru without him noticing.

Satoru notices the plate of mochi he was devouring earlier. He reaches out and holds it in front of Gullna. "*Tono mag ess so...so...*" *Would you like to eat some...some...*Satoru struggles to think of how to say mochi. He isn't sure this word exists. "*So...feiy...nol?*" *Some...rice...sweets?* Satoru thinks is what he said.

Unexpectedly, Gullna's solemn mouth turns up slightly into a smile as he struggles to hide some laughter. There is a slight sparkle in his sapphire eyes.

Little did Satoru realise that what he just said was, *Would you like to eat some hamsters?*

The golden-haired boy reaches out and takes a mochi before popping it in his mouth. His small cheeks are puffy as he chews. He then looks at Satoru.

"Ciena," he whispers. *Hello.* The boy is barely audible.

Satoru stares back, stunned.

"Mei ileumya Arubeto Leonei." My name is Albert Leon.

CHAPTER NINETEEN

The Deal

IT WAS VERY LATE IN the night by the time Satoru finished bathing himself and recovered from the embarrassment of the Mutoren's mischievous schemes. Once composed, he commanded Ryota and the palace guards to filter through every single signed acceptance letter from every lady's household until they found the one which belonged to the last candidate at the introductory ceremony. He had ordered for it to be delivered straight to his chamber door and now he waits on his bed staring at nothing.

His ears perk up as soon as he hears something slide underneath his door. He gets up in such a hurry, he nearly trips over.

Satoru bends and hastily picks up the piece of parchment. He strides back to his bed and sits. Just as he is about to unfold it, he suddenly stops, and then wonders why he is hesitating. He takes a breath and unfolds it slowly.

His eyes glance over the generic announcement from the palace until it reaches the bottom line. There, signed in rough, un-lady-like script, is a name.

Sana Harlande.

Satoru gulps as he drops the parchment onto his crossed legs and snaps his eyes forwards. He looks at the wavering flame of his candle and remembers the day when it suddenly went out—the day he and the Mutoren first met in his very chamber.

He glances back down at the script. It looks like it was written quickly and carelessly.

Sana Harlande, he repeats to himself inside his head.

He leans back and lets his mind wander. Since the Mutoren case first began, he had been obsessed with it. It was his main focus amidst the many cases he worked on . . . at least until the dead bodies started to appear.

After so many years thinking about the Mutoren,

he'd thought he had uncovered so much, but it seems he was wrong.

He tries to organise his mind. *Sana Harlande, is it?* he thinks. *The radiant one. This contradicts the darkness of the Mutoren.*

He folds up the piece of parchment and tucks it into his dressing table drawer along with the rest of the Mutoren pile he has accumulated over the years. He takes out his bamboo flute, makes his way towards his window, and climbs out onto the roof.

The night breeze flows into the thin silks of his night clothes and through his long, soft hair. The cold is refreshing and he plays a soulful tune that is carried into the trees of the forests.

✤

Satoru wakes up before sunrise the next morning and hurries to his dressing table to ready himself for the day. Today, he wears a dark green robe laced with silver, and his long, black hair is braided into a sleek plait. He has decided that he will get straight to the point to speed things up. He already knows what he wants and he needs to get this over and done with. He will select the Mutoren and find a way to keep her here.

He needs to obtain as much information from her

as possible.

"Ryota!" Satoru commands.

His door opens immediately.

"Good morning, Your Majesty!" Ryota bows.

"I will make this quick and simple. I have my eye mainly on the last one who turned up yesterday. I will conduct her interview and combative demonstration to confirm my decisions. Thank the rest of the ladies and organise carriages to send them home today."

Ryota nods ferociously. "Yes, Your Majesty!" He salutes.

"When I am ready, ensure that girl is present."

"Yes, Your Majesty!" Ryota closes the door.

By the time the sun has risen higher in the sky, Satoru has finished three days' worth of paperwork already. The embarrassment of what happened is making him get through his tasks much more quickly as he tries to shake off that feeling. He puts down his calligraphy brush and makes his way out of his chamber, taking long strides towards the outside of the palace. He heads towards the Central Training Ground.

As he nears the clearing, he notices high wooden beams with a covering that overlooks the training ground—a place constructed for him to sit and spectate. He makes his way up the wooden stairs and spots Ryota

sitting in the middle, awaiting him.

Ryota stands up immediately and bows. “Your Majesty! We are ready for you, whenever you are ready.”

“I thank you for your help, Ryota,” Satoru replies. He sits down next to his guard. “Is the girl here?”

“She must be waiting in the interview room,” Ryota replies. “We asked her to wait until you were ready.”

“Bring her straight here. I am here now, so we will start her with combat.”

“Yes, Your Majesty.” Ryota stands and bows before asking another guard to fetch the young girl.

A few moments later, Satoru sees her.

Mutoren.

Today, she is dressed in the colour of slate. Her hair is braided differently, running from the crown of her head to the nape of her neck and secured with a red ribbon.

Satoru leans forward. “Lishuah,” he commands.

She kneels on one knee like she did before. “Your Majesty,” she answers calmly.

“When I raise my hand, that is the signal to show off your skills. Please, be prepared for anything,” Satoru states.

“Your Majesty, are you not going to introduce each

stage?" Ryota hurriedly whispers next to Satoru.

Satoru holds up a hand and Ryota quiets. He wants to see her fight.

"Bring out number one, please," Satoru states.

"One!" a guard shouts.

In a split second, twelve hand spears appear in all directions, headed straight for the girl. She is as still as stone and Satoru watches her round, obsidian eyes scan the area before she simply somersaults into the air, just in time for the spears to hit each other and fall to the ground. She lands softly on her feet next to them.

"Nice one," Ryota comments.

"Two, please," Satoru says.

A guard then shouts.

A strong, tall man of six-foot-five appears and lunges towards the girl. It is Liam, one of the palace training helpers, who often helps with testing the guards when it comes to strength and power. He swings out a large fist towards the girl.

Ryota covers his eyes. Satoru looks on, face full of concentration, his chin resting between his fingers.

The young girl moves her head to the side and dodges the fist before jumping up and twisting his neck ever so slightly with her feet—just enough to cause him discomfort and break his balance.

Liam falls to the ground before getting back up and patting his knees. Satoru notices a smirk on the girl's face, as if she is finding all of this too easy. He also notices that her movements are very different to how the Mutoren was that night.

Satoru frowns. "Three, please."

Ten men charge in all directions towards her. The Mutoren is as light as a feather on her feet. Her movements are swift and quick, and she manages to take all ten of them down, one by one, with softness and grace.

Ryota's eyes are wide.

Satoru continues to frown. *Is she putting on a show?* he thinks to himself. *This is not how the Mutoren fights. Where are her bizarre, spider-like movements?*

"Get me a spear, Ryota," Satoru commands.

"Sorry, Your Majesty?"

"A spear, please. Make that two."

Ryota blinks in alarm, but hurriedly gets up and orders that the prince's requests should be fulfilled. When a guard comes back with two spears, Satoru takes hold of them both and starts to walk down the wooden stairs towards the girl.

She bows.

"Lishuah," Satoru commands. "If you want to be my

first-hand guard, you will need to know how to fight with this." He throws a spear in her direction and watches as she catches it. It looks nearly twice her height.

"Show me what you have," Satoru states.

He lunges into the duel. His eyes are on the Mutoren. He is watching her, trying to calculate and pre-empt her actions. He studies her movements carefully now that they are in the daylight.

The Mutoren's grasp on the spear and the way she turns it are a little clumsy at first, but she picks it up very quickly.

Satoru notices that the Mutoren's flow, although amateur, is slick and adaptable. He is somewhat impressed that she can duel against him using a weapon she has not used much before. She is creative, making her an interesting opponent and making this duel different to all the duels Satoru has been in in the past. He is starting to enjoy this.

"Impressive," Ryota comments to himself from the wooden beams. "The last time I've seen a fight this exquisite was the one at the Showman Training Ground."

As the two of them duel, the Mutoren's face comes close to Satoru's as she tries to use her spear to defend against his advances. Their eyes meet briefly as they try

to overpower each other and, for a second, a thud throbs inside Satoru's head, causing him to lose concentration.

This happens just as the Mutoren moves back and swings her leg towards him. She almost gets into contact with Satoru, however, she lets herself swing back around without striking him, and as Satoru snaps back into this moment, he seizes this opportunity to trip her over by dislodging her spear.

She falls onto her back as Satoru knocks the spear out of her hand.

Why did she do that? Satoru thinks, as he looks upon her face, panting. She looks straight back at him with a smirk. It is almost as if Satoru can hear what she is saying through her eyes.

I let you win.

Satoru holds out a hand to help the girl up, but she brushes it aside and jumps back onto her feet without taking it.

Satoru takes a moment to breathe. "Please, guards. Let us go to the interviews," he commands. He thinks through the questions that he had planned.

✽

The prince's mind races as he makes his way towards the interview room. Why is he feeling so impatient?

Satoru and his guards sit down and the Mutoren follows, sitting opposite. She stares at him, straight on.

Satoru's mind goes blank and he forgets all the questions he had planned. "Lishuah, you say you are from Shinrin, is that correct?"

"Yes, Your Majesty."

"And your age . . . twenty, is it?"

"Yes, Your Majesty."

Ryota looks back and forth at the prince and the young girl. He has never heard the prince speak in such a harsh tone before and wonders if he is in a bad mood.

The prince frowns. "Are you studying?"

"Yes, Your Majesty."

"Studying what, please?"

"Music, Your Majesty."

Satoru raises an eyebrow. He isn't sure if anything he is hearing is true. He is unsure why he cannot think of anything important to ask.

Or does he feel like he is unable to say anything because there are too many people here?

"And do you do anything outside of your studies?"

"I practice my combat skills," she says simply. "As you can see."

Satoru stands abruptly, making the guards and Ryota jump. He looks like he is not having it.

"I am going to have to conduct the rest of this interview alone," he states, surprising the guards. "Follow me, girl." He gets up and leaves the room.

Ryota blinks a few times and shrinks back in his seat. "Is he angry?" he whispers to a guard sitting next to him.

The Mutoren carefully follows behind Satoru. Her eyes dart in all directions as she tries to figure out what will happen next.

Satoru leads her into an empty room further down the hallway. He watches as the girl steps inside before he closes the door.

Hopefully this works, Satoru thinks to himself. He had taken one of the hand blades from the training ground earlier. In a split second, he takes it out from his sleeve and throws it straight at the girl.

She disappears in a flash.

Satoru looks up, and there she is: spider-like, upside down, and hanging from the ceiling on her hands and feet.

He smirks. *This is more like it. Pesky Mutoren.*

Sana looks at him carefully. He wants another challenge *now*, does he?

"We meet again, Mutoren," Satoru says, picking up the blade. He looks up at her. "Stomach ache, is it?" He

raises an eyebrow.

"Took you some time," she replies. Her braid dangles down from the ceiling and there is a glint in her eyes.

Satoru senses no fear from her. Is she always this confident?

"Come down. I cannot speak to you when you are upside down—"

Without warning, the girl lunges at the prince, a foot aimed right at his face. Satoru's eyes widen as he dodges her just in time, before the Mutoren crawls like a spider along the floor at the speed of light, right towards him. Her limbs bend at odd angles and carry her across the floor. She then jumps up into a double spin before extending the back of her leg, again aiming at his head. A hook-kick.

As Satoru dodges her second attack, he throws a few kicks and strikes at her with speed in various directions, putting in trick moves at times to try and trip her up. He studies her quick reactions and notices how she is rapid with her defences. At times, she anticipates his moves, and at times, she falls into his traps, but her movements are so swift that, each time, she can defend and dodge, no matter what Satoru throws at her.

As the two of them duel, Satoru struggles to find a

way to describe her style of fighting. Her bizarre, yet impressive, movements do not appear to fall into any category of martial art that he is aware of, yet sometimes, she will throw out a round house kick or spinning axe kick, same as the traditional arts which he is much too familiar with.

Her ability to utilise space is something that has also caught Satoru's attention. At times, she is on the wall, and at times, she is on the floor. Unlike the traditional way of fighting upright and head-on, she is like an unpredictable, wild creature, moving and bending at angles he didn't know were possible. It is a different feeling, fighting with her in the daylight.

Sana's eyes are wide and blazing. The more they duel, the brighter the gleam in her eyes. Her mouth turns into a terrifying smile, displaying the excitement she is feeling. It is as if their fighting is lighting a fire inside her.

"Mutoren, I've come to ask you for a compromise," Satoru manages to say between pants as he tries to catch his breath whilst throwing a fist strike towards the girl's head.

She blocks him and holds out against his strength.

For a moment, the two of them are eye to eye. Then, the gleam in her eyes suddenly diminishes and,

as if deliberately, she lets go, causing Satoru to fall forwards towards her.

Satoru briskly holds out his hand as he falls towards the girl onto the floor, bracing himself from hitting her.

They are face to face as Satoru pants. She looks up at him.

Why is she smiling? For a moment, Satoru blinks at her.

"We seem to always end up like this, do we not?" she asks.

"Mutoren," Satoru says as seriousness returns in his voice. "I have revealed your identity, but as you can see, I have kept it hidden from the world."

"How courteous of you."

"You do know that you have committed a serious crime? Not just one, in fact, but many."

The Mutoren remains silent.

"Under normal circumstances, you would have been locked away in palace confinement and received the most serious punishment," Satoru states.

For the briefest of moments, Satoru notices a slight uneasiness creep over the Mutoren's eyes. She writhes slightly underneath him, as if wanting to get away. Satoru keeps his hand planted into the ground, pinning her with his weight. He looks straight into her eyes to

show that he means exactly what he says.

The uneasiness in the Mutoren's eyes disappears. She looks back at him with the indifferent, yet confident, expression she usually holds and speaks in her minimal and flat tone. "But?" she asks.

"But I have decided that you may be spared. Only if you remain as my first-hand guard for now and answer any questions I have," Satoru replies.

"And?"

"If you work with me, I will also not only ensure your family's welfare remains at the utmost, I will keep your identity sealed. I will not penalise you for your crimes, *Harlande.*"

Sana's eyes widen at the mention of her name. She ponders briefly and stares on as the prince holds his gaze, his green eyes burning into hers.

"Deal?" he asks.

There is a pause. Sana does not move an inch. Her eyes catch onto the emerald jewels embedded into the prince's hair.

"Deal," she whispers.

Satoru relaxes a little, before suddenly, the girl reaches out and plucks the emerald jewel out from his raven strands, taking him by surprise. Before he has time to react, there is an overwhelming smack as the girl

headbutts him on his forehead.

Satoru sits up in shock, just as the girl jumps onto her feet and disappears out of the door. As it closes behind her, there is the sound of a wooden beam falling with a thud to land horizontally across the door.

As Satoru holds a hand to his throbbing forehead, his other hand reaches onto the door handle, and he tries to push it open. It does not budge. He pauses and pushes again. The door does not open.

She locked me inside? Satoru thinks, exasperated.

He shakes his head and holds his hand across his temples, closing his eyes. He needs a moment. He sighs as he thinks about how to command his guards to come and open the door.

Honestly, this girl is something else.

CHAPTER TWENTY

Journey to Qieta

A YOUNG ALBERT WATCHES IN horror as the most frightening creature he has ever seen barges towards him. Her eyes are blazing red, her claws are the length of his arms, and her teeth are sharp daggers, ready to devour his soul.

"*Arubeto, tono himeta*!" *Albert, hide!* His sister screams at him as she pushes him to the side.

She stands in front of the creature and turns around to look at Albert as he tumbles. Her crystal blue eyes are wide with fear and the wind from the storm outside is

racing through her long, golden hair.

The creature's claws extend towards the girl and, in a flash, she swipes her out of sight.

"Aratas!" Astra! Albert screams.

✻

Albert jolts upright. His clothes are drenched. His eyes are wide. He pants and pants. After a while, his breathing starts to settle down.

He looks across him and his horse, Erwin, is curled up on the deck next to him, fast asleep. His white belly rises and falls.

Albert leans back and rests his head against the wall of the boat, breathing deeply.

It has been a long time since he has had this nightmare. He must really be feeling the fatigue from the past few weeks. He remembers the times as a child when he would have this nightmare multiple times a night.

It was the last time he ever saw his sister, and that scene would not stop replaying in his mind, haunting him in his sleep for years. Often, he would wake up screaming and crying, and on some occasions, he even wet the bed.

Each time, the prince would rush into his room and

comfort him until he calmed down.

Albert peers out of the window of the boat. The night sky is clear and the sea is calm. The stars glisten like jewels and remind him of his sister, Astra—they are just like her name. She is at peace now amongst the cosmos, along with his mother and father.

As he watches the stars sparkle, he suddenly wonders if he will ever go back to Cerne. He has not been there since he left at the age of eight. He wonders how it is there now. He says a small prayer to his family and shifts his mind to the journey ahead.

He departed on a boat to Qieta, as Prince Takashi requested. He wonders how the prince is doing and if there is any news about the dead bodies or the Mutoren. Once he reaches the island, he should send Prince Takashi a Kaidara as soon as possible.

The boat halts. One of the commanders of the boat walks down the deck and shouts through each window.

"Please, passengers for Qieta will need to disembark here!"

Albert gently wakes his horse before exiting his compartment and getting off the boat. It appears he and Erwin are the only ones leaving.

"To Qieta, sir?" a young man asks Albert.

"Yes," Albert answers.

The young man beckons for Albert to follow him. He leads him off and around the deck.

Albert is unsure where he is.

They walk a small distance and reach a white, sandy shore that connects to some shallow water. There is a small, wooden canoe with a young boy standing in it. There is something mystical about him. He has navy-coloured hair tucked behind his ears and he wears a white robe, very different to the usual robes in Shinrin. He holds onto a long, wooden paddle.

"You will have to board here," the young man advises Albert. "This is the only way into Qieta." He points at the canoe and the young boy.

Before Albert has a chance to respond, the young man hurries back the way they came and disappears.

Albert is unsure if the small, wooden boat will take the weight of both him and his horse, but the young boy holds Erwin by his reins and leads him aboard. The boat barely moves. He beckons for Albert to join them.

Albert steps onto the boat slowly and then sits. He is a little overwhelmed, as he has never journeyed so far out before. The journey had been quite tiring, and everything he is seeing is so unfamiliar.

The young boy remains standing at the very edge of the boat. He puts his long, wooden paddle into the

water and, soon enough, the boat drifts offshore.

They travel silently on the water, heading towards what appears to be a cave. As they enter, his vision struggles to make out a single thing in the complete darkness. Albert reaches out towards Erwin and holds his head close.

A speck of green light appears. It glows. The light expands, then diminishes. It then glows again. As Albert looks around, the whole of the inside of the cave slowly begins to illuminate with both green and cyan blobs of light. Albert turns to see Erwin looking around curiously. A single speck of light lands between his nostrils. Erwin looks down, his large beady eyes going cross-eyed.

"Fireflies?" Albert asks quietly. He has read about these magical insects in the scriptures, but never seen one in real life.

He turns to look at the young boy. The boy looks straight ahead, slowly paddling through the water. He does not respond. Albert continues to look around curiously, just like his ivory companion, and the two of them watch in awe as the glowing blobs circle around them and light up the mysterious path ahead.

Suddenly, the glowing lights above their heads disappear as the small canoe drifts out into the open.

Albert is under a night sky full of stars and a stripe of a glittery cloud stretches like a band above them.

The sky looks almost amethyst and it reflects onto the clearest waters he has ever seen. He looks down into the transparent sea surrounding the boat and curiously dips his fingertips inside.

Unexpectedly, the water is strangely mild—not cold like he assumed. There are schools of fish swimming past, the size of them about the length of Albert's palm. They leave white trails that glow behind them as they glide through the water.

Erwin's head arches close towards the sea as he also watches the fish glimmer in front of him. His tail swishes against the wooden boards of the boat as he watches excitedly, taking in the strange, new, yet calming environment around them.

Albert looks ahead and notices that they are now approaching land. There are large stone—or perhaps marble?—stairs arising from the transparent sea, leading onto the white landing of a mystical piece of architecture held up by porcelain pillars. Some pillars have fallen amongst the waters in a damaged but beautiful way.

The boat approaches the stairs. The young boy steadies the boat and steps down. His feet are bare and

they enter the water. He beckons to Erwin and helps him off the boat before looking towards Albert and nodding towards him, gesturing for him to follow. He bows and motions to them to continue ahead.

Albert steps onto the landing and takes a few steps forwards. He holds Erwin's reins tightly. He is unsure where to go or what to do.

He notices a young man walk towards him. He appears no older than his early twenties, and has long, sleek, jet-black hair that falls to his waist. He wears an elegant, ivory robe, tied in a way Albert has never seen before. An elegant, thin, silver headpiece is wired around his head.

"Sir Albert Leon, is it?" the young man asks.

Albert nods. He feels reassured that the young man appears to be expecting him. Prince Takashi had sent Albert a Ketu claiming he would find a way to send a message to Qieta via a Kaidara to alert them that Albert was coming.

The young man bows. "Follow me," he says.

Albert and his horse's footsteps are loud against the marble floor as they weave their way between the pillars and follow the young man. Soon, they find themselves standing in a grand, marble hallway with a tall, arched ceiling.

"Wait here. I will inform Liuana Pharlos of your arrival," the young man advises, before disappearing into the distance.

Albert stands patiently, holding onto Erwin's reins, and waits, taking in his new surroundings. There is certainly something very mystical about this place.

A few moments later, the young man returns alongside an elderly man; they take some time to reach him. His face is graced with lines of wisdom. He hobbles slowly, holding onto a silver staff that is twisted around a glowing lilac and blue orb which sits at the top. He wears an elegant, navy-and-silver robe with sleeves so long they drape along the ground. A few strands of white hair are all that is left on his head, and bushy white eyebrows cover his eyes.

The young man looks towards Albert and speaks. "Liuana is the honorific title we give to our spiritual guiders of the highest rank," he explains. "And Liuana Pharlos is one of the most highly respected." He bows.

The old man continues to shuffle towards Albert and stops when he reaches him. He strains his neck to meet Albert's gaze. "Hello, young Sir Leon of Shinrin," he says, as his bushy white eyebrows rise and reveal two, gleaming, shiny eyes. "Welcome to Qieta."

CHAPTER TWENTY-ONE

Lilium Sidereum

A YOUNGER DELWYN SETS HIS basket by the edge of the river and opens his small, cloth bag as he prepares his tools. He crouches on the grass and ties the laces of his left boot. It appears to have come undone during his journey here.

His wife, Elian, had fallen ill the past few days and is currently suffering a high fever. This winter had been particularly cold and unrelenting, but as a devoted botanist, Delwyn is grateful that his knowledge has

allowed him help treat his wife without having to request a visit from one of the village healers.

Due to the increasing number of villagers falling sick, healers have been in extremely high demand in recent months. As such, one request for a healer to visit may take days, if not weeks. Although Delwyn is unsure what may be causing his wife's illness, he knows that the Sadore plant, when brewed into tea, has properties to bring down a fever.

Today, he has travelled a few miles on foot from their home in Akamatsu to a nearby river, where Sadore flowers grow despite the cold temperatures. He spots a few swaying in the wind just at the edge of the waters.

"Father! Ducks!" a four-year-old Eirlys shouts. Her breath makes small puffs of mist in the cold, crisp air.

Young Eirlys had insisted on journeying with her father today, instead of staying home.

Delwyn's eyes follow his daughter's chubby pointing finger, and he sees four white ducks paddling down the river. His daughter runs along the bank towards the birds. Her little honey-coloured braids flap in the wind. He feels blessed to have such a wonderful daughter.

Eirlys turns around and shouts, "Father, are they not cold?"

"They look very content to me," Delwyn replies, and smiles. He gets to work and begins to pick out the Sadore flowers, putting them into his basket and then carefully plucking off the fragile, white petals. He pops them into small, glass bottles and secures each of them with a cork.

"Don't run too far from me, Eirlys," Delwyn gives a gentle warning as he continues to work. He looks up and notices his daughter's honey-coloured hair poking out above some long blades of grass further down the river. "Eirlys," Delwyn repeats more sternly this time.

His daughter does not move. Delwyn puts down his tools and begins to make his way towards her. As he approaches, her daughter pokes her little face out.

"Father," she says with wide eyes. Her little mouth is shaped into a surprised 'O.'

Delwyn suddenly hears the sound of a baby's cry. He raises his eyebrows in astonishment and hurries closer. There, he sees a small, brown basket trapped between the rocks of the river, containing something moving and tussling underneath some soft, blue blankets.

"My goodness," Delwyn says. "Eirlys, stay here," he says to his daughter.

He begins to make his way carefully towards the

basket, climbing onto the rocks. They are cold and mossy, and Delwyn gets onto his hands and feet to stabilise himself. The cold waters bite at his skin and his feet slide on the slippery boulders. He takes his time as his daughter looks on, worried.

Delwyn approaches the bundle and, sure enough, he finds himself looking at a tiny child nestled in the blankets. She squirms and cries.

Delwyn shakes his head in awe. "It is a miracle you are still alive," he whispers. He reaches out and holds the basket carefully, before slowly descending back down the rocks, his heart beating heavily in his chest.

Delwyn manages to make it onto the ground safely. He crouches next to his daughter before putting down the basket. As the baby shifts, the blankets fall to the side, revealing a copper chain tied loosely around her. He peers closely at the small feather carved onto it. There is also a sapphire lily laid next to her.

"My, is that lilium sidereum?" Delwyn asks curiously.

His daughter peers at the crying baby and then looks towards him. "She has a moon behind her ear!" Eirlys exclaims, pointing at the baby.

Delwyn looks towards his daughter's chubby finger and sees that, sure enough, there is a birthmark behind

the child's left ear. It looks like a crescent moon with slightly jagged edges.

Delwyn scoops up the child and opens his cloak. He holds her close to his chest, wrapping his cloak around the both of them to try to keep her warm. He picks up his baskets and tools bag in his other hand and beckons to his daughter.

"Let's make our way home," he says to Eirlys.

The two of them begin their long walk back to their village of Akamatsu.

✾

That night, Delwyn sits at his study. He peers through his reading spectacles at the pages in front of him. Earlier, he had brewed some Sadore tea for his wife, and both she and Eirlys are now sleeping soundly.

He looks at the sapphire lily laid on his desk before blowing out the candle and heading towards the window with the flower in his hand. He holds the stem carefully under the moonlight.

Slowly but surely, the blue petals open, revealing a delicate, soft, velvety inside. They are cobalt in colour and tinged with lilac in the centre. It glows beautifully.

Delwyn's eyes are wide as he looks at the flower in awe. "Lilium sidereum indeed," he whispers.

He hurries back towards his desk and places the flower carefully on a stand under a glass jar, then sets it next to the many mysterious and beautiful plants on his shelf. He then re-lights his candle and continues reading.

Lilium sidereum, the Starry Lily, also known more commonly as the Midnight Jewel, is a magical flower from the island of Qieta. This beautiful flower blooms only at night under the starry skies and gives off an ethereal, lilac glow. When given from one to another, this flower holds the meaning of the deepest love, respect, and sincerity.

Delwyn's eyes scan the text on the parchment quickly. He never thought he would see this magical flower in real life.

He holds a magnifying glass close to the petals and examines it. He then looks over at his couch. The mysterious child is now fast asleep in the warmth of their house. He ponders why such an innocent, helpless child would be abandoned in the harsh cold of the outside environment. He then wonders what she has to do with a magical, glowing flower.

His heart beats as he looks at her with a strong sense of love and protection. He wonders what magic has created this miracle, for they have been blessed with another daughter this day.

CHAPTER TWENTY-TWO

Connections

SINCE THE FOREST HAKKAN HAD begun laying down malachite over the walls of the kingdom two months ago, Satoru had not heard of any more news of the killings. He is unsure if this means his strategy is working or not, but at least, for the time being, his kingdom is at peace.

He makes his way to the palace tea rooms. Two guards by the entrance to the guest tearoom bow simultaneously.

"Prince Takashi!" they shout in unison.

"Good afternoon," Satoru says, and nods towards them.

The guards slide the two bamboo doors—lined with parchment screens—in opposite directions. Inside, an elderly man and woman dressed in smart robes kneel on soft plump cushions by the tea table. They immediately stand and bend forwards into deep bows.

"Your Majesty," they both say.

"Good afternoon, Mr. and Mrs. Tanaka," Satoru says. "Thank you so much for coming."

"It is our absolute pleasure," Kenta replies. "We are honoured to be invited."

"I am honoured to have you both as my guests," Satoru replies. He kneels onto a soft cushion opposite them. "Please, what tea would you like?"

Kenta looks at his wife.

"Oh, anything will do," Shizuko answers humbly.

Satoru looks towards the servant standing by the wall. "Please, may you ask for the assorted tea tray and desserts to be brought out for our guests?" Satoru requests.

The servant bows and immediately marches off. Soon enough, he returns with a large wooden tray.

Shizuko and Kenta peer at the rectangular box in

front of them. It is divided into small squares—twenty at the very least—each with different dried leaves and flowers inside.

"Please, help yourself," Satoru says.

The elderly couple are unsure which to choose, as they have not seen most of them before. Shizuko points at a square that contains tea leaves mixed with petals of sunset orange and magenta.

"Lotus flower tea," Satoru answers their curious expressions. "Good choice."

The servant uses a small, wooden spoon and puts a heap of the chosen tea into both the elderly couple's cups, before pouring hot water into them. They watch as the petals slowly open and expand, giving off a very aromatic scent.

"Your Majesty?" the servant asks.

"Jasmine, please," Satoru answers.

The servant responds to his request.

As Kenta and his wife both take a sip of tea, Satoru begins. "Mr. and Mrs. Tanaka, I believe Sir Leon had the pleasure of staying at your inn."

"Oh, he was the most pleasant man! It was an absolute honour to have him," Shizuko replies.

"He tells me you were both residents of Qieta, once," Satoru answers.

"Indeed, we were," Kenta replies. "We were explorers sent to the land, back in the day."

"You both must have heard about the killings," Satoru continues as the elderly couple nods. "It appears something similar may have happened in Qieta many years ago. Is that right?"

"Indeed, Your Majesty," Kenta agrees. "We were there when the disasters struck."

Satoru listens with anticipation. Perhaps they can give him some valuable information right now. "Tell me more of what you remember about the disasters, Mr. Tanaka."

"First of all, Your Majesty," Kenta begins slowly, "the skies would turn crimson red. Then bodies kept appearing by the waters of the island. There came a never-ending storm, which swallowed most of the Kingdom. The king and queen began to command the civilians to flee. We were lucky to have survived it, in all honesty."

"The bodies . . . how did they look?"

"Gouged eyes and internal organs missing, Your Majesty. It was the same every time."

"Interesting." Satoru nods, holding his chin in his hand. He pauses to take a sip of tea. "It is exactly the same."

History must be repeating itself, indeed.

“Unfortunately, we do not know much more about these killings, nor what caused them. We left the land before any answers were found,” Shizuko says.

“That is quite alright,” Satoru answers. The anticipation inside him shrinks slightly. It seems he will have to wait for Albert’s return to find out this information after all.

“How many years were you residents of the island, Mrs. and Mr. Tanaka?” Satoru asks.

“Thirty, at least, Your Majesty,” Shizuko answers.

Satoru ponders for a moment. That is quite some years. “Tell me, what is the kingdom like? How are the people and how is the climate?” Perhaps knowing more about the land itself might give him some clues as to when and how the attacks occur.

“Oh, the people are the loveliest,” Shizuko says proudly. “Hard-working, genuine, friendly, and close-knit. The king and queen were righteous rulers.”

“There’s something interesting about that, actually,” Kenta pipes up. “The land of Qieta does not have sunlight. I could not quite believe it at first. You would think this would make a place dark and miserable, but in fact, it is the complete opposite. It is such a mystical and bustling place. The moon shines ever so brightly,

and the population has all sorts of light sources from fireflies, to their magical plants and creatures, to various special lanterns. It is such a fascinating land."

"And the population of Qieta," Satoru asks, "is not very mixed like it is here in Shinrin, I take it? They speak Qietian there?"

"Yes, most of them are ethnically Qietian, Your Majesty," Shizuko replies. "It is a land so far away and secluded, mostly filled with people who have pale skin, dark hair, and dark eyes. Surprisingly, most of the population can speak both Qietian and the common language."

Satoru nods as he takes in the information. The elderly couple are expanding some of the knowledge he has obtained from Sir Koberic's volumes.

The servant reappears again and places a large, dessert bowl containing tangyuan onto the table. Kenta's eyes sparkle underneath his bushy eyebrows and Shizuko struggles to hide laughter.

Satoru smiles at the old man as he notices the glint in his eyes. "Please, help yourselves."

"The architecture there is also something else," Kenta continues as he helps himself to the dessert. He chuckles and bobs his head as he watches the white and pink chewy rice blobs swirl around in his bowl of sweet

soup. "Unlike the broad, flat wooden houses and cottages—or even the bamboo huts you usually see here in Shinrin—their houses are thin and tall, usually made from stone or marble."

"And their transport!" Shizuko joins in enthusiastically as she suddenly remembers. "In Shinrin, we have horses and carts, but there, they had something so advanced we had never seen before. They had tracks along their shallow waters and large carriages which ran along them. They could carry many passengers and these 'roads' went all the way around the island. You could even sleep on them overnight."

"And the waters there were ever so clear. I've never seen anything like it. The creatures and fish glow as they swim by. It was so tranquil and truly splendid," Kenta adds.

Satoru looks at the elderly couple who are both starry eyed as they remember the magical memories of this island. They are both clearly very fond of it.

"It certainly sounds magnificent," Satoru says.

Indeed, it does sound like a fascinating place, one very different from the forests of Shinrin that he is used to.

He smiles as he watches Kenta and Shizuko enjoy the tea and the dessert. Something about this elderly couple

makes his heart very warm.

✾

That night, Satoru lies propped up on his bed as he thinks about what the Tanaka couple told him. His mind is forming various links to the Mutoren from what they had said, although he is unsure if any of them are truly connected.

The fact that the kingdom exists only in the night—the Mutoren had only ever appeared on nights with a full moon, and she sees extraordinarily well in the dark. The Qietian people have pale skin, dark hair, and dark eyes. His excuse for the palace announcement on how those traits could lead to better night vision could be somewhat true, after all.

Mutoren, are you Qietian? Satoru wonders. *Do you know anything more about these killings? Do you have anything to do with them?* He ponders on this thought.

Satoru leans his head back and thinks about her. Since the day the deal was made, he has organised for her to stay in the large guest room. He managed to command his guards to come and unlock the door, after which he found her back in the interview room sitting innocently, like a harmless vedeir.

Satoru is due to have a formal dinner with her

tomorrow evening, as part of introducing her to the palace. He contemplates about the duties he can assign her as his new first-hand guard and the questions to ask her about the killings.

It has been another long day and recently, Satoru feels constantly tired. With a sigh, he closes his eyes, and tries to drift off to sleep.

CHAPTER TWENTY-THREE

The Last Meal

AIYLA AND SAKO ARE USHERED with the rest of the children into a large, battered wooden building.

"Single file, kids!" a red-masked soldier shouts unkindly. "Last meal of the day, and then you'll get to work!"

The children notice that the inside of the building is filled with shabby, wooden tables and benches. They are overcrowded with scruffy-looking children; each has a bowl in front of them. It looks like some sort of run-

down dining hall.

As the pair approach, they see stacks of bowls piled upside down. The children in front of them pick one up each and turn them right side up. Aiyla and Sako copy them and do the same. Aiyla notices how the bowl is chipped at the edges and how it is grey with rims of dark brown and black stains inside. It looks unwashed and unhygienic. She pulls a face and swallows down disgust.

They then reach a large, cauldron-like pot. A round man stands behind it with a big, wooden spoon. His face is vacant. He dunks his spoon into the pot and fills each child's bowl, like a machine. The line of children moves along gradually.

When Sako and Aiyla reach, their bowls are loaded with some brown liquid from the pot. It splashes over onto their hands as the man fills them carelessly. The children then look around, unsure where to sit.

Aiyla glances towards the far corner and Sako's eyes drift towards where she is looking. By the window, on the edge of one of the long wooden benches, a boy sits further away from the rest of the children. He has his back turned and is looking outside. He rests his head on his hand. His platinum, short blond hair stands out in the dark room.

Sako and Aiyla look at each other and decide to sit

with the boy. They make their way across the room and, as they plop their bowls down onto the table, the pale-haired boy turns around suddenly and looks up.

He looks young, perhaps around Aiyla's age. He has sharp, grey eyes and a tall nose. His eyebrows turn downwards into a small frown. His mouth remains flat and expressionless.

"Newbies, huh?" the boy asks flatly. His pale skin is scruffy with dirt and his arms are covered in scratches and bruises. He has barely any muscle—it is just skin wrapped on bones.

Sako looks at Aiyla.

"Hi, I am Aiyla," she says quietly.

"I'm Sako," Sako follows.

"Claus." The boy gives a short nod. He pauses. "I guess you are both as unfortunate as I am, to end up here."

Aiyla looks at him curiously. "Are you from Hinoki, too?"

"I have no idea where that is," he replies. "I'm from Neril."

There is something about this boy that makes his demeanour seem a lot more mature than he physically appears. Aiyla blinks at him. She then looks down at her bowl. It looks like liquid mud. A single piece of carrot

tragically floats across the top.

Claus notices her facial expression. "This is what you'll both have to get used to, sadly," he comments. "We get one meal a day . . . and that is if we do enough work. What you are having today is a luxury."

Sako looks at him, eyebrows furrowed with worry. "What are we expected to do here?"

"You've both come to the mines. We spend most of our day digging for gemstones—either that, or sheen, which is a rock with some sort of glitter inside. I can show you when we get to work. Those idiots expect a minimum of three baskets full of either, each day, from each of us." He pauses and marks out a circle about twice the size of the bowls in front of them with his hands. "About this size," he continues. "And if we do, we get food. If not, we don't."

Aiyla and Sako gulp as they take in this new information. Aiyla wonders if they are going to die here. Will she ever see her parents and brother Akalin ever again? A cold shiver runs through her, and she looks down at the table. She would do anything to be back home with her family right now.

"This place is a hell hole," Claus says bluntly. "Sorry you guys are here."

"Who was it that brought us here? Why are they

making us do this?" Aiyla asks.

"No idea," Claus answers, "but I plan to find out." He stops for a second. "Each day, just make sure you guys get back out of those holes. Kids keep disappearing. My guess is that they get lost in the darkness and die down there."

Aiyla and Sako look at each other, eyes full of terror.

So, we really might die here, Aiyla thinks. She swallows uncomfortably and begins to tremble slightly in her seat.

"How long have you been here?" Sako whispers.

Claus shrugs. "Heaven knows. You lose track of time once you're here." He pauses and looks at Aiyla. His frown softens a little. "Nice hair," he says. "You remind me of my little sister. She had silver hair like you. It's a rare colour. She was probably around your same age, too."

"Is she here?" Aiyla whispers.

"No." Claus's eyebrows turn back into his frown. "She's dead," he says flatly.

Aiyla is taken aback. "Sorry," she whispers.

"It's fine." Claus is indifferent. "She died in these blasted mines." He shuts his eyes and exhales, folding his arms behind his head. "I only know this for sure because I carried her back out and buried her with my own hands. A gigantic rock fell on her." He sighs. "I don't

care about anything anymore. I just have to get out of here. I will find the grand idiot who started all this and kill them." Claus then opens his eyes. "By the way, how old are you guys?" he asks, changing the topic.

"Nine," Aiyla replies.

"Thirteen," Sako follows.

"You guys are young," Claus nods. "I'm sixteen."

This surprises both Aiyla and Sako. He appears so much younger than he is.

Before the children can say anything else, a soldier bursts through the door. "Out, kids!" he shouts. "Get to work!"

Various children start scrambling, frightened, as several more soldiers enter and start shooing them out of the building.

Claus looks at Aiyla and Sako, eyes wide. He points at the mud soup in front of them. "Drink it!" he urges. "You don't know when you'll be able to eat again!"

In a hurry, both Sako and Aiyla gulp down the brown sludge. Aiyla chokes as the stench hits her and the muck drips down the back of her throat. The tragic carrot tastes like a piece of dry board. Sako wipes his mouth with the back of his hand and pinches his nose to try and dampen down the taste.

Soon enough, one of the soldiers approaches them

and shoves them hard in their backs, forcing them to join the mob of scrambling children.

Aiyla looks at the soldier with an intense hatred in her eyes. These people destroyed her home and massacred the people of her village. They separated her from her parents; she does not know if they are dead or alive. She decides in that moment that she, too, will find out who is behind all this, and—along with Sako and Claus—she will take revenge.

CHAPTER TWENTY-FOUR

Meness

THE DISCOMFORT OF AKALIN'S ARMOUR digs into his skin. He is not used to wearing something so rigid. His eyes are wide as he tries to take in everything he is seeing. He frowns behind his mask, which is suffocating him.

The children were offloaded from the boat into a cart housing a large cage; now, he and Samuel sit silently on the outside of the carriage, listening to the muffled cries of the frightened children. The cart wobbles from

side to side as they are carried up the high, midnight cliffs of Keska.

They reach the top of the cliff and Akalin stares on as the poor children, chained up in a straight line, walk fearfully along flimsy, wooden beams. He follows behind them as they approach a stony clearing.

His heart is absolutely crippling with rage.

A soldier—wearing the same armour as the rest—approaches him and Samuel. Akalin notices however, that he does not wear a cloth over his face and the fabric tied to the front of his chest appears to be maroon, rather than red.

"Montine. Lorenz." He nods at them both.

Akalin eyes him carefully and gives a brief nod.

Samuel bows down to him. "Sir Koslov," Samuel says, his eyes fixed to the floor.

The man looks at Akalin suspiciously. "Your duties for this round are done. Make way."

"Yes, sir!" Samuel salutes to him and bows again.

Akalin eyes the man carefully again and slowly lowers his head. "Yes, sir," Akalin replies.

The man frowns and he takes a step towards Akalin. Suddenly, he grabs him by the red cloth tied near his neck, pulling Akalin towards him threateningly.

"Have you forgotten how to salute your seniors?" He

spits at Akalin's face.

For a split second, despite it feeling suffocating, Akalin is grateful there is a piece of fabric between them. His rage then triples and his hands automatically turn into fists. However, after a short moment, he relaxes his hands and keeps his composure.

"My apologies," Akalin manages to say through gritted teeth. His voice is stone cold.

The man shoves hard and Akalin stumbles slightly. He steadies himself. Sir Koslov turns and walks away without a second glance.

Samuel looks at Akalin, his eyes shaking with concern. "That was harsh of him, and I'm sorry, but we should go." He hurriedly takes a few steps forwards.

Akalin follows behind him, still eyeing everything carefully. This completely new and strange environment is keeping his senses on maximum alert. He wonders how he will be able to hide his identity here.

After walking along the gravelly tracks for a while, they reach a large, wooden cabin situated next to a forest. Samuel opens the door and, inside, there are more doors stretching down an endless corridor. They walk to the end, where Samuel pulls out a metal key from his armour, unlocks the door, and pushes it open.

Inside is a very simple room with a bunk bed. A

small, square window on the wall allows some sunlight into the room and, under the patch of light, some specks of dust float in the air.

Samuel takes off his helmet and shakes his head, as if to get some air. He then takes off his armour and walks to the side before hanging it up onto the small hooks embedded into the wall.

Akalin sees that Samuel is a young man—perhaps around his age—with clear, umber skin, short black hair, and kind, brown eyes. He has a strong facial structure and thick, dark eyebrows. He wears a simple, white shirt and black trousers.

He looks up at Akalin, confused. "Are you not warm?" he asks.

Akalin stands still in his armour. He is trying to decide what to do next. This man in front of him still has not realised that he is not his comrade, Lucas. What will he do when he finds out? Scream for help? Call for attention?

That is the last thing Akalin wants.

He sighs. Since leaving Hinoki, he has had to make choices that go against his morals. But there doesn't seem to be any other choice.

In a split second, Akalin is behind Samuel. He puts his forearm around Samuel's neck and his other hand

on the side of his head, threateningly.

Samuel's eyes widen in a panic and Akalin can feel the fear in his neck as he swallows.

"I—I am sorry Lucas—whatever I have done—"

"I am not Lucas," Akalin answers coldly. "I killed him."

Samuel breathes heavily.

"Do not think of screaming or shouting for anyone," Akalin continues. "If you stay quiet, I will not harm you."

"I—I won't," Samuel manages to say. "I pro–mise."

Akalin lets go of him and Samuel falls in a heap onto the floor, panting. He then turns to face Akalin, the muscles on his face trembling with fear.

He shuffles backwards slightly. "Wh–Who are you?" he asks, his lips shaking. He gazes up at Akalin.

"I need to hide here," Akalin replies. He is sorry for terrorizing the young man.

Samuel nods ferociously and gulps.

Akalin sighs. After a moment, he slowly removes the red cloth covering his face and the heavy metal helmet over his head. His long, silver hair flows out from behind him. Samuel stares at him, taking it in.

"Lucas tried to kill me," Akalin says. "If I did not defend myself, I would have been the one who died that night."

"T–To be ho–nest, I kind of gathered," Samuel says quietly. His eyes are still wide, and his chest rises and falls as he breathes. There is a silence, before Samuel suddenly says, "I hated him. He was a wicked man and a bully. I have never known a heart as vile as his."

Akalin remains silent and eyes him suspiciously—when did Samuel realise Akalin was an imposter, and why didn't he say anything?

"Lucas killed my parents right in front of me," Samuel continues, unable to stop. "It's his fault I got dragged into this evil, corrupt universe. I never wanted any of this." The more he remembers Lucas's evil actions, the angrier he becomes. "He was mentally unstable. He beat me when he felt like it and told me I am nothing but a useless pawn who will continue to do this until the day I die."

Akalin continues to listen. All information will be helpful to save his sister.

Samuel then laughs and looks at Akalin again. "I told myself I would get revenge on him one day and save these children. But it looks like you have done half of it for me already. I thank you for it," he says.

Akalin slowly sits on the floor, maintaining his distance. Perhaps his instinct that the man in front of him has a good heart is correct after all . . . but he still

needs to keep his guard up. He leans against the wall and rests his right arm over his bent knee.

"I am not surprised he tried to kill you," Samuel continues. "He was evil. Pure evil."

"You two share this room?" Akalin asks, changing the subject. He eyes Samuel, maintaining his vigilance.

"Unfortunately, I was allocated this room with him. It's been torture. It was like my life depended on his mood."

"What happens to these children?" Akalin asks, wanting to get to the point. He needs to know where he may find his sister. But he also needs to consider that the man in front of him might be a potential ally.

"Unfortunately, I do not know much. I know the gang has been abducting children from various places and sending them here. It has been going on for a while. There are mines back there—" He points in a direction behind him. "—and the small ones are made to work. They dig for gems or for sheen. The bigger ones are chained to the large grinder, where they crush the rocks containing the sheen so it can be made into fancy stuff, like jewels and things. Thing is though, I feel like some children are disappearing. I have a good memory and each time I am rotated to work in the kitchens, some faces are missing."

“And who is behind this?” Akalin asks.

“I am not sure. I suspect Princess Lore has something to do with it.”

“Princess Lore?” Akalin raises an eyebrow. He has never heard of this name.

“Yes. She comes here every so often to check how things are getting on. And all the soldiers follow her orders. She’s supposedly powerful, and—” Samuel clasps his hand over his mouth.

Akalin raises an eyebrow, wondering what has happened.

“I just remembered. She is coming tomorrow,” Samuel says, eyes wide. “Please, sir. You will have to be careful.”

“Tell me, what I should be concerned about?”

“She likes good-looking men, and you, sir, are exquisite—”

Akalin is taken aback by the sudden compliment.

“—Every time she visits, she does this thing where she makes all the soldiers line up in a row and she will pick one. Every man she has picked, I have never seen again.” Samuel’s eyebrows furrow with concern and he trembles as he talks.

“The other soldiers are always excited when she comes. They say that not only is she beautiful, but she’s

also powerful. They say that any man would be lucky to be picked, for she will grant one a lifetime of abundance. But she makes me feel so unsettled. There is something very wrong, I swear. I think I have only made it this far because I look rather plain."

Akalin blinks, taking in this information. He leans back against the wall and sighs. "You are fine the way you are," Akalin answers quietly. He wonders why this young man is being so forthcoming with this information.

"Sir, why have you come all this way?" Samuel asks him.

"I have come to save my sister," Akalin answers. Hearing this out loud causes a heaviness to sink inside his heart.

Samuel's eyebrows raise in surprise. "She is here?"

"My village was destroyed by these men. They massacred the citizens and stole the children. I do not even know if my parents nor my sister are alive, but I have hope." He pauses. "As such, I am here."

"What does she look like? How old is she?"

Akalin thinks about Aiyla and the pain in his heart intensifies as he pictures her face. Although he is somewhat uncertain about the soldier in front of him, part of Akalin tells him that this Samuel may be of help.

"Little." Akalin gestures the approximate height with his hand. "Bronze skin, purple eyes, and silver hair that is a bit lighter than mine. She is nine years old."

Samuel nods ferociously again. "Sir, I never introduced myself properly," he says suddenly. "My name is Samuel Lorenz. I am from Keska, the land itself. And what about you, sir?"

"I am—" Akalin pauses. "Perhaps it is better if you do not know."

"You can tell me," Samuel says as he leans in eagerly. "I want to help you."

"Perhaps a later time," Akalin answers.

"Then I will have to give you a name," Samuel replies, not pressing further. "To me, you look like a Sir Meness, because of your hair. It means moon in my mother tongue, Keskan."

Akalin raises his eyebrows in surprise. Samuel quickly takes a few steps towards him, and then kneels as he clasps onto his hands.

"Sir Meness, Samuel Lorenz at your service." He looks into Akalin's eyes with deep sincerity. "You look like a good man and I will help to find your little Meness. *Your little moon.* You can count on me."

Akalin looks back at him and, for the first time in many months, the pain in his heart slightly eases. He

almost smiles.

CHAPTER TWENTY-FIVE

A Meal With the Prince

SANA SITS AT THE DRESSING table in the large guest chamber as she gets herself ready. She had received an invitation from the prince inviting her to a formal dinner tonight.

For some reason, she feels a little strange. Why is Prince Takashi treating her like she has done something great? Did she not strike, attack, and lock him up inside a room? Did she not make a fool of him in front of everyone in the palace?

Part of her still wants to make him forget their encounter. However, since they have made the deal, something inside her has been telling her not to. The fact that the prince promised to keep her family safe was the main reason she accepted his deal. She also still needs to reclaim her emblem.

Although the prince appears to be someone who is true to his words, is he still up to something? He may still lock her up at any point. She frowns suspiciously.

. . . Or perhaps that is how he is, forever righteous, always pure, and perfect.

She scoffs. Does he really think that by keeping her here and by being nice to her, she will return the treasures? How naive.

She sighs. *I do not have much time left,* Sana thinks. This thought has been plaguing her mind persistently in recent days.

But now, she is stuck inside the prince's palace. It is going to take time for her to get out of this situation if she goes against her initial plan.

Sana holds the emerald jewel she took from him that day up to the chandelier and closes one eye, turning the gemstone in various directions to watch the light bounce off at different angles. She then looks around her room.

Elegantly carved furniture, a luscious, soft bed with the most delicate fabrics—large enough to fit five of her—and various ornaments that are probably worth more than what she will be ever able to have in three lifetimes are placed around the room, just because they are pleasing to look at. So, is this what living like royalty feels like?

There is a *tap tap* on the window.

Sana turns to face the glass and notices a furry creature sitting outside on the ledge. The creature reaches a grey paw onto the glass and scratches at it, as if trying to come inside.

A stray cat?

Sana slides the window open slightly, and the fluffy grey creature jumps onto the floor of her room. Sana notices it has a slight limp; something seems to be wrong with the cat's back leg. It doesn't stop her from immediately brushing against Sana's ankles as she purrs.

Sana squats. "Well, aren't you a clever girl?" she asks, patting her head. "If you don't have a home to go to, the royal palace isn't a bad start for sure."

Sana is fond of animals. They have a purity that makes her heart feel refreshed. The cat closes her eyes, face full of content.

Sana gets up and walks towards the bed, picking up

one of the small pillows there. It has fancy golden tassels on all four corners. She squats back down and dangles one of the corners in front of the cat.

The creature's large, amber eyes focus with full concentration, and she starts to swat at it with her paws. Sana smiles as she wobbles the pillow left and right, watching the cat jump from one end to another. It is endearing.

"I am going to name you Luna," Sana decides, "because you look like a Luna to me."

There is a knock at the door.

"Lady Lishuah," a voice comes from the outside.

Sana laughs silently. She has given herself a new name.

Sana pats the creature's head again. "I'll bring some food back for you." She stands and makes her way towards the door, opening it. A guard stands outside.

He immediately bows. "Lady Lishuah, the prince is ready for you," he says.

Sana nods and follows behind him as he leads the way towards the grand dining hall. The grey creature sits and watches them walk away before deciding to follow behind.

Sana glances at the corridor walls as she strides behind the guard, looking at the various paintings in

fancy, golden frames. They reach another grand door and she is then advised to wait while the guard enters.

She peers at one of the paintings. Elegant, simple, yet impressive brush strokes make up two birds—sparrows perhaps—on a branch of a cherry blossom tree. Sana admires the talent that must have gone into this work of art.

"These are Prince Takashi's works," a voice appears behind her. "He is quite an artist."

Sana turns around. There is still one more guard standing outside the grand door. He is tall and has short, soft dark hair and dark eyes. A slight beard trims his jawline. She recognises him as the young man who was standing behind the prince that day she fought with the spear.

He bows. "Good evening. My name is Ryota Yasui, first doorman guard to Prince Takashi," he says.

"Lishuah," Sana replies, nodding. She suppresses a laugh as she hears herself say her made up name out loud.

The door opens, and the guard from earlier reappears. "Please," he says, as he gestures for Sana to enter.

Sana steps inside the room to find an enormous dining table full of colourful and enticing-looking food.

She has not seen such abundance in her life in a very long time.

Prince Takashi sits opposite, wearing a grand, black-and-golden robe, trimmed with white at the sleeves and at the collar. His long, black hair is tied half up, half down, and is secured in place with a golden headpiece. He looks rather extravagant.

Sana wonders how hard it must be to move around wearing all those things and how much time he must have spent on making himself look like that. She commends him for making it look easy.

"Take a seat," Prince Takashi says.

Sana sits down in front of him. Her legs do not reach the ground and dangle off the chair. Her garment is a simpler version of his own—a black-and-white robe with balloon trousers, a simple red ribbon tied at her waist, and her hair pulled up into a high ponytail.

"Please, start." Satoru gestures towards her.

Sana is suddenly slightly overwhelmed. She glances from bamboo steamer baskets to various plates, unsure where to even begin. If this was any other day, she would have likely jumped on the opportunity to fill her stomach. Yet today, she stares blankly at the feast in front of her. Part of her feels like, any moment now, guards may burst through the door and attack her.

Sana notices the prince's eyes on her as she gapes at the food. With his chopsticks, he reaches out to three different plates and places one of each item into the bowl. He thinks for a moment before putting the bowl onto the rotating surface in front of him. He spins it slowly until it reaches her.

"These are starters," Satoru explains. "Dumplings of various types."

Sana continues to stare. Is the prince trying to distract her with food?

Prince Takashi laughs slightly. "Have you not tried these before?" he asks. "Guotie," he says, pointing to pan fried dumplings. "And yujiao," he says, pointing to deep fried taro dumplings next to it.

There are others that Sana has never seen before.

She looks at the enticing food and relaxes a little. Perhaps she really is just here for a dinner after all. She looks at the yujiao. It looks golden and crispy. She picks it up with her chopsticks and takes a bite. Her cheeks puff out as she chews. Her eyes light up and she takes another bite.

The corner of the prince's mouth turns up slightly with amusement as he watches her reaction. He takes a moment before speaking again. "I have a few things I need to discuss with you," Satoru begins.

Sana is barely listening. She devours the third dumpling in her bowl.

"It's about the killings, Lishuah. I am sure you have heard about them?" Satoru asks.

Sana nods and reaches out towards a different plate, wanting to try a fourth dumpling.

"What do you know about them, please?" the prince continues.

"Not much," Sana replies. She munches away.

Satoru holds a hand up to the guards inside the room, gesturing that he would like them to step out. They immediately bow and leave the room.

Sana notices that the prince's bowl remains empty. He pours some tea into the cup in front of him gracefully and gestures to her, silently asking if she would like some. Before she responds, he pours some in a second cup anyway and puts it onto the rotating surface to spin it towards her.

"Pu'erh tea," the prince says. "Mutoren . . . these killings also occurred in the land of Qieta many years ago. Did you know that?"

"Perhaps," Sana answers, wondering where this is going.

"Any idea why they are now appearing in Shinrin? Any thoughts on who could be behind this?"

"No idea," Sana replies. She pauses. "If I did, I would have tried to stop it by now."

Satoru raises an eyebrow. "So, you have been looking into it as well, have you?" he asks suspiciously, before taking a sip of tea from his cup.

"Perhaps," Sana replies again.

Satoru frowns, as if expecting her to say more. He waits a little before speaking again. "Mutoren, from what I have learned, these bodies were not killed recently despite them showing up over the last few months. I admit, I am not sure how that is possible."

"I believe they are from Qieta," Sana replies.

Satoru's eyebrows raise in surprise. He finally takes a small dumpling and pops it into his mouth. Even when chewing, he manages to do so with elegance. A glow seems to radiate from him no matter what he does.

Sana blinks a few times, wondering why she is noticing these things.

"In truth," Satoru continues, "I have commanded the forest Hakkan to strengthen the defence walls with malachite. Since then, we have not heard of anymore new sightings. It has been more than two months. The lack of new bodies is nice, but I must find the perpetrators."

Sana ponders for a moment. Does she truly want to

help the prince? It is unclear. But there is a chance that learning what all he has done to protect the kingdom may help her instead.

"What I've noticed," Sana says slowly, "is that the bodies always appear where there is water. The walls may be a way to halt their appearance, but I wonder if the bodies are appearing from underground. Rather than on the surface. If you understand what I mean."

Satoru narrows his eyes. He takes in this information, pausing to think.

"I too, have noticed this," Satoru says, "and the method of death does seem somewhat related to drowning. But it is odd that, every single time, the condition of the bodies is identical—all missing eyes and organs as well as that none of the victims died recently."

"Perhaps something is feeding off them," Sana suggests.

"Feeding off them?" Satoru asks.

"Feeding off the organs. Or removing them," Sana continues. "Although I don't know how to explain that the bodies were not killed recently."

"Perhaps so. Professor Asante, our medical examiner, has mentioned that a creature may be devouring the organs of these victims," Satoru follows. He rests his

chin in his hand.

"Right," Sana answers.

"I suppose the next time I meet with the professor, I ought to invite you too, Mutoren. I believe you may be able to help."

Sana blinks at the prince, wondering why he believes this.

After a while, the prince speaks once more. "Tell me, Mutoren, what is your link to Qieta?" Satoru asks. He looks at her and leans in towards the table as he awaits her response.

"I'm not sure," Sana answers. Why is he asking? Is it because of the emblem? Does he have it with him?

"Are you from Qieta, Mutoren?"

"What makes you think that?" Sana asks in response.

Before Satoru has a chance to continue, there is a knock at the door. "Yes, come in," Satoru answers.

The door edges open. One of the chefs pokes his head inside. "Your Majesty, how are the starters getting on? Are you ready for the soup?"

"Yes. Please ask them to bring it, Sora," Satoru replies.

The chef bows immediately. "Yes, Your Majesty."

The prince appears to have lost his trail of thought. He looks at the Mutoren. "You seem to like these," he

says, nodding at the dumplings in front of them.

"What do you do with any food that is left over?" Sana asks, changing the subject. She wonders if they just throw it away. *What a waste.*

"We wrap them and donate them to the shelters and people who need them," Satoru answers, taking her by surprise.

Do they really? Sana wonders if the prince has a perfect answer for everything.

"Sora is one of the finest chefs here in the palace," Satoru continues. "His cuisine is exquisite. What we will have next is udon noodles in miso soup."

Soon enough, there is another knock at the door. It opens slightly and one of the cooks steps inside with a metal tray on wheels. A large, round, brown clay pot sits on top with steam drifting off its surface. The pot is placed alarmingly close to the edge of the tray, and it wobbles as it is pushed towards the dining table.

Sana realises it is because the cook wanted to make some room to collect some of the empty plates.

Someone bursts through the door in a panic with another tray on wheels that carries another brown pot.

"Vina! You brought the wrong one!" the second cook shouts. "That is the one Sora said wasn't done well enough!"

The cook, Vina, turns in a panic and profusely apologises. “Oh! My apologies, Prince Takashi!”

“It is quite alright—”

Vina turns around too abruptly and knocks the brown pot to the floor.

At the same time, Sana suddenly senses something come near her. She turns around briskly and is surprised to see a furry grey creature. *Luna*?

She is limping slowly across the floor, right where the pot is about to tip. The hot liquid almost pauses in the air as it is about to make its way down.

Sana somersaults onto the floor, rolls like a barrel rolling down a hill towards her new companion, and jumps up just in time to pick the cat up out of harm’s way with her right hand, whilst her left hand steadies the heavy clay pot back onto the tray.

The soup gushes over the rim and onto Sana’s hand, scalding it. There is a sudden pain but she continues to hold onto the pot tightly, her fingers still immersed inside the boiling liquid. She pants as her eyes remain fixated on the cat.

In another second, she finds herself in the prince’s arms. He half kneels on the floor, carrying her in his left arm, and there is a firm grasp on her left wrist as he hurriedly pulls it out of the pot.

Satoru turns towards the cooks. "Please, someone fetch some cold water. Now!" he commands. He turns back to face the Mutoren, his hand still firmly holding onto her. Her eyes are wide with shock and her wrists feel tiny in his grasp.

Sana's eyes remain round and stunned as Prince Takashi's sage eyes blaze back into hers. They are wide, like emerald jewels, and filled with genuine concern and shock. She is like a fish out of water, flopped over in his arms.

Someone runs into the room with a porcelain bowl of cold water and some cloths. Satoru immediately soaks the fabric in it and wraps it onto her left hand. It stings. He then sits her up and immerses her hand into the bowl.

Sana looks at him. His face is close to hers. There is a slight yellow blur on his forehead and Sana realises it is a fading bruise from when she headbutted him. She suddenly feels a twinge of guilt.

The prince looks at her, as if wondering what she is looking at. He reaches towards his head and pushes the jewel in his hair deeper inside, as if anticipating that the Mutoren may be about to steal it like she did last time.

"Are you alright?" he asks.

Sana blinks back.

Vina suddenly squats down next to them, hastily trying to pick things up. “Oh! Milady! I am so terribly sorry! Prince Takashi—”

“It is alright,” Sana whispers.

“Please, you need to be more careful,” Prince Takashi says to Vina.

The cook is almost sobbing.

Sana is suddenly wary of all the attention that is on her. She looks at Vina. “Calm down,” Sana whispers. “I am not hurt.” Her hand however, stings.

Satoru turns and looks up at the door.

Ryota has come running inside. “Master Takashi, I brought some bandages. I will call for the palace healer,” Ryota says.

“There is no need,” Satoru replies. “I can do it. Please, help to clean this up.”

Ryota bows and he and the cooks immediately start to clean up the disaster.

“Well, that was dramatic,” Sana whispers.

“Hold onto this with your other hand,” Satoru says to her, gesturing to the porcelain bowl.

Sana does as she is told and is suddenly lifted in the prince’s arms. He picks her up with ease before lowering her onto the chair gently.

“How is it?” he asks, gesturing towards her hand.

"It is alright," she answers. She unwraps the soaked cloth and looks at her palm and fingers. They look red. She tries to make a fist slowly. It stings again. She grimaces slightly but tries to act indifferent.

"It is good that it hurts," Satoru says as he sits down on a chair next to her. "I know it is painful, but that means it is superficial. It should heal by itself soon without any problems. I will give you an ointment to speed it up." He hands her a dry cloth. "Please."

Sana takes it and dries her hand slowly while the prince rolls out the white bandage onto his lap.

"Please," he says again, nodding towards his lap.

Sana places her hand on top, wondering why she is following his commands so obediently. She then watches as he skilfully bandages her hand, as if he has done it many times before. His movements are delicate, yet proficient.

Suddenly, a memory flashes across Sana's mind. Her eyes widen slightly as an overwhelming pain stabs right through her heart. Cold sweat begins to gather on the sides of her head. She closes her eyes tightly for a brief second before opening them again. The feeling subsides and she continues to look on.

Satoru notices her watching. "I may be a prince," he says, "but I am able to do things myself."

Sana remains silent.

"In fact, I know how to do this all too well," he continues as he ties a knot. "Back when I was younger, I was constantly hurting myself after training. This was like a daily ritual for me."

"Is that so?" Sana whispers.

She allows herself to think back to her younger years when she, too, was training and constantly hurting herself. The pain in her heart throbs slightly once more. Sana's eyes soften as she glances at the prince.

Perhaps he is not as pampered as she assumed.

Perhaps he is not here to lock her up.

✾

Later that evening, Sana returns to her chamber to find Luna laying sprawled out on her bed.

"Luna!" Sana shouts.

The fluffy creature immediately jumps up and hobbles towards her, purring.

"You little troublemaker," Sana says, as she strokes her furry back. "Look at what you did to me," she continues, as she holds up her bandaged hand towards the ceiling.

There is a knock at her door. Sana opens the door slightly.

The guard outside, Shou, immediately bows. "Milady," he says, as he hands her a box wrapped in a cloth.

Sana thanks him and places it on the bed before untying the crimson fabric. She finds herself looking at a wooden box containing a roll of bandages and a small pot of ointment. A folded piece of parchment is tucked in the side.

She opens it up.

Use it when you wake up and before you go to sleep.

Sana reads the prince's elegant script. She then lies down on the bed, holding her left hand. It still stings. She stares up at the ceiling, unsure of what she is staring at and ponders about the events that happened earlier that evening.

CHAPTER TWENTY-SIX

Princess Lore

ON THE DAY AKALIN ARRIVED in Keska, Samuel helped to hide him in their room.

Akalin is somewhat suspicious, not wanting to trust the man fully. However, there is not much else he can do in this new and unfamiliar environment.

The door creaks open and Samuel quickly steps inside before shutting it again.

"Sir Meness," he says, plopping his cloth bag onto the ground, "I brought you some food. I took some

bread and fruits."

Sure enough, he takes out a few slices of bread, an apple, and a banana. He places them on the table.

Akalin looks at the man in front of him. He is grateful for his help but feels somewhat unsettled.

"Why are you helping me?" Akalin asks.

"Because I can tell you are a good man. You want to come and save your sister. A person with a bad heart would not do that. Also, in a sense, you saved me. You accomplished half of my revenge for me, as well."

Akalin eyes him and takes a piece of bread before taking a small bite. His stomach growls. He is ravenous.

"Thing is, we need to think things through properly. People are already asking where Lucas is," Samuel continues. "When I went to the meal house, everyone was asking me where he is. I said that he isn't feeling well, and that I would take food back for him."

Akalin thinks. He can sense that his hideout is not going to last very long.

"Also, tomorrow, Princess Lore will be here. I was thinking that you can just hide here, at least until she leaves. But again, people will be asking where Lucas is."

Akalin continues to devour the piece of bread and reaches out for a second piece.

"So, the only thing I can think of," Samuel goes on,

"is if you just pretend that you are Lucas and get it over and done with. The line thing that she makes us do usually doesn't last long, and I am sure if we cover you up properly, she won't even notice you."

"When is she coming?" Akalin asks.

"She comes first thing in the morning."

"And you really have no idea what happens to the men she takes with her?"

This Princess Lore certainly sounds worrying to Akalin.

"No, Sir Meness. All I know is that I never see them again."

"Samuel, I think you have to look out for your own safety as well," Akalin replies. This man has been so forthcoming with so much information, and Akalin is beginning to feel that Samuel is putting himself in danger.

"It is not a problem, Sir Meness. I have been here a while and have an idea of how things work."

Akalin ponders. He does not like the sound of this. One danger leads to another.

Will it ever end?

✾

The next morning, Samuel and Akalin are getting ready

and putting on their armour.

A soldier creeps quietly towards the cabin from the outside, ducking out of sight. He hears a muffled conversation coming from the inside but cannot tell what is being said. He looks up at the window, but a curtain is drawn across it. He tries to peer inside through the gaps of the wooden planks.

"Where is Montine?" the soldier asks himself.

He struggles to see anything. He then takes out a fine metal tool and slots it between one of the gaps. Using some force, he tries to pry it open. The gap widens just a tiny bit, enough for him to catch a glimpse of a man with long silver hair a split second before he puts on his helmet.

"Heavens," he whispers to himself. "We have an intruder. I must inform Sir Koslov." He immediately takes a few steps back and runs off into the distance.

Inside the room, Akalin suddenly senses something behind him, as if someone is watching him. He briskly turns his back and puts his helmet on in a haste. He does not feel safe at all in this environment.

He covers most of his face with the red cloth, leaving only the tiniest gap, just enough for his eyes to see. He then follows Samuel out of the cabin, and they head towards the clearing.

There are two lines of soldiers facing each other. Akalin and Samuel quickly join the line.

One soldier, who is unmasked with a maroon cloth tied on the front of his chest, starts to shout commands.

"Good morning, soldiers!" he shouts.

"Sir Jensen!" the soldiers shout in unison as they salute.

"As we all know," Sir Jensen continues, "this morning, we will be expecting Princess Lore! You know the drill. Line up and stand up straight! One lucky man will not be returning tonight, for they will be leaving with the princess, and have their lifetime catered to!"

Muffled chuckles and excitement fill the air. Akalin wonders why these men appear so excited when a chill runs through his spine. He scans the scene and then looks at Samuel, who is standing next to him.

Samuel looks back, his eyes stern and serious.

Soon, the sound of a cart and horses' hooves can be heard. An elaborate looking cart appears in the clearing. The horses and the cart are covered with crimson-and-golden embellishments. The rider hops down and opens the cart door, bowing.

A lady steps out. The soldiers crane their necks to see her.

From afar, Akalin can see she wears an extravagant

crimson-and-golden dress that matches the cart, and her hair, wrists, and neck are covered in jewellery that clink and clank as she walks. A white piece of fur is draped over her shoulders and she exudes an aura of excessive wealth.

She strides towards the line of soldiers, and peers at them one by one, taking slow steps.

"My," she says. "I do find this exciting each time I come. Aren't you all so well behaved?" She giggles as she eyes each soldier.

Akalin stares straight ahead. His heart begins to thud. He has no idea what is going on, but he prays that she will leave him alone. He thinks of his father, his mother, and Aiyla. He thinks of Satoru. He thinks of Albert.

Before he knows it, the lady is standing right in front of him. An intense scent of perfume hits his senses.

Princess Lore peers at Akalin curiously. Her dark hair is tied into an extravagant hairstyle and pearls dangle from her ears. Her large, crimson eyes lock onto him, and her lips spread into a smile. "Wow," she says dreamily. "I think I've found the one."

Something inside Akalin's heart sinks while she continues to peer at him.

"Isn't it amazing," she continues, "that despite the fact I can barely see anything of you, I can just tell that

you are wonderful?" She takes a step back and looks him up and down.

The hairs on the back of Akalin's neck stand up.

"Well, I guess it is a quick decision for me today," Princess Lore says happily. "I don't need to see the rest. I'll take him." She points at Akalin.

His heart sinks further. He looks at her pointy, crimson nail and beads of sweat begin to form around his temples.

Sir Jensen nods from afar, and Princess Lore immediately links her arm through Akalin's, taking him by surprise. She begins to walk towards her cart.

Akalin turns around and looks at Samuel in a panic.

Samuel's eyes are wide and distressed. They cannot speak, but Akalin can almost hear what he is trying to say. *Sir Meness, I am sorry. Stay safe. I will find your sister.*

Princess Lore hums to herself as she holds onto Akalin and the two of them walk towards the cart. The cart door opens.

"Please," the lady says to Akalin, gesturing for him to board.

Akalin slowly steps inside and sits. He tries to sit as far away from her as he can, but when the door shuts, the princess immediately squishes up right against him. Her eyes are wide as she stares at him.

"My, you do have beautiful eyes," she says. "They look like . . . amethysts." She sits back down and wriggles the fingers on her right hand. "Would be nice if I had a ring that colour, don't you think?" She then leans close to him. Her finger lightly touches Akalin's jawline and she trails it across his chin before holding gently onto the red cloth that is covering his face.

Akalin is about to throw up.

"I wonder what you look like," she whispers. She pauses as she lifts the cloth slightly. "I am a very lucky lady," she says softly. She then lets go of the cloth suddenly, as if she has changed her mind about something.

"Never mind," she whispers. "I'll leave it for later. It is like unwrapping a present. It makes it even more exciting." She giggles and leans back into the seat, wraps her hands back around Akalin's left arm, and leans into him, sighing in content.

Akalin stiffens uncomfortably and closes his eyes, praying to whatever—if anything—is watching over him.

Please, dear lord, what have I gotten myself into?

CHAPTER TWENTY-SEVEN

On the Rooftop

IN THE LATE HOURS OF the night, Satoru storms across the palace grounds, wearing a heavy, black cloak and carrying a lantern which is emitting an orange glow. He is making his way back towards his chamber.

"Master Takashi." Ryota bows to him as soon as he nears.

"Ryota." Satoru nods and acknowledges him before stepping inside. He takes off his shoes and cloak, lights a few candles inside his room, and blows out the flame

in his lantern.

Satoru trudges towards his desk and steadies himself with his left arm, giving himself a moment. He looks down at the wooden markings on his desk and sighs. He then slumps in his chair and holds his head in his hands.

Two more villagers have been found dead along the shallow rivers of Ajisai Village. Satoru had immediately gone in person to investigate the matter. Once again, the corpses had mottled skin with organs missing.

Although he was having trouble finding the perpetrators, he thought his plan with the malachite had at least managed to keep them out of Shinrin for now. After all, he had had some months of peace without any sightings.

Now, he must ask for these victims' bodies to be retrieved and once again have them analysed. There are more investigations to do.

Is this all an indication that he is beginning to fail as a leader? Under his reign, Shinrin seems to be falling into more and more danger.

He can already sense how the public will panic as soon as news breaks out that more bodies have been discovered. Why is it that, after so long, he feels like he has barely made any progress on this case?

A pounding headache is starting to constrict around Satoru's head. He knows this feeling all too well. The stress is getting to him again. Recently, he had been feeling particularly exhausted. Major incidents keep occurring—such as the Hinoki massacre—which is adding a heavy load onto his already existing pressures.

Since becoming the ruler of Shinrin, Satoru has had nothing but constant duties and felt a suffocating pressure to remain impeccable in everything he does. He has had to carry all these responsibilities on his shoulders. He is aware that the citizens think very highly of him and that the things he has accomplished during his reign have given him the finest recognition and reputation.

However, did he want any of this?

Aged six-and-twenty, Satoru is now the Emperor of Shinrin, but he never formally took on the title. Instead, he remained a prince as this gave him a slight comfort. "Prince" was the title he had when his family was still around; some part of him thought that, if he formally took on the title of an Emperor, it would emphasise the fact that he is truly the lone ruler of this kingdom.

Satoru wishes his older brother were here right now. He would do anything to hear his comforting words and to have his guidance.

Satoshi, born ten years before Satoru, had always been a role model, an exemplar, and a source of reassurance. He is someone who Satoru held dear to his heart and always looked up to, but to this day, he still does not understand why he suddenly disappeared.

He misses his brother.

Thinking of Satoshi reminds Satoru suddenly of his flute. In times of stress, Satoru often climbs onto his roof to play his bamboo flute. It reminds him of the times when he and his family were still together, and it brings him comfort, which helps to take the pain and the stress away.

Satoshi had gifted this flute when Satoru was still a child. It is a beautiful, delicate, chestnut-and-golden-coloured instrument, which Satoru took to like duck to water. He enjoys composing his own music, and the ability to transcribe his deep emotions into soulful tunes is something that has helped him get through difficult times.

Satoru makes his way towards his dressing table and pulls out the drawer, reaching for the box encasing his flute. He takes it out and leaps out of his window before hopping onto his roof. This is his special place of tranquillity.

He breathes in the cold, crisp air and the wind flows

through his hair as he closes his eyes for a few seconds. He thinks about one of the deep, emotional tunes he wrote for his brother and begins to play.

✾

Sana puts on a thick, brown robe and blue trousers. It looks cold outside.

She has decided to go and look for Prince Takashi to see if she can convince him to give her back her emblem. Is it too late in the night? Perhaps the prince will be in his chamber. She decides to give it a try, nonetheless.

She looks at Luna, who is currently snoozing on a pillow by her bed.

Sana opens the guest chamber window, and a gust of cold wind sweeps against her face. She tucks a few strands of hair behind her ears and jumps onto a neighbouring tree. It sways, and Sana uses this motion to jump onto the next branch. She continues to do so until she reaches the outside of the prince's chamber.

There are no guards on his window balcony today. She wonders where they are.

A glow comes from his window. She gently slides open the glass and creeps inside onto his ceiling, hanging upside down.

Sana takes a moment to look around from above. Although a few candles are lit, the prince is nowhere to be seen.

Where is he? She blinks. *Oh, perhaps he is in the bathroom.*

A sharp sound suddenly comes from above, then screeches. It sounds like an inconsistent, frustrated cry.

Sana realises it is the sound of a flute, coming from the roof. Like a spider, she crawls along the ceiling back towards the window and hops silently onto the rooftop. Prince Takashi has his back to her.

Sana wonders why his music sounds like a murder scene. *What is going on?*

✤

Satoru takes a breath and tries again. What is happening today? His beautiful, soulful tune refuses to flow no matter how hard he tries. This is ridiculous. Has he forgotten how to play his flute? Heavens, he might as well say he doesn't understand any music at all.

Again, Satoru takes another breath, and attempts once more. A piercing, ghastly screech. He tries again. An ear-splitting shrill. The frustration expands inside him as he takes a moment to try and compose himself. He grasps onto the flute with his left hand, so firmly that

he is shaking. He tries to inhale, but his stress is spiralling out of control.

Satoru, calm down.

Alright, one more time.

He takes a breath.

The sound which comes out is an unsightly, hideous scream.

The disgruntlement inside him overspills. In a split second, Satoru grasps his bamboo flute and hurls it down with all his force as his frustration explodes.

The delicate instrument hits the rooftop and immediately snaps. The two pieces roll their way down the rooftop and fall into the gutter.

Satoru bends forwards, his hands on his thighs. His eyes are wide, and he is panting. He blinks as he hears his own breath. He suddenly realises what he has done and, in a flurry, he runs towards the gutter and picks up the two pieces of his beloved possession in his hands.

His hands shake as he looks at his instrument, fragile and shattered.

His brother's flute.

There is a sudden crack in his heart as he remembers the time when he received it. A time when his brother, mother and father were still around him.

The whites of Satoru's emerald eyes redden as he

takes in what he has just done. He squeezes his eyes shut and inhales, gripping onto the broken pieces.

After a while, he opens his eyes. He swallows down his emotions and slowly begins to try to piece together the fragments.

He has to fix what he has just done.

✻

The prince's back is turned. Are those screeches coming from his flute? Sana has heard him play it before. When she was analysing her target of the emerald necklace, she had sat in the trees and heard his music a few times. Each time, his music had been soulful, beautiful, and emotional. She wonders what has happened today.

Should she alert him that she is here? She takes a few silent steps and crawls to the side of the roof; she startles when she notices the fury in the prince's eyes, and can only watch as he suddenly propels his instrument down onto the roof. The snap is crisp and loud.

Sana's eyes widen and a hand covers her mouth as she watches the unexpected scene unfold in front of her.

She has never seen the prince like this. His usual calm and courteous composure have been replaced by intense and profound emotions that have just exploded.

Sana watches as the prince realises what he has done and runs towards the broken pieces before picking them up. The pain in his eyes is indescribable and she can almost feel the agony in his heart. His frustration suddenly diminishes as he holds his flute in his hands, which are shaking. After he takes a breath, his usual collected manner returns in his eyes as he tries to piece the fragments back together.

Sana takes a few steps towards him.

✾

Satoru suddenly senses that there is something behind him. He turns slowly and sees her.

Mutoren?

"Hey," Sana whispers.

Satoru wonders how much she saw.

She slowly sits down beside him. Her legs dangle off the edge of the roof.

"Hey," Satoru answers quietly. The informal softness in his voice still exudes the pain of what he was experiencing earlier. The rawness of his emotions cling to the air around him.

Behind his outer shell of perfection, it appears the prince is only human, after all.

"What are you doing here, Mutoren?" Satoru asks

softly. His eyes stare into the distance.

Sana thinks about why she is here. She decides to keep it quiet. "Just stumbled by," she answers.

The two of them sit in silence.

"The Mutoren has a name," Sana suddenly says, breaking the silence.

Satoru looks at her. "Yes, stomach-ache."

Sana laughs. She looks at the prince, who is still holding onto the broken fragments of his instrument.

"I am sure there is someone in the palace who will be able to fix that," Sana says quietly.

Satoru manages a small laugh. "I guess, but it was embarrassing and immature of me," he whispers.

"You are only human, after all," Sana tells him.

For a moment, Satoru looks at her. His forest eyes linger on her round, obsidian ones. He then looks away.

"My brother gave me this flute," Satoru continues. "It is one of my most prized possessions.

"I can see it means a lot to you."

Satoru suddenly thinks of something. "You mentioned you do music, is that correct?" he asks her softly.

Sana nods. "I do indeed." She pauses, then points in the distance. "At Hida."

Hida Academy is one of the institutions in Shinrin,

notable for producing the finest musicians.

Satoru nods. “And you play?”

“Harp.”

Satoru is impressed. The girl must have quite a substantial level of musical expertise to be accepted into Hida.

“Right,” he acknowledges. He notices the bandages on her left hand. It looks messy and appears to be falling off. “How is your hand?”

“Oh, it’s alright. The ointment really helped.” Sana pauses and notices the prince looking at the bandages. “I can’t do it as well as you,” she admits.

“Perhaps that is a good thing. It means you were not getting hurt as much as I was.”

“Oh, trust me. I was,” Sana answers, “if not more. I just didn’t have anything to cover it—most of the time.”

Satoru looks at her and wonders about her past. The girl in front of him is nothing short of mysterious. The frightening and formidable Mutoren. Yet in this moment of tranquillity, he feels he is somewhat enjoying her company.

“Why did you steal all these treasures?” Satoru asks.

Sana takes a second before speaking. “Because I can.”

Satoru raises an eyebrow. It seems she is back to her usual short, vague answers.

"Where did you learn your martial arts—" Satoru ponders for a second on whether to continue calling her Mutoren, "—Harlande?"

The sudden use of her name surprises them both.

"I've never seen anything like it," Satoru adds.

"From somewhere special," Sana replies simply. Her eyes, however, reflect a flicker of emotion, as if she is remembering something.

Satoru laughs. Indeed—short, vague answers from the Mutoren once again.

"Our land is in danger," Satoru comments. "I have already ordered heightened soldier training in case we need to be prepared for battle." He looks at her. "You are very versatile in your way of fighting. Perhaps you can take on the role of a knight and train our soldiers. I believe it would be an invaluable addition. Do you think you can do that?"

"Perhaps," Sana answers after a moment at the sudden request. "But not in the style of the Mutoren." She turns to face the prince.

"No," he agrees. "In the style of Harlande."

The cold wind breezes through them and Satoru watches as the girl's hair flows around her. She looks somewhat beautiful. His heart thuds a little.

"It is cold and late. You should go back," he says to

her.

"And you should get some rest," Sana replies. She stands and, with a simple hop, she lands on the railings of the prince's chamber balcony.

Satoru takes a moment to catch up.

Sana looks at him and gives him a short salute. "Good night, Prince Takashi," she says softly.

Hearing her say his name tugs slightly at strings in his heart. By the time Satoru reaches her, Sana leans backwards and lets herself fall into the darkness.

Satoru lunges forwards and holds onto his balcony railings, looking down. He sees nothing.

The Mutoren has disappeared into the night.

CHAPTER TWENTY-EIGHT

An Old Man's Tale

ALBERT KNEELS ON THE SOFT cushion in front of him by a large, round, porcelain table.

Liuana Pharlos sits opposite him, cross-legged. He nods towards the young man who greeted Albert earlier, and smiles. "Introduce yourself," the old man says.

"Ilkari Xandyr." The young man bows towards Albert. "I am one of the spiritual followers and the first advisor of Liuana Pharlos."

"Very nice to meet you. I am Albert Leon." Albert nods in return.

"Ilkari, please. Prepare some tea and refreshments for our guest," the old man says to him.

The young man quickly strides off in the opposite direction.

Albert looks around. They are sitting near a round, open altar, surrounded by a few ivory pillars. The ceiling above them is open with fragile metal bars forming a dome. It holds together pieces of different coloured glass, which allow the moonlight to cast various colours down onto the table and the ground where they sit.

"It is an honour to have you as our guest, Sir Leon," Liuana Pharlos begins. "You have made quite a journey having come all the way from Shinrin."

"Thank you so much, Liuana Pharlos," Albert replies.

"I have been notified by the prince of Shinrin that you are here to investigate the great disaster of Qieta. Is that correct?"

"Very much so."

"I hear the disaster has come to Shinrin."

Albert nods.

"How awful," the old man answers.

Ilkari returns with a few transparent glasses and a transparent teapot full of an amber liquid. He places a tray of light refreshments on the table. After he pours a glass, Liuana Pharlos takes it and places it in front of Albert.

“This is Seta tea, one of the most authentic teas we have here in Qieta. It comes from our Setang plant.”

Albert holds the glass in his hands and thanks him.

“Sir Leon, you have come to an island of magic,” Liuana Pharlos continues. “It will be a pleasure to help you gain the information you seek, but first, let me tell you more about our land.”

Albert sits up and listens intently. He looks at the fine lines of wisdom on the old man’s face, and how his eyes sparkle as he speaks.

“First of all, I would like to warn you that you may have some strange dreams here,” he explains.

Albert cocks his head to one side. “Strange dreams?”

“Yes. Have you heard of Lilium Sidereum?”

“I have not.”

“It is a magical blue flower native to our land. It glows in the moonlight, and one of its strange properties is that it causes us to have dreams. But not just any dreams.” The old man leans closer to Albert. “These dreams are so realistic that it is hard to distinguish

between what is real and what is not while you are in them. Of course, once you wake up, you realise the things are not true."

Albert is still confused. He blinks.

The old man sees this expression and chuckles. "It is a strange concept for one who has never experienced it," he answers. "For example, do you have a wife, Sir Leon?"

"I do not." Albert is taken aback. Why is he asking?

"Well, you may dream that you have one. And it will seem so real that it almost feels as if you have known this lady your whole lifetime . . . until you wake up and realise it was actually a dream."

"That is very strange, indeed," Albert says.

"We are all used to it here. And, because these flowers are so deeply rooted into our soils, its effects flow through the entire island. In fact, the citizens quite enjoy it. We say it is a chance for another adventure while we sleep." The old man winks at Albert.

Albert takes a sip of the tea. It tastes mild, but sweet—similar to something his mother used to make when he was still a young child in Cerne.

"There are no royal rulers here?" Albert asks, wondering why there has been no mention of a king or queen.

"In the great disaster many, many years ago," Liuana Pharlos replies, "the king and queen unfortunately passed away." The old man looks up at the colours casting down onto the table. There is some pain in his eyes. "There were no royal survivors and, since then, Qieta has become a land without royalty."

"You must have experienced the disaster first-hand," Albert says quietly.

The old man closes his eyes and takes a breath. "Oh, yes." He opens his eyes. "Soon after the killings began to occur, there came a never-ending storm. The sea swept over most of the island. Something must have been watching over me for me to have survived. It is hard to believe it has been so many years since then."

Albert nods, taking in his story. He thinks through the things Prince Takashi asked him to find out. "When did this disaster take place, Liuana Pharlos?"

"Twenty-two years ago, to be exact," the old man replies.

Albert nods.

"Although most of the land was destroyed, we tried to restore what we could." Liuana Pharlos looks at Albert and his eyes gleam under the moonlight. "When you have faith in what watches over us," he says, "it gives you strength."

Albert feels heavy at the grief in the old man's voice.

"There were not many survivors," Liuana Pharlos continues. "But using what was left, we rebuilt the spiritual grounds and reconstructed some of the villages. And now, we carry on our humble lives." He takes a sip of tea. "Would you like to try these?" He points to the small tray containing the refreshments, and takes out a flat, round item that is pale green in colour. "These are called Morelle, made from our Moti berries. Try one." He smiles as he hands it to Albert.

Albert bows slightly as he receives it with both hands. He looks at the round, flattened, pale green snack and the sugar dusted over it before taking a small bite. The chewiness of the inside comes as a surprise and his eyes light up. It reminds him of the rice cakes back in Shinrin. He takes a moment to swallow before speaking.

"This is wonderful." Albert gestures to the small dessert on his hand. "I must ask, Liuana Pharlos . . . were you ever able to find out who or what was behind those killings? Is it true that the sky turns crimson red before the killings occur?"

For the slightest second, the old man has a flicker of surprise in his eyes. The white hairs of his eyebrows raise ever so slightly. "Yes. The horrific killings," he begins. "The ones with missing organs—that is what you

are talking about, correct?"

Albert nods.

"It took me some time to discover what was behind it," he says slowly.

Albert awaits his response.

"There is an evil soul amongst us." There is a pause. "A soul who possesses dark magic. There was never a proven sighting of him during the disaster itself, however, he is who takes the lives of innocent civilians. He feeds off their organs and he is in search for something that will heighten his power."

"Is that so?" Albert's eyes widen. *So, it is a human who is behind all of this?* He focuses back on the conversation. "Then why are the bodies now appearing in Shinrin?" Albert whispers. "Are they victims from all these years ago? How have the bodies not decomposed?"

"The waters of our world are connected," Liuana Pharlos explains. "The victims lost their lives to his dark magic and their bodies have been infiltrated with it. His dark magic runs through the waters of our world."

"I still do not fully understand how, but the fact that these killings are now appearing in a land as far as Shinrin . . . perhaps this is a sign he has commenced his deeds once more." The old man frowns and strokes his beard.

Albert is unsure of what to make of what he is hearing. He fidgets on his cushion and adjusts his position. This talk about dark magic is making him feel unsettled.

"This soul . . . do we have any idea where he is?" Albert whispers.

"I have met him, once," Liuana Pharlos replies. "Perhaps a month or so after the disaster, he appeared once by the shores up North. As a group, we spiritual guiders stood together and used our power of light and purity to banish him. He retreated into his dark haven and thus far, we have managed to keep him at bay. There has not been another report of a killing or a sighting of him since."

"And how did you get to know these things?" Albert asks.

Liuana Pharlos smiles. He turns slightly and picks up the silver staff which lays next to him. He shows Albert the glowing lilac and blue orb which sits at the top.

"This, young Sir Leon, is a gift from the above which I have had my whole life," the old man explains. "It allows me to see things, sometimes before they occur." He holds his hand over the orb and it glows slightly brighter. "My duty is to defend and to protect the innocent. Although he is among us, I believe that with

true purity and grace, we can win over any evil."

Liuana Pharlos starts to stand up slowly; his elderly body takes time to straighten up.

Albert startles and considers helping him, but the man makes it to his feet before he can.

"Come, young Sir Leon," he says. "Let me take you to some of the villages and show you around. I will ask Ilkari to bring your stallion a little later. I shall introduce you to the innkeepers as well. They will be honoured to have a royal figure stay in their guest houses tonight." He smiles at Albert and gestures for him to follow as he takes a few steps and leads him out into the open, Qietian night.

✿

Albert follows behind Liuana Pharlos as they weave between the ivory pillars of the spiritual grounds. As they do so, another old man wearing a long, white gown with long sleeves— similar to Liuana Pharlos—appears and walks by them.

Liuana Pharlos bows to the other old man. "Liuana Ophair," Liuana greets him.

"Liuana Pharlos," the man replies. He disappears in the opposite direction.

Soon, they reach the outside. The night air is mild

and the stars shine like diamonds in the sky. The gentle waves of the crystal clear waters flow by the ivory stairs of the building, and a few brightly coloured fish swim by. They leave trails of glowing silver light behind them.

"Follow me." Liuana Pharlos smiles at Albert as he watches him take in the scenery. He hobbles in the opposite direction from the waters, using his silver staff to help him walk. "Qieta is very different to the rich forests of Shinrin, I take it?"

"Different, but very beautiful, nonetheless," Albert replies. He looks up into the night and it suddenly reminds him of something Kenta from Tanaka Inn had mentioned. "Is it true that sunlight does not exist on this island?" Albert asks.

"Indeed," the old man replies as they continue. "Qieta has only moonlight. We do not have days, but only nights. But as you can see—" He gestures to their surroundings. "—our land is far from dark."

Albert looks around. Sure enough, the moon shines brilliantly along with the scattered, silver stars in the amethyst sky. The sound of flapping wings draws close, and Albert looks up to see a glowing, sage-coloured bird fly over his head.

It is certainly a beautiful sight.

As they walk further away from the spiritual

grounds, a white and grey cobbled path begins to appear. There are rectangular ivory buildings of different heights on both sides, and a few villagers are dotted about, going about their usual day.

They look up to Albert as they pass by, smiling. They put their palms together and nod towards Liuana Pharlos.

✤

After Liuana Pharlos shows Albert around the village some more, he soon comes to a stop. They stand in front of one of the ivory buildings, one with an old, wooden door. A bunch of glowing, blue lilies are tied and they hang upside down at the front of the entrance.

"These are lilium sidereum." Liuana Pharlos points to the glowing lilies. He takes the round, metal knocker and taps lightly three times. "Let me introduce you to Mister Jayler's Inn," Liuana Pharlos explains. "He is a good man and this will be a nice place for you to stay tonight."

"Thank you." Albert smiles. He looks at the glowing lilies as they wait for someone to open the door.

"I hope you are enjoying your first few moments here in Qieta, Sir Leon. Let us continue our talks tomorrow." He winks at Albert. "And make sure you get

some good rest tonight."

CHAPTER TWENTY-NINE

A Fresh Kill

SATORU STANDS BY ONE OF the stone surfaces. A white sheet is draped over the body that lays underneath. He waits for Professor Asante to begin.

"Prince Takashi." The Professor bows as he approaches. He gestures at the body. "You see—"

The room turns dark.

Satoru turns to find that the professor is nowhere to be seen. An explosion rocks the space and the glass windows of the examination chamber shatter all at once.

Satoru's eyes widen in shock. Out of nowhere, a frighteningly forceful—yet perishingly cold grasp—suddenly latches onto his left wrist.

There is a mottled hand gripping him. He is unable to shake it off. The white sheet rustles as the body underneath begins to move. The sheet falls to the floor and the body snaps upright, her face only an inch from the prince's.

The bloody sockets of the eyes are dark and terrifying as they stare right into Satoru's soul. Satoru's heart beats wildly in his chest and he is unable to turn away from this half-decaying and terrifying face. The corpse's void-filled eyes widen, and thick, crimson blood begins to collect at the bottom of the rims before it drips down her face and onto Satoru's arm.

It burns into his skin like ice. Her face nears and her mouth widens into an impossible, horrifying grimace. She screams.

Satoru jolts awake.

He jolts so hard that he is now sitting bolt upright in his royal bed. His forehead is wet with perspiration and his breathing is hard and heavy. It takes him a moment to come back to his senses and to shake the terrifying image from his mind. He briskly lifts his bed sheets to one side and stumbles out of his bed. Something tells

him that he must pay a visit to the Hakkan.

Now.

He lights his lantern and pulls on his cloak in a haste before he pushes open his chamber door.

"Master Takashi!" His night doorman guard, Akira, bows immediately.

"Akira." Satoru nods and paces out of his chamber.

"Your Majesty!" Akira exclaims. "Where may you be going at this hour?"

Satoru is already halfway down the corridor. The guards who line either side of the hallway all bow immediately.

"I must see the Hakkan. I shall be back soon," Satoru states.

The urgency is evident in his voice. The prince paces down more stairs and hallways until he reaches the open night.

Satoru continues until he reaches the palace stables. The image of the bloody voids is haunting his mind. A cold shiver permeates every inch of his body. A feeling of impending doom lingers inside him.

I feel like something extremely bad is about to happen, Satoru thinks to himself, his breathing heavy.

These killings are escalating out of control. He has still not been able to find the perpetrators, but since that

day when he was on the rooftop with the Mutoren, the killings have started to appear once more. Darkness is draping over the kingdom of Shinrin and he can feel it.

Perhaps the Hakkan will be able to do something.

Satoru reaches his stallion. He is a tall, midnight creature with a glossy, raven mane, and he pokes his head out as soon as he notices the prince.

"Yonaka," Satoru says. He swings open the stable door.

His horse takes a few steps forwards and Satoru immediately leaps onto his back without so much as a saddle nor reins. They journey in a haste into the Shirinese forests.

The night air is crisp and the moon is a silver crescent in the sky. After a while, they reach the forests of Oku, where tall grand oak trees stand. In the centre, there is a small lake surrounded by huge, stone boulders. The rocks are grey and white, covered in rich green moss. The lake glistens a cyan glow. Crickets chime away in the trees.

Satoru hops down from his horse and nearly stumbles over. His breath creates mist in the night air. He strides towards the boulders and stops. He presses two fingers gently against the surface, although he wobbles slightly. He then holds his two fingers a little in

front of his face and closes his eyes as he begins to mumble a chant in the ancient tongue of Shinrin. He steps back.

Soon enough, various green-and-cyan glowing symbols appear all over the giant boulders. The ground begins to shake and bits of small rock roll onto the ground. The boulders rumble as they begin to turn. They arrange themselves until the side of a huge giant's face can be seen, half-embedded into the forest ground.

"You have woken the Hakkan," comes a deep, booming voice. It echoes through the forests and some birds rustle out of the trees, flying into the night.

"My apologies for waking you," Satoru begins. His heart is still beating heavily inside his chest. He prays the Hakkan will be able to help. He was hoping more than one of them would wake up.

He readies himself to face the giant—they are not easy to talk to.

"Does one have a good reason for waking the Hakkan?" the slow, booming voice continues.

Satoru looks at the sideways half of the giant's face protruding from the earth.

"Prince Takashi," the voice vibrates. "You may be the ruler of Shinrin, but the Hakkan still do not like to be awakened."

"I respect that, and I apologise," Satoru answers. "However, I must speak with you."

"I sense urgency in your voice, Prince Takashi."

"I understand the Hakkan has already helped us to lay down malachite across the entire walls of our kingdom," Satoru says, hoping that this acknowledgement will make the Hakkan more tolerating.

"Yet the prince has come to ask us for more?" the giant booms, unimpressed. "The last time we were woken—prior to the malachite laying—was a century ago."

"Please, Hakkan," Satoru urges. "You are a part of the walls and landscapes of our land. You must have sensed something." Satoru leans in towards the giant's face. "There are new bodies appearing in our kingdom since the malachite laying. Where could they be coming from and what could possibly behind this?"

"Did the prince awaken the Hakkan just to satisfy a small question he thought of in the middle of the night?" the giant's voice thunders. "We have already done you a huge favour. We do not care about little human bodies."

The ground shakes as boulders begins to move. It appears that the giant is trying to turn his head back around and to return to sleep.

"Wait," Satoru pleads. "Please! Tell me what you know." Satoru feels like he is hitting a wall. Why is it that each time he tries to get more information on this case, it is proving itself to be difficult? The frustration inside him expands.

"We do not know anything, Prince Takashi," the giant booms. "We laid down your malachite, yet the bodies still appear. My guess is that you should dry up the lakes and the rivers for it to stop."

"So, you are confirming that these bodies arise from the waters?" Satoru presses. "I had a terrifying dream where the bodies woke up. Have you sensed anything prior to the appearance of the victims?"

"We do not know," the giant says to Satoru's disappointment. "Now leave us in peace and do not wake us for something so trivial," the Hakkan's deep voice rumbles through the earth of the forests.

The boulders turn and the ground shakes once again. Satoru stretches out his arm to tell the giant to wait to no avail. He soon finds himself staring at the plain, mossy boulders of the forests.

The Hakkan has gone back to sleep.

Satoru stands in the forest, his eyes wide and his breathing still heavy. He listens to his own breath as his eyes drift into the distance and he catches sight of the

cyan lake, glowing under the stars. The breeze forms gentle ripples along the surface of the water.

Suddenly, there is an overwhelming flash in the sky, like lightning.

Satoru instinctively holds his arms above his head as he ducks. A few seconds later, a deafening boom rattles through the sky like thunder.

He looks up to find the sky is crimson red.

This colour reflects upon his wide, emerald eyes, and his heart beats so hard that it is as though it is going to explode out of his chest.

Soon, the midnight sky returns to its normal colour. Satoru stares at it, trying to understand what is happening. His eyes dart towards the lake.

Something moves and—between one blink and the next—something emerges on the shore.

Is that a body? His heart sinks as he hurries towards the oddity.

As Satoru approaches, he notices something squatting next to the body. It has its back turned, and its hands are inside the victim's abdomen. Satoru frowns as he peers at what is happening from behind a tree.

The creature has its legs bent out at sharp angles and it appears to be digging inside the victim. Suddenly, its head straightens up, as if it has sensed something, and

its hands emerge out of the body.

These hands are covered in blood.

The creature turns to face the prince.

A shadow casts over its face and Satoru is unable to make out its appearance. However, its form reminds him so much of her.

Mutoren?

Satoru leaps forwards and before he has a chance to catch a second glimpse of the creature, it immediately scurries into the water.

By the time Satoru catches up, the creature is nowhere to be seen. He pants, looking at the dead body in front of him, sickness rising in his stomach.

He squats next to it, taking in the horrific sight, unsurprised to find gouged eyes and missing organs once again. Satoru places the back of his hand against the victim's wrist. It is warm.

A fresh kill? Satoru thinks in alarm. His mind is spinning as he tries to piece together what he just saw. He shakes his head. In a panic, he hurries back towards his horse.

"Yonaka!" he commands, before jumping back onto his companion and rushing back towards the palace in a haste.

As Satoru rides through the night, something eats at

his heart. *It can't be*, he thinks.

As soon as he reaches the palace, he jumps off his horse and dashes towards the guest chamber.

The palace guards bow immediately as Satoru rushes past them. "Prince Takashi!" they say in unison.

Satoru does not have time to acknowledge them. He reaches the guest chamber door and before Shou—the guard by the entrance—has a chance to react, Satoru knocks loudly on the door.

There is no response.

He knocks again and waits.

No response still.

"Please excuse me," Satoru says as he pushes the door open with slight urgency. He is unsure why something is eating away at his heart so much so.

He finds himself facing the empty bed of the guest chamber. *Where is she?*

The window is slightly open and the curtains flap in the night breeze. A small lantern is lit and placed by the bedside and a furry grey cat lies on the pillow, curled up. He takes a moment to take in this scene.

Suddenly, the gap of the open window widens. The young girl appears on the windowsill and starts to enter the chamber.

Satoru's eyes widen. *Mutoren.*

She immediately notices the prince. She blinks at him as she makes her way inside.

"Please, close the door," Satoru commands to the guards outside.

"Yes, Your Majesty!" they say. The door shuts instantly.

There is a silence.

"Evening," the Mutoren says as she gives a short nod. Her eyes tell Satoru that she is wondering why he is in her chamber.

Satoru takes a few steps towards her. His wide eyes are fixed on her with an expression of disbelief. "Harlande," Satoru says, catching his breath.

"Your Majesty?" Sana replies.

"Where were you, please?" Satoru asks.

He looks at the Mutoren. Her raven hair is braided loosely and falls over her shoulder as she looks back at him. Her eyes are round and innocent like a vedeir.

"What brings you here?" Sana replies.

"Answer me, Harlande." *It can't have been you by the lake earlier.*

Sana frowns. She pauses. "I was out."

Satoru's eyes narrow. Short, vague responses again. "Where, please?" Satoru asks sternly.

Sana's frown deepens. "At the palace kitchens."

Satoru isn't sure what to think.

The Mutoren reaches into her outer robe to take something out from underneath her arm.

His body reacts instantly and, before he knows it, he finds himself grasping onto the girl's wrist, stopping her in her tracks.

Sana looks at her wrist, then back into the prince's eyes. "What are you doing? Please let go. I do not want it to fall."

Satoru blinks at her as she shrugs off her outer robe, letting it fall to the floor. Sure enough, underneath her arm, is a wooden box.

Satoru can see she is trying to keep it as level as possible. He drops her wrist.

Sana places the box onto a small table that stands on the side of her chamber. She removes the lid and some light smoke drifts from it. The scent of a warm, comforting bowl of soup hits their senses. A piece of soft bread lays next to it.

"I got a bit hungry. That is all," Sana says. She blinks at the prince.

There is a long pause. Satoru looks at her innocent face. Should he tell her what he just witnessed? What was it that he really saw in the Oku Forests?

"Did you hear the loud thunder earlier?" Satoru asks.

"Oh, earlier?" Sana replies. "I heard it just as I was about to come out of the palace kitchens. Thought I would be caught up in rain but—" She peers back out into the window and up into the sky. "—Hmm, it does not appear to be raining." She leans back inside.

"Did you see the colour of the sky?" Satoru presses. "When you heard the thunder?"

"No, I was inside," Sana replies. She cocks her head to one side, as if wondering where all these questions are coming from.

Satoru exhales. He leans back against the wall and takes a moment. For sure, it cannot have been the Mutoren who was by the lake.

. . . Right?

"May I eat now?" Sana asks, a little impatient. She rubs her nose. Her sleeve brushes past her face.

Satoru suddenly notices the simple, beige pyjamas that she is wearing. The trousers are a little short. Her feet are small and bare. She appears so delicate and harmless.

Satoru straightens abruptly. "My apologies for intruding into a lady's chamber," Satoru says, realising that he had entered without her permission. His cheeks warm.

There is a silence. He strides towards the door and

reaches out for the door handle.

"Goodnight then, Prince Takashi," Sana says.

Satoru's hand stops mid-air. He blinks as he suddenly remembers the night on the rooftop. Something pulls slightly inside his heart once more.

"Goodnight," he replies, before nodding and briskly making his way out.

✾

After entering his chamber, Satoru pulls off his cloak and collapses onto his bed face down. His heart is still beating hard inside his chest. What made him rush into the guest chamber with such urgency?

The image of the creature lifting its blood-covered hands replays in Satoru's mind. He turns over briskly and stares at the ceiling.

Things are accelerating. What did he see earlier? Who was it at the lake? He had just witnessed a fresh kill—the first one he has come to know of in Shinrin. He will need to have this body retrieved and analysed.

Is he going to have to dry out all the lakes and rivers of the kingdom? Will that stop whatever is happening? Already, there is talk amongst the citizens that an evil spirit is lurking in the waters. Parents forbid their children to play by the riverbanks.

But how is he going to dry up the lakes and rivers?

Satoru shakes his head. Things are getting worse and worse.

Satoru wonders what exactly happened during the disaster of Qieta. Was it like this? He thinks of Albert suddenly. Has he reached Qieta? It has been quite a few months, yet he has not received a Kaidara from him.

Perhaps he should visit the aviary as soon as he gets the opportunity to. He sighs before pulling the bed covers over his head and closing his eyes tightly.

CHAPTER THIRTY

The Private Chamber

SAMUEL SITS ON THE FLOOR of his room, his head in his hands. He has an awful feeling. Why, out of all people, was Sir Meness the one who was chosen? Should he have just told him to hide here, like he'd initially thought?

Was it his fault Sir Meness was taken?

Samuel squeezes his eyes shut. His saviour—a sliver of hope who unexpectedly appeared in his life out of nowhere—did not last more than a day before he was

taken away from him.

His stomach turns at the thought of Princess Lore taking Sir Meness into her cart. What is going to happen to him? Will he ever see him again?

He must do everything he can to find Sir Meness as well as his sister.

Suddenly, there is a huge bang. Samuel turns briskly to see a soldier has kicked down his door. His eyes widen with shock. Have the soldiers discovered that Lucas is dead? Is he in trouble?

Immediately, more soldiers burst through into his room and restrain him by his arms.

Samuel struggles against the force, but there are too many of them.

Something hits him in the back of the neck, and he immediately falls unconscious.

✾

Samuel wakes. There is a terrible throbbing inside his head. He struggles to open his eyes—at first, everything around him looks blurry but things slowly start to fade into focus.

He is in a darkened room. He tries to stand, before realising that he has been tied to a chair. He cannot move his arms. His eyes widen in panic.

“Good morning,” a voice says.

Samuel turns to the voice and sees a soldier. He cannot make out who is speaking, as the man’s face is covered with a black cloth. Perhaps they have never met before.

Another voice comes from behind him. “I didn’t think you would be the type to betray us,” the voice says. Another soldier appears from behind. His face, too, is covered with a black cloth. He has angry, piercing grey eyes. “Where is Montine?”

Samuel looks at him. “I don’t know,” he answers quietly. The pace of his breathing increases.

“Did you kill him?” the soldier asks.

Samuel remains silent.

“Strike him,” the soldier orders.

His comrade immediately slaps Samuel across his face with overwhelming force. The pain is staggering. Samuel closes his eyes and swallows his fear.

“It appears you let an intruder into our organisation,” the soldier continues. “A man with silver hair.”

There is a thud inside Samuel’s heart. How did they find out? Do they not know that Princess Lore has taken him?

“Where is he?” the soldier continues.

Samuel looks at those cold, grey eyes—eyes that remind him of Lucas. He frowns and keeps his lips tightly sealed.

"Strike him again," the soldier commands.

His comrade takes out a metal pole and forcefully hits Samuel against his left shin.

Samuel almost feels something inside him break.

"I asked a question, Lorenz," the soldier snarls. "Where is the silver-haired bastard?"

Samuel flinches at the unkind remark. He stares back at the man, with intense hatred in his eyes. If he is going to be beaten to death tonight, he will do so with honour. He is sick of the corrupt, unjust universe he has somehow found himself in.

He will not let them have any satisfaction.

The soldier suddenly grabs Samuel by his jaw and leans frighteningly close to him, his eyes boring into his soul. "Where is he?" he repeats.

Samuel remains silent once again.

"You little bugger." The soldier laughs, then kicks Samuel forcefully in the stomach.

Samuel falls backwards in the wooden chair he is tied to, and hits the cold, hard floor. Pain throbs all over his body and eats at him.

Everything turns black and he loses consciousness

once again.

✾

Akalin has no idea where he is. Is he still in Keska?

After a long journey in the cart—one where he felt like his stomach learned how to do somersaults—he arrived at some sort of elaborate palace and was led into a room that resembles a chamber.

Now, he paces around inside, extremely unsettled. His head is dizzy and the odour of concentrated perfume appears to have cemented itself inside his nose.

Someone opens the door, and Akalin immediately snaps his eyes towards the entrance. He has never felt so on guard in his life.

A man wearing a robe, different to the traditional Shirinese style which Akalin is familiar with, steps inside. He places a violet-and-silver robe—an extravagant version in the same style as his own—onto the bed.

He then looks at Akalin. "Evening, sir. Please put this on and wait to be called."

Akalin looks at him and does not move an inch.

"Please do as you are told, sir," the man says. "Someone will call you soon." He then steps out and shuts the door.

Sickness rises inside Akalin's stomach. He tries to

shake the feeling from his mind, although deep inside, he is extremely uneasy about what may be about to happen.

He paces in the room, thinking about what he can do, listening to his own shallow breaths.

He is a very good fighter. However, he is trapped in a completely unfamiliar place with unfamiliar people and has no weapons. With the size of this palace, the staff likely outnumbers him.

Akalin is truly alone.

He reluctantly makes his way over to the amethyst piece of clothing, removes his armour, and puts it on.

After a while, his door opens once more.

Do people not knock here?

The man from earlier beckons him. "Please come with me, sir. Princess Lore is ready for you."

The sickness inside Akalin's stomach intensifies. He slowly walks behind the man, his senses on full alert.

Akalin is led to a grand, ornate door, covered with various intricate carvings.

The man knocks slightly. "Princess Lore," the man says.

Oh, so for the Princess, *they knock.*

"Yes, bring him in, my lovely," Akalin hears her respond in her high-pitched voice.

The man pushes the door open and gestures for Akalin to enter.

Akalin slowly steps inside and immediately realises he must be in Lore's private chamber. The strong scent of perfume hits him once more. The room is full of extravagant decorations, soft, silken furniture, and an enormous, lustrous bed is laid out in the centre.

He remains as close to the door as he can, even as it closes behind him.

Princess Lore has her back facing Akalin. She is perched on a couch and appears to be looking in a mirror, dabbing something onto her eyelids. She turns and sees Akalin.

Her mouth breaks into a smile. "My prince," she says softly. "Please, come sit." She gestures to the couch opposite her.

Akalin looks around the room. There is a window here, there, and behind that way—possible escape routes. The door is there, but at least four or five men stand outside. His mind works quickly.

Princess Lore finishes doing whatever she is doing and turns to fully face Akalin as he sits. She has changed into soft, golden fabrics that drape over her and cling to her frame.

Akalin decides that, if he has to fight to escape here,

he will do so.

“My, how adorable.” Princess Lore giggles. “You still have the red piece of cloth over your face.” She stands, strides towards Akalin, and sits next to him, again, uncomfortably close.

“I think it is time we meet properly,” she whispers, as she slowly tugs the cloth covering Akalin’s face.

Akalin braces himself as it peels away. His face is about to be revealed and he may be eaten alive.

The princess’s scarlet eyes widen. “Wow. You are . . . exquisite,” she whispers, looking into his eyes and admiring his face. “Not only exquisite but . . . charming . . . almost ethereal.” She leans back and continues to admire him. “The robe really brings out the amethyst in your eyes. You are a true work of art.”

Akalin remains silent. He is almost crying silent tears inside. He wants to do a million somersaults off the trees in Shinrin’s forests to shake the feeling of disgust looming over him.

“Let us talk a bit first,” the princess decides.

To Akalin’s relief, she sits back on the couch opposite. His relief is short-lived when she crosses her legs in an inappropriate, intentional way.

The fabrics fall to the side.

“I want to begin with a question, my prince,”

Princess Lore says as she gazes softly at him. "Tell me, is it dangerous in the lands outside of Keska?"

Akalin raises an eyebrow. *What is she on about? The most dangerous land I know of right now is Keska itself.* He looks at her and does not say a word, wondering what she is doing.

The princess looks at Akalin, blinking her large eyes, and smiles. She bats her eyelashes.

"I don't know what you are talking about," Akalin mutters. To his surprise, Princess Lore's eyes widen and her smile grows even larger.

"You are a lucky man," she begins, "because I have chosen you. So, for the rest of your life, you will have everything you've ever dreamed of." She winks.

Akalin has never felt more trapped in his life.

"I like you, so I have brought you straight to my private chamber. And I am a lucky lady, because *you* have one of the most beautiful faces I have ever laid eyes upon."

Alarmingly, she gets up and moves behind Akalin, placing her hands on his shoulders.

Akalin stiffens. Should he fight now? What if she calls for her men before he can get away?

Princess Lore leans against his left ear. "As you know already, I am Princess Lore," she whispers. "But . . . you

can call me Suyin. That is my first name. It will make us feel more . . . intimate." She giggles. "What is your name?"

Akalin remains silent. *Please go away.*

"Your name, my prince?" she whispers once more.

"Meness," Akalin answers coldly.

The princess runs her hand through Akalin's long, silver hair. "Moon, like your hair. I like that." She wraps his silver strands around her wrist and admires them, before placing her hand on Akalin's waist.

The sudden touch makes him flinch.

She trails her hand down further, and then towards his inner thigh—

Akalin has had enough. Like a flash of lightning, he swiftly grasps onto her wrist, stopping her in her tracks. He does so with so much force, it makes her yelp.

He turns to face her, his eyes burning with disgust. "You are a princess," Akalin says coldly. "Where are your manners?" He drops her wrist.

Princess Lore is stunned, and she collapses onto the floor, shaking. "How—how could you —"

"I should hope a lady would be better taught than this," Akalin says.

His heart beats hard inside his chest. The princess may be about to call for her guards any second now, but he is not going to let himself get hurt. The adrenaline

pulsates inside him as his breathing accelerates.

The princess stammers. “You—” She takes a second to breathe. “You do not understand how lucky you are. Men would die to be in your position. I grant true happiness, and men would do anything to be with me—”

“Men who want your body and your wealth,” Akalin snaps, intimidating her. “I am not sure what sort of men you surround yourself with, but if this is what you call true happiness, I pity you.”

Inside, Akalin is about to vomit. Fear threatens to consume him.

Princess Lore stares at the floor, breathing heavily, her face an expression of shock. Some memories flash across her eyes. She looks up at him, as tears begin to form.

She looks back down at the floor and manages a small laugh. “Well, you are a true gentleman, aren’t you?” she asks, barely managing a whisper.

A few of her round tears drop to the floor.

CHAPTER THIRTY-ONE

An Identified Victim

SOMETHING TAPS ON THE WINDOW of Satoru's study just as he is about to meet Professor Asante. The prince turns to see a bright, yellow bird with dark, splotchy patterns on his head. It holds a folded piece of parchment in his beak and blinks at him.

Is that a Cabib? Satoru thinks. He gently pulls the parchment from the bird's beak and unfolds it before scanning the writing.

Prince Takashi,

Recently, dead bodies have been discovered in the Kingdom of Rheahldere. I have heard that something similar may be happening in Shinrin, although I do not have much information. I wonder if you may provide us with some insight.

I plan to pay a visit to Shinrin soon.

Regards,
Saeya Saeldis

Something drops inside Satoru's heart. The dead bodies have started appearing in Rheahldere as well? The message from Queen Saeya was completely unexpected.

He quickly scribbles a response before heading down to the examination chambers.

✤

Satoru pushes open the heavy stone door of the examination chamber.

Professor Asante immediately bows to him. "Good day, Prince Takashi."

"Professor Asante." Satoru nods. "I am eager to learn what news you have for me."

He prays that the Professor will bring him some good news. Recently, things have truly been getting out of hand.

He stops for a second. "Where is Knight Lishuah?"

"I am not sure, Your Majesty," the Professor replies.

Satoru wonders where she is. He had called for her to attend this meeting in the hopes that she could help him and reveal more information. It is unlike her to be late.

"Please begin," Satoru says. "I do not want to use up too much of your time. She may join us if she appears later."

"Very well, Prince Takashi," Professor Asante answers.

Satoru scans the room. There are now a few more bodies lying under white sheets. He suddenly remembers his dream and glances at the window, hoping the glass will not shatter.

"Prince Takashi," Dimak begins as he adjusts his spectacles, "although I cannot explain how, the conclusion I can draw from the original victims is that they did not actually die from drowning."

"Is that so?" Satoru asks, surprised.

"All of them have been in contact with the same substance, although I am unsure what it is. However, after studying each of them closely, I believe each of them were first murdered through strangulation. After that, their organs were removed—or devoured—and then they were thrown into the waters."

Satoru takes in this new information.

"I believe the mottled pattern on the skin and hair I explained to you before is a result of whichever common thing they have come into contact with," Dimak continues. "Whatever it is seems to leave a residue once it's been immersed in water for a long period of time."

"My goodness," Satoru says.

"I still do not understand why the bodies appear on our riverbanks, or where they came from, however," Dimak replies.

"Do you still believe they are Qietian?" Satoru enquires.

"That is my best guess."

"And what about the newest victim?" Satoru asks.

"This one, unfortunately, is a Shirinese citizen. I have identified him as Mr. David Yale, a four-and-fifty-year-old gentleman who works as an entomologist."

Satoru's eyes widen.

"According to his family, he was out that evening in search for some of the nocturnal insects he was studying. He leaves behind a wife and a daughter. His family are currently grieving," Professor Asante explains, his expression sombre.

"This is terrible," Satoru says. He pauses. "In truth, I witnessed something that night. There was a creature by Mr. Yale. From afar, it appeared that the creature was removing his organs."

"Yes, I remember you telling me, Your Majesty," Dimak replies.

"Have you found any evidence for who the perpetrator may be?"

"There were some remnants of saliva on the wound edges," Dimak answers. "It appears Mr. Yale was strangled and his body ripped open by the mouth of the perpetrator."

"And you still believe this perpetrator is a creature—rather than a human?" Satoru asks.

"Yes, Your Majesty," Dimak replies. "I am inclined to say that it appears more animal-like than human."

Satoru inhales. "I thank you for your expertise once again, Professor Asante."

"I will continue to do my best, Prince Takashi," Professor Asante replies. "I must say, this is the most

intriguing—yet horrifying—case I have ever worked on."

"Indeed."

Satoru thinks through what he may need to do. Perhaps he will need to set up something by the shores of the riverbanks to try and catch this creature the next time it strikes.

✾

After some time more time has passed, the stone door of the examination chamber slowly edges open. The professor and the prince both turn towards it.

The Mutoren slowly steps inside. "My apologies for being late," Sana says.

Satoru looks at her. Today, she wears a simple black robe with white trousers. Her hair is loose. She looks slightly pale and perhaps a little tired. The usual glint in her eyes appears to be absent.

"Knight Lishuah," Satoru says.

"Your Majesty," Sana replies.

"You are late indeed."

"My apologies," Sana whispers, slightly out of breath.

The professor bows to them both. "Good day, Knight Lishuah."

Satoru's eyes narrow. "I thank you again, Professor

Asante," Satoru says. "We shall let you continue your work." He begins making his way to the exit. "Lishuah," Satoru says. "Let us go back."

Sana does not respond. She slowly walks behind the prince and watches as he closes the large stone door. She continues to trail behind him as they walk down the long corridor.

"Where were you?" Satoru asks. He pauses to allow her to catch up.

She doesn't respond.

"It is unlike you to be late," Satoru says.

Sana still does not respond. She continues to walk down the corridor, although it seems to take a lot of effort. "Let's go," she whispers.

Satoru looks at her again. His eyebrows furrow with some suspicion and concern. He puts his hand on her shoulder to stop her. "Harlande—"

Sana turns slowly to look at him. Everything is aching. She catches a glimpse of Prince Takashi's eyes just before a heavy weight consumes her, and she falls backwards.

Satoru holds out his arms in alarm, just in time to catch her. He kneels instantly with her in his arms, eyes wide. "Harlande?" Satoru repeats, the tone of his voice changing.

Sana manages to open her eyes slowly. With effort, she attempts to get back to her feet.

"It is all right," Sana manages to whisper.

Satoru presses the back of his hand to her forehead. "Harlande, you are burning up."

Sana only notices him touching her. It feels light and cool. She closes her eyes.

Urgency rises in Satoru. He immediately stands and lifts the girl in his arms with ease before racing down the rest of the corridor towards the guest chamber.

"Prince Takashi!" some of the guards lining up by the hallway greet him and bow instantly.

"Please, call for the palace healer," Satoru commands, before he continues his way towards the guest chamber.

Sana feels like everything is weighing her body down. Every inch of her is aching. Every next breath is a struggle. She has no idea what is happening and her eyelids are too heavy for her to open them. There are strong arms around her. Something warm is against her cheek. There is a *thump thump* which she can hear, although the pace of it is quickening.

Is that the prince's heartbeat? It feels somewhat comforting.

As soon as Satoru reaches the guest chamber, Shou

greets him and bows before opening the door hastily. Satoru lays the Mutoren down onto her bed. He looks at her as she lies limply, his heart pounding with worry.

Sana begins to cough. She winces as pain radiates through her chest.

Satoru immediately scoops her into his arms before sitting her on the bed and propping her upright with some pillows. He takes out a handkerchief from his robe and holds it in front of her mouth as he waits for the moment to pass.

"Trust you to always surprise me, Harlande," Satoru comments, his eyebrows furrowed with concern.

Sana takes a breath before she leans back, exhausted.

Satoru's eyes widen. Something cracks inside his heart.

The white handkerchief he held by her face is covered in bright red blood.

CHAPTER THIRTY-TWO

The Red Thread of Fate

THE DOOR OF SATORU'S CHAMBER swings open. An eight-year-old Satoru turns around to see his older brother running inside, arms wide and ready to scoop him up.

"Satoru!" Satoshi shouts cheerfully as he picks him up and spins him around.

Satoru's little mouth breaks into a wide smile. "Brother Satoshi!" he exclaims cheerfully.

His brother puts him down. "Ah." He sighs happily

as he collapses to the floor in a heap. “It’s good to be back.”

Satoru sits next to his brother. Satoshi, his dear brother, is ten years older than him. He boasts a handsome face—something that seems to run in the Takashi family—and the same long, raven locks as his younger brother, Satoru. His eyes, however, are amethyst, like orchids.

“Let me tell you,” Satoshi begins. “Enjoy being a child.”

Satoru looks at his brother, confused.

Satoshi sits up. “Once you get to a certain age, Satoru,” his brother explains, “you will start getting ladies all over the place who want to marry you.”

Satoru’s small face scrunches up into a twist. “Ew. Who likes girls?”

“Honestly!” Satoshi continues. “It’s exhausting. People say it is a privilege to have so many beautiful ladies lining up and wanting to take your hand, but—” He sighs and throws his palm against his forehead. “—I barely know any of them. How am I supposed to marry someone I don’t know?”

“Don’t ask me.” Satoru shrugs innocently.

“I truly believe,” Satoshi continues, looking up at the sunlight which is pouring through Satoru’s chamber

window, "you cannot force these things. If it is meant to be, then it is meant to be."

Satoru looks at his brother. Sometimes, he goes off into these trances and Satoru feels like he does not know what he is talking about.

"Have you heard of the red thread of fate, Brother?" Satoshi asks.

Satoru shakes his head.

"There is a saying that, between some people, there is a red thread which connects them. You cannot see it, but it is there."

Satoru blinks.

"It connects two people who are meant to be together."

"Is that so?" Satoru asks.

"Yes. They may be miles apart—perhaps even universes apart—but if they are connected, they will find each other, somewhere. Somehow."

Satoru cocks his head to one side. "Hmm . . ."

"The thread may stretch, it may twist, or even get tangled, but one day, they will be led to each other at last."

Satoru thinks for a moment. "So, it is like a strong bond, is it?"

"I guess you could say that."

Satoru nods. "I understand." He then looks at his brother, his forest eyes wide and playful. "That means the red thread connects us two!"

Satoshi laughs. He pats his brother on the head. "Satoru," he says. "When you grow up, do not let anyone tell you who you should or should not marry. Find someone who touches your heart. Someone who sees a side of you that no one else sees, and who brings out a side of you that no one else can bring out. Do it for yourself. Do not settle for someone you can live with, but rather . . . be with someone you cannot live without. May it be a lady, or a gentleman, or, whatever!"

"I see."

"Or, if you are like me, someone who is currently perfectly content being by himself," Satoshi says, "that is also, perfectly fine." He ruffles his hand through Satoru's hair.

Satoru draws his knees against his chest, his face suddenly solemn.

"What is it, Brother?" Satoshi asks.

Satoru looks at him but remains silent.

"Satoru?"

"Mother said—" Satoru inhales. "Mother said . . . soon you will have to leave. Is that true?"

Satoshi pauses for a moment and blinks. His facial

expression softens and he puts his arm around his little brother. “She told you?” he asks.

Satoru nods.

“I won’t be gone for long,” Satoshi says to his brother.

“Where are you going?” Satoru asks.

Satoshi holds his brother and brings him even closer towards him. “On an adventure.” He winks. He then looks slightly more serious. “One day, you will understand, Brother,” he says, looking into Satoru’s eyes. “Sometimes, we have to do things for the people we love.”

Satoru feels like his brother is going into one of his trances again, saying deep things that do not quite make sense.

“How is Albert settling in?” Satoshi says, changing the subject.

“He gets nightmares and wets the bed,” Satoru says honestly. “He wakes up crying in the night.”

“The kid must have gone through a lot,” Satoshi says. “Be kind to him, Brother.”

“I am,” Satoru replies, defensively.

“Of course.” Satoshi ruffles his hand through Satoru’s hair once more. “You are such a good boy.”

Satoru holds his brother’s arm and leans his head

against his shoulder. There is an ache inside his heart, although he is unsure why.

Satoshi feels his little brother's grip tighten around his arm. His heart sinks a little and he takes the moment to cherish the time he has left with him.

CHAPTER THIRTY-THREE

Heartbreak

THAT NIGHT, PRINCESS LORE LIES on her silken bed. The back of her hand rests over her forehead and her eyes are closed. Tears roll from her eyes onto her bed sheets, forming circles of dampness.

Her mind drifts back to her memories from many, many years ago. The amethyst eyes of the man with the silver hair have reminded her of someone she holds close to her heart.

The only man she ever truly had feelings for, even

if they were ultimately unrequited.

"Satoshi Takashi," she whispers to herself.

Hearing this name out loud sends a warm, but painful, ache through her heart. She has not allowed herself to think of him in a very long time.

She wonders where he is now.

✾

When Suyin was still a young girl, she was constantly bombarded by arranged meetings with various Keskan men of nobility, as well as many other kingdoms. Her parents, the king and queen of Keska, were determined—even obsessed—with the idea of forming alliances, and they were willing to do anything to ensure constant abundance and wealth for their land.

They told Suyin that the world outside of Keska is a dangerous place, and that if she is to marry, the man must come and reside with her in Keska—the safest kingdom in Neputa.

Her life was miserable. The countless men were so much older than her and most of them made her uncomfortable. They seemed to want her for the wrong reasons.

While there were countless men lining up outside her door daily, all wanting to get to know her and to

marry her, there was one particular land who rejected an invitation to come to Keska to discuss marriage.

Shinrin.

However, Shinrin was the largest, if not one of the most powerful lands in Neputa. The king and queen believed that, if they could form an alliance with Shinrin, they would achieve ultimate success and the epitome of power and wealth. They had told Suyin that Shinrin was one of the rare, safe kingdoms. As such, they arranged for her to go to Shinrin for a few days to meet their royalty instead.

When Suyin reached Shinrin, she was treated with so much respect she felt as if—for the first time—she was enjoying her life. She was shocked at how beautiful the land was.

And then, she met Prince Takashi. He was only two years older than her at that time and she felt as if she fell in love with him at first sight.

He had the most beautiful, orchid-coloured eyes and long, raven black hair. But what Suyin found the most attractive was his courteous, elegant manner, and his mind of wisdom. He was everything she would want in a man: knowledgeable, well-spoken, chivalrous, and patient. He was like a breathtakingly beautiful angel who had been carved from perfection.

She thinks back to a conversation she has embedded inside her heart.

✾

"Prince Takashi," a sixteen-year-old Suyin says as they walk through the gardens of the Shinrin palace. "I must say, I have never met a man as wonderful as you."

Satoshi laughs. "You need to get out and see the world more, Princess Lore," he replies.

"My parents say the world is a dangerous place. They want me to marry. Every day I am being pushed to meet people I do not care about."

"I know how that feels," Satoshi replies, "although it is not that my parents are forcing me . . . it is more that these ladies keep lining up outside our kingdom without being invited." Satoshi then realises what he has just said, and he covers his mouth. "I mean—"

"I guess you are not interested in marriage, Prince Takashi?" Suyin asks, realising that she is another burden on top of the countless women who push themselves towards him.

"There is a lot more to life than marriage," Satoshi answers her. "Princess Lore, think of this," he says. "Look around you. What do you know and what do you *not* know? What do you want to find out? What do you

want to do with your life?"

The sudden number of questions stun her a little. She has never thought much about the world outside of Keska, as she had always been told it is too dangerous.

"There is so much to do, so much to see, and so much to explore," Satoshi continues. "Marriage can be a part of life, but it is only a small part of what makes your life whole. You are young and you have a lot left ahead of you. You should do things for yourself and not for others."

Suyin takes a moment to absorb what Prince Takashi is saying to her.

"It must be frustrating to be pushed into doing something you do not want to do. But you should marry someone because you love them and because they love you. Be with someone who will treat you like a queen and who will cherish you. Find someone who would die for you. Not because your parents tell you to."

Suyin blinks a few times. "My, Prince Takashi . . . where did you learn this from?"

"My lovely mother and father," he replies. He then looks at her and she blushes. "We are but a small speck of dust in this universe, Princess Lore," he says. "Get out there and see the world."

Suyin takes a breath. "But . . . Prince Takashi, is the

world not a dangerous place?"

"Does it look dangerous to you?" Satoshi replies gently, gesturing at the environment around them.

"Shinrin is truly beautiful," Suyin admits, "but I'm afraid of how the rest of the world may be."

"Then, you have clearly not experienced it." Satoshi smiles at her. Suyin takes a moment to take in his words. She suddenly realises, there is so much she does not know. She does not want to return to Keska just yet.

"Prince Takashi . . . I am due to leave tomorrow." An intense feeling of sadness sweeps over her.

"Then, you should go and live your life."

"Prince Takashi, I—" Suyin stutters. She looks at his violet eyes and her heart throbs. "I know it has only been a few days, but I have such strong feelings for you. Could we please—May you please—Could you possibly consider me?"

"Princess Lore," Satoshi says to her softly. "I thank you for making the journey all the way here to Shinrin and I thank you for your time. But marriage is not something I want now."

"Prince Takashi, I have never felt this way before about anyone. I believe I am utterly in love with you," Suyin pleads. Tears are starting to well up in her eyes.

Satoshi blinks in alarm. "Princess Lore," he says

again, trying to comfort her. "One day, you will realise that there is so much more to life. You will do things that will make you happy and you will realise that I am not the one for you. I will become nothing more than a memory that will fade away."

"I will never forget you, Prince Takashi." Suyin wipes a tear from her eye. She wonders how the man in front of her, a man who is only two years older, can be so perfect, so wise, and so unattainable.

A soft, white handkerchief appears in front of her. She looks up.

"Here," Satoshi says softly.

Suyin takes the soft handkerchief from his hands and looks at the small, emerald leaf embroidered on it.

"Keep it," Satoshi says. "And don't cry anymore."

✾

When Suyin returned to Keska, she and her parents got into a terrible dispute. She refused to marry anyone and went on to refuse anything her parents asked of her. In a fury, they locked her up in the palace, claiming that it was to keep her safe. They forbade her to leave after she announced that she was going to, "Go and see the world."

As the years went on, Suyin became more and more

withdrawn. Her parents continued to build up the Keskan empire, doing anything they could to maintain its wealth.

Their most recent accomplishment was the Keskan mines. Suyin was aware that children were being abducted and enslaved to maintain this organisation, but something inside her had faded and she no longer felt anything such as guilt nor remorse.

For a few years now, she has been taking the small opportunity of being allowed out of the palace to bring a soldier into her chambers. She would pick someone who she believed may have seen the world. She hoped that he would be able to help her escape the castle. The men who appeared to be madly in love with her also gave her a strange feeling of power and control, something that helped cover up the pain consuming her.

Suyin had hoped that she would be able to ignite the flame she had once felt for Prince Takashi for someone else. However, none of the men had been able to fill the void in her heart, nor did they have any knowledge about the outside world—

Until this man with silver hair and amethyst eyes appeared.

His eyes remind her so much of Prince Takashi. His

brief answer to her question also tells her that he knows about the world outside of Keska.

Something inside her heart twinges once more.

✾

Suyin suddenly sits up on her bed, eyes wide with worry.

Every so often, her father will appear and take away whichever soldier she has chosen, as if to punish her for what happened so many years ago. To this day, she still does not know where they are taken.

Something in her heart tells her that she must not let this happen to the man with silver hair.

In a flurry, she flings open the door of her chamber and runs towards the room housing her new guest. She bursts through his door, only to see him balancing on the windowsill, as if he is looking for a method of escape.

"Meness," she demands.

Akalin looks at her. *What now?*

"I am a princess," she says, repeating the words the man in front of her said earlier. "And I order you to come with me. Now."

CHAPTER THIRTY-FOUR

Azrael

"THANK YOU FOR HAVING OUR little Satoru over," Satoru's mother and father say to Albert's parents.

The sun is beginning to set and the sky is a warm, orange haze.

"Come again soon!" Albert's eleven-year-old sister, Astra, says.

"Did you have fun?" Satoru's mother asks her son.

Satoru nods furiously. "We made cakes together today, Mother!" he says proudly, holding a cloth bag up

towards her. "You and father can try when we get home! Also, Albert showed me how to fold a frog from parchment!"

"How lovely," his mother answers.

She looks at Albert's mother and they both smile as they watch their children wave goodbye to each other.

✽

Albert sits up from his bed. *A dream?*

He rubs his eyes. It takes a while for him to recognise where he is. He realises he is in one of the guest houses in Qieta; Liuana Pharlos brought him here the day before.

He thinks about his dream and realises he now understands what the old man was trying to explain. The dream had felt incredibly real, so much so that when Albert woke up, he still felt as if he and Prince Takashi's family had really met when they were children.

The reality of his own deceased family hits him.

He decides that today, he must find out how to send a Kaidara to Prince Takashi—back to his homeland of Shinrin—to let him know he arrived in Qieta.

Albert gets himself ready and heads out into the common room. The innkeeper whom he met yesterday

is there.

Albert greets him. “Good morning, Mister Jayler.”

The middle-aged man greets him immediately and bows. “Good morning, Sir Leon of Shinrin,” he replies. “Did you sleep well?”

“Very much so.”

“Please, take a seat while I get some breakfast ready for you.”

Albert thanks him and sits on one of the chairs by a round wooden table. He peers out of the window. The sky is dark. Moonlight shines through onto the ground.

“Any interesting dreams last night?” Mister Jayler asks cheerfully from behind.

“Oh, this is something I will have to get used to,” Albert replies.

The innkeeper chuckles.

Albert decides to ask another question. “Mister Jayler,” he enquires, “may you remind me again what symbol represents your land?”

The innkeeper dries a few glasses and, as he puts them away, he says, “It is our native flower. The lilium sidereum.”

Albert ponders on this. Didn’t Prince Takashi say that the Qietian symbol is a circle with a Kaidara feather? He wonders why there is an inconsistency.

"And how about Shinrin?" the man asks.

"It is an emerald leaf," Albert replies. "One that represents our magnificent forests."

"Very nice," the innkeeper acknowledges. He smiles. "I do hope I can visit one day. Shinrin is a land that is very highly spoken of." He walks behind the counter and into the small room behind.

Before Albert can reply, someone bursts through the door. Albert turns towards it just as Mister Jayler also steps back out with Albert's breakfast tray in his hands.

"Sir Xandyr," Albert says, his expression is one of surprise, "Are you alright?"

"Sir Leon," Ilkari says, his voice etched with worry. He takes a moment to catch his breath. "Liuana Pharlos has requested that you please come to the spiritual foundations immediately."

✾

Albert does not even have time to wish his horse, Erwin, a proper good morning before Ilkari urges him to leave. The two of them leap onto their horses and journey quickly towards the spiritual towers.

As they approach, Albert notices Liuana Pharlos standing by the entrance.

"Young Sir Leon," the old man says to him, his eyes

wide with fear. The fine lines on his forehead deepen. "I am so glad you are here. Please, you must come with me."

"What is happening, Liuana Pharlos?" Albert asks quickly.

Erwin begins to neigh and shake his head ferociously, his ivory mane swishing in a panic. Albert has never seen his stallion like this. He holds Erwin's head close to him and strokes his forehead to calm him down.

"What is it, Erwin?" Albert asks gently, although he is aware that he should be hurrying. His horse looks at him with his large, beady eyes and breathes rapidly.

Erwin does not settle down at all.

"He must feel it as well," the old man interjects. "Please, Ilkari, bring the horses inside while we continue on," he urges.

Sir Xandyr immediately takes the reins of both horses and starts to lead them aside.

Albert turns to look at Erwin one last time; he is somewhat unsettled without his horse by his side.

Liuana Pharlos begins to walk at a rapid pace and Albert has no choice but to follow him. He is surprised that the old man can stride so quickly.

"Please, Liuana Pharlos, what is going on?" Albert

asks, feeling uneasy.

"Young Sir Leon," the old man answers as they continue walking, "my orb brought me a vision last night. It appears Azrael sensed that a new man came to Qieta and that he has come out of his dark haven to look for you." His eyes are wide with panic.

"Azrael?" Albert asks. *Is that the evil soul? The one behind the killings?*

Albert continues following the old man as they weave between ivory pillar after ivory pillar.

"Yes. Azrael is the evil soul who devours the organs of innocent civilians."

"Why is he looking for me?"

"I do not know, young Sir Leon," the old man answers. "Perhaps he feels that you are an intruder. An outsider. Or perhaps he is curious. He is unpredictable."

Albert tries to process this information. He is struggling to make sense of what is happening.

"We need to go to the centre of our grounds," the old man continues, "for it is the safest there. And please, young Sir Leon—stay behind me and watch out for your safety."

Soon enough, the ivory pillars stop and converge to form a large clear, circumferential area. The multicoloured glass dome above gives a prismatic effect,

casting down various shades of coloured light onto the ground. There is a large, porcelain structure in the middle—perhaps a throne of some sort—and a man is already sitting there comfortably, as if he has been awaiting them for some time.

Even when sitting, Albert can see that he boasts a tall frame. He wears a long, luxurious, high-collared robe inlaid with black-and-maroon patterns. He rests his head in his right hand as he smiles elegantly, crossing his left leg over his right.

The old man's eyes widen. He shakes his head in disbelief. "Azrael," he gasps. "He is here already." Liuana Pharlos holds up his silver staff horizontally, as if trying to ward Azrael off. He turns towards Albert. "Stay behind me, my child!" the old man shouts.

Albert looks at the man in front of him. His sapphire eyes widen, first in confusion and then with disbelief. He looks at Azrael's long, raven black hair, half braided at the top, with the ends flowing loosely over his shoulders. His amethyst eyes look back at him softly.

"B–Brother Satoshi?" Albert whispers.

The man looks at him and smiles, as if finding all this quite amusing. "Albert Leon." He nods slowly. His voice is deep and silky. "Long time no see."

About the Author

Dr. Ting-Wei Wu, known by her peers as Tina Wu, was born in Taiwan and moved to the United Kingdom in 2001. As a little girl with a big imagination, The *Quest for Qieta* series has lived in her mind since she was sixteen. At last, over a decade later, she has put pen to paper to bring the universe of Neputa to life.

www.thequestforqieta.com

THE QUEST FOR QIETA

For information contact:
Website; http://www.thequestforqieta.com
Instagram/X/tiktok; @tinainqieta

Cover design by Antonio Cesar
Book Formatting by Derek Murphy

First Edition: September 2023

ISBN: 978-1-7395297-0-3

To So

The Quest for Qieta

Dr. T. Wu

Helene und der Kater Karajan

Die Klassenzicke und der adelige Kater aus Paris – da fliegen die Fetzen! Und wenn sie lange genug die Krallen gezeigt haben, schnurren sie wieder friedlich wie zwei kleine Kätzchen …

Silas und das Krokodil Rick

Silas reißt seine Klappe oft viel zu weit auf. Genau wie Rick. Zwei Freunde mit Biss!

Finja und das Koalamädchen Sydney

Seit die zarte Finja einen Koala zum Kuscheln hat, fühlt sie sich nicht mehr einsam. Und duftet herrlich nach Hustenbonbons …

Viele Tiere, viele Kinder …
Wer wird wohl der Nächste sein?

Inhaltsverzeichnis

Die Schule der magischen Tiere

Top oder Flop!

E-Mail, abgeschickt von einem Internetcafé in Canterbury, England

Von: mortimer.morrison@fly.com

An: teacher-mary@mail.com

Hi Sister,

viele Grüße von der Insel! Schön mal wieder hier zu sein! Ich fahre mit meinem Omnibus durch das Land oder wandere ein bisschen im Regen. Gerade hab ich versucht ein paar Schafe für die magische Zoohandlung zu begeistern, aber die haben nur verwirrt geblökt und mir die Butterkekse weggefuttert. Pinkie will unbedingt nach London und die Kronjuwelen angucken. Hoffentlich löst sie keinen Alarm aus, meiner Elster traue ich alles zu.
Wie läuft es an der Wintersteinschule? Wie kommst du mit Agent Y zurecht? Pass gut auf ihn auf, ich glaube, die Vogelspinne ist ein bisschen schüchtern.
Hoffentlich finden wir bald ein nettes Kind für ihn!

See you, Mortimer

Der Linksverkehr trieb Mortimer Morrison in den Wahnsinn! Schwarze Taxis überholten ihn von hinten rechts. Ein roter Doppeldeckerbus hupte ihn wild zur Seite.

„Ich hasse Städte“, knurrte Mr. Morrison vor sich hin.

Seine Elster Pinkie hingegen, die auf dem Beifahrersitz des alten Omnibusses saß, hatte blendende Laune.

„Ich kann es kaum erwarten, die herrlichen Funkeldinger zu besichtigen!“, jauchzte sie. „Hui, wird das schön!“

„Hab's ja schon kapiert“, brummte Mortimer Morrison und kämpfte sich weiter durch den Großstadtverkehr.

Nur der Elster zuliebe kurvte der Inhaber der magischen Zoohandlung durch die Straßen von London. Kronen, Zepter und Ringe – das wollte sich Pinkie auf keinen Fall entgehen lassen. Allein die Krone von Königin Victoria bestand aus 1300 Diamanten!

Mortimer Morrison fuhr über die Tower Bridge, links ragte bereits die mächtige Burganlage in den Himmel. Mist, wo war die richtige Einfahrt?

Auf einer Verkehrsinsel hoppelten ein paar Kaninchen.

„He, ihr Kleinen!“, rief Mr. Morrison aus dem Fenster. „Wollt ihr mitkommen in die magische Zoohandlung?“

Aber die Kaninchen rümpften nur ihre Näschen.

„Dann eben nicht“, murrte Mr. Morrison.

Endlich hatten sie es geschafft. Da war der Parkplatz.

„Abflug!“, kommandierte Mortimer und öffnete die Beifahrertür. „Aber mach keinen Unsinn, verstanden?“

„Ich doch nicht!“ Die Elster legte den Kopf schief und sah den Inhaber der magischen Zoohandlung treuherzig an. „Niemals!“ Und damit flatterte Pinkie davon, um ein offenes Fenster im Tower of London zu suchen.

„Wir treffen uns in einer Stunde!“, rief Mortimer der Elster hinterher.

Ein unwiderstehlicher Duft stieg Mr. Morrison in die Nase. Pommes und Backfisch … Sein Magen knurrte. Hier musste irgendwo ein „Fish'n'Chips“-Laden sein!

Eine Rolltreppe führte ihn in den Untergrund.

Tatsächlich – da war ein Imbiss! Mr. Morrison drängte sich durch die Menge. In der U-Bahn-Station war es laut und stickig. Menschen hasteten vorbei und quasselten in ihre Handys.

Ob es hier Tiere gab? Magische Tiere?

Eine U-Bahn fuhr ein. Bremsen quietschten. Plötzlich sah Mortimer Morrison zwischen den Gleisen zwei schwarze, neugierige Augen aufblitzen. „Cool, Baby!“, staunte eine freche Stimme.

Was war das? Ein Marder?

„Ich glaub's einfach nicht!"
Ein Schatten huschte über die Gleise. Er verschwand in einem Rohr – und kam direkt am Imbissstand wieder rausgekrabbelt.
„Mortimer höchstpersönlich! Cool, Baby!", rief das Tierchen.
„Wer bist du denn?", gluckste Mortimer und bückte sich.
Das Tier blinzelte. „Ich bin Cooper, die schlauste Ratte Londons! Und weit und breit die einzige Ratte, die sprechen kann!"
Mortimer lächelte. „Dann bist du bei mir genau richtig."
Cooper hüpfte in Mortimers Jackentasche. Sie bestellten eine doppelte Portion Pommes mit Essig und marschierten fröhlich zurück zum Omnibus.
Vor dem Tower of London standen Polizeiwagen mit Blaulicht. Polizeibeamte liefen hektisch hin und her. Irgendjemand musste die Alarmanlage ausgelöst haben.
Auf dem Beifahrersitz wartete schon Pinkie.
„Na, endlich bist du da!", seufzte die Elster. Sie beachtete das neue magische Tier gar nicht, sondern wirkte reichlich nervös. „Können wir bitte rasch von hier verschwinden?"
„Nichts lieber als das", antwortete Mr. Morrison und legte den Rückwärtsgang ein.

FISH 'N' CHIPS
UNDERGROUND
OPEN

1. Kapitel

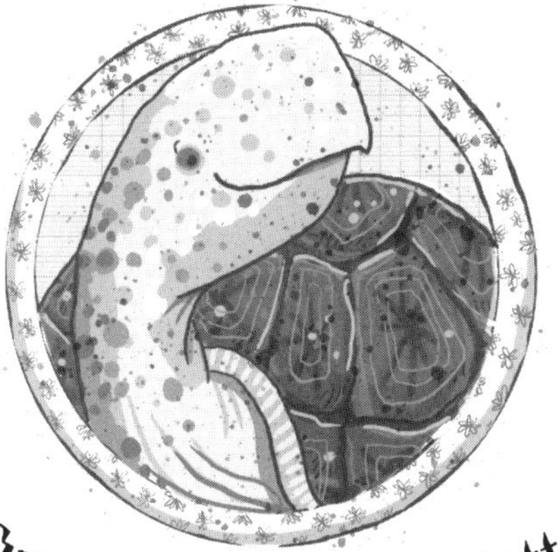

Turnstunde mit Henrietta

„Hoch den Popo, hoch den Popo!“, kommandierte Henrietta. Es war Montagvormittag. Die Schildkröte stand mit ihren Stummelbeinen auf dem Sportplatz der Wintersteinschule und reckte ihr Köpfchen in die Luft. Die magischen Tiere standen um sie herum und stöhnten. Henrietta hatte sich ein flottes Trainingsprogramm ausgedacht!

„Nicht so lahm, Peperoni!“, mahnte Henrietta.

Das pummelige Pinselohrschwein sank erschöpft auf den Boden. „Ich kann nicht mehr!“

„Die letzten drei Liegestütze!“, rief Henrietta vergnügt und schaute in die Runde.

Neun Tiere tummelten sich auf der roten Laufbahn: ein Fuchs und eine Schildkröte. Ein Pinguin und ein Chamäleon. Ein Pinselohrschwein und eine Fledermaus. Ein Kater und ein Krokodil. Und Sydney, das Koalamädchen.

Sie waren magische Tiere und konnten miteinander sprechen. Miteinander – und mit ihren menschlichen Gefährten. Denn die Tiere gehörten zu den neun Kindern, die gerade in der Turnhalle Sport hatten: Ida, Benni, Jo, Anna-Lena, Schoki, Eddie, Helene, Silas und Finja.

Die Schildkröte war eine gute Trainerin und alle Tiere waren mit Feuereifer dabei.

Fast alle. Während Rabbat, der Fuchs, seine schlanken Glieder dehnte und Koalabär Sydney zehn Klimmzüge am Stück machte, schleckte sich Kater Karajan gelangweilt die Pfote.

„Sport ist Mord“, sagte er nun schon zum dritten Mal von der Mauer herab. Eugenia, die Fledermaus, baumelte kopfüber an der oberen Latte des Fußballtors und ließ sich im Wind hin- und herschaukeln.
„Jetzt den linken Arm nach vorne strecken!“, rief Henrietta fröhlich. „Eins, zwei, drei, vier … Eine Runde Bauchtanz“, kicherte sie und ließ ihren Panzer kreisen.
Das war nun doch etwas viel verlangt. Rabbat, der Fuchs, brummte: „Ich hoffe, zur Belohnung gibt es Schokokekse.“

Während die Tiere auf der Wiese mit dem Bauch wackelten, spielten die Kinder aus Miss Cornfields Klasse eine Runde Jägerball.
Wer den Ball besaß, durfte abschießen. Wurde ein Kind getroffen, schied es aus. Yannik, ein Junge mit roter Turnhose, war dran. Er donnerte den Ball mit so viel Wucht durch die Halle, als wollte er ein Fenster in die Wand werfen.

„Aua!“ Finja rieb sich das linke Ohr. „Das hat voll wehgetan!“, jammerte sie. Ihre Freundinnen Helene und Katinka warfen Yannik grimmige Blicke zu.
„Ausgeschieden!“, rief Yannik. Mit dem Ball in der Hand rannte er im Zickzack übers Spielfeld und stolperte dabei über Schokis Beine. Beide purzelten übereinander.
„Yannik, reiß dich zusammen!“, schimpfte Frau Bergmann, die Sportlehrerin.
Yannik rappelte sich wieder hoch. Ohne Schoki aufzuhelfen, rannte er weiter. Und Schuss!
Jetzt bekam Anna-Lena den Ball mit voller Geschwindigkeit in die Seite. „Raus bist du!“, jubelte Yannik und schnappte sich gleich noch mal den Ball.
Wütend setzte sich Anna-Lena neben Finja. Sie rieb sich ihre Knochen. „Mann, tut das weh!“, schimpfte sie. „Blöder Idiot!“ So sauer hatte die Klasse Anna-Lena selten erlebt.
Yannik grinste nur und grölte: „Weiber! Können einfach nicht verlieren.“
Silas klatschte mit Yannik ab.

Helene spurtete auf Yannik zu. Sie eroberte den Ball und warf ihn zu Ida. Ida holte weit aus – und traf Yannik genau am Po.
„Treffer, versenkt!", freute sie sich und klatschte mit Helene ab.
„Das war unfair!", schnaufte Yannik. Jetzt hatten ihn doch tatsächlich zwei Mädchen abgeschossen. „Ihr habt zusammengeholfen!"
„Ist nicht verboten", antwortete Helene seelenruhig und prellte den Ball lässig auf den Boden. „Musst du jetzt weinen? Warte, ich bring dir ein Taschentuch!"
Wütend rannte Yannik nach draußen.
Frau Bergmann blickte ratlos hinterher. Dieser Schüler machte ihr es wirklich schwer! Yannik hatte so viel Energie wie ein Pingpongball. Nur leider konnte er mit seiner Kraft nicht haushalten. Frau Bergmann seufzte. Wirklich schade.
Das Spiel gewann am Ende Jo. Er konnte schnell rennen und zielte genau. Aber er warf im Gegensatz zu Yannik auf die Beine der Mitspieler und nicht auf ihren Kopf. Alle gönnten ihm den Sieg.

Verschwitzt schlenderten die Jungen und Mädchen in die Umkleideräume.
Und was tat Yannik? Der hatte wütend seinen Rucksack geschultert und war aus der Turnhalle gestürmt. Nun rannte er über den Sportplatz und boxte mit aller Kraft in die Luft. Mann, hatte er eine Wut im Bauch! Helene war so eine dumme Ziege! Yannik rannte zum Basketballkorb und versuchte hochzuspringen. Das klappte nicht. Also kletterte er. Er kletterte schnell. Wie Spiderman, dachte Yannik, als er sich das letzte Stück hochzog. Doch plötzlich – blieb Spiderman stecken!
Im Basketballkorb!
„He!", rief Yannik. Er war so ungeschickt in den Metallring des Basketballkorbs gerutscht, dass er mit seinem Rucksack feststeckte. Hilflos zappelte er mit den Beinen. „So ein Mist!", fluchte er. Mann, war das peinlich!
Er strampelte und strampelte. Da, jetzt bewegte sich was. Yannik strampelte weiter, als – ratsch! – die Turnhose riss.

„Verflixte Hühnerkacke", murmelte Yannik.
Yanniks Wut verwandelte sich in Verzweiflung. Er drehte sich nach links und nach rechts und zerriss dabei das Netz des Basketballkorbs. Auch das noch. Und noch immer steckte er fest.
In dieser aussichtslosen Lage entdeckten ihn die magischen Tiere.
„Coole Nummer!", staunte Rick, das Krokodil.
„Was macht er da oben?", wunderte sich Juri, der Pinguin.
„Er ist in Not", erkannte die Schildkröte Henrietta.
Von oben konnte Yannik sehen, wie Rabbat, der Fuchs, im Umkleideraum der Mädchen verschwand.
„Oh nein!", stöhnte er. „Alles, nur das nicht!" Er hatte das ungute Gefühl, dass alles noch schlimmer werden würde. Und genauso war es.
Helene kam als Erste angeschlendert. Neben ihr spazierte ihr magischer Kater Karajan. Beide hatten ein breites Grinsen auf dem Gesicht.
„Oh, da hängt ja unser Superman!" Helene prustete los. „Wie ist die Luft da oben?"

„Hübsche Unterhose!“, kicherte Ida, die zusammen mit den anderen Mädchen nachgekommen war. „Sind das die Zwerge von Schneewittchen, die da abgebildet sind?“

Yannik fühlte sich wie eine Fliege, die hilflos in einem Spinnennetz zappelte. „Das sind die Schlümpfe“, quetschte Yannik hervor und ballte die Fäuste. Die konnte er immerhin noch bewegen.

„Taschentuch?“, fragte Helene. „Oder brauchst du eher eine Kotztüte? Du bist schon ganz grün im Gesicht.“

Yanniks Puls raste. Er schaute nach unten. Wie kam er nur aus diesem Spinnennetz raus? Er zappelte und zappelte und die Mädchen sahen ihm ungerührt zu.

Also gut. Yannik gab sich einen Ruck. Es half alles nichts.

„Kann mir vielleicht mal jemand helfen?“, fragte er zögernd.

Ida legte nachdenklich ihren Zeigefinger an die Nasenspitze.

„Nee, wir sind nur Weiber. Zum Helfen sind wir viel zu schwach.“

„Hab ich irgendwo das Wort ‚bitte‘ gehört?“, fragte Finja.

„Ich könnte mir meine Fingernägel abbrechen“, flötete Helene und schüttelte den Kopf.

„Zicken!“, zischte Yannik und wusste nicht, was er machen sollte. Schließlich war es Anna-Lena, die beim Hausmeister Willi Wondraschek eine Leiter besorgte. Yannik kletterte herunter, quetschte ein „Danke“ hervor und verschwand, so schnell er konnte, im Umkleideraum der Jungen.

2. Kapitel

Rabbats Überraschungsparty

„Keine Schokokekse!", jammerte Rabbat. Der Fuchs zog enttäuscht die Schnauze aus Idas Schultasche. Dabei hatte er sich nach all dem Sport doch eine Belohnung verdient …

Sie warteten zusammen im Klassenzimmer auf Miss Cornfield, ihre Lehrerin.

Karajan saß auf dem Fensterbrett. „Isch hätte auch nischts gegen ein wenig Konfekt …"

„Du hast doch gar nicht mitgeturnt“, erinnerte ihn Caspar, das Chamäleon. Er erholte sich auf Anna-Lenas Matheheft von den Liegestützen.
„Sport ist was für Schluffis.“ Karajan streckte sich. „Das habe ich nischt nötig.“
„Schokolade!“, japste Peperoni. „Ich will Schokolade! Trauben-Nuss! Und Marzipan!“
Auch Rick hatte Hunger: „Ich könnte eine ganze Packung Fischstäbchen auf einmal verputzen. Uaaah!“ Er öffnete seinen Mund, so dass man sogar die hintersten Zähne sehen konnte.
Henrietta kicherte, als Rick jetzt noch einmal ihre Lieblingsübung wiederholte: „Hoch den Popo, hoch den Popo!“
Angst hatte niemand vor dem Krokodil. Sie hatten schon so viel zusammen erlebt, dass jeder wusste: Rick riss zwar gern mal sein Maul weit auf, doch im Grunde war er ein lieber Kerl. Genauso wie sein Gefährte Silas.
„Also bei Ida zu Hause sind noch jede Menge Schokokekse“, sagte Rabbat. „Im Küchenschrank

liegen mindestens fünf Packungen, hab ich gestern erst gesehen. Wenn ihr was Süßes wollt, kommt doch heute Nachmittag vorbei!"

Der Fuchs warf einen aufgeregten Blick zu Ida hinüber. Je länger er nachdachte, desto besser fand er die Idee. In letzter Zeit hockte Ida viel zu viel allein herum. Sie lernte andauernd und steckte mit der Nase nur noch in Schulbüchern und Übungsheften. Ein Treffen mit ihren Freunden würde ihr guttun!

Ida bekam von der Einladung nichts mit. Sie stand bei den anderen Mädchen.

„Yanniks Mami sollte öfter mal mit ihrem Sohnemann auf den Spielplatz gehen", stichelte Helene. „Da gibt es ein Klettergerüst zum Üben. Aber Vorsicht, Yannik: sehr hoch!"

Die Mädchen kicherten. Yannik tat so, als würde er nichts hören.

Als Miss Cornfield endlich mit zehn Minuten Verspätung das Klassenzimmer betrat, warf sie Yannik einen strengen Blick zu.

„Herr Wondraschek ist stinksauer", teilte sie Yannik

mit. „Der Korb war nagelneu. Wie es aussieht, musst du den Schaden bezahlen.“ Sie seufzte. „Der Hausmeister will sich an den Direktor wenden und der wird sich dann mit deinen Eltern … hoppla!“
Der Lehrerin entfuhr ein Lächeln. Sie war über das Krokodil gestolpert, das wie so oft im Weg herumlag.
Dann verteilte sie Deutsch-Arbeitsblätter. Die Klasse musste Doppellaute üben und trennen: Map-pe, Pap-pe, Hüh-ner-stall.
„Möpse, Pampe, Hühnerknall“, half Henrietta, die neben Benni saß und ebenfalls ins Arbeitsblatt hineinguckte.
Seit Wochen versuchte er seiner Schildkröte lesen beizubringen. So richtig gut klappte das noch nicht.

Ida wunderte sich, als es kurz nach drei an der Haustür klingelte. Wollten die Besucher zu ihren Eltern? Der „Friseursalon Elfriede“ lag im Erdgeschoss, die Wohnung der Kronenbergs im ersten Stock.

Aber nein, es waren Finja und ihr Koalamädchen Sydney.
Eine Minute später klingelte es schon wieder. Und noch mal. Und wieder. Um Viertel nach drei saßen neun Tiere und zehn Kinder in Idas Kinderzimmer. Außer den Kindern, die magische Tiere besaßen, war auch noch Max mitgekommen. Schoki hatte ihn zufällig auf der Straße getroffen.
„Wo kommt ihr denn alle auf einmal her?“ Ida guckte sich verblüfft in ihrem Zimmer um. Auf jedem freien Fleck hockte ein Kind oder ein Tier.
„Tolle Überraschung, Rotschopf, oder?“ Rabbat lächelte seine Gefährtin etwas unsicher an. „Diese Einladung war meine Idee.“
„Rabbat, wie konntest du …“ Einen kurzen Moment lang war Ida sauer. Sie mochte es nicht, wenn jemand über ihren Kopf hinweg bestimmte. Aber Rabbat blinzelte sie aus seinen bernsteinfarben glänzenden Fuchsaugen an – und da konnte Ida einfach nicht mehr böse sein.
Sie holte alle Schokokekse, die sie finden konnte, und

Rabbat und Peperoni machten sich sofort darüber her. Schoki hatte Mühe, selbst noch eine Packung zu ergattern.
Silas warf Rick einen Keks nach dem anderen ins Maul. Sydney teilte sich eine Packung mit Caspar, der nur kleine Miniportionen knabberte. Alle futterten vergnügt vor sich hin, nur Kater Karajan beschwerte sich: „Die sind ja nischt mal selbst gebacken!"
Sie spielten eine Runde Uno und lachten, als Eugenia eine Spielkarte aus dem Stapel zupfte und damit durchs Zimmer flatterte. Sie unterhielten sich über die Schule und die magische Zoohandlung und rätselten, wer wohl als Nächster ein magisches Tier bekommen würde.
„Vielleicht ja ich?", überlegte Max. „Ich könnte dem Tier sicher viel beibringen." Er trug den Spitznamen „der Professor", weil er der Klassenbeste war, natürlich dicht gefolgt von Ida.
„Hey, habt ihr mal auf die Uhr geschaut?", unterbrach Benni die Grübelei. „Gleich kommt *Top oder Flop* im Fernsehen!"

Fast jeder aus der Klasse guckte die Sendung. Sie lief jeden Montag um 16 Uhr auf Kids-Quiz-TV. Jede Show wurde live aus einem Schulhaus gesendet. Als Kandidaten traten Kinder in ihrem Alter an. Es machte Spaß mitzuraten und noch mehr Spaß, den Kandidaten zuzugucken – denn die stellten sich manchmal ziemlich dämlich an!
Ida und ihre Freunde zogen ins Wohnzimmer um und machten es sich vor dem Fernseher bequem.
Ida schaltete genau im richtigen Moment ein. Gerade wurde die Sendung angekündigt: „Topf ohne Klops", entzifferte Henrietta und Benni lachte.
Jetzt wurde der Name des Moderators eingeblendet, er hieß Karsten Markoni. Was aber las Henrietta? „Käse Makkaroni!" Alle kringelten sich vor Lachen, als Benni es ihnen erzählte.
Das Titellied erklang, das Publikum trampelte mit den Füßen. Es ging los!
„*Top oder Flop*, die lustigste, spannendste und verrückteste Schulshow aller Zeiten!", rief der Moderator und sprang wie ein Clown durch die Luft.

Diesmal wurde aus der Aula einer Leipziger Schule gesendet. Allerdings sah die Aula überhaupt nicht mehr wie eine Schule aus, sondern wie eine tropische Badelandschaft. Die Filmleute hatten einen Sandstrand aufgeschüttet und in der Mitte ein Wasserbecken aufgebaut. Es gab eine Bar und Liegestühle. Die Kandidaten trugen rote und blaue T-Shirts und zappelten aufgeregt herum.
Der Moderator ließ sich an der Bar einen Drink mixen, dann setzte er sich in einen Liegestuhl und verkündete die erste Aufgabe: „Ihr müsst aus einem riesigen Blatt Papier ein Boot falten.“ Er schlug lässig seine Beine übereinander. „Welchem Dreier-Team wird es gelingen, damit im Wasserbecken herumzupaddeln, ohne unterzugehen? Zeit läuft!“
Die beiden Teams legten los. Sie hatten fünf Minuten Zeit, eine große Uhr an der Hallendecke zählte die Sekunden herunter.
Die erste Gruppe war fertig. Sie setzte ihr Boot ins Wasser. Kaum zu glauben, es hielt das Gewicht von drei Kindern aus!

Juri, der Pinguin, und Rick, das Krokodil, starrten auf den Bildschirm.
„Das würde ich auch gern machen", seufzte Juri.
„Herr Wondraschek würde ausflippen, wenn er das aufbauen müsste", lachte Jo.
Eine Assistentin reichte den Kindern ein Paddel. Auch das zweite Team war jetzt im Wasser.
„Schnel-ler, schnel-ler!", feuerten die Zuschauer ihre Kandidaten an. Die Kinder mit den blauen T-Shirts gingen prustend unter. Rick sah neidisch zu, wie sie abtauchten.
Das rote Team hatte gewonnen.
Nach der Wasserübung kamen die Wissensfragen dran. Der Moderator trug inzwischen einen Strohhut und stand barfuß im Sand. Mit bunten Karteikarten in der Hand feuerte er eine Frage nach der anderen ab.
„Wer ist der reichste Mann der Welt?"
Ida musste nicht lange überlegen. „Bill Gates. Sein Vermögen beträgt 70 Milliarden." Damit war sie schneller als das Mädchen im Fernsehen – und schneller als Max. Der biss sich auf die Lippen.

Stolz kraulte Ida Rabbats Ohr, ohne den Blick vom Fernseher zu lösen. Mit roten Flecken auf den Wangen wartete sie auf die zweite Frage. Da war sie auch schon!

„Wie heißt der höchste Berg der Welt?"

„Mount Everest, 8848 Meter!" Diesmal war Max der Erste.

Karsten Markoni zückte die nächste Karte.

„Was versteht man unter Sudoku?"

Während der Junge im Fernsehen etwas von „asiatischem Kampfsport" faselte, riefen Ida und Max gleichzeitig: „Japanisches Zahlenrätsel!"

Die magischen Tiere staunten. „Die beiden sind wirklich gut!"

Rabbat glühte vor Stolz.

Bei der nächsten Aufgabe mussten die Kandidaten Holzkisten übereinanderstapeln. Die Kinder waren mit Seilen gesichert, trotzdem sah die Übung ziemlich schwierig aus – und gefährlich.

Ein Junge stellte sich so ungeschickt an, dass er auf die

dicke Matratze plumpste. Während er fiel, erwischte er mit dem Bein den Turm seines Teams, der schon fast bis zur Decke ragte. Polternd flogen die Kisten zu Boden.

„Satz mit x, war wohl nix“, spottete Karsten Markoni. Das blaue Team war zerknirscht, das Publikum lachte.

„Blöder Makkaroni“, schimpfte Henrietta. „Ist der fies!“

Als sich die Kinder später von Ida verabschiedeten und sich für den schönen Nachmittag bedankten, hatten alle gute Laune. Und ein Kind hatte eine Idee.

3. Kapitel

Die Idee des Professors

Kurz vor acht sauste Max, der Professor, ins Klassenzimmer. Er hatte fünf Blätter in der Hand und wedelte wichtigtuerisch damit herum. „Ich war gestern noch am Computer, und wisst ihr was?“

Keiner hörte zu.

Benni und Henrietta spielten mal wieder Verstecken. Die Schildkröte verschwand gerade im Bücherregal hinter „Drei Vampire auf Klassenfahrt“.

Silas schrieb bei Jo die Mathehausaufgaben ab. Helene zeigte ihren Freundinnen ein Musikvideo auf ihrem Handy. Schoki teilte sich mit Peperoni einen Schokokaba.
Yannik nahm gar nichts um sich herum wahr. Er starrte auf das aufgeschlagene Mathebuch. In Gedanken aber war er bei dem kaputten Basketballkorb. Er hatte sich nicht getraut seinen Eltern davon zu erzählen und Direktor Siegmann hatte auch nicht bei ihm zu Hause angerufen. Noch nicht …
Pünktlich mit dem Gongschlag betrat Miss Cornfield das Klassenzimmer. Unter dem Arm trug sie einen Stoß Arbeitsblätter. Die Klasse stöhnte. Sie würden doch nicht etwa eine Probe schreiben?
Max schnippte mit den Fingern. „Miss Cornfield, ich würde gern …"
„Nicht jetzt." Die Lehrerin stoppte den Schüler mit einem strengen Blick. „Erst wird gerechnet."
Sie hob ein Blatt in die Höhe und schrieb an die Tafel: „Multiplizieren im Hunderterraum".
Henrietta las: „Mutti putzt im Hundeturnraum."

Aber Benni konnte diesmal nicht lachen.
Auf eine Matheprobe war er überhaupt nicht vorbereitet. Auch Yannik kam ins Schwitzen. Seine Noten waren nicht so besonders …
Ida und Max dagegen hatten Spaß an den schwierigen Aufgaben. Ihre gespitzten Bleistifte flitzten übers Papier: 3 × 26 = 78, 5 × 45 = 225, 186 × 4 = 744.
Doch wie so oft war es jemand anders, der als Erstes mit den Rechenaufgaben fertig war. Franka, die allein in der hintersten Bank saß.
„Babykram", brummte sie. Sie drehte das Blatt um und holte dann ein Buch aus ihrer Tasche, „Kennwort Morgenrot" stand darauf. Ein Agenten-Roman: Zwei Mädchen streiften durch London und lösten knifflige Zahlenrätsel. Im Nu war Franka ganz woanders …

Miss Cornfield saß im Schneidersitz auf ihrem Pult.
Ihr Blick ruhte auf Franka.
Das Mädchen machte ihr Sorgen. Ja, Franka war herausragend in Mathe, aber sonst?

Sie kapselte sich ab, verbrachte die Pausen allein … Es war, als lebte sie in einer ganz eigenen Welt.
Die Lehrerin stand auf und ging durch die Reihen. Momentan lief es nicht besonders in der Klasse. Die Mädchen bildeten Grüppchen und stritten mit den Jungs herum. Dabei waren sie auf der Klassenfahrt so eine gute Gemeinschaft gewesen! Fünf Tage und vier Nächte hatten sie miteinander im „Haus Steinfels" verbracht, das hatte die Klasse richtig zusammengeschweißt. Von der guten Stimmung war nicht mehr viel übrig.
Yannik kippelte nervös auf seinem Stuhl hin und her. Anscheinend hatte er Schwierigkeiten mit den Aufgaben.
„Nicht zappeln, Yannik!", mahnte Miss Cornfield. Sie lehnte sich wieder gegen ihr Pult.
Plötzlich fühlte sie ein feines Kribbeln am Bein. Unter ihrem Rock kroch eine Vogelspinne hervor. Eine magische Vogelspinne!
„Agent Y!", zischte die Lehrerin. „Was machst du denn hier?"

Anscheinend hatte sich das magische Tier in Miss Cornfields Schultasche geschmuggelt. Wollte es sich im Klassenzimmer nach einem Freund fürs Leben umsehen?
Miss Cornfield verstand die Sprache der magischen Tiere nicht, aber Mortimer Morrison hatte ihr von den Sehnsüchten der Vogelspinne erzählt. Agent Y wollte nichts mehr als einen Gefährten. „Sogar dieser dämliche Kater hat eine Freundin“, sagte er zu Mortimer Morrison. „Nur ich hocke tagein, tagaus in deiner magischen Zoohandlung herum …“
Jetzt krabbelte Agent Y über ihr Handgelenk. Oh, wie das kitzelte! Fast musste die Lehrerin kichern. Sie riss sich zusammen und sah sich vorsichtig um. Hatte eines der Kinder die Spinne entdeckt?
Nein, alle hatten ihre Köpfe übers Pult gebeugt.
„Kusch, Spinne, rein mit dir!“
Schnell setzte sie das Krabbeltier zurück in ihre Ledertasche.

Während die Lehrerin die Arbeitsblätter einsammelte, meldete sich Max wieder zu Wort.
„Miss Cornfield, Sie kennen doch sicher diese Kinder-Quizshow, die jeden Montag im Fernsehen kommt?"
„*Top oder Flop*", warf jemand ein. „Mit Karsten Markoni."
„Käse Makkaroni", grummelte Henrietta.
„Der ist cool!", rief Yannik. „War super gestern!"
Miss Cornfield nickte aufmerksam.
„Da sind kluge Köpfe gefragt", berichtete Max. „Und Supersportler."
Silas und Jo trommelten sich auf die Brust. „Wie wir!", grölte Silas und Rick schnappte zustimmend mit dem Krokodilmaul.
Max sprach weiter. „Ich habe ein Plakat von der Show ausgedruckt, in Farbe. Darf ich?" Ohne eine Antwort abzuwarten, stand er auf. Er hängte das Poster an die Pinnwand, gleich neben den Spinnen-Steckbrief, den sie im Sachkundeunterricht angefertigt hatten. Ein breit grinsender Moderator war darauf abgebildet und zwei Kinder mit einem goldenen Pokal.

Max ging zurück zu seinem Platz. Die Klasse sah ihn erwartungsvoll an. „Und wisst ihr, was das ist?“ Wieder wedelte er mit Papier herum. „Das sind die Bewerbungsunterlagen! Für das Bewerbungsvideo!“

Plötzlich redeten alle in der Klasse durcheinander.

„Ein Video drehen? Cool!“, rief jemand von hinten.

„Los, versuchen wir's!“, kam es von der Seite.

„Ich will Kameramann sein!“, rief Schoki. „Oder Beleuchter!“

Henrietta stupste Benni an. „Ich helfe dir“, sagte Benni schnell.

„Wir können den Hip-Hop-Tanz zeigen, den wir in der Tanz-AG gelernt haben“, schlug Finja vor.

„Henry soll sein Saxofon mitbringen!“

„Und Franka kann etwas vorrechnen“, ergänzte Miss Cornfield. Sie nahm Max die Unterlagen aus der Hand und las sie aufmerksam durch. Da war von „Zusammenhalt“ die Rede, von „Teamgeist“ und „gegenseitigem Vertrauen“.

Die Lehrerin überlegte: Vielleicht war die Bewerbung bei Kids-Quiz-TV eine gute Gelegenheit, um die Klassengemeinschaft zu stärken?
Sie las weiter. Und runzelte die Stirn. „Oh, die Bewerbungsfrist endet schon morgen! Punkt Mitternacht. Schaffen wir das?“
Die Klasse, die aus 24 Schülern bestand, stimmte ab. Mit einem klaren Ergebnis: 23 Kinder und neun magische Tiere stimmten für die Quizshow. Ein Mädchen stimmte dagegen.
Das Mädchen war Franka. „Ich lass mich doch nicht beim Rechnen filmen!“ Sie verzog das Gesicht. Und auf diese peinliche Quizshow hatte sie erst recht keine Lust. „Das ist total bescheuert. Ohne mich!“

4. Kapitel

Yannik bekommt eine Nachricht

Miss Cornfield hatte den Ablauf bereits mit dem Direktor Heribert Siegmann besprochen und auch der Hausmeister wusste Bescheid.

Herr Siegmann fand die Idee seiner „lieben, geschätzten Kollegin“, wie er gleich mehrmals betonte, „ganz entzückend“. Der Gedanke, dass die Wintersteinschule im Fernsehen gezeigt werden würde, gefiel ihm. Vor einem Millionenpublikum!

Der Hausmeister Willi Wondraschek war dagegen. So eine Veranstaltung bedeutete eine Menge Arbeit für ihn. Aber seine Meinung zählte ja nicht …

An diesem Mittwoch kamen alle Kinder überpünktlich zur Schule. Sogar Eddie, der morgens nur schwer aus den Federn kam, war rechtzeitig da. Seine kleine Fledermaus hatte ihn geweckt.

Ein Video zu drehen machte mehr Spaß als Matheunterricht! Die Kinder standen in Grüppchen zusammen und bereiteten sich auf ihren Auftritt vor. Bälle aus der Turnhalle und Instrumente aus dem Musikzimmer lagen bereit. Die Mädchen aus der Tanz-AG ließen sich von Helene schminken, Henry packte sein Saxofon aus. Juri putzte sein Gefieder, Karajan das seidige Fell.

Ida schrieb noch schnell einen Ablaufplan und notierte, wer wann an die Reihe kam. Sie selbst wollte bei der Nummer „Superhirn gesucht" auftreten.

Gerade kamen Benni, Schoki und Yannik vom Hausmeister zurück, schwer bepackt mit Kamera, Lampen, Kabeln und Mikrofon.

Benni nahm die Kamera, Schoki kümmerte sich um das Licht. Yannik sollte der Tonmann sein, hatte Miss Cornfield entschieden.
Yannik warf einen sehnsüchtigen Blick auf seine Jonglierbälle und griff seufzend zur Tonangel, einem langen Stab, an dessen Ende ein Mikrofon steckte.
Miss Cornfield nickte ihm aufmunternd zu: „Jetzt setz noch den Kopfhörer auf und pass auf, dass nichts rauscht. Alles muss gut zu verstehen sein."
Yannik nickte. Er hatte sich vorgenommen heute alles richtig zu machen. Noch immer hatte der Direktor sich nicht bei seinen Eltern gemeldet. Vielleicht kam er ja noch mal davon?

Der Dreh konnte beginnen!
Benni schwenkte die Kamera durchs Klassenzimmer. Helene und Max wechselten sich als Moderatoren ab. Max hatte sich zur Feier des Tages ein Jackett angezogen.
„Du bist ja fast so schick wie Juri", zog Jo ihn auf.

Die beiden Moderatoren führten Interviews mit dem Direktor und dem Hausmeister. Zwischendurch machten Benni und Schoki Außenaufnahmen vom Schulgarten, dem Teich und dem hübschen Schulgebäude mit seinen zwei Türmen.
Und die magischen Tiere? Henrietta studierte den Ablaufplan, sie wollte im richtigen Moment das Licht anknipsen. Juri übte Seilspringen, verhedderte sich und plumpste auf den Boden. Krokodil Rick lag wie immer im Weg herum. Fledermaus Eugenia gab Ratschläge von oben: „Eddie, schieb das Hemderich in die Hose! Du bist gleich dranerich!"
Miss Cornfield beobachtete ihre Klasse und lächelte still in sich hinein. So gut wie heute war die Stimmung schon lang nicht mehr gewesen! Dass die magischen Tiere ständig um die Moderatoren herumhopsten, störte sie nicht. In dem Film würden die Tiere aussehen wie harmlose Kuscheltiere. „Versteinern", so hieß der Trick, den ihnen Mr. Morrison beigebracht hatte. Die Tiere wandten ihn automatisch an, sobald fremde Augen sie musterten.

Die Schule war vorgestellt, nun ging es an die einzelnen Vorführungen.
Den Anfang machte Schoki. Er wollte mit verbundenen Augen jede Schokoladensorte erraten, die es im Supermarkt zu kaufen gab.
Die Idee stammte von Peperoni und natürlich hatten sie gestern Nachmittag noch eifrig geübt.
Schoki gab den Scheinwerfer für seinen Auftritt an Eddie ab und zog sich die Strickmütze über die Augen. Ida überprüfte mit ein paar Handbewegungen, dass er auch wirklich nichts sah, und schon ging es los.

„Kamera läuft!“, rief Benni und drückte auf den Knopf. Henry spielte ein paar Takte auf dem Saxofon, die Schildkröte Henrietta knipste mit dem Fuß eine Lampe an.

„Hier kommt Schoki, der beste Süßigkeitentester der Welt!“, rief Helene.

Ida hielt die erste Tafel in die Kamera, riss die Verpackung auf und reichte Schoki ein kleines Stück Schokolade. „Granatapfel, Kakaogehalt 85 Prozent“, antwortete Schoki und leckte sich die Lippen. Peperoni grunzte bestätigend.

Es folgten „Erdbeer-Joghurt“, „Karamell in weißer Schokolade“ und die Sorte „Zartherb mit Meersalz“.

Kein Problem für Schoki! Er erriet sogar „Blaubeer-Lavendel, unendlich zartschmelzend“ und „Vollmilch mit klein gehackten Piemont-Haselnüssen“.
Die Klasse klatschte und jubelte.
Als Nächstes kamen die Mädchen von der Tanz-AG dran. Karajan drückte auf Helenes CD-Spieler und die Musik ging los. Max übernahm die Moderation.
Helene, Finja, Anna-Lena und Luna schleuderten ihre Beine in so atemberaubendem Tempo durch die Luft, dass Benni fast vom Zusehen schlecht wurde. Und schon stellte Helene den nächsten Schüler vor: „Max, das Superhirn!“
„Suppenbirne“, kicherte Henrietta. So hatte *sie* es auf Idas Ablaufplan gelesen.
Der Professor ratterte die Namen sämtlicher Nobelpreisträger der letzten drei Jahre herunter.
Ida schrieb schwierige Worte ohne Rechtschreibfehler von A bis Z an die Tafel: Atmosphäre, Biorhythmus, Chamäleon, Dynamit.
Henrietta starrte Ida mit offenem Mund an. „*Sie* ist die Suppenbirne“, sagte sie zu Benni und las staunend:

„Autofähre, Birnenmus, Clä… Clon…“ Weiter kam sie einfach nicht.

Jo und Silas machten Klimmzüge am Türrahmen.

Alle halfen zusammen.

Außer Franka.

Als Einzige aus der Klasse nahm sie von den Filmaufnahmen keinerlei Notiz. Mit ihren schwarzen Klamotten saß sie am Boden und las seelenruhig in ihrem Agenten-Buch. Neben ihr lag ein Totenkopf-Lesezeichen. Die beiden Spioninnen waren kurz davor, am Computer ein Passwort zu knacken. Gleich würden sie in den Tresorraum der British Royal Bank vordringen und dort auf gefälschte Gemälde stoßen. Das Buch war viel spannender als dieses Babyvideo!

„Kannst du nicht bitte was vorrechnen?“, fragte Anna-Lena sie.

„Komm schon, Franka“, bat Benni. Aber Franka gähnte ihn nur an und las weiter.

Da hatte Henrietta eine Idee. „Stell die Kamera auf dein Skateboard.“ Benni folgte ihr. „Und jetzt einen Schubs!“ Schon rollte die Kamera auf Franka zu.

Sie kam näher und näher, zeigte erst das schwarz gekleidete Mädchen, dann ihre Stiefel und am Schluss nur noch die Hände, die das Buch hielten. Franka sah aus wie ein Bücherwurm, der sich durch nichts aus der Ruhe bringen ließ.
Benni filmte und filmte. Als auch er ins Bild musste, gab er die Kamera Schoki und machte einen Purzelbaum. Er wurde ziemlich schief, Henrietta rief trotzdem: „Super!"
Und auf einmal war Yannik im Bild. Eine Stunde hatte er sich still um den Ton gekümmert, dann hielt er es nicht mehr aus. Er jonglierte vor der Kamera und hörte nicht auf, als längst jemand anders an der Reihe war. So viele Sportgeräte lagen herum – Yannik konnte nicht widerstehen. Er kickte einen Fußball mit dem Knie auf und ab, ließ einen Tischtennisball auf dem Schläger tanzen und übte Handstand, während Eddie vor laufender Kamera Comics malte.
Niemand bekam mit, dass vor dem Klassenzimmerfenster ein Baum wackelte. Äste schwankten hin und her und das Laub raschelte.

Wenn Yannik noch auf seinem Stuhl gesessen hätte, hätte er den Kletterkünstler gesehen, der gerade die alte Linde erklomm. Aber was machte Yannik? Luftgitarre spielen.

Dass er sich eigentlich um die Tonaufnahmen kümmern sollte, hatte Yannik komplett vergessen. Und so verpasste er eine wichtige Nachricht. Sie kam aus dem Kopfhörer, der herrenlos über der Stuhllehne baumelte.

Die Nachricht lautete:

An Yannik Nowak!
Die magische Zoohandlung teilt mit: Das Auswahlverfahren läuft. Bald wirst du dein magisches Tier bekommen. Halte dich bereit.
Viele Grüße!
Die magische Zoohandlung

Die Stimme verhallte im Nirgendwo.

5. Kapitel

„Gestatten, Morrison!“

Helene wollte die nächste Nummer ankündigen, als es an der Tür klopfte. „Herein!“, rief sie zusammen mit Miss Cornfield.

Was für eine Überraschung! Es war Mortimer Morrison, der Inhaber der magischen Zoohandlung. Mr. Morrison, der die magischen Tiere überreichte! Auf seiner Schulter saß wie immer Pinkie, die freche Elster.

Benni stellte die Kamera zurück auf den Ständer und räumte mit Schoki die Spielgeräte zur Seite, damit sich der Besucher einen Weg durchs Klassenzimmer bahnen konnte.
Mr. Morrison marschierte in Richtung Lehrerpult und verbeugte sich: „Gestatten, Morrison!" Auch Pinkie verneigte sich, ein wenig wackelig allerdings.
Alle warteten gespannt. Wer hatte eine Nachricht erhalten? Wer bekam heute einen Gefährten?
Die 15 Kinder, die noch kein magisches Tier besaßen, reckten neugierig ihre Köpfe: Mr. Morrison hatte keinen Käfig dabei …
„Ich will ein Meerschweinchen", seufzte jemand.
„Ich warte schon sooo lange auf mein Pony", jammerte jemand anders.
„Ein Weißkopfseeadler wäre interessant", meinte Max.
Doch Mr. Morrison schüttelte den Kopf. „Nein, heute kommt ein anderer dran." Miss Cornfield nickte lächelnd.
Silas und Rick, die am Boden saßen, sahen, wie ein kleines Tier aus Mr. Morrisons Lederstiefel krabbelte.

Sie blinzelten neugierig. Da waren Wollfäden, die ineinander verknotet waren. Die Wollfäden lösten sich, wurden zu Beinen …

„Eine Vogelspinne?“, rief Silas und sprang auf.

„Iiih, eine Spinne!“, kreischte Finja und flüchtete auf einen Stuhl. Sydney kletterte hinterher.

Anna-Lena und Katinka sprangen auf ihr Pult. Eddie, Jo und Ida hüpften aufs Fensterbrett. Ida zog die Beine auf den Stuhl und vergrub die Nase im weichen Fell ihres Fuchses. Jo und Juri drängten sich aneinander.

„Ist das eine Kraushaar- oder eine Rotknievogelspinne?“ Max kam neugierig näher. „Wie lang sind denn die Giftklauen?“

Die Spinne huschte über den Parkettboden und versteckte sich hinter dem rosaroten Prinzessinnenrucksack, der Helene gehörte. Helene schrie und rannte in die Ecke. „Tun Sie die da weg!“, rief sie empört.

„Das ist Agent Y“, sagte Mr. Morrison stolz.

„Aus dem Tal des Todes in Kalifornien“, ergänzte die Spinne. Doch das konnte nur Mr. Morrison hören.

„Wow!“, staunte Jo beeindruckt. „Eine Agenten-Spinne!“
„Beißt sie auch Lehrerinnen?“, fragte Silas unschuldig und kraulte sein Krokodil am Kopf. Miss Cornfield räusperte sich, Rick grinste.
„Ich habe Agent Y bei meiner letzten Amerikareise eingesammelt.“ Mr. Morrison lächelte. „Na ja, eigentlich hat sie sich selbst eingesammelt.“
Agent Y krabbelte inzwischen quer durchs Klassenzimmer.
Während die anderen Kinder sich kichernd gruselten und in großem Bogen von der Spinne weghopsten, stand Franka wie gelähmt in der hintersten Ecke. Sie drückte sich an die Wand und ließ Agent Y nicht aus den Augen. Das Herz schlug ihr bis zum Hals. Hoffentlich beobachtete sie keiner. Niemand sollte sehen, welche Angst sie vor Spinnen hatte. Sie konnte ja noch nicht mal diesen Spinnen-Steckbrief ansehen, der an der Pinnwand hing. Franka hatte am ganzen Körper Gänsehaut …
„Nun reicht es“, sagte Miss Cornfield streng.

Mr. Morrison stiefelte der Spinne hinterher und nahm sie zärtlich hoch. „Hab ich dich, du Schlitzohr!“ Er ließ das Tier in seinem Ärmel verschwinden. „Du bleibst bei mir, mein Freundchen! Zumindest vorerst.“

Ein erleichterter Seufzer breitete sich aus.

Franka atmete auf.

Miss Cornfield stellte sich vor die Klasse. „Bevor Mr. Morrison uns das nächste magische Tier anvertraut, müsst ihr schwören das Geheimnis zu bewahren.“

Alle nickten und machten sich bereit.

An der Tafel erschienen neongrüne Buchstaben.

Die Kinder begannen mit feierlicher Stimme zu sprechen:

„Niemals, niemals sprechen wir
mit anderen über das magische Tier.
Die magische Zoohandlung ist streng geheim,
so soll es für immer und ewig sein."

Während die Kinder den Schwur murmelten, blickten sie einander an. Die meisten aus der Klasse warteten ruhig, nur Yannik wippte wie immer mit den Füßen vor und zurück. Ida und Benni tauschten einen rätselnden Blick: Wer hatte die Nachricht bekommen?
Mr. Morrison ging zum Fenster und beugte sich nach draußen. „Tingo, komm rein! Yannik kann es kaum erwarten, dich zu sehen!"
Yannik riss die Augen auf. Was? Er bekam ein magisches Tier?
Yannik, der nie stillhalten konnte, blieb einen Moment stocksteif stehen. Dann atmete er kräftig ein und aus, stieß seine rechte Faust in die Luft, brüllte „Tschakka!" und begann jubelnd und johlend durchs Klassenzimmer zu tanzen. Alle Sorgen verschwanden mit einem Mal in weite Ferne.

Die schlechten Noten? Egal.
Der Basketballkorb? Egal!
Er bekam ein magisches Tier! Unglaublich!
Freudig taumelte er zum Fenster und suchte die Umgebung ab.
Den Teich. Wartete eine Wasserschlange auf ihn?
Die Bäume. Saß ein Papagei im Baum?
Die Schulwiese. Hüpfte dort ein Känguru herum? Oh, ein Känguru wäre lustig!
Plötzlich raschelte es im Baum.
Der Blätterwald teilte sich. Heraus schwang sich – ein Schimpanse! Er turnte hin und her, löste den Griff und landete mit einem Satz im Klassenzimmer.
Yannik schnappte nach Luft. Und in der Klasse brach fröhliches Gelächter aus. Das Äffchen war einfach zu putzig! Es kratzte sich am Kopf und grinste von einem Ohr zum anderen.
„Ist der süüüß!“, jubelten alle.
„Tadaaaa! Tingo ist da!“ Der Schimpanse sprang vom Boden aus in Yanniks Arme. „Ich freu mich so, dass ich bei dir bin!“

Yannik drückte den Schimpansen fest an sich. Und während er das weiche Fell seines Gefährten spürte, breitete sich ein warmes Gefühl von Glück in seinem Körper aus. Er hörte das Herz seines neuen Freundes aufgeregt pochen, dicht an seinem eigenen, und auf einmal wusste er, dass alles gut werden würde. Die Klasse applaudierte.

Mr. Morrison winkte noch einmal freundlich, dann stapfte er in Richtung Tür. Pinkie flatterte neben ihm her. „Tschüssikowski!", flötete sie.

„Entschuldigung, Mr. Morrison!", rief Anna-Lena ihm nach. „Sind Sie denn heute gar nicht mit dem Omnibus gekommen?" Sie hatte kein Knattern gehört.

Mr. Morrison lächelte. „Och, die alte Kiste ist mal wieder in der Werkstatt. Alle zwei Jahre wird sie überprüft. Aber keine Sorge – die Karre schnurrt tadellos. Für Nachschub an magischen Tieren ist gesorgt. Bis bald!"

Der Schimpanse sprang von Tisch zu Tisch.
„Oho, ein Chamäleon!" Er verbeugte sich vor Caspar.
„Wie hübsch, ein Pinguin!" Juri lächelte geschmeichelt.
Tingo tätschelte Peperoni und stolperte über Rick, das Krokodil. Henrietta begrüßte er mit den Worten: „Hallo, altes Haus!"
Er winkte Eugenia und Sydney zu, stellte sich Karajan und Rabbat vor. Er zupfte an der Krawatte des Professors herum und blickte Franka über die Schulter: „Spannendes Buch!"
Yannik bemerkte staunend, dass er tatsächlich der Einzige unter den Kindern war, der Tingos Worte verstehen konnte. Schon hopste sein neuer Freund weiter.
Die Klasse sah ihm lachend zu.
Als Miss Cornfield streng den Kopf schüttelte, sprang der Schimpanse zurück in Yanniks Arme. „So, und wofür ist jetzt die Kamera?", fragte er neugierig. „Für mich?"

Yannik grinste. „Nicht ganz, die Kamera …“
„Die Kamera!“, rief Benni. „Die läuft ja noch!“ Hektisch drückte er auf den „Aus“-Knopf.
Oh weh! Die Übergabe, der Schwur, Tingos Begrüßungsrunde – die Kamera hatte alles aufgezeichnet. Die Kinder sahen Miss Cornfield erschrocken an.
Aber Max winkte lässig ab. „Ist doch nicht schlimm. Wir bearbeiten den Film sowieso am Computer. Die Stellen mit Mr. Morrison lassen wir einfach weg. Post-Produktion nennt man das beim Film.“
Durch den Besuch von Mr. Morrison war viel Zeit verstrichen. Wenn sie das Video noch fertigkriegen wollten, mussten sie sich beeilen. Miss Cornfield klatschte in die Hände.
„Alle auf ihre Plätze! Das gilt auch für dich, Tingo!“
Der Schimpanse war gerade dabei, vor Yanniks Pult ein Rad zu schlagen.
Der Schimpanse schnappte sich noch schnell eine Banane aus Finjas Schultasche, dann setzte er sich bei Yannik auf den Schoß.

„Um 13 Uhr ist Schulschluss!", rief die Lehrerin. „Bis dann müssen alle Aufnahmen im Kasten sein. Zeit läuft!"

Die Mädchen schwangen Hula-Hoop-Reifen, während Yannik im Hintergrund jonglierte – zusammen mit Tingo. Sie warfen sich gegenseitig die Bälle zu, so fröhlich und unbeschwert, dass Miss Cornfield es nicht übers Herz brachte, die beiden zu stoppen.

Dann knackste es im Lautsprecher. „Miss Cornfield, bitte in mein Büro." Es war der Direktor, Herr Siegmann.

„Ausgerechnet jetzt", seufzte Miss Cornfield und wandte sich zur Tür. „Keinen Unfug machen, ja?"

Kaum war die Lehrerin draußen, ging es im Klassenzimmer drunter und drüber.

Yannik und Tingo holten sich einen Softball und kickten ihn hin und her. Jo und Silas machten begeistert mit. Dann klinkte sich Katinka ein und auf einmal waren auch die anderen Mädchen dabei. Die Tafel wurde zum Tor, Henry war der Torwart. Rabbat jagte Tingo den Ball ab und spielte ihn weiter zu Ida.

Ida schob den Ball zu Anna-Lena, die gab ihn an Katinka, und als Helene ein Tor schoss, riss Yannik die Hände hoch und rief vergnügt: „1:0 für die Weiber!"
Dann drückte Yannik Tingo einen Tischtennisschläger in die Hand und zeigte ihm, wie man auf einem Schultisch Pingpong spielte. „Die Federmäppchen sind das Netz. Los!"
Der Schimpanse schwang den Schläger wie ein Profi. Eugenia spielte den Schiedsrichter: „4:2 für Tingorich!", rief die Fledermaus von der Lampe herab. Benni und Schoki nahmen alles mit der Kamera auf.
Als Miss Cornfield zurückkam, hatten sie alle Szenen im Kasten. Kinder und Tiere saßen brav auf ihren Plätzen.
„Herr Siegmann will das Bewerbungsvideo sehen, bevor es an den Fernsehsender geht", erläuterte die Lehrerin und schwang sich auf ihr Pult. „Er ist bis 17 Uhr in seinem Büro. Bringt ihm das Video vorbei, er guckt es sich an und schickt die Datei dann per Mail weiter an den Fernsehsender. Und jetzt holt bitte eure Deutschhefte raus."

Die Klasse ächzte.

Es waren nur noch 15 Minuten bis Schulschluss. Die Lehrerin nutzte sie, um ein Diktat zu schreiben. „Der berühmte Seefahrer Christoph Kolumbus wurde 1451 in Genua in Italien geboren …“, diktierte Miss Cornfield. Alle stöhnten.

6. Kapitel

Zack, zack, zack

Vier Kinder aus Miss Cornfields Klasse verabredeten sich für drei Uhr nachmittags im Computerraum: Ida, Benni, Max und Yannik. Yannik hatte sich freiwillig gemeldet, weil er weitere Pluspunkte sammeln wollte. Max betrachtete sich als Chef des Projekts, schließlich hatte er die Idee gehabt. Ida musste kontrollieren, ob die anderen auch alles richtig machten, und Benni? Den hatte Henrietta überredet.

Yannik ging in der Mittagspause nicht wie die anderen Kinder nach Hause, seine Eltern waren sowieso bei der Arbeit.
„Gut festhalten“, sagte er zu Tingo. „Wir erforschen den Stadtpark!“ Wie einen Rucksack trug er den Schimpansen auf dem Rücken: Die langen Arme waren die Riemen, die Beine der Hüftgurt.
Sie tobten herum und die Zeit verging wie im Flug.
Hand in Hand spazierten sie in die Wintersteinschule, wo sich die anderen gerade vom Hausmeister den Computerraum aufschließen ließen.
Max setzte sich an den Schulcomputer, bevor Ida es tun konnte. Er tippte das Kennwort ein und hielt Benni die Hand hin.
„Den Chip“, sagte er knapp.
Benni musste lange in der Hosentasche kramen, bis er ihn fand, und erntete dafür einen strengen Blick von Max.
Sie lachten viel, als sie das Filmmaterial sichteten. Der Professor sah ulkig aus in seinem Jackett und Helene war eine großartige Moderatorin.

Yannik war ständig irgendwo im Bild und auch die Tiere waren überall zu sehen. Eine Fledermaus flatterte um den Kartenständer herum. Ein Pinselohrschwein hüpfte durch einen Hula-Hoop-Reifen. Max stolperte über ein Krokodil, ein Koala knabberte an einer Grünpflanze. Nur Caspar, das Chamäleon, war nirgendwo zu entdecken, er war wie so oft unsichtbar. Tingo hüpfte begeistert auf dem Stuhl auf und ab, während sie das Material durchsahen. „Ich wusste gar nicht, dass Schule so lustig ist. Mr. Morrison hat mir was ganz anderes erzählt …"

Sie sichteten fast zwei Stunden Filmmaterial. Und mussten radikal kürzen. „An die Arbeit", sagte Ida. Max bediente die Computermaus. Ida und Benni saßen neben ihm und achteten streng darauf, dass alle Szenen herausgeschnitten wurden, in denen Mr. Morrison zu sehen war.

Die Szenen, in denen die versteinerten magischen Tiere zu sehen waren, blieben drin. Für die Jury von Kids-Quiz-TV würden sie aussehen wie ganz normale Plüschtiere.

Das Video durfte nicht länger als drei Minuten sein. „Macht für jeden 7,5 Sekunden", hatte Ida blitzschnell ausgerechnet. Aber allein die Aufzählung der Nobelpreisträger dauerte mehr als 20 Sekunden! Die Aufnahmen von der Schule und die Interviews mit Direktor und Hausmeister mussten ebenfalls bleiben. Zack, zack, zack.
Max war superschnell am Computer. Er kürzte wild entschlossen Bennis schiefen Purzelbaum auf zwei Sekunden, klaute Ida bei ihrer Rechtschreibübung vier Sekunden und schnitt Schokis Schokotest auf zehn Sekunden zusammen.
Ida runzelte die Stirn. Sie wollte protestieren. Aber Max rief „fertig" und Benni sagte „super", also ließ sie es sein.
Max drückte auf Speichern.
Erschöpft lehnten sich die Kinder in ihren Stühlen zurück.
„Ich brauche dringend frische Luft!", stöhnte Ida.
Rabbat, der am Boden fast eingeschlafen war, sprang sofort auf. Er liebte den Schulgarten!

„Gute Idee", sagte Max. „Wer kümmert sich um die Kopien?"
„Wir machen das", antwortete Yannik. „Komm, Tingo!" Er setzte Tingo auf seinen Schoß und die beiden fuhren eine Runde Karussell auf dem Drehstuhl.
„Wir brauchen eine Kopie für Herrn Siegmann und eine für Miss Cornfield", erinnerte ihn Ida.
„Und eine für uns?" Henrietta lächelte Benni an. „Dann können wir heute Abend zusammen den Film angucken!"
„Klar", sagte Benni. „Es sind ja genug CDs da." Sie beschlossen insgesamt sechs Scheiben zu brennen: für Herrn Siegmann, für Miss Cornfield, für Benni, Ida, Max und Yannik.
Yannik legte die CDs ein, Tingo half ihm dabei.
Sie klopften übermütig auf den Tasten herum und Yannik sang seinem Freund Dschungellieder vor: „*Wer hat die Kokosnuss, wer hat die Kokosnuss, wer hat die Kokosnuss geklau-a-aut?*"
Ida, Rabbat und die anderen verschwanden genervt nach draußen.

Im Hinausgehen fragte Benni Max: „Hättest du auch gern ein magisches Tier?“

Max blieb stehen.

„*Die Affen rasen durch den Wald …*“, sang Yannik, so laut er konnte. Tingo schnatterte dazu.

Max schnaubte: „Also einen Schimpansen bestimmt nicht! Was für eine Nervensäge.“

Fünf Minuten später war alles fertig. Während die Tiere im Schulgarten warteten, huschten die vier Kinder hinauf zu Herrn Siegmann.

Der Direktor zog sich gerade die Jacke an. „Das Bewerbungsvideo für *Top oder Flop?* Wunderbar!“ Er nahm die CD und legte sie auf seinen Schreibtisch. „Ich muss noch schnell Besorgungen machen. Briefmarken.“ Herr Siegmann wurde rot.

Die Kinder wussten: Immer wenn er rot wurde, dachte er an seine geliebte Dolores. Er hatte sie im Schullandheim kennengelernt, wo sie Herbergsmutter war.

„Wenn ich zurück bin, sehe ich es mir sofort an.“

Gemeinsam gingen sie nach unten. Auf der Schulwiese blieb Herr Siegmann plötzlich stehen.
„Was machen denn all diese Plüschtiere hier?" Verblüfft deutete er auf eine Bank. Ein Fuchs, ein Schimpanse und eine Schildkröte saßen brav nebeneinander.
„Macht die Post nicht gleich zu?", fragte Ida rasch.
„Stimmt", nickte der Direktor. Er errötete und eilte zu seinem Auto.

7. Kapitel

Tingo

Normalerweise fuhr Yannik mit dem Bus nach Hause. Aber jetzt hatte er Tingo. Und Tingo hopste lieber. Also gingen sie zu Fuß.
In der Lindenallee kletterte Tingo eine Straßenlaterne hoch und rutschte gleich darauf wieder hinunter. Zum Glück waren gerade keine Fußgänger da, die ihn beobachten konnten. Wofür würden sie Tingo halten? Für einen ferngesteuerten Spielzeugaffen?

Wie elegant sich Tingo von einem Baum zum nächsten schwang! Er wusste bestimmt, wie man auf ein Basketballgerüst kletterte, ohne darin stecken zu bleiben.

Yannik seufzte. Die peinliche Aktion auf dem Sportplatz hatte er in der ganzen Aufregung beinahe vergessen. Aber jetzt war es wieder da, dieses bohrende Gefühl im Bauch … Yannik seufzte noch einmal.

Plötzlich lief Tingo artig neben ihm her. „Alles klar?"

„Hhm", machte Yannik und griff nach Tingos Hand. Sie fühlte sich warm und vertraut an.

„So lustig wie vorhin ist es wohl nicht immer an der Wintersteinschule, oder?", fragte Tingo vorsichtig.

„Nee, echt nicht." Yannik grinste schief. „Normalerweise rechnen wir. Und halten Referate. Wir üben Rechtschreibung und Lesen, Stunde um Stunde. Das zieht sich, kann ich dir sagen."

Tingo nickte verständnisvoll. „Wie in einem Käfig, das ist schlimm. Dürft ihr denn nie raus aus dem Klassenzimmer?"

„Doch, doch", beeilte sich Yannik zu sagen. „Wir haben Pausen und Sportunterricht –" Er brach ab. „Stell dir vor, was mir am Montag passiert ist …"
Yannik schüttete seinem neuen Freund das Herz aus: wie peinlich es war, in einem kaputten Basketballkorb zu hocken. Wie schrecklich es sich angefühlt hatte, als die Mädchen über ihn lachten. Und dass seine Eltern wohl ziemlich mit ihm schimpfen würden, wenn sie von dem Schaden erfuhren, den sie bezahlen mussten.
„Gestern habe ich sogar mein Sparschwein geplündert", gestand Yannik. „Es waren aber nur acht Euro und elf Cent drin. Viel zu wenig."
„Armer Yannik", seufzte Tingo mitfühlend.
Hand in Hand schlenderten sie durch den Stadtpark. Auch jetzt, am späten Nachmittag, war es dort wunderschön. Die Wiesen waren mit gelben Löwenzahnblüten übersät, das Laub leuchtete in hellem Grün.
Sie hopsten über Baumstämme, jagten über Wiesen und versteckten sich in Büschen. Sie baumelten an Ästen und ließen sich ins Gras plumpsen.

Als Tingo der Magen knurrte, kramte Yannik aus seinem Rucksack zwei Müsliriegel hervor.
„Oh, das hat Spaß gemacht!“, schmatzte Tingo glücklich.
Aber Yannik hatte noch lange nicht genug. „Wer als Erster zu Hause in der Heinemannstraße ist!“
Erst an der Haustür holte der Schimpanse Yannik ein.
„Du hast ganz schön viel Ausdauer“, japste er.
Yannik schloss auf und lauschte.
Kein Laut war zu hören.
Anscheinend waren seine Eltern noch unterwegs. Sein Vater hielt als Politiker ständig irgendwo Reden. Und wenn er keine Rede hielt, saß er in einer Besprechung. Und wenn er nicht in einer Besprechung saß, hatte er eine Telefonkonferenz. Bei Yanniks Mutter sah es als Anwältin nicht viel anders aus.
„Hallo, jemand zu Hause?“, rief Yannik in Richtung Wohnzimmer.
Er bekam keine Antwort.
„Na dann – zeig mir deine Hütte!“ Tingo nahm Yanniks Hand.

Der Schimpanse bewunderte den Wintergarten, der voller Palmen, Bananenstauden und Bambus war und ihn ein wenig an seine Heimat Tansania erinnerte. Er klimperte auf dem Klavier im Wohnzimmer herum – nicht sehr melodisch allerdings –, öffnete den Kühlschrank in der Küche und nahm sich einen Bananenjoghurt.

Im Elternschlafzimmer hopste er auf das große Bett. Dazu sang er laut: „*Der Affenonkel, welch ein Graus, reißt alle Urwaldbäume aus!*" Und Yannik fiel mit ein: „*Die ganze Affenbande brüllt: Wer hat die Kokosnuss, wer hat die Kokosnuss, wer hat die Kokosnuss gekla-a-aut …*"

Hand in Hand marschierten sie in Yanniks Zimmer. „Aha, du hast auch so eine Computerkiste." Tingo deutete auf Yanniks Schreibtisch. „Gucken wir uns den Film an? Euer Video?"

Yannik zögerte. Singen, hopsen, Filme gucken – alles machte mehr Spaß als Mathelernen. Aber morgen hatten sie eine Probe und er hatte noch gar nichts geübt.

„Später, Tingo, später“, versprach er.
Er holte sein Heft und begann das kleine Einmaleins zu wiederholen.
2 × 8 = 16.
3 × 8 = 24.
4 × 8 = 32.
Tingo fummelte währenddessen an den Knöpfen des Computers herum und hämmerte auf die Tasten. „*Der Affenmilchmann, dieser Knilch, der wartet auf die Kokosmilch*“, sang er.
Yannik versuchte sich zu konzentrieren.
5 × 8 = 40.
6 × 8 = 48.
„*Die ganze Af-fen-baaan-deee brüüüüüllt …*“ Tingo schunkelte jetzt auf dem Stuhl, wurde beim Singen langsamer und sah Yannik auffordernd an.
Yannik musste lachen. Was machte er da überhaupt? Er hatte heute ein magisches Tier bekommen! Einen Freund fürs Leben! Wie konnte er da an Mathe denken? Anstatt das Einmaleins zu üben, sollte er besser mit Tingo spielen!

Er klappte sein Heft zu und zusammen sangen sie den Refrain: „*Wer hat die Kokosnuss …*“

Dann spielten sie eine Runde Fangen, quer durchs Zimmer. Und eine Runde Hopsen. Vom Stuhl zum Bett, vom Bett aufs Fensterbrett und von dort in den Kleiderhaufen.

Tingo begann den Haufen zu durchwühlen und zog ein paar Sachen heraus. „Die könnte mir passen!“, rief der Schimpanse übermütig und schlüpfte in eine von Yanniks Trainingsjacken. Er fand eine Schirmmütze und eine Sonnenbrille und setzte beides auf. „Guck mal, Yannik!“

Yannik prustete los.
„Können wir jetzt euren Film sehen?“ Der Schimpanse schob seine Schirmmütze zurecht. „Den, in dem du so toll die Bälle durch die Luft wirfst?“
„Klar!“, rief Yannik.
Er legte die CD ein und Tingo hüpfte auf seinen Schoß. Die erste Einstellung zeigte die Wintersteinschule von außen. Es folgten der Direktor, der überschwänglich seine Schule lobte, und der Hausmeister, der erklärte, dass alles „tipptopp“ sei. Dann kam Helene, die die einzelnen Nummern ankündigte.
„Angeberin“, murmelte Yannik.
„Ich finde, sie macht das total gut“, sagte Tingo.
Tingo sah genau zu, wie Jo und Juri ihre acht Klimmzüge machten. „Wir beide hätten doppelt so viel geschafft, Yannik!“
Was dann folgte, raubte Yannik den Atem.
Mr. Morrison stapfte zur Tür herein.
Auf seiner Schulter saß Pinkie.
Die Vogelspinne plumpste aus dem Ärmel, die Klasse sprach gemeinsam den Schwur …

Manchmal wurde das Bild unscharf und der Text war nicht immer zu verstehen. Damit war klar: Was sie sich hier anguckten, war nicht das Bewerbungsvideo. Das war die Rohfassung!
„Oh nein!“, stöhnte Yannik. „Wir haben den falschen Film kopiert!“
Er sprang auf, Tingo landete auf dem Boden. „Tingo, wir stecken tief in der Patsche. Ganz, ganz tief!“
Der Schimpanse starrte Yannik mit großen Augen an. „Was ist denn, Yannik?“, flüsterte er erschrocken.
Yannik standen die Schweißperlen auf dem Gesicht: „Der Direktor darf das nicht sehen. Niemals!“
„Auweia“, stöhnte Tingo. Sein Bauch krampfte sich zusammen. Hätte er doch im Computerraum nicht die ganze Zeit Quatsch gemacht!
„Ich bin schuld“, flüsterte er. „Ich hab dich abgelenkt.“
Yannik hörte ihn gar nicht. Wie gelähmt starrte er auf die Szene, wo er Tingo in die Arme schloss. Was, wenn Mr. Morrison davon erfuhr, dass er den Schwur gebrochen und das Geheimnis verraten hatte? Ob er sein magisches Tier wieder abgeben musste?

Und ihr Auftritt bei *Top oder Flop* war damit auch gelaufen. Selbst wenn Herr Siegmann das Video weiterleitete, ohne es anzusehen – die Fernsehleute würden ihre Klasse für völlig bekloppt halten … Max und Helene würden stinksauer auf ihn sein! Die beiden hatten sich so viel Mühe gegeben …
Yannik konnte nicht anders, er begann zu weinen.
Tingo sah ihn bestürzt an.
„Jetzt ist alles vorbei“, schniefte Yannik. „Miss Cornfield kriegt Ärger, die anderen sind sauer, ich bin erledigt …“
Tingo überlegte und überlegte.
Nach einer Weile fragte er vorsichtig: „So lange ist es doch noch gar nicht her, dass wir das Video abgegeben haben. Vielleicht hat Herr Siegmann es noch gar nicht angesehen? Wir könnten es doch einfach austauschen.“
„Austauschen gegen was?“, schniefte Yannik. „Dazu müssen wir erst einmal eine Kopie vom richtigen Film machen. Und dafür müssen wir in den Computerraum der Schule. Wie sollen wir das schaffen?“ Er sackte

zusammen. „Ich Idiot weiß ja noch nicht mal das Kennwort vom Computer. Ich hab nie aufgepasst."
„Hm", sagte Tingo. Er überlegte und überlegte.
„Die anderen machen Hackfleisch aus mir!", jammerte Yannik. „Morgen melde ich mich krank!"
„Nichts da", protestierte Tingo und sprang auf. „So schnell geben wir beide nicht auf. Ich hab eine Idee."
Mit wenigen Sätzen erklärte er seinen Plan. Erst nickte Yannik eifrig – doch dann verschränkte er die Arme vor der Brust. „Vergiss es. Ich frag doch kein Mädchen um Hilfe!" Er schnaubte. „Und ausgerechnet Franka! Die ist nicht gerade berühmt für ihre große Hilfsbereitschaft ..."
Tingo sah seinen Freund herausfordernd an. „Du brauchst jemanden, der das Passwort kennt und dich nicht verpetzt. Richtig?"
Yannik nickte stumm.
Tingo fuhr fort: „Franka hat was in der Birne, das sieht jeder sofort. Und sie quasselt nicht so viel wie Ida oder Max. Franka kann schweigen wie ein Goldfisch."
Yannik staunte, wie genau Tingo seine Klassen-

kameraden beobachtet hatte. Aber Franka um Hilfe bitten? „Ich weiß nicht …“, sagte er gequält.

„Hast du eine bessere Idee?“ Tingo trommelte ungeduldig mit den Fingern auf den Tisch. „Willst du Max anrufen? Oder Ida?“

„Nein“, stammelte Yannik. „Bloß nicht.“

Tingo schob Yannik zur Tür hinaus: „Auf zu Franka.“

8. Kapitel

Drei Einbrecher

Es war schon kurz nach sieben, als Yannik sein Fahrrad abstellte und an Frankas Tür klingelte. Die Adresse hatte er aus der Klassenliste: Luisenstraße 32.
Als Franka öffnete, sagte sie kein Wort.
Sie stand einfach nur da und wartete, ob Yannik den Mund aufkriegen würde.
Zunächst sah es nicht danach aus.
Bis Tingo ihn in die Seite knuffte.

„Aua!“, sagte Yannik empört. Franka grinste. Und Yannik holte tief Luft.
„Äh … Du kennst dich doch mit den Schulcomputern aus, oder?“, stammelte er. „Das Video, du weißt schon …“ So nach und nach gelang es ihm, die Sache zu erklären. „Wir haben dem Direktor den falschen Film gegeben. Den, auf dem alles drauf ist. Mr. Morrison, der Schwur, einfach alles.“
Frankas Blick wanderte zwischen Yannik und seinem Schimpansen hin und her. Es fiel Yannik schwer, die nächsten Sätze auszusprechen: „Bitte, Franka.“ Er schluckte. „Kannst du uns helfen? Es ist ein echter Notfall!“
Franka sagte immer noch nichts. Doch dann rang sie sich immerhin vier Worte ab: „Was krieg ich dafür?“
Yannik warf einen Hilfe suchenden Blick zu Tingo. Der überlegte und überlegte. „Vielleicht könntest du sie ins Kino einladen?“, flüsterte er. „In einen Agentenfilm?“
„Vergiss es“, flüsterte Yannik zurück.
Mit einem Mal wurde Franka richtig gesprächig. „Am Samstag will ich mein Zimmer streichen. In Schwarz.

Meine Eltern dürfen nichts davon wissen. Es muss ganz schnell gehen. Wenn du mir streichen hilfst, dann helfe ich euch." Sie ging in die Knie und lächelte Tingo an. „Dein neuer Freund kann gern mitkommen."
„Mach schon", raunte Tingo Yannik zu.
„Geht klar", murmelte Yannik.
Franka streckte ihm die Handfläche entgegen. Yannik schlug ein.
„Dann auf zur Wintersteinschule!", rief Tingo. „Und zwar in einem Affenzahn!"

Yannik zitterte, als er sein Fahrrad in den Fahrradständer stellte. Tingo hatte die Arme fest um seinen Rücken geschlungen. Der warme Körper des Schimpansen tröstete ihn ein wenig.
Die Eingangstür der Schule war abgeschlossen.
„Soll ich den Hausmeister holen?", fragte Yannik. Inzwischen war es halb acht. Der Hausmeister wohnte in einem Bungalow hinter der Schulwiese. Bestimmt hockte er gerade vor dem Fernseher.

„Quatsch." Franka schüttelte den Kopf. „Tingo kann doch klettern, oder?"
Sie deutete nach oben. Im zweiten Stock stand ein Fenster zur Toilette offen.
Yannik gab Tingo ein Zeichen und Tingo sauste los. Erst auf den Baum, vom Baum zum Fensterbrett und vom Fensterbrett hinein ins Schulgebäude. Eine Minute später öffnete er im Erdgeschoss ein Fenster und winkte ihnen zu.
Franka hob den Daumen.
„Super gemacht, Tingo", freute sich Yannik und fasste ein wenig Mut. Schnell kletterten die beiden Kinder ins Schulhaus.
Sie lauschten.
Alles war still.
„Merkwürdig abends allein hier zu sein", murmelte Franka.
Yannik wollte so schnell wie möglich weiter. „Los, zum Computerraum!", raunte er.
Sie hatten Glück – Herr Wondraschek hatte ihn nicht wieder abgesperrt.

Franka fuhr den Computer hoch, tippte „wintersteinschule“ und schon erschienen verschiedene Symbole.

Tingo starrte Yannik verdattert an. „So einfach ist das?“

Yannik wäre vor Scham am liebsten im Boden versunken.

Franka drückte drei Tasten, öffnete die richtige Datei, schob eine CD ins Fach, drückte auf „Speichern unter“. Innerhalb von 30 Sekunden kopierte sie den richtigen Film.

„Sie ist wirklich gut“, flüsterte Yannik Tingo zu.

„Sag ich doch“, antwortete Tingo. „Und nett ist sie auch. Das wirst du sehen, wenn du am Samstag ihr Zimmer streichst!“

„Du kommst doch hoffentlich mit!?“, rief Yannik erschrocken.

„Mal sehen ...“ Tingo kräuselte seine Nase. „Eigentlich soll ich am Samstag Mr. Morrison in der magischen Zoohandlung helfen ...“ Doch dann rief er schnell: „Reingefallen!“, und Yannik seufzte erleichtert auf.

Zu dritt liefen sie hoch zu Herrn Siegmanns Büro. Yannik klopfte an der Tür. Er wusste nicht, was lauter war: sein Herzklopfen oder das Klopfen an der Tür. Er flehte, dass Herr Siegmann den falschen Film noch nicht angesehen hatte. Vielleicht bekam er noch eine Chance!

Klopf, klopf.

Keine Antwort.

Tingo drückte die Klinke nach unten.

„Niemand da", flüsterte er.

Die Kinder schlichen hinein. Yannik sah auf den ersten Blick, dass die CD nicht mehr auf Herrn Siegmanns Schreibtisch lag.

„Wir kommen zu spät", stöhnte Yannik.

„Klappe!", knurrte Franka.

Sie setzte sich und starrte auf den dunklen Bildschirm.

„Wir müssen Herrn Siegmanns E-Mail-Konto knacken." Franka rieb sich nachdenklich die Nase. „Wir haben drei Versuche. Hast du eine Idee, welches Passwort er verwendet?"

„Wintersteinschule?", schlug Yannik vor.

Franka sparte sich jeden Kommentar.
„Null Punkte“, nuschelte Tingo.
Franka ließ ihren Blick durchs Büro wandern. Ein Foto an der Wand zeigte einen freudestrahlenden Direktor mit einem riesigen Kohlrabi in der Hand. Herr Siegmann hatte einmal an einem Wettbewerb teilgenommen und war Kohlrabikönig geworden. Darauf war er mächtig stolz.
Franka tippte: „kohlrabi“.
Auf dem Bildschirm blinkte ein Fenster auf:

Passwort ungültig

„Noch zwei Versuche“, murmelte sie.
Yannik wusste nicht, was er tun sollte. Er wollte hier weg, der Direktor konnte jeden Moment zurückkommen. Aber er wollte auch keinen falschen Vorschlag machen.
Im Büro lagen Comichefte herum, eine ganze Sammlung.
Yannik hielt eins hoch und Franka schrieb: „asterix“.

Als Nächstes wollte sie „obelix“ versuchen, aber Yannik stoppte sie.
„He, schau mal hier!“
Er hatte eine Postkarte entdeckt. Sie stammte von Dolores, Herrn Siegmanns Freundin. Jeder aus der Klasse wusste, wie sehr er sie mochte. Wahrscheinlich saß er gerade in einem Café und schrieb ihr eine Postkarte. Natürlich in Reimen, was ziemlich lange dauern konnte …
Franka lächelte und tippte: „dolores“. Eine Melodie erklang und das Postfach öffnete sich.
In Windeseile ging Franka die Liste der Mails durch.
„Keine Nachricht an Kids-Quiz-TV!“, rief sie.
Yannik machte einen Luftsprung. Er war gerettet! Am liebsten wäre er mit Tingo durchs Büro getanzt!
„Aber wo ist die CD?“, zischte Franka und blätterte durch die Papierstapel auf dem Schreibtisch.
Yannik erschrak. Nein, noch waren sie nicht gerettet.
„Im Dings an der Computerkiste?“ Das magische Tier hüpfte zum Rechner.

„Meinst du das CD-Laufwerk?“, fragte Yannik überrascht. Tingo lernte wirklich schnell!
Im selben Moment hörten die Kinder ein Geräusch.
Schritte.
Und das Klappern eines Schlüsselbunds.
Herr Siegmann!
Tingo schnatterte erschrocken los und hielt sich gleich darauf den Mund zu.
Yanniks Herz raste.
Selbst Franka bekam rote Flecken im Gesicht. Trotzdem öffnete sie mit ruhiger Bewegung das CD-Fach.
Tatsächlich! Da war ihr Film.
Die Schritte kamen näher.
Franka tauschte die CD aus.
Mann, war sie cool! Yannik war beeindruckt, ob er wollte oder nicht.
Die Schritte erklangen nun direkt vor der Tür.
Yannik überlegte gerade, ob er sich im Schrank verstecken sollte, als draußen ein Handy klingelte.
„Oh Dolores, wie schön, dass du zurückrufst! – Ja, ich habe es zweimal versucht.“

Franka deutete zum Fenster.
Vor dem Büro stand eine
Buche mit starken Ästen.
Als Erstes schwang sich Tingo
nach draußen.
Dann Yannik.
Und schließlich Franka.
„Sportlich ist sie auch noch“,
schwärmte Tingo und Yannik
nahm sich vor in Zukunft ein
bisschen weniger auf „die blöden
Weiber“ zu schimpfen.

9. Kapitel

Ein Totenkopf blinkt

Am Donnerstag saß Yannik mucksmäuschenstill auf seinem Stuhl im Klassenzimmer. Neben ihm saß Tingo. Auch er hatte seine Handflächen artig auf den Tisch gelegt. „Stell dir vor, dein Po ist mit Superkleber festgepappt“, flüsterte der Schimpanse seinem Gefährten zu. Die beiden hatten sich fest vorgenommen heute keinen Unsinn zu machen.
Max kam herein. „Na, alles klar?“

Yannik nickte. Anscheinend hatte Max gestern seine CD nicht mehr angesehen.
Helene und Karajan waren die Nächsten. „Ist der Film gut geworden?"
„Logo", antwortete Yannik, nun schon etwas lockerer.
Franka schlenderte im schwarzen Schlabberpullover ins Klassenzimmer. Sie sah Yannik nicht einmal an, sondern ging einfach an ihren Platz in der letzten Reihe und schlug ihr Buch auf.
„Der Goldfisch ist da", kicherte Tingo.
„He! Keine Witze über Mädchen", wies ihn Yannik grinsend zurecht.
Franka war in Gedanken längst bei ihrem neuen Krimi. Gespannt blätterte sie in ihrem Buch, rückte ihr Totenkopf-Lesezeichen zurecht – und stutzte.
Der Totenkopf auf dem Lesezeichen blinkte.
Und darunter stand in winzigen Buchstaben:

An Franka Lindbergh!
Die magische Zoohandlung teilt mit: Das Auswahlverfahren läuft. Du bist die Nächste, die ein magisches Tier bekommen wird. Halte dich bereit. Viele Grüße!
Die magische Zoohandlung

Franka schlug entsetzt das Buch zu.
Ihr wurde heiß und kalt zugleich.
Die Vogelspinne!
Agent Y aus dem Tal des Todes!
Franka bekam schweißnasse Hände. „Wenn ich nur nicht solche Angst vor Spinnen hätte", flüsterte sie so leise, dass es keiner hören konnte.
Oh nein, oh nein, oh nein.
Oder hatte sie sich verlesen? Sie schlug erneut das Buch auf und wagte einen zweiten Blick.
Der Totenkopf blinkte unverdrossen:

An Franka Lindbergh!
Die magische Zoohandlung teilt mit

Es gab keinen Zweifel.
Ob man sein magisches Tier auch umtauschen konnte?
Ausnahmsweise?
Franka blickte auf und ließ ihren Blick durch die Klasse schweifen. Gerade kam Eddie herein, über seinem Wuschelkopf kreiste Eugenia. Was gäbe sie für eine Fledermaus!

Der Schulgong ertönte und Miss Cornfield rauschte in den Raum.
„Einen wunderschönen guten Morgen!" Die Lehrerin strahlte die Klasse an. „Soeben habe ich mit Herrn Siegmann gesprochen. Er ist begeistert von eurem Video. Ich wiederhole: *begeistert!* Die Bewerbung ging pünktlich raus und die Schule hat sogar schon eine Antwort von Kids-Quiz-TV bekommen: Wir sind in der engeren Auswahl!"
Die Mädchen von der Tanz-AG sprangen auf und umarmten sich. Einige Jungs trampelten mit den Füßen. Max klatschte am allerlautesten. Yannik und Tingo vergaßen ihre eigene Superkleber-Regel und tobten durchs Klassenzimmer.
Miss Cornfield kämpfte gegen den Lärm an: „Morgen um zehn Uhr erfahren wir, ob wir dabei sind!"
„Nicht übel, gar nicht übel", freute sich Henrietta. „Benni, du warst ein sooo toller Kameramann!"
Benni streichelte zärtlich das Köpfchen seiner Schildkröte. „Und du hast sooo toll das Licht an- und ausgeknipst", lobte er sie.

Peperoni grunzte zufrieden. „Machen wir bald wieder einen Schokotest? Ich bin dran!“
Miss Cornfield klatschte in die Hände. „Vorerst können wir nichts anderes tun, als abzuwarten. Holt bitte eure Hefte raus, Hausaufgabenkontrolle!“ Sie ging von Bank zu Bank und ließ sich die Hefte zeigen.
Yannik und Tingo saßen längst wieder brav auf ihren Plätzen. Doch das nützte nichts, wenn man die Hausaufgaben nicht gemacht hatte.
Yannik kassierte einen Strich und eine strenge Ermahnung. „Schon zum zweiten Mal in dieser Woche! Das geht nicht, Yannik!“
Und im Mathetest lief es nicht besser. Yannik kaute ratlos an seinem Bleistift herum: „Zeichne ein gleichschenkliges Dreieck …“ Wenigstens konnte er das Einmaleins so einigermaßen.
Oder doch nicht? Als Miss Cornfield die Blätter einsammelte, schüttelte sie enttäuscht den Kopf: „Yannik, so kann das nicht weitergehen. Dein magisches Tier soll dich unterstützen! Wenn es dich vom Lernen abhält, haben wir ein Problem.“

Tingo und Yannik erschraken. Ein paar Minuten lang waren sie beide zerknirscht, doch dann kitzelte Tingo Yannik am Ohr. „Nicht aufgeben!“, flüsterte er. „Heute Nachmittag wird geübt, dass es kracht. Zur Not klebe ich dich wirklich am Stuhl fest. Wie viel ist 6 × 7?“
Da musste Yannik lachen und seine gute Laune kehrte zurück.

Und Yannik und Tingo hielten sich an ihre Abmachung!
Am Nachmittag tobten sie erst mal eine halbe Stunde im Garten herum. Danach setzte sich Yannik an den Schreibtisch. Allein. Tingo döste währenddessen im Wintergarten unter Palmen vor sich hin.
Als er nach seinem Schläfchen nach Yannik sah, saß der immer noch da und lernte.
„Wie viel ist 9 × 9?“, fragte Tingo geradeheraus. Der clevere Schimpanse konnte nicht nur lesen, sondern auch rechnen.
„81“, antwortete Yannik.

Tingo warf ihm zur Belohnung eine Socke ins Gesicht. Danach brachten sie Ordnung in Yanniks Kleiderhaufen. Und beinahe stritten sie darüber, wer die Sonnenbrille tragen durfte. Sie stand beiden richtig gut, das hatten sie vor dem Spiegel ausprobiert.

„Weißt du was?“, schlug Tingo vor. „An geraden Tagen trägst du sie, an ungeraden ich.“

„Geht klar“, lachte Yannik.

Sie spielten Sackhüpfen mit zwei Bettbezügen und lernten später das komplette Siebener-Einmaleins. Tingo fragte ab und Yannik antwortete. Jede richtige Antwort belohnte Tingo mit einem Sockenwurf.

Als Yanniks Eltern spät am Abend nach Hause kamen, saß Yannik auf dem Wohnzimmersofa und las in einem Buch. Es hieß: „Tansania – Land der Träume“ …

Im Arm hielt er ein Kuscheltier. Frau Nowak musste lächeln, als sie ihren Sohn so dasitzen sah. Sie konnte sich gar nicht erinnern, wann sie ihm den Plüschaffen geschenkt hatte. Wahrscheinlich stammte er noch aus der Kindergartenzeit.

„Hallo mein Schatz", rief sie und Yannik blickte auf.
„Hallo Mama, weißt du, was heute in der Schule …"
Aber Yanniks Mutter war schon in der Küche, um das Abendessen vorzubereiten.
Herr Nowak telefonierte, während er zur Tür hereinkam.
„Ja, sag ihm, dass die Abstimmung schon morgen ist. – Hallo, Yannik. – Was? Ja, er soll die Zahlen überprüfen, ich geh auch noch mal drüber …" Yanniks Vater drehte sich zur Seite. „Ja, ich weiß", sprach er ins Telefon. „Die Zufahrt zu der Tiefgarage ist noch ungeklärt, aber …"
Yannik hörte gar nicht hin.
Er hatte in dem Buch Fotos entdeckt, die in einer Forscherstation aufgenommen worden waren. Ein Schimpanse ordnete Zahlen der Reihe nach. „Sogar deine Kollegen im Dschungel können rechnen", staunte Yannik.
„Aber nicht so gut wie ich!" Tingo zog Yannik eine Socke vom Fuß und warf sie ihm an den Kopf. „Wie viel ist 7 × 7?"

„49“, antwortete Yannik und fing die Socke auf.
Yanniks Mutter klapperte in der Küche mit Tellern und Besteck, wurde aber ebenfalls von einem Anruf unterbrochen: „Was, die Frau will morgen nicht vor Gericht erscheinen? Grippe? Ach du meine Güte … Also gut, pass auf: Wir müssen unbedingt daran denken, dass …“ Sie klemmte sich den Hörer hinters Ohr, während sie Brote schmierte.
Tingo schmiegte sich näher an Yannik.
Kurz darauf servierte Yanniks Mutter Käsebrote mit Gemüsesticks. Aber gemütliche Familienstimmung kam trotzdem nicht auf. Erst sprang Yanniks Mutter auf, weil sie das Mineralwasser vergessen hatte. Dann Yanniks Vater, weil er sich einen Espresso machen wollte. Kaum saßen alle zusammen, klingelte schon wieder ein Handy. Während Frau Nowak telefonierte, sah Herr Nowak am Computer seine Mails durch. Schließlich löste sich Tingo aus seiner Versteinerung und angelte nach einer Karotte. „Es achtet sowieso niemand auf uns“, mümmelte er und kuschelte sich eng an Yannik.

10. Kapitel

Kandidaten gesucht!

Der Freitag begann mit einer Sensation.

Der Schullautsprecher knackste und Herrn Siegmanns Stimme überschlug sich fast vor Begeisterung.

„Ich bin entzückt“, tönte es aus dem Lautsprecher. „Die Wintersteinschule hat es geschafft! Wir wurden für *Top oder Flop* ausgewählt. Am kommenden Montag sendet Kids-Quiz-TV live aus unserer Schule! Am Vormittag reist Starmoderator Karsten Markoni mit seinem Team an, um in der Pausenhalle alles vorzubereiten. Um 16 Uhr beginnt die Show! Freunde und Familienangehörige sind herzlich eingeladen, uns anzufeuern. Ich danke Miss Cornfield für ihren unermüdlichen Einsatz und ihrer Klasse für die vielen guten Ideen. Ich werde später vorbeikommen, um persönlich die Begründung der Jury vorzulesen."

Einen kurzen Moment lang hörte es sich im Lautsprecher an, als würden im Büro des Direktors die Sektkorken knallen.

Und im Klassenzimmer? Jubelten die magischen Tiere los.

Tingo vergaß mal wieder den Superkleber und hopste durchs Klassenzimmer. „Schule ist aufregend! Schule ist lustig!"

Eugenia quietschte: „Juhuherich!"

In der Klasse begann sofort die Diskussion, welche Kinder als Kandidaten antreten sollten.

„Drei Mädchen, drei Jungs!", rief Max, der die Bewerbungsunterlagen studiert hatte. „Das ist immer so."

Die anderen nickten. Sie brauchten sechs Kandidaten und zum Schluss kam eine Klassenaufgabe, bei der alle mitmachen durften. Es gab Wissensfragen, sportliche Herausforderungen, Geschicklichkeitsübungen und Quatschaufgaben. Und es gab superknifflige Rechenaufgaben!

„Möchtest du mitmachen, Franka?“, fragte Miss Cornfield und blickte in die letzte Bank.

Franka schreckte auf. „Auf gar keinen Fall!“, wiegelte sie ab.

„Och Menno“, raunte Tingo. „Sie ist so gut!“

„Jetzt übertreib mal nicht“, knurrte Yannik, fand es aber insgeheim auch ein bisschen schade.

Die Klasse einigte sich: Für die Wissensfragen und Rechenaufgaben wurden Ida und Max ausgewählt.

Wer war der beste Kandidat für Sport?

Die Klasse zögerte: Silas oder Jo?

Bei der Abstimmung hoben fast alle Mädchen für Jo die Hand.

„Er sieht einfach am besten aus“, flüsterte Helene Karajan zu. „Ist ja schließlich eine Fernsehshow.“

„Pah", schnaubte der Kater.
Das Ergebnis war eindeutig: Silas war draußen.
„Also gut", knurrte Silas. „Aber wehe, du versaust es!", fügte er spaßhaft hinzu und boxte seinem Freund in den Arm.
Und wer war der Beste für die Quatschaufgabe?
In dem Moment klopfte es.
Franka sackte in ihrem Stuhl zusammen. Oh nein! War das Mr. Morrison?
Es war nur der Direktor.
Voll Stolz wedelte er mit einem Blatt. Dann las er vor: „Die vielen witzigen Ideen haben die Jury überzeugt. Die blonde Moderatorin ist ein echtes Showtalent!" Der Direktor blickte anerkennend zu Helene. „Die Klasse glänzt durch ihr umfangreiches Expertenwissen. Wer kennt schon sämtliche Namen der Nobelpreisträger der letzten drei Jahre? Ausgezeichnet!"
Max wuchs in die Höhe, Ida ärgerte sich. Ihre superschwere Rechtschreibübung wurde nicht erwähnt! Dabei hatte sie so lange dafür geübt.
Heribert Siegmann wippte auf seinen Zehenspitzen.

„Besonders haben der Jury die Auftritte des äußerst aktiven, jonglierenden Jungen im Hintergrund gefallen! Und die vielen witzigen Plüschtiere im Video … Respekt für diese Gemeinschaftsleistung!“

Es folgten ein paar Hinweise für Montag. Zum Schluss las Herr Siegmann Grüße von Karsten Markoni vor: „Kids-Quiz-TV ist happy und freut sich auf die große Show am Montag. Dann könnt ihr zeigen, was ihr draufhabt! Badesachen nicht vergessen! Servus und bye-bye. Euer Karsten Markoni!“

Der Direktor senkte das Blatt. Er hatte rote Backen vor Aufregung.

„Käse-Makkaroni“, muffelte Henrietta. „Können die nicht jemand anders schicken?“

„Nicht so laut“, ermahnte Benni seine Schildkröte. „Die anderen finden ihn toll. Ist doch super, wenn er an unsere Schule kommt!“

„Weiß nicht, weiß nicht“, nuschelte Henrietta und verzog sich in ihren Schuhkarton.

Zum Abschluss rief der Direktor noch: „Das wird ein großer Tag für die Wintersteinschule!“

Dann schlug er die Füße zusammen und verschwand.
Die Kinder blickten sich an. „Bestimmt gibt's eine Wasserschlacht! Coooool!"
Plötzlich waren alle in der Klasse dafür, dass Yannik der beste Kandidat für die Quatschaufgabe war. Schließlich war er ausdrücklich von der Jury gelobt worden. Ebenso Helene. Auch sie gehörte jetzt zum Team.
Miss Cornfield stellte erleichtert fest, dass die Klasse sich einig war. Helene war manchmal recht vorlaut, aber seit sie ein magisches Tier bekommen hatte, war sie viel netter geworden. Anscheinend empfanden das auch ihre Mitschüler so.
Schwungvoll schrieb Miss Cornfield die Namen der fünf Kandidaten an die Tafel: Ida, Helene, Max, Jo und Yannik. Fehlte noch ein Mädchen.
Es klopfte schon wieder. Hatte Herr Siegmann etwas vergessen?
Nein, diesmal war es Mr. Morrison.
Franka hielt sich entsetzt die Hand vor den Mund.
Es ging ganz schnell.

Mr. Morrison verbeugte sich, Pinkie ebenso.
Es wurde ruhig im Klassenzimmer. Tingo griff nach der Hand seines Gefährten. Und die Kinder standen auf.
Gemeinsam sprachen sie den Schwur:

„Niemals, niemals sprechen wir
mit anderen über das magische Tier.
Die magische Zoohandlung ist streng geheim,
so soll es für immer und ewig sein.“

Alle warteten gespannt.
Franka zitterte.
Mr. Morrison räusperte sich. „Bereit, Franka?“
Durch die Klasse ging ein Ruck. Ausgerechnet Franka sollte ein magisches Tier bekommen?
Mr. Morrison ging in die Knie und zupfte an seinem Ärmel herum. Gleich würde Agent Y herauskrabbeln.
Franka hob abwehrend die Hände.
„Franka?“, fragte Miss Cornfield besorgt. „Alles in Ordnung?“

Das Mädchen brachte kein Wort heraus.
„He, wo bist du denn?“ Verärgert schüttelte Mr. Morrison seine Jacke. „Komm endlich raus, Cooper!“
Cooper?
Franka senkte die Hände.
Cooper?
Schon hielt ihr Mr. Morrison mit flacher Hand das magische Tier entgegen. Es war – eine Ratte! Eine braun gefleckte, bezaubernde Ratte!

Frankas Augen wurden kugelrund. Eine Ratte hatte sie sich schon immer gewünscht!
Dem magischen Tier schien es ganz genauso zu gehen. „Cool, Baby!" Cooper blickte direkt in Frankas Augen. „Hab ich ein Glück!"
Mit einem Satz sprang er von Mr. Morrisons Handfläche auf Frankas Schulter und knabberte begeistert an ihren schwarzen Haaren. Franka ließ es verdutzt mit sich geschehen. Die Ratte raunte: „Nicht einmal in London gibt es so coole Girls, echt!"
Franka strahlte von einem Ohr zum anderen. Sie konnte es einfach nicht glauben. Wow! Sie hatte eine Ratte bekommen! Eine sprechende Ratte! Aus London! Keiner in der Klasse hatte das schlecht gelaunte Mädchen je so glücklich gesehen.
Cooper blickte sich mit seinen munteren Knopfaugen um. „Was geht denn hier ab?" Er sah die Kamera, die noch immer im Klassenzimmer stand. Er sah die Scheinwerfer. Er sah das Plakat von der Quizshow und er sah die Namen an der Tafel. Er zählte eins und eins zusammen und stellte sich empört auf die Hinterbeine.

„Hey, ihr Tulpen! Geht es hier um eine Fernsehshow? Wieso steht mein cooles Girl nicht drauf, hä?"
Franka wurde rot. Auf einmal kam ihr ihre Absage dumm vor. Sie hob die Hand und meldete sich für die Matheaufgabe. Und damit war das Team komplett.

11. Kapitel

Cooper

Nach der Schule kaufte Franka ein großes Stück Käse. „Englischen Hartkäse mag ich am liebsten“, verriet Cooper und reckte seine rosa Nase in die Luft. Er saß auf Frankas Schulter.

Franka hatte keine beste Freundin. Ihr fiel es schwer, anderen von sich zu erzählen. Aber ihrem magischen Tier vertraute sie vom ersten Augenblick an. Auf dem Nachhauseweg erzählte sie Cooper einfach alles.

In der Klasse hatte sie das Gefühl, dass keiner sie verstand. „Die sind alle so kindisch." Und zu Hause fand ihre ältere Schwester Kaja *sie* kindisch und sperrte sich ständig allein mit lauter Musik in ihrem Zimmer ein. „Die hält mich für ein Baby."
Cooper berichtete von seinem Leben in London zwischen Mülltonnen und Abwasserrohren.
„Und dann kam Mr. Morrison in seinem Omnibus vorbei und hat dich abgeholt?", erkundigte sich Franka und wechselte die Straßenseite. Fast waren sie da.
„Jep", bestätigte die Ratte. „Auf der Fahrt habe ich ständig mit Pinkie über die Musik gestritten. Pinkie wollte Schlager, ich Punkrock."
Franka lachte. „Und, wer hat gewonnen?"
„Was glaubst du denn?" Cooper zwinkerte ihr zu.

In Frankas Zimmer wunderte sich Cooper über den schwarzen Farbeimer in der Ecke.
„Morgen wird das hier eine dunkle Räuberhöhle", kündigte Franka an.

Die Ratte staunte. „Alles wird schwarz? Echt? Von oben bis unten?“ Franka nickte und Cooper pfiff durch die Zähne. „Cool, Baby! Dann lebe ich bald wieder in der Dunkelheit. Du hättest dich nicht besser auf meine Ankunft vorbereiten können. Hast du dich sehr gefreut, als du die Nachricht von Mr. Morrison bekommen hast?“

„Äh … Also, i-ich … wusste ja nicht so recht …“, stammelte Franka. Dann holte sie Luft. Egal. Sie erzählte Cooper, wie viel Angst sie vor der Übergabe gehabt hatte. Wie hatte sie nur so misstrauisch sein können? Mr. Morrison und Miss Cornfield suchten immer genau das Tier aus, das am besten zu einem passte.

Ob Leonie tatsächlich eines Tages das Pony bekommen würde, nach dem sie sich so sehnte? Bisher hatte Franka Leonie immer für eine Heulsuse gehalten. Aber auf einmal wünschte sie es ihr von ganzem Herzen.

„Wer gehört noch zu deiner Familie?“, wollte Cooper wissen. „Mama, Papa, Kaja, weiter?“

„Na, das reicht doch wohl“, antwortete Franka.

Sie saßen nebeneinander auf dem Bett und mümmelten Rosinen: eine für Franka, eine für Cooper, eine für Franka …

„Ich hab ungefähr 96 Brüder und Schwestern", berichtete Cooper. „Wir haben uns komplett aus den Augen verloren. Jeder macht sein eigenes Ding. Schade eigentlich." Er spielte mit seiner Schwanzspitze. „Aber jetzt bin ich bei dir! Ich hab ein neues Zuhause!"

„Und ob!" Franka strahlte. „Hilfst du mir beim Zimmerstreichen?"

„Klar. Aber warum machst du es heimlich?", fragte Cooper. „Willst du Kaja beeindrucken?"

Frankas Stimme wurde leiser. „Vielleicht nimmt sie mich dann ja endlich mal ernst." Sie räusperte sich. „Sie hat ja auch Recht. Ich meine, es ist doch wirklich albern, Kids-Quiz-TV zu schauen, beim Schulkonzert Blockflöte zu spielen oder für Senioren ein Theaterstück einzustudieren. Kennst du Yannik schon? Das ist der Junge mit dem Schimpansen. Der ist neulich einen Basketballkorb hochgeklettert und kam nicht mehr runter. Alle haben ihn ausgelacht!"

„Und damit dir das nicht passiert, machst du lieber gar nichts?“, erkundigte sich Cooper.
„Genau.“ Franka nickte eifrig. „Kaja sagt einfach: Keinen Bock, keine Lust, egal, weiß nicht, chill mal. Damit kommt sie überall durch.“
„Ist sie gerade zu Hause, deine große Schwester?“, wollte Cooper wissen. Er hatte eine Idee!
Franka lauschte. In der Wohnung war keine Musik zu hören.
Sie schüttelte den Kopf. „Glaub nicht.“
„Dann könnten wir doch jetzt ein wenig Quatsch machen, oder?“ Die Ratte hüpfte aufs Fensterbrett. Franka wohnte im zweiten Stock. Ihr Fenster stand offen und draußen gab es eine Regenrinne. Die Regenrinne führte über den Balkon und machte eine Kurve. Die perfekte Rutsche!
„Cool, Babyyy!“, brüllte Cooper, streckte die Beine nach vorne und schwups, war er weg.
Unten landete er mitten in der Regentonne.
„Das macht Spaß!“, jauchzte Cooper und planschte vergnügt.

Franka rannte nach unten, fischte den tropfnassen Cooper aus dem Wasserfass und trug ihn wieder nach oben. „Das nennt man wohl Wasserratte", sagte Franka und grinste.

Cooper schüttelte sein Fell. „Und jetzt mit Zeitstoppen!", rief er.

Nach ein paar Runden kramte Franka eine Puppe hervor, die sie von Kaja geerbt hatte. Kaja hatte nie mit ihr gespielt, aber Franka fand Bella Dracula ganz witzig. Sie trug schwarz-lila Klamotten und ihre Beine konnte man abknicken. Jetzt hatte Cooper eine Rutschgefährtin!

Schwupp, die Puppe verschwand im Rohr und landete im Regenfass. „Sieben Sekunden!", staunte Cooper. Er schaffte es in fünf.

Sie spielten fast eine Stunde lang Wettrutschen. Mal gewann Bella Dracula, mal gewann Cooper. Am Schluss hängte Franka die Puppe zum Trocknen an die Wäscheleine auf dem Balkon.

„Gut, dass Kaja das nicht gesehen hat", sagte Franka und blinzelte gegen die Sonne.

„Ach, Franka." Die Ratte lächelte. „Hör doch auf, dich mit deiner großen Schwester zu vergleichen. Du hast deinen eigenen Kopf. Zum Glück!"
Die Sonne war für die Ratte zu grell, Cooper verkroch sich hinter einem Blumentopf. Nur die rosa Nasenspitze guckte hervor. „Und morgen streichen wir dein Zimmer, ja? Wirklich in Schwarz?"
„In Schwarz", antwortete Franka.

12. Kapitel

Das Wochenende vor der Show

Helene, Jo, Ida, Max, Franka und Yannik hatten drei Tage Zeit, um sich auf *Top oder Flop* vorzubereiten. Helene stand vor dem Spiegel und übte verschiedene Gesichtsausdrücke. Sie guckte oft Sendungen im Fernsehen, bei denen Nachwuchsstars gesucht wurden. Mädchen balancierten auf hohen Schuhen über lange Laufstege, Jungs sangen Popsongs. Helene war überzeugt, dass sie das gut hinkriegen würde.

Sie probierte ihren ganzen Kleiderschrank mehrmals durch. Karajan gab ihr Ratschläge. Nach drei Stunden war entschieden, was sie am Montag tragen wollte: ein Glitzeroberteil, schwarze Ballerinas und ihren Lieblingsrock.
Karajan strahlte. „Du wirst die Schönste sein!"

Jo traf sich mit Silas. Sie hatten beschlossen zusammen mit ihren Tieren ins Fitnessstudio zu gehen. Jos Vater hatte dort ein Abo, die Kinder durften kostenlos rein.
Jo stemmte Gewichte und Juri zählte dazu: „Eins, zwei, drei!"
Danach ging es aufs Laufband. Sogar Rick machte mit. Es sah lustig aus, wie das grüne Krokodil über das schwarze Laufband joggte und ein Pinguin daneben das Tempo vorgab: „Noch einen Kilometer, gleich geschafft!"

Ida las ihr Kinderlexikon von A bis Z durch. Immer wieder. Sie startete bei „Aal“ und las weiter, bis sie bei „Zylinder“ angekommen war.

Rabbat versuchte seine Freundin abzulenken. „Du bist doch die Klügste von allen, Rotschopf! Du musst nicht immerzu lernen. Lass uns lieber zusammen rausgehen.“

Ida seufzte. „Aber nur eine kleine Runde.“

Sie spazierten an der großen Kastanie vorbei über den Johannisplatz, winkten Leonardo, dem Streifenhörnchen, zu und bummelten weiter zur Lerchenfeldstraße. Hier rollte Benni mit seinem Skateboard auf und ab. Hintendrauf saß Henrietta.

„Na, schon aufgeregt?“, rief Benni ihnen fröhlich zu.

„Gar nicht!“, antwortete Ida.

„Null Komma null“, behauptete Rabbat.

Aber Benni und Henrietta glaubten ihnen kein Wort.

Max entspannte sich, indem er die Hieroglyphen in seinem Buch über das alte Ägypten studierte. Er liebte es, die geheimnisvollen Zeichen zu betrachten und daraus Worte zu bilden. Hoffentlich kamen am Montag Fragen aus dem alten Ägypten dran. Darüber wusste er alles!

Zur Vorbereitung sah er sich alte *Top oder Flop*-Sendungen auf dem Computer an und wunderte sich, wie leicht die Fragen waren.

„Wie lang ist der Äquator?“, lautete eine und Max wusste es sofort: 40.000 Kilometer.

Schwieriger fand er die Geschicklichkeitsaufgabe. Zwei Jungen sollten Papierflieger basteln. Das Modell „Wolkenschneider“ segelte acht Meter weit, während Modell „Kondor“ in einer Pfütze landete. Der Kandidat rutschte aus und landete mit dem Po im Wasser. Karsten Markoni lachte und das Publikum klopfte sich auf die Schenkel vor Begeisterung.

Zu jeder Mahlzeit trank Max ein Glas Milch: Er hatte gelesen, dass Milch die Gehirnzellen in Schwung hielt. Konnte ja nicht schaden.

Und was machten Yannik und Franka?
Yannik stand in Frankas Zimmer und tauchte seinen Pinsel in schwarze Farbe. Neben ihm arbeitete Tingo. Franka war ungewöhnlich gesprächig. Jetzt, wo sie Cooper hatte, war sie viel lockerer. „Wir haben genau eine Stunde, um das Zimmer zu streichen", machte Franka unmissverständlich klar. „So lange sind meine Eltern weg. Hau rein!"
Yannik pinselte und pinselte. Er hatte sich von zu Hause eine alte Hose und ein altes Hemd mitgenommen. Tingo half, so gut er konnte. Das war gar nicht so einfach für einen Schimpansen mit Sonnenbrille. Heute war nämlich ein ungerader Tag. Tingo kletterte die Leiter hoch und strich die Decke. Aus dem hellen Mädchenzimmer wurde ein dunkler U-Bahn-Schacht.

„Cool, Baby!", rief Cooper. Er hielt einen dünnen Pinsel aus Frankas Schulmalkasten in den Pfoten und malte die Zimmerecken aus. „Deine Eltern werden begeistert sein."
„Oh nein!", lachte Franka und drehte das Radio lauter, das sie heimlich aus dem Zimmer ihrer Schwester geholt hatte. „Sie werden mir den Kopf abreißen! Was meint ihr, warum ich euch um Hilfe gebeten habe? Hau rein, Yannik!"
Sie strichen wie die Weltmeister und waren kurz vor drei tatsächlich fertig.
Obwohl Yannik ziemlich erschöpft war, beeilte er sich nach Hause zu kommen. Er war nicht gerade wild darauf, Frankas Eltern über den Weg zu laufen ….

Zu Hause blätterten sie „Tansania – Land der Träume" durch und richteten sich ein gemütliches Lager im Wintergarten her. Tingo hatte Yannik gestanden, dass er sich dort am allerwohlsten fühlte.

Schon bald war der Schimpanse eingeschlafen. Er kuschelte sich eng an Yannik und Yannik spürte seinen Atem. Er wurde ganz ruhig und fühlte sich so gut aufgehoben wie schon lange nicht mehr. Er freute sich auf morgen: Dann durfte er die Sonnenbrille haben.

Und er freute sich auf übermorgen: Dann war die Quizshow!

Und er freute sich auf überübermorgen und alle darauffolgenden Tage. Denn jetzt hatte er Tingo und mit Tingo war das Leben einfach nur fabelhaft!

13. Kapitel

Das Fernsehen kommt

Als die Kinder aus Miss Cornfields Klasse am Montag zur Schule strömten, parkten drei riesige Trucks vor dem Schulgebäude. Darauf stand: „*Top oder Flop* – Die Kinderquizshow mit Millionenpublikum".
Benni und Henrietta rollten auf dem Skateboard zur Schule. Silas kam mit Rick unterm Arm auf dem Rennrad angesaust und Schoki und Peperoni fuhren mit dem Bus.

Anna-Lena und Caspar marschierten die Lindenallee entlang und stießen dort auf Eddie, aus dessen Ärmel eine Fledermaus hervorlugte. An der Kreuzung warteten Jo und Juri. Alle waren schrecklich aufgeregt. Sogar die Zeitung hatte das Ereignis angekündigt, mit einer fetten Schlagzeile auf der ersten Seite: „*Top oder Flop* – heute live an der Wintersteinschule!“ Und darunter stand: „Nun heißt es Daumen drücken für die Wintersteinschule! Sie tritt an gegen die Watzkeschule aus Berlin.“

Helene wurde in letzter Sekunde von ihrer Mutter im Geländewagen gebracht. „Ich bin ja so stolz auf dich, meine Süße!“ Die Mutter warf der Tochter eine Kusshand hinterher. „Ich komme nachher zur Show. Bussi!“

Die Pausenhalle war kaum wiederzuerkennen. Mitarbeiter von Kids-Quiz-TV eilten hin und her und riefen sich Anweisungen zu. Bunte Schaumstoffwürfel wurden übereinandergestapelt, Strahler angeschleppt. Sie waren dreimal so groß wie die, die Benni und Schoki verwendet hatten.

Frauen rollten Teppiche aus. Männer steckten lange Plastikröhren ineinander. Für die Regie wurde ein Pult aufgestellt.

Da quetschten sich auch Ida und Rabbat durch die Eingangstür. Ida war todmüde und aufgekratzt zugleich. Sie hatte kaum geschlafen. Ob ihr die richtigen Antworten einfallen würden? Rabbat hielt sich dicht bei ihr.

Max überholte sie mit schnellen Schritten. Er trug einen braunen Anzug mit Pullunder darunter. „Na, Ida, alles klar? Hast du am Wochenende auch alte Sendungen angeguckt? Mann, die Fragen waren babyleicht."

Zusammen trabten sie in den ersten Stock, wo Jo schon wartete. Auf Juris Rat hin hatte er sich einen neuen Pulli gekauft mit der Aufschrift „Cool guy", was nichts anderes als „Cooler Junge" hieß. „Die Mädchen aus Berlin werden in Ohnmacht fallen, wenn sie dich sehen", hatte der Pinguin gesagt.

Ida fiel auf, dass Jo sich noch öfter als sonst die Haare aus dem Gesicht strich. War er etwa auch nervös?

Neben Jo stand Franka in schwarzen Stiefeln und Röckchen. Sie war die Ruhe selbst. Ihre Ratte saß auf der Schulter.
„Sie ist so cool!“, flüsterte Ida ihrem Fuchs zu.
Von oben konnten die Kinder gut in die Pausenhalle gucken. Yannik und Tingo kamen herein. Tingo hatte eine Sonnenbrille auf und klaute sich aus dem Obstkorb der Fernsehleute eine Banane.
Eine Tribüne wurde aufgebaut. Die Plätze waren für Presse, Familie, Freunde und den Fanklub der auswärtigen Gäste reserviert.
Natürlich hatten alle Kinder aus Miss Cornfields Klasse am Wochenende wild herumtelefoniert. Jeder, der es irgendwie einrichten konnte, kam zur Wintersteinschule. Der Rest hatte versprochen sich um Punkt vier Uhr vor den Fernseher zu setzen. Alle fieberten mit!
Herr Siegmann stolzierte in der Halle auf und ab. Wie schade, dass Dolores nicht hier war! Aber vielleicht konnte er sie grüßen? Ah, da war ja der Moderator, dieser Karsten Markoni!

Herr Siegmann steuerte auf ihn zu. Herr Markoni saß in Jogginghose auf einem Barhocker und nippte gelangweilt an einem Pappbecher.
„Herr Markoni, wie schön Sie an der Wintersteinschule begrüßen zu dürfen!" Der Direktor schüttelte die Hand des Mannes so heftig, dass der Moderator seinen Kaffee verschüttete.
Karsten Markoni sprang auf. „He! Können Sie nicht aufpassen? Das ist Markenkleidung!"
Miss Cornfield, die sich gerade in der Pausenhalle umsah, eilte herbei und tupfte hektisch mit einem Taschentuch auf der Hose des Moderators herum. „Ich bin Mary Cornfield, die Klassenlehrerin." Sie errötete. „Wenn Sie Hilfe brauchen, Herr Markoni – ich bin für Sie da. Jederzeit!"
Die Zähne des Showmasters blitzten auf. „Das ist schön!" Er fuhr sich durch das schwarze Haar und zwinkerte der Lehrerin zu. „Und wenn *Sie* etwas brauchen, bin *ich* auch für *Sie* da!"
Dann warf er Herrn Siegmann einen bösen Blick zu und stolzierte davon.

An Unterricht war an diesem Montagvormittag nicht zu denken.

Miss Cornfield dachte zunächst, sie könnte die Klasse mit Arbeitsblättern beschäftigen, gab jedoch bald auf.

Max versuchte einen Papierflieger zu falten, Silas half ihm dabei.

Ida zerriss ein Arbeitsblatt gedankenverloren in kleine Papierschnipsel und Anna-Lena war so aufgeregt, dass sie ihr Chamäleon Caspar mit einem Radiergummi bewarf. Das kickte ihn verdutzt zurück.

Yannik und Tingo hopsten durchs Klassenzimmer, die Superkleber-Nummer funktionierte heute überhaupt nicht.

Henrietta verkroch sich in ihrem Schuhkarton. Ihr war der Trubel zu viel.

Franka starrte in ihr Mathe-Buch. Zwischendurch sagte sie Primzahlen auf: 2, 3, 5, 7, 11, 13, 17 …

Cooper knabberte beruhigend an ihrem Ohrläppchen.

Max rutschte auf seinem Stuhl hin und her und ratterte die Einwohnerzahlen der europäischen Hauptstädte herunter. Rom: 2,8 Millionen. London: 8,2 Millionen …

Helene wippte mit den Füßen, spielte mit ihren Haaren und tupfte sich ständig neues Lipgloss auf die Lippen.

„Hoffentlich fängt die Show bald an“, knurrte Karajan.

Auch Willi Wondraschek, der Hausmeister, war gereizt. Hatte er es doch gewusst! Die Fernsehleute brachten viel zu viel Unruhe in seine Schule! Die Röhren in der Pausenhalle wurden zu einer riesigen Wasserrutsche zusammengesteckt. Schläuche wurden ausgerollt, ein Planschbecken aufgebaut.

Der Hausmeisterkiosk in der Pausenhalle wurde gerade mit Folie zugeklebt. Er sollte dem Team der Wintersteinschule als Aufenthaltsraum während der Show dienen. Für die Kandidaten aus Berlin wurde ein Klassenzimmer im Erdgeschoss vorbereitet.

Jetzt wollte Karsten Markoni auch noch das Lehrerzimmer haben, als persönlichen Umkleideraum. Der hatte vielleicht Nerven!

Keiner der Schüler aus Miss Cornfields Klasse ging zum Mittagessen nach Hause. Sie hatten sich Brote und Obst mitgebracht und trafen sich im Schulgarten zum gemeinsamen Picknick. Die Lehrerin leistete ihnen Gesellschaft.
Als Karsten Markoni zufällig vorbeikam, um aus dem Truck etwas zu holen, sprang Miss Cornfield auf und bat um ein Autogramm.
„Für eine hübsche Dame immer gern", antwortete der Moderator und zückte den Stift.
Als auch Benni ihn nach einem Autogramm fragte, schob er ihn zur Seite. „Keine Zeit!", fauchte er.
„Blöder Makkaroni", stänkerte Henrietta.
Die Lehrerin sah dem Mann nach, der im Lastwagen verschwand. „Wahrscheinlich ist er genauso nervös wie ihr."

Keiner der sechs Kandidaten hatte Appetit.
„Ihr werdet eure Sache gut machen“, versuchte Miss Cornfield sie zu beruhigen. „Und selbst wenn ihr Zweiter werdet: Dabei sein ist alles!“
Max sah das anders. Er wollte unbedingt gewinnen! Es gab einen Pokal und einen Geldpreis für die Klassenkasse. Millionen Menschen sahen heute live zu, wenn er im Rampenlicht stand. Sie alle würden sehen, wie klug er war!

Um 14 Uhr fuhr ein Reisebus vor und eine Menge Kinder quollen heraus: die Gegenkandidaten von der Watzkeschule aus Berlin. Sie marschierten schnurstracks aufs Schulgebäude zu.
Die Kinder aus Miss Cornfields Klasse packten ihr Essen zusammen. Nun wurde es ernst!
Ein Junge aus Berlin ging vorbei. Er trug ein Muskelshirt und war einen Kopf größer als Jo. Er sah wirklich fit aus. Bestimmt der Kandidat für die Sportnummer!

Juri schluckte. „Keine Angst, Jo! Der tut nur so, als wäre er stark."
Eine Mitarbeiterin des Fernsehteams scheuchte die Kinder ins Klassenzimmer. „Bald geht's los!"
Sie gingen nach oben und warteten.
Aber nichts passierte.
Nicht nur Helene wurde nervös. „Die müssen uns doch langsam mal schminken und so", schimpfte sie. „Die kümmern sich die ganze Zeit nur um die Klasse aus Berlin!"

Gerade wollte sie sich beschweren, als die Tür aufflog. Karsten Markoni höchstpersönlich steckte seinen Kopf herein. Er trug jetzt gelbe Jeans, schwarzes Sakko und Sonnenbrille.
Henrietta musterte den Mann misstrauisch unter ihrem Panzer. Sie konnte ihn einfach nicht leiden. Sie beobachtete, wie sich Karsten Markoni im Klassenzimmer umsah. Er betrachtete schmunzelnd die Kuscheltiere, die sich auf Stühlen, Tischen und Fensterbrettern tummelten, und erschauerte, als er den Spinnen-Steckbrief neben der Tür entdeckte.
Henrietta kicherte leise in sich hinein. Aha, das Großmaul hatte also Angst vor Spinnen!
„Kleine Planänderung!", verkündete Karsten Markoni und warf der verdutzten Ida fünf rote T-Shirts zu. „Eine Nummer wird gestrichen, weil ein Mitarbeiter krank geworden ist. Heute brauchen wir nur fünf Kandidaten! Einer fliegt raus!"
Er wollte verschwinden, aber Helene hielt ihn am Ärmel fest. „Was soll das denn heißen?", fragte sie empört. „Wir haben uns doch alle vorbereitet!"

Der Moderator grinste breit. „Regt euch ab, ist doch nur ein Spiel, Kiddys! Aber wenn ihr euch nicht einigen könnt, stelle ich gern eine Entscheidungsfrage. Top oder Flop!“ Er zog eine Karteikarte aus seinem Sakko und schob sich seine Sonnenbrille ins schwarze Haar. „Wer von euch wollte bei den Wissensfragen antreten?“

„Ich!“, rief Max.

„Und ich“, piepste Ida.

Beide traten vor.

Der Moderator warf einen kurzen Blick auf die Karteikarte und fragte: „Wie heißt der längste Fluss der Welt?“

„Nil“, rief Ida.

„Amazonas“, antwortete Max.

„Der Junge hat Recht.“ Der Moderator stolzierte zur Tür hinaus. „Die Kleine ist raus.“

Ida blickte dem Mann sprachlos hinterher. Zum Glück war Rabbat sofort an ihrer Seite und leckte ihr die Hand. „Mach dir nichts draus“, tröstete er seine Gefährtin. „Der Typ ist doof.“

„Kannst du laut sagen", schniefte Ida. „Nil ist richtig, das weiß ich genau! Steht in meinem Lexikon. Nur Doofmänner nennen den Amazonas! Weil er so viele Seitenarme hat und keiner genau weiß, wo die Quelle liegt."

„Meine Siegerin", sagte Rabbat und sprang auf Idas Schoß.

14. Kapitel

Bauchplatscher für die Wintersteinschule

Um 15:45 Uhr durften sie endlich aus dem Klassenzimmer. Die Pausenhalle war nicht wiederzuerkennen. Überall leuchteten Scheinwerfer. Auf den Tribünen saßen dicht gedrängt die Zuschauer. In der Mitte der Pausenhalle lag ein roter, runder Teppich. Und vom obersten Stock wand sich spiralförmig eine Rutsche nach unten und endete in einem Wasserbecken.

Rick wäre am liebsten sofort mit Silas hineingehüpft. Auch Cooper juckte es in den Pfoten, aber er blieb natürlich bei Franka, die immer noch am gelassensten von ihnen allen war. Juri watschelte stolz neben Jo. Wie die anderen Kandidaten trug auch Jo das rote T-Shirt von Kids-Quiz-TV und es stand ihm hervorragend.

Miss Cornfield und die Klasse nahmen ihre Plätze auf der Tribüne ein und die fünf Kandidaten bahnten sich den Weg zum Hausmeisterkiosk, der ihnen als Umkleide diente. Max suchte die Reihen nach seinen Eltern ab. Wo steckten die beiden nur? Sie hatten fest versprochen rechtzeitig da zu sein …

Helene winkte ihrer Mutter im Publikum zu. „Denkst du an das Autogramm von Karsten Markoni?“, rief Frau May quer durch die Pausenhalle. „Bussi!“ Frau May war die einzige Person, die im Gebäude eine Sonnenbrille trug. Außer Karsten Markoni natürlich – und Tingo, weil heute ein ungerader Tag war.

Auf der Tribüne hatte sich bereits der Fanklub aus Berlin breitgemacht. Ida suchte nach einem Platz.

Als sie Mr. Morrison in der zweiten Reihe entdeckte, fühlte sie sich gleich ein bisschen besser.
„Gibt's was Neues vom Omnibus?", erkundigte sie sich, als sie sich mit Rabbat neben den Inhaber der magischen Zoohandlung quetschte.
„Der ist noch in der Werkstatt", brummelte Mr. Morrison. „Wird mal wieder teurer als gedacht …" Er seufzte. Und Pinkie auf seinem Schlapphut nickte sorgenvoll.
Die magischen Tiere nutzten die Zeit bis zum Beginn der Show, um Pinkie ein wenig auszufragen.
„Gibt's neue Tiere in der magischen Zoohandlung?", erkundigte sich Rick. „Elch? Kröte? Zebra?"
„Verrat ich nicht", kicherte die Elster.
„Bist du allein hier?", fragte Rabbat und hielt Ausschau nach Ashanti, der Schwarzen Mamba. Das würde einen Tumult geben, wenn die Riesenschlange hier in der Schule ausbüxte!
„Sag ich nicht", flötete die Elster und zwinkerte Rabbat zu. „Aber du weißt doch: Für seine Lieblingstiere hat der Boss immer Platz."

Im selben Moment sah Henrietta, wie unter dem Ärmel von Mortimer Morrisons Mantel die Beine einer Vogelspinne hervorspitzten.

Es wurde dunkel in der Pausenhalle. Scheinwerfer flammten auf, laute Musik ertönte. Die Tiere zuckten zusammen.
Ein Assistent deutete mit einem Leuchtpfeil auf die riesige Digitaluhr, die in der Mitte der Pausenhalle hing. Er zählte rückwärts: „10 – 9 – 8 – 7 – 6 – 5 – 4 – 3 – 2 – 1 – Zero!"
Die Titelmelodie erklang und Kinderstimmen sangen: *„Top oder Flop, hopp oder top, welche Klasse kriegt den Pott …"*
Der Showmaster joggte auf die Bühne, es sollte so wirken, als hätte er gerade einen rasanten Spurt hingelegt. Dabei waren es gerade mal fünf Meter, die er laufen musste.
Die Zuschauer klatschten höflich. Auf einmal war Ida froh, dass sie nicht mitmachen musste.

„Sehr verehrtes Pupslikum!“ Der Moderator verbeugte sich. Keiner lachte über den Witz. Erst als eine Assistentin ein Schild in die Luft reckte, auf dem „Applaus“ stand, begannen die Leute zu klatschen.
„Das ist doch total künstlich“, murmelte Ida.
„Wir freuen uns sehr, dass wir heute in der Winterfeldschule sein dürfen …“
„Das heißt Wintersteinschule!“, rief Herr Siegmann empört, der an der Seite stand.
Applaus-Schilder erschienen und wieder klatschten alle.
„Mann, ist der schlecht vorbereitet!“, japste Henrietta.
„Wir begrüßen unsere Kandidaten!“
Es wurde eine Sekunde dunkel, dann erschien ein blauer Lichtkegel. Die Musik wurde dramatisch, wie bei einem Boxkampf. Die fünf Kandidaten aus Berlin trugen blaue T-Shirts und rollten auf Einrädern herein. Es sah ziemlich spektakulär aus.
„Wow!“ Rick ließ die Zähne blitzen. „Hoffentlich kann unser Team da mithalten. Wären wir zwei doch nur angetreten …“, raunte er Silas zu.

Die Kinder aus Berlin stiegen lässig von ihren Einrädern.
„Und jetzt die Kinder der Winterbein-, äh, Wintersteinschule!“ Wieder ertönte Musik. Doch diesmal klang es wie ein Kindergartensong: *„Dackel Waldi, komm doch baldi aus dem Waldi …“*
Helene ließ sich nicht beirren. Mit selbstbewussten Schritten betrat sie die Bühne. Das Glitzeroberteil stand ihr gut, auch wenn sie inzwischen ein rotes T-Shirt darüber trug. An ihrer Seite stolzierte mit hoch erhobenem Kopf ein schwarzer Kater. Karajan hatte beschlossen sich heute nicht an die Versteinerungsregel zu halten. Er wollte seine Gefährtin nach Kräften unterstützen und das ging am besten, wenn er lebendig war. Helenes Mutter klatschte lauter als alle anderen.
Etwas widerwillig trat auch Franka auf die Bühne. Auf ihrer Schulter saß eine Ratte. Im Gegenlicht erkannte sie ihre Eltern im Publikum. Sogar Kaja war dabei! Nun freute sie sich doch. Mann, waren ihre Eltern am Samstag sauer auf sie gewesen!

Ihr Vater war sofort in den Keller gerannt und hatte nach irgendeiner Farbe gesucht, um das Schwarz zu überstreichen, hatte aber nichts gefunden. Kaja hatte blöde gegrinst und sie kein bisschen verteidigt. Nur Cooper hatte zu ihr gehalten. „Ich find's cool, Baby", versicherte er wieder und wieder, während Frankas Mutter verzweifelt ihre Psychologin angerufen hatte.
Aber nun drückten ihr alle drei die Daumen. Über Frankas Gesicht huschte ein kleines Lächeln.
Jetzt fehlten noch die drei Jungs: Max erntete Applaus, als er im Anzug den Teppich betrat. Das rote T-Shirt hatte er einfach unter das Jackett gezogen.
Yannik trug Tingo huckepack, Jo und Juri gingen Hand in Hand.
„Haha, jetzt kommen unsere Kandidaten mit den Kuscheltieren!", fuhr der Moderator fort. „Bei euren Tieren könnt ihr euch ausweinen, wenn eine Aufgabe nicht klappt. Und euer Papa trägt wohl einen Anzug, ja? Hahaha!" Er deutete auf den Professor, der drei Schritte entfernt stand und knallrot wurde.

Ida ballte die Fäuste. Mann, war der Typ fies!
„Na, habt ihr alle frische Windeln an oder wollt ihr noch mal wechseln?“ Der Moderator grinste. „Wir warten gern.“
Niemand rührte sich. Die Kinder in den blauen T-Shirts stupsten sich gegenseitig an und kicherten.
„Na dann …“ Der Moderator machte eine Handbewegung. Ein Trommelwirbel ertönte.
Das Publikum wartete gespannt. Schilder, Applaus!
Und Karsten Markoni grinste in die Kamera: „Die Show beginnt!“
Als der Applaus verebbt war, zwinkerte der Moderator der Kamera zu. „Wir starten mit der Aufgabe für die Supersportler. Zeigt her eure Füße, zeigt her eure Badehosen! Hahaha!“ Karsten Markoni streckte seine Füße in die Höhe, um seine Markenschuhe in die Kamera zu halten.
„He! Werbung ist an meiner Schule verboten!“, knurrte Herr Siegmann. „Das war nicht abgesprochen!“ Der Direktor wurde wütend. Das würde noch ein Nachspiel haben!

Jo, der Supersportler, musste sich umziehen.
Idas Herz klopfte. Hoffentlich klappte alles.
„Wir beginnen mit dem fantastikulären Wasserrutschen-Race!"
Es wurde für einen Moment dunkel, und als das Licht mit dramatischem Trommelwirbel wieder anging, stand der Moderator in Badehose da. Die Frauen im Publikum johlten begeistert.
Jo joggte in Badehose aus dem Hausmeisterkiosk. Die Mädchen im Publikum tuschelten.
„Und natürlich tragen wir Badekappen! Hihi!"
Eine Assistentin huschte auf die Bühne und hielt zwei Bademützen in der Hand.
Der Junge aus Berlin schnappte sich rasch die schwarze Kappe mit goldenen Sternen.
Übrig war eine rosarote Kappe. Solche Bademützen trugen ältere Damen im Hallenbad. Jo machte das Beste draus. Er zupfte seine Haare zurecht und lachte sein unwiderstehliches Lachen.
„Applaus für Turbo-Jo!", rief Silas. Ida und die anderen klatschten wie verrückt.

„Wir haben in die Röhren einen Geschwindigkeitsmesser eingebaut." Der Moderator deutete auf die Digitaluhr an der Decke. „Und eine Kamera. Nicht dass einer unserer Kandidaten einen Düsenantrieb zündet, hohoho!"
Jo packte Juri unter den Arm und rannte die Treppe hoch. Ida sah, wie sie tuschelten.

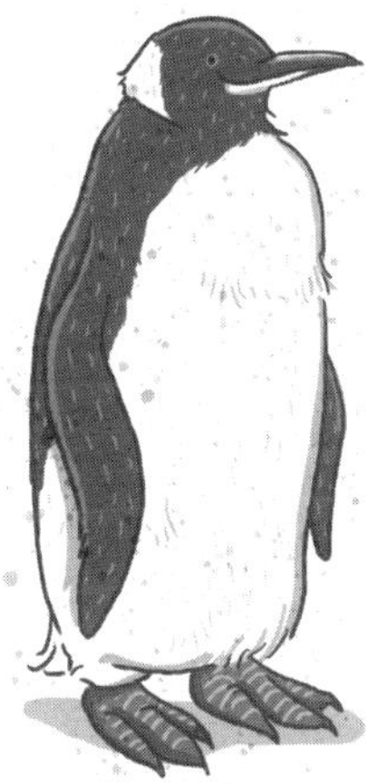

„Nimm dein Kuscheltier ruhig mit in die Röhre!", rief der Moderator ihm höhnisch nach.
Jo achtete gar nicht auf ihn. Er stand barfuß oben an der Treppe und prägte sich die Tipps ein, die ihm Juri gab. Der Pinguin hatte viel Übung vom Eisschollenrutschen in der Antarktis.
„Ellenbogen anwinkeln, Fersen fest in den Boden drücken. Ist gebongt. Und weißt du, was ich noch für einen Spezialtipp kenne?" Er flüsterte Juri etwas ins Ohr.
Der Pinguin kicherte. „Du wirst gewinnen, Jo!"

Doch zunächst war der Junge aus Berlin an der Reihe. Es war tatsächlich der Muskelprotz, den die Kinder vor dem Bus gesehen hatten.
„Zeig's ihm, Jo", knurrte Silas.
Durch einen Lautsprecher kam das Kommando: „Auf die Plätze, fertig, los!"
Der Junge sprang in die Röhre und sauste davon.
„Schnel-ler! Schnel-ler!", jubelte das Publikum. Mit einem großen Platsch landete der Junge im Becken. Rick, der auf der Tribüne in der ersten Reihe saß, wurde nass gespritzt.
„Noch mal!", juchzte das Krokodil begeistert.
„4,1 Sekunden!", rief der Moderator in Badehose. Sein braun gebrannter Bauch glänzte im Scheinwerferlicht.
„Selbstbräuner", grummelte Helene, die alles mit den anderen Kandidaten vom Hausmeisterkiosk aus beobachtete.
„Pst!", wies Max sie zurecht.
Jo war an der Reihe!
Und wieder schallte es durch den Lautsprecher: „Auf die Plätze, fertig, los!"

Juri und Jo sprangen in die Röhre und los ging's. Juri sauste vorneweg und quietschte vor Vergnügen.
Jo schoss hinterher.
Er war blitzschnell.
Er hatte die perfekte Technik.
Vor allem aber hatte er noch seinen Spezialtrick: Kurz vor dem Absprung hatte er sich die Badehose zwischen die Pobacken geklemmt. Im Freibad machte das jeder: Weniger Stoff bedeutete weniger Reibung.
„Schneller, schneller", feuerte er sich selbst an.
Jo drückte die Fersen in den Boden und sauste mit dem Wasserschwall nach unten. Es spritzte so sehr, dass er die Augen zusammenkneifen musste. Seine Kurvenlage war allererste Sahne!
„3,8 Sekunden", rief der Moderator und Ida trommelte wie verrückt mit ihren Füßen. „Die Wintersteigschule geht in Führung!"
Ida lachte erleichtert auf. Vielleicht wurde die Show ja doch noch ganz lustig.
In dem Moment kam ein Assistent auf die Bühne und flüsterte dem Showmaster etwas ins Ohr.

„Kleine Korrektur!", rief Karsten Markoni. „Wir werfen einen Blick auf die Überwachungskamera!"
Mitten in der Pausenhalle entrollte sich eine Leinwand. Ein kurzer Film wurde eingespielt. Er zeigte Jo, wie er an seiner Badehose zupfte. Seine blanken Pobacken waren zu sehen!
„Der rosarote Kandidat hat sich selbst disqualifiziert!", verkündete der Moderator. „Alle Punkte gehen an die Gäste aus Berlin!"
Eine Hälfte des Publikums jubelte.

15. Kapitel

Drei knifflige Aufgaben

Auf der Leinwand erschien die nächste Aufgabe: „Schönheitswettbewerb". Karsten Markoni verschwand, um sich umzuziehen, und die fünf Kandidaten wurden wieder in den Hausmeisterkiosk geschickt.

Der Fernsehsender schaltete auf Werbung.

In der Pausenhalle baute das Filmteam in Windeseile die Rutsche ab, das Wasserbecken aber blieb.

Über das Becken legten sie ein schmales Brett, mit Leuchtbändern eingefasst. Eine Assistentin kippte grünen Badeschaum ins Becken.
Bei der nächsten Aufgabe ging es darum, sich wie ein Fotomodell zu bewegen und das Publikum zu verzaubern.
„Das wird eine Kleinischkeit für dich“, sagte Karajan zu Helene. Die stimmte ihrem Kater selbstbewusst zu: „Die nächsten Punkte haben wir sicher!“
Das konnte Jo aber nicht trösten. Er hatte es vermasselt. Mit hängenden Schultern und nassen Haaren ließ er Max’ anklagende Blicke über sich ergehen.
„Ich hätte es genauso gemacht“, tröstete ihn Yannik. „Du kannst nichts dafür, diese Regel ist total bescheuert.“
Helene spitzte aus der Tür heraus.
Der Moderator schlitterte gerade mit roten Lackschuhen und schwarzer Lederhose auf die Bühne. Die Sonnenbrille hatte er diesmal in der Garderobe gelassen.

„Im nächsten Wettbewerb", er machte einen großen Schritt nach vorne und breitete die Hände aus, „will ich zwei Königinnen sehen!"
Er zauberte aus einer Kiste zwei Silberkrönchen hervor. Eine bekam Helene, eine ihre Gegenkandidatin aus Berlin. Helenes Mutter zückte das Handy.
„Damit werdet ihr unsere Schlosstreppe hinunterlaufen", er deutete auf eine steile, mit Gold beklebte Holztreppe, „und über den Laufsteg balancieren." Karsten Markoni zeigte auf das schmale Brett über dem Schwimmbecken, an dem nun die Neonbänder aufleuchteten. „Immer lächeln, meine Damen, immer lächeln!"
Er schob die beiden in Richtung Treppe.
Das Mädchen aus Berlin machte sich auf den Weg nach oben. Jemand reichte ihr ein Paar Stöckelschuhe.
Ton ab! Und los!
Unsicher stakste die Kandidatin nach unten.
Vor dem Pool bekam sie neue Schuhe, deren Absätze noch mal drei Zentimeter höher waren. Damit musste sie über den schmalen Steg.

Helene sah, wie das Mädchen zitterte. Ihre Krone verrutschte und saß nun schief auf ihrem Kopf. Das Mädchen starrte auf das Brett und tastete sich Schritt für Schritt voran.
Pah! Das konnte sie besser! Helene freute sich schon auf ihren Einsatz. Das Mädchen kam heil ins Ziel, das Publikum klatschte höflich.
Erleichtert streifte sich ihre Konkurrentin die Schuhe von den Füßen.
Jetzt war Helene dran. Auch sie schlüpfte in die Hackenschuhe.
Ton ab!
Mit sicheren Schritten schritt Helene die Treppe hinunter. Sie sah toll aus! Ihr Rock wippte unter dem roten T-Shirt und die Prinzessinnenkrone saß fest auf ihrem Kopf. Dass sie von einem schwarzen Kater begleitet wurde, kam bei den Zuschauern besonders gut an.
Helene winkte strahlend ins Publikum. Helenes Mutter wusste gar nicht, wohin mit ihren Händen: klatschen oder filmen?

Beim Wasserbecken bekam auch Helene neue, höhere Schuhe. Sie schlüpfte hinein. Und erschrak. Die Schuhe waren viel zu groß!
„He, was soll d…“ Es war niemand mehr in ihrer Nähe. Die Assistentin war weg.
„Und los geht's, hopp, hopp!“, dröhnte der Moderator. Also ging Helene los. Es war zum Verzweifeln! Sie konnte nur schlurfen und krallte sich mit ihren Zehen fest, um die Schuhe nicht zu verlieren. Immerhin, die Krone blieb oben. Karajan versuchte die Blicke auf sich zu lenken, indem er kleine Hüpfer einbaute, während er über das Brett lief. Helene lächelte tapfer, auch wenn ihr nach Heulen zu Mute war.
„Arme Helene“, flüsterte Ida. Sie hatte auf einmal das Gefühl, dass es bei dieser Sendung nicht mit rechten Dingen zuging. Irgendetwas stimmte nicht. Hatten die Gegner aus Berlin etwa die Schuhe vertauscht?
Plötzlich ertönte ein neues Lied, so laut und mit so starkem Bass, dass das dünne Brett unter Helenes Füßen wackelte. Helene erschrak. Sie verlor das Gleichgewicht – und landete im Pool!

Als sie auftauchte, hatte sie einen grünen Schaumbart. Die Prinzessinnenkrone schwamm im Wasser.
„Applaus für das Sumpfmonster aus der Winterschule!“, rief Karsten Markoni. Das Publikum klatschte verunsichert.

Sämtliche Punkte gingen an Berlin.
Triefend und zitternd verschwand Helene im Hausmeisterkiosk. Karajan hüpfte empört auf und ab.
„Unverschämtheit! Wir wurden reingelegt!“, zeterte er.

Es half nichts. Als Nächstes musste Franka ran, zur großen „Super-Duper-Knobel-Nummer“. Ohne eine Spur von Nervosität stapfte sie mit Cooper auf der Schulter auf die Bühne. Ihre Gegenkandidatin stand schon bereit.
Diesmal ging es auch um Schnelligkeit. Wer die Lösung wusste, sollte auf einen roten Knopf drücken und die Antwort sagen.
„13 × 12?“, feuerte der Moderator los, noch bevor Franka am Pult war.
Franka hechtete zum Knopf und rief: „156“.
Das stimmte, die Punkte gingen an die Wintersteinschule.

Die nächste Frage war eine Fangfrage: „20 Sänger brauchen für ein Lied zwei Minuten. Wie lange brauchen 40 Sänger?“ Das Mädchen aus Berlin fiel darauf herein. Es drückte auf den Knopf und rief: „Vier Minuten!“ Das Publikum lachte.

Die Wurzel aus 1089? „33!“, rief Franka.

Aber sie hatte vergessen den Knopf zu drücken! Es gab keinen Punkt.

Der Moderator machte schnell weiter: „Wie viele Nullen hat eine Million?“

„Sechs“, antwortete Franka, und weil Cooper sie diesmal rechtzeitig ins Ohr zwickte und sie ganz schnell am Knopf war, gingen die Punkte an die Wintersteinschule.

Karsten Markoni guckte säuerlich. Ida beobachtete ihn: Gönnte er der Wintersteinschule nicht, dass sie aufholte?

„Und jetzt die Masterfrage für Berlin!“, rief Karsten Markoni. „Sie zählt doppelt.“ Er nickte dem Mädchen im blauen T-Shirt aufmunternd zu.

Die Aufgabe war ganz schön knifflig. Sie lautete: „Im

Zoo leben Flamingos und Zebras im selben Gehege. Zusammen haben sie 12 Köpfe und 40 Beine. Wie viele Flamingos und Zebras sind es?“

Das Mädchen rechnete ewig vor sich hin. Es nahm seine Finger zur Hilfe, kratzte sich am Kopf, auf der Stirn bildeten sich Schweißtropfen. Sie sagte erst: „Sechs Flamingos und sechs Zebras“, das war falsch. Doch zwei Sekunden später verbesserte sie sich und sagte: „Acht Zebras und vier Flamingos.“

„Richtig“, lobte der Moderator und gab ihr die volle Punktzahl.

„Das ist unfair!“, kreischte Cooper.

„Locker bleiben“, antwortete Franka.

Sie war dran mit der Masterfrage! Der Showmaster ließ sich von hinten einen großen Pappkarton reichen. Darauf stand:

8 + 8 = 91

Er schaute Franka an. „Ist diese Antwort richtig oder falsch?“

„Falsch, falsch!“, japste Cooper.
Aber Franka antwortete seelenruhig: „Wenn Sie den Karton umdrehen, ist sie richtig!“
Sie nahm dem Showmaster den Karton aus der Hand und streckte ihn nach oben. Jetzt stand da:

16 = 8 + 8

„Cool, Baby!“, staunte Cooper.
Sogar der Fanklub aus Berlin klatschte diesmal mit und Frankas Schwester Kaja trommelte mit den Füßen. Franka hatte die „Super-Duper-Knobel-Nummer“ gewonnen!
Wenn Max nach der Werbepause die Wissensaufgabe schaffte, gab es Gleichstand. Ida biss sich vor Aufregung auf die Lippe. War das spannend!

Im Hausmeisterkiosk herrschte übermütige Stimmung.
„Franka, das war großartig!“, rief Helene neidlos.
„Max kann den Ausgleich schaffen“, nickte Jo.

Der Professor polierte ein letztes Mal seine Brille. „Keine Sorge, Leute!“ Er ging auf die Bühne.
Sein Gegenkandidat brauchte anscheinend etwas länger, um sich fertig zu machen. Also gut. Kein Problem. Er konnte warten.
Er versuchte seine Eltern in der Menschenmenge zu entdecken. Keine Chance. Die Scheinwerfer blendeten und strahlten warm in sein Gesicht. Puh, war das eine Hitze hier! Hätte er doch Hemd und Pullunder unter dem roten T-Shirt ausgezogen …
Er fühlte sich ganz komisch. Ziffern und Buchstaben schwirrten wild durcheinander durch seinen Kopf. Ägyptische Schriftzeichen mischten sich mit mathematischen Formeln. Nichts ergab einen Sinn. „Reiß dich zusammen“, ermahnte er sich und atmete tief ein und aus. In der Pausenhalle war es stickig, nur ein kleines Fenster stand offen. Er sah sich Hilfe suchend um. „Könnte ich vielleicht ein Glas Wasser haben?“ Niemand kümmerte sich um ihn.
Endlich kam der Junge aus Berlin. Der Moderator zückte seine bunten Karteikarten und legte los.

„Wie heißt der größte Planet unseres Sonnensystems?"
Max drückte auf den roten Knopf. „Jupiter!"
Das war richtig.
„Wer wurde im Jahr 2006 Fußballweltmeister?"
„Italien", brüllte der Junge aus Berlin.
„Wie viele Diamanten zieren die Krone von Königin Victoria in England?"
Pinkie, die noch immer auf Mr. Morrisons Schlapphut saß, klapperte aufgeregt mit dem Schnabel: „Die Krone kenn ich! Es sind 1300 Glitzersteine! Jetzt sag schon, Max! Schnell!"
Aber Max konnte die Elster nicht verstehen.
In seinem Kopf drehte sich alles. „Die Queen heißt doch Elizabeth", murmelte er. „Ich versteh die Frage nicht!" Er schwitzte.
Miss Cornfield betrachtete ihn sorgenvoll. Was war mit ihrem Klassenprimus los?
Weil auch der Gegenkandidat die Antwort nicht wusste, bekam keiner einen Punkt.
Die nächste Frage verwirrte Max noch mehr: „Wo wurde der Entdecker Amerikas geboren?"

Miss Cornfield verstand die Welt nicht mehr. Warum zögerte Max? Christoph Kolumbus wurde in Genua geboren. Sie hatten gerade ein Diktat darüber geschrieben! Sie wusste, dass Max die Antwort wusste. Max wurde weiß. Dann wurde er rot. Miss Cornfield beugte sich zu Mr. Morrison und tuschelte mit ihm.
Es gab einen lauten Knall. Max fiel zu Boden und blieb reglos liegen.
Das Publikum wurde unruhig.
Der Moderator rief: „Kleine Musikeinlage!"
Eine Sekunde später schallte es durch die Halle:
„Dackel Waldi, komm doch baldi aus dem Waldi …"
Die Lehrerin stürzte nach vorn.
Max lag auf dem roten Teppich und fühlte sich hilflos wie noch nie zuvor in seinem Leben. Sein Kopf war auf einmal wie leer gepustet! Er wollte doch unbedingt gewinnen! Was würden die anderen sagen, wenn er die Superhirn-Nummer nicht schaffte?
Miss Cornfield beugte sich über ihren Schüler. Und wunderte sich: Max blinzelte! Er täuschte die Ohnmacht nur vor! Hatte er Angst, zu versagen?

In dem Moment machte Max die Augen auf und sah seine Lehrerin an. Auf einmal wusste er, was zu tun war: „Ida soll mich vertreten“, flüsterte er. „Sie kann das viel besser als ich.“
Erleichtert wollte er sich aufrichten – da sah er etwas Merkwürdiges. Auf der Leinwand, wo eben noch „Wissensfragen für Superhirne“ gestanden hatte, war jetzt zu lesen:

AN MAX KRAMER!
DIE MAGISCHE ZOOHANDLUNG TEILT MIT: DU BIST DER NÄCHSTE, DER EIN MAGISCHES TIER BEKOMMEN WIRD. HALTE DICH BEREIT.
VIELE GRÜSSE!
DIE MAGISCHE ZOOHANDLUNG

Und dann fiel er tatsächlich in Ohnmacht.

16. Kapitel

Muriel

Miss Cornfield blickte zum Fenster. Viel Zeit war nicht. Die Fernsehleute warteten schon ungeduldig, der Aufnahmeleiter kommandierte hektisch herum. Also gut, dann sollte jetzt eben Ida einspringen. Sie winkte das Mädchen nach vorn. Ida schüttelte erst den Kopf – doch dann gab ihr Rabbat einen sanften Stups und gemeinsam machten sie sich auf den Weg zur Bühne.

Der Moderator runzelte die Stirn. „Miss Neunmalklug-ich-weiß-die-richtige-Antwort-nicht? Was willst du denn hier?“ Aber weil die Show irgendwie weitergehen musste, ließ er sich von hinten ein rotes T-Shirt geben und warf es Ida zu.

Ida atmete tief durch. „Du schaffst das“, raunte Rabbat. Um Max kümmerten sich währenddessen die Schulsanitäter. Sie trugen ihn auf einer Liege zur Seite, wo er blinzelnd zu sich kam.

Henrietta krabbelte zu Mr. Morrison und stupste ihn an.

Der Inhaber der magischen Zoohandlung nahm die Schildkröte verwundert hoch.
Mr. Morrison lächelte, als Henrietta ihm von ihrer Idee erzählte. Und wackelte mit dem Arm.
Schon sauste eine Vogelspinne in Richtung Karsten Markoni. Genau vor den roten Lackschuhen des Käse-Makkaronis blieb sie stehen und versteinerte.
Dann passierten mehrere Dinge gleichzeitig:
Karsten Markoni begann zu kreischen. Seine Karteikarten flogen zu Boden.
Durch das offen stehende Fenster flog eine Eule herein und landete auf Max' Bauch.

Ida bückte sich und sammelte die Karteikarten ein, die der Moderator verloren hatte. Ihr Blick fiel auf eine der Karten und ihr Herz begann zu rasen. Die Karten waren gekennzeichnet in „Gewinner-Fragen“ und „Verlierer-Fragen“! Der Sieger der Show war von Anfang an vorgegeben!

Ida konnte es nicht glauben. Die ganze Show war von vorn bis hinten Betrug!

Während Markoni wimmernd vor Angst am Boden saß und den Blick nicht von der Vogelspinne lösen konnte, zeigte Ida die Karten Miss Cornfield.

„Da! Wir wurden reingelegt!“ Sie warf dem Moderator einen zornigen Blick zu. Der kauerte immer noch schweißgebadet am Boden. Der Selbstbräuner löste sich auf und rann in langen Schlieren über sein Gesicht. Karsten Markoni sah gar nicht mehr wie ein Fernsehstar aus.

Die Fernsehleute hatten das auch schon festgestellt und filmten lieber das Publikum.

Der Mann aus der Regie ließ einen Werbefilm mit der Titelmusik spielen:

„Top oder Flop, hopp oder top,
welche Klasse kriegt den Pott?
Top oder Flop, Start oder Stopp,
welche Klasse hat mehr Bock …“

Die Zuschauer hatten keine Ahnung, was gerade auf der Bühne vor sich ging. Ida und Miss Cornfield aber, die hatten alles durchschaut.
Helene hatte absichtlich zu große Schuhe bekommen! Und zwar nicht von den Gegenkandidaten, sondern von einer Assistentin von Kids-Quiz-TV!
Franka hatte absichtlich besonders schwere Fragen bekommen, „unlösbar“ stand als Kategorie auf der Karte. Ha, und trotzdem hatte sie die „Super-Duper-Knobel-Nummer“ gemeistert!
Die boshaften Bemerkungen, die fiesen Fragen – alles stand genau auf den Karteikarten. Und nun sollte auch bei den Wissensfragen die Klasse aus Berlin gewinnen!
Miss Cornfield und Ida wechselten einen Blick: „Ida, sag dem anderen Team, was hier gespielt wird. Und dann tretet ihr gegeneinander an wie geplant.“

Sie nickte dem Mädchen aufmunternd zu. „Sportlich und fair!"
Rabbat stupste seine Gefährtin an: „Zeig's ihnen, Rotschopf!"
Miss Cornfield sammelte seelenruhig die Vogelspinne ein. „Ist doch nur ein Plüschtier", sagte sie zum Moderator und hielt ihm das Tier unter die Nase. „Alles nur Show."
Er zuckte panisch zurück.
Miss Cornfield warf einen langen Blick auf die Karteikarten, dann reichte sie sie weiter an Karsten Markoni. Mehr war nicht nötig. Der Moderator wusste, dass er entlarvt war.
Und Max? Der schaute währenddessen in zwei freundliche Eulenaugen. Er fühlte sich immer noch ein wenig schwummerig und war sich nicht sicher, ob er das alles vielleicht nur träumte.
„Ich heiße Muriel und werde dir helfen", versprach die Eule. „Steh auf."
Folgsam rappelte sich Max hoch. „Ich hab's versemmelt", stammelte er.

Es war das erste Mal in seinem Leben, dass er diesen Satz sagte. Er dachte daran, wie überheblich er sich in den letzten Tagen Ida und den anderen gegenüber verhalten hatte, und schämte sich. „Die werden mich in der Luft zerreißen. Und weißt du was? Es geschieht mir ganz recht." Er knirschte mit den Zähnen.
„Jetzt komm schon!" Die Eule hüpfte auf seinen Schoß. „Noch ist nichts verloren! Streng deine kleinen grauen Zellen an! Für die Wintersteinschule! Los!"
Sie lächelte ihrem neuen Gefährten aufmunternd zu.
Max' Finger kribbelten. Das Federknäuel hockte dicht bei ihm. Erst jetzt wurde ihm klar, was gerade passiert war: Er hatte ein magisches Tier bekommen! Eine kluge Eule!
„Du hast Recht!", rief er und seine Augen strahlten. „Du hast so was von Recht!"
Er sprang auf die Beine und stellte sich neben Karsten Markoni. „Bin wieder da, Herr Makkaroni!"
Ida prustete los und auch der Berliner Kandidat grinste: „Ihr seid jetzt ein Zweierteam, oder was? Also gut, euch schaff ich mit links!"

Karsten Markoni sagte gar nichts. Als die Scheinwerfer ihn anstrahlten, ordnete er notdürftig seine Frisur.
In diesem Moment sah Max, wie die Tür aufging.
Seine Eltern stürzten herein. Sie bahnten sich einen Weg nach vorn und winkten ihrem Sohn aufgeregt zu.
Max lächelte glücklich zurück.
Das Publikum war froh, dass es weiterging, und der Moderator leierte seine Fragen herunter. Von seiner Selbstsicherheit war nicht viel übrig geblieben.
„Welche Form haben Eiskristalle?"
„Sechseckig." Idas Antwort kam schnell wie der Blitz.
„Wie heißt der griechische Gott des Meeres?"
„Poseidon", rief Max. Muriel pikste ihm vor Freude ins Ohr. Die Eltern von Max streckten begeistert ihre Daumen in die Luft.
So ging es Frage um Frage.
Mal wusste Ida oder Max die Antwort, mal kannte sich der Kandidat aus Berlin besser aus. Alle freuten sich, dass Max wieder in Bestform war.
„Wie heißt der weiße Fleck, den ein Reh am Po hat?"
„Spiegel!", rief Max und Muriel nickte eifrig.

„Welches Säugetier kann fliegen?"
„Icherich!", rief aufgeregt ein kleines Wesen, das mit ihrem Gefährten von der dritten Reihe aus das Geschehen verfolgte.
Max konnte Eugenia zwar nicht verstehen, wusste aber trotzdem die richtige Antwort. Er trug schließlich nicht umsonst den Namen Professor!
„Die Fledermaus", freute er sich.
Die Kinder ballerten eine richtige Antwort nach der anderen raus. Auch das Publikum machte mit und rief Antworten hinein. Es war ein fröhliches Durcheinander. Allen war es vollkommen egal, wer gewinnen würde.
Die Fernsehleute verstanden nicht, was mit ihrem Starmoderator los war. Sollten sie jetzt Applaus-Schilder hochhalten oder welche, auf denen „Buh!" stand?
Karsten Markoni grinste zwischendurch immer wieder in die Kamera, ohne etwas zu sagen, und machte dann einfach weiter. Er wollte nur irgendwie die Show zu Ende bringen.

Miss Cornfield achtete darauf, dass sie immer so dastand, dass der Moderator sie sehen konnte. Sie und Agent Y. Die Vogelspinne saß stolz auf dem Handrücken der Lehrerin und freute sich sehr, dass sie ins Fernsehen kam!

17. Kapitel

Der Bananentrick

Ida wusste, worin die letzte Aufgabe bestand. Sie hatte sich die Karteikarte durchgelesen. Es war eine Kletteraufgabe, Yannik sollte antreten.

Die Aufgabe war nicht zu schaffen, das sah Ida sofort. Auf der Karte stand: „Anweisung an die Kameras: Bitte die Matten filmen! Die Kinder werden reihenweise hinunterpurzeln. Die Zuschauer sollen was zu lachen haben.“

Die Mitarbeiter von Kids-Quiz-TV legten die Bühne mit dicken blauen Matten aus. Dann schleppten sie drei Meter hohe Gummipalmen heran, an denen Plastikbananen hingen. Sie waren nur mit Klettverschluss angeklebt. Die Aufgabe bestand darin, die Bananen zu pflücken und in einen Korb werfen.
Ida sah sofort, dass die Palmen zu hoch waren und die Bananen viel zu weit voneinander entfernt hingen.
Rabbat zuckte mit der Schnauze. „Ich hab eine Idee!" Er flüsterte Ida etwas ins Ohr.
Ida nickte erst, dann schüttelte sie den Kopf. „Das geht nicht, das ist gegen die Regeln."
Rabbat sah das anders: „Was der Moderator kann, können wir schon lange. Nun komm, Rotschopf!"
Aber Ida blieb hart.

„Jetzt kommt eine Übung für Kletterprofis", kündigte der Moderator nach der nächsten Werbepause an. Er wirkte wieder selbstsicher wie eh und je und grinste breit: „Eine echte Herausforderung!"

Trommelwirbel erklang. Die Lichter gingen aus.
Alle hielten den Atem an.
Die Scheinwerfer gingen wieder an.
Der Junge aus Berlin begann. Es war ein zierlicher, aber sehr gelenkiger Junge. Er erklomm eine Palme, versuchte eine Banane zu erwischen, streckte sich – und plumpste auf die Matte.
„Buh!“-Schilder wurden in die Luft gestreckt, die aber niemand beachtete.
Stattdessen rief jemand aus dem Publikum: „Versuch’s gleich noch mal!“
Diesmal kam der Junge ein gutes Stück weiter. Er japste und schnaufte. Die Banane erwischte er wieder nicht. Er fiel.
„Noch mal, noch mal!“, feuerte das Publikum ihn an.
Ida und Rabbat beobachteten, wie der Moderator dem Jungen aus Berlin etwas zuflüsterte.
„Was soll das?“, fragte Ida.
Rabbat spitzte die Ohren und berichtete, was Karsten Markoni sagte: „Diese verrückte Lehrerin bringt mich ganz durcheinander. Siehst du die Vogelspinne auf

ihrer Hand? Diese ganze Klasse mit ihren Kuscheltieren ist völlig durchgeknallt. Die reden nur Unsinn! Die schummeln! Diese Kinder dürfen auf keinen Fall gewinnen. Wenn du mitmachst, erhöhe ich das Preisgeld für deine Klasse."

Ida schnappte nach Luft. „Von wegen, *die* schummeln doch!", rief sie. „Und tun sich jetzt sogar noch zusammen! Voll fies!"

Rabbat sah seine Freundin an. „Findest du meinen Plan immer noch so schlecht?"

Sie beobachteten, wie der Moderator unauffällig eine Banane aus seiner Sakkotasche zog. Dann gingen die Lichter aus. Karsten Markoni wurde von der Dunkelheit verschluckt.

„Und jetzt", verkündete er mit grollender Stimme, „der letzte und finale Versuch unseres erfolgreichen Teams aus Berlin!" Kleine Lichter blitzten um den Moderator auf.

Ida behielt die Palmen im Auge. Und konnte in der Finsternis erkennen, dass der Junge auf eine Palme kletterte und die Banane mit Klettverschluss befestigte.

Ganz nah, ganz leicht zu erreichen. Dann sprang er wieder nach unten.

Ida schickte Rabbat zum Hausmeisterkiosk. „Mach schnell!“

Der Fuchs sauste davon.

Trommelwirbel!

Die Lichter gingen wieder an.

Der Junge begann zu klettern, erwischte die Banane und warf sie in den Korb. Er traf und bekam alle Punkte.

Zufrieden klatschte Karsten Markoni in die Hände. „Großartig, Applaus, Applaus! Und nun der Kandidat aus der Winterleinschule!“

Ida biss sich nervös auf die Unterlippe. Ob Rabbats Plan aufging?

Der Applaus verebbte.

Und wieder wurde es dunkel.

Trommelwirbel.

Spot an!

Eine kleine Gestalt hüpfte aus dem Hausmeisterkiosk. Sie trug ein rotes T-Shirt und eine Sonnenbrille.

In Windeseile erklomm der Kandidat die erste Palme, so schnell, dass man ihn kaum sah. Er schwang sich lässig von einer Gummipalme zur nächsten, pflückte eine Frucht nach der anderen und warf sie zielsicher in den Korb. Das Publikum staunte und applaudierte. Immer mehr Bananen landeten im Korb. Der Moderator glotzte.

Die letzte Banane aber, die wollte der Kletterkünstler behalten. Er versuchte die Schale abzumachen. Es ging nicht. Sie war aus Plastik. Enttäuscht schleuderte der Kandidat die Plastikbanane durch die Luft. Sie landete genau am Kopf des Moderators. Der taumelte kurz und fiel auf eine blaue Matratze. Die Kameras nahmen alles auf, genau so, wie es ihre Anweisung war.

„Toll gemacht, Tingo!“, riefen Franka, Helene, Max, Jo und Yannik, als der Kletterkünstler wieder im Hausmeisterkiosk ankam, und klopften ihm begeistert auf die Schulter.

Tingo lugte zur Tür hinaus und zwinkerte Rabbat zu.

18. Kapitel

Das große Finale

Karsten Markoni schaute auf die Uhr. Die Sendung dauerte noch zehn Minuten. Das große Finale wartete. Das ganze Filmteam sehnte das Ende der Show herbei. Diesmal lief überhaupt nichts nach Plan.
Die Kinder trugen nun Badesachen, außerdem die T-Shirts in der Farbe ihrer Mannschaft.
Von der Decke baumelten jetzt zwei Seile. Aus dem Wasserbecken war ein Schlammbecken geworden.

Die Kinder von der Watzkeschule und die Kinder von der Wintersteinschule kamen nach vorn.
Peperoni quietschte vergnügt, als er die braune, nach Lehm duftende Masse sah. Am liebsten hätte er sich sofort darin gewälzt. Schoki konnte ihn nur mit Mühe zurückhalten.
Auch Cooper war voller Vorfreude. „Cool, Baby!“, japste er und machte sich zum Kopfsprung von Frankas Schulter bereit.
Franka war so gut gelaunt wie schon lange nicht mehr. Seit sie Cooper hatte, lief alles viel besser! Sie winkte ihrer Familie zu und fing eine Kusshand ihrer Schwester auf.
Der Moderator senkte seine Stimme und sagte die letzte Nummer an: „Stellt euch vor, ihr seid im Dschungel. Es geht um euer Überleben. Ihr müsst euch mit dem Seil über den schlammigen Abgrund schwingen! Im Wasser schwimmen Krokodile …“
Schwups, schon schwamm tatsächlich ein Gummikrokodil im Schlammbecken. Das war natürlich Rick.

Der Moderator rieb sich die Augen, das Publikum lachte. Ein Kameramann richtete die Kamera auf das Krokodil. Jetzt riss es sogar sein Maul auf!
„… und giftige Wasserschlangen“, fuhr der Moderator fort.
Ida hielt die Luft an. Würde gleich Ashanti auftauchen? Sie wunderte sich heute über gar nichts mehr.
Aber anscheinend hatte Mr. Morrison die Giftschlange in der magischen Zoohandlung zurückgelassen.
Stattdessen paddelte auf einmal eine Schildkröte neben dem Krokodil. Die Kameras surrten.
„Schwingt die Hufe! Jeder, der das Ziel erreicht, bekommt einen Punkt.“ Der Moderator trat zur Seite. Zirkusmusik erklang.
Zunächst wechselten sich die Klassen ab.
Jo machte den Anfang. Anlauf, schwups, schon war er drüben.
„Ein Punkt für die Winterkleidschule“, rief der Moderator. Herr Siegmann knurrte.
Ein Kind nach dem anderen versuchte ans andere Ufer zu kommen.

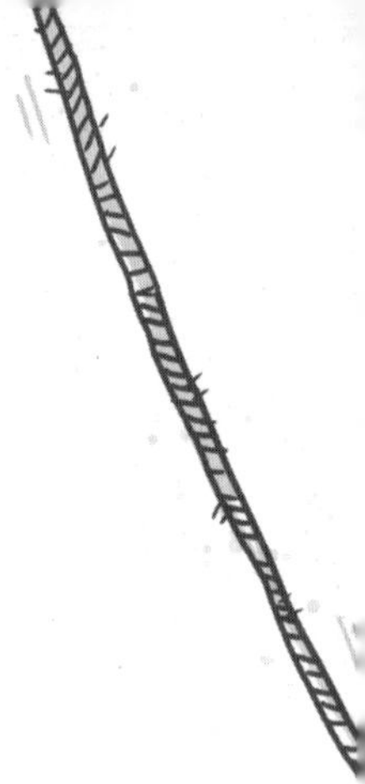

Ein Mädchen aus Berlin landete im Becken und lachte.
Ein Typ mit Sonnenbrille schnappte sich das Seil und holte einen Punkt. Yannik war der Nächste. Auch er war in null Komma nichts drüben. Das Berliner Team holte drei Punkte nacheinander. Schoki ließ sich absichtlich fallen, dicht gefolgt von Eddie und Benni.
„He, ihr Dreckmonster!“, quietschte Eugenia, die über dem Becken kreiste. „Wollt ihr nicht lieber ein paar Punkteriche holen?“
„Das macht Tingo für uns!“, antwortete Eddie fröhlich und formte mit den Händen einen Lehmknödel.
Und irgendwann hielt sich niemand mehr an die Reihenfolge. Es ging wild durcheinander. Eine übermütige Schlammschlacht begann.

Die Leute von Kids-Quiz-TV kamen mit dem Zählen längst nicht mehr mit.
Finja und Sydney holten gleich drei Punkte für ihre Schule, Anna-Lena und Caspar immerhin einen. Cooper paddelte längst zusammen mit Rick und Henrietta im Schlamm. „Komm rein, Franka!“, rief er und bewarf seine Freundin mit einem Matschbällchen.

Aber Franka holte lieber ein paar Punkte für ihre Schule. Ihre Eltern und Kaja applaudierten wie verrückt.

Helene und Karajan weigerten sich mitzumachen. Auf keinen Fall wollten sie sich schmutzig machen.
Der Moderator hatte vollkommen den Überblick verloren.
Aber zum Glück gab es Ida und die hatte mitgezählt: Es stand 75 zu 70 für die Wintersteinschule! Ein Mann von der Regie, der sich das ganze Spektakel noch mal in Zeitlupe ansah, bestätigte das Ergebnis.
Miss Cornfields Klasse hatte gewonnen! Das Preisgeld und der Pokal gingen an die Wintersteinschule!
Eine feierliche Musik erklang. Noch drei Minuten, dann war die Show zu Ende.
Vor dem Schlammbecken wurde in Windeseile ein Podest aufgebaut. Karsten Markoni machte sich zur Siegerehrung bereit. Auf dem Podest standen, Arm in Arm: Max, Jo und Yannik, Helene und Franka. Sie strahlten von einem Ohr bis zum anderen.
Begleitet wurden die Kinder von einer Eule, einem Pinguin, einem Schimpansen, einem Kater und einer Ratte. Max wollte unbedingt, dass auch Ida mit aufs Siegertreppchen kam, aber sie winkte lachend ab.

Ein Zeitungsreporter sprang herbei.
Der Moderator trug inzwischen einen hellen Leinenanzug und bemühte sich um gute Laune. „Eine super-duper Show!“, rief er. „Und ein tolles Publikum! Danke an die Winterschweinschule!“
Herr Siegmann hatte genug.
Er setzte sich in Bewegung. Bis zum Schlammbecken waren es nur sieben Schritte. Ganz beiläufig gab er dem Moderator einen kleinen Schubs. Karsten Markoni taumelte – und fiel kopfüber ins Schlammbecken. Das letzte Fernsehbild, bevor die Titelmelodie einsetzte, zeigte ein schlammiges Wesen, das mit den Armen ruderte. Und dann war die Sendung aus.

19. Kapitel

Franka wird bunt

Willi Wondraschek hatte geschimpft und gezetert. „Dem Sender schreibe ich eine saftige Rechnung!“, hatte er angekündigt und Herr Siegmann hatte eifrig genickt. Die Fernsehleute hatten nur rasch ihren eigenen Kram gepackt und waren mit den drei Trucks abgedampft. Übrig blieb ein einziges Chaos.
Also halfen die Kinder tapfer mit: aufräumen, schrubben und Stühle schleppen.

Franka und Cooper waren völlig erschöpft, als sie endlich nach Hause kamen. Frankas Familie erwartete sie in der Küche mit Häppchen und Orangensaft.
„Echt super, wie du das gemacht hast, Franky!“, sagte Kaja stolz. „Das Rätsel mit den umgedrehten Zahlen hätte ich nie geknackt!“
„Du hast Nerven wie Stahlseile, meine Süße!“ Ihre Mutter nahm sie in den Arm. „Ich glaube, ich wäre in Ohnmacht gefallen vor Aufregung, wie dieser Junge, wie heißt er noch mal?“
„Max“, murmelte Franka und nahm ein Glas Orangensaft. „Prost!“
Es wurde eine lustige Küchenparty und niemand störte sich daran, dass eine Plüschratte auffallend nah an dem Teller mit den Käsebrötchen hockte.
„Du kannst ja Bella Dracula noch dazuholen“, schlug Kaja vor.
„Und du deinen Lolli“, lachte Franka. Lolli, das war Kajas Teddy aus Kindergartenzeiten.
Genau das machten die zwei Schwestern. Sie setzten die Puppe und den Teddy rechts und links neben Cooper.

Ihre Eltern freuten sich, dass sich ihre beiden Mädchen so gut verstanden.
„Weißt du, eigentlich finde ich dein schwarzes Zimmer ziemlich kultig", sagte Frankas Vater und schenkte sich ein zweites Glas Sekt ein. „Ich wollte als Jugendlicher auch immer ein schwarzes Zimmer haben. Durfte ich aber nicht, und ich braver Bubi hab meinen Eltern natürlich gefolgt."
Kaja und Franka bekamen einen Kicheranfall. Sie stellten sich gerade ihren Papa als braven Bubi vor.

Doch komisch. Als Franka später zurück in ihre Räuberhöhle ging, fand sie ihr Zimmer auf einmal – ziemlich düster.
Cooper ging es genauso. Die Ratte legte den Kopf schief und meinte: „Ein paar Sterne, ein paar Streifen – die Flagge von Großbritannien würde sich doch gut über deinem Bett machen, oder?"
„Hmm", meinte Franka und streifte sich die Stiefel von den Füßen.

Plötzlich begannen ihre Augen zu leuchten. „Graffiti! Wir sprühen Graffiti an die Wand. Gleich morgen machen wir uns an die Arbeit."
„Genial", freute sich Cooper. „Wollen wir Yannik und Tingo fragen, ob sie helfen wollen?"
Franka nickte eifrig. „Und Eddie, der kann toll zeichnen! Mit der süßen Eugenia natürlich!" Auf einmal fand sie ihre Mitschüler überhaupt nicht mehr doof oder kindisch.
Und dann schmiedeten sie weitere Pläne.
Cooper versuchte Franka zu überreden, dass sie zumindest ab und zu etwas Buntes anziehen sollte. „Immer nur Schwarz ist langweilig. Schau dir mal mein Fell an, sind die bunten Flecken nicht hübsch?"
„Wunderhübsch", lachte Franka.
„Willst du nicht auch bunte Haarsträhnen in dein Fell?", fragte Cooper.
„Warum eigentlich nicht ..." Franka überlegte. „Idas Eltern haben doch einen Friseursalon, da frag ich mal ... Ida hat auf jeden Fall immer total schöne Frisuren."

Sie kuschelten sich in Frankas Bett und schliefen bald ein.
Franka träumte von wilden Graffiti-Mustern in ihrem Zimmer.
Cooper träumte von einem Berg Käsebällchen. Eine Hälfte verspeiste er. Die andere Hälfte schleuderte er gegen die Stirn von Starmoderator Karsten Markoni. Natürlich nur im Traum.

Letztes Kapitel

Abrechnung

Es war ein herrlicher Dienstagmorgen, die Sonne brach hinter den Wolken hervor. Miss Cornfields Klassenzimmer war lichtdurchflutet.
Die Lehrerin saß auf ihrem Pult. Um den Hals trug sie Ashanti, die Schlange.
Vergnügt blickte sie in 24 strahlende Gesichter.
Yannik saß auf seinem Stuhl und rutschte nur ein ganz kleines bisschen hin und her. Er hatte seine Hefte

ordentlich vor sich liegen. Der Schimpanse saß neben ihm und spitzte eifrig Yanniks Stifte.
Yannik und Tingo waren zu Fuß zur Schule gehopst. Das wollten sie jeden Tag so machen. Dann konnten sie danach besser stillsitzen.
Franka tuschelte mit Ida wegen eines freien Termins im Friseursalon. Sie trug eine neongelbe Bluse zu schwarzen Jeans und heimste anerkennende Blicke von Jo und Helene ein. Die Bluse hatte sie sich von ihrer Schwester geliehen.
Cooper fragte: „Du, Rabbat, wollen wir in der Pause zusammen die Mülltonnen plündern?"
Und Rabbat antwortete: „Aber nur, wenn ich die Schokokekse bekomme, Kleiner!"
Miss Cornfield freute sich, wie gut wieder alle miteinander auskamen. Die Aufregung der Fernsehshow hatte die Klasse zusammengeschweißt.
Auf Max' Tisch saß nun eine wunderschöne, prächtige Eule. Max strich ihr über das Gefieder, während er mit Yannik flüsterte: „Klar kann ich dir Geo erklären", sagte er leise. „Soll ich heute bei dir vorbeikommen?"

„Erst später“, antwortete Yannik knapp, denn Miss Cornfield räusperte sich. „Eddie und ich helfen Franka, ihr Zimmer bunt zu machen. Mit Spraydosen!“
Max nahm sich vor in der Pause zu fragen, ob er auch mitmachen durfte.

Direktor Siegmann war ebenfalls sehr zufrieden. Er saß in seinem Büro und nahm Gratulationen entgegen. Studienfreunde und Kollegen von anderen Schulen – alle hatten die Sendung im Fernsehen verfolgt und auch die Zeitung hatte groß über *Top oder Flop* berichtet.
Kids-Quiz-TV schickte eine E-Mail und teilte die Einschaltquote mit: 1,2 Millionen Menschen hatten zugesehen. Das war ein neuer Rekord. Außerdem kündigte der Sender an, sein Konzept zu überarbeiten. Für die nächste Staffel wurde ein neuer Quizmaster gesucht. „Wir wünschen uns jemanden, der besser auf die Bedürfnisse von Kindern eingehen kann“, hieß es in der Mail.

Am meisten freute sich Heribert Siegmann über den Anruf von Dolores. Sie lobte die Klasse, die so selbstbewusst die Ehre der Wintersteinschule verteidigt hatte. „Der Sturz des Moderators ins Schlammbecken am Schluss war das Beste. Köstlich!“

Nur eine Sache bereitete ihm doch ein wenig Kummer. Inzwischen war die Rechnung für den Basketballkorb eingetroffen. Die Versicherung hatte sich geweigert den Schaden zu bezahlen. Sie sprach von „mutwilliger Sachbeschädigung“. Ein neues Netz kostete 74,50 Euro.

Der Hausmeister wollte, dass Yanniks Familie die Rechnung übernahm. Aber Herrn Siegmann war das nicht recht. Gestern war der Junge so eifrig von Palme zu Palme gehüpft und hatte den Sieg für die Wintersteinschule geholt. Da war die Kletterei auf dem Basketballkorb doch schon fast eine Art Training gewesen! Und jetzt sollte er ihm eine Rechnung unter die Nase halten?

Die Schüler arbeiteten mucksmäuschenstill vor sich hin, als es klopfte.
„Herein“, rief Miss Cornfield, die einen kurzen Moment lang glaubte, Mr. Morrison käme zu Besuch. Aber es war der Direktor, der den Raum betrat, mit einem Blatt Papier in der Hand. Er hüstelte.
„Yannik, ich muss leider ein unangenehmes Thema anschneiden. Ich habe hier die Rechnung für den kaputten Basketballkorb, 74,50 Euro. Dumme Geschichte …“ Er seufzte. „Könntest du bitte deinen Eltern …“
Da schnippte Max mit den Fingern. „Wir haben doch gestern das Preisgeld gewonnen. Eine ganze Menge. Wie wäre es, wenn wir davon die Rechnung bezahlen?“

Miss Cornfield hob überrascht den Kopf. „Das ist ein wunderbarer Vorschlag, aber natürlich müssen die anderen zustimmen."

Sofort flogen 23 Finger in die Luft. „Einverstanden!"

Yannik, der nicht mit abgestimmt hatte, wusste gar nicht, wie ihm geschah. „Danke", stammelte er.

Tingo wäre am liebsten aufgesprungen, aber er war versteinert. Wie die anderen magischen Tiere auch. Schließlich war gerade der Direktor im Raum.

Miss Cornfield strahlte. Was hatte sie nur für eine nette Klasse! „Und was machen wir mit dem restlichen Geld?", fragte sie.

„Den Rest kriegt …", begann Benni.

„… Mr. Morrison für seinen Omnibus!", rief Anna-Lena.

Zum Glück war Herr Siegmann in diesem Moment schon wieder draußen.

Und dann ließ Miss Cornfield die Köpfe ordentlich rauchen. Sie stellte knifflige Aufgaben: von Zebras, die im Zoo wohnten, vier Beine hatten und sich mit Tausendfüßlern ein Gehege teilten.

Sie lösten Sachaufgaben über Ameisen, die mit einer Geschwindigkeit von 2 Zentimetern pro Sekunde von A nach B krochen. Wie lange brauchten sie für 100 Meter?

Die Stifte flogen übers Papier.

Wenn jemand nicht weiterwusste, bat Miss Cornfield Franka um Unterstützung. Sie stand dann auf und half den anderen.

Die Kinder zählten zusammen, wie viele Flöhe auf Hundeköpfen saßen, wenn auf dem ersten 22, dem zweiten 107 und dem dritten 11 hockten. Und schließlich dachte sich Miss Cornfield folgende Sachaufgabe aus:

„Der Inhaber der magischen Zoohandlung fährt mit 90 Stundenkilometern durch die Welt. Immer wieder macht er halt, um magische Tiere einzusammeln. Er fährt nach Italien, durchquert die Sahara und schließlich landet er in Kenia. Wie lange ist er unterwegs?"

Die Kinder holten Atlas und Lineal hervor und begannen zu messen.

Auch die magischen Tiere steuerten kluge Gedanken bei: „Das macht drei Tage extra, weil Mr. Morrison sich in Italien an den Strand legt!", rief Henrietta. „In der Wüste hat der Omnibus bestimmterich eine Pannerich", quietschte Eugenia, die kopfüber am Kleiderständer baumelte. „Zähl zwei Tage dazuerich, Eddie!"

Die Kinder rechneten und radierten. Die Aufgabe war unlösbar. Keiner wusste, welche Umwege Mr. Morrison fuhr und wo er eine Pause einlegte. Machte er an der Küste einen Tauchkurs, weil er endlich einmal ein Wassertier mitbringen wollte? Kletterte er auf einen Gipfel, um eine Bergziege einzusammeln? Und während die Kinder rechneten und radierten, wirbelte allen der gleiche Gedanke durch den Kopf: Wer bekam wohl als Nächstes ein magisches Tier?

Mortimer Morrison trommelte mit den Fingern auf dem Lenkrad herum. Sein Omnibus stand mitten in Kenia in der Savanne.

Der Motor dampfte und qualmte, keinen Meter konnte er weiterfahren. Er brauchte dringend neues Kühlwasser.

Das Wasserloch lag nur etwa hundert Meter von ihm entfernt, aber es war von Flusspferden belagert. Und die interessierten sich leider überhaupt nicht für seine Notlage.

Pinkie, die Elster, drückte ungeduldig auf die Hupe. „Platz da, ihr dicken Dinger!“, rief sie.

Ein paar Tiere drehten die Köpfe.

„Hör auf damit!“, fuhr Mr. Morrison die Elster an. „Flusspferde sind gefährlich! Wir müssen warten, bis sie das Wasserloch verlassen haben.“

Aus der Savanne kamen weitere Tiere angetrabt.

„Das ist gar nicht gut“, murmelte Mr. Morrison und hielt das Lenkrad umklammert. Der Inhaber der magischen Zoohandlung wusste: Nilpferde trampelten alles nieder, was ihnen auf dem Weg zum Wasserloch in die Quere kam. Auch Omnibusse.

Ein Flusspferd stieß mit seinem breiten Maul gegen die Beifahrertür. Ein zweites donnerte gegen die Radkappe.

„Schnell, mach die Scheibe hoch!“, rief Pinkie voller Panik. „Beeilung, Boss!“

Mortimer Morrison kurbelte, so schnell er konnte. Einen Spalt ließ er allerdings offen. Auf seiner Stirn bildeten sich Schweißperlen. Die Tiere würden den Omnibus umwerfen. Dann war er verloren!

„Ist denn kein magisches Nilpferd unter euch?“, rief er verzweifelt. „Ich bin’s doch: Mortimer Morrison von der magischen Zoohandlung!“

Plötzlich drehten die Flusspferde ihre dicken Köpfe zur Seite. Das Ruckeln hörte auf.

Und mit leisen Schritten näherte sich aus der Steppe ein Leopard.

Mortimer Morrison hielt den Atem an. „Na gute Nacht“, flüsterte er. Pinkie versteckte sich unter dem Mantel, der auf dem Beifahrersitz lag.

Das elegante Tier kam auf den Omnibus zu – und sprang auf die Kühlerhaube. Er schaute Mr. Morrison direkt in die Augen.

„Hilfe“, piepte Pinkie unter dem Mantel hervor.

Da begann der Leopard zu sprechen, mit samtig weicher Stimme. „Keine Sorge, Mortimer“, sagte das schöne Tier. „Ich bin’s, Leander.“ Er fauchte die Flusspferde an, die träge davontrabten.

Erleichtert öffnete der Inhaber der magischen Zoohandlung die Fahrertür. Der Leopard sprang mit einem Satz in den Bus und machte es sich auf der Rückbank gemütlich.

„Na dann, auf geht's!“, schnurrte Leander. „Ab nach Hause!“

SMS, abgeschickt von der Oasenstadt Tamanrasset, Algerien
Von: Mortimer Morrison
An: Mary Cornfield

Hallo Mary,
habmir dashandy eines touristenausgliehen. Beimeinem ist der Akkuleer. Du wirst staunen, wen ich diesmal mitrbinge. Meinneues Tier macht geradeeinen Spaziergang und wird tausendfachfotografiert. Ich glaub, dasmag er nicht. Er schaut schonganz grimmig. Mussschnellhin, sonst frisster einen Touristen. Bin baldzuhause. Hpüfe initalien vielleichtnochkurz ins Meer. Machsgut. M.

Wow!
Ein Leopard!
Ob dieses magische Tier
in Miss Cornfields Klasse einen Freund findet?
Oder hat Mr. Morrison vielleicht
noch ein ganz anderes Mitbringsel aus Afrika?

Lies auch das nächste Abenteuer
aus der Schule der magischen Tiere!

Die Schule der magischen Tiere

Nass und nasser!

DIE SCHULE DER
MAGISCHEN TIERE
Nass und nasser
Margit Auer
CARLSEN

Leseprobe aus

DIE SCHULE DER MAGISCHEN TIERE

Nass und nasser!

Die Haushälterin öffnete – und begann sofort zu schimpfen. Und zwar noch viel schlimmer, als Benni vorhergesagt hatte! „Noch mehr Kinder! In meiner letzten Arbeitswoche muss ich mich noch mit einer Kinderbande herumplagen."
„Hallo, Frau Rettich!", rief Hatice und winkte ihr zu.
„Hach!" Frau Rettich biss unwillig die Lippen zusammen.
Ihr Blick fiel auf Peperoni: „Hat der Läuse?"
Schoki schüttelte empört den Kopf.
„Flöhe?" Der Rettich musterte Rabbat.
„Quatsch!", zischte Ida.
„Wie geht es Henry?", fragte Benni.
Das Gesicht der Haushälterin lief rot an. „Du schon wieder!", rief sie. „Gestern musste ich noch mal durchwischen!"

Helene stemmte die Hände in die Seiten. „Wir sollen Henry die Hausaufgaben bringen“, stellte sie klar. „Im Auftrag unserer Lehrerin.“
„Danke sehr, auf Wiedersehen“, schnappte der Rettich und wollte Benni wie gestern die Blätter aus der Hand reißen. Aber diesmal war Benni darauf vorbereitet.
„Ich bringe sie Henry selbst!“, rief Benni und Henrietta warf ihm einen bewundernden Blick zu. Wie mutig Benni war!
Der Rettich schüttelte den Kopf. „Kommt nicht in Frage“, knurrte sie.
Während Benni und Frau Rettich miteinander zankten, gaben Max und Eddie ihren magischen Tieren einen Wink. Schon flatterten Eule und Fledermaus hinter Frau Rettichs Rücken ins Haus und durchsuchten zügig ein Zimmer nach dem anderen. Die Haushälterin bekam nichts davon mit.
„Henry ist weg“, rief Muriel, als sie zurückkehrte.
„Sein Bett ist so was von leererich“, zwitscherte Eugenia.
„Da hat nicht malerich eine Windpocke Platz.“
Benni drückte der Haushälterin die Blätter in die Hand.
Erleichtert schloss der Rettich die Tür.
Die Kinder marschierten ratlos zurück.

Margit Auer

Als Kind wollte Margit Auer Postbotin werden und mit einem gelben Fahrrad Briefe verteilen – aber dann kam alles ganz anders. Sie wurde Journalistin und schrieb viele Artikel für Zeitungen. Als ihre drei Söhne zur Welt kamen, las sie jede Menge Kinderbücher und beschloss, selbst welche zu schreiben. Trotzdem findet sie es immer noch toll, wenn jemand Post verteilt. In ihrer Bestseller-Reihe „Die Schule der magischen Tiere" macht das Mr. Morrison. Welches Tier würde sie selbst sich wünschen? Einen Esel!

Nina Dulleck

Die Illustration Nina Dulleck zeichnet und malt, seit sie Stift und Pinsel halten kann. Sie lebt mit ihrer Familie am Rhein inmitten von Weinbergen und Kirschbaumplantagen. Dort illustriert sie viele, viele Kinderbücher und lässt sich dabei von dem Rotkehlchen in ihrem Garten schöne Lieder vorsingen. Fast könnte man meinen, es wäre magisch.

MAGISCHE TIERFREUNDE

Band 1:
DIE SCHULE DER MAGISCHEN TIERE
ISBN 978-3-551-65271-3

Band 2:
VOLLER LÖCHER!
ISBN 978-3-551-65272-0

Band 3:
LICHT AUS!
ISBN 978-3-551-65273-7

Band 4:
ABGEFAHREN!
ISBN 978-3-551-65274-4

Band 5:
TOP ODER FLOP!
ISBN 978-3-551-65275-1

Band 6:
NASS UND NASSER
ISBN 978-3-551-65276-8

Band 7:
WO IST MR. M?
ISBN 978-3-551-65277-5

Band 8:
VOLL VERKNALLT!
ISBN 978-3-551-65278-2

Band 9:
VERSTEINERT!
ISBN 978-3-551-65279-9

Band 10:
HIN UND WEG!
ISBN 978-3-551-65280-5

Band 11:
WILDER, WILDER WALD!
ISBN 978-3-551-65361-1

EINGESCHNEIT!
EIN WINTERABENTEUER
ISBN 978-3-551-65046-7

WWW.CARLSEN.DE

CARLSEN

WER SIND DEINE
MAGISCHEN FREUNDE?

Margit Auer
DIE SCHULE DER MAGISCHEN TIERE: MEINE FREUNDE (FREUNDEBUCH)
Mit Bildern von Nina Dulleck
Hardcover
128 Seiten
ISBN 978-3-551-65033-7

IN DER SCHULE DER MAGISCHEN TIERE FINDET JEDES KIND einen besten Freund! Wer sind deine Freunde? Hier erfährst du alles, was du schon immer über sie wissen wolltest! Welches magische Tier sie gern hätten, welche Filme sie mögen und was sie später mal werden wollen ... Auch Ida und Rabbat, Benni und Henrietta, Jo, Helene und ihre magischen Tiere haben schon eingetragen! Viele magische Nachrichten warten auf dich!

Die Abenteuer der „Schule der magischen Tiere“

gibt es überall im Buchhandel sowie auf www.carlsen.de

Kennst du schon unsere Internetseite rund um die Schule der magischen Tiere?

→ Hol dir jetzt den Newsletter!

www.carlsen.de/newsletter-magischetiere

www.carlsen.de/kinderbuecher/schuledermagischentiere

Willst du dein eigenes magisches Tier zeichnen?

Nina Dulleck zeigt dir in ihrem Youtube-Kanal, wie es geht!

Wir produzieren nachhaltig

- Klimaneutrales Produkt
- Papiere aus nachhaltigen und kontrollierten Quellen
- Hergestellt in Deutschland

FSC www.fsc.org MIX Papier | Fördert gute Waldnutzung FSC® C014496

Völckersstraße 14–20, 22765 Hamburg

Umschlag und Innenillustrationen: Nina Dulleck

Umschlaggrafik: Sabine Reddig

Lektorat: Claudia Scharf

Herstellung: Constanze Hinz

Layout: Eva Grimme, Stuttgart

Lithografie: Margit Dittes Media, Hamburg

Satz: Dörlemann Satz, Lemförde

ISBN 978-3-551-65275-1

Winter
ist